The Whole She-Bang Triplets: Three Aren't One Collection

Dani Haviland
USA Today Bestselling Author

Presenting the first five stories in the
   TRIPLETS: THREE AREN'T ONE *series:*

THE SET UP
DIAMONDS AREN'T FOR EVERYONE
THAT MAGIC TOUCH
HOW LOVE GROWS
THEY CALL ME SHERLOCK

I would say the complete collection – and it is as of March 2023 – but who knows when the voices in my head will whisper the ladies' further adventures to me.

Enjoy!
Dani Haviland

Contents

The Set Up

Triplets: Three Aren't One

Book One

The Set Up

Just before high school graduation, life seemed perfect. Grace is suddenly knocked into a harsh reality by her manipulative mother who demands absolute obedience.
Everything changes when the three Armstrong brothers come into her life.
Will she ever get back to her one true love?
And will he want her again if he finds out what she's done?

Chapter 1: Mother Knows Best

"Are you sure we should be doing this?" Dusty asked breathlessly.

With hormone-induced strength and determination, Grace wrapped her fingers around his and pried his protective hand away from his half-unbuttoned fly. "Yes, I'm sure," she cooed seductively.

"But...but...what if you get pregnant?" he whispered. "Can't you just do the grab and tug thing again?"

"You may like that, but it doesn't do a thing for me except give me sticky fingers. And not the good kind like after eating a giant cinnamon roll with extra glaze. Now, come on! We're both old enough now. At eighteen, no one can say anything." Grace tucked her fallen hair behind her ear and straightened her shoulders. "We're consenting adults."

"But...but... Oh, man..." Dusty slumped back into the couch cushions, defeated in his battle to keep her virginity intact. His virginity, too. He was about to be both a winner and a loser in the battle of fear of and desire for the greatest treasure the human body had to offer.

Grace pulled her tank top off over her head, then shimmied out of her jeans, standing before him: the goddess of female perfection in lace and lust. "You still have that condom, don't you? I think you've been carrying that around since you were thirteen!"

"Oh, yeah..." Dusty reached into his hip pocket and pulled out his wallet. He fumbled through his single dollar bills until he found it. Hastily, he tore open the pale blue packet, then moaned as it fell apart in his fingers.

Tears welled up in his eyes as he looked up to her.

"What?" she asked. She took it from him and held it under the lamp on the end table. "Oh, shit!" She huffed and grunted in frustration, then looked up to see his reaction.

Eyes red with stifled tears, Dusty wiped under his nose, trying to compose himself. His emotions had fallen apart, but the message hadn't been relayed to his male member, still hard and ready to procreate.

Grace gently touched the firmness in his red knit boxer shorts, so different now that she knew it was about to be hers. She leaned over and whispered, "Don't worry. I'm a virgin, so since it's the first time, I can't get pregnant." She took in the size of his erection — longer than the length of her hand — and winced, a slight groan escaping. "At least, that's what Shawna said. Plus, just to make sure, you can pull out at the last minute or second or whatever. Shawna said it's messy, but she's had sex lots of times and she's not pregnant."

"Well, if you're sure..." Dusty rolled sideways and sat up, fumbling with

1

his jeans. "I'll do this part. I know zippers are easier for you, but I didn't think we were going to be doing anything like this tonight." He stopped at the last button. "Are you sure your parents are gone for the whole weekend?"

Grace leaned against the wall, watching the awkward striptease by the young man who had fascinated her since he had started working with his father as a groundskeeper. Dusty was still gawky and lean but had the broadest shoulders of any man she'd ever seen without wearing full football regalia. He didn't play for her school, but she didn't care. That just meant he wasn't stuck on himself like the guys at her private academy.

"Um…" Dusty paused and looked around the guest house living room that doubled as the game room. "Aren't we supposed to have a bed or something? I really don't know what I'm doing here."

"We'll figure it out. At least we're not in the back of a car. You're not only my best guy friend," Grace said, shaking from both the chilly air and nerves, "you're my first lover."

Dusty stepped on the hem of the pant leg still tangled around his ankle. "And your last lover, too," he added hastily and lifted his leg up, nearly toppling over. "Because I don't ever want to lose you."

Grace moved to his side quickly, shoring him up. "Kind of hard to lose someone who never wants to leave your side." She glanced down and saw he was still ready for her. "Or your front," she added with a giggle.

"You know, there's no reason to rush into this…"

"Dusty, I've been waiting for two years, at least!" Grace reached around and unhooked her bra, freeing her perky breasts that didn't really need a brassiere. "Tonight's the first time we've been alone together, and I want you bad! I mean, I want you good. Or want you great. Oh, hell!"

Grace tossed her bra onto the couch and wrapped both arms around her sinewy wannabe lover, rubbing her belly against his, feeling with her abdomen what she had only touched with her hands. "Couch?" she panted.

"Oh, yeah…"

The teenage couple stumbled to the green damask-covered sofa, arms and legs bumping into each other as throw pillows were tossed aside, fingers fumbling to grab body parts and place them where their overstimulated hormones directed.

"Oh, man," Dusty groaned, submitting to her climbing on top of his naked body. She scooted forward, trying to find a place to set her knee in the couch. Making the most out of the awkward situation, she bent forward and kissed him as she reached back to find his cock. She rubbed it against the fuzziness of her pubic hair and tried to straddle him.

"I don't think I can stop…" he moaned as his back arched, trying to penetrate her.

"Then don't," she whispered.

2

"Huh?" he asked, paralyzed in fear that she had changed her mind.

"Don't stop, I mean. Please." She found her moist opening and gently sat back on his dick, wiggling to get it in all the way. "I want you so bad I ache!"

Dusty pushed up further, eliciting a squeak from his partner. "Does it hurt?" he asked, pausing.

"No. I…I…" She lifted her hips and came back down on him, slowly, then lifted up again, her lady muscles automatically squeezing as she moved up, relaxing as she sat back down. "Oh, man…"

The two quickly found their rhythm. "Oh, oh, oh!" Grace squealed as an orgasm approached.

"Should I stop?" he asked.

She squirmed on top of him, enjoying her last shudder, then sighed in completion. "Not yet, but let's change places."

The two disengaged and Dusty climbed on top. They started again slowly, the music on the CD player setting them up with a new pace. Gradually, their movements increased to a drum roll speed, the rock tune unheard. Suddenly, he paused, eyes wide in shock.

"Ah, shit!" he shrieked and quickly pulled out, squirting his load on the couch.

"Huh?" she asked, confused at the abrupt loss of physical contact.

"Babies," he panted. "Not today. I hope."

"Oh, yeah. I forgot."

"I'm glad I didn't. Just a sec." Dusty stood up and retrieved his boxers from the pile of abandoned clothing. "I'll clean this up." He wiped the spilled seed from between her legs. Let's hope the coach was wrong. He said whenever you have sex could be the time you make a baby. I guess I shouldn't tell her that word is that Shawna's already had two abortions.

"Um, can we do it again? I mean, I thought it was going to hurt the first time."

"For me or for you?" Dusty asked. "Because it sure didn't hurt me!"

"For me. I guess that time I fell on my cousin's bike rail did make a difference. I remember my mom saying something about how it popped my cherry."

"Huh?"

"That virgin piece that gets in the way and is pierced the first time a woman has sex. I think it's called the hymen or hybrid or something like that. Anyhow, I broke it when I was six. I remember when it happened, it hurt like I'd been slammed down there with a hammer. I bled, too. It stopped hurting a few hours later, though. I guess it was a small sacrifice. Oh, and hey! I think I had my first orgasm."

"Really? What was it like?" Dusty asked, grateful for the pause in activities so he could recover.

3

"Um, you know how when you ride on the Ferris wheel you get all tingly down there?"

"Oh, yeah. I thought only guys got that. I mean, it can give a guy a boner if he's not careful."

Grace giggled at the word boner, then composed herself. "So, did you have an orgasm, too?"

"Well, with a guy it's different. There's a visible spurt when he has one. Kind of hard to fake." He held up the shorts he'd used as a washcloth. "Proof positive."

"Keep that close at hand," she said. "I think we'll need to use it at least once more. Sex is fun. Now I know why everyone likes it so much."

"Anything for you, Gracie. Anything."

***

"Oh, shoot! Look at the time! I gotta get home or my dad will clobber me. We have to start work at six tomorrow. I hope I can sneak in without him seeing me."

Grace rolled off his outstretched arm. "It's three o'clock? Yeah, I guess I'd better get busy and clean up this place. I don't think my folks will be back until tonight, but I was supposed to be staying with Shawna. We kinda-sorta made a mess in here."

The two cuddled close to each other on the couch, their eyes following the trail of clothes and scattered magazines from the coffee table, the pool cues and chalk now on the floor, the pool table cover wadded into a pillow on top of their impromptu bed.

"I'll never forget this night," Dusty said and stood up. "But I really have to leave. You're okay with cleaning this up by yourself?"

"Pbbt! Of course I am." She got up and turned her face into his chest, giving him a quick kiss on his sparse chest hairs, inhaling deeply to memorize his musky scent. "Give me a call later if you can."

"I'll do better than that. If we finish early, I'll drop by and see you. But I can't get done early if I don't make a good showing for the old man." Dusty stepped into his jeans and quickly jumped up twice to get them all the way on.

Giggling behind her hand at his male parts bouncing with the quick-dress movement, Grace suddenly remembered his skivvies. She looked over at the very well-used cleanup cloth. "Um, I think you forgot something…"

His face brightened red in embarrassment. "Just throw them away. The next time, I'll make sure we have something more suitable."

"Ah," Gracie sighed, her hand brought up to caress her breast in recall. "The next time."

Dusty pulled his tee-shirt on over his head, grabbed his socks from the floor and stuffed them in his pants pocket, then stepped into his tennis shoes. He gave her a quick kiss, groaned, then bent in to embrace her with a full-body hug and smooch. "I can't wait to have you every morning, noon, and night for the rest of my life. But it's going to have to wait. I really do love you, you know."

"Yeah, me too," Grace said. "On everything." She patted him on the shoulder and urged him to the door. "Go. Now. If you don't, I won't let you out of my sight again. Ever."

"All right. Tonight, if I can. And if I can't, I'll find a way."

"Find a way..." Grace said, and moved him out the door, shutting and deadbolting it behind him. "Because I'll be waiting," she said to herself softly. She looked at the daunting task of cleaning up the normally tidy room, then decided it could wait a few hours. She picked up one of the throw pillows from the floor and cuddled up with it on the couch. "I can't imagine life without you now."

***

"What in the hell happened in here?"

Grace awoke disoriented, her mother's shrill voice like tiny knives in her head, trying to carve their way out of her brain through her ears. She shook her head, struggling to remember where and who she was.

"Well? Answer me!"

Still clutching the pillow close, Grace realized she was naked, in a room not her own, and her mother was back almost a day earlier than planned. The first two dilemmas weren't as bad as the last one. If Mother was home early, that meant her parents had had another major blow-up. Would Dad finally get fed up and leave? And if he did, where would she go? She still had two weeks of school left until she graduated.

Grace felt her mother's cold, bony hand grab her chin, bringing her out of her daze. "I asked you," she said icily, her eyes piercing, looking for the telltale signs of lying. "What happened here?"

"I didn't want to go to Shawna's," she said honestly, hoping her talent for storytelling was wide awake and creative. "I put on some loud music, shot pool until three in the morning, then got tired." All true except I used the pool table for a different purpose.

"And your clothes..."

"Bra was too tight after binging on chips and soda. Plus, it was hot." Grace quickly scanned the room, looking for more fodder for her fabrication. "You know, you really ought to have that handyman check out the heating and cooling system in here. One minute, everything's fine, the next minute, I'm sweating like a boxer."

And then she saw them, lying next to the trash can she had thrown them at and missed. Grace quickly looked away and focused on the pool table, hoping her mother hadn't followed her gaze to see Dusty's left-behind red underwear.

"Speaking of boxers," her mother said. She walked over and kicked at the wadded shorts. She noticed the stiff and shiny spots where body fluids had dried and her blood pressure skyrocketed. "It looks like you had company," she said through clenched teeth.

"What are those doing there?" Grace asked, trying to look shocked rather than embarrassed. Yeah, what are those doing there? They should have made it to the bottom of the trash, at least!

"I don't know what I did to have such an ungrateful daughter. I put up with your father's pawing and whining just so you can have a nice home and the finer things in life. A home to be proud of, not to bring horny boys to for a good time. How many times? How long has this been going on?" Victoria asked, her nails digging in as she clenched her daughter's upper arm. "It was that gardener's kid, wasn't it?"

"Let go! You're hurting me," Grace yelped, shoulder dipping as she tried to twist out of her mother's angry grasp. She knew it was useless, though. Her mother always got to have her own way through intimidation and, lately, her physical prowess. All those hours she spent at the gym were good for more than sporting the tightest abs and best-toned legs of any woman in her forties. She could twist the freckles off a frog if she had a mind to.

Grace had made her mother angry many times in the past but this time, she was livid. Was it because sex was involved or had she had a spectacularly horrid time with Dad and come back early, ready to blame someone – anyone –for her miserable existence? This time, Mother hadn't even tried to lecture her. She had gone straight to screaming and grabbing.

Slap!

"What was that for?" Grace asked, her hand up to cover her stinging cheek.

"Who was it? No, never mind. I'm pretty sure it was that lowlife without prospects for a decent future." Victoria paced the room, walking and plotting, pausing to snort in indignation, then stopped suddenly. Her eyes brightened and a conniving smile spread across her face as she realized she could still make this work in her favor. Grace had just sped up the time frame. Her daughter would just have to skip college and go straight to a well-contrived marriage. She had saved the family a fortune in tuition, sorority fees, living expenses and probably a trip to Europe or two.

Grace watched her mother pace but didn't engage her. Instead, she stooped to pick up her clothes and got dressed, stealing sidelong glances to keep track of the mercurial moods. She had just set the pool table straight when she saw Mother's devilish smirk appear. Crap!

"I guess this situation is still salvageable, but you're going to have to do everything I say." She looked at Grace and saw her cheek was still crimson from being slapped. She hadn't done that in ages. She didn't regret it but did feel bad that it would probably leave a mark for more than an hour.

"Sorry about that," Victoria said, trying for sincerity but knowing Grace could see right through her. "I kind of lost my cool when I found out you'd been

6

sleeping around. I guess it doesn't make a difference how many times you've done it or with whom. What you need to do now is find a Mr. Right who has a brother. I want you to sleep with both of them. It'd be better if we can find a family with three available brothers."

"What are you babbling about?"

"Three brothers and who cares if one, or even two, are married? As long as one is single so you can marry him. Actually, multiples might be better. Throw in a little family drama and we might get a six-figure buyout. If you're pregnant, eh? We'll deal with that later."

"I'm not pregnant," Grace said. "We were careful. And I don't want to sleep around. I want to marry Du…"

Grace's eyes widened, shocked that her mother's hand was on her face again. This time, it wasn't a slap, but a firm grip over her mouth to keep her from speaking.

"You will do as I say," Victoria said, glaring at her daughter. "I didn't want to have you to begin with, but you did give me a comfortable existence for the past nineteen years. If you don't do as I say, I will have your little boyfriend arrested for rape."

Grace twisted her head and escaped her mother's grasp. "I'm eighteen and you know it! He is, too. There's no way…"

Humph!

Grace doubled over with the punch to the gut, then looked up, shocked and amazed at the new level of physical violence her mother had sunk to. "What? Why?" she gasped.

"Birth certificates are so easy to fake. All I have to do is make a few calls and the police will be out here, looking for the man who raped my seventeen-year-old daughter."

"But it wasn't…"

Fwap! Thunk!

Two more punches – one to the face, another to the belly – and Grace was on the floor.

"Care for a few more?" her mother asked snidely. "If you give in now and do as I say, he won't be arrested for rape, assault with intent to kill, robbery… Give me a minute and I can think of a few more charges. Looks like I have corroborating evidence on who the culprit was, too." Victoria grabbed one of the pool cues and lifted up the underwear loaded with DNA samples.

Grace remained on the carpet to avoid more of her mother's painful blows, considering her options as she held her pain and rage in check with the slow, steady breathing techniques she had learned in yoga classes.

If I play along, Dusty will be safe. Whether I have to be the docile daughter for a week, a month, or a year, it's still better than losing the love of my life to prison. Even if I can convince a judge that it wasn't rape and he isn't convicted,

7

just being charged will smear his – our – life with a record.

Victoria watched as her daughter considered her choices. She knew she had brought up a smart girl who would come to the right conclusion. Still, a few pugilistic blows would show the little rebel that Mother was still bigger, stronger, and more determined to control a situation than she could ever be.

"Yes, do as I say," Victoria said using her low and sultry no-nonsense voice, "and both lover boy's record and your reputation will remain clean. No matter how innocent a girl is when she's 'taken advantage of,' having that event in her life will always be a stigma. You will be marked as that beautiful blonde who allowed herself to be raped.

"I also want you to consider what this would do to your father and his business if this debacle ever became known. Your name spread all over the newspapers, his clients avoiding the man whose daughter was violated. One look at your pretty little boyfriend, and they'll think you either lured him in or lied about the rape. Either way, everyone loses."

"And your way?" Grace asked, sniffing back her tears, hoping they weren't visible or were thought to be from the physical pain, not the loss of the life she had hoped for.

"You target a well-to-do young man and his brother. Or brothers. I'll help scout out the right ones. All you have to do is be pretty and make yourself available. Once you get one brother's interest, flirt with the other or others. Figure out which one you want to marry and you're set. Oh, and I don't care how 'careful' you were, the women in my family are extremely fertile. Unless you went behind my back and got an IUD or are on the pill, you're probably already pregnant."

"Why brothers?" Grace asked, forgoing a conversation on her level of fertility or method of contraception.

"Why not? Increase your chances of getting a better provider. Oh, and you have to sleep with both of them within the first week or two. It's leverage for the future. You may not ever need to use that secret against either one of them but consider it an insurance policy. No condoms, either. If you have sex with the brothers in the first month, you'll be pregnant and guaranteed a hurry-up wedding."

Victoria reached her hand out to help Grace from the floor, her fake smile not even beginning to cover her sneer of disgust. "It was bound to happen one way or another. You blew your chance at four years at an Ivy League college, scouting for Mr. Right. You'll have to settle for four weeks of hoping for a not-too-disgusting Mr. Right Now."

Grace rolled to her side and got up from the floor without assistance, ignoring her mother's hand. "If you don't mind, I'll finish cleaning up in here. Then I want to take a shower."

"You can scrub until sunset but the stink of messing up your life with a night of legs spread for the wrong man will never leave. We'll just have to make sure your Mr. Right Now is the same height and coloring as that gardener's son you've been drooling over for the last three years. At least you succumbed to someone of the right color."

Grace used every ounce of control – and the recent memory of being pummeled by the woman who claimed to love her – to keep from pivoting in place and spearing her mother with the pool cue she had just picked up. Instead, she bent over and gathered a fallen cube of cue chalk, crushing it between her thumb and fingers before dumping the clumpy blue powder into the trash. One day at a time. One second at a time. Don't stoop to her level of assaulting from anger. Make a plan and keep to it. Protecting Dusty is worth it.

Chapter 2: Surviving the Day

How could life have been so perfect at three in the morning and not worth living four hours later?

Grace rinsed the last of the shampoo from her hair, then watched as the bubbles slipped down the drain, disappearing into the blackness of the unknown just like her life. She tapped the stopper with her foot, allowing the tub to start filling. Mother said she wanted to talk when she was done but hadn't given her a deadline. She'd take every bit of time she could and give herself the full treatment including a hair masque and a few minutes with the jacuzzi. She patted herself gently between her legs. The swelling had gone down, but she was still tender. She'd set the jets on low for now.

A warm, comforting tingle ran up her spine at the memory of how she had become sore and how she had sprinted into womanhood, sharing her body and soul with the man she had chosen to spend forever with. Her smile and glow suddenly evaporated as a stream of water from the showerhead hit her cheek just wrong. She flinched at the pain, a reminder of her mother's harsh slap.

Why had that vile woman who birthed her dash her hopes and plans, sealing her dissertation with a one-two punch and a non-negotiable threat? Was it jealousy at her fading beauty or rage at her own failed marital relationship?

Grace turned off the shower and let the tub fill from the waterspout, the flow not too hot but warm enough to keep her from getting chilled. She squirted hair conditioner into the palm of her hand and new memories of the passions of the night before flooded in at the sight of the white creamy fluid. A shudder of mixed emotions – the recall of pleasure with and the despair at the loss of – Dusty overwhelmed her. She mindlessly applied the conditioner to the ends of her long hair, twisting the dark blonde tresses together, pressing the mass close to her scalp. Bending forward, she wrapped the works into a towel turban, letting the warmth of her head seal in the oils and botanicals. The cotton wrap cushioned her head as she lay back, ready for the tub level to rise so she could push the start button and bubble away her problems. For a few minutes, at least.

Thunk! Thunk! Thunk!

"Are you going to be in there all day?" Victoria hollered.

"No, just shaving my legs," Grace lied. She ran her hand up her calf to her thigh, feeling the smoothness she had insured the day before. Had it only been twelve hours since she had primped, shaved, and oiled her body to perfection for her 'first time'? And less than six hours since she had kissed Dusty goodbye, the two of them talking about their 'next time' and a shared forever?

"I want you downstairs and dressed in ten minutes. We have work to do," Victoria said, then smacked the door again to punctuate her command.

"Yes, Mother," Grace replied dispassionately, then pushed the Jacuzzi pump button, obliterating the chance of hearing anything else from her ruthless parent. She looked at the digital clock on the sink counter, noting the time. "I won't be late."

Sinking down to her towel-wrapped hair, Grace let the water jets work their magic on her tense muscles. "Minute by minute," she reminded herself, inhaling deeply, recalling the scent of her lover's musky chest, the feel of two of his five chest hairs as they tickled her nose. Her eyes closed for a moment, then popped open to see the time.

"Crap!" She scooted down in the tub, ran her fingers through her hair to work out as much conditioner as she could in ten seconds, then stood up, hastily drying as much of her hair and body as she could before grabbing the dressing gown hanging on the hook. Thirty seconds left!

She rushed downstairs and slowed two steps before the kitchen door, catching her breath and reminding herself to keep her remarks to herself.

"Is that how you plan on finding a husband?" Victoria sneered, eyeing Grace head to flip-flop shod toes, then taking another drag off her cigarette.

"You said dressed and I am. I didn't know it was for an interview. If you'd like, I can go back and change."

Victoria flicked invisible ash from the end of her cigarette into the marble ashtray, then picked up her demitasse cup of coffee, pinkie extended. "No. Don't bother. This is just the first step. We need to peruse these to find one who looks more or less like your little boy toy. I really can't remember much about him other than he was fair-skinned and as lanky as a two-by-four clothesline. His build had promise with those broad shoulders, but as the son of a groundskeeper, he may as well have been a twenty-year-old garden rake."

Keep quiet. Don't comment. Get through this conversation. She'll wear out eventually. Or she'll find something else to keep her occupied. Remember, minute by minute.

Picking up the photo album at her elbow, Victoria opened it to the tab marked 'B.' "If you had been accepted – or your father and I had purchased your acceptance – into a top tier college, the 'A' list men would have been an option. Not as many to choose from as the 'B' list, but their pedigree and net worth are so much more desirable."

Grace couldn't help it. She hissed the harsh words even before they had formed them in her head. "Is that all love and marriage are to you?"

Undaunted by the context but surprised that Grace had lost her cool so soon after her first 'attitude adjustment,' Victoria decided to let this one slide. Her daughter had, after all, been sleep deprived and was still in shock at her new status in life as an adult. "Marriage is a social arrangement - a legal business contract. Love is something that comes and goes; a fondness for a cute puppy that quickly grows into frustration with an uncontrollable, mangy cur. Men are nothing but skirt-chasing, turd-dropping burdens who ruin your holidays."

"Oh, so that's what this is about; you're mad at Daddy?"

In a flash, Victoria was on her feet, her diamond-ringed fist clenching Grace's throat. "You know, it really isn't too late for more rape injuries to be inflicted. I have a wine bottle or two that could do some real damage."

Just as quickly as she had grabbed her, Victoria released her, dropping her hand to her side, settling back into the chair at the table as if nothing had happened, scanning the newspaper clippings of the men on the first page of the 'B' candidates.

Grace was stunned by the sudden assault, the physical result of choking even worse than the emotional distress. She tried to relax her throat muscles, doing everything she could not to puke and humiliate herself further. I gotta get out of here!

"Oh, and don't even think about leaving," Victoria said as if reading her thoughts. "Remember, I know your little boy toy's daddy. It wouldn't take much to ruin both of them with the accusation of a father and son rape. After all, some men might like that kind of thing. You know, sharing a woman. Or a girl. After all, you are only seventeen," she said, then added a sinister smirk.

Don't talk. She's baiting you. You already had this conversation. She wants you to argue. Facts mean nothing. She can manipulate anything.

"Ah, obedient silence," Victoria said. "I like that. Keep it up and we'll get along just fine. Now, come sit next to Mother and point out which ones you think would work for you. Mind the notes in the margin: net worth, location, and height. We'll have to read through the text to see how many siblings. Those who don't have any at all are in the 'C' list. Let's hope we don't have to sink that far."

I've already sunk that far…

"How about this one?" Victoria asked.

Grace turned the binder around and glanced at the society page photo of a man who seemed to be similar in looks to Dusty. The notes said, 'Stockbroker, two brothers, one possibly gay, the other an architect.

"Sure. Why not?" Grace said, then sunk back in the chair and looked at the wine chiller, stocked with bottles for the week's meals. You may become my next best friend.

Chapter 3: Setting the Bait

Victoria picked up her black leather-bound monthly planner, checked the annual calendar on the back page for reference, then switched back and forth to the current month, comparing notes. "Well, it looks like we're in luck. You'll have to skip a couple of days of school, but I think we can make it. I'll just say I forgot to bring our invitations."

"Make it to what?" Grace asked, reaching for one of the fresh-baked muffins.

Victoria smacked her hand. "None of that until we find your Mister Right. If you're on the skinny side, a man will feel sorry for you and want to take you under his wing and fatten you up."

"Like a calf? Lucky me."

Victoria's jaw clenched and her hand flew up, ready to instill an obedience adjustment when she heard the housekeeper shuffling toward the breakfast nook. Her fingers fluttered down, settling harmlessly to the side of her head, pushing some of her perfectly coifed hair behind her ear, her attention back to her social events scheduler.

The housekeeper looked around, sensing the tension. "What's the matter, Missy?" she asked, and briefly set her hand on Grace's shoulder to reassure her. She patted it twice, then brought the platter of muffins closer, setting a clean plate in front of the young woman she had looked after for over a decade. "I baked these just for you this morning. I know how much you love them." She paused and looked around at the sparsely set table. "Oh, that's right. You like them with lots of butter. Here, I'll get some out of the pantry for you."

"Oh, don't bother, Sally," Grace said. "I'm not ready for breakfast yet. Thanks anyhow. I'm sure they'll be just as great at lunch."

"Ooh, that does sound good. Maybe with a bit of cream cheese and preserves? Makes me hungry all over again and I already ate two of them."

"Good morning, everyone," Hal said brightly, swatting Sally's ample rear end playfully with the rolled-up newspaper. "The Times isn't good for much else," he said to her, then set the paper on the table. "You're not going to call sexual harassment on me, are you?" he whispered in her ear.

"Not as long as you keep giving me those big Christmas bonuses, I won't," she said, grabbing a plate for him. "Care to join your family?"

Hal glanced at Victoria and a chill shot up his spine. She was tenser than usual, her bony shoulders pulled further back, chin higher in the air. She was wearing her iron maiden attitude, ready for battle with whoever was nearby.

Then he noticed Grace. She was biting her bottom lip, blinking back tears, avoiding looking up at him. He'd seen that look before but not since her Sweet Sixteen party. Victoria had made her miserable, embarrassed her in front of all her friends, then acted like Grace was overreacting when her friends decided they'd better leave early. Apparently, something had just happened between the two. He swallowed hard and looked at Sally to see if she had noticed.

The robust housekeeper and cook had taken two mini bran muffins and added them to a plate of fresh orange slices. "I made some small ones so I wouldn't feel too bad if I ate four of them. Try these! I added dried cherries instead of raisins to this batch. It really kicked them up a notch."

Grace looked over at her former nanny and a genuine smile emerged. Sally looked back at Hal and gave him one of her all-knowing winks. *That woman won't bedevil your daughter while both of us are here.*

With the wink, Hal scooted back and relaxed into the chair he'd been sitting on the edge of. Sally was a decent cook, a passable housekeeper, but also the most nurturing woman he'd ever encountered. He wasn't in love with her but was eternally grateful that she was in his life. Or at least, in Grace's life.

"So, I was thinking of taking Grace to the regatta next week," Victoria said, her voice more assertive than usual.

"I don't think that's a good idea," Hal said. He poured a cup of coffee, knowing she'd have a retort. As soon as she cleared her voice to speak, he continued his thought, intentionally talking over her. "It's her last week of school before graduation. It's one of the most socially active times of her high school experience. This is her last chance to spend time with the friends she grew up with before she takes off to college. Bryn Mawr is so lucky to get you."

"What?" Grace squealed, popping up out of her chair and her doldrums.

"Yup, they're lucky to get you. You see, since my mother went there, you're a legacy. One generation removed, but that was close enough when I offered an endowment." Hal looked away, paused, then caught his daughter's eye. "Nah. Just messing with you..."

Her glee popped like a soap bubble, Grace sat back in the cushioned kitchen chair, ready to set her chin on her knuckles.

"Whoa! Wait!" he said, rushing over to hold her close, clutching her in a half-hug. "I wasn't joking about being accepted at Bryn Mawr; just the endowment part."

He pulled away and looked at her. He saw her tears fall then felt them reappear on his face. "You got in on your grades and extracurricular activities. The acceptance letter was mailed months ago, but for some reason, it never got here. I called about it, wanted to know if they had made their determinations and if so, did they possibly have some wiggle room for the daughter of a son of a daughter of Bryn Mawr. They were surprised by the call. They figured you had accepted somewhere else."

Hal shot a glare at Victoria but remained mute. He didn't need to let everyone know that the college told him they had received a letter of declination signed by Grace. By his daughter's ecstatic reaction on hearing she was accepted, he knew someone in the house had drafted a fake response and forged

14

the signature. One hundred to one it wasn't Sally or anyone else not married to him.

Getting Grace out of the house and away from her toxic mother couldn't come soon enough. His face reddened as he choked down his frustration. His wife's jealousy of her own daughter was bad enough, but she had taken it a giant step beyond that. Ever since he could remember, she had been presenting Grace with a skewed outlook on life. She insisted that women of their social status should consider the importance of improving, or at least maintaining, the breeding line. Suggestions were constantly being dropped to Grace that she needed to enhance her face and figure with surgeries and silicone to ensure she was attractive to a suitable mate. A good marriage was the only way she would be able to afford a comfortable existence and a place for dear mommy if and when said mommy was kicked to the curb.

Hal knew that it was only a matter of time before Victoria screwed up and he caught her having an affair. He needed to catch her literally with her pants down if not in the act itself. If he even hinted at a separation or divorce, she'd bleed him beyond death, leaving him as empty as a desiccated corpse without even a beggar's cup for Grace. He didn't have any valid grounds against her. Yet. As soon as she was caught being unfaithful or deceitful or any of those other 'fuls' with a negative connotation, he'd have her in divorce court so fast, her two-faced head would spin off her skinny neck. He blessed his mother daily for insisting on an ironclad prenuptial. It was the only thing that kept him sane. Hope. Hope for him and his daughter.

"No," Victoria said pointedly, then lit another cigarette.

Hal coughed at the smoke and pushed the battery-powered smoke eater towards her. "If you don't mind," he said. *And even if you do...*

"No, what?" Grace asked, peering hopefully at her mother.

"No, you won't be attending the last few days of school. We had an agreement, remember?"

"What's all this about?" Hal asked, standing close to his daughter, hand on her shoulder in reassurance.

Victoria's scowl deepened as she glared at Grace. When Grace didn't flinch, she picked up a wine bottle and ran her hand up and down the neck of it. "I think we should have *coq au vin* tonight, don't you, Sally?" she asked. "I'd like the bottle when you're done with it..."

Grace's eyes widened in shock. You'd rape your own daughter with a wine bottle just to get your own way? And ruin the lives of two others at the same time, both of them innocent?

Victoria smirked and shook her head at Grace. You can't win. You play my game and let me win; or you fight me and you, your boyfriend, and his lawn-cutting daddy all lose. Which one?

Grace looked up at her father, letting a shadow of disappointment show.

15

"Mother and I were talking about this earlier," she said truthfully, knowing she was a lousy liar. "She made some very strong points for taking off before school was out. I'm sure my friends will have a good time without me." *Even if I'm going to be setting myself up for a miserable existence, seeking out whatever husband she decides is right for me. Oh, for an early death!*

***

"Not bad," Victoria said as she looked over the linen-covered tables laden with silver chafing dishes of hot meats and sauces, and cut-crystal platters of fresh fruits, canapes, and intricately carved and formed vegetables. "Just make sure you pick up something quick to chew and swallow that won't stick in your teeth or stain them. Better yet, just grab some celery to play with. Give them a little preview of how sweet your long fingers will look, running up and down…"

"Mother!" Grace hissed. She cleared her throat, nodding to a worried man who looked to be the butler or someone else in charge of keeping order. She quickly got her embarrassment under control and asked, "You did get the invitation situation cleared up, I hope." *Oh, Lord, I hope you didn't get it cleared up. If they throw us out, we'll be ruined. Even F-list men won't want me. I'll be free again!*

"Silas!" Victoria gushed, her hand out, ready to paw the arm of the man in charge of checking invitations. "I didn't know you worked in this neighborhood. Nice digs," she added, nodding to the elaborate ice sculptures on the tables, then the young men rushing back and forth with trays of champagne flutes.

"I'm doing well, thank you for asking," Silas said guilelessly, then looked aside, as if he wished she hadn't spotted him.

"Oh, and this is my daughter, Grace. Say hello to Silas, dear," she prompted. Her hand lay on Grace's forearm, fingers clutching gently, reminding her to play her part.

Grace looked to make sure her mother was turned away, watching for available suitors, before she said, "Hello, Silas," then mouthed the word, 'dear.'

Silas's mouth twitched in a grin as she playfully repeated what her mother had told her to, then quickly returned to somber when he saw Victoria look back at them. "It's a pleasure," he said. He turned to Victoria and added, "If there's anything I can do for you, Mrs. Stillwater, please don't hesitate to ask."

"Well, now that you mention it, Silas," she said, her hands leaving Grace and settling on his upper arm. "We would love an introduction to one, or all, of the Armstrong brothers. You see, it doesn't really make a difference which one we meet *first*," Victoria said. "I hear they're all such interesting men."

Silas flashed his phony smile, acknowledging the truth of what she had just said, but hiding his true feelings from her. His stomach knotted at being near this social lamprey who was obviously siccing her disinterested daughter on whichever of the rich brothers took a fancy to her.

The gentleman's gentleman had first encountered Victoria Stillwater years

16

ago when he was working for another family and she was still a newlywed. She was slobbering drunk at the time, and he had only been employed by the banker and his family for a week when she hit on him. She rubbed her bony fanny up against him, then turned and grabbed him in the crotch when she thought no one was looking. He covered up the shock of her fumbled clutch, pretending he had a sudden gut pain, but his boss had seen the whole episode. The only good that had come out of her botched flirt was his employer had seen that he was capable of discretion under pressure.

He stayed with the banker until he died, enjoying a comfortable relationship with the confirmed bachelor. In appreciation, the old man left him his huge house and a very comfortable inheritance.

Silas no longer *had* to work but still very much enjoyed the people watching – the social sambas and tangos – that blossomed at galas and parties. He let it be known to local families that he would be available for big events where a cool head and discerning eye were needed – situations like tonight where multiple party-crashers had already dropped in. Some of the revelers were looking for introductions, others to pinch a silver salver or two, a few just wanting free food and drink. Discretion in ejecting wayward sorts was a top priority; bad publicity and the need for law enforcement was to be avoided.

He looked up, presumably searching for one of the young Armstrong men, but really trying to read the beautiful young girl with dark blonde hair. She couldn't be more than a recent high school graduate, a gentle soul who appeared to have no interest in her mother's hunt for a husband for her. The sadness behind the young girl's eyes couldn't be hidden by the expert application of makeup or the feigned smile that was fading as the moments passed.

Yes, his gut impression was right. It was the mother who was on the prowl, seeking a mate for her pup. It was obvious to him that the humbled lass had her sights set on someone who was not in this thoroughbred stable. More than likely, she had chosen an open range mustang and Mom had shotgunned him out of the territory, scared him away with emasculating threats.

"Oh, isn't that one of the sons?" Victoria exclaimed, grabbing Silas's arm, bringing him out of his introspection. She realized what she had done, glad that she had only nodded in Alex's direction and not pointed. "Isn't that Armando?" she asked.

"No, ma'am," Silas said, enunciating the generic salutation, refusing to call her by name. "That is Alexander, although I don't think anyone ever calls him by his full name. I suggest Alex for addressing him."

"Oh, yes," Victoria agreed. "Al is such a common name. It sounds like the name of a plumber or car mechanic, not an architect."

Silas glanced over at the young woman. She was suppressing a grin at her mother's obvious prejudice when it came to names, snapping back to primness when her mother turned her way.

"It looks like he's ready for a fresh drink," Silas said. "Let me see if he's available."

As soon as her social coordinator was out of earshot, Victoria clutched Grace's arm, her fingers digging into the bare flesh. Grace flinched and her mother relaxed her grip, hoping she hadn't inadvertently left a mark. "Remember to let him do the talking. It's fine to give him prompts. Ask him about his latest project, where he likes to vacation, anything positive." She looked up and saw Silas speaking with him, then glancing her way. "Smile, Grace. Show him your perfect teeth, but don't open your mouth too wide. I don't want you to appear too eager."

Grace smiled at the irony. Eager? I'm the opposite of eager. Her slight smile widened as she noticed the eye roll of the party manager. Looks like Silas has us pegged. I may be missing the parties with my friends, but if Mother gets her comeuppance at this gala, it will be worth it.

Perfectly at peace for the first time since her mother had 'caught and broke' her, Grace was radiant in her momentary serenity as the two men approached. She briefly caught the scent of her mother's perfume, her body's nervous sweat setting off the high-dollar aroma. *Better her than me. She's a nervous wreck! And I am so enjoying her discomfort...*

"Mrs. Victoria Stillwater," Silas said, positioning himself between the two parties. "May I introduce the first son of our host. This is Alexander Armstrong," winking at the man when he used the full version of his first name.

"Alex," he said, winking back, then accepted the proffered hand. He reached to shake it, then realized Victoria was holding it up for him to kiss. He stifled his chuckle at the formality and brushed his lips across her cold knuckles. He stood up and looked at the young woman beside her. "And you are?"

"I'm sorry," Silas said. "I didn't get your name, Miss."

"I'm Grace Elizabeth Stillwater, but Grace or 'Hey, you!' will get my attention," she said, making sure she didn't laugh out loud at her own joke.

"Well, then, Grace it is," Alex said, now totally intrigued with the good-looking party crasher. "Silas, why don't you show Mrs. Stillwater to the more comfortable seating inside. I think Grace and I would like to take a walk. You would like to see the stables, wouldn't you?"

"You have horses?" Grace asked, then playfully smacked her forehead. "Let's hope so. I don't think you have stables for camels or ostriches...or do you?"

Alex put his arm across her shoulder. "Where have you been all my life?" he asked, then looked back to make sure they wouldn't be followed.

Silas's hand was on Victoria's elbow, urging her toward the pavilion. "Let's leave them alone, shall we?"

Victoria took a step to follow the young couple, then halted. She'd have to trust Grace not to blow her first chance at bedding the billionaire's son. Then again, there were still two more brothers. It would serve the brat right if she did choose the wrong one the first time.

Chapter 4: Alex the Architect

"I don't think I've ever seen you before at one of these events," Alex said to Grace, snagging a glass of champagne from the server's tray as he passed. He handed it to her and smiled.

She accepted it reluctantly, holding it by the stem, pinkie extended like it might bite her if she approached it wrong. "I'm not sure about the law in Massachusetts, but I'm only eighteen. Actually, I don't think I'm old enough to drink in any state," she said and handed the flute back to the shocked server.

Alex whispered in her ear. "No one's carding tonight. If you'd like one, go ahead. If not, let me know, and I'll have Sam bring you whatever your heart desires."

Grace giggled. "Does he have access to root beer?"

"With or without ice cream?"

An abbreviated chuckle escaped, then she took a deep breath, using the moment to figure out what she should do. "Surprise me. Mother would have a fit if she saw me eating or drinking sweets. She already thinks I'm too fat."

Alex eyed her up and down, adding an exaggerated frown of disapproval. "I'd say fewer bagels in the morning might take care of that belly roll. Oh, and skipping the cream cheese might help erase one or two of those extra chins."

"You're hilarious," Grace said. "And here I thought I was going to be miserable tonight."

"Hey, the night's still young." He looked over at his father and shook his head.

"Someone you know?" Grace asked, noticing his sudden change in demeanor.

"Yup. All my life."

Grace moved over to his other side and noticed her mother fawning over the man Alex had been eyeing. He was tall and handsome; except for the silver hair, an older version of the man beside her. "Yup. Parents. What are you going to do with 'em? You can't claim they're not yours with DNA tests getting more and more accurate, and they refuse to run away from home."

"Yeah," Alex replied in the same dry tone. "And no matter how much you scream or pout or try to distract them, they keep trying to live your life for you."

"Amen to that!" Grace said, then grabbed Alex's glass of champagne and chugged the contents.

"I thought you were too young to drink."

"I am. But I'm not too young to have my mother totally ruin my life." She saw her dilemma waving at her and returned her gesture with the empty glass. "And yours?"

"Don't have one. Mom died a long time ago," Alex said. He took the champagne flute from her. "And I may not be *your* parent, but I do think you're too young to drink. Sorry, I don't mean to be bossing you around or telling you what to do, but I'd protect a stranger the same way if she was walking in front of a truck."

"Yup. That's my mother. A highjacked firetruck, rushing in to take over someone's situation with loud noises and flashing bling. Always trying to alter the course of people's lives whether it's any of her business or not."

"Wow! You're pretty sharp. I take it she's already trying to commandeer your life?"

"Already? Try the word still. My father and nanny did as much as they could to insulate me from her, but once I turned eighteen, my nanny was out the door. Or she would have been if my father hadn't decided that we needed a full-time housekeeper and cook. She was already doing those jobs, too, but Mother wanted my warm-blooded comforter and confidant gone. Dad insisted she stay but did give in a little. She's only part-time now. That leaves way too many hours in the day that I'm vulnerable."

"What about your father? Are your parents still married? I mean, it'd be a miracle if they were."

"Yes, they're still married. No, it's not a miracle. It's called an ironclad pre-nuptial agreement. I think my father wishes he'd never had it drafted that way. It was to protect him from the poor money-grabber who was carrying his child. Me. Yes, I have plenty of guilt with that one. He'd have his freedom now except they're supposed to be active in each other's lives, blah, blah, blah. I guess he thought he loved her at some point. I've seen what it really was with other couples since, though. He didn't love her; he loved the child she was carrying. Yup. Still me. I don't know if they've even had sex in the last however many years. She tenses up when he gets near, even though he's not the least bit attentive to her."

"Maybe with some therapy…"

"No way, José," Grace said, laughing out loud. She looked over at her mother and noticed she had moved to the other side of their host, making sure she could observe the young couple in their first encounter even if she couldn't supervise or direct them. "She says therapy is for losers; that there isn't a problem that can't be solved with a few bottles of wine and a gold card. I'd tell you more, but this is a party and we're supposed to be having fun. Or celebrating something. I'm not sure which."

"Come on, Grace," Alex said, his arm around her shoulder. "Let's get some real food into that cute little belly of yours. Alcohol on an empty stomach is just inviting trouble."

Rather than move away from the man she had just met, Grace leaned into him, appreciating the warmth and solidness of his body, a reminder that there was someone who could literally stand between her and her abusive mother. "I assume you know the way?" she asked whimsically.

"If I didn't, I'd still find sustenance for you. You're as skinny as a maverick separated from the herd."

Thunk!

His soft-spoken comment was a reminder of her mother's advice to be thin to get a man's attention – to entice him to want to take care of little girl lost. Alex had certainly meant nothing by it, but it still made her feel as if her heart was a six-pound stone that had been dropped into a puddle of mud – dirty and worthless.

Grace was in a daze of disappointment as her broad-shouldered champion led her through the maze of gala attendees. Most of the chatter among the couples and small groups was about the upcoming regatta. Evidently, Robert Van der Cleft's wife was to make an appearance. Bets were being taken as to whether she'd be as stunning as she had been in the past. The woman was due to have a baby by Christmas. She insisted that regaining her figure would be 'no big deal;' that women who didn't take care of themselves were just lazy.

"I saw Zelda Van der Cleft last week," Alex said, holding his hands out to indicate a big belly. "I don't know much about pregnancies and babies, but if she can shrink down to a bikini body two months after she delivers, she deserves her husband's money."

"What's a shapely figure have to do with anything?" Grace asked, accepting the plate from the caterer with a nod and a quick smile. "Do you think a woman has to be built like a brick shithouse to be worthy of her husband's money…or his affections?"

"No, no, that's not what I meant. Oh, crap," Alex said, looking into the crowd, trying to find a reason to leave the uncomfortable conversation. "Hey, I see someone I have to speak with," he lied. "Would you excuse me?"

"Of course. I don't have any claim on you. It's your party. I'm just the teenager whose mother decided…" She blanched at her near confession, turned away, and swallowed her groan.

Certainly, he already knew or suspected that her mother had brought her to the party of rich single men to find a husband. What did he care about her and her feelings as long as he had a good time? She was just a warm garage he hoped to park his hot rod in before the night was over. If she wasn't available, there were plenty of other skinny, painted females around.

"What happened to him?"

Grace tensed at her mother's hissed question, the canapes and curled carrot sticks slipping off her plate onto the grass. She quietly counted to five, then answered, "He had to speak with someone. Why?"

"What? Why?" Victoria sputtered. She looked around to make sure they didn't have an audience, then whispered harshly through a fake smile, "You're here to make a good impression on at least two if not all three of the brothers. You haven't been here twenty minutes and you've already scared him off!"

"*Au, contraire, Mama.*" Grace stepped back to the ornate expanse of *hors d'oeuvres,* picked out a couple of crab puffs and at the same time, kicked her spilled food under the table. "He and I were connecting very well before he spotted an important business associate. You don't want him to lose his wealth by spending all his time with the new love of his life, do you?" Grace nodded to Alex who was speaking with an elderly gentleman. She gave a perfect Miss America wave to him, her smile as inviting as an engraved invitation.

Alex paused his conversation with his father's chauffeur when he saw Grace waving at him. He waved back. It looks like she needs to be saved from Mother Imperator. Rescue the damsel and I still might get lucky after all.

"Excuse me, Gregory," Alex said, accepting the fob with two keys. "This should do for tonight. Thanks for letting me in. I know it's supposed to be reserved for special occasions for Dad, but tonight is special for me. Or I hope it is."

Gregory followed Alex's gaze. The innocent standing beside Victoria Stillwater must be her daughter. He hadn't seen her since she was in grade school. If she was who Alex was planning to devour, he'd better make sure the young man spoke with his father first. There was more at stake than just a little romp in the rose garden.

"By the way," Gregory said, his hand covering Alex's key-clutching fist. "I believe your father wanted to speak with you on a very important matter before you get carried away. Make sure you let him know you'll be using the garden house, too. Oh, and he'll be interested to know that you've made the acquaintance of Hal Stillwater's daughter. Those two go way back. I'm sure he'll be thrilled at the prospect of a family alliance."

Alex's hand went limp at the hint of what was in store if he dallied with this new infatuation. Now he knew why Gregory had made the odd gesture of holding onto him. He would have dropped the keys like they were molten metal if he had known. "Why?"

"Does it make a difference if you're already attracted to her? She's a wonderful young lady. Her mother, not so much. Your father will let you know more. I do believe he's at the boathouse now."

"I smell a skunk," Alex said, his lips pursed in frustration.

"No, not a skunk," Gregory said. "That's Chuck. He's down the way, smoking with a few of the guests."

"Let's hope Dad doesn't have much to say. If I'm more than a few minutes, would you make sure Grace knows I won't be long?"

Gregory smiled devilishly. "I think I'll go over there now and make your excuse. I'd love to trade jabs with Victoria. I have no attraction to that woman at all, but it would almost be worth having an affair with her just to get it on tape. Having proof like that is the only way Hal would be able to divorce her."

"What are you talking about, Gregory? Have you been smoking with

23

Chuck and the boys? Your brain-mouth filter seems to be missing."

"As a matter of fact, I am slightly stoned. Of course, if I weren't, I wouldn't be admitting it. Nevertheless, talk to your father. You'll see why tonight my restraints are made of tissue, not leather or steel."

"Thanks for the warning." Alex reached up and patted Gregory on the shoulder with his free hand, letting the long-time chauffeur and family friend know that he'd regained his composure. "And see if you can insulate Grace from that monster mother of hers. I hate to say it, but that skinny Medusa is the number one reason I wouldn't want to get serious about Grace. She gives me the shivers."

"You and me both."

It didn't take long for Alex to find his father. Evidently, he had been watching for him. As soon as the son was over the rise and in view of the boathouse, 'Papa Doc' Armstrong was out from the shadows of the painted wood enclosure and out in the open.

"How's my favorite eldest son tonight?" his father asked brightly.

"I'm fine. Gregory said you wanted to talk to me. He also said to make sure to tell you that I've taken a shine to Hal Stillwater's daughter. She and I might be spending more time together," Alex said, then brought the cabin's keys up and jingled them.

"Hal Stillwater?" Papa Doc asked with a frown, then a smile rose as he remembered who he was. "Oh, I so would appreciate you getting along with his daughter. Her name's Faith, isn't it?"

"Close. It's Grace. She's here with her mother tonight. I have the sneaking suspicion that they crashed the party. At least, that's what I read in Silas's face."

"Yes, that man has a way of hiding his true feelings but letting what he wants to say be read with a twitch or sneer or lift of an eyebrow."

"So, Dad, what's going on? Gregory said you wanted to speak with me about something."

His father sighed and shook his head, the harbinger of bad news. "Looks like the big C might be back. I'm okay for right now, but I might need your help in making some transitions. I don't trust Ben farther than I can shove him, and Chuck has no interest in the business. In other words, the funds ain't what they used to be so don't go buying any new houses or Picassos."

"Dad, I haven't used your money for anything since I got the firm going. My architectural designs are in high demand. I didn't expect to be this successful for years. And if I'm reading you right, you're saying that all those high risk-great rewards stocks my sweet brother Ben told you to buy were not only duds, they were devastating."

"It wouldn't be so bad, but after the first round went south, he tried to get me to make it up with another investment. I finally had to say no when he tried to salvage it with a third swing. 'Three strikes and I'll be out,' I told him. I finally had to walk away. Anyhow, it can be repaired. If I can entice Stillwater to joint venture with me, we'll both be sitting pretty. There was some bad blood between us a few years back. And by that, I mean nearly twenty years ago. It had to do with that evil woman he wound up marrying." Papa Doc shuddered as he recalled her seducing him right after her honeymoon. "How he could live with that evil witch is beyond me."

"I'm in agreement there, even if I've never met him. You might want to stay here for a while. Sweet Grace is up there with her now. You don't want to bump into her."

"Thanks for the warning. Be nice to Grace. If you two spark up a romance, be polite. And careful. Not that I wouldn't want a grandchild or two, but if our two families are going to be working together, I don't want there to be animosity over a soured affair."

"Our family businesses working together," Alex corrected. "And I'm always gentle in my goodbyes. I learned from the master." He reached over and gave his father a quick hug. "And Master, please stop acting on Ben's crazy schemes. You can listen to him; just don't sign anything or give him money. Remind him that you started with nothing and have the world." He spread his hands out, indicating the vast properties. "He, on the other hand, started out with millions and is winding up with nothing."

"Well, just don't go rubbing it in. He already has short bald-man syndrome. He doesn't need any more insecurities. Now, go put a smile on that young woman's face. And see if you can get one of those *paparazzi* to get a picture of the two of you for the tabloids. That will definitely work in our favor."

"No problem there. I'm sure Old Mother Stillwater has already nudged them in that direction. Plus, all I'd have to do is look like I'm trying to avoid them, and they'll be on me like gnats on a jelly donut. I'll tell you all about it at lunch tomorrow. Or not, depending on how the evening goes."

"Go! No details required," Papa Doc said. Just don't do anything that would piss off her father.

Alex half-walked, half-sprinted up the hill, his pace quickening when he saw Grace turn to watch him approach.

"I thought you'd ditched me," she said, her eyes squinted in playful admonishment.

"I couldn't get back here fast enough," Alex said, glad to see that Mother had left the immediate area. "One important conversation led to another. By the way, the last one was with my father. He remembers you from long ago. Did we ever meet?"

"Not that I recall," Grace answered. "I don't think I've ever met any of my father's friends or their families. All social events are coordinated by Mother. Maybe she knows your father."

"Shush," Alex said, then winked. "Let's not talk about parents tonight, shall we? How about a walk. I have something special I'd like to show you."

"If you mean ditch my mother, I'm all in, even if it's just to watch windmills turn."

"Not quite as exciting," Alex said drolly, then kissed the side of her hair. "Sorry, I probably shouldn't have done that. Must be the champagne."

"I'd like to think at least a little bit of it was me."

"All of it was you. The alcohol removed the last little bit of inhibition. Come on, let's split. If your mother tries to give you any flack, just tell her the host wanted you to mingle. Or to show you off, depending on how she feels about me."

Grace opened her mouth to continue the playful banter, then shut it again and silently considered what to say. She decided it was best to remain mysterious; to squeeze his arm playfully and remain mum. She'd let him lead. Anything was better than going back to Mother.

Ah, smart woman. Not too gabby. She knows it's better to be coy and mysterious than chatty and annoying. Alex looked around for the ever-present society photographers. Drat! The one time he wanted them in his face, they were taking a bathroom break. Or with the marijuana smokers.

"Let's walk this way," Alex suggested, rerouting them to the garden house via the shrubbery maze where the pot party was.

A hundred yards into their trek, Grace couldn't help but ask, her nose twitching, "Are there skunks around here?"

"Are you kidding? This is a high society party. There are dozens of skunks!" Alex laughed at his own joke, glad that she was chuckling, too. And then he saw them: two of the most ambitious *paparazzi* on the eastern seaboard. He looked over and caught Jimmy's eye and winked. *Got one for you. It's okay to follow.*

Jimmy nudged his partner, causing the man to quickly drop the joint and step on it, hiding his evidence. "Huh? Oh, yeah. Good find. They're going to eat this one up," he whispered. "She's a hottie. Young, too. Do you know who she is?"

"Not a clue," Jimmy answered. "I'll let Jaylene figure that one out. She knows everyone and their kids. Let's just hope for his sake that's she's legal. Looks like he's taking her up to the garden house."

"Yup," the assistant whispered. "The infamous house of deflowering."

Jimmy glared at him and he rephrased the comment. "Okay, so most of the gals who go up there aren't innocent, but quite a few petals have been pushed and poked within those four walls."

"Yeah," Jimmy chuckled, "what I wouldn't give to have a spy camera in there. We'd never have to chase society snobs and actors again."

Jimmy started following the couple, knowing his backup cameraman was running ahead, snapping photos of their approach to the hideaway. *And if I can sneak in after their tryst, odds are that there's already a hidden video camera. All I have to do is snag the tape. I don't even have to sell it to the highest bidder. I'll just let it be known that I have it and get a monthly blackmail check from the family!*

"And here's one of the most beautiful gardens on the eastern seaboard," Alex said, opening the gate of the white picket fence.

"How beautiful!" Grace said. "Is this where you stay or is this just for *special* occasions?" she asked, winking at him.

Alex moved closer, changing the atmosphere of their casual friendship with his nearness, their skin-to-skin contact hopefully leading them into the lover zone. "I think you still have a little champagne in your system," he cooed into her hair, nuzzling her ear, making sure there wasn't a tree or building in the way of the photographer's lens.

"Very little," Grace said softly and turned to look at him in the soft light afforded by the garden's floodlamp. "And I think I could get used to the taste. Do you happen to have more inside?"

"Ooh, I like that," Alex said. He gently touched her elbow again, leading her to the front porch. He pushed in the access code and opened the door. Looking back into nothingness, he shook his head briefly, letting Jimmy know the photoshoot was over. The rest of the evening was just for him and his latest lady love.

"Are you ready for what waits inside?" he asked.

Grace's fake smile fell as fear covered her in a nervous sweat. It hadn't been too bad – the teasing had actually been kind of fun – but now it was pay-up time. Could she be intimate with someone other than Dusty? Her blank features darkened as she considered her options. Or her single option. It was either spread her legs for the handsome and charming man or go home with Mother. Try to find as many likable aspects of the billionaire's son or listen to her abusive parent chastise her for being a failure. Or worse: feel her mother's blows. Yes, bring on the liquor. Hopefully, it would make it all tolerable. At least Mother wasn't trying to hook her up with some ancient rich widower.

    ***

"Are you sure she knew where I was?" Grace asked, pulling the sheets up over the bottom of her face to contain her morning breath.

"Positive," Alex said. "I texted Silas and asked him to tell your mother that you and I had made plans for the rest of the evening."

"What kind of plans did you say?"

"I didn't. I left that up to him. He's pretty creative. He reads people well. He'd be able to tell if she needed to hear that I was flying you up to New York City to watch the opening of a highly acclaimed off-Broadway show or take you out for a midnight sail. Or anything else."

"So, this is a usual party night for you? Find a sweet young thing and have your way with her?"

"No," Alex said, then chuckled. "Now, come on. We're both adults. Or at least you did tell me you were eighteen. That means that legally you're an adult, even if you don't have a lot of life experience under your belt." He looked over at her clothes laid over the chair beside the bed. "Or lack of belt. No, most of the women who come up here are older and more experienced. I try to stay away from anyone who is marriageable if that even is a word."

"I believe it is," Grace said dryly, remembering that she still had to bed at least one more of the brothers. "Does that mean the women you usually 'entertain' are already married?"

"I should be ashamed to admit it, but I'm not. Yes, married women are very good lovers. They know what they're doing. Or rather, they are more adventurous. From what they tell me, once they've married, their love life goes downhill. It's the same three-minute special for sex, once or twice a month. Maybe more often if she has an extensive library of porn videos and exotic apparel and knows how to put on a show."

"Ew! Really? You'd think that being in love with your mate would be enough," Grace said. The words echoed in her head as she realized where she was and with whom. She had just played the whore. She was no better than the horny man in front of her who took advantage of cheating wives by giving them an afternoon or evening of carnal kicks. There hadn't been any love involved in what she had done last night. It was strictly booze and friction. And frustration.

"Love and marriage don't necessarily go hand in hand," Alex said as casually as if he was telling her how to spell cat. "And I hate to say it, but from where I stand, the love a couple has in the beginning quickly fades after being married. Maybe it never was love but only an infatuation. Then again, it could be it's the commitment itself – feeling trapped with only one sex partner, home, or life goal. Or it could also be that the added responsibility of living up to your mate's expectations sucks the pleasure out of everything."

"Or maybe marriage really is just money and obligations," Grace said, her stomach churning as she thought about her parents.

"Marriage? Money and obligations? How novel," Alex said, then popped up out of bed. "Be back in a flash, then you can take all the time you need in the bathroom. I'll call in for breakfast to be brought over unless you want to go out somewhere. Options are to the big house or anywhere in the world the family jet flies to."

"I'll let you know after freshening up," Grace said, then rolled over and pulled the satin sheets over her head. How did I wind up here? And how can I get myself out of this mess? What did my mother do to Dusty? Ah, crap! Will he even want me back after this? I might as well be dead!

True to his word, Alex was out of the bathroom in a short two minutes. He

28

stood above her shield of sheets and realized he felt guilty. *She didn't want this, I know she didn't. I need to help her get her head straight or there could be trouble. The last thing Dad needs is another fiasco. Ben's given him enough to deal with. If I can get her feeling good about herself, at least she won't be a liability.*

"Would you like coffee when you get out of the shower?" he asked. "I have a little espresso machine here. I make a killer cappuccino."

Grace peered up at him, a smile emerging despite her dire circumstances. His confident voice was a helping hand, offering to help her out of her world of shame. He was a bulwark between her and her mother. She'd be smart to make use of him until she had to face her mother again. She sat up, pulling the sheet over her breasts as she did, then realized he had seen and touched pretty much every bit of flesh and hair on her body the night before. Why hide herself now?

"Coffee? Sure, why not. I feel bad that I don't have any clean clothes to wear. I think my little black dress is a little overkill for breakfast attire," she said, giggling at the thought.

"Don't worry about it." Alex pulled open the hall closet door, exposing a long line of color-coordinated jogging suits. "Just pick your color and length. It's not that I'm a Lothario…"

"Just accommodating," Grace finished. "You know, you really are a nice person. I mean…"

"Nothing you say before your first cup of coffee can be held against you. Take as long as you want to get ready, but sooner is better. It looks like someone forgot to stock the breadbox with fresh pastries." His stomach growled at the word. "Cappuccino with extra cream is going to have to suffice for a while."

She dropped the sheet and stood up. "I didn't bring any makeup, either. Not that I wear much when I do bother with it." She strutted to the closet, suddenly feeling brazen. She swiped aside the neutral-tone clothes and picked out a neon pink suit, checking the length of the pants. "This will do."

"There are a few dozen pairs of new panties in the top drawer there. Sorry. I don't do bras."

Grace stuck out her chest, proud of her perky breasts. "I don't either. I think I'll pass on the panties, too." She saw his drop-jawed stare, taking in her perfect form. "You'd better get started with the coffee, dear. I'm very low maintenance. As long as there's soap and a towel, I'm set."

"Huh? Oh, yeah. It's all in there," he stammered. *Maybe she is worth keeping around…*

Chapter 5: The Morning After

"You're right. You do make a great cappuccino," Grace said, sipping the hot contents, leaning forward just in case, cautious of spilling it on her borrowed clothes. Or new clothes. Certainly they weren't passed back and forth between liaisons!

"Where to for the real food?" she asked, eager to get out of her head and away from all the drama that lived there.

"There's usually a big morning-after brunch up at the main house. I doubt if anywhere we go would be able to match it. Plus, it's closer; just a quick jaunt up the hill."

"How about a slow stroll up the hill; with sunglasses," Grace suggested. "I think I have my first hangover."

"Ah, I have a remedy for that. A little crème de menthe will complement the cappuccino plus cool it down. Sorry, I got a little distracted when I was steaming the milk. I would say, 'Where have you been all my life,' but besides sounding trite, you were a minor when I was really looking for someone to…to travel with."

Grace caught his little stutter of infatuation but figured she'd let it slide. After all, neither one of them had eaten yet and a few hours earlier, he had expended a lot of energy with his lovemaking.

Scratch that. With having sex. Despite just having stepped out of the shower, Grace suddenly felt dirty. What she needed now was oblivion. "Will there be mimosas?"

Alex's unexpectedly bright outlook on life suddenly muddied with the mention of alcohol. Had she always been a lush and hidden it? Or was she just confused and scared, ready to hide behind any substance that masked the real world? A glimmer of hope peeked in as he recalled her mother. "Orange juice, fresh squeezed, with or without the champagne, will be available," he said. "But this time, let's make sure you eat something before drinking. It's just my family around this morning. You can eat all you'd like without anyone *mother*-henning you."

Relief flooded over Grace with his spot-on words of assurance. She stuck her hand into the crook of his elbow and snuggled close to him, her spiked cappuccino held out at arm's length so neither of them got splashed. "You'd better watch yourself, Alexander Armstrong. I'm beginning to like you."

"Back at ya, Babe," he said and kissed the top of the head. "Come on. Let's go meet more of my family."

***

"Looks like you had company last night," the thirty-something-year-old man with a shaved head and a cocky attitude said.

"Hello, Ben," Alex said, his voice suddenly chilled and formal.

Grace, still holding him close, gently squeezed his arm, letting him know she wouldn't let the cad dressed like he was going to a photoshoot for the local yacht club intimidate her.

Alex sighed with relief at her show of confidence, his feigned smile becoming real with having a friend so near.

"Aren't you going to introduce me to your latest lady love?" Ben sneered, refusing to hold back with his words of intimidation.

"Whoa there, sons," Papa Doc said, stepping between the two, gently elbowing Ben away. "Alex, who is this charming young lady? I don't think I've had the pleasure of being introduced."

"Dad, this is Grace Stillwater. Grace, this is my father, Alexander Benjamin Charles Armstrong, usually called Papa Doc."

"A.B.C. Armstrong," Grace said, accepting his hand. "Don't tell me you have a sister named Deborah Elizabeth Frances Armstrong," she added with a grin.

"Close. Very close. Her first name is Delores, but you got the other names right. Dad said he was going to have a whole alphabet full of children. Mom did her best to shorten the list by giving us all three names."

"Did your dad make it to Xerxes Yosef Zachariah?" Grace asked brightly, then sipped her coffee.

"Nope. After my sister and me, he decided two children were enough for any family. Now, Alex said your last name was Stillwater. You don't happen to be Hal's little girl, do you?"

Grace stood up tall, straightened her shoulders, then playfully stood on her tiptoes, leaning into Alex to try and squeeze another half-inch of height. "Not so little anymore. I'm five foot seven in my bare feet."

"Well, you're bright and bold enough to bring a true smile to my son's face. He's never brought a friend to a morning-after breakfast. Welcome to the inner circle, Grace," Papa Doc said, saluting her with his cup of coffee.

Just as she saluted back, Ben said, "Oh, puh-lease..." and turned away.

"Is he always that cheerful?" Grace whispered sarcastically.

"Don't pay any attention to him," Alex said. "We don't. He's perpetually in a bad mood."

"Oh, Gracie dear!" a woman's shrill voice called from afar.

Grace dropped her cup, stepping back so she didn't get splashed. "Mother!" she hissed, then realized only Alex and Papa Doc had heard her guttural reaction of disgust.

Now it was Alex's turn to give her arm a squeeze of reassurance. He pulled her close and at the same time, looked to his father. "We might need some help here, Dad."

"Don't worry. I've known Victoria for years." He turned to Grace and whispered. "No offense, but she's a pain!"

"You have no idea," Grace whispered back, then stood up tall to face her intimidator, knowing she had at least two strong men at her back. No need to fear the fists today. At least, right now.

Victoria was adorned in the classiest workout wear available, but her hair and makeup were styled for an evening soiree. She behaved as if she was ready for a run on the beach – reaching up and stretching before making her final approach – but Grace and probably everyone else knew she was here to make a social appearance.

"I was sorry to hear you suddenly got ill last night," Victoria said. She lunged forward to stretch her leg, and the sudden movement in her direction caused Grace to take a step back.

A quick smile of domination flitted across Victoria's face at the fear shown. "I hope these wonderful men took good care of you," the caustic matriarch said, adding a wink to Alex.

Alex clenched his jaw, silently counted to three, but before he had composed himself enough to say a word, his father stepped in and took control. "I think it may have been a bit of food poisoning," Papa Doc said. "I insisted she stay the night. I take it Silas got the word to you?"

Now it was Victoria's turn to take a step back. "Oh, yes, he did. I hope I'm not intruding," she said, looking at the spread of food.

"Oh, no, no, no." Papa Doc took Victoria by the inner elbow, sternly but politely leading her away from the young couple and toward the chef making omelets to order. "Let's see what we can put together for you."

Papa Doc felt an inner glow of hope. Until Victoria showed up, it looked like Alex and Grace were only pausing for sustenance, ready to go back to the garden house and enjoy the weekend with each other. He'd been hoping for a solid relationship for Alex with a single woman. Grace was quite young but seemed to be down-to-earth; not flighty like women twice her age. Yes, he'd do whatever needed to keep Victoria the Viper away from the young couple and their blossoming relationship. He didn't know how much time he had left, but if he could be a grandpa before he died, his life would be complete.

Alex set his hand gently on Grace's shoulder and whispered in her ear, "Do you want to just grab a few pastries and take off? We can go anywhere you'd like. Maybe lunch on the Seine?"

"No passport. How about somewhere closer?" Grace looked to the garden house and grinned, then heard her mother's cackling laugh. "But not too close."

"Motorcycle, car, boat, or helicopter?" he asked.

"Really? I mean, how about helicopter? And how long until a pilot shows up?"

Alex used the silver tongs to add two croissants and a few pieces of roast beef and cheddar to his plate. "You're looking at him, sweetie."

Grace let go of his elbow and picked up a plate. "Oh, I am so ready to leave." She grabbed two cream cheese Danishes and said, "Now all I need is a cup of coffee to go."

"Whoop, whoop!" Alex said, mimicking a helicopter's rotor. "I sure didn't see this happening when I got my arm twisted into coming here last night. Best guilt trip ever."

"Ditto!"

∗

Alex rolled off of Grace. "I'm sorry. Sort of. I really hadn't meant to get anything started. It's just… Damn, woman! You're putting off some extra strong vibes or pheromones or something!"

"You have something going on there, too," Grace said, then started to chuckle. *Yeah, if I keep you in bed or at least wanting to have sex with me, I won't have to go back to my mother.* Her smile and her mirth evaporated as soon as she realized if she left her mother, she'd be giving up on her father and Sally, too.

"All right," Alex said, then took a quick drink of water from the bedside table. "First, what was so funny, and then how come it got so *unfunny* all of a sudden?"

Grace brought her chin up and decided she was done with lying. She wouldn't – couldn't – tell him everything, but what she told him would be the truth.

"Do you promise not to kick me out of bed – or at least your life – if I tell you a secret?"

"Cross my heart, hope to go broke…"

"You're so silly. That's one of the many characteristics I like about you." She took a deep breath, shut her eyes so she wasn't looking at him, and said, "My mother set us up. Or she kinda sorta made me at least try to seduce you. But…"

"Yeah, so," Alex said, then put his hand on her cheek. "Look at me."

Grimacing with embarrassment, Grace opened one eye and saw his concern, then opened her other eye.

"But," he prompted.

"But I didn't think I was going to like you. At least this much. You're a blast to be around. I mean, I have – or had – a boyfriend, and I'm pals with lots of guys at school, but you're nothing like them."

"I hope I have a few years of maturity on them. I'm sure most of them will grow up eventually. So, does this mean you're hanging around with me because you want to now, and not because your mother wants you to? It was kind of obvious when she dropped by that she was making sure the mouse had taken the bait."

"You, my dear friend," Grace said, crisscrossing the curly hairs on his chest, "are not a mouse. You are more of a man than I thought I could ever have.

33

So, now that I've said that, did I just cook the goose that laid the golden egg? Are you going to take me for a quick trip in your helicopter, and then I'll never hear from you again?"

"Nope."

"I mean, you'll probably have someone send me a Christmas card..."

"Grace, I'd like to spend Christmas Eve with you. I'm not a gambling man, but unless the world comes crashing down around us, I don't see any reason why we can't spend Christmas week in Sydney then sailing the warm waters toward Tahiti."

"Or making snowmen in Tahoe?"

"Tahoe or Tibet or wherever you want. But I really would like to take off before it gets too late. I can't fly at night yet. That's another level of certification. I was going to take a few more hours of class, but I think I just found another passion. Flying will have to wait."

Chapter 6: Ben the Broken Broker

Sunday morning

Alex received the call just moments after they had taken off. Grace could only hear one side of the conversation, but the scowl on his face made it clear that he'd received bad news. He turned the helicopter back to his starting point and set it down.

"That was the quickest touch and go I've ever made. I'm sorry about this. There's been a disaster at the job site. If there was any way I could get out of it, I would. This is too big to pass on to the job supervisor. My reputation as an architect and engineer, and the integrity of my company are at stake. Plus, the safety of the building's other wing might have been compromised with the collapse, and I might lose a few million bucks by missing a deadline... Promise me we can continue this weekend later?"

"I'm not going anywhere. At least, I hope you'll allow me to stay in the garden house. I sure don't want to go back to 'her!'"

"You can stay there, or you can have my suite at the big house. I'd rather you were there where my father can look out for you, though. Silas has been spending a lot of time with the old man lately. He's a good bouncer when need be. Both of them know your mother and will isolate you from 'her.' Besides, I think my dad has a little crush on you."

"If he does, it's a daddy crush. I've seen it before. He only had sons, right?"

"Yes, you're right. He's really excited about having you in the family," Alex said, then closed his eyes tight and groaned softly. "I mean..."

"No explanation required. I think we're both in happy shock. Don't spoil it with making excuses. Let's just go with the flow."

"Works for me. Just know that I'm a raging river right now. There's not a dam in the world that could stop me. But I do have to put everything on pause."

"Understood. And just for the record, I have those same surging, rushing feelings for you."

"No dam built..." Alex said, then paused, waiting for her to finish his thought.

"Could stop this feeling," she continued, then tiptoed up and kissed him. "I'll be waiting for you. Be safe."

***

Two days later

Back at the garden house to grab a change of clothes, Grace stopped looking through the colorful row of jogging suits to answer the door.

The chronically cranky and dour brother was there, dressed in a cable knit sweater and beige pleated slacks, a captain's hat on his shaved head. "Alex told me to come get you and bring you out to the job site. He felt really bad that he had to ruin your weekend and all," Ben said, his eye twitching.

Grace saw the tic but didn't know him well enough to discern whether he was lying or had a nervous disorder. It was true that Alex had felt horrible about cutting their trip short. She still didn't know if he had found out whether it was defective material – the supplier's fault – or a poor design – his fault. He'd been so busy that he hadn't had time to call. Just a few short texts of constant apologies. Maybe going to see him would help him relax and assuage his guilt.

"Don't worry about grabbing an overnight bag. I think he already has everything you need," Ben said, then turned away and whispered, "Hanging between his legs."

Grace glanced up and saw Ben's reflection in the mirror. She quickly looked away as soon as she saw what he had said. The last thing she needed was this weirdo finding out she had seen what he said.

"Oh, I'd like to stop in at the big house and say goodbye to your father and Silas," Grace said, looking around the room to see if she was forgetting something. She spotted her new sunglasses and grabbed them. "One more thing. I'll be right out," and went into the bathroom.

For no other reason than she had watched a parody of horror movies with her two favorite old men the night before – Papa Doc and Uncle Silas - Grace decided to leave a note just in case something weird was going on. She found one of the many pads and pens Alex kept scattered around for inspired notes or designs on the counter.

'1105 AM Tuesday. Ben picked me up to bring me to see you. You make me so happy!' Her hand twitched as she started to sign it. "Ah, what the heck." *'Love, Gracie.'*

"Is everything okay in there?" Ben asked.

Chills ran up Grace's arms at his voice. He was right outside the door, listening to her use the bathroom. What kind of pervert wanted to hear a woman pee? Another shiver. There were lots of weirdos out there. Money, power, and social status had nothing to do with that part of a person's personality. Nor did how wonderful his brother was.

Grace flushed the toilet and turned on the faucet. The note was on the vanity top, in plain sight. She opened the drawer containing Alex's shaving supplies and set the notepad and pen on top of his razor, underneath his comb. He'd find the note when he least expected it. Plus, the housekeeper didn't need to see their love notes.

"I'll be out in a sec. Would you grab a couple of bottles of water for me? Grab one for yourself, too. Alex says you never know if they'll have any on the job site."

Ben bit his bottom lip in frustration. This was taking a lot longer than he thought. He wanted to slip in and out before anyone saw his car. "I'm on it," he said. *And I'll be on you soon!*

The bathroom door popped open, startling Ben as he dropped the last of the water bottles into a cloth grocery bag. Looking up, he saw Grace with her arms in the air, securing her ponytail with a bright pink scrunchy. He felt himself harden at the thought of how he'd soon be with her, holding onto her bound hands as he...

"Are you okay?" Grace asked. "You look flushed."

"No, no. I mean, yes, I'm okay. I'm just in a hurry. Stress and blood pressure, you know. Or maybe you don't know. You've never been out in the real world, have you?" Ben said, holding the bag in front of his now bulging Dockers.

"I'm young but that doesn't mean I haven't experienced some of life's ups and downs. I'm ready; are you?"

Ben nodded, holding his lips together to keep back his smirk. *Oh, I am so ready for the ups and downs...*

***

"This doesn't look like a construction site." Grace said.

Ben pulled into his assigned parking spot at the suburban apartments he'd been downsized into. "Um, I need to grab a few things," he said, his eye twitching again. "Why don't you come up and see the place?"

Warning sirens blared in Grace's head. Whether the eye tic was lying or nerves, either one was a potential danger. "No, thanks. I'll wait for you out here." Grace reached over and pushed the window button. "Is this broken?"

"No. It won't work unless the key is in. Now, I want you to come up and see my apartment. It's not as nice as the garden house, but I think you'll enjoy it."

"I'd rather wait," Grace said and smiled, hoping he didn't see that he was scaring the piss out of her.

Ben reached in his pocket and felt the small handgun. He really didn't want to resort to it yet. "Suit yourself. It's just that I was able to convince Alex to break away for an hour. He's up there waiting for you now."

Grace leaned forward and looked around the parking lot. "I don't see his car."

"He had one of the guys on the job drop him off while I went to pick you up. I'll take off and let you two have some time together. You'd better make it quick, though. He only gets an hour, then his ride will return to take him back."

Anticipation at seeing the new love of her life overrode Grace's common sense. "Are you sure?"

"Why would I lie?" Ben said, then turned away before she could see his eye twitching again. He opened his door and stepped out. "Go ahead and stay here if you'd rather. I'll be right back. I have to tell him you didn't want to see him."

"No, don't do that," Grace said, then paused. "Hey. Why doesn't he come out?"

"Oh, dear sweet innocent," Ben said, his head shaking back and forth in mild admonishment. "That would mean he'd have to get dressed again. As I said, he only has an hour."

"Okay. If you say so."

Ben hurried toward the outside stairs, almost running to the first step, then taking them two at a time to unlock the door. He knocked on it twice, said, "We're here, Alex," then opened it.

Grace followed behind him, her face aglow with anticipation as she stepped inside.

Ben jerked her by the arm, making sure she was completely in, then slammed the door, deadbolting the extra lock with a black key.

"Where's Alex?" she asked. She looked around the living room. A cheap futon couch and cardboard moving boxes were the only furnishings. "And why did you lock the door? You aren't sticking around to watch, I hope."

"Alex is in here," he said, leading her to the bedroom. "And I won't be here to watch." He opened the door and shoved her in. "I'm here to participate," he growled.

Grace stumbled and fell to the floor, catching herself before she did a face plant. "What? What's going on?"

"This room's all set up for you. Just you. I bet you like this sort of stuff. Cuffs, whips, and bondage. I even guessed at your size and bought you a cute little outfit to wear. Not that there was much sizing required for a thong and push up bra. You can do without the boots, I suppose. I'm more of a toe man, anyhow."

Grace gasped at the array. Black leather and metal studded bands and chains hung from eyebolts in the ceiling, belts and braided twists of whips and what looked like collars were draped from the spindles of the four-poster double bed. "What? Couldn't afford a king-sized bed?" she asked in nervous fear.

"Why spend the bucks when I'll be on top of you? That's where you really belong, you know: beneath me. Quivering with anticipation. Waiting for the next lash of my whip…" Ben reached up and grabbed her ponytail and twisted, pulling her head down to his face. "If you ever want to see that big brother of mine alive, you'll do as I say. Oh, and in that department," he patted his bulging trousers with his free hand, "I'm the big brother. You are so gonna love The Dominator."

Grace pivoted away from him, then reached up and punched his elbow, bending it the wrong direction. Ben yelped and released his grip in pained reflex. "You bitch!" he screamed, swinging wildly with his undamaged arm.

"I will not be hurt again," she growled. "You are so wrong about me. I *hate* pain and I have no desire to be underneath you or even see

38

your…your…dominator dick!"

"Ah, but you are fond of my brother, are you not? Did you ever wonder why you haven't heard from him? Anyone can send a text from his phone." Ben held up Alex's cellphone.

"Where is he? If you've hurt him, I swear I'll…"

"You'll what? If you want to see him, you'll do as I say."

"How do I know you haven't done something to him already? Give me some assurance and I'll comply."

Ben shrugged one shoulder, still cradling his hyperextended elbow. "Sounds reasonable. If it will make you more *accommodating…*"

He opened the closet door and kicked twice, awakening his hostage.

"Umph!"

Alex was bound and gagged; his eyes squinted in anger at seeing his brother. His captor.

"I brought you a surprise," Ben said, then moved aside, allowing him to view Grace.

"Omph!" Alex squealed, squirming with ferocity, trying again to escape his bindings.

"I just thought it was time for a little payback. After all these years of watching my older brother - Daddy's tall, smart, and handsome pride and joy – get all the best in life, I figured it was time for him to see how I roll."

Ben turned to Grace – now aghast and pale – and grinned in delight. "Get dressed," he said, nodding to the black leather bra and thong hanging on the footboard. "But first, strip slowly. I want to watch both you and dear brother squirm."

Alex rocked back and forth, grunting in renewed frustration at being bound and gagged. His hands and feet were numb, his neck and jaw a cold, dull ache. No doubt Ben would shoot him before his jealousy-fueled revenge was complete. How else could he get rid of the evidence of kidnap and rape? Whether he lost his hands and feet didn't matter now. He'd chew through his brother's neck if he had to. What he had to do was spare Grace. He'd heard the rumors that Ben's movie library was stacked with videos of bondage and sadism. He couldn't wait to see if his brother would try to re-enact the perversions. He had to try to do something.

"Ooh, look at his wiggle," Ben said, then kicked at Alex again.

"Leave him alone," Grace said, rushing forward to intercede.

"Nuh, uh, uh," Ben said, pulling the gun from his trouser pocket. "You wouldn't want to make love to me with his brains all spattered over the walls, would you?"

"I'll never make love to you!" Grace hissed. She paused, realizing her voice was all she had left. "Help! Rape! Fire!"

Ben put the pistol back in his pocket so he could use both hands, then tackled Grace to the bed. He shoved his forearm over her throat, throttling her, choking off both her breath and ability to scream. "If you make one more noise above a whisper, I'll shoot you and make him watch. You do know what necrophilia is, don't you?"

Alex had been stunned by the attack on his girlfriend, the woman he had decided to marry. Now that her life was on the line, his protective instincts were back, recharged with more adrenaline. He pitched himself forward and rolled towards the bed as his brother lectured.

"Necrophilia," Ben explained, his voice deepening with the excitement of being all-powerful, "is having sex with a corpse. Abuse of a corpse they call it if you get caught. Of course, I have plans for both of you. They'll never find your remains. I'm going to get big bucks for this movie." He looked up at the video camera mounted on a tripod in the corner. "Not only bondage but a snuff movie, too. That ought to be enough to finance a fresh start in Thailand. I understand they're a lot more flexible in their sexual mores. Lots of movie opportunities for an experienced director and producer. And well-hung American actor."

Grace gasped and sputtered, trying to catch a breath as he held her down. "Oh, I don't want to stifle you yet," he said, pulling his arm away just enough for her to breathe. "We have to get you aroused and satisfied before we get rid of you."

"Why?" Grace whispered hoarsely.

"Why? Revenge, of course. Don't you know that success is the best revenge there is? I plan on making more money than either of my brothers. Not that Chuck is worth a dime. That faggot does nothing but work in free clinics and give away all he owns. You see, rumor is that the old man is ready to kick the bucket. Haven't you noticed how gray he is? He's eaten up with cancer. I'll be the successful son now, even if I live in another country. I guess it doesn't matter whether I get an inheritance from him or not. As long as Alex doesn't, I'll be happy. He already has too much of everything. Including you."

Grace couldn't hear Alex struggle, so he was either passed out – unlikely – or up to something. She needed to keep Ben talking. "So, does that mean that you don't want Alex around anymore? What are you going to do with him? He's bigger than you. That's a lot to haul away."

"I told you," Ben hissed in her face, his spittle of rage sprinkling her, making her flinch. "I'm bigger, not him!"

"Haven't you heard," Grace said, an ethereal calm coming over her at the prospect of rescue by her bound lover, "that bigger isn't better? A woman craves tenderness."

Ben's face flushed with anger. He sat up and straddled Grace, then bent forward, his arms pushing her shoulders deep into the bed. "You know what? I really don't care what you or any other woman wants. All I care about is me! Why haven't you figured that out yet?"

Grace panted in renewed fear, his firmness on her belly, her arms pinned by the pressure to her shoulders. She was immobile.

But he was also fully dressed and so was she. Those two impediments would allow Alex time to rescue her before she was raped. Or he was murdered.

"Oh, you think I didn't hear my *little* brother coming up behind me?" Ben sneered, then hopped off of Grace and the bed. He kicked at Alex, knocking him from his belly crawl position onto his back like an upturned turtle bound in duct tape and rope. "There. You'll have a better view that way. Strip, woman. Now! And make it worth my while or I'll start making a bloody mess out of his miserable body."

"No, no! You're better than this, Ben," Grace pled, her hands up in supplication. "Please don't. This situation is recoverable. We can get you help. You're just under a lot of stress. Your business might be in trouble but your father…"

Ben's fist flew out and punched Grace in the mouth as the word father began to form, her plea ended with the solid tooth-loosening smack.

Alex rolled back over, the gag in his mouth tighter with his struggles. "Don't you listen, boy!" Ben hollered, kicking him onto his back again. This time he left his booted foot on Alex's throat. "It wouldn't take much to finish you off, but I want you to watch."

"Leave him alone! I'll do whatever you want. Just let him live. No. I mean, let him live whole. Don't hurt him. We'll both keep this whole fias…event a secret. Please."

Tears fell from Grace's face, her fear and begging giving Ben the sexual arousal he craved. This was better than he had ever dreamed. It wasn't some old hag his brother was involved with. This one was young, barely broke in. She might even still be a teenager. His cock grew harder at the thought.

"You're mine," he hissed, then stomped on Alex's throat, shutting out the noisome grumbles and whimpers his brother still managed to make. "No distractions. Even if he doesn't get to watch a live performance, I'll set it on auto replay. He can watch me plow your sweet little pussy until he draws his last breath…"

Thunk! Crash! Slam!

"What in the hell is going on here?"

Ben screeched, "Chuck?" then scrambled to his feet.

Grace rolled off the bed and onto the floor, furiously grasping at the duct tape and rope that bound Alex. Her fingers couldn't find a weak spot, so she jumped up and ran to the kitchen. Just about everyone in the world had a knife in there.

Suddenly, she was aware of loud voices, contentious yelling and body thunks as the two men fought. She didn't care. Grace had one mission: get Alex unbound so he could breathe. "Finally!" she huffed, grabbing a steak knife from the scatter of silverware in a kitchen drawer. She rushed into the bedroom, ducking just as Ben swung wide, missing the hero, the momentum causing the sadist to fall backward.

"I got you, Alex," Grace soothed, ignoring the fist falls and thuds, her fingers searching for a spot to slip the knife under. "Ah, crap." She turned his blue face to the side and began sawing atop his duct-taped neck, trying not to go all the way through to his skin.

"Here, let me," the stranger said, then whipped out his own knife and deftly sliced through the cut Grace had started. He ripped the tape away, then turned Alex's head back and began mouth-to-mouth resuscitation.

"Do you know CPR?" he asked between breaths.

"No, but I'll try," she said.

"Not yet," he replied, then handed her the knife. "Cut."

Grace bent to the task of slicing through yards of duct tape and twisted nylon rope, glad for the diversion the task gave her but frustrated that she couldn't do more. When she got up to unbind his other side, she glanced around the small apartment, looking for Ben. He was laid out on the floor by the front door, his leg askew. It was either broken or his knee was trashed – or both. Her assailant's mouth hung open, his chest rising and falling slowly. Knocked out but not dead. Either way, he wasn't going anywhere on his own power.

"Did you call 911?" she asked.

"Would you? There has to be a phone around here somewhere."

Grace laid Alex's hands out straight, hoping the sudden rush of blood didn't injure them further. Her initial search for the phone was cautious - she didn't want to disturb anything that might be evidence – then suddenly became desperate. Lamps and boxes were knocked over as she looked for a phone.

"Check the walls for the outlet," the man said, then he bent back to breathing for Alex. "If you can't find it, run to a neighbor's. He's in rough shape."

Grace looked at every wall outlet but when she finally found the one for a phone line, it was empty. "I'll be right back," she said. "And thanks."

She knocked on three doors before anyone answered. "Yes," the older woman drawled, then looked up and saw Grace's battered face. "Oh, my. Are you all right?"

"No," Grace said, then shoved her way past the concerned crone. "Where's the phone? My friend needs an ambulance."

"Right there on the counter, dear. Help yourself, but please don't make any long distance...

Grace tuned out the woman as she dialed emergency services. "Yes, ma'am. I need an ambulance. No, I don't know the address, but it's two doors down from the one I'm calling from. Just send the medics and I'll wait in the parking lot and show them which apartment. Please hurry. Yes. His name is

Alexander Armstrong. Shoot, I don't know his medical history. He's been strangled. Someone's up there giving him CPR right now. No, I don't want to hold. There's nothing I can tell you other than his name. Yes, go ahead and send a police officer, too. Yes, there was a crime committed. I just hope it wasn't murder."

Chapter 7: Chuck the Invisible

"There's nothing more we can do for him now," the man said as they watched the ambulance pull away, wishing he could reach out and comfort her. "Damn! I wish I'd been here sooner!"

"I'm sorry. Who are you?"

"Don't be sorry," he replied, wiping away his tears. "I'm Chuck. The other brother. The one no one talks about."

"You gave mouth-to-mouth to one brother and beat the snot out of the other?" Grace remarked, then snorted in disbelief. "Um, I think they're going to be talking about you for a long time."

Chuck laughed and shook his head. "I doubt it. Actually, I prefer a low profile. I take it you're Grace."

"How'd you know?"

"I may not be tight with my brothers, but Dad and I are close. The other two just don't pay attention to us. Alex is a workaholic and partier who just found the love of his life. And Ben is the investment broker who is always going after the next bigger, better stock or IPO, then brooding for months when it doesn't pan out."

"Actually, from what little I know about Ben, you're being quite generous in your description." Grace paused. "Wait! You said Alex just found the love of his life. You mean me?"

"Duh! He and I didn't get a chance to talk after he met you, but Dad and Silas went on and on about how they've never seen him so happy. Actually, they were both concerned and that's why I'm here."

"I was wondering about that…"

"It seems that no one has heard from Alex for two days. I know he has one of those new cellphones that can send messages like a pager."

"Yes. He gave me one, too. I left it at the house. He sent me a few text messages, but he never called me."

"Yup. That's what Dad said, too. That doesn't sound like him. I called his office and they said he had a new girlfriend and would be incommunicado for a week. That didn't sound like him, either. New girlfriends are usually bored wives and never last more than a few hours at a time."

Grace raised her eyebrows but remained mute.

"Sorry. That was probably too much information. So, missing brother number one and mystic message on my answering machine from brother number two."

"What was the message?"

"'Do you know where I can get a hurry-up passport and visa to Thailand? Something's just come up.' That meant to me that he was probably in trouble with the securities exchange commission again and had to leave the country. I came over here to see if I could help. I certainly didn't find what I expected!"

"Do you think he's going to be okay? I mean, can we go to the hospital and wait there?"

Chuck looked up and saw the apartment door was open, police tape draped across it. "Let me make sure they don't have any more questions for me. Or you. You don't mind if I speak for both of us, do you?"

"Actually, I'd appreciate it. I don't know what I'm doing."

Chuck reached up and touched her forehead. "A little clammy. You might be in shock. We'll get some fluids in you; maybe a little juice or soda. The sugar will do you good. Wait here."

Grace glanced up at the apartment and got a shiver. "Yeah, staying here's fine."

A short minute later, Chuck was back. "I gave him my number and said he could contact both of us there."

Her back straightened in terror at Chuck's words. He noticed it and changed his approach. "I gave him my pager number. I figure we'll both be at the hospital until Alex is out of trouble. After that, I hope you plan on staying with Dad. That is unless you have another place. Sorry, I don't know anything about you other than everyone who meets you is infatuated with you."

"I'm beginning to hate the word infatuated."

"Well, Ben's screwed no matter what. I don't think you'll ever have to worry about him. I don't think there's a death sentence in this state for kidnapping or attempted murder, but a life sentence sounds like a definite possibility."

"Or life in a mental institution."

"I pity the poor doctors there," Chuck said, then nodded to the dinged and faded van. "My chariot awaits."

"You're sure you're part of this family?" Grace asked, suddenly wary. Then she remembered how he had just come in and literally saved the day for her. "But even if you're not, thanks for what you did."

"I had about twenty years of getting-even punches pent up. It was definitely my pleasure. I just wish I'd been here sooner."

Grace accepted his help getting in, then reached out and put her hand on his forearm. "I'm just glad you weren't a minute later."

Chuck gasped and straightened up as he realized what he could have walked in on. "Oh, Lord. I didn't even think of it that way…"

"Come on." Grace pulled the seatbelt across her and clicked it in. "Let's get to the hospital."

***

"We can go through this way," Chuck said, leading her through the emergency room, past the nurses' station.

"Hey, Baby Doc! What are you doing on this side of town?"

"Slummin'!" Chuck answered back, slapping his hand down on the counter and grinning. "Nah, I got someone special in here I want to see."

"Hey, is that your girlfriend?" one of the younger nurses asked.

"Maybe," he said, then touched Grace's elbow. "Play along," he whispered, then led her through the corridor.

As soon as they were out of earshot, Grace pulled away. "Play along?" she asked. "What? Who?"

"You're going to hear about it sooner or later," Chuck said, looking around to make sure they were alone. He saw the chapel and pulled her into it. "I'm gay but still in the closet, shall we say. A few of the nurses have been hitting on me. Actually, both male and female nurses. If I pretend to have a girlfriend, both groups will leave me alone."

"Groups? You have groups of nurses hitting on you?"

"Not really groups. Let's just say factions. I think they're all just fishing, trying to get me to come out one way or the other."

"Sorry, Chuck, but I've led a very sheltered life. I've read some stories about gay people. You're just regular folks with yens for the same gender, right?"

"Wow. That's blunt. Blunt but accurate."

"Yeah, well, you should hear my mother rant and rave about how queers are ruining America. I figured if she was that adamant about it, something had to be wrong." Grace looked around the small chapel and saw the clock. "Do you think he's out of surgery now?"

"If they had to perform surgery, he's probably still there. Or at least, in post-op. The only thing he might have needed would be a tracheotomy." Chuck pointed to the soft spot under his Adam's Apple. "Ben messed him up pretty good."

"I was worried about his hands but being able to breathe is way more important."

"Come on. I'll see what I can find out."

"Won't they tell me anything?" Grace asked.

"Nope. You're not his wife or mother or sister and probably don't have medical power of attorney. You don't, do you?"

"Alex and I weren't together that long; just long enough to know that neither of us saw an end to our relationship."

"That's good to hear. He was due to have a good woman. At least, one he didn't have to share…Sorry, that was crass. I think I have a little shock going on, too."

"Here," Grace said, offering him her can of soda. "I'm not afraid of your cooties."

"Yeah, being queer ain't contagious, darling," Chuck said, then took a long swallow of the lemon-lime soda. He handed it back to her and put a comforting arm around her shoulder. "I'll never hit on you, but right now, I need you next to me more than you'll ever know."

"Back at ya," Grace said and snuggled into him.

***

The two walked down the hall, their easy pace identical and comfortable. "So, how come everyone knows you here?" Grace asked.

"I'm a doctor. I don't operate out of here, but I do have courtesy privileges."

"Which means?"

"Which means if I ask, they'll tell. I'm not a surgeon, anyhow. I mean, I can cut and sew, but I run a clinic on the other end of town. You know, the proverbial wrong side of the tracks?"

"Helping those who can't afford to pay?"

"Pretty much. Say, look up. See who's here?"

Papa Doc was as gray as dirty springtime snow and just as precarious as he stood up, Silas quick at his side to steady him. "Any word yet?"

"I was just going to ask you the same thing, Dad."

"And you?" Papa Doc asked Grace. His hand gently explored the side of her face where Ben had punched her. "Ouch. Looks like a good chunk of steak would help that. Did he, um, do anything else?"

"Other than just about kill Alex, no. Pretty much intimidation. He would have, though, if Chuck hadn't interceded."

Grace looked up and saw Chuck in a different light. Yes, he was still the tall, good-looking man who had come to the rescue, but he also looked like a younger version of his father. All the men in the family had broad shoulders, strong jawlines, and bright blue eyes, but Alex had darker hair and a more robust nose. Chuck's nose was finer, almost feminine. She shuddered as she started to consider Ben, then blocked him out. He couldn't bully her anymore, even as a memory. She wouldn't allow it.

"Are you all right?" Chuck asked, feeling her falter. He squeezed her close again. "We have you: Dad, Silas, and me. And Alex when he gets better. All of us are here for you. You know that, right?"

Grace nodded, the tears starting to slip out. "I just want this day to be over. I want to go back in time to three days ago..."

"Oh, Gracie! Hello, Gracie, dear."

Grace slumped at the sound of her mother's voice. She looked up at Chuck. "Tell me I'm hallucinating. That isn't my mother, is it?"

Chuck looked up at the ultra-thin woman walking down the hall, rushing but trying to look like she was on a catwalk, one foot placed in front of the other in a practiced manner. "It's a woman, but nothing about her reminds me of you."

"Yeah, that's her mother," Silas said. "Put on your shit boots."

Papa Doc and Grace both sniggered into their hands, then looked at each

47

other, comfortable in their identical reaction to Silas's spot-on declaration.

"Boots on, strapped, and tied," Chuck said softly through a clenched smile as he watched the woman approach. He gave Grace a quick cuddle of assurance then waited for the drama that was sure to come.

"Gracie, darling. Where have you been? I went to the Armstrong's to see if you'd recovered. I was sure you'd be better by now."

Chuck looked down, his movement causing Grace to look up. She had a moment of clarity, realizing this woman had nothing on her now. "Why are you here, Mother?"

"Oh…I…ahem. I thought that if you were severely sick, you would have been admitted to the hospital."

"You could have called," Grace said, her voice icy. "Certainly, they would have told a mother if her daughter was a patient; no medical power of attorney required."

Victoria gasped at the remark, surprised that her little girl – so easily intimidated four days ago – was suddenly secure and independent. Or at least had found no less than three strong men to protect her. "Oh, and your little friend Dusty came by looking for you," she lied, an evil glint in her eye. *Don't mess with me, Missy! I can still play dirty.*

Grace tensed, held her breath, then let it out. "That's funny," Grace lied back. "I talked to him just yesterday. He said he joined the army because his dad got a new job upstate. I wished him well and that was that. Are you sure it was Dusty who called?" *I know you're lying. Get out of my life and out of my head!*

"Actually," Victoria said, strutting over to sit next to Papa Doc, "I heard that Alex had been involved in an accident. He didn't crash his helicopter, did he?"

Papa Doc and Silas looked at each other, wondering how she could know Alex was in the hospital. A smile started to bloom on Silas's face. "You've been talking to Jimmy, haven't you?" he asked.

"Well, I may have met him at coffee this morning…" Victoria said, a sudden blush rising to show through her three layers of foundation.

"Victoria, Victoria, Victoria," Papa Doc said condescendingly, patting her hand like she was a six-year-old. "You have to quit following after the *paparazzi*. You'll get more gray hairs than Lady Clairol can keep up with." He looked at her temple, noticing the telltale smear of a recent dye job that hadn't been completely cleaned up. "All is fine here. It was just a little incident. Nothing major. Grace has agreed to stay at the house and keep him company while he recovers."

"What happened?" Victoria asked.

Chuck stepped in. "That's private," he said. "Family only. Now, if you don't mind, I had asked everyone here for a family meeting and we were just getting started."

48

"And who are you?" Victoria snapped. Her eyes widened as she realized that he looked just like Papa Doc had thirty years ago. "You're not…"

"Oh, yes, I am. I'm Chuck, the youngest Armstrong son." He moved away from Grace, nudging her gently, nodding toward Silas and his father. "So, now that you've seen Grace is in good hands, I'm sure you'll allow us a little privacy." He put his elbow out, enjoining her wordlessly to follow him.

Grace sat between the two older men, one hand on each man's arm, clutching them with her fingertips until Chuck and her mother were out of sight. She lay her head on Papa Doc's shoulder, ready to share. "I think I need to tell you something," she said softly.

"You mean that your mother set you up with Alex; that it wasn't your idea to come to the party?"

"Did Alex tell you?" she asked, sitting up straight with surprise sprinkled with irritation.

"Sweetheart," Papa Doc said, "that's the way things go in this crazy world. Whether rich or poor, mothers have been setting up their daughters with good 'finds' for centuries. She's no different than any other mother."

"Well, maybe," Silas and Grace said at the same time. Silas nodded to her, urging her to continue.

Grace shrugged. "She's horrid. I came to the event under duress. She threatened my friend Dusty. Or rather, she threatened me with what she'd do to Dusty and his father if I didn't do what she said."

"And the other thing you're not telling me?" Papa Doc asked. He turned her head to the side and traced over the yellowing bruise. "If I'm not mistaken, this is a woman's handprint and it's a few days old. That means she physically and emotionally coerced you into crashing the party."

Grace nodded, the tears spilling as she relived the horror of her mother threatening to rape her with a wine bottle and blame it on Dusty and his father if she didn't obey her. "Why couldn't it have been her, not Alex? She doesn't deserve to live and he does."

"He'll be fine," Silas soothed, then looked up. "Here comes Chuck. Maybe he found something out."

Chuck saw the apprehension in the men's eyes and the tears on Grace's cheeks. That meant they hadn't heard anything about Alex yet, but also that Grace had just revealed something intense. "Remember, Grace," he said, kneeling down in front of her, "We're here for you."

"You know what's the worst part? I've lost my father. I mean, he's not dead, but I can't get to him without going through her."

"Don't worry about him," Silas said. "In case you haven't heard, I'm the miracle worker when it comes to social *imbroglios*. I'll get in touch and let him know whatever you want to share or where you want to meet. *And* I'll hold back whatever you want to keep private. It looks like I'm going to have to have another talk with Jimmy and his new assistant. He'll get nothing if he starts playing me against Victoria."

"Wow. This really is a different world," Grace said, wiping her tears with the cloth Silas offered.

"And now you know why I keep away," Chuck said so softly, he was certain the men wouldn't hear him.

Grace looked up at him and winked. "And I'm here for you, too."

***

"How long have we been here?" Grace asked, suddenly awake from the nap she hadn't planned on taking.

Chuck rubbed his eyes and looked down at his watch. "Almost three hours. Something's not right here. We should have received an update." He unwrapped his arm from around her shoulders and sat up. "Excuse me a minute while I check this out."

Grace watched as he walked away, stretching his arms, working the kinks out of his neck and shoulders from holding her close.

"Yeah, he's a keeper," Silas said. "No disrespect to his dad, but two out of three ain't bad when it comes to having stellar kids. I don't know what went wrong with Ben. He never was wired right. Even as a kid, he'd torment cats and dogs, and even his little brother. Alex was always there for Chuck, though. Stepping in, thrashing him like brothers do when someone's picking on a kid brother. Didn't make any difference to him whether it was his own brother or a neighbor kid."

"Why should it?" Papa Doc asked, now awake. "I mean, it was a straightforward case of the big beating on the little. That's probably one reason Chuck has such a big heart. He didn't have a younger sibling to protect. He learned how to do it from Alex and transferred that skill to taking care of the poor folks on the other side of town."

Silas patted Papa Doc on the shoulder. "Now, now. Don't cut yourself short. You had a little influence on that, too."

"Are you a real doctor?" Grace asked. "I mean, I thought folks were calling you Papa Dog at first, not Papa Doc."

Both men laughed. "Yes, I was a doctor. I guess I still am if the need arises. I haven't practiced in ten years, at least. My health started going downhill, so I decided to slow down. You know, get rid of the stress."

"Plus, it's not as if you had to work," Silas said.

Papa Doc glared at his words, then he relaxed and sat back. "Well, if she's going to be family, she might as well know. I still have a few bucks stashed away in the Old Money piggy bank. I kept pulling more and more out of it, trying to keep Ben from going under. Alex would put more back in every time he got a chance. It's not as if it was near empty, but he finally took me aside and explained it so it made sense. Ben would never grow up and take responsibility

50

for his screw-ups if we kept bailing him out. He'd keep sticking his finger in the blades as long as we kept pulling the fan back. We had to walk away so he'd know that if he stuck it in there again, it was going to hurt."

Chuck walked in on the conversation, ready to add, "Ben's just an ass," then decided it was best to stay still. He sat down on the other side of his father and leaned back, trying to make some sense out of how messed up the day had become.

"So, he got mad and decided he'd make Alex pay?" Grace asked. "He not only wanted him to hurt physically but emotionally, too. From what you all have told me, I'm the first real...um...lady friend Alex has had any interest in."

"Excuse me," a man in blue scrubs said. "You are the Armstrong's, right?" he asked.

Chuck sat up straight, then stood up, nodding to the surgeon.

"Oh, hi, Chuck. I didn't see you there. Shoot! Was Alex your brother?"

"Was?" Grace gasped, then fell back in the chair, glad she hadn't been standing. She held her hand over her mouth, willing herself not to puke, her breathing slow and deliberate.

"Shit," the surgeon huffed. "I'm sorry. I'm really, really sorry. We did everything we could. He was on a breathing machine. We thought everything was going to be fine, and then his blood pressure went sky high. It was a stroke."

Chuck focused on his father's face as the surgeon spoke the words. He'd had a three-second heads-up that Alex had passed. He wasn't psychic, but he had seen the grief in the doctor's eyes when he came out, looking for the next of kin. It would have been worse if he had asked everyone into a private room. That would only have prolonged the agony for everyone, including the surgeon.

His father was in shock. They'd better get him to a room right away. He knew he had finished chemo the week before, but he wasn't totally out of the woods. "Can we get him a bed?" Chuck asked the surgeon, nodding to his father. "I want to make sure he's doing okay."

"Oh, yeah. Of course. Let's go down the hall to the ER. I'll grab a wheelchair."

The combination of the two stresses – losing Alex and watching Papa Doc falter before her eyes – was too much. Grace grabbed the trash can next to her and lost her resolve to keep it all together, puking up streams of bile and soda, her shoulders heaving, nose running as she broke down sobbing without caring who saw her.

"Make that a double room and two wheelchairs," Silas called out, rushing to Grace with a box of tissues.

Chapter 8: Recuperating

Late June 1991

"Are you sure it isn't the flu?" Grace asked Papa Doc.

"You're the one who came to me. Have you taken a pregnancy test yet?"

"Yeah, well, you know those things aren't that accurate," she said, then sighed in resignation and shook her head. "Now what?"

"Looks like you get to make me a grandpa," he said.

"But there was one other. I mean, it wasn't just Alex."

"You mean Chuck?" he asked, then laughed. "Now that would really be a miracle."

Grace glared at him, trying to keep her resolve, then giggled at the inside joke. She had been living with Chuck as boyfriend and girlfriend to the outside world, but as brother and sister to those who knew them.

"Ben never got to you, did he?" he asked, suddenly concerned. "Because if he did, I'm gonna whack that spaghetti noodle dick of his off at the base."

"They wouldn't let you into prison to do that," Chuck said. "Sorry, I didn't mean to eavesdrop. You just didn't hear me come in."

"Yes, I did," Papa Doc said. "She didn't, though."

"Little Miss Superwoman ears didn't hear me? She must have been distracted," Chuck said, then leaned over and gave her a quick kiss.

Grace grinned at the kiss, then pouted again. "Yes, I was distracted. I think I'm pregnant."

"Of course, you're pregnant."

"What? When did you find out?" she asked.

"Duh! We live in the same house. I empty the trash occasionally, you know."

"Every day," Grace said. "You have got to be the cleanest housekeeper I've ever known. You could give Sally lessons."

"Who's she?"

"She was my nanny growing up. When my mother decided I didn't need one, she canned her. Dad knew how close I was to her, so he gave her a job as housekeeper and light cook."

"How do you cook light?" Papa Doc asked, then slapped his knee. "I still got it."

"Yeah, and I hope I don't get it," Silas said. "So, what's this I hear that I'm gonna be a grandpa?"

"You guys are making this difficult for me," Grace said in a huff.

"Honey," Papa Doc said, his hand on hers. "We don't ever want to make your life difficult. On the contrary. Now, whether I am the biological grandfather of the child you're carrying or not, I am still going to claim her as mine. I mean, you're not my biological daughter, but I'd fight whoever challenged my love for you with a fistfight. Of course, I would have to try and win by intimidation first because I'm as weak as any man twice my age, but I'm certain of my love for you."

"Ditto," Silas said. "And Papa Doc and I aren't a couple but who says this little girl can't have three granddads?"

Grace's grin swished side-to-side as she tried to figure out if she wanted to laugh or cry. "Thanks for keeping my first dad in the loop. I'll let him know about it in person when he comes by on Tuesday. And please, don't anyone let my mother know. Promise me, right now, each and every one of you three, that you won't so much as let my mother touch my child. She can see a picture of him or her, but no touching. After what she did to me - and threatened me with – I couldn't…wouldn't…"

"Calm down," Chuck said. "We won't let her near you or our baby. Oh, and yes, we can get married if you'd like."

"Chuck!" Silas and Papa Doc screeched at the same time.

"That's not how you ask a woman to marry you, son," Papa Doc said sternly.

"Tsk, tsk," Silas muttered, then returned to making cucumber sandwiches for lunch.

"What? I just wanted to let her have an easy out if she wanted," Chuck said. "Are you putting pickles on those sandwiches, Silas?"

"They're cucumber sandwiches which means they're already pickles. Or at least, could be."

"Chuck, you know I love you," Grace said. "And if I had anything but sisterly feelings for you," she rolled her eyes, "you could be my Mr. Right. However, there's a chance that this baby could be someone else's. Remember I said something to you all about my mother threatening my friend, Dusty?"

"The one you said joined the army?" Papa Doc asked.

"Well, Mother lied about him, so I did, too. I don't know where he is. Lord, I hope she didn't concoct some lie and have him and his dad thrown in jail."

"Why would she do that?" Silas asked, then set down the knife. "Oh, wait. She's Victoria Stillwater. She doesn't have to have a reason, right?"

"Yes and no," Grace said. "She's crazy, but I think she'd do it just to be mean to me."

"Why is she so mean to you?" Chuck asked.

"Because she's Victoria Stillwater," Papa Doc and Silas said at the same time.

"So, I'm pregnant, unmarried, one potential father is dead and the other is missing…" Grace sniffed, looked around for something to wipe her nose with, then realized that 'Always There For You' Chuck had a box of tissues ready.

Silas cleared his throat to bring the attention away from her as she cleaned up the physical remnants of her distress. "Yes, all that's true. One of those three statements is wonderful: the pregnancy. One is horrific: Alex is dead. The other is an unknown, totally fixable by someone I know who is a fantastic detective."

"Who's that?" Papa Doc asked. Chuck frowned as he nudged his father and grunted. "Oh! Yeah, that would be you, right, Silas?"

"Correct. So, we have a baby coming, a fantastic support network of three mostly able-bodied men," he looked Chuck up and down, "some more so than the others, but all of us are willing to help you through this."

"But how do I keep my mother from finding out?"

Papa Doc gave her a quick squeeze. "Your father's already sneaking over here to see you once a week. I doubt we'll be able to keep your impending motherhood a secret for long. If he's been able to keep his visits a secret, I'm sure he'll be able to handle the ultimate discretion: another addition to his family tree."

"What would I do without you?" Grace asked, her tears starting anew.

"We'll never know because we'll always be here for you," Chuck said.

"As long as I have a breath left in this old body…" Papa Doc started, then corrected himself. "I guess it's a good time to tell you. I'm clear. At least, so far, so good."

Chuck smacked him on the back playfully. "Didn't I tell you that attitude made all the difference in treating cancer? All those good vibes streaming through your body kicked the bad ones out."

"And this coming from a medical professional?" Papa Doc teased. "You're right, though. So, let's get down to business. Grace, you tell Silas everything you know about Dusty and his father: friends, schools, hangouts, barber, the works. From there, he'll set out his guys. Mark my words, it won't be long and he'll be joining this family."

"Huh?" Grace asked.

"You don't think I'm going to ever give you up, do you? I own enough businesses around this country that I'm sure he'll fit in with one of them. A good manager is always in demand. At least, I still believe in nepotism."

"Nepo-what?" she asked.

"That just means he believes in hiring his relatives," Chuck said. "Except his sons were as independent as he is. Let's hope that finding family outside the bloodlines will work."

"Amen to that," Papa Doc said. "Now, what's for lunch? Only good food from now on. I'm going to take better care of my body this time around. Not everyone gets a second chance."

Grace rubbed her belly, melancholy despite the pep talk and dynamic support team surrounding her. *Eighteen, unmarried, and pregnant. If Mother knew, she'd be howling in bitter delight.*

Mid-July 1991

Victoria Stillwater looked over her ladies' club's bank statement again. It had been two months and he still hadn't cashed that check. Looking through the window, she wondered where that boy and his father had fled to. The new gardener was decent to watch – broad-shouldered but with that inbred flaming red hair. His manager was a pain to deal with, always wanting to be paid upfront. She'd have to call the agency and have a new landscaper sent out for next week.

She didn't know whether Dusty had believed her or not when she told him that Grace was upset, so traumatized by something that had happened the week before that she didn't want to talk about it. She alluded that it had something to do with him, adding the stinger that Grace had asked her to tell him not to ever contact her again.

Maybe saying she was so hurt that she didn't even want to bother with graduation – that she wanted a fresh start in Europe – was overkill, but she wanted Dusty completely out of Grace's life. When he insisted he could make everything right if he could just speak to her, it was time to bring out the checkbook. Money, the great negotiator.

"You seem like a nice young man. You're a hard worker. You could have a comfortable life with some college under your belt. How about I help with some tuition? Consider it an investment in your future. You can do the same for someone else when you're well off. Ten thousand dollars will get you through junior college. Keep your grades up, and you'll be able to transfer over to a first-class university and maybe get a scholarship. Go west. Try California. There are plenty of great schools out there, plus the weather is so much nicer."

"Listen to her, son," his father had said. "Chances like this don't happen often."

Dusty slapped the check onto his palm a couple of times, pondering his future. Ten thousand dollars would be more than enough to start his own business. Lawn and garden care in the summer; snow plowing and private drive maintenance in the winter. He felt his father's hand on his, folding his fingers over the check.

"Take it, son," he asked more than instructed, biting his bottom lip, hoping his son would be able to have a better future than his.

"Thank you," Dusty said to Mrs. Stillwater, then nodded, not wanting to insult the elitist woman with a handshake from a working man.

"Well, it looks like he's still deciding what to do or he's lost the check. Damn! And here I was hoping I could get him for theft and forgery." Victoria looked over the carbon copy of the check she had written, intentionally changing the angle of her signature and misspelling her own last name. "He must have lost it. I doubt he has the balls to come back and ask for another one. At least, he's gone."

"Good afternoon, Victoria," Hal said as he walked into the den. "Checking the balances on all those bank accounts you keep?"

"How'd you know… I mean, yes, I'm doing some bookkeeping. Why do you ask?"

"Just wondering if you've heard from our daughter." Hal sat down in the recliner and held a magazine up so she couldn't see his face if he happened to break character. "I was hoping she'd send us a postcard or two. Europe in the summer can be divine."

"Oh, she called last night, just after you went to the club. She's been keeping busy with her new friends," Victoria said, then moved papers over her bank statements so he couldn't see the numbers.

"Where is she this week?" Hal asked.

"I believe she was in Paris."

"Let's see, I left at eight, so that means it was sometime after two in the morning in Paris."

"I think she may have been calling from London."

"Really, Victoria. I wish you'd let me speak with her when she calls. I miss my little girl. I don't think we've ever gone more than a week without chatting."

"Well…well," Victoria said, trying not to stutter but suddenly at a loss for words. "Well, she's getting older now. She's in Europe, with a new group of friends, and a whole new way of life."

Hal shrugged, knowing she could see his gesture but kept his National Geographic held high, his grin of glee at terrorizing her hid behind it. "Just let me know if she needs money. I can wire it to her. I don't want her going without."

"As a matter of fact," Victoria began, but Hal cut her off.

"But tell her I want postcards or a phone call first. No money until I get proof she's still alive."

"I think you're being ridiculous," Victoria huffed, frustrated that she'd once again been thwarted in getting more money out of her husband.

Hal put the magazine down and glared at her. "Ridiculous? No, I'm not," he said. "And get dressed. We're going out tonight. You committed us to an appearance at a fundraiser for the hospital. If you said we'd be there, we will."

***

"Hey, Sweetie Pie," Hal said. "Are you feeling better today?"

"Oh, Daddy," she cried, reaching out for a much-needed hug, then stopped as she felt her gorge rise. She held her hand up and ran to the bathroom.

"How long is this going to last?" Hal asked Chuck.

"Dad said each woman and each pregnancy is different. I want to get her in for an ultrasound. It's kind of hard doing it under the radar. Are you sure this is the right way to go?"

Hal nodded. "I'm going to respect Grace's wish to keep her mother out of her life. As it is, that woman's haunting hospitals, police departments, and even insane asylums looking for her. And no telling how many private eyes she's hired."

Silas walked in, his arms loaded with groceries. "All she has to do is have the *paparazzi* sniff around."

"Oh, she has those guys eating out of her hand," Hal said. "She's spread the word that Grace has fled to the Balkans with some Romanoff heir, that the two of them are seeking the true meaning of life…or some other horseshit. Those boys aren't stupid. They're looking, but they won't print anything without a picture. Actually, she's pretty smart there. She's getting at least Jimmy and his crew for free. They're pretty thorough."

"Yup," Silas said, "and that's why we want to keep her here. No one gets into this compound without permission. She has plenty of activities to entertain her, good food," he held up a head of romaine lettuce and two large tomatoes, "fresh air…"

"And fantastic company," Grace said, completing the often-heard soliloquy on how she needed to stay put.

"Plus your dear old dad has been seeing you more now than when you were living at home! Come here and give your old man a hug," Hal said, arms opened wide as he walked toward her.

"Are you really okay?" he whispered in her ear.

She pulled out of the embrace and nodded. "If I get the urge to go shopping or talk to someone new, all I have to do is think of her coming at me, her shrill voice belittling me, or telling me how worthless my friends are."

"So, she did hit you then?" Hal asked.

Grace took a deep breath and looked at Chuck, then Papa Doc. She was done protecting her. She nodded and felt the tears come. She blinked them back. She'd never let her mother make her cry again.

"No need for details," Hal said. "I'm sure I'll find a way out of our marriage."

Silas started chuckling despite the somberness of the conversation.

"What's so funny, Silas," Hal asked crossly. "You wouldn't be laughing if you were the one who had to see her face every morning!"

"No, you're right there. I just remembered hearing Robert Van der Cleft tell about the masseuse his wife had come make house calls. Evidently, our dear Robert has video cameras set up all over the house. Zelda knows about most of them because they're hidden just enough so she can find them and turn them off. He set her up with André the Giant."

"The wrestler? He's a masseuse?" Chuck asked.

"Not the same guy. This one is called the giant because of his monster sausage. If you'd like, I can get his number. You just figure out which room or rooms sweet little Victoria is most likely to want a *personal* massage in, and we can send him right over." Silas shifted in his shirt, slightly uncomfortable with the proposition. "On second thought, we – or I – might have to have one of her lady friends set up first. Without the camera, of course. If the idea comes from one of her confidants, she's more likely to take the bait."

"What? Are you André's pimp or something?" Chuck asked with a nervous chuckle.

"Nope," Silas said with a wide smirk. "I'm just one of the three who claim your little angel. I want Grace protected. One way to help is to get that Mad Medusa out of her life so she doesn't have to live under house arrest."

"Yeah, well, even if it is the most magnificent place on earth to be incarcerated, I still can't come and go at will. What do you say, Dad? Is it time to finally get your freedom?" Grace asked, suddenly happier than she'd been in weeks.

"Oh, yeah… Silas, let's make a plan."

***

August 1991

"There's a mobile ultrasound unit in DC, but we can't bring it here. We're going to have to sneak you out in disguise, give you an assumed name, and hope that Jimmy or one of his boys isn't watching," Papa Doc said.

"No," Grace said, then rolled back over in bed, pulling the sheet over her head.

"But honey, we need to see if there's something going on in there."

She rolled her head and shoulders back just enough to look him in the eye. "Chuck and I discussed what might be going on. He doesn't suspect anything tragic. There *would* be a tragedy, though, if she found out where I was and my condition. I only have six more months of this and then the pregnancy is over. Whether I'm having one or two babies, the health care stays the same: eat right, drink plenty of fluids, and get lots of rest. It's just the curiosity factor that will be satisfied. I won't risk it."

"But don't you want to know?"

"Of course I want to know, but I don't want my mother in my face gloating. She'd find a way to claim credit for me being so fertile…" Grace paused, then groaned in defeat. "She already claimed credit. As soon as she found out I had sex, she said I was pregnant; that women in her family were ultra-fertile or something like that. Great. I can't even claim or blame being pregnant without her interference."

"How's my girl doing?" Chuck asked, joining the conversation when he heard Grace's refusal to get an ultrasound.

"Still pregnant," she said, then reached for the trash can. She coughed up the little bit of lunch she had managed to eat, then set the can back down. "Sorry."

58

"No worries," Chuck said. He pulled out the plastic trash can liner, added it to the sealed trash receptacle in the closet, then relined her barf bucket. "And still pregnant is a good thing. Don't worry about getting an ultrasound. You're right: nothing's going to change on the number of babies. Women have been having twins for eons without tests. Pretty soon, I'll be able to hear one heartbeat or two. I am concerned, though, about your nausea. I did a little research on traditional remedies for morning sickness."

"You mean you asked some of the ladies who come in to see you at the clinic?" Papa Doc suggested.

"Research, local consultants, *kaffeeklatsch* group: same thing. It seems the best remedy is not legal yet but very prevalent and effective. Now, I know you don't care for smoking, but until you can get your tummy settled down enough to eat some Alice P. Toklas brownies, you'll have to take a puff or two." Chuck pulled a joint out of his shirt pocket. "Courtesy of some of Plymouth's finest."

"You mean, smoke it in here?" Grace asked, elbowing her way up to a seated position, getting a burst of energy at the prospect of finding a cure for her nausea.

"Sure, why not? Who's going to bust you? Dad?"

"Nope, not me," Papa Doc said. "Oh, and it's B. Toklas, not P. Toklas."

The window halfway lifted open, Chuck stopped and looked back. "Dad?"

"You didn't know I had baking skills, did you, son? How do you think I got through three rounds of chemo? After you take a puff - maybe two - Grace, let me have that doobie. I don't want you to get plastered. If you've never smoked, it might knock you on your butt."

"I'm already knocked on my butt," Grace said. "Would you start this, Papa Doc. I don't know what I'm doing."

"I thought you'd never ask," he said, then pulled a lighter out of his pocket. "I was hoping you'd figure this out by yourself, Chuck. I've been wanting to suggest it for weeks but didn't know if her doctor would approve."

"Well, as her doctor," Chuck said, "I did both field and medical research. She's in more danger by not smoking and becoming dehydrated and malnourished than inhaling a little smoke with cannabinoids. Plus, when I asked one of the mothers if she got morning sickness with her children, she said, 'Every time.' She said smoking a little weed to start the day settled her tummy plus made managing her crew of eight a lot easier."

"Eight? Oh, no way am I going through this again. And I'm not even halfway through the pregnancy!"

"Hold it like this," Chuck said, then lit the end of the marijuana cigarette, and inhaled. "Wow! It's been a long time..." he said while holding his breath, then exhaled and handed it to her.

Grace took a novice-sized puff but swallowed the smoke rather than inhaled it. "That wasn't too bad."

59

"Yeah, well, you didn't pull it into your lungs," Papa Doc said. "Here, watch me."

He demonstrated, then looked up and saw Silas in the doorway. His eyes widened but he didn't lose breath control. He turned and blew the smoke toward the window. "Hey, Silas."

"You guys gonna turn her into a pothead?" he asked with a frown and a glower.

"If that's what it takes to keep food and fluids in her," Chuck said.

"Hmm. Well, then I'm all for it. Do you think that stuff will cure my rheumatism?"

"Maybe," Papa Doc said. "But one of us better stay straight in case we have to drive somewhere."

"Good plan," Silas said. "Next time, you're the designated driver."

"Are you gonna hang onto that thing all day or let me see if I can find the ultimate cure to morning sickness?" Grace said sternly, then started giggling. "Maybe I did get some of it the first time. At least, I don't feel like I'm going to puke. Still, let's make sure."

Grace pinched the reefer with her fingers, pinkie extended, while Chuck lit it. "Watch it," he said. "I think I'd better get you a pipe. I don't want you getting burned."

"I'll let her use my bong," Papa Doc said. "It makes the smoke smoother. It's less harsh when it runs through water."

"Well, aren't you full of surprises," Silas said. "And here I thought I had you all figured out."

"Let's hope you never figure out all my secrets, Silas. Come on. Help me fix supper. I have a feeling there will be four at the dinner table tonight."

***

October 1991

"Anybody home?" Hal sang out.

"Shoot! Busted!" Grace said, then rushed to hide the bong in the closet.

Papa Doc hollered, "Be right out," then opened the window the rest of the way and clicked on the fan.

Grace picked up an aerosol can and spritzed a wide swath of rose scent. "Just a sec," she said, then giggled as she realized that both she and Papa Doc were calling from her bedroom, asking for a little more time.

Hal didn't say a word when the two walked into the living room, stifling guilty grins. He took a deep breath, then let it out slowly. *Ah, the skunk's back in the rose garden. As long as both of them can eat again, who cares what settles their stomachs or gives them an appetite?*

"We're here. What's up, Dad?"

"I have some news for you," he said, then looked around. "Where is everyone?"

"Right here," Papa Doc said, then started laughing for no apparent reason.

"You know, Doc," Hal said, shaking his head in disbelief. "I know what you two do in there. I mean, I wasn't born yesterday and I did do two tours in Vietnam."

"Huh?" Grace asked.

"He means he recognizes the smell of marijuana," Doc said. "So, is it good news? And do you want a toke to celebrate? Or is it bad news, and you want a toke to chill?"

"Neither on the smoking. Victoria can smell a fart before it comes out a gnat's ass. I don't dare even walk past the perfume counter at Nordstrom's for fear she'll accuse me of having a girlfriend who wears Chanel No. 5."

"Yup, that's Mother! So, good or bad – great or horrid – on the news?"

"It's fantastically great news! Silas worked his magic. Turns out that Victoria was so turned on by the idea of a guy coming over to give her a little personal relief that she didn't even look for a camera in the spa room. I have two angles of her getting the thousand-dollar treatment by this guy." Hal took a deep breath and stifled a blush. "Excuse me, but he really does deserve the name André the Giant."

"When are you going to file for divorce?" Grace asked.

"I'm not in any hurry now. I've got a comfortable routine. My office crew doesn't need me breathing down their necks to do a good job. Plus, coming out here a couple times a week might not be so easy if I'm loaded up with lawyers' appointments."

"Don't you want a life, Dad?"

"I do, but on my terms. But, do you want to know the real reason I'm willing to wait? Or at least a major one?"

Papa Doc and Grace nodded, then started giggling again from being high.

"This guy she's screwing charges a fortune, but she keeps calling him over! We've had separate bank accounts for years, but she isn't aware that I can watch where her money goes. I know she's pilfered from your college trust and a few other funds over the years, but I'm watching and keeping track of everything for when I file for divorce. I know exactly how much she's taken and from which accounts, and how much she has left in her personal one. And you know what? Her funds are finite. She has no way of embezzling another nickel now that I froze your accounts. I also cut off her allowance when she got mouthy beyond my tolerance. She'll be single with no job or skills to get one. Broke and stuck with a lawyer-proof prenuptial agreement.

"Oh, and to add a little spice to the pizza, I let Sally go. I gave her the option of taking a two-month vacation with a bonus or I'd help her find a new job. I just wanted her away from the house so your mother's trysts with André could continue. Not only is the upkeep of the house now your mother's responsibility, but she's almost broke. All I have to do is keep the VCRs loaded

61

with blank tapes and multiple backups of the recorded ones in case of theft or fire. Speaking of that, I have one set of them on the porch right now."

"Well, that sounds like good news to me. The impending divorce – not the homemade porn movies," Papa Doc said. "Silas has a vault we can put them in. You might not ever need them, though. Just letting her know where the cameras are after the fact may be enough."

"Ew, my mother a potential porn star," Grace said, then giggled. "I don't think anything I can do will top that one."

"Let's hope not," Hal said. "I'm just sorry you've had such a miserable time. I certainly didn't know she was so bad. I really did do the best I could."

"You did and I knew it. Plus, you kept Sally in my life. Now all I have to do is get through this pregnancy."

Papa Doc started laughing out loud. "So, you think that all your troubles are going to end with childbirth? Sweetheart, they're just beginning."

Grace stilled suddenly, her secret choking her. *How am I going to give this child or children up for adoption with these men so eager to be grandpas? I have to get an advocate.*

Chapter 9: The Secret

December 2, 1991

"I can't take it any longer," Grace groaned. "I can't possibly get any bigger, either. Look at these stretch marks! Even with a pound a cocoa butter a day, my skin's practically ripping apart! Not to mention my boobs look like hot water bottles on top of a medicine ball."

Chuck brought out the blood pressure cuff and wrapped it around her upper arm, silently counting her rants and raves. *Eighty-four today. Not even noon and she's beat her personal best on complaints.*

"We don't use a pound of cocoa butter," he said, squeezing the bulb to inflate the cuff.

"Ouch! Do you have to make it so tight?"

"Actually, yes, I do. If we can't get your blood pressure down, you're going to have to have an emergency C-section. That means going to the hospital and loss of your anonymity. Is that what you want?"

"No," Grace said, quickly switching her rant to a pout.

"Still too high. How's your appetite? Have you eaten anything today?"

"You know everything I eat and drink. You may not weigh it out, but that calculating mind of yours catalogs everything."

Chuck bent forward and gave her a kiss on the top of the head. "You say that like it's a bad thing. Now, do you want to try walking a little?"

Taking his outstretched arm, Grace sat up as straight as she could and swung her legs over the edge of the hospital bed he had brought in for her. "Look at my feet; they're huge! I look like I have cankles, not ankles."

"Cankles?"

"My leg goes from knee to foot, the calf and ankle the same size."

"Well," Chuck said, still trying to switch up her grumbling, "at least you have a matched pair."

Grace's face squeezed into an exaggerated pout that burst into a full laugh when she looked up and saw him waiting for her reaction. "How do you do that? I mean, I'm so emotionally pissed and physically miserable, and you can still make me laugh."

"You're worth it, Grace. Don't let anyone ever tell you differently. You are, and always will be, my best friend. You have to know that."

"I do," she said, then let him help her to a standing position. "So, does that mean I can share my inner fears and hopes and stupid ideas with you without being judged?"

"Yup. Now watch the threshold. We're not going outside, but I want to see how well you can ride in a vehicle. Just in case."

"There's no way I'm going anywhere in that ground-hugging Ferrari of

Papa Doc's."

Chuck swung the door open completely and let her take it in. "An ambulance? Where in the hell did that come from?"

"The ambulance stork delivered it last night," he said drolly, grinning.

"Do you really want me to get in it?" she asked, suddenly fearful.

"No, I just wanted to let you know that if we can't get you to calm down and stop being so angry at the world, this is what you'll be riding in to the hospital. The babies will certainly be too small to survive on their own. They'll be in incubators with tubes stuck down their throats, cotton pads over their eyes, little shunts in their veins…"

"Stop it!" Grace whispered harshly. "I get it. I mean, bringing an ambulance home is a little overkill, don't you think?"

"How many times have I told you to take a chill pill? You said you didn't want to smoke anymore because you wanted to embrace your rage. Let. It. Go! Life sucks sometimes. Other times, like this, what you see as a hardship is just a stretch of your life that it's hard to get through. You have support, though. Between me and the three grandpas, that's four people who'd do anything in the world for you. Do you know how rare that it?"

"But my babies don't have a father…"

"I hear your words, but what I understand is that you're saying you don't have a husband. I've told you dozens of times, we can get married."

"Chuck, I love you, I really do, but you and I both know that you may be plumbed like a man who'd be a great husband, but you're not wired the right way. I mean…"

"Yes, I know what you mean," Chuck said. "I'm queer."

"Don't say that like you're ashamed of it. I really do wish you'd come out of the closet. It's not as if it's wrong. So, you're like a minority of the human population, not the majority. Only cruel people have decided that there's something wrong with it, okay?"

Chuck looked at her and shook his head in awe. "How can you be straight and have such a profound insight on life and still be only eighteen years old?"

"I'm either blessed or cursed. Take your pick."

"Kind of like me?"

Grace's shoulders slumped as she realized they had so much in common despite age, background, and current physical condition. "Okay, my 'oh so not identical twin,' you've helped me with everything else so far, I want to ask one more favor. And it's a biggie."

"Anything for you," Chuck said aloud, hoping she didn't hear the '*Ah, shit! What now?*' gut response he had stifled.

Grace shut her eyes and paused. How could she ask? She imagined the words written on a blackboard in chalk and read them aloud, "I want you to take the babies and give them up for adoption."

"Whoa! Wait! What? Huh?" Chuck sputtered. "I mean, you don't want your own children?"

"Not now. Not with the way my life is."

"Oh, no, no, no. You can't just say, 'I don't want you because it's not convenient. I'll come back for you when I get my head on straight.'"

"You don't understand…"

"Oh, yes I do understand," Chuck said, his hands on her cheeks, forcing her to look him in the eye. "You are under the influence of a double dose of pregnancy hormones. You want out of this situation completely, to walk away from everything and get your perky little figure back so you can hit the road and find your long-lost Dusty. Well, I've got news for you. It isn't that easy. This isn't playable with the hand you've been dealt. These two babies will be loved and cherished beyond what ninety-nine percent of two-parent families can provide."

"My mother will find a way to mess this up, no matter how careful you and the others have been. I feel it in my bones. I have to protect these little guys or gals. I'm not asking you to help me give them away because I don't love them. It's just the opposite. I'm doing it because I *do* love them. Please, I can't reach out and find the right parents with Papa Doc, Silas, and my dad watching me. You're sharp and have excellent taste. I have one request. I'd prefer a family from a lower-income bracket unless it's a stellar man, woman, or couple who want to adopt, and then I don't care. At least poor folks love each other for who they are, not what they have or will inherit."

"You sound like you've been planning this for a while. Any other restrictions?"

"Other than the obvious: don't let my mother know anything about me having twins."

"So, since you've thought this whole thing out, how are we going to hide it from the men?"

"When the time comes, take me away, deliver them, and tell the guys that the babies died. I'll be distraught no matter what. I'm sure you will be, too. We won't have to fake anything."

"You're not leaving me much time for this. You know your blood pressure is sky-high. You shouldn't even be at home."

"If I was in a hospital, what would you be doing for me?"

"I told you. I'd take the babies early and hope for the best for them, all while trying to save your life."

"What? You mean my life's in danger?" Grace asked, stumbling toward the special lift recliner her father had bought for her.

"Isn't that what I've been telling you?"

"No, it isn't. So, if you want me to stop stressing, the first thing you have to do is take away my reason: the future of these twins. Promise me right now you'll find homes for these two and not let the men know about it."

"You know, for not being intimate, you sure have my balls in a vice…"

"Promise me or there's no way I can stop stressing."

"And you're turning the handle, ready to emasculate me."

"I'll let up. All you have to do is say the word."

"All right. I promise you I will find homes for your two babies and will not tell anyone about them."

"Anyone, especially our dads and Silas," Grace prompted.

"I promise. Cross my heart, hope to die, pinky swear and all that. Geez, Grace. Isn't my word enough?"

"Yes, it is. I just wanted to watch you squirm."

"Yeah, well, when it's delivery time, I'll get my payback. I've only delivered twins once. I have to tell you, the mother looked most uncomfortable."

"I'm sure you're understating the event. If it's at all possible, knock me out."

Ring! Ring! Ring!

"Saved by the bell. Let me answer that. Don't run away," Chuck said.

Grace put a hand on each arm of the recliner as if to get up, then changed her mind and settled back into the chair. "Couldn't even if I wanted."

"Hello. She what? Oh, tell me you're pulling my leg. How close is she? How did she find out? No, I didn't tell a soul, either. Okay. I'll go to plan B. I don't want to say it in case this line is tapped. Hey, I gotta scoot. Oh, and thanks in advance. Bye."

"Who was that?" Grace asked, her finger now pressing the chair lift button, rising up.

Chuck ran his fingers through his hair, exasperated and confused, not knowing what to do first. He looked over at her. "Yes, get up. Shoot, you don't even have time to change clothes. I'll grab the keys and your bag while you make your way to the garage. I'll help you get in the ambulance. You can ride in the front, can't you? I don't want you in the back alone."

"You're babbling, but that means the shit has hit the fan. Yes, I'd rather ride in front."

Chuck snatched his keys from the rack in the kitchen, dashed into Grace's room and grabbed her overnight bag, and was at the pantry door to the garage by the time she had reached it. "Watch your step."

"Are you going to tell me what's going on?"

"Not until we're on the road."

"Crap. That means my mother found out, right?"

"I wish you weren't so perceptive sometimes. Yes, but we have it under control. Come on, let's go. I don't know how much time we have."

He opened the passenger door of the ambulance, threw the overnight bag behind the seats, scooted the seat back a couple more notches, then offered her a hand up. After trying three times to hoist herself up with the grab bar, she admitted defeat and asked, "Help, please."

Chuck boosted her fanny up and over, into the seat. "Seatbelt," he said, offering the extended buckle to the now breathless woman. She tucked the nylon strap under her belly, then leaned back and tried to catch her breath. Chuck ran around the ambulance and jumped in, his nervous energy practically radiating as sparks.

Grace bit at the cuticle of her fingernail as Chuck strummed on the steering wheel, both anxious for the garage door to hurry up and open. As soon as there was clearance for the rooftop beacons, Chuck stomped the accelerator. Backing off the gas, he carefully negotiated the curves of the long icy driveway, slowing to a crawl at the bottom of the hill, looking for other vehicles. There weren't any. Victoria wasn't around. He stopped ten feet before the gatehouse and put the ambulance in park.

Grace started to chew on her finger again, thought better of it, and tried to put her hand under her armpit. When the seat belt got in her way, she settled on interlacing her fingers and resting them on her belly. "Damn! Why did you stop? And where did you say we're going?"

"The first thing I want to do is see what happened to the guard."

"Wait. You mean my mother's not here? I thought that's why we were hightailing it out of here."

"Dad's security team has a truck they use. Can you see *any* vehicles around here, because I can't?"

Grace twisted in her seat and looked out her side window. "Nope. Nothing here. Maybe the guard went out for a pizza or something."

Suddenly, a light flipped on inside the gatehouse and a broad-shouldered man with dark curly hair pulled back in a queue stepped outside. Grace didn't know who the usual guard was, but the uniform this man was wearing was at least two sizes too small, the few buttons that were fastened, strained.

"Good evening, sir," he said. He paused then looked through the driver's window, squinting past Chuck to check out Grace.

Chuck leaned forward, doing his best to block the man's view. "What happened to Caleb? I thought he was working tonight."

"Who? Oh, Caleb?" the replacement guard said to Chuck with a slight French accent. "Yes, he had a stomach pain and chose to leave. The agency sent me over," he explained, then looked behind Chuck to check out Grace again.

Chuck took his foot off the brake, driving forward slowly as he spoke. "No worries," he said, denying the guard the chance of seeing more of Grace than he already had.

"Let me guess. That wasn't the regular guy and you smelled a rat?" Grace asked as they pulled away.

"Worse," Chuck growled as he drove onto the access road to the highway.

"That was André."

"Who's André? Oh, wait. You mean the man my mother was having sex with? How do you know what he looks like?"

Chuck glanced over at her – grimaced but didn't say a word – then returned to watching the road.

"Chuck?"

"Okay. I was curious. I skimmed through one of the videos before I locked them away."

Grace giggled. "Well, he can't have been that impressive if you know what his face looks like…"

Chuck's somber face of embarrassment cracked and three seconds later, he was laughing along with her. "So, it looks like the best hung Canadian in town may have caught a glimpse of your pregnant body. I doubt that he took a second job as a guard, especially if he's making as much per session as your dad says he is. I'd say Victoria's either conned him into getting blackmail information on you or he was here to try to kidnap you. Since the regular guards are nowhere to be seen, I'd say he either bribed someone to stay away or he has the regular guy tied up somewhere."

"I sure hope it isn't worse than that. You don't think he'd kill anyone, do you?"

"I doubt it, but then again, I tend to think the best about everyone. I'm PollyAndy, remember?"

"Well, since my dad said he cut my mother off, I wouldn't put it past her to have taken out a life insurance policy or two on me with her as beneficiary…"

Chuck reached over reflexively to protect her, one hand on the steering wheel, the other on her left arm that was resting across her belly. "You don't think she'd really do that, do you?"

"Chuck, you didn't see the way she looked at me when she was fingering that wine bottle, ready to rape me with it and blame it on my boyfriend. I don't think she cares about anyone other than herself."

"We have to get you out of this town. Time for Plan C. Sorry, but we're going to have to let our guys worry for a while. We may have a mole or rat or someone's wiretapped the house. Right now, it's just you and me, kid."

Grace glanced at her side mirror again, noticing the distinctive headlights getting closer and closer. "Not exactly. I think there's a Jaguar on our tail. I'm sure there's more than one in the area, but this one's a classic."

"Your mother's?" Chuck asked, checking his mirror to verify.

"Yup. How many people do you think would tailgate an ambulance?"

"Hold on, Grace," Chuck said, reaching up to flip on the siren and rotating beacon. "It's time to clear the roads ahead and hope your mother can't corner worth a damn without studded tires."

Grace reached out and grabbed the door and his armrest. "Let's go, Mario!"

Chapter 10: The Shootout

"Crap!" Chuck steered into the spin, but the heavy, awkward, and boxy vehicle still wound up slipping off the road, pointed in the wrong direction.

"Is she still following us?" Grace asked.

"I don't know. I lost track of her. If she is, she has her headlights off." He put his hand on the door handle, ready to open it. "Wait here. I want to see if I have enough room to turn around and get us out of here."

"Be careful," Grace said.

"Always."

Using a flashlight, Chuck looked under the ambulance and saw that he hadn't high-centered it. He could put it in reverse and – if he got enough traction – get back onto the road, make a three-point turn, and be pointed in the right direction in less than a minute. If he hadn't looked first and just driven forward, he would have been stuck. A screwed sitting duck. "Glad I trusted my instincts and checked."

Crunch! Crunch!

Chuck switched off the flashlight and froze at the sound of the icy ground breaking apart under approaching footsteps.

Pop! Pop!

He dropped to the pavement, away from the silenced gunshots, his back pressed close to the ambulance.

Click! Slam! Thunk, rumble. Omph!

"Get in and drive!" Gracie shouted to him from her window.

Chuck sprang to his feet and jumped in, ready to stomp on the gas, then remembered to back up first or be stuck. He grunted as he turned the steering wheel hard, making do with a two-point turn, back onto the road with an emotionally charged and frantic getaway. He watched the side mirror as he sped away. The stunned thin person on the ground rose slowly, waving a fist in rage, any words absorbed by the crackle of studded tires and road noise as he sped away.

"Who or what just happened?" he asked.

"That was my mother. She fired two shots into the window, so I slam-opened the door and knocked her ass down."

"What?" Chuck leaned forward and looked over at her but the dashboard lights were too dim for him to see if any damage had been done. "I can't see. Did she hit you? How bad?"

Grace kept a tight grip on her right upper arm with her left hand. "Yes, she hit me, but I don't know how bad it is. I'm afraid to look. I'm sure I'll live but it hurts like hell."

"Here, put pressure on it with this." Chuck grabbed the sweatshirt hanging behind him and tossed it to her. "And if it hurts, that's a good thing. The ones you don't feel are the really bad ones."

Grace adjusted the bulky sweatshirt so it was against the two holes in the window, blocking the freezing air and also pressing against her wound or wounds. "Okay. I got this. So, to distract me, please tell me what Plan C is. And keep talking."

"I'm going to take you to a friend I met in an online chat room. That's an internet thing if you don't already know."

"So, have you met him in person before. I assume it's a guy and not a girl."

"Yes, he's a guy; you're the only girl in my life. We've kicked it up a couple notches, exchanging real names and pictures. I checked him out thoroughly. Actually, I've talked to him on the phone a few times, too. As in, I called his office and asked to speak with him, using my Chat Room username for the first time. He's a decent guy, has a practice in New Hampshire, and most importantly, he's discreet."

"Pardon my naivety, but what does that mean? Is it a gay thing?"

"We're both still in the closet, but that's not what I mean. It means he can treat your bullet wound and not report it to the authorities."

"You mean, my mother is going to get away with shooting me?" Grace asked, her voice ending on a high note of frustration.

"Do you want to go to the police and press charges? You do know that you and your huge pregnant belly would be thrown into the spotlight immediately, right? Everyone would want to know what's been going on in the life of Victoria Stillwell's missing daughter. Being an unwed mother may or may not make a difference to many but having a wife who shot his daughter might just mess up your father's business big time."

"Okay. Let's keep him out of this for now. Besides, if it's known I'm pregnant, I'll pretty much have to keep the babies. I'm still positive that they'd have a better life away from me. Even more so now that their grandmother is a felon, that she tried to murder her own daughter. The twins would never live down that stigma."

Grace shuddered, then realized it wasn't just the emotions causing a chill. "Can you turn up the heater? I'm cold."

"It's like a hundred degrees in here… Oh, crap. How much blood have you lost?"

"How in the hell should I know? It's not as if I have a meter running on this thing. Shit! I can't even see it."

Chuck reached over, ready to turn on the lights, then stopped at her screech. "Don't! What difference does it make? We're going wherever we're going as fast as possible, right? One or both of us is going to freak out if I've lost too much blood. We can't do anything about it anyhow unless you have a pint of blood in the back and can pump it into me and drive at the same time."

"Grace, sometimes your logic amazes me. Just chill and leave getting there to me. At least, we don't have a tail anymore," Chuck said, quickly glancing into the side mirror to confirm.

"I just hope the door broke her nose and blacked an eye or two. So much for honoring my mother."

"Well, look on the bright side: at least you still have one good parent left."

"All right, PollyAndy. Let's pass the time talking about something else. Tell me about your cyber lover."

Chuck sighed in resignation. He'd share anything with her to keep her mind off her dilemma. They had over a hundred miles ahead of them, and a winter storm was coming in. It was going to be a long night.

***

Chuck looked over and saw the conversation had stopped because Grace had fallen asleep in mid-sentence. He reached over and touched her cheek. Warm and dry, her breathing regular. According to the road signs and odometer, he only had twenty miles to go. He pulled the cellphone out of his front pocket, flipped it open, and started punching numbers.

"Hello? Buddy? Yeah, this is Chuck. I know, we were due for a chat an hour ago but life suddenly got complicated. I'm on the road with a very pregnant and gun-shot woman. Yes, it's Grace. Her crazy mother fired at her twice, and at least one bullet caught her in the arm. Can I come to your clinic? Yes, your in-home clinic would definitely be better. I'm driving an ambulance, so I'll be easy to spot coming in. Just tell me whether I should come in with lights, siren, or silent. Okay, silent it is. Duh! Especially if we're going to your house. Do you have a garage this beast will fit in? I don't want it spotted on the road. No, it's legal – bought and paid for. I'm pretty sure no one's following me or even knows my destination. Nope. Only you and I know where we'll be. She already signed the affidavit for the adoptions, but we didn't have a witness. I'd rather start from scratch with one signed in New Hampshire. Sort of wish you were a notary, too. You are? Aren't you a bundle of surprises? Yeah, we'll find out more about those surprises later. We need to take care of her before we get to know each other better *that* way. All right. See you soon. *Ciao!"*

The hypnotic drone of studded tires on asphalt and the gentle swaying of dips and curves disappeared suddenly as the ambulance slowed to a stop at the traffic light,
waking up Grace.

"Hey, there, sleepyhead. How ya' doing?"

Grace blinked and looked around to see where she was, trying to orient herself. *Chuck. Okay, but why are we in a car? Why do these traffic lights and buildings look different?* "Where are we?"

"Someplace safe. How's your arm?"

Pulling herself upright, Grace squeaked in pain. "Ouch! What? Wait just a sec. It's coming back to me…shot in the arm by my own mother. Damn!

Where's one of your dad's brownies when I need one?"

"I packed lots of your special comfort food and smokes for you, so don't worry. But we'll have to wait a few minutes." Chuck picked up the map from the center console and flipped on the light, verified his location, then went dark again. "Two more blocks to go and we're safe. Buddy's a doctor, too. Actually, he's an obstetrician. Now, before we get there, are you still certain you want to give these two babies up for adoption?"

"Why do you keep asking me? Yes, I'm certain. I already signed those papers you drew up. I want them safe, out of the spotlight, and in a nice boring community, away from Mother."

"The only reason I ask is because we never had those papers notarized. I can print up another set and have Buddy notarize them. He has several good couples looking to adopt. You can even interview them if you want."

"No. I'd prefer it if you would do that part. That is if you don't mind. Damn. You've already cleared half your workdays and all of your weekends for me. Are you going to stay here with me until I deliver, or are you just dumping me on this Dr. Buddy?"

"I'm not dumping you. This is sudden, though. I may have to get an imaginary exotic and highly contagious disease to explain my absence."

"I'm sure you can think of something. Plus, that would be a good reason for you to stay away from our dads and Silas, too. And as far as my disappearance, why don't you just leave it alone? If the cops start snooping, they'll figure out my mother and André are involved and bust them for kidnapping. I wouldn't put it past her to have already sent a ransom note to my dad."

"You know, you're pretty smart for only eighteen."

"I read a lot of mystery novels."

"Well, your life would be a good one, at least the last seven months. Hey, look up ahead!"

Grace saw a beautiful house directly ahead, the garage door opening at 3 AM, apparently for them. "Is this the place?"

"I think so," Chuck said, leaning forward to catch a glimpse of the address on the gatepost. "Yup. We're home. At least, home for the next month or so."

Grace sighed and leaned back into the seat. "God, I hope time flies. I am so ready for all this to be over."

Chuck pulled into the driveway, not commenting aloud on her remark. *Me, too, Gracie. Me, too.*

A tall dark-skinned man with slicked-back hair in navy blue pajamas pointed the way to the designated parking spot in the large subterranean garage. The stranger waited on the passenger side of the ambulance as Chuck pulled in, his hand raised in a fist to indicate stop. Smiling and nodding a quick silent greeting, he opened the door for Grace. Instinctively, the medic held fast the bloodied sweatshirt being used as a bandage. Ignoring the perfunctory medical attention he had just provided her, he said, "Greetings. You must be Grace."

"That's me," she answered. Grace reached for the dash, using her good hand to help pivot her in the seat, ready to get out.

"Please allow me to assist. I'm sure it's been a long ride." Hand out, ready to help her stand, he said, "Your legs may not be ready for your weight."

Grace stumbled as she exited the vehicle, embarrassed both that he had been right and that he had to catch her to keep her from falling. "What a first impression," she grumbled, then straightened up. "You must be Buddy."

Buddy put his arm around her back and under her arm. "My full name is Guamtam Deepak Jeet, but yes, please call me Buddy." He looked up and saw Chuck watching them. "And you must be Chuck."

"Charles Darwin Armstrong, but if you call for Charles, I'll think I'm in trouble and won't answer."

"All right, Chuck. If you would, just inside that door, you'll find a wheelchair. It might be easier on the lady if she rides."

"I'm no lady. I mean, I'd prefer it if you called me Grace. I'd rather walk, but I'm afraid my legs don't agree." She suddenly reached around and clutched at a back spasm, grunting with the unexpected pain. "Back's a deal-breaker. Bring out the wheelchair."

"You must let us take care of you," Buddy said, resisting the urge to give her a hug. "You are a special, strong lady and we want to help you. I will call you Grace, though."

"Not for long, though. I mean, no offense, but I hope we're done once this baby thing is over and I'm back…"

Grace sat down hard in the wheelchair, not bothering to finish her sentence. Where was she going after this was over? She had no life now. She still had her father, but how long would she be able to continue to lie about the twins and where they had disappeared to? He'd be heartbroken beyond repair.

"Chuck, can I have a brownie or two?" she asked, then twinged with a fake back spasm. "I'm hurting pretty bad here."

Buddy looked up at Chuck, curious about what she was asking about.

"Let's get you checked out first," Chuck said. "It appears you only have a flesh wound on your arm, but I want to look over everything. It's been a long journey in more than one way."

***

December 5, 1991

"Are you sure this is the best place to meet her?" Hal asked Silas.

"A public place, lots of witnesses, plus she's less likely to run you over with a truck inside a building."

"We both know she's desperate, Silas, but I don't think she'd ever lower herself to drive a work vehicle."

"Besides the fact that she'd have to step *up* to get in a truck, from what Grace told me, she's more of an intimidation expert who likes to throw sneaky punches. Too bad I can't frisk her before she sits down. Let's just hope she's not desperate enough to shoot you for a life insurance policy."

"Grace is my beneficiary, not her," Hal said, sipping his coffee, his eyes still focused on the front door.

"That doesn't mean she didn't take out a new policy on you. She could do that as your wife."

Hal turned back and looked at him, wide-eyed.

"Hey, just saying…"

Ding! Ding!

The brass bell on the diner door announced another person coming in. Or two. Victoria had arrived, swathed in a dark blue scarf, sporting oversized sunglasses. André was at her back, holding the door open for her. "Thank you, dear," she said, looking up to the exotic bodybuilder and smiling with feigned sincerity.

She glanced around the room, spotted Hal and Silas in the corner, then sauntered over to their table, leaving André at the door. After waiting a moment for the men to stand up and acknowledge her or offer a seat, she pulled a chair out for herself and sat down gingerly.

The first thing Hal noticed was her nose. It wasn't the sunglasses that made it look so big, it really was swollen and was painted with a thick coat of foundation. "What happened?" he asked, then chuckled. "Get too close to a mirror?"

"I'm here about our daughter, Grace," she said haughtily, totally ignoring his comment.

"Since we only have one daughter, I would assume it's Grace. So, what did you do to her? Where is she?"

Silas noticed Victoria flinch when Hal asked what she had done to Grace, then blanch in confusion at where she was. Apparently, she had done something to her but didn't know where she was. *Keep up the interrogation, Hal. You're doing great.*

"I know Grace is pregnant. Very pregnant. She needs to see a doctor. I made a few calls and my gynecologist can clear his afternoon to see her today." Victoria babbled her practiced spiel, then paused. Her whole face – save her heavily-painted nose – reddened in embarrassment as she realized what Hal had said. *Where is she? She didn't come home? He doesn't know anything… I've just been given a blank check! He thinks I have her!*

"Isn't anyone going to offer me coffee?" she asked, looking for a waitress, avoiding the truth-seeking stares of Hal and Silas.

Silas took the setting from an empty table, then walked behind the counter and grabbed a full pot of coffee. He set the cup and saucer down with a clatter, then splashed the hot black liquid into it, intentionally overfilling the cup and making a mess. "Better?" he snarled.

Victoria looked up at him with disdain, then down at the cup. She huffed and decided to ignore his rude acquiescence and continue. His impromptu dramatic production had given her enough time to devise a plan. "If you'd like to see our daughter again, you'll transfer five million dollars into my personal account. I know you have the routing numbers. You've been watching it for years," she said, ending her demand with a slight nervous twitch of her upper lip.

Hal sprung up with rage, knocking the table toward her, the cup of coffee spilling into her lap, causing her to jump, too. He grabbed her by the throat. "Where is she? What did you do to her?" he repeated, this time at full volume, spittle flying from his mouth in uncontrolled rage.

André rushed to her defense, but Silas stepped in front of him. He wasn't as tall or beefy as the wannabe pornstar boyfriend – and was twice as old – but he had more experience as a bodyguard and it showed. "Don't!" he commanded, chin out in defiance.

The frightened lover took a step back, hands dropping to his sides in defeat. He'd attached himself to another nut. Defeated and frustrated, he shook his head at the woman who had both run out of money and plans to get more. Time to shut the book on this one.

Ding! Ding!

Hal loosened his grip, brought back to his senses by the sound of the doorbell. He looked away from the terrorized Victoria and saw André leaving, his head still shaking back and forth in disgust. "Looks like someone else is fed up with your lies," Hal said. "You'll be hearing from my lawyer very soon. He's 'cleared his afternoon' for me," he added snidely.

"And that's a cut!" Silas said suddenly and dramatically. He looked around the room as if making sure everything was in place, saluting the non-existent hidden cameras. "Thank you, ladies and gentlemen. You've just participated in a scene from The Plymouth Chronicles. Watch for it in a theater near you the summer of '92."

Hal walked over to the waitress, wearing a grin of embarrassment. "Here," he said, pressing three hundred-dollar bills into her hand. "I don't think anything more than a cup or saucer was broken, but we did make a mess. Don't worry. We won't be back."

She looked down at the money, spreading the bills apart to count them. "Come back any time!" she said enthusiastically. "And she really did seem like a bitch. Hope all goes well with the divorce. Oh, and that you find your daughter…"

"Yeah, me, too," Hal said. "Me, too."

"What now?" Silas asked once they were out of the café.

"All we can do is hope that Chuck calls in. I really did think that Grace was kidnapped after you found the gatekeeper tied up. Oh, and great call on making my attack on Victoria look like a scene from a movie. That was an Oscar-worthy performance."

"Yeah, well one thing bothers me – other than where in the hell did Chuck and Grace disappear to and why – is how did Victoria get a broken nose? Lord, I hope Grace did it," Silas said, opening his car door.

"That would be nice, wouldn't it?" Hal looked at his watch. "I have time to drop in on my lawyer. I'll meet you at the compound for dinner. Should I bring fish, beef, or salad?"

"I'll pick up some crab. You go ahead and grab salad makings. I'm pretty sure there are enough steaks in the freezer for everyone if we want to get that crazy. No telling when Doc's coming home. He's making a personal appearance at Chuck's downtown clinic. Lots of folks remember him from way back when. If Chuck left a clue to where he went, Papa Doc will sniff it out."

"Yeah, well, according to him, he learned from the best. See you at supper."

***

Papa Doc pulled up to the gate and rolled down the window. "How's the head?" he asked the guard.

"I still have a headache, but the embarrassment is the worst part. I've been working here for ten years, Doctor Armstrong, and never a lick of trouble. Then one woman comes in and blindsides me."

"Don't worry about it. I'm just glad it wasn't something more serious. Let me know if you see either Victoria or that boyfriend of hers snooping around. Don't engage them; just call me immediately and we'll go from there. Oh, and anything on my number three son?"

"No, sir. I haven't heard from or seen him in about a week."

"All right. I'm in for the evening," Papa Doc said, then drove up to the house, frustrated, defeated, but still hopeful.

As soon as he walked in the door, Silas looked up, suddenly crestfallen that Doc was alone. "So, I guess it's just three old bachelors for dinner? Anyhow, what did you find out downtown?"

"Chuck sent a fax in from a restricted phone number. 'We've been exposed to Ebola virus. Must stay isolated to protect all. Chuck.'" Papa Doc crumpled up the copy of the fax and tossed it into the trash.

"Hey, maybe there's a clue or two on there," Silas said.

"Already found it. Chuck's saying, 'Leave us alone for a while. We have some crap we have to work through.' Damn. I know he cares a lot for that woman, even if he is gay. Still, he's taking her away from her father," Doc said, looking at Hal.

"I've seen those two together," Hal said. "He's doing it because she wants

76

him to, not the other way around. All we can do is be patient. If we stir up crap, this place will be a feeding frenzy for the press. Keep on keeping on so the roads remain clear and unwatched, ready for them when they decide to come home."

"Them and the babies," Papa Doc said hopefully.

Hal and Silas looked at each other and winced. Either Doc hadn't noticed that Grace hadn't ordered one piece of baby clothing or furniture, or he was choosing to ignore that glaring fact. Either way, neither of them would bring it up.

Chapter 11: Oblivion

December 3, 1991

"Not much needed for that," Chuck said, sealing the gauze on Grace's upper arm with adhesive tape. "You were lucky."

"Will it scar?"

"Probably," Chuck said, "but you can say you walked into a sharp branch or fell on a piece of pipe if you don't want bragging rights about being shot at close range by a crazy woman." He kissed her on top of the head. "Now, how is everything else?"

"I hurt everywhere. I feel like I'm a gray whale trapped in a harbor seal's body: bloated and ugly and ready to pop out of my skin no matter what." Grace looked over at Buddy, waiting silently on a stool in the corner. She knew he was letting Chuck take care of her injury before intruding on her emotionally delicate situation. Both men were handsome, gentle, and considerate: no wonder they were attracted to each other.

"Buddy, do you want to check me out so you two can have some time getting acquainted? I'm sure you have a place for me to sleep when you're done. Or at least, try to sleep. I can't find a comfortable position these days, but I'm still willing to look for one."

"Yes, I have a room. How about you lie back, so I can listen to those three heartbeats."

"Three?" Grace squealed.

Chuck, standing behind Grace and out of her line of sight, frowned at Buddy. "Three," Buddy clarified with a nervous smile. "The two babies and yours."

"Oh, yeah. I guess I wasn't thinking of it like that."

"Can I check her BP for you?" Chuck asked, trying not to flirt but still remain helpful and close at the same time.

"Yes, please," Buddy said. "May I?" he asked Grace, his hand on the hem of her maternity shirt.

"Go for it," she said, then tried to relax into the examination table. "Chuck said twins usually come early. Please tell me he's right? I don't want to wait six more weeks."

"Usually two weeks early is fine. As long as the babies are around five pounds each, they should be healthy enough to live outside of the mother. The lungs are usually developed by then."

"Four more weeks to go?"

"Yes, but I can make your wait much more comfortable. Hold still a moment and let me listen to heartbeats. Then I have a surprise for you; one you will be very happy with."

Buddy traversed her belly with hands and stethoscope, verifying the babies' body positions so he could find their heartbeats. He tried to keep his face stoic, but when he heard the third strong and rapid fetal heart, he allowed a smile to escape. "One more," he said, then offered her his hand to help her sit up. "Breathe normally," and checked her lungs, too.

"Perfect." He looked at Chuck. "Her blood pressure?" he asked.

Chuck grimaced slightly. "Too high. I don't like it, but after what she's just been through, I think anyone would have those kinds of numbers."

"Come with me, Grace. It's time for your surprise." Buddy helped her get off the examination table and back into the wheelchair.

"Now you really got me going," Chuck said as he followed them down the hall.

"What? You don't know where we're going?" Grace asked, frightened all over again.

"No, but I trust him, and you should, too," Chuck said, patting her shoulder in reassurance.

"What do I have to lose?" Grace relaxed back into the wheelchair, then grumbled, "I have nothing."

When they came to a stop outside a room with an industrial-sized door, Chuck squatted down beside her. "You will always have me. Always, or as long as you want me in your life."

Grace quickly looked over at Buddy, avoiding eye contact with Chuck's new beau apparent, letting Chuck know that she was referring to his new friend.

"I can love more than one person at a time. I just won't be sleeping with both of you," he whispered.

"You can sleep with him as long as you leave me with Alice P."

"Alice B.," he corrected. "Yes, I'll make sure you're well-stocked with sweets and smokes of oblivion."

"Right in here," Buddy said, opening the door to the inner room. "It's an immersion tank, filled with magnesium sulfate."

"Huh?" Grace asked, pulling back, trying to move away from the tomb-like enclosure.

"Wow. I like it," Chuck said, then explained it to Grace. "It's a giant Epsom salts bath. You won't feel the weight or pressure of the pregnancy while you're in there. Plus, your body is probably deficient in magnesium. That might be another reason you hurt all the time. This will help take care of that. And if you're not hurting, your blood pressure should come down. Win-win-win situation."

"Can I use the bathroom before I go in? And I guess you two don't care that I don't have a bathing suit, do you? I mean, you're both gay, right?"

"Aye," Chuck said, "we're both fairies. But more importantly, we're both doctors. The only way we're interested in your body is to make sure you stay

79

healthy and keep those babies inside of you long enough that they can survive in the outside world. Any other concerns?"

"Minute by minute," Grace said. "Potty break then a bath. After that, maybe a bite to eat and a warm place to sleep. What more could anyone ask?"

"A healthy delivery and a new life for you. Silas is still searching for Dusty. I know we never talk about it so we don't stress you. I just want to make sure you know that he's still searching."

"Thanks. I needed that."

***

Knock! Knock!

"Come in."

"How'd you sleep?" Buddy asked, balancing the breakfast tray one-handed as he opened the door.

"I can't believe I slept so long. I'll bet I was out for three hours straight at least once. If I didn't have to get up to pee so much, I would have slept straight through. Still, if this clock is right, I've been out of it for twelve hours!"

"The clock is right. Chuck said you didn't care for coffee, but I thought you might like some herbal tea. Normally, I'd advocate exercise, but I'd rather you rest every chance you get. Only get up for bathroom breaks. You can ring that bell and someone will come and take you via wheelchair to the float tank or into the library to choose a book or videotape. No walking beyond the bathroom. Oh," Buddy held out a colorful cotton thong with a pendant on it. "Press this if you fall and can't reach the bell."

"Where's Chuck?"

"He said he had an errand to run."

Grace lifted an eyebrow in doubt and shook her head. "If we're all going to get along for the next month or so, you'd better tell me the whole truth."

"He wanted to have that paper we all signed last night filed as soon as possible."

"I'm not going to change my mind," Grace said.

"Even if your Dusty shows up?" Buddy asked, using the same raised-eyebrow gesture.

"Do you think he's going to want this blimp of a body?"

"Grace, men love the person, in here," he thumped his chest, "not the fabric-wrapped flesh container. Now, I might be ruining the prospects of two couples getting a child by speaking with you like this, but I don't want you to have regrets."

"Did Chuck put you up to this? Is he standing outside, waiting to hear me recant so he can tear up the release of parental rights, then take the babies back to our fathers to raise as one giant dysfunctional family?"

"Eat. Please. You have low blood sugar. If you can't do it for yourself, do it for the people who are going to take these babies home next month. If you

80

don't keep your 'flesh container' healthy, all this will have been for nothing. We'll be burying little corpses, then sending you on your way a few weeks sooner. Is that what you want?"

Grace glowered at him, angry that he had gotten through her thick skin, then grabbed a piece of toast and stuffed it in her mouth rather than answer his question. "Go away," she said with cheeks full. "I have some babies to build."

Buddy closed the door behind him, then let a smile escape. The chances of the babies surviving just went up.

Chapter 12: Shopping

Late December 1991
The Mall of New Hampshire

Chuck pulled into the mega-mall's parking lot driving his new old ride: an all-wheel-drive van. It was boxy but discreet, an electrician's work vehicle that had been converted into a mini-home on wheels. It had a bed, cabinets, propane stove and refrigerator. It didn't have a bathroom but did have a battery-powered water pump and basin for quick clean-ups. The seller assured him that a five-gallon bucket with trash bag liners would work for any long stretches between gas station pit stops. The young man was more than happy to make a swap for the ambulance – an exotic and hard-to-find vehicle. He had given Chuck his full asking price, plus marked down the trade-in value of his van because it needed a paint job. Both buyer and seller walked away happy with the transaction.

"A low-profile ride and enough cash in my pocket to outfit my cross-country motorhome with a nursery and supplies for at least a month. No need to use that trackable, traceable credit card yet. The stars are aligning, Chuck. You're doing great."

The mall seemed to be even larger on the inside than it was on the outside. He looked for a mall directory, couldn't find one, so walked into the biggest store on his end of the building. "Excuse me, but do you know where I can find clothing for preemies?"

The bleached blonde at the jewelry counter looked Chuck up and down like he was an idiot, batting her long fake eyelashes at him as if shooing him away. "We don't have that in this store, sir," she replied haughtily.

Chuck started to explain that he just wanted to know if there even was such a store in the mall or where a directory was so he could figure it out himself, then realized that if it didn't pertain to her or her commission, she probably didn't want to hear about it.

Suddenly, he felt a soft hand on his elbow, trying to get his attention. "I know where one is, and I'm going that way." The friendly lady in a sporty mauve business suit was all smiles at the prospect of helping him, proving that classy clothes and good grooming didn't make a snob. "Care to join me?"

"Yes, I'd like that. My name's Chuck and I'm new in town," he explained as they walked down the corridor. "I have no idea where to shop. I'm looking for items for a premature little girl."

"How much did she weigh?" asked the woman, stopping suddenly, her hand grasping his upper arm.

Momentarily stunned by her intense reaction, Chuck quickly realized that she was genuinely interested, eager to hear any information or hints about tiny baby girls. "She hasn't been born yet," he said, "but I know she'll be under term weight."

"Same here," she replied, then pulled him along with a renewed excitement. "I'm Gloria Thornwhistle, by the way. I'm getting a daughter in one week, maybe sooner. We couldn't conceive so decided to adopt. We just heard that she'd be available soon. I thought we had more time, so didn't have anything for her yet. Well, except for the nanny. I made sure I had the best one in New England on retainer as soon as I even considered marrying Roger."

"How does he feel about the adoption?"

"Oh, he's over the roof with joy. He's the greatest uncle in the world to his sister's two boys. At first, I thought we were going to have to wait until a baby boy became available, but Roger said he'd always wanted a daughter. I guess the stars are aligning for us now..."

"Funny, I was thinking the same thing just a few minutes ago. So, tell me; you said this baby became available suddenly. I thought waiting lists were years out."

"Well, they are," the woman said, then dropped her voice to a whisper, forcing Chuck to lean close to hear her, "unless you know the right people. Or rather, the right doctor. We're paying over $50,000 plus expenses for this child. He's making a mint off delivering white babies to desperate folks like me. He has a few birthing homes stashed around the country, I hear."

"Can you tell me his name? This little girl might want a sister," Chuck asked, curious about the black market for white babies.

"It's some odd Indian or Pakistani name: Jeet or Peet or something like that. We just call him Dr. Buddy. His latest client is having triplets, but he's only making money on two of them. Apparently, the person who brought him the mother gets the runt of the litter. I'm getting the biggest one, he said. Since there's no guarantees, she'll have a better chance of survival. All the post-care is up to me. He's an obstetrician. As he's so fond of saying, 'I just pull them out. After that, the kid's all yours and the pediatrician's.'"

Gloria picked out a frilly pink dress, then set it back. "Maybe later. My sister-in-law said to keep away from ruffles and lace until they're older. It just scratches and itches their tender little skin. She's so excited about this baby. When she found out there was an extra one to adopt, she wanted her. But she was too late. That would have been so awesome: identical cousins."

"I'm sorry. I'm not following you," Chuck said, forcibly scowling in confusion to cover his ire.

"You see, the babies are identical! Three identical little girls..." Gloria sighed, her smile of contentment stealing any more words.

"Maybe you can find out who the other parents are. You know, keep in touch to see how much the girls look and act alike over the years."

"I'm one step ahead of you. I'm pretty sure I know who the one parent is. Luther has been a friend of mine for years. He and his wife Leanne have been wanting children for ages. He's some world-famous botanist, frustrated that he can get corn to grow on a rock but can't do anything about his wife's infertility. Yes, I'm sure they'll be great parents, too."

"How about this?" Chuck said, intentionally shutting off the thread of conversation by showing her a soft cotton sleeping gown. He already had the full name of one parent and enough information about the other adoptive family to get their last name. Not that he wanted to take the girls away from their new parents, but it would be nice to confirm that they were safe and loved.

A salesclerk followed Gloria around as she selected clothing and accessories while Chuck investigated the other side of the store, trying to keep the chitchat to a minimum. He didn't want to seem too curious, even though he did want to know what she knew about the person getting the 'finder's fee.'

He set three boxes of diapers and a carton containing a small portable bassinette by the register, then toted around an infant car seat by the handle, using it as a shopping basket, tossing in assorted gowns, blankets, bottles, and cans of powdered formula.

"You might want a couple of these," Gloria said, holding up three different styles of pacifiers. "My sister-in-law says they're a lifesaver. You'd better get all three, though. No telling which one she'll prefer."

He added the trio to the rest of his bounty on the counter, then took one more look around the store. "Am I missing anything?" he asked the clerk.

She pawed through the contents, looking down at his choice of bassinette, then nodded. "Yup. Unless this is a plastic doll, I suggest baby wipes." She pointed to the display on the end cap. "Make sure you get the unscented kind. Oh, and have plenty of plastic bags on hand for disposal. Babies are little, but they make a big stink!"

"And distilled water," Grace said, coming up beside him. "You don't want to use tap water." She set her business card on the counter in front of him.

"I don't know who you are or anything about you, but I kind of have that zing feeling with you, Chuck. Stay in touch. And if there is anything you need, let me know. I don't know when our little girls are going to be born, but it sounds as if they might wind up being zodiac twins."

"Gloria, I didn't say this was my baby. I'm not even married," Chuck said, adding a wink.

"If she's not yours, you want her to be. Whether you're Daddy or Uncle Chuck, there's no doubt in my mind that you already love her."

"That'll be $374.36, sir," the cashier said.

"It's on me," Gloria said, handing the clerk her gold charge card. "Her first gift from her silent godmother."

Chuck took a deep breath, then bent forward and hugged the generous woman, ending his thanks with a firm kiss on the cheek. "You're going to be a great mother, too," he said. "Thanks for giving that little girl a good home."

"My pleasure," she said, tears welling. "My pleasure."

Chapter 13: Arrivals

January 3, 1992

Cups and plates skittered across the room as Grace threw another tantrum, a spoon ricocheting off the TV stand and hitting Chuck in the head.

"Oh, God! I can't take it anymore! I'm serious," she cried, wiping her runny nose on the shoulder of her hospital gown, the only clothing that fit her. "Nothing is helping anymore!"

"Well, it looks like it's a good thing we cut you off from forks and knives," Chuck said as he cleaned raspberry jam from his forehead with a found napkin. He rose from the recliner that had become his domicile and office after he added obstetrician and nurse maid's duties to those of best friend. The oversized and overstuffed chair was his bed, dinner table, and research library.

"Are you done yet or have you found something else you can throw? Earrings, underwire bra, false teeth?"

Grace blanched as Chuck wiped the red stickiness from his head, then realized it was jam. She still felt bad for having struck him, even if unintentionally. "I'm sorry, Chuck. You've been a positive saint about all this. Scratch that. I think saints should take lessons in patience and sacrifice from you. I'm serious, though. Can we get the babies out now? They're big enough, aren't they? I overheard one of the nurses tell Buddy that the test results said the lungs were functional."

"You did? When was that? He didn't say anything to me."

"I overheard him the day before yesterday. He thought I was still sedated. He seemed really excited, too, when he looked at the sonogram measurements. He babbled something about 2200 something or other, and then I was out again."

"Grams?"

"Yeah, that's it," Grace said, then winced as a spasm hit. "He said they should all be over 2200 grams now. Does he mean that's how much they weigh?"

"Maybe." Chuck hit the volume up button on the TV remote and grabbed Grace's hairbrush. "Here, let me fix you up a little." He leaned close to her ear and whispered, "Yup, he's been keeping data from me. I'm pretty sure this room is monitored. I don't think he wanted you to know that they were ready to be born. I'm sure it's to keep you calm. Your blood pressure is still pretty high."

Grace turned toward him and gave a quizzical look. "What is it you're not saying? Are you worried about something?" she asked, her eyes shifting back and forth indicating their whole environment.

"Hey, Grace. Remember, as long as you have me, you'll be fine. Now, are you ready for this? It's too risky for you to deliver naturally. Lots of women would be jealous of the fact that you don't have to go through labor. Buddy has it under control, I'm sure. I've checked everything out and he has a fantastic operating room and neonatal clinic." *I just hope his postpartum recovery program is as great.*

Knock, knock, knock.

"Greetings and good day to you both," Buddy said, his teeth shining bright with a wide smile. "Are you ready to deliver?"

"Duh! I was ready two months ago, but I guess the question should be, 'Are the babies ready to deliver?'"

"Yes," Buddy looked down at the clipboard he held close to his chest, "according to the information from the last ultrasound and amniocentesis, the babies have attained a healthy weight and their lungs are fully developed."

He paused, looking at the scattered dishes on the floor, the oatmeal trail ending at an upside-down bowl. "So, how much breakfast did you eat today?" he asked, stifling a smirk.

"I didn't," Grace said with a pout of embarrassment. "Sorry about the mess. I had a bad night."

Buddy raised one eyebrow and looked at Chuck who replied with a shoulder shrug. He added, "She has a hard time sleeping. Considering all she's been through lately, I'd say the damage is minimal. And yes, unless she has a pizza under her pillow and has been sneaking bites of it, all she's consumed in the last twelve hours was a little jello last night and water. She's ready for surgery and so am I. I'd still like to assist."

Bottom lip stuck out in thought, Buddy paused then nodded. "Yes, I think I could use an extra pair of hands. Grab a cup of coffee and a bite to eat from the kitchen if you need to, then I'll meet you in the surgery in thirty minutes. I think you'll find everything you need in there."

"But...but..." Grace sputtered, her hand on Chuck's arm, holding him back.

"Hey, this is what you've been wanting, isn't it? I just need to eat a little breakfast, so I don't get the shakes or pass out. Someone should be coming in to scrub you up a little, and then roll you down the hall to the operating room. By lunchtime, you'll be able to see your toes again. Tonight you can sleep, and by summer, you'll have your bikini-beautiful body back, your thin little cesarean scar invisible to onlookers."

"And all these stretch marks?" she asked, frowning.

"Believe me, those are minimal," Chuck said. "If they're even visible at all in six months, they'll just be little silver threads. Most women develop them at some time in their lives anyhow."

"And many men," Buddy added. "You probably just never looked. If they bother you, wear a one-piece suit. One last time, you do want to give up these babies up for adoption, correct? And you still don't want to see them or know their gender?"

Grace nodded as the tears fell again. "Damn! How long until these pregnancy hormones get out of my system? I've cried more in the last month than I have in my whole life!"

"A month or two. Give it time. Eat plenty of fresh vegetables and fruits, drink lots of water, exercise more than you thought possible, and you will have a speedy restoration to your pre-pregnancy body and attitude. Don't skip any of those, though, or depression will try to steal your life. I have medications for that, but good body maintenance works best." Buddy patted her on the shoulder. "Leave it to me and your friend. Chuck has your best interests at heart."

Chuck flipped his wrist, checking his watch. "Gotta jet, Grace. I'll be back in a flash. Don't go anywhere without me."

"Yeah, right, said the Galapagos tortoise to the Arizona jackrabbit. Have a good breakfast."

Chapter 14: Road Trip

January 3, 1992
Armstrong Estate, Massachusetts

"I found him!" Silas shouted out as he walked through the front door, fist-pumping the air in victory.

"Him? You mean them?" Papa Doc asked. "Chuck and Grace?"

"Nope, him as in Dusty. Damn! I know if Grace knew I found her old beau, she'd come out of hiding. How many weeks until she's due?"

"You know as well as I do that she's still three weeks out," Hal said.

"Yeah, well, she is having twins," Papa Doc said, "so by my experience, she's about a week out. Chuck won't let those babies get too big. Two eight-pounders is more than enough for even a seasoned mother to carry and way too much for an eighteen-year-old heifer."

"Do not refer to my daughter as a heifer," Hal said, "but I agree. Can't we just haunt all the hospitals in the area?"

"I've been doing that ever since they disappeared," Silas said. "I'm expanding the area now, just in case they migrated north or south."

"Who'd want to go north in the winter?" Hal asked. "No, wait. It doesn't matter. Sometimes I don't even know why we bother to look."

"Because she's our daughter and those are our grandchildren she's carrying," Papa Doc said. "And don't even think about contesting Silas's interest in her. Even if they aren't Alex's babies, I can't help but think of them as my grandchildren, too."

"Yeah, well, I'm more than happy to share the grandpa duties with all of you," Hal said. "These babies may not have a grandma worth claiming, but they'll make up for it with a bounty of grandpas."

"So, tell us, Silas, where's Dusty now, and where has he been hiding all these months?" Hal asked. "I never knew the kid beyond seeing him work with his father cutting grass or trimming hedges, but he seemed decent enough."

"So, you knew he was your landscaper?" Silas asked.

Hal nodded. "Yeah, for the last few years or so."

"Well, that would have been a good thing to know and might have made my search a lot easier. Or not. Anyhow, that's what he's doing now."

"It's winter! How in the heck is he a gardener now?" Hal asked.

"I'll let you ask him. He's clearing the drives as we speak. I told him to come up to the big house to get paid, that I had a bonus for him if his work was better than the last guy's."

"How much does he have left to plow? Do you think we should ask him to dinner? Does he know that Grace was staying here until last month? Oh, good grief! Does he even know she's pregnant? Shoot! Speak up, Silas," Papa Doc said. "Inquiring minds want to know!"

Hal and Silas burst out laughing at Doc's blathering and frustration. "I guess it wouldn't hurt to set another plate out."

"It's a good thing we're having chili and cornbread tonight. Plenty to share," Doc said, grabbing another place setting. "So, are we telling him about the babies or just pretending Grace has been hanging out here for the heck of it?"

Suddenly, Papa Doc and everyone else was silent, totally at a loss for words or sassy remarks.

Ding! Dong!

"I'll get it," Silas said. "You two do the talking. I did my part in finding him."

"I'm beginning to think he had the easy part," Papa Doc whispered to Hal.

"I agree. Toss you for it – loser gets the dishes." Hal flipped a coin. "Call it."

"Heads."

"Heads it is," Hal said. "That means I lose and have to wash the dishes."

"You mean, you win and get to wash the dishes," Papa Doc groaned.

"Oh, Mr. Stillwater! Good evening," Dusty said with genuine shock and enthusiasm, his hand reached out to shake his. "You're the last person I expected to see." Dusty suddenly blushed and became tongue-tied. "I...um...was wondering, how's your daughter? I mean, I haven't seen Grace in nearly eight months. Her mother said she was mad at me and never wanted to see or hear from me again..."

"She what?" Hal bellowed.

"I win twice," Papa Doc whispered, then sat back and smiled, curious about how Hal was going to handle the explanation.

"Mrs. Stillwater was insistent that I keep away from Grace. I think she felt kind of bad about it. I mean, I think she knew how fond I was of Grace. She even gave me a ten-thousand-dollar check to use toward college so I could get a better education and maybe start a new life! For some reason, though, she thought I would do better if I moved to the west coast... Anyhow, I felt bad about taking her money, so I just held onto it. Plus, there was no way I was going to move so far away that I'd never see Grace when she was out and about. I mean, if I could just see her and talk to her now, I know I could make everything right."

"So, what *have* you been doing?" Hal asked, stalling for time.

"Well, I really didn't want to go to college, but I wasn't going to take your wife's money if I wouldn't be using it for what she intended. So, I decided to use the check as collateral for a business loan. I bought a good used plow truck, a trailer, and some good second-hand mowers and gas-powered trimmers. I was right, too, about people willing to pay upfront for a contract to keep their driveways plowed in the winter and yards green and well-landscaped in the summer. I was able to pay back the loan in six months."

Dusty reached into his hip pocket and pulled out his wallet. "Oh, here. Please give this to your wife, sir. I got it back from the bank when the loan was satisfied."

Hal turned over the check, saw that it hadn't been endorsed, then verified the routing number. He took a deep breath, then decided to keep the fact that Dusty might have been in trouble if he had tried to cash a check on an account that Victoria had no legal rights to. "I'm proud of you, son," he said. "That was very clever, starting your own business like that. Um, I haven't seen Grace for quite a while. She took off on a… What would you call it, men? Maybe a journey of self-discovery?"

Silas and Papa Doc laughed nervously, glad that they didn't have to explain anything. "Yes," Silas said. "We haven't had any contact with her in quite a while, either."

"Well, I thank you for your business, Mr. Armstrong. I've heard good things about you. If you do hear from Grace, would you tell her I'd move heaven and earth just to talk to her for one minute." He paused, reflecting on what he had just said. "I'm serious. If I could just talk to her for one single minute, I'd give her everything I own…"

"No need to fret about that," Hal said, patting Dusty on the arm. "I tell you what, I'll make sure that as soon as we see her, we'll tell her she needs to talk to you. No ifs, ands, or 'I'm mad at him still's' accepted."

"I appreciate it, sir. Oh, and here's your invoice. I accept cash or check. I'm not set up for credit cards yet, but if you'd like to set up an account, I'll take you at your word and can send you a monthly statement."

"Yes, yes, Dusty," Papa Doc said, sniffing back tears of hope that there was still someone honorable and special waiting for Grace, even if it wasn't one of his 'good' sons. "If you'd consider me one of your regular customers, I'll breathe easier every snowfall."

"And summer? I still do groundskeeping. You can ask Mr. Stillwater here if he was happy with the work my father and I did."

"Most definitely consider us a year-round client," Papa Doc said.

Brrinng! Brrinng!

"Would you care to stay for some dinner?" Silas asked, picking up the conversation while Doc went into the kitchen to answer the phone. "Chili and cornbread. We're just getting ready to eat."

"I don't want to intrude…" Dusty paused, then sniffed the comfort food. "It does smell great, though."

"Just the right thing to warm your bones," Hal said, grabbing the extra place setting and arranging it next to his.

"Normally I wouldn't do this," Dusty said, "but I'm done for the afternoon.

Plus, I skipped lunch."

"Coffee or hot cider?" Silas asked, holding up two carafes.

"Coffee, black, sounds good."

Papa Doc burst through the kitchen doors, excitement radiating from him like electricity from a three-foot plasma ball. "Hey, everyone. I hate to crash my own party, but we'll have to pack up this spread in to-go cups. We have to leave – like right now!"

"What?" Silas asked, setting down the coffee.

"We don't have a four-wheel-drive vehicle that will fit four, do we?" Papa Doc asked.

"You're talking crazy," Hal said. "What's going on?"

"That was Chuck. We have to go to New Hampshire and get Grace – and I mean right now!"

Dusty raised his hand like a first-grader eager to get his teacher's attention. "I have a four-wheel-drive crewcab truck outside. I fueled up just before I got here. Let me go, too, and I'll drive."

The older men looked at each other, each one nodding to the other. "Grab the coffee and some granola bars and let's go!" Hal announced. "My baby's comin' home."

***

Delivery/Operating Room, New Hampshire

"How are you doing, Dad?" Buddy asked.

Chuck grinned under his surgical mask, then realized Buddy couldn't see it. "Nervous as any other first-time father, I suppose. How'd she do?" he asked the anesthesiologist seated at Grace's head.

"She was a little nervous, but they all are. I made an excuse for your absence. If she asks, tell her you got over your stomach cramps; that it wasn't the flu." The bald and rotund knock-out specialist laughed. "Actually, I told her you had a sudden attack of morning sickness but not to worry. You'd be over it in nine months or sooner."

"How'd she take that?"

"Eh! Not too impressed, so I turned on the juice and let her sleep. She's young. She'll do fine."

Scalpel held up, Buddy said, "Here we go," then bent to his task.

Chuck had seen several cesarean section procedures, so knew what to expect. He was at the ready in case he was needed, but the surgical nurse was experienced and anticipated every clamp and suture Buddy needed. One, two, and the first babies were out, the two neo-natal nurses grasping their charges, then bringing them to the warming table to do their thing. Buddy maneuvered the afterbirth out of the way, then handed the last and smallest little girl to Chuck.

"She's small but viable," Buddy said.

Chuck glanced from his newborn to the doctor and saw an impossible-to-read expression in the Pakistani's dark eyebrows. "Thank you," he said sincerely, then took his daughter to the same neo-natal area, glad that he had taken time to make his phone call before the procedure.

Although the older nurse had given him a crash refresher course in post-delivery care of a preemie, his instincts took over as he did the quick assessments and ran through the procedures. Goosebumps rose at her squalls, verifying that her lungs were clear and working well. "Four pounds, eight ounces," he announced, echoing the brevity of the other nurses' announcements of five, six and five, eight. "In case anyone's taking notes."

"Nope," the younger nurse next to him said, then looked over to make sure Buddy was still concentrating on finishing up putting Grace back together. "This one's totally off the radar. As far as anyone knows, she had twins." She paused, waiting for Chuck to look at her. Seeing his eyes, she shoved her mask down with the back of her glove and mouthed, 'We need to talk,' then slipped the mask back in place. "Congratulations, Dad," she said aloud. "She's definitely a keeper."

***

"How soon can Grace be moved to the post-care apartment?" Chuck asked Buddy as they cleaned up and changed out of their scrubs.

"Soon, very soon. I've found it's better if they come out of anesthesia in a different environment. I make sure they're comfortable. A nurse is with them when they wake up to take care of any complications and make sure they have food and aren't alone. After that, it's up to them when to leave. Most don't stay around more than a day. As soon as they can walk, they've called a friend or family member, and then they're back into their lives as if nothing happened."

"Do they ever come back?" Chuck asked, concern furrowing his eyebrows. "I mean, do you ever deliver the same woman more than once?"

"No, but then I've only been doing this for a year. If you're interested, I can set you up." Buddy put his hand on Chuck's. "I know it didn't work out between the two of us on a personal level, but we could be business partners. You're already a physician with a wonderful bedside manner. That's so important, that the girls trust you. It's so easy to find rich wannabe parents, willing to pay anything to have a healthy white child. There are plenty of babies coming from overseas, but they're usually Asian. White parents want white babies; it's as simple as that."

Chuck swallowed back his disgust and faked a smile of interest. "I'll have to get back to you on that. I need to make sure Grace gets back to her family. If you don't mind, can I ask one of the nurses to keep an eye on my daughter for a minute while I check on her?"

"I don't mind at all," Buddy said, a sly smile arising. "There are two; take your pick."

Chuck approached the nurse who had given him the non-verbal warning, certain that she would help him and be discreet. Plus, a little alone time would give her a chance to speak with him. "Hi, I guess you already know my name is Chuck. I was wondering," he said, his eyes looking around the room to let her know he hadn't forgotten their interaction, but he needed to wait a bit for that, "if you could watch my daughter while I check on Grace."

He smiled as he said the words 'my daughter.' "I never thought I'd have a child. Do you know how wonderful it is for a gay man to be able to say, 'my daughter'?" he asked.

"Not the gay man part," the nurse said, "but I know about having a daughter and how good that feels, even if she was only alive for a short while. Sorry, we haven't been introduced. My name is Grace, too."

"Grace Two? That makes it easy for me. Well, Grace Two, would you watch Rhianna for me?" nodding to the smallest of the babies, now topped with a white knit cap, swaddled in pale yellow flannel.

"Nice to officially meet you." She reached out and shook his hand, pressing a small slip of paper in his at the same time, a slight frown of admonishment to be discreet marking her otherwise unreadable features. "I'm pretty sure I can look after two babies at the same time. Ellen has Baby One under control," she said, canting her head toward the hefty, older nurse beside her.

"I'll be back in a jiff, Grace Two," he said with a wink.

"Sure 'nuff," she replied. *Just read the note before you get back.*

Chuck pushed through the doors, his smile of joy shining for the security cameras that he was sure were everywhere. He ducked into the bathroom and into the shower stall, verifying that there wasn't a spot where a camera could be hidden. As an extra measure of privacy, he turned on the hot water, letting a cloud of steam form before he took out his note.

They're taking her to 11348 Mountain View after you see her. Have her picked up ASAP. Babies are getting moved soon. Take yours and scram!

Chuck collapsed against the shower wall, then slumped onto the shower seat, still fully dressed. He looked at the note again, then stuffed it back in his pocket. He pulled out his phone and texted his father again, this time with the new address.

"Are you all right?" Buddy hollered from the outer bathroom area.

"Yeah," Chuck replied. "I just needed a little shot of steam. You know, dry winter air and all. I'll have to remember to pick up a humidifier."

"How's Grace?" Buddy asked, his eye twitching and smile uncertain.

"Don't know yet," Chuck said as he walked up to him. He patted Buddy on the back. "I didn't want to greet her with a stuffy nose. She's probably still unconscious anyhow. Thanks for helping us out. Life is sure going to be different as a father, but it's a journey I'm looking forward to. I have to make

94

sure Grace is set before I leave, though. Where did you say she was going?"

"She'll wake up completely at the apartment we keep in Skyline. I never send mail there but it's right on the corner of Oak and Main," Buddy said.

"Just making sure," Chuck said. "If Rhianna's still stable, I'm going to head out after I see how Grace is doing. Goodbyes are hard enough for me. I don't think I'll be able to tell her that this is goodbye forever. After she gets to the Skyline apartment, would you tell her I had an emergency or something? After a few weeks of not hearing from me, she'll figure it out."

Buddy breathed a visible sigh of relief. *Great! No interference from best friend!*

The change in attitude confirmed what Chuck had suspected. *Liar! You were planning on hiding her from me. Now, you're relieved that I won't still be glued to her elbow!*

"Yes, if she wants to stay in this part of the country," Buddy said, "I have a very good friend at an employment agency. I'm sure he can find something for her."

"Thanks again," Chuck said, then rushed out the door and into the hall before he threw up.

Pausing at the water cooler to compose himself, Chuck slowly sipped a cup of plain hot water. *Be strong. The dads will be there for her. I know they will. This is what's best for her.*

He tossed the paper cup in the trash and braced himself for one of the hardest tasks in his life: saying good-bye.

"Hey, Grace," Chuck said, standing beside her gurney.

Grace remained motionless as she feigned being asleep. The sense of immense loss was something no one had warned her about. The constant kicking and change of pressure on her internal organs were missing. The new stillness was as scary as a sudden loss of sight or hearing. Those uncomfortable and unpredictable sensations she had endured for the last six months were gone, never to be recovered – their memory, too intense to be forgotten.

"It's going to be all right, Grace," Chuck whispered, then sat next to her, his hand gentle on her shoulder. "I feel like a coward, but I'm afraid every time you see me, you'll remember this, these last few months. I told you that I'd always be here for you. Now, it's by leaving that I'm doing you the biggest favor. You're stronger than you know; braver and more generous than anyone I've ever met. Keep being you and you'll conquer this world and all the evils in it. I do love you, Grace. You've been the biggest, brightest star in my life. And you've given me more than I ever thought possible."

Chuck stood up, then bent over her and kissed her on the cheek. Tears had left a shiny trail from the corners of her eyes down her temples and into her hair. "Good-bye, my sweet. And good luck."

Rushing out the door, Chuck was hit with nausea again. *Coward! You can't turn around and steal her away now. Don't chicken out and do the easy thing. She needs to be free. She can't – won't and didn't – change her mind. Seeing Rhianna would tear her up. She's out of your life now. All you can do is make sure she's safe.*

"Oh, there you are," Grace Two said, halting her nervous pacing when she saw him walk back into the neo-natal area.

"Sorry, it took longer than I thought. I…um…ran into Buddy and we had a little chat."

Grace Two's eyes widened but Chuck's minimal head shake settled her fear. She looked to Ellen. "Can you watch all three for a minute? I want to go outside for a smoke."

"No problem. I'll let you spell me when you get back," the other nurse said. "Not for a smoke, though…"

Chuck's new confidant took him by the elbow and ushered him down the hall and out an exit. She glanced around, verified they were alone, then whispered, "There's going to be a bust here by morning. I talked the feds into waiting until these babies were delivered and had a few hours to adjust before whisking them away. They're all fine, but Buddy's going to get arrested for white slavery and a few more charges. He was going to use your Grace for breeding stock."

"What?" Chuck squeaked, quickly bringing down the volume as the word escaped.

"Surrogate mother. She's proven she can carry three babies and deliver them at a viable weight. Lots of rich couples are eager to have their fertilized zygotes implanted. Buddy will keep her around to recover as long as he can, ply her with a high paying, low skills job; then whisk her off to his birthing house. White slavery still exists. I want to end it right now."

"How do… How do you know this?" Chuck asked.

"I was one of them. He trusts me. In reality, I was just waiting until I could gain that confidence so I could bring him down. You're different. You were doing this for her, to get her out of a bind."

"Wait. The babies…"

"He's going to whisk them off and 'resell' them several times over. The promised parents will be told the babies died, that their fifty grand purchase price for a baby is non-refundable."

"I'm going to make a call," Chuck said, his hand on her shoulder – his emotional grounding rod. "Do you think you can help me get all these babies out of here? I have a van all set up for one baby. I think they'll all fit in the one bassinette, though. At least, until we can clear ground zero."

Grace Two looked at her watch. "He takes off to be with his wife at the big house at seven every evening, come rain, shine, or blizzard. If you can have your vehicle here and warmed up ten minutes later, we should be able to stay out of the shit storm. What about your Grace?"

"Buddy has a wife?" he gasped. "That explains a lot. Anyhow, her ride's already enroute. I just texted the new address to them. I hope the message comes through in time. They're driving up from Massachusetts."

"Well, make your other call fast then come in. He's going to suspect something if you're not spending every moment you can with your baby. Oh, and cell reception is best up there," Grace Two said, pointing to a cleared area at the end of the patio. "And no cameras."

Chuck took his cellphone out of his pocket as he walked away, glad that he had taken the time and expense to buy one. He took the business card out of his wallet and dialed.

"Hey, Gloria. This is Chuck. From the baby store. You're my daughter's godmother, remember? Yeah? Really? Mine was, too. No, she didn't die, too. They're all fine. Shoot. I suppose there's no holding back. Our daughters are sisters. At least, they're biological sisters. So, here's the deal. You need to be at the gas station on Sherlock and Hemingway at seven twenty tonight. I don't care if you're in the middle of the biggest dinner party in the world…well, it's a good thing you're both home. Anyhow, you and your botanist friend who has dibs on the other baby need to come and grab your daughters then. No, I promise you they're not dead. They're all perfectly healthy. Well, don't let Buddy know I called you. I think he's in big trouble. Yeah, well, telling you the babies died should be enough for you to doubt everything he says. I'll be in a plain white van – you know, the kind electricians use? Yeah, well it's a conversion. I'll have all the babies with me. Just give me the password 'Woodstock' and either I or the nurse will let you in. All right. Bundle up and bring car seats. I only have the one you bought for Rhianna."

"Rhianna," Gloria mused as she set down the phone. "Well, they both can't have that name. We'll have to find a different one. Roger!" she called upstairs. "Come on down. You got that miracle you were praying for. Let's go get her!"

"She's alive?" the red-eyed man asked, sniffing back leftover tears as he rushed down the stairs.

"Yup. You got me convinced that prayers work. Grab your coat and warm up the car. I'm calling Luther and Leanne and giving them the good news, too. I'm sure glad we left the car seat and welcome home goodies where they were. We're less than an hour away from holding our baby."

Chapter 15: The Shit Storm

Enroute to save Grace
January 3, 1992

"You know, a lot may have gone on during the last few months, Dusty. It's been how long since you've seen her?" Hal asked.

"It's been two-hundred-thirty-three days, sir. Sorry. I'm a little obsessive about the loss."

"Well, it's been a month and a day since we've seen her. All was fine and dandy at breakfast, then the next thing you know, she and my son had disappeared. Poof!"

"Um, Mr. Armstrong. I don't mean to sound rude," Dusty said, his foot off the accelerator as he thought of how he should word his concern without losing his new customer. "But don't you think it would have been a good idea to tell me that my girlfriend ran away with another man? You made it seem like…"

"Excuse me, son," Silas said. "We're in a hurry here. If you can't put the pedal to the metal, pull over and let me drive. Don't worry about Chuck. He's *Doctor* Armstrong's youngest son. He's a doctor, too. He's the one who's been taking care of her."

"Are you sure they didn't fall in love or something?" Dusty asked. "I mean, she's a wonderful woman, and beautiful, too."

"Pretty sure," Papa Doc said.

Silas leaned over and whispered, "Plus he's gay."

"He is? Oh, thank heaven!" Dusty blurted out, his foot now heavy on the accelerator. "I mean, that's good for me. And for her, too. I hope."

"And him eventually," Papa Doc added, comforted by the pat on the shoulder by Hal.

"So, Dusty, I don't mean to be a downer," Hal said, "but she has been gone for a long time. Would you still love her if she, say, gained a lot of weight?"

"Mr. Stillwater, I'd still love your daughter if she was a deaf-mute quadriplegic."

"And what if she committed a crime like maybe stole something big?" Silas asked.

Dusty sighed deeply, his foot coming off the gas again.

"Keep up your speed, son," Silas warned.

"Oh, yes, sir. Sorry about that. You see, though, she already is a thief. She stole my heart. She's who I think about when I fall asleep at night, and my first thoughts in the morning are of her, too. We were going to get married. I mean, we hadn't set a date or anything, but we knew we wanted to be in each other's lives forever and ever."

"Sounds like someone's been watching too many animated fairy tales,"

Hal whispered to Papa Doc.

"I heard that," Dusty said. "But yes, I do believe in happy ever afters. I know not everyone gets one, but I know that if we can just talk for a minute, I can convince Grace that we can have ours. I'm on the right track with this new career. She can help me with it, doing the books and all. We can get our own little apartment to start with, then maybe save up enough money for a down payment on a…"

"Just drive," Silas said. "We all know what a happy ever after is. We're just as eager to find out what's happened in the last month, too."

"It's been nearly eight months for me, sir. I'm sure she's just as beautiful and sweet as ever, though."

"Anyone for coffee and a granola bar?" Papa Doc asked to redirect the conversation. "I didn't bring the chili. Not a good idea in close quarters, if you know what I mean."

"Granola bar and coffee sounds good to me," Silas said. "Why don't you pull over and I'll drive. Speed limits were meant to be flexible in extreme circumstances. I can drink and drive legally as long as it's coffee. Come on, kid. You've been working all day. You need to rest up at least a little so you're in top shape to see her." *And don't pass out on the spot when you see she's either pregnant or a new mother of twins!*

***

Three hours later

"Wake up, Sleeping Beauty," Hal said, nudging the dozing Dusty who had fallen asleep. "We're at the rendezvous spot."

"Huh? We're where?" Dusty looked around, blinking moisture into his eyes as he tried to figure out where he was and who these old men were. A smile erupted on his face, splitting his dry bottom lip. He licked it and brought his elation down to an earthly level. "She's here? Now? Where?"

"I guess they haven't got here yet," Silas said. "The text said he'd let us know when she was on the road. Whatever that means."

"What does that mean?" asked Dusty.

"If I knew, I'd tell you. Just keep your eyes open. Now, Dusty," Silas said, turning sideways in the seat to face the anxious young man, "she might look a little different…"

Hal and Papa Doc snickered at the same time, then brought their hands up to contain their explosive reactions to a very pregnant Grace looking a 'little' different. "Sorry," Papa Doc sputtered.

Dusty gulped audibly, then reached for the thermos of coffee and poured a splash into his cup. "There's a little left if anyone else wants some," he said. He gulped it down, waiting for more comments. When none came, he voiced his suspicion. "I'm beginning to think that you all know something big and don't want to tell me."

"Big?" Hal whispered, then Papa Doc started snickering again.

"So, what did she do, go on an eating binge and she's as big as a house now? You think that just because she got fat, I won't love her?" Dusty fumed. "Because that's what it sounds like you're trying *not* to say!"

Silas lay his hand on Dusty's shoulder. "You'd make a good investigator, son," he said. "Yes, we're trying not to tell you that she got big. Last time we saw her, she *was* big as a house. Well, not a real house, but so big she could hardly walk."

"But why would she keep overeating if she couldn't even... Oh, shit! Is she pregnant? Is that why she's so big? Is that why she ran away from me? She's having our baby and..."

Dusty stopped when he felt Silas squeeze his shoulder. "What? Are you doing that because I'm right or I'm wrong?"

"The last time we saw her," Silas said, his voice slow while he chose his words, "she was pregnant. Very pregnant."

"Well, we did have sex, so I guess that means using the pull method doesn't work..."

Hal harrumphed but didn't say a word.

"Sorry, Mr. Stillwater. I guess we were a little early on the honeymoon part, but we are going to get married. I promise you. If Grace will have me, we'll get married right away."

"A lot went on after you saw her last," Papa Doc said. "It seems she and my eldest son were sort of an item, so to say."

"What? But she loved me! I know she did!"

"Yes," Hal said, his indignation overridden by compassion for the confused young man. "And her mother forbade her to see you again, then set her up with a new beau. Sorry, Doc, but we all know it's true. Grace wouldn't have slept with Alex if her mother hadn't essentially blackmailed her."

"How could she blackmail her own daughter? Grace didn't have any money that Mrs. Stillwater couldn't have taken anyhow."

"She blackmailed Grace with you. She was going to have you and your father arrested for... Let's just say my wife was ready to make up false charges against you and your father that would have put you two in prison for a long time. Grace pretty much had to become intimate with a stranger to protect you. I believe that she did it out of love for you."

Dusty's face skewed up. "You mean she had sex with another man because she loved me? That is what you're saying, isn't it?"

All the men hemmed and mumbled, but it was Papa Doc who spoke up. "She may have been coerced into it, but she knew she could never go back to you. Not because of you but because of what her mother would do. She had to start anew. What she hadn't planned on was falling in love with my son, Alex."

"But you guys said he was gay – that she ran away with your son the gay doctor."

"No," Papa Doc corrected. "Different son."

"Okay. So, maybe the baby's his. I'll challenge him, though. Even if that isn't my baby, it's hers. We can bring him or her up together. Where is he? I want a duel or at least a chance to win her back."

"First off," Hal said, "whether she goes with you or not is totally her decision. At least, you say you love her no matter what."

"And second," Papa Doc said, "I wish there was a way you and Alex could duel or duke it out or just sit down and talk about it, but you can't."

"Why not?"

"Because he's dead," Silas said. He turned around and saw he was right to answer for Doc. His best friend was crying all over again, recalling the loss of his son.

"I'm sorry, sir," Dusty said. "Truly, I am. But I swear to everyone in this car, that no matter who's the father, I'll take care of both Grace and the baby."

"Babies," Hal corrected. "They're twins."

"What? I'm going to be the father of twins?" Dusty screeched excitedly, dropping his empty cup on the floorboards. "That's great! I mean, it might be a little crowded in my trailer for a while, but we can..."

"Hold on there, Champ," Silas said, physically holding the excited man down with a shoulder grip. "I don't think it's going to be that easy. If it was, Grace would have stayed where she was with us. And we wouldn't be making a middle-of-the-night exodus into New Hampshire based on one phone call and a couple of texts. Something screwy's going on. You and I and everyone else need to keep a level head. Let me take the lead on this. The worst thing you could do is burst out of this truck as soon as you see her, scaring the Bejesus out of her."

"Yeah, I guess you're right," Dusty mumbled. "Damn it."

***

"My van's warmed up and ready to go. Do you have a plan or am I just winging it?"

Grace Two looked up at the clock. "You're a little early, Chuck, but that might be a good thing. Do you feel that itchy, crawly vibe in the air?"

"Yup, that's why I buzzed out half an hour early to get ready. No telling if we'll get another opportunity." Chuck looked over at the three babies, their isolettes pushed together under the warming lights, their little bodies swaddled in pink, aqua, and yellow to tell them apart.

"Come look at this," he said, canting his head so she'd follow him as he walked to the tropical zone. "Do you have a place to go?" he whispered, "because I could really use your help with Rhianna."

"Do I have a place? No," she said softly. "But I'm always ready. All I ever need is packed in the gym bag I've been bringing into work with me for the last three years."

"How big's that gym bag?" Chuck asked, a twinkle in his eye.

"I always knew you were smart, Chuck. Yup. It's insulated, padded, and will work great for transporting them for a short distance."

"I wish I had thought of picking up some baby dolls at the mall when I was there. They had some little ones that looked so real..."

"What do you think is taking up space in my gym bag right now?" Grace Two said, then nudged him with her elbow.

Chuck took a deep sigh of relief. He raised an arm, ready to give her a hug of gratitude, then quickly redirected the movement to scratch his temple. *Cameras!*

"So, how about we see what's in the kitchen for breakfast," he said in a normal tone. "I make a great omelet."

She looked up at the clock. They had half an hour until Buddy was due to take off to see his wife. "Go ahead and start prepping. An everything-but-the-kitchen-sink omelet sounds great. Ellen's due back from her break pretty soon."

Chuck sang 'Oh, what a beautiful morning' as he strolled down the halls, pausing at the thermostat to check the temperature. Making sure his back was to the security camera, he surreptitiously turned up the temperature to high. He flipped the lights off in every room down the corridor before cranking up those thermostats and leaving, appearing to be energy conscious but actually trying to suck up as much juice from the electrical panel as possible. In the bathroom, he fumbled through the drawers, found and plugged in the two high-volume hairdryers, and set them to max heat. Leaving them running on the counter, he popped into the shower room and turned on the infrared heat lamp, then walked out, ready to start breakfast. How long would it take to shut down the thirty-amp breakers and which would pop first? He grinned. He didn't care as long as they shut down in the next ten minutes.

"Mega omelets," he said, acting engaged for the security cameras that were everywhere. He fished through the refrigerator shelves, looking for eggs, meat, onions, and peppers for his supposed creation, adjusting the regulator to its coldest setting as he pushed aside different foods.

"Let's see," he said, thinking out loud. He pulled out two pans and set them on the stove, turning all four burners to high and cranking the oven to broil at the same time.

Grabbing a cleaver from the butcher block, he started chopping, making quick work of the ham, onions, and peppers. He glanced up at the clock. Less than five minutes. That ought to be enough time to pop a circuit breaker or two. Or set off a smoke alarm if something shorted out or caught fire. He cracked four eggs into the bowl, then bent over forward and clutched his belly. "Oh, no... Not again!" he said, then ran out of the room, leaving everything where it was.

Chuck pushed open the outside door and looked down the drive, making sure his vehicle was still running. That was the plus side to Buddy being in an upscale neighborhood: no car thieves. Besides, who would want an old service van, even if it was four-wheel-drive and freshly painted?

The rumble of the garage door opening brought him out of his introspection. Watching from his secluded spot at the side of the house, he remembered to bend over and pretend to gag in case there were cameras he wasn't aware of. Buddy was pulling out, his white Cadillac squealing tires as it backed up hurriedly, as if he was late for an appointment.

"Crap!"

Chuck ran back inside, directly to Grace Two and the babies. He took a moment to catch his breath, one finger up asking her to wait a moment.

"Are you all right?" she asked, seeing that he was also flushed.

"Zero hour," he panted, then bent forward, this time truly ill but with nerves. "Get your bag. Stat."

The unlicensed but experienced neonatal nurse didn't waste a moment questioning him. She dashed down the hall, not concerned if she looked like she was crazy or not. It really was zero hour in more ways than one. She'd have her freedom, too.

As soon as she was back, her gym bag opened and ready, the lights went out with a *thunk!*

"Crap!" she huffed.

Chuck shined a flashlight on her bag. "Need a light?" he asked.

"Yeah," she said sarcastically. "What did you do?"

"I overloaded the circuits to give us a little element of surprise," he said. He squatted down beside her and helped her rewrap the dolls in the babies' spare blankets.

"Here," she said, pulling out a drawer under one isolette, handing him a fistful of knit caps. "We have lots of them."

Chuck finished dressing the dolls, then joined her at the warming station.

"I need light," she said, fidgeting with the babies under the glow of the battery-operated emergency light mounted in the corner of the ceiling.

He shone his flashlight on the little girls. She had already moved them to one isolette, the bassinette's thin bedding folded up around them like a taco shell. He held the bag open, the flashlight in his mouth showing her the spot to settle them in. The shuffling around had upset them, their little squalls now drowned out by the sudden blare of smoke alarms.

"Overloaded the circuits?" she repeated as a question.

He took the flashlight out of his mouth. "And I may have left a few burners on high without anything in the pans." He sniffed the air. "Pee Ew!"

"Ready, Dad?"

"Which door?" he asked.

"You take the babies. I know the secret exit."

103

Chuck wiped the flashlight off under his arm, handed it to her, then took the bag. "At least, we know we won't be running into Buddy. He already split. He left early and seemed to be in a hurry."

Grace Two shone the light on the floor, leading him in what felt like the wrong direction "That must be why I felt the tension in the air," she said. "He probably got a heads up. Damn!"

The two plus the babies wound up exiting where he had just experienced his pretend stomach distress. "There's the van." He looked to the right. "Uh, oh. We'd better jet. Looks like we have incoming..." he said, and scurried down the rise, leading the way.

"Quick," she said. "Give them to me, then you jump the fence."

"What?"

"It's only three feet high. Shit! Just step here..." She stepped on the well-hidden but strategically placed cinderblock next to the stucco perimeter fence, sat down and swung her legs over, stepping on another block before hitting the ground. "Give them to me, then you come over."

Chuck repositioned the strap and holding the babies close, was up and over the fence in a flash. "Got it. Sorry. I'm a little possessive."

"No worries, Dad," she said. She took two steps, then put up her hand, stopping him.

"Is everything all right there?" a voice called out.

"Yes, sir," Chuck answered. He squinted to see who it was, then put his arm around Grace Two's shoulder and pulled her close. "We're eloping!" he declared to the man in the FBI jacket. "Do you need to see ID?" he said, fumbling in his pocket, his smile wide.

"Heading out at this time of night?"

"Yes, sir," he replied. Chuck held up the gym bag and pointed to the van, obviously warmed up. "We were just staying with some friends on our way cross country. It's another three days to Vegas, but we were hoping to make the Lincoln Memorial by morning."

The officer looked at Chuck, all giddy with excitement, not nervous and scared as a white slaver would be, then made the snap decision to let them go. They'd just slow him down with paperwork.

"Have a safe trip," the FBI agent said. "And don't gamble!"

"Hey," Chuck quipped. "I can't say that! I'm getting married, aren't I?"

"Well, then, be safe."

"Thanks, we will," Chuck said, then gave Grace Two an extra squeeze of joy at their second victory: deception.

The two took their time walking the rest of the way to the van, holding hands, swinging them back and forth like schoolchildren to perpetuate the ruse. The joy was real. They were almost free!

Chuck unlocked and opened the side door, then handed her the bag. "Do you have this or do you want me to come back there and help you?"

"That might look a little suspicious. Even if it didn't, I want to get the hell away from here. Just watch out for bumps and sharp curves. I don't want to move them to the bassinette yet. They're snug and comfortable where they are."

"Kind of like they were still in the womb?" Chuck asked.

"Exactly."

"Then we're off to play stork to two very lucky couples."

"Honk, honk," Grace Two said, then chuckled. "I think I may like hanging around with you, Chuck. Just don't ever make a pass at me or I'll castrate you."

"Oh, me putting my arm around you and saying we were eloping?" he asked, suddenly concerned. "Is that what you mean? That was me insuring our exit. What were *you* going to do to get away? Bring out a shotgun?"

Grace Two grunted. "No. I'm sorry. If you can't tell, I've had a rough life..." She paused, then said, "Really. I'm sorry. I don't think I could have pulled this off without you. At least, getting these two to the parents. You did say they were good folks, right?"

"First, you can decide on whether you think they're good or not for yourself. We'll be meeting up with them in less than five minutes. Second, I'll never make a pass at you. Third, no further apologies or explanations expected or required."

"Got it." Grace settled herself on the bed, the babies in the bag held close to her midsection, her feet up, knees brought up around them. "Stork One, ready for takeoff."

Chuck checked his mirrors and put the van in drive. "Baby Drop gas station, here we come."

***

"Oh, my God," Dusty said, peering into the night. "Is that her?"

A matronly woman in a heavy winter coat had her arm around Grace, partially supporting her weight with her shoulder, an overnight bag dragging behind her. The *whoop! whoop!* sound of a cop car trying to get someone's attention frightened her, her head spinning like a demon as she looked to see where the sound had come from. Without a word, Nurse Ellen dropped the bag and ducked out from under Grace's shoulder, leaving her where she was, wavering in confusion.

The panicked nurse rushed back to the sedan and took off, tires spinning on the icy pavement. Left behind was a stunned and still semi-sedated Grace wearing a hospital gown, wavering in the snowy driveway with nothing but house slippers and a blanket around her shoulders to keep her warm in the sub-freezing weather.

"I ain't waiting, guys," Dusty said, and bolted out of the truck, hopping over hedges to get to her before she collapsed.

"I got you," he said. He wrapped the sagging blanket around her tighter,

105

then held her close. Tears of joy streamed from his eyes at her nearness. He hadn't been able to see her face clearly in the dimness of the streetlight, but he knew it was her. He started to pick her up to carry her back to the truck but stopped at her yelp of pain.

"Are you okay?" he asked.

"No," she sobbed, leaning into his shoulder. She sniffed back the tears, then realized it was Dusty's scent, not Chuck's, that she smelled. "Dusty?" She blinked rapidly, lifting one hand up to wipe her eyes. "Is that you?"

"Yes, it's me, Dusty. I'll never let you out of my sight again."

Hal, Papa Doc, and Silas rushed over to join the reunion. "We got you, sweetheart," Hal said, crying just as much as they were, his arms wrapped around them both. "I promise, one of us will always be with you."

"But Mother..." she pined.

"Gone. Out of the picture. Divorce is in the works. I have some really stinky dirt on her now. I doubt she'll ever bother us again."

"But...but...they're gone. The nurse told me they died. They were fine at first, and then they died."

"Our babies?" Dusty asked. "They died? Both of them?"

Grace nodded, tears streaming, nose running, shoulders heaving, and without the energy to say another word.

"Let's go home," Papa Doc said, then moved in between Dusty and Hal to help bolster Grace. "There's plenty of room for all of us at the big house."

***

"Is that them?" Gloria asked her husband, clinging to his arm, tiptoeing to try for a better look.

Roger gave her hand a comforting pat, then moved away from the group so he could see the station wagon pull up to the gas pumps. "I don't know. Did he tell you what he'd be driving?"

"Oh, yeah. He said he'd be driving a white van," Gloria said. "Remember the password, 'Woodstock.'"

"Sounds like my kind of guy," Luther, the other father, remarked. He hugged his wife around the shoulders. "Remember when we were there?"

"How could I forget," Leanne giggled. "Over twenty years ago, and now our baby is finally here. That's a long gestation!"

"There's Chuck!" Gloria exclaimed, hopping up and down with joy, her hands tucked under her chin at seeing his familiar face behind the steering wheel of the white van.

"Settle down," Roger said. "You don't want to bring attention to us."

"Two middle-aged couples, snuggled up against the wind, looking like vultures ready to pounce... I'd say we were already suspicious," Luther said.

Chuck looked beyond the gas pumps and saw the two couples standing by the stack of bundled firewood, their smiles of anticipation marking them as the new parents. He rolled past them and came to a stop at the side of the mini-store, out of sight of anything but owls searching for dinner. "Tranquility base: Stork One and Stork Two have landed," he said, then opened the door and got out.

"Hey, there," he said to the huddled foursome. "Anyone for a game of golf? Know a good course around here?"

"How about Woodstock?" Gloria said, then ran up to Chuck and gave him a big hug. "Are they inside? Are they okay? I thought I was going to have a total meltdown when Dr. Buddy called and said that Grace had died, and they couldn't get the babies out in time. That they had all passed."

Chuck's eyes widened. "Grace was alive when I left." He opened the side door, exposing his new traveling nursemaid and the gym bag full of babies.

"I'm still alive," Grace Two said indignantly, then groaned softly as she realized it was a misunderstanding about the shared name. "I think you'd better call me Nanny." She looked at the eager parents, crowded around the open door, the women squeezed in front of their husbands to keep away from the chill. "Why don't you ladies come inside?"

Gloria led the way. "Which one is ours?" she asked once inside, peering into the unzipped bag.

"It's up to you two who gets Aqua and who gets Pinkie. The yellow-wrapped sweetheart is mine," Chuck said, watching the allocation of babies from the front seat.

"Oh, my God!" Leanne exclaimed. "They are identical! I can't believe it. How will we know whose is whose?"

Little Pinkie opened her eyes, started to squall, then caught sight of Gloria and smiled. "I don't care if she's the biggest or not; this one's mine."

"Then that must mean she's ours. Oh, I can't believe it. I swear I feel a tingling in my breasts. I'm as barren as a moon rock, but I swear she's kicked in a bucket load of estrogen." Leanne looked at Nanny. "Can I take her home now?"

"That's the plan. Oh, and don't even try to get in touch with Dr. Buddy. Either of you. If they didn't catch him, they will. You're lucky Chuck and I got in the middle of this or you wouldn't be celebrating motherhood tonight."

"Thank you, Nanny," Gloria said. "Chuck has my number. If you two run into any trouble or need a few bucks, just give me a call." She unzipped her jacket and put the swaddled baby inside. "Come on Vickie. You're coming home."

Leanne copied Gloria's tactic of carrying the baby inside the coat. "And you, too, Tori Lynn. Daddy's waiting outside."

Leanne stepped out of the van, then suddenly yipped. "She latched on! Oh, my Lord! I'm going to see if Luther can set me up with some of those plant estrogens. I may be able to nurse my baby still! Sing hallelujah!"

***

"I need to get some fuel before we head out of town," Silas said. "I'll pull in up here. Anyone need anything?"

"Gracie, do you want something to eat or drink?" Dusty asked.

"Something to drink," she said. "Maybe water?"

"Get her some chocolate milk and pick up a gallon of water, too. She needs some calories and we all could use the water," Papa Doc said. "You go ahead inside." He reached in his pocket and pulled out a fifty-dollar bill. "Get whatever you want, too. I'll stay with her."

"But…" Dusty started to protest, then saw how Grace was snuggled into Hal. Right now, she needed her father more than anyone else. "Thanks, Doc."

Silas pulled into the gas station at Hemingway and Sherlock. It seemed busy, but then he noticed that the three vehicles weren't getting fuel but were having some sort of meeting at the side of the building. "Drug dealers," he muttered when he got out, then saw that the men huddled by the side door were older. "Just pot," he added with a chuckle, then turned away to fuel both tanks on Dusty's truck.

"Do you want a coffee, Silas?" Dusty asked. "Doc's buying."

"Sure. Black, no sugar. And get me the biggest chocolate bar you can find, too."

"Gotcha," Dusty said, then walked into the mini market, grinning wide in uninhibited joy at finally reconnecting with the love of his life.

***

"That went well," Chuck said after the two couples had left. "Are you ready to hit the road, Nanny? Hmm. I really do like that name. It fits you. No nonsense, but nurturing."

Grace Two, now renamed Nanny, couldn't help but smile. "New name, new beginning. Works for me. Did you remember to pick up distilled water for mixing the formula? I didn't see any in here."

"Oh, shoot! I'm glad you noticed. No, I forgot. I'll run in and get some right now. Do you want a soda or coffee or anything?"

"Coffee, black, would be great."

"I'll get you something else, too. Stress eats up calories and we have a long way to go," Chuck said, then mumbled under his breath, "Wherever it is we're heading."

Chuck walked in and looked around. "Where do you keep the water?" he asked the clerk.

"What is this? There's a real run on bottled water tonight. Back there. See that kid with the ball cap? Yeah, right next to him."

"Thanks. And is the coffee fresh?"

"Just made a pot. Don't tell me; you want a giant chocolate bar, too," the clerk said, adding a chuckle.

"Hey, that does sound good."

"Just follow the kid. He's after the same stuff."

Chuck went to the back of the store where the young man was and found the water. "Dang!" he said, checking the label, then noticed the kid had picked out a bottle with a different colored cap. "You got the last distilled water, didn't you?"

Dusty lifted up his jug of water. "Shoot. I don't want this kind. Here, I'll swap you. I was after spring water for drinking."

"Thanks," Chuck said, then headed to the coffee kiosk. "What did we do before convenience store coffees?" he commented.

"Shoot. I don't know," Dusty answered. "I don't think I was born yet. For me, they've always been around. I didn't even know what a rotary phone was until I was clearing out my dad's attic. I can't imagine having to stay in one room while talking, tethered to a six-foot curly cord."

Chuck blew out a breath, stopping short of a full laugh, and shook his head. "Yeah, our folks really had to rough it. Have a good night, what's left of it," he said and saluted the young man in farewell.

"Yeah, you, too," Dusty said. "I know it's going to get better because I just found my woman. Thank you, Lord!"

Chuck paid for the water, coffee, and candy then walked to the side of the building and rapped on the side door of the van. "What's the name of Snoopy's bird?" he asked.

Click.

Nanny opened the door and let him in. "Do we have to keep doing that?" she asked.

"No, probably not. I'm just trying to bring a little levity to this harrowing evening. I know my emotions are all over the place. Elation at getting out of there with all three babies alive; fear of either being caught by Buddy's crew or being charged as an accomplice by the FBI; excitement with being able to help two couples get the daughters they were told were dead; and absolute sadness and loss at having to walk away from Grace. Lord, I hope the guys got her. Oh, shit!" he said, his voice loud as if he'd just been pinched. "I can text them!"

Chuck pulled his cellphone out of his front pocket and tap, tap, tapped the quick message to his father. 'Did U get her?'

***

"Here you go, Mr. Stillwater," Dusty said, handing the gallon of drinking water and chocolate milk to Hal.

"Seeing as you've been through so much hell and still seem pretty set on marrying my daughter, you can go ahead and call me Dad or Hal, whichever feels more comfortable."

Beep! Beep!

"What was that?" Dusty asked, looking around.

"My cellphone," Papa Doc said. "I got what they call a personalized alert tone for my incoming texts." He took the phone out of his shirt pocket, tapped a few buttons, and then put it back in his pocket. He looked at Hal and grimaced. "Someone just checking to make sure all went well on our end," and nodded at Grace.

"It's going to take time for all of us to heal," Hal said. "Some losses take longer to get over. Let's hope you haven't lost Chuck because of all of this."

"Only for a little time. My son has a nurturing soul and is a gentleman. I think he's just stepping back so Dusty can help her heal."

"What do you mean? He didn't know Dusty was coming with us or that we even found him. That was last minute, remember?" Hal said.

"Yeah, I wouldn't know your son if I sat on him," Dusty said. "Hey, does anyone want some chocolate?"

Grace listened to the men banter back and forth, their voices rising and lowering with their emotions and concerns. She hadn't heard her father and two surrogate uncles in a month and didn't realize until now how much she had missed them. She looked out the window. The world was getting better, itty bit by itty bit. Dusty was here. Would he accept her as she was? The way he had held her – sobbing uncontrollably with joy – when he rescued her after she had been abandoned by Nurse Ellen, she knew he'd do anything for her. He seemed to be sharing her feeling of loss for the babies, too. All her men could mourn with her. And they would heal together, too.

All but Chuck. Where was he? She closed her eyes tight and tried to find a thread of recent memory, struggling to recall the last words he had said to her. There it was. An echo of his words. He was leaving her, he said – leaving so she wouldn't associate him with her loss.

Which would have been worse, the loss of the babies to adoption or death? Definitely death. With adoption, they would still have been happy little people with families who cared for and cherished them. Now with death, they were just little corpses. Was it her fault they had died? Did she do something wrong?

Grace looked at Dusty, blinking back the tears that had returned. A familiar movement out of the corner of her eye caught her attention. She leaned over him to watch the man coming out of the convenience store. "Who's that?" she asked, pointing out the window.

Dusty recognized him as the man he had swapped jugs of water with. "Just some guy from the store. He got coffee and water, too. Why? Do you know him?"

She sighed then leaned back into his arm. "I thought I did…"

"Grace, I know it's not exactly romantic – my timing and all – but I want to make a new life with you as my wife. I have a lot going on now. I have my own business and everything. I still want to marry you and always will. We can start again with a family as soon as you say the word. I kinda know what went on with the other guy, and it doesn't matter to me. I mean, I know you have been

110

hurt in about a million different ways, but I want to help you heal. Would you let me? I mean, I'd do it however you want, but I'd rather do it as your husband than as your best friend."

Grace leaned into Dusty and inhaled his unique scent of boy and man. She felt the first smile in ages come to her face. She looked up. "Yeah, I think I'd like you better as a husband. Let me get healed up, and then let's get married. But if you don't mind, I'd still like to live with Papa Doc and Silas for a while. And hang out with my dad, too."

"And me?"

"Duh! You'd be living with us, too. One great big dysfunctional family."

"With a live-in groundskeeper," Dusty added.

***

"One month today," Papa Doc said. "Do you think we ought to have a candle or something for this cake?"

"Nope," Silas said. "That's just calling attention to what happened a month ago. You can put sparklers on it, though."

"Why? What for?"

"I was going to let Hal tell you, but his divorce is final. I talked him into sharing the news with everyone at dinner tonight."

"Hey, there!" Grace said as she walked into the kitchen and gave both men a hug. "I was just wondering... And I want you to tell me the truth now. No sparing my feelings because if you do that when I ask a direct question, I'll take that as lying to me."

"Fair enough," Doc said. "Shoot."

"It's been a month since...well... I haven't heard from Chuck in a month. Have either of you? Or do you know of anyone who has? And that includes texts, emails, phone calls, or rumors of any or all of the above."

"Wow," Silas said, chuckling. "You don't give a creative guy any wiggle room for shaving warts off the truth, do you?"

"Answer the question, because by that answer, it sounds like you don't want to tell me something."

"Grace, if my son called, you'd probably hear me yell at him from here to Canada, giving him hell for ditching you. No. Not a hint, whisper, cyber-sent word or letter. I don't even know if he's dead or alive. I know that sounds harsh, but yes, I'm concerned. I have a bucket of hope that he's just giving you and Dusty time to get reacquainted and settled. Maybe he thinks if you see him, you'll remember all you went through together."

"Hmph!" Grace frowned, then turned to the other man in the room. "Silas..."

"Ditto what he said except I haven't been sitting around waiting for him to contact us. I've been scouring the east coast looking for him. I have his credit card info, and there's not so much as a five-dollar charge for a burger. He's gone dark. He's off the radar."

"And don't even think to say that he's dead," Papa Doc piped in, his voice high with protest. "If something bad happened to him, they'd notify next of kin, and that's me. Nope, that man could give a shadow hints on how to hide in a spotlight."

He came over to Grace and put his arm around her. "He's given you the gift of a fresh start. Don't stomp on it by looking for him. One of these days, he'll show up. Mark my words. I feel it in my bones."

"Me, too," Silas said. "And it isn't my rheumatism acting up, either. You and Dusty are doing great together. I appreciate you two hanging around here, but if you want to go somewhere to make a home of your own, let me know. I have a few bucks held back and I'm not bashful about sharing them with my adopted daughter and her husband."

"Here, here!" Hal said, popping through the back door and saluting the group with a bottle of champagne. "It's my emancipation day! The divorce is final! As a show of good riddance and thanks for not hanging around to make any more bad memories, I bought Victoria a one-way ticket – non-refundable – to Costa Rica."

"And she took it?" Papa Doc asked.

"All I had to do was wave a blank VHS tape in her face, the box marked 'My Good Times with André the Giant.' Man, I wish I had a picture of the look on her face!" Hal wrapped his arm around Grace's shoulder. "She's out of our lives for good. I am so, so sorry that I couldn't get rid of her sooner."

"Well, as my old friend PollyAndy would say, 'Better today than tomorrow.'"

"Come join us in a toast," Hal said when he saw Dusty walk in the door. "Here's to friends, family, and joyous tomorrows!"

"But, I'm not old enough..." Dusty stammered.

"No one's carding tonight," Silas said. "Cheers!"

"Cheers to all of us!" Grace said. "Happy Independence Day, Dad."

"And to all a long life!"

Conclusion of THE SET UP
**Next up is, DIAMONDS AREN'T FOR EVERYONE, Book Two in the series TRIPLETS: THREE AREN'T ONE.

Diamonds Aren't for Everyone

Triplets: Three Aren't One
Book Two

Copyright

Diamonds Aren't For Everyone

Birthday mayhem turns into a hunt for her parents' blackmailers.
Will a handsome young rich heir ruin Vickie's plans?

Chapter 1: New Old Parents

January 3, 1992

"Is anyone following us?" Gloria asked, checking the side mirror of their Cadillac.

"Why would they be? We didn't do anything wrong," her husband said, now worried too.

"Other than adopt a baby without papers or even the birthmother's okay."

"First off…" Roger paused a moment to collect his wits and recheck the rearview mirror, then started again. "I seriously doubt that birth mothers are ever around when their babies are adopted out. Plus, I don't think Dr. Buddy would have let all three of her babies go without getting her permission."

"Dr. Buddy lied to us, though," she said. "Remember? Maybe he tricked the mother and lied to her, too. Imagine, getting over $80,000 from us upfront for his fee and expenses, and then telling us the mother and babies had died. I'm so glad Chuck came to our rescue. I only met him a couple of times, but I don't think he'd steal three babies from a mother who wanted them. She must have been overwhelmed. I mean, really? Can you imagine how daunting it would be to raise three babies all at once?"

"I watched my sister with just one at a time," Roger said. "No, I can't imagine twins, much less triplets. There must be more to the story. I have the feeling that Chuck knows more about what's going on but he's sparing us."

"So, do you think people will really believe I'm her natural mother?" Gloria asked, pulling down the visor to examine the faint crow's feet at the corners of her eyes.

"My dear wife, you're only forty years old. Lots of women your age give birth. More than anything, they'll wonder how you got your figure back so soon. Or even how you hid a pregnancy so well. You're as much a fox now as you were twenty years ago."

"Well, I'll simply say I didn't want to announce the pregnancy, just in case something went wrong. Of course, since the baby is so small, I can say that's why I recovered my shape so quickly." Gloria flipped the mirror up out of the way, then pulled the zipper down on her ski jacket to look inside at the face of her newborn treasure again. "She is so beautiful…"

"Yes, she is," Roger agreed. "Let's cancel all our social engagements for the next month or two. I want to spend as much time with her as…"

"But…but…"

"No buts. Hear me out. If we're off everyone's radar for a while, we can say we've been taking care of our new addition. That will be the truth, won't it?"

"Well, the two of us plus the nanny..."

"Fine. With or without the nanny, we'll make sure we get lots of pictures of us which should help support our absence. I think it's ridiculous to pretend she's our natural child, but if that's what you really want to do," Roger said, then sighed. "Nobody needs to know whether the adoption was through an agency or out the side door of a converted utility van. And before you ask for the seventh time in ten minutes, you're plenty young enough to have a child. If only those fertility shots had worked for you."

"They made us both crazy. Or rather, they made me over the hills hormonal and irrational and that almost drove you crazy. I didn't want to risk losing you because of it."

"Well, those *were* four very emotionally charged months," Roger agreed, recalling the screaming, crying, and knife-throwing episodes.

"How many times am I going to have to apologize..." Grace began, then stopped when she saw his head shaking. "Oh, you weren't looking for an apology."

"Let's move forward, shall we? Just you and me and baby makes three. Are you sure you want to name her Victoria, though?"

"Victoria like my sister? Heavens, no!" Gloria exclaimed, startling the baby snuggled next to her.

She brought her voice down and soothed the hours-old baby she had disturbed, "There, there, Vickie Lynn. You'll be home to a nice warm bottle in about three minutes. Mommy's here for you."

Roger glanced over at the two of them and grinned. Content. Happier now than he ever thought possible. "I'm glad to hear you call yourself Mommy. Mother sounds so stilted and formal. I never could understand why *she* insisted Grace call her Mother. Her own, biological daughter... That sounds so stoic and sterile."

"Grrr," Gloria groaned. "*She's* the reason I hate the name Victoria so much. The name on her birth certificate read Vickie but she hated it. 'Vickie' is such a common name,' she argued. 'It really should be Victoria. I'm like a queen – I'll be remembered long after I'm gone.' She whined so much about it that Dad changed it legally to Victoria for her twelfth birthday. I think it may have been part of the reason our mom had a heart attack. She loved her Grandma Vickie so much that it was an emotional slap in the face to just throw out the name like that. You couldn't prove to me that Victoria didn't agitate her on purpose with stunts like that. She knew Mom had a weak heart. Damn *Victoria* still!" she said with disdain.

"You won't hear me argue that one," Roger said. "I lost my favorite cousin and best friend in the whole world because of her, but as I was just saying, we have a fresh start, right?"

Gloria reached up and patted her husband on the shoulder. "You may have been second in line for my hand, but you were and still are the best man for me, Roger Stillwater Thornwhistle."

"And you for me, Gloria Lynn Thornwhistle."

***

"Oh, dear," Gloria fretted, pacing back and forth, trying to soothe the squalling baby. "I think I need to call the nanny right now. Something's wrong. She won't quit crying."

"Hold on a sec," Roger said patiently, holding back his frustration. One of them losing it was one too many.

Ding!

Roger took the bottle of water out of the microwave, stirred in the suggested amount of formula, swirled it around, and then capped the bottle.

"Here," Gloria said, grabbing for it.

"Nope," he said, pulling it away. He tipped a small amount of formula on the inside of his wrist, verifying the temperature, then handed it to her. "Perfect. Body temp."

Gloria snuggled Vickie close then clumsily tried to feed her the bottle. "Damn! I think I need my reading glasses just to find her mouth!"

The baby's mouth turned and latched onto the nipple that had struck her cheek, leaving a milky mess. Roger grabbed a tissue and wiped it clean. "Smart girl. She'll find the food. Just get it in the general area, but make sure it's not too hot or too cold."

"How did you know that?"

"I read up on it, plus I did hang out with my sister's sons every once in a while. Just keep her warm, dry, and well-fed and she'll soon be our little princess in satin and lace."

"She can be our princess in satin right now," Gloria said, "but lace will have to wait until her skin isn't so tender. See. I hung out with your sister a bit, too."

***

Two weeks before Christmas, 1995
Nearly four years later

"Where'd she go?" Gloria asked in a panic.

"What do you mean, 'Where'd she go'?" Roger huffed. "I thought you had her!"

"I did! She said she was going to see you. I looked up, there you were, and now she's gone!"

"You go that way; I'll check over in the toys," Roger said. "I don't believe

117

in tethers, but I wish I had her on one right now."

***

Near the carousel

"I remember when you were little," Hal said, his arm around Grace's shoulder. "I'd bring you here to ride the pink unicorn. No matter how long I let you ride, you'd always ask for 'one more turn.' It'd irritate your mother to no end if she was here with us, too."

"I think I remember that," Grace said. "She'd stomp her foot and walk away when you gave into me."

Hal chuckled at the memory but didn't add to the story.

"And if I remember right, you'd let me ride until I wet my pants."

"Hey, that wasn't my fault. You didn't tell me you had to go."

"Yeah, well, you should have known. When we'd come here, you'd let me have anything I wanted. I wonder if they still have those orange juice and ice cream milkshakes…"

"Here you go, Dad," Dusty said, handing Hal his 'orange-sicle' drink. "And I got the largest size they made for Grace."

"You remembered!" Grace said, accepting the giant cup.

"It's still good for you: juice and milk. Add a few bacon bits and strudel crumbles and you have all four food groups," Hal said, smiling.

Grace looked toward the carousel and blanched in horror. She clumsily set her cup down and rushed to the flimsy security fence, swooping up the little blonde, sparing the tyke a disastrous tumble into the twirling ride.

"Whoa there, honey," Grace soothed, holding her close. "You have to wait until it stops to get on."

"I want to ride the pink ooni-corn," Vickie said, reaching out.

"Okay. Let's wait for it to stop, and then I'll ride with you. Will that be all okay?"

Vickie looked up at Grace and squinted, studying her features, then back at the twirling ride that was slowing down.

"Again?"

"Well, for me it will be again," Grace said. She looked back at her dad and Dusty. "Call security and tell them they have a lost little girl at the carousel. Maybe they can find her parents."

Hal stared at the duo, frozen in shock at the resemblance of the little blonde beauty to Grace when she was that age. She could have been a pint-sized clone of her.

"Um, Dad? Do you want me to go tell them or do you want to?" Dusty asked. When Hal didn't respond, he said, "Okay. I'll go."

"This was my favorite when I was your age, too," Grace said, hoping she didn't scare the little girl. "How old are you?"

"Vickie Lynn."

118

Grace realized the girl was confused, so she tried the other oft-asked question. "What's your name?"

"I'm this many tomorrow," she said, holding up four fingers, using her other hand to keep her thumb from popping up

"And what's your Mommy's name?"

"Vickie Lynn January Third."

The carousel came to a stop beside them. "Here's the unicorn," Grace said, hoisting her up. "This was my favorite one, too. So, is your name Vickie Lynn?"

The little girl in the pink satin coat trimmed with a real white fur clung to the bronze pole in the middle of her magical creature, rising up and down, oblivious of the questions trying to intrude on her quest to find the rest of the unicorns in fantasy land.

Grace put her interrogation on pause, letting the little girl enjoy the ride. Certainly, her parents would be found soon. Who would let someone so precious out of their sight? Then again, she'd never let anyone get in her way of riding the pink 'oonicorn' when she was that age, either. Tears welled in her eyes as she realized that her twins would have been this age if she had kept them. Why had she balked? Given up on them even before she let them know her? Maybe they wouldn't have died if she had had them in a hospital, not at Dr. Buddy's birthing center?

Her smile dropped as the reasons smacked her in the gut like one-two punches. Those threats to Dusty and his father were why. Victoria – she refused to even think of her as Mother – was long gone now, a resident of Costa Rica thanks to Dad's not-too-subtle threat of blackmail. Dusty was back in her life – safe – and her husband for almost four years now. If she would have known that circumstances would be in her favor, she wouldn't have given up hope and the twins. No looking back on that now. Hopefully, the fertility specialist had a solution to her recent sterility and they could start anew with more children.

"Again! Again!" Vickie Lynn demanded, bouncing up and down.

"I got it," Hal called from below, nodding to the carousel operator who had been given a healthy tip to keep the ride going for the blonde pair clinging to the magical animal of fiberglass and pink resin.

Hal sighed at the beautiful blondes, so much like a mother and daughter in looks and favorite animals. *I wonder if the twins were girls? I know it shouldn't make a difference because they're dead, but it does. If I had only seen them for a moment, even an ultrasound of their little feet kicking, their little bodies twisting and turning, their little bottoms showing off which gender they were...*

"Oh, thank God!" Roger said, stopping short at the sight of his young daughter with a beautiful blonde supporting her on the carousel.

"I take it she's yours," Hal said, then blanched as he looked back and saw who was speaking. "Roger?"

"Hal?" Roger asked. He glanced back momentarily to verify the voice belonged to his cousin, then was focused back on Vickie. "It's been… Yes, that's my daughter. She bolted when my wife looked away."

"Gloria?"

"Yes, Gloria," Roger said, looking back at Hal, his eyes narrowed.

"She's a wonderful woman. I'm glad you could have children. I know she always wanted them," Hal said, swallowing hard. *And if she's the mother, I wonder who the real father is!*

Roger quickly moved to Hal's side. "She's adopted and if you tell a soul, I'll hunt you down and castrate you," he whispered harshly.

"I see the family resemblance," Hal said, non-plussed by the threat. "That's my Grace up there with her now." He patted Roger on the shoulder. "Your secret never left my lips," he whispered, "and never will. No hard feelings, I hope."

Roger's shoulders slumped in embarrassment. "I'm sorry. Really, I am, Hal. I heard through the rumor mill that *she* is gone. I never should have let her get between us."

"Divorced and it didn't cost me a dime," Hal said softly. "Other than a one-way ticket to Costa Rica. Congratulations on having a daughter. They're the greatest joy but can give you the greatest scares, too. I lost Grace for a while there, but she's back. That's her husband coming over to watch them now. Come on. Let me introduce you."

"Daddy!" Vickie squealed, lunging for her father, ignoring the gap between him and her pink pony.

Grace caught her and held her tight, memorizing the feel of the soft yet sturdy body in her arms, the scent of shampoo and excitement, the sound of her squeals at being reunited with a parent. A sound she'd never hear from the children she'd lost.

The group walked away from the carousel, Vickie now clutching her daddy close. "Join us for a drink?" Hal asked. "We have plenty."

"I'll go get some little cups," Dusty offered, then went back to the concession stand.

"Don't ever do that again," Roger scolded Vickie, his face furrowed with concern, a tear escaping from the corner of his eye at the thought of losing his treasure. "You scared your mother and me… Oh, shoot. Stay here with Uncle Hal and Cousin Gracie. I have to call Mommy and let her know I found you."

Grace held onto the four-year-old as they watched Dusty pour the thick peach-colored confection into the cup. "Be careful," she warned. "It's messy. And don't drink it too fast."

"Brain freeze!" Vickie said, then giggled. "That really hurts, huh?"

Hal sat back and watched the pair interact, fantasizing of how it would be when Grace and Dusty had their own child. Or would have been if Grace's twins had survived…

120

He shook his head. No bad thoughts today. Reunited with an estranged cousin: one huge blessing. Grace and Dusty discovering a new relative, another big blessing. Maybe this encounter would kick Grace's hormones into gear, or realign whatever was keeping her from getting pregnant. Dusty had already been tested and verified as potent. The results from her visit with the fertility specialist this morning would be back in less than two weeks. Now all they could do was wait. And pray.

Roger handed Hal his business card that he had added his home and cellphone numbers to. "Call me anytime. We can get together. At least, if it isn't too uncomfortable with you and Gloria."

"Um," Hal stalled, trying not to think of the woman he had wanted to marry but instead thinking of the opportunity for Grace to have 'good' family to get to know. "I think it would be fine. I know Grace has had some trouble conceiving. Maybe she and Gloria can share a few secrets. Or not. I'll leave it up to you." Hal pulled a card out of his wallet, scribbled his personal contact info on the back, and handed it to Roger. "We're still just outside of Plymouth. I let the kids have my place. I'm up the road at the bachelor's pad. You remember Doc Armstrong and Silas, right?"

Roger paled, then nodded. "Doc had three sons, didn't he? And didn't they start calling him Papa Doc after one of them became a doctor, too?"

"Yup. But a heads up if you come out to see us. He's kinda, sorta out of sons. The first one was murdered by the second one – who's in prison doing life – and the third one has been missing for four years. A little family drama there; not worth going into. I'm sure Chuck will come around again one of these days."

"Yeah, family is family. When you least expect it, we're there for each other. How many years has it been for us?" Roger asked.

"Way too many," Hal said. "Tell Gloria I said hi, and congratulations to both of you for having one of the most beautiful daughters in the world. I'm a little prejudiced there, though. I don't think you saw Grace when she was that age, but your little Vickie could be her clone. They're identical all the way down to those little ears that stick out just enough to be precious. Little angel ears, I call them."

"Must come down the mother's line, then," Roger said with a wink. *Keep the adoption part a secret, Cousin. We can still claim these two girls are related without referring to Victoria the Viper-mother and aunt.*

Chapter 2: Bad News & a Birthday

Two weeks later

"Did we have to come into the city for this?" Dusty asked. "I mean, couldn't the doctor just tell us what was wrong over the phone or call in a prescription or something?"

"I know they usually want to have a little visual going on at the same time. Posters and plastic models and such," Grace said, then brought up her finger, ready to chew on her cuticle again.

Dusty caught her eye, then grinned. "Tabasco," he whispered.

"Don't you dare!" she hissed, then giggled. "Just the thought of it keeps me from doing it. But you're right. I need a little reminder every once in a while. Nervous energy is not good. I think I'll bring my crocheting with me next time. I can't keep my hands still."

"We have so many afghans now, I think we're going to have to start giving them away."

"I already did," Grace said. "You only see the ones I make in the evening when you're home. I make at least three shawls a week and take them right to the hospital for newborns and mommies."

"Shawls for babies?" Dusty asked.

"Shawls for the mommies to use while they're nursing the babies…" Grace sighed in longing and frustration, then huffed. "What's taking them so long?"

"It's a doctor's office. That's what they do."

Grace looked around and saw that she wasn't the only one with the anxious pallor and tight lips. She tried to smile at another woman whose eye she had caught, then realized they were both grimacing at what was sure to be bad news for both of them. She shrugged and looked down at her hands, then twiddled her thumbs. Another clinic. Another doctor.

Dusty set his hand on top of hers. "Just a few more minutes, and then we'll know. I'm sure it's good news or they wouldn't make us wait so long," he said, hoping his wishful speculation was more fact than fantasy.

"Mr. and Mrs. Rhodes?" the nurse called out, scanning the room. "Come on back."

Grace got to her feet, then faltered, nerves taking away her ability to lock her knees. "I got you," Dusty whispered, his arm around her waist.

"That's the only thing that keeps me going," Grace whispered back.

The nurse ushered the couple into the doctor's office, totally bypassing the exam rooms. "Uh, oh," Dusty whispered. "I don't know if this is good or bad."

"Bad," Grace said, covering her mouth to keep from losing the light breakfast she'd eaten.

Dusty leaned forward and looked for a trash can, but was stilled by Grace's hand. "I got it," she said, then sat back, composed. "It is what it is."

The bald and rotund doctor came in and greeted the young couple. "Let me be blunt," he said. "I see from your records that you were delivered of twins approximately four years ago via cesarean section. There were no hospital records that we could find..." he said, waiting for Grace to complete his thought.

"It was a private clinic," she said. "The doctor told me the twins died. That's why I know I'm not barren. I've conceived before."

"Uh, huh..."

"And my husband was tested three years ago. He's got very active sperm. They even wanted him as a donor!" Grace tried to contain her anger and frustration but it spilled out. "So, if I can conceive twins and carry them to over eight months gestation," she said vehemently, "and my husband has swimmers that are so active that the fertility folks wanted his boys for building tall blond babies, why can't we have a baby together? I mean, we did it before!"

"Because, my dear," the doctor said with as much compassion as he could, "the doctor or nurse or whoever delivered you, tied your tubes when he was in there. You had a tubal ligation. You have healthy eggs but no way for them to get to the uterus."

"I'll kill him," Grace hissed. "If I ever see that Dr. Buddy again, I swear to God and to anything holy or unholy, I'll kill him!"

"Oh...Dr. Buddy..." the doctor said.

"You know him?" Grace asked, turning back to Dusty. He shrugged and shook his head, clueless.

"He was arrested about three, maybe four, years ago. He had a series of birthing clinics all up and down the east coast. He'd bring in pregnant women who wanted to give their babies up for adoption, give them a wonderful place to stay while gestating, then deliver them."

"Yeah. That's pretty much what happened to me. So, that's illegal?" Grace asked.

"What came next was. He'd deliver healthy babies, sell them – which is illegal – to desperate families, then tell the new parents the baby had died. Of course, that meant that he had a child he could resell many times over."

"The scum!" Dusty hissed.

"Ah," the doctor continued, "but it didn't stop there. He sedated the mothers so they didn't know their babies were still alive. While he was in them, he sterilized them, just as he did with you."

"But why?" Grace asked.

"Not only sterilized them but kept them as breeding stock. This way, he could promote a healthy vessel to prospective parents looking for surrogates. No chance of the mother having a child from her own eggs. He was a white slaver. You're lucky to be free. Many young women who went to his clinics to deliver children for adoption are still missing."

"Yeah, well, there was some intervention there. My friend got in the middle of that," Grace said, then looked at Dusty and grimaced.

"Was he an accomplice?" the doctor asked, leaning forward in his seat, eager to hear her answer. "Because if he was, he might have information that will help the authorities find these missing women."

"No, he didn't aid and abet or anything like that, I'm sure. I don't know where he is, though. I do know he's the reason I'm free. From what my father told me, they were setting me up in a recovery house but told him I was going to be somewhere else. He found out where I was and sent my dad and Dusty to come and get me. So, back to my fertility…"

"Yes…"

"Does that mean that I can be my own surrogate or whatever you call it?"

"Yes, we can fertilize the eggs outside of your body and implant them. It's called *in vitro fertilization*. We've been doing it since the late 70s. It's pricey but relatively safe. It doesn't work every time, but we can use your own eggs and his sperm. Does this sound like something you'd like to pursue?"

A sudden chill went up Grace's arms. She looked at Dusty and saw that he looked like he was the one ready to vomit this time. "Not right now," she said. "We'll get back to you."

Grace stood up and reached for Dusty's hand. "Come on. I want to go home." She looked at the doctor and blinked twice. A glimmer of familiarity sparked between them and then was gone. "Thanks for your time."

She reached out for her queasy husband. "Come on," she said and led him out of the office.

Once in the hallway, a dazed Dusty made his way to the fountain. "Just a sec. I'm thirsty."

"Sure. Why don't you go in the john and splash some water on your face, too. That might help."

Grace paced while she waited outside the men's bathroom. Nerves on edge, her hand flew towards her mouth. "Ah, to hell with it," she grumbled, then chewed at her cuticle. "Damn baby thieves!"

"What's wrong?" Dusty asked, seeing that she was back to her bad habit but positive that now was not the time to say, 'Tabasco.'

"I think this doctor was in cahoots with Dr. Buddy. Did you see the way he was positively radiant when he said Buddy had been busted? He wants to find those baby-making mamas for himself! He's got dozens, scores of couples looking for a ripe place to plant seeded eggs. I wouldn't trust him to put my egg with your sperm back into my body, even if I watched the procedure from start to finish. Damn! Damn! Damn!"

"Grace, you're going to have to trust someone, sometime," Dusty said, his hand on her shoulder.

"Yeah, well, I trust you, my dad, Silas, and Papa Doc. Even if he's been gone for four years, I'd trust Chuck, too. I know Papa Doc thinks he's still alive, but I can't believe he wouldn't at least check in on me."

"Um, Gracie, I think we need to talk," Dusty said. "But not here. Let's take a walk. You got me paranoid about security cameras now."

"I do? When did I ever talk about security cameras?"

"Walk," Dusty said. He put his arm around her shoulder, not willing to accept any discussion on the subject. "Outside, fresh air." *Traffic noises, people walking past us...*

"Can we even get to the parking garage this way?" Grace asked.

"Yup," Dusty said, pushing the door open for her.

"Why are you being so weird?"

Dusty put his hand on her shoulder and led her toward the little city park across the street. "Wait to talk."

He spotted an empty picnic table and used a found newspaper to sweep off the bench seat. "Did you realize that after what he just said, our babies may still be alive?"

"Wait! What? Oh, my God! No! I mean, yes! They could still be alive?"

"Sounds reasonable to me. I know you got the chills talking to him. Did you recognize him or something?"

"Yes. I was sedated a lot of the time. Come to think of it, I remember going under and the anesthesiologist made a crack about Chuck's upset stomach being morning sickness. Shit! He knows who I am!"

"Well, for right now, I'm going to agree with you about no invasive procedures to make a baby. Let's give it a year or so and see if we can find our children," Dusty said.

"I don't know if it's delayed maternal hormones or not, but I'm on a roll now!" Grace said.

Yeah, and now I don't feel obligated to tell you that Chuck really is alive and well. That secret can come out later. I just hope I don't trip myself up! The guys would kill me if I spilled the beans!

***

January 2, 1996

"Hal? Yeah, this is Roger. Hey, I hate to do this to you at the last minute like this, but we're having a birthday party for Vickie Lynn tomorrow and wanted to know if you and your beautiful daughter and her husband wanted to come by and say hi. Yeah, well, I would have said something when I saw you, but Gloria was organizing it, and I didn't want to step on her toes. Neither one of us thought about you until Vickie Lynn asked if we were going to go see that 'ooni-corn' lady again. Yeah, Grace really made an impression on her. Well, we're still at the same place. Light snacks around four-ish if you don't have to work too late. I thought you and those old guys might want to pop in and sing happy birthday to my little miracle baby, too. There won't be that many kiddos around but there'll be plenty of *hors d'oeuvres*, cake, and sangria for everyone. Bring the gang. No, don't worry about upsetting anyone or stirring up hard feelings. I think Gloria wants to see if you're still the hunk you were in college. Yeah, well, put a hat on so that shiny bald spot doesn't blind her. Hey! Someone in the family had to keep all his hair! All right. See at least three of you tomorrow, then."

***

Knock! Knock!

"Hey, Dad. What's going on?" Dusty asked Hal. "You look like you just sold your portfolio at twice its estimated value."

"Nah, I'm not even thinking about work until half-way into January. This being semi-retired at forty-five is great! Hey, how's Gracie doing?"

"She's still bummed that she was sterilized, but she does have a fire under her that keeps her getting up in the morning. She's up at daylight or earlier, searching the internet for news stories about *in vitro fertilization* procedures in other countries. At least it's keeping her from depression. I'd rather see her fuming than a lump under the covers."

"Yeah," Hal agreed. "You and me and everyone else. Three years was enough! So, the reason I'm so perky is that we've been invited to a birthday party. Remember Grace's little cousin we met at the carousel a couple of weeks ago?"

"Your cousin's daughter?"

"Yup. She's four-years-old tomorrow. Roger and his wife invited us over for her birthday party."

"Um, Dad… You do know what tomorrow is, don't you?"

"The day after today?" Hal quipped, then looked down at his watch to verify the date. "Oh, crap."

"Yup, it's the day she lost the babies. Oh, and before you tell her what's going on, can I tell you something?"

"Of course." Hal pulled out a kitchen chair and sat down. "Do you need anything? Are the guys downtown giving you fits?"

"No, they're cool. They got over me being a blue-collar guy right after I pointed out the holes in their proposals. Now they call me The Natural."

"Good for you. Now, what's on your mind?"

"We told you about the doctor's visit. Sort of. What Grace didn't tell you was that the specialist she saw was the anesthetist who was there when she had the babies. He was sort of fishing for where Chuck was. You see…Well, this is a biggie. This guy said that this Dr. Buddy who delivered Grace would tell the adopting parents that the babies had died. This way, he got to keep all their money, and still had babies to sell to other parents."

"Oh, shit!" Hal slumped sideways in his chair, nearly fainting while seated.

"And you think that maybe her twins didn't die? That they're out there somewhere?"

"That's the first thing I thought of, too. It didn't hit her right away, though. She'd already been dealing with so much guilt about doing something wrong while pregnant and that's why they died, that she couldn't see the proverbial forest for the trees when he mentioned it. So, somewhere out there, there might be a couple of her children."

"And we don't even know if they're boys or girls or one of each..." Hal said.

"I was, and still am, going to let her tell you my suspicions in her own time. She didn't ask me *not* to tell you, so I'm not betraying a confidence. Still, I'd appreciate it if you didn't let on we already had this conversation."

"So, she's really searching the internet for clues about her babies?"

"Not the babies, per se, but Dr. Buddy and his cohorts. It seems they had – or still have – a series of homes where they keep women to carry surrogate babies."

"White slavery still exists," Hal said softly. "Damn!"

"Hey! What are you doing here, Dad?" Grace asked.

Startled, Hal sat up and took a deep breath to compose himself, then grinned, remembering the original purpose of his visit. "Just talking with The Natural here. We're invited to a birthday party tomorrow. Your little second cousin is having a birthday party, and we're invited."

"Vickie Lynn? Oh, that's right! She's so cute. She's at that age where when you ask her name, she gives you her age. Ask her age, and she gives you her name. Is she going to be four or five? She showed me four fingers, but I don't know if they taught her how old she was or would be."

Hal shook his head and said, "I guess we'll find out tomorrow when we count the candles, won't we? Anyone for a shopping trip into the city to find her a gift?"

"We don't need to," Grace said. "I already have the perfect one. I have a stuffed pink unicorn that she's going to love. I'll just clean it up and add a big ribbon, and she's good to go. As a matter of fact..."

Hal and Dusty watched as Grace's face twitched in recall. "Yes..." Hal prompted.

"I got that doll for my fifth birthday! I've had it for nearly twenty years. Pinkie's ready for a new home. She looks great on the shelf, but really needs someone to play with."

Dusty and Hal both noticed her tears escaping but didn't comment. They both knew Grace had been saving that magical stuffed animal for her own child. Giving it away – whether to a relative or not – meant that she was finally moving on.

"You're right," Hal said, standing up to hug her. "The perfect gift."

"Here goes nothing," Hal mumbled so only Papa Doc could hear.

Or so he thought.

"If only we could be that lucky," Silas said softly. "I remember the last time I was here…"

The door opened swiftly at the soft tap of the brass knocker, as if someone was standing behind it, waiting. "Hey, there!" Roger said, hand out ready to greet whoever he saw first with a hearty handshake.

"Long time, no see," Papa Doc said, then moved away so Silas could have his own moment of personal discomfort.

"Sounds like congratulations are about four – or is it five? – years too late," Silas said, returning the firm grip with a minimal pump of the traditional handshake.

"Four. Vickie Lynn is four-years-old today. It doesn't seem like it, though. Sometimes it seems like it was only yesterday she came into our lives. The next minute, it's like she's always been a part of our family. I can't imagine what it's going to be like when she grows up and moves away."

"Do your best not to think about it," Hal said, then stepped back.

"Enjoy them every minute," Papa Doc added, his eyes misting. "One minute, they're under your feet and you can't wait for them to take off to school, the next, you're wondering where they are."

"Or worse," Silas whispered, then grimaced, thinking of Papa Doc's first son dead, killed by the second one who was in prison, the third one – Chuck – lying low and living off the grid somewhere in the backwoods of America.

Roger saw the familial interaction, like a visible electric current, a common thought moving from one man to the other. All four of them had been acquainted for more than twenty years, but those three now seemed more like the cousins he and Hal used to be. One man's reflections were shared by the other two. Like an old married couple, these three were in sync, comfortable in their lives.

"I brought something for Vickie Lynn," Grace said, holding up a bright bag stuffed with pink tissue paper. "It used to be mine but I'm sure she'll love it."

"She'll love it even more, then," Roger said, ushering her in. "A family heirloom."

"Hello there, Dusty, is it?" he asked, letting the last of the family group in.

"Yes, sir," Dusty said, then craned his neck to catch sight of the little birthday girl. "We love children and hope to have some of our own soon."

"Well, I hope you don't have to wait as long as Gloria and I did. Over fifteen years of trying and then, boom! A baby. Of course," he whispered loud enough so the men could hear, "the trying was fun."

Dusty felt his face redden, so held one finger up in agreement, covering most of his glow with the gesture.

"Oh, my!" Grace said, looking around the room. Dozens of unicorns filled the area, from piñatas to posters to the ice sculpture in the middle of a fountain of pink punch.

"Well, I *may* have gone a little overboard," Gloria said, coming up to greet Grace.

"Yeah, well, they're only young once. She may not appreciate this much attention when she's a teenager, but for now, enjoy it."

"Oh, I do enjoy it! I feel as if I'm in my second childhood. Oh, and you probably don't remember me. I'm your Aunt Gloria, but please, just call me Gloria. No one needs to know we're related *that way.*"

Grace chuckled, glad that Gloria didn't want to bring up that her sister, Victoria, was her mother. "Yes, my father's cousin's wife is close enough to being my aunt, but Gloria works for me, too. Where's our birthday girl?"

"Oh, she's upstairs. I just got a nanny for her. Not that she really needs a nanny. Roger and I did everything for her since the day she was born. Elsa is more of her tutor. Most parents send their children away to preschool at four, but I'm not ready to part with her. Besides," she whispered, "you never know what the children they're associating with will be like. It's not really the kids so much…" She shook her head and pursed her lips. "But some children's parents…"

"Tell me about it. Or rather, let's not. Where should I put this?"

Gloria took the bag Grace offered and set it on the table laden with exotically-wrapped gifts, a miniature battery-powered Rolls Royce with a huge pink ribbon parked beneath it.

"I'd say it sucks having a birthday so close to Christmas," Grace said, "but it looks like she still managed to do well."

Roger came over and put his hand on Grace's shoulder. "I think my wife gives her too much in the way of material goods, but we tell Vickie Lynn that she has to take care of what she has or we'll give it away to someone who will appreciate it. So far, so good."

"And here she comes now," Gloria said, her smile bright at watching the young girl come down the steps one-by-one, poised as a real princess, her hand gently waving to the fifteen or so adults and half dozen children at the bottom of the stairs.

"Wow! What an entrance! And where did you get that dress?" Grace asked.

"One of my friends is a close friend of Christian Dior. He designed it for her. It's my gift to her."

"Oh, my. You might want to get her a life-sized doll made so when she grows out of it, the dress won't go to waste."

"Already commissioned," Gloria said. "She's getting a real twin…"

Gloria started coughing as soon as the word was out of her mouth, gagging on the memory that somewhere in the backwoods of Oregon and California, her daughter really did have a twin. Or rather, two.

Grace wrapped her arm around Gloria's waist, ready to help her to a chair when she was waved off. "No, I'm fine. I just swallowed wrong," she whispered hoarsely then looked up to watch her daughter continue her entrance.

Vickie Lynn was still taking her time descending the staircase, heeding the prompts from the nanny three feet behind her. "Smile, little one. Show those perfect teeth."

However, when the miniature beauty queen spotted Grace, all poise and charm blew up into unbridled excitement and passion, arms waving and voice squealing. "Ooni-corn Lady! You came!"

Rushing down the last four steps, Vickie Lynn tumbled forward, her foot catching on the leading edge of the gown of pink chiffon, seed pearls, and lace. Six adults rushed to catch her, but it was Grace who wound up with her in her arms. "Are you all right?"

"You came!" Vickie Lynn said, swiping the curled ringlets out of her face with a sputter. "I asked Daddy for you for my present and he said you'd come. Maybe. But if you came, I couldn't keep you. Are you sure you don't want to live with me, Ooni-corn Lady? We can go ride the carousel all day long. That is if you drive us there. I got a car from my Aunt, but I can't go past the front yard, Mommy said."

Grace brushed the curls behind Vickie's ears, noticing they stuck out just like hers. "I can't stay here all the time, but I can come and see you whenever your mommy and daddy say I can. I do have to work sometimes, though."

"Is she okay?" Roger asked, his bottom lip sucked in with fear.

"She just messed up her hair a bit. You should be an acrobat. You landed on your feet pretty fast," Grace said. "Here, honey. Give your daddy a big hug and a squeeze. You scared him."

Roger picked her up and held her close, pivoting so he could see Gloria. His head shook minimally, a silent admonishment that her overzealousness for a show had almost injured their daughter.

'I'm sorry,' Gloria mouthed, her watery eyes proving her sincerity.

"Thank you for bringing Ooni-corn Lady, Daddy," Vickie said, reaching out to touch her.

"My name is Grace," she said. "Do you know what my name means?"

"Ooni-corn Lady!" Vickie Lynn declared.

"Yeah, I think it does," Roger said, then winked at Grace. "Thanks for coming. Double thanks since that's twice you've saved her from falling on her face."

"I'll be there for her anytime you need me," Grace said. "And I babysit for free," and added a wink.

"I'm not a baby," Vickie said.

"Okay. I 'pretty little girl' sit for free," Grace said.

Everyone within earshot laughed, then started milling around. Excitement for Act One was over. Excitement for Act Two – the opening of presents and eating of cake – was coming soon.

***

Eight years later

Elsa looked at the slip of paper with the phone number. She hated to bring anyone else into her world of extortion but after eight years, her garden of blackmail sources was depleted. She needed more information. Or proof for some of her suspicions. After all these years of operating solo, she didn't want to admit she needed anyone, especially a man. She snorted in frustration and dialed.

"Hello, Jimmy? Yes, you don't know me. but you come highly recommended. No, I'm not the police or a lawyer. I want photos if you can get them, but I also hear you have a directional microphone. There's a certain young woman I want you to follow. No, not all the time. I'll give you a heads up when she's with the Thornwhistle's daughter. Oh, so you do know that family. Yes, their only child is twelve-and-a-half years old. I suspect that a certain Grace Rhodes is her biological mother. Yes. I want you to listen in on the pair's conversations. Do you think you can do that? Well, I don't give a flying fart about anyone else. I pay well. You won't have to trail behind pop stars and aging country singers anymore. I have your number. I'll give you a call the next time they're together. No. You don't need to know my name. Just call this number with any information."

Click.

"That should restart the revenue stream," Elsa said with a sneer of perverted pleasure. "Try and get rid of me when she starts high school, will you, Roger Thornwhistle! I've just begun to harvest your wealth!"

Chapter 3: Growing Up is Hard to Do

January 3, 2005

"Are you sure she wants us at her birthday party?" Dusty asked. He helped himself to a cup of coffee and croissant from the buffet the Thornwhistles always had set up for visitors. He pulled up a chair and sat next to Grace. "I mean, she's thirteen years old now. She's sure to want just friends her own age. Old folks hanging around are just boring."

"No, we're worse, even if we aren't that old. We're embarrassing. That's my job: to make her blush in front of her friends."

"Grace!" Dusty yelped.

"No, I'm messing with you. I remember how giddy and ridiculous I was at that age. I knew everything." Grace blanched and shook her head, trying to forget the sneers and mean words her mother tormented her with when she was growing up.

"Are you all right?" Dusty asked. "You look all pasty – like you had another one of those flashbacks."

"Yeah, I did. In my mother's opinion, everything I did, said, or wore was stupid or ugly." She snorted in derision. "I never would have made it this far if it hadn't been for my father and Sally, the housekeeper. Dad would literally tell me *not* to listen to anything she said. Well, except they did agree on one thing…"

"What's that?"

"They both said don't have sex until I was married. And not to get married until after I had finished college." Grace rolled her eyes. "I guess that's two things. Oh, well. So much for going to college. Now with the internet, I can do all the studying and research I want online."

"I was glad I could skip right to starting a business. All I needed was a little direction from your dad and a foot in the door with the right advertising firms and bankers. Rhodes and Gardens made it onto the Fortune 500 this month, too! Who thought creating a franchise for groundskeeping and snowplowing would work? Hey, is it true that your Dad and the guys are going to Nepal this year?"

"Nope."

"What do you mean, nope?"

"They just started that rumor to flush out some of the *paparazzi* who have started nosing around again."

"Who are they following and why?" Dusty asked, picking up the croissant to dunk in his coffee.

"Me," Grace said. "And before you ask again, I don't know why."

"Maybe it's because you spend a lot of time with Vickie Lynn and you two just happen to look a lot like…" Dusty suggested, his eyes squinted in anticipation of another argument.

"Like mother and daughter? Hey, as long as Gloria's busy with her charities and Roger says it's all right, I want to spend as much time I can with her during her formative years. That snide bitch of a nanny they insist on keeping around keeps poisoning Vickie's outlook on just about everything. Did you know I heard her actually lecture Vickie on how poor people are dumb? That if they were smart, they'd have money?"

"What?"

Grace nodded her head, eyebrows furrowed as if she was boring a hole through Nanny Elsa's forehead. "I can't explain it, but I have an intense hatred for that woman."

"Well, poisoning our daughter's outlook on life is a biggie. Maybe I can have a word with Roger…"

"Don't. We agreed a long time ago to stay in the background in Vickie's life. There's no way I could tear her away from them. I know you can't measure love, but if you could, I'd say it was an absolute four-way tie on which one of us loved Vickie the most. Besides, there's no way I want to alienate anyone and not even be a spectator to what's going on in her life."

"So, do you think that one of the *paparazzi* suspects you're the biological mother?"

"That's what the Dads think. Silas said he was sure that the fat bald guy is Jimmy grown old ungracefully. Remember I told you that my mother knew I was pregnant, that she saw me just before Chuck got me to Dr. Buddy's home clinic?"

"Yeah, and then she shot you!" Dusty said, his fists balled up on either side of his coffee cup.

"All she'd have to do is tell Jimmy to follow me and eavesdrop with one of those fancy mics; listen for me to say something revealing to Vickie. Of course, I never would, so there's no story there. Those guys are a nuisance, but there's nothing to record or sell to the tabloids. If there *was* something that proved we were Vickie Lynn's parents, one of us would have found it years ago."

"And what would we have done with it if we had found it?" Dusty asked, wiping the crumbs off his fingers.

"Even if I found it today, I'd still do absolutely nothing. I have to wonder if Gloria and Roger know who adopted the other twin, though. Something tells me they do."

"I agree there. That lifesize twin doll she keeps in her office, dressed in the Dior Vickie wore on her fourth birthday, is kind of spooky."

"No, what's spooky is the way she glances back and forth between it and Vickie when she's in the room. I was only there once when it happened. Gloria noticed me watching her. I must have looked stunned or shocked or something because she remarked about it. "Just like she had a twin, huh?"

"I was there, remember?" Dusty said. He pushed his coffee cup away, uncomfortable at recalling their loss. "There's no doubt in my mind that she knows there's a twin. We just have to make sure she doesn't know that we know. I don't want to lose our unofficial godparents status."

"Amen to that," Grace said. "But that doesn't mean I'm going to stop looking."

"Back at ya on that amen."

"Do I look pretty?" Vickie asked, startling them as she came into the room unannounced. She turned around slowly to present her lace over satin pale blue gown, the tight bodice and pushup bra creating a body beyond her thirteen years of age. Earrings dripping with jewels and a matching diamond and sapphire necklace pointed to the spot where cleavage would be in a few years. A simple diamond tiara was nestled in the coif of curls piled on top of her head, a reluctant smile on her face.

"Pretty is too tame a word," Grace said. "You're stunning!"

"Uh, huh!" Dusty proclaimed. "But you're only thirteen. I mean, you look much older. Or, rather, you're dressed like it."

Vickie came over to the table with them and plopped down, very unladylike. "I hate it. I know I should be grateful, but diamonds aren't for everyone. I'd rather have ripped denim jeans, a tank top, and a flannel shirt. I know I could order them – and I have in the past – but as soon as Nanny Elsa finds them, they're in the trash. Or even worse – she burns them in the incinerator! Then I have to listen to her lecture for a week about how we need to show our best side to everyone all the time, how rich people are better and need to remind the lower class."

"You don't believe her, do you?" Grace asked.

"No. I rarely believe anything she says. If it's not in one of my school books, I just take it as her opinion, not fact."

"Opinions are like belly buttons," Grace said. "Everyone has one."

Vickie started to giggle. "That's almost the same thing Daddy says only he uses another part of the human anatomy."

"Yeah, well, I didn't want to say asshole," Grace said, then giggled, too.

"Tell you what," Dusty said, acknowledging the old joke with a grin and a head shake of 'enough, already,' now wanting to change the subject. "You go ahead and let Grace know what you want for clothes. We'll order them and you can wear them when you hang out with us. Maybe we can talk your parents into letting you come camping with us for the weekend. Would you like to learn how to fish?"

"Really? I mean, yeah! That would be the best birthday present ever! Just don't let Nanny Elsa know. She's sure to find a way to ruin it for us."

"Our secret," Dusty said.

"Ours and your parents," Grace added. "I'm sure they agree that Nanny Elsa doesn't have to rule your whole life."

"I can't wait to go to high school, just so she's out of my life." Vickie reached up and took out her earrings. "And these things are so heavy! I want to wear little gold hoops like you, Grace."

"We'll get you some of those to wear when you're camping, too," Dusty said. "Country chic."

"Now I'll look just like you, Grace!" Vickie said more brightly than usual. *Just like the mom who gave birth to me!*

Grace looked at Dusty looked and shrugged, the mischievous twinkle in Vickie's eye not missed by either of the 'godparents.' *She suspects! Don't you say a word, and I won't either.*

***

January 3, 2008
Three years later

"Can you believe our little girl is going to be sixteen?" Roger asked Gloria.

His wife leaned closer to the mirror, then pulled back, scowling. "As of today, she *is* sixteen. Hmm. It used to be that the closer I got to the mirror, the better I could see. Now I have to move back. And reading is even more difficult. My arms are almost too short to read the newspaper now."

"Well," Roger said, chuckling, "There's nothing but crap and gossip in that society section you're so fond of. And if you can't get far enough away from the mirror to inspect for new wrinkles, that's a good thing."

"What? Why?"

"Which one? Both. It's good you can't read that garbage *and* that your brain isn't being poisoned by someone else's opinion of our friends and business associates. Plus, it's great that you're not stressing about itty bitty laugh lines." Roger leaned over his wife and gave her a kiss on top of the head. "You always have been and always will be the most beautiful woman in the world."

"What about Vickie Lynn?" Gloria asked.

"You, my dear, have the benefit of your beauty being enhanced by my true love for and devotion to you. Our daughter has raw beauty and innocence. She's simply the most beautiful *young* woman in the world."

Gloria snorted in frustration. "She and her two sisters. I really do wish Chuck and Leanne and Luther would reach out again. It's been how many years since Leanne and Luther sent a family picture?"

"That was only two years ago," Roger said.

"Well, that one didn't count. Tori Lynn was wearing a ski mask. We couldn't see what she looked like. Plus she was wearing a snowsuit. Who knows if she's fat or skinny or…"

"Slow down, Gloria," Roger said, standing behind her to look in the mirror. "I think your hormones are getting in the way of common sense again. Luther and Leanne are great parents. For God's sake, they're botanists! They're feeding her the best natural foods on the planet. That girl has probably never even had a bite of junk food in her life! They're all happy. Let them bring her up their way."

"Yes, but we've never even seen Chuck's little girl. Not even a fuzzy snapshot."

"So, when was the last time you heard from him?" Roger asked, adjusting his tie.

"Probably two years ago. He sent a money order from West Virginia. He did include a little note, telling me thanks for the loan – we should be caught up now."

"I wish he hadn't done that," Roger said. "I was more than happy to help him out until he could get his mobile clinic established. You did burn it, didn't you?"

"The clinic?" Gloria asked.

"The money order."

"You asked me to, didn't you?" Gloria replied, not wanting to let him know she had kept it as a memento – her one link to their daughter's other triplet sister.

Roger nodded and sighed. He wouldn't push her. She had saved it. Just like every other photo or scrap of contact pertaining to the other two girls. Whether she was being obsessive, compulsive, or just a little bit nuts, it was who she was – his Gloria.

***

"Nanny Elsa, how do I look?" Vickie asked.

"A little chubby, but not too bad," the stern taskmaster said, pushing the girl's waistline in with her bony index finger.

"If I eat any less, I'll lose all my boobs! As it is, I'm only eating eight hundred calories a day. And not even one carb! If I ever smell tuna again, I think I'm going to puke!"

"Puking's good," Elsa said. "You can enjoy the food, then purge it without adding a calorie. Just make sure you rinse your mouth afterward or it will eat the enamel from your teeth."

"But my boobs!"

"You can buy boobs. Just ask your father for a nice set of double-D's as another birthday present. I'm sure he'll say yes. All men like big boobs."

"I don't know about that…" Vickie said, looking in the mirror at her reshaped ears. "He and Mama both threw a fit when I asked to have my ears fixed. I know you said they looked horrid the way they stuck out, but Mom and Dad always said they were so cute. Angel ears they called them. Are you sure they won't throw a fit when they find out you took me to the doctor and had them clipped?"

"Your mother and I have an agreement. She won't discharge me," Elsa said, her smirk of control uninhibited.

"She must really like you. Most of my friends lost their live-in nannies and tutors by middle school. It seems your only duty these days is that of personal dresser and confidant."

"It keeps me busy," Elsa said. *And rich!*

Vickie twisted her curly locks together and set the bundle on top of her head, then let it go. "Do you think I should wear my hair up or down?"

"Ah, wear it up to show off those new ears that lay so flat to the side of your head."

"But won't my parents notice?"

Elsa shrugged, her smirk of domination returning. "What are they going to do about it? The deed has been done. It's your body, isn't it?"

Vickie slumped on the stool, depressed that she had let anyone talk her into changing her looks. She was insecure enough about her body image. All her life, her parents had told her how beautiful she was. Now every freckle and curve were under intense scrutiny and criticism from Nanny Elsa. Sometimes she felt as if she'd be better off without her. At least her self-esteem wouldn't be under constant attack. Still, she was only sixteen. Just two more years until she could make her own decisions. She was doing well on class credits. She'd graduate early – at the semester break – and hit the road as soon as she was eighteen. That would probably be the only way to get rid of that skinny Swedish gray-haired guilt dispenser!

"Here, let me arrange your hair. I'll loan you this antique comb for the evening. It's been in my family for generations. It should set off the tresses perfectly."

Vickie Lynn sat at her dressing table and watched as Elsa deftly arranged her curling iron-enhanced curls into a cascade atop her head, letting a few tresses drift down one side, then securing them with the gem-encrusted heirloom her father had told her would be hers one day. *Why did Nanny Elsa say it was hers? Now is not the time to challenge her ownership. Then again, it never is a good time to contest anything she says.*

Vickie picked up the mirror and turned around to look at the back of her coif. She glanced down and saw the incision the doctor had cut in the back of her ear. The cut itself was nearly invisible, but the area around it was red and swollen. Nanny had lied! She said there was no chance of infection. She resisted the urge to touch it and verify it was fevered. It was best to play ignorant than acknowledge both the inflammation and the fact she'd been lied to. Unless her iron-willed matron was out of the room, she was watching her. Shoot! Even then, she felt as if she was a test subject under observation. She probably had nanny cams stashed everywhere.

For years, she'd felt like a flesh and blood android: told how to stand, sit, eat and speak. Life had been a blast when she was younger: riding her battery-powered Rolls Royce all through the house and gardens, going to the carousel with Mom and Dad, Grace and Dusty. Their weekly get-togethers were the highlight of growing up. When had all the fun stopped?

She didn't know the day because she wasn't aware of calendars and dates back then, but she did remember when. It was the day her mother introduced her to her nanny. Nanny Elsa.

"We'd like to keep you at home as much as possible," Mom had said, "so rather than go to pre-school with all those children who have cold and flu germs, we've hired a special teacher for you. This is Nanny Elsa. She's going to be living with us, too."

Mom tried to look happy about it but even at that early age – four or five – Vickie could tell the smile was fake. Dad didn't even try to smile. He kept bringing up the newspaper, pretending to look at it or turn the pages, then shake it and set it down, frowning. Vickie thought it was because he wasn't happy to have someone taking his place. Now that she knew Nanny Elsa, though, she knew it wasn't the nanny part he objected to; it was the Elsa part.

Suddenly, Vickie felt ill. The infection might be a part of it. Nearly starving herself for the last three weeks – so she could shrink down to the twenty-two-inch waistline Nanny Elsa insisted was essential for a young woman of breeding like herself – could be another contributing factor. But what really soured her stomach was seeing how she and her parents had been manipulated by Nanny Elsa for years. She knew the why for her: because she was a child. She knew she had to listen or would have to pay the consequences. Mom and Dad never saw the bruises from being pinched because they no longer helped with bathing. The one time Mom had seen the bruise on her backside when changing into her bathing suit at the beach house, Nanny Elsa made up a lie, saying she had bumped into the dresser.

Vickie set down the mirror and saw she was practically under a microscope again. Elsa was staring at her, her wire-rimmed glasses slipping down her nose. The warden pushed them back up. "Is something amiss?" she asked caustically – as if she could smell rebellion in the works.

"My stomach feels queasy. I don't know if I want to go…"

Elsa took three determined steps up to Vickie and grasped her chin, bringing it up to face her. "This is your sixteenth birthday party. Some very important people will be here this evening. You *will* be in attendance. And you *will* be on your best behavior. And you *won't* eat more than a carrot stick or drink more than sparkling water. Do. You. Understand?"

Vickie's heart felt like it was coming up through her mouth. Beating so hard, it felt like it had pumped itself up to basketball size and was rising, threatening to choke off her breath. She managed a nod, then Nanny Elsa let go. "Put some concealer on that chin. There's a red spot right there," she said, thumping the spot she had just let go of.

"Yes, Nanny Elsa," Grace said. *Do all sixteen-year-old daughters of billionaires wish they were dead or is it only me?*

***

"Here she comes," Dusty said, saluting Vickie Lynn with a glass of champagne.

"Our little girl is almost all grown up," Grace whispered. "Isn't she beautiful?"

Dusty sighed. "I'm sorry, but when I see her, I can't help but wonder if her twin was a girl or a boy. Can you imagine two young women that beautiful existing in the same world?"

"If I could just ask Gloria about it, and then rewind time so she didn't remember me asking – or even knowing that I was aware Vickie had a twin – I would. The way she looks at the life-size doll, though, my bet is that it was another girl."

"So, do you ever regret not having the procedure?"

"You mean in vitro fertilization? No. I keep busy enough with the human trafficking research. At least I was able to get Dr. Fat Boy busted and his clinic shut down. He may have been unsure about who I was when we went there for the test results, but he won't ever forget me now."

Grace set her champagne flute down and picked up a sparkling water with a lime wedge. "Plus, I really do believe that one of these days, we'll find our other twin. In the meantime, being the favorite aunt-type godmother and second cousin is good enough for me."

Dusty hugged her. "Me, too."

"Good evening." Vickie didn't even try to make her fake smile look real for Grace and Dusty. Her left eye twitched as a tear tried to form. "Thank you for coming this evening," she added mechanically, then bit her bottom lip, impending tears choking back her ability to even try for a real conversation.

Grace looked around the room quickly and spotted the iron maiden in the corner, her eyes like binoculars fixed on Vickie. She suddenly reached out and grabbed for Vickie, clutching for her as if she felt faint and needed her help. "Ladies room," she gasped.

Vickie totally forgot her problems and held onto Grace, supporting her. "I have you," she said.

"Here, let me help," Dusty offered, then caught the quick scowl from his wife. "Well, if you're sure you have her," he added, stepping back.

"Lady stuff," Grace gasped.

Vickie Lynn led her to the bathroom off her father's downstairs office, bypassing the rooms set aside for the guests. "Are you all right? Are you

139

pregnant? You look a little weird. I mean…" she babbled, concerned for Grace.

Grace stood up straight and stared Vickie in the eye. "What's wrong," she asked, then walked around her slowly, inspecting her for damages. She came back to stand in front of Vickie and noticed the smudge. She wiped the excess foundation away with her thumb, verifying the signs of abuse.

"I don't think your mother or father ever has or ever will lay a hand on you. That leaves only one person. Did that bitch Elsa do that to you?"

Vickie's mouth twitched into a smile as she sniffed. "You called her a bitch," she said, then allowed a small chuckle to escape.

"Well… I guess that means she did. I guess if she asks if you told anyone, you can truthfully say you didn't. Just nod if yes."

Vickie nodded, then the tears started falling.

"I'd say don't cry or you'll spoil your makeup," Grace said. "But if it makes you feel better, cry away. This isn't how a sixteenth birthday party is supposed to be. It should be a celebration, not a cover-up for a tyrant. So, yes or no question: do you know what Elsa has over your parents?"

"Huh?"

"I'll take that as a no. Look, you're enough of an adult that I can tell you a few things, including that there has to be some reason why your parents keep Elsa employed. I've seen the way your father looks at her. He absolutely loathes her. Your mother doesn't feel too kindly towards her, either. I mean, as far as I can tell, she barely tolerates her. And I know they'd do anything for you, but I really don't think they're keeping Elsa here because *you* want her."

"Oh, Lord in Heaven, no!"

"Well, I'll see what I can find out later. I know I had the most horrid mother in the world. I wanted someone to rescue me from her. My dad did the best he could to insulate me from her…"

"But my mother isn't horrid," Vickie interrupted.

"I know, I know. She's sort of in the position my dad was. I don't know what hold Elsa has over them, but I'm sure it's something."

"Grace, I know it's supposed to be a secret, but I have to ask you…"

Grace's eyes widened and her skin flushed. *Dear Lord in Heaven, did she find out I am her mother?* "Sweetheart, you can ask me anything." *I might not be able to give you an answer but before I start saying too much, let me hear your question.*

"Is my mother your mother's sister? I mean, everyone knows that your dad and my dad are first-cousins, but are you and I related, too?"

A wave of relief washed over Grace, a veritable horde of tingle gremlins rushing over her skin. "Yes, we are very much related. We are blood kin. And yes, your mother and my mother are sisters." *And how I wish I could tell you I'm your birth mother and only your cousin by virtue of adoption.*

"Wouldn't that make us double cousins or something?"

140

"Um, I'm not sure how that goes. If our fathers were brothers, then we'd be double cousins. Let's just say we're closely related. But let's keep that between you and me. As I said, I am not fond of my mother. She and Elsa are – or were – very much alike."

"Is she still alive?"

"Don't know. Don't really care. My dad said the only good thing that ever came out of her was me."

Vickie laughed at the old joke, causing Grace to give in to the giggles, too. "Are you ready to go back to your birthday bash?"

"Bash? For my birthday, I wish someone would bash her!"

"Ach. Don't worry. The night is young and Dusty's drinking champagne. Anything's possible."

The two interlocked elbows and came out together, all smiles and relief.

"Here they come!" Dusty said, walking briskly over to the now dimpled duo. "Are you all right?" he whispered.

"She just had a little gas," Vickie said, laughing anew at the thought of Dusty punching Elsa.

"There's my little girl. I guess you're not so little anymore now, though, are you?" Roger said, walking over to give her a big hug. He looked down and saw the heirloom hair comb in Vickie's hair, the latest piece of jewelry Elsa had blackmailed Gloria into giving her. His face reddened. *One of these days. I swear, one of these days I'm going to strangle that Swedish bitch!*

"Are you all right, Dad?"

"Yeah, are you all right, Roger?" Hal seconded. "First my daughter scoots out of the room before I even get the chance to say hello, and then you're all puce-colored."

Roger took three deep breaths, willing his blood pressure and rage down to socially acceptable levels, then remembered how important this night was for Vickie: his daughter's sweet sixteen party. He'd suck down just about anything for her.

"Yes, I'm fine. I might have to start taking blood pressure medicine, though. I didn't realize that the ladies had invited so many people – so many young men. Good Lord, I think every man of means from the east coast and his son is here tonight. What was Gloria thinking?"

Gloria came up behind him, her lips drawn tight, and tugged his elbow to get his attention. "It wasn't me," she hissed. "*Someone* decided she needed to take over the guest list and arrangements."

Roger felt his face start to redden again and immediately began the yoga breathing technique his doctor had suggested.

"Are you having a fit or something?" Hal asked, stepping in front of his cousin to block him from the view of the guests.

"No, it's an alternative method for controlling high blood pressure and

141

anger management. It was either this or a pocketful of pills with a long list of side effects."

Hal watched as Roger's eyes narrowed in sheer loathing. He quickly turned around and looked behind him to see the target of the hatred. Yup, just as he suspected. The nanny, Elsa. "Why don't you just up and fire her?" Hal whispered.

Roger took another deep breath then blew it out. "I would if I could, but I can't. It's complicated."

"Well, you know if there's anything I can do to help you out of your *predicament*, I'm here for you." Hal paused as he realized there was something he could do. "Give me all the information you have on her: name, birthdate, where she was born, former employers, everything. Silas can probably even find out what toilet paper brand she used when she was twenty!"

Roger snorted with laughter, softly at first, then at a roar.

"It wasn't that funny," Hal said softly, now embarrassed at Roger's exaggerated reaction.

"Thanks. I needed that. The visual image of her wiping her ass... Yup, just what I needed." Roger playfully punched him in the upper arm, then moved around him. "Come on. Let's mingle."

"Roger and Hal! I haven't seen you since I was five foot three and two-hundred pounds. Remember me? Little Ricky Rickman?"

The guest who looked like he should be selling fine wines in a commercial laughed at the identical gap-mouthed reaction of his former classmates, two of the dozen or more males who had taunted him about his size when he was growing up. "No hard feelings, guys," he said, offering a sincere handshake.

"Ricky? What happened to you? I mean," Hal sputtered, "where did you go? One day you're there on the ballfield with us, huffing and puffing, trying to kick that damned soccer ball into the goal, and the next day – *poof*! – you're gone, and your locker and desk are empty."

"I would try to make you – and everyone else who went to that damned privileged academy – feel bad by saying I had a nervous breakdown, but the truth is, my dad got transferred to London. Once there, I really got into playing soccer, or as they call it, football. Plus, with only blood pudding and other traditional British food to eat, I stopped overeating and grew into my weight. I thank my lucky stars that Dad wasn't sent to Paris. Can you imagine what I'd look like if I had free range of all those French pastries?"

Roger and Hal laughed nervously at the image. The man before them was not only fit, he seemed to be the model of health for men in their sixties. Broad-shouldered and with thick hair that shone like polished silver – he was an Adonis for any age.

"I'm sorry," Roger said. "Not to be rude, but why are you here? I haven't seen you in generations. Literally!"

"My son and I were invited to your daughter's birthday party." He pulled out the invitation and showed it to Roger. "I thought it was a little unconventional, but when I saw your name on it, I decided we had to come and see if it was for real or a prank. It took a little arm-twisting on my part to get him here, but we made it."

Roger scanned the invitation, immediately disgusted that it had a provocative photo of his daughter printed on the inside. Draped in furs, she was leaning forward to show cleavage, wearing at least ten carats of diamonds and an uncomfortable smile that looked more like a pained grimace to him. He blinked back his disgust and read:

You are invited to Vickie Lynn Thornwhistle's Sixteenth Birthday Gala.

Meet the young lady who is heir to the largest distributor of fine arts on the east coast.

Take this opportunity to find out if your child is compatible with ours. A merger or joint venture might be in your son or daughter's future.

RSVP E. E. Swensen for Roger and Gloria Thornwhistle

"Didn't your wife tell you she had invited me? Oh, that's right. She may not have known we were acquainted when we were younger."

"First off, I had nothing to do with this tacky and tawdry invitation. Second, I'm sure my wife is also unaware of it. Third," Roger scanned the room for either a *doppelganger* to Rick or a short rotund boy, "you have a son here?"

"He's the young man speaking with the lady over there. Is *that* your wife?"

Hal and Roger followed Rick's nod that directed them to a tall, handsome young man listening to Nanny Elsa. Her face was shiny with nervous sweat, her hands flicking about, fidgeting with her hair, then landing on the guest's arm. "Her?" Roger squeaked. "My wife? Oh, good God, no!"

Hal didn't even try to contain his laugh but did bring the quick outburst down to a chuckle, earning a sneer from Roger.

Feeling the need for payback, Roger bent forward and squinted in her direction, pretending to focus on her face. "She's not mine, but isn't that *your* wife, Hal?" he asked, elbowing Hal in the ribs, flipping the joke back on him.

Hal growled at being punked, then shook his head and gave in to the levity. "If you don't remember, Rick, Roger and I are cousins. It must be all these youthful hormones in the air. I feel like I'm sixteen again. How old is your son?"

"Rich is twenty. He's attending Harvard. So, if she isn't your wife, do you know who she is? That woman seems to have an unnaturally keen interest in my son."

The three men watched in disgust as the skinny gray-haired crone moved her hand up and down Rich's arm seductively, the sly grin on her face followed by her tongue rimming her upper lip.

"I think I'm going to be ill..." Roger said. "Excuse me, Rick. It looks like your son's being quite the gentleman but enough is enough. He's in need of a rescue."

Hal reached out and held Rickman back. "Let him handle it. She's his daughter's nanny. That Swedish witch has been giving him fits for years. She may have just crossed the line with hitting on your son, though."

The younger Rickman squirmed uncomfortably under the hag's touch; her graphic description of her sexual skills unbelievable. "Excuse me," he said, tactfully removing the crazy old woman's grasp from his arm. "I think I'll have to pass. I think I see the guest of honor..."

Elsa's hand reached out and grabbed his, ready to bring it to her silicone-enhanced breast. "We can share the pleasures of my Scandinavian..."

"Excuse me a moment," Roger said, stepping between the couple. An awkward three-way scuffle ensued as Rich disentangled himself from Elsa's clutch. As he backed away, she moved closer, trying for a more controlling hold, at the same time trying to nudge Roger out of the way.

Elsa became aware of the murmurs and realized she was desperately clinging to a man a third her age and let go. Her embarrassed slump-shouldered posture changed in a flicker to standing bold and upright; stoic and authoritative. "I hope you have a good reason for interrupting our conversation," she said, teeth clenched and eyes afire.

"Indeed, I do," he answered. "Rich, I see you've met my daughter's nanny. She's been around for," he sighed deeply, trying for the most caustic way to offend her without it making even more of a scene. "Well, let's just say that big oak tree was a cast aside acorn when she came to work for our family. Come, let me introduce you to my daughter, Vickie Lynn."

Elsa stuck her chest out, momentarily dumbstruck at Roger's nerve. By the time she thought of a scathing retort, her moment had passed. The men were already halfway across the room. *You'll pay for that, Mr. Moneybags. I don't take being cast as an aging servant lightly!*

"I don't think we've been introduced," Rich said, reaching out to shake Roger's hand. "Oh, and thanks for the rescue," he added in a whisper.

"Don't worry about it," he replied in the same tone, then spoke up. "I'm Roger Thornwhistle. Your father and I went to school together many, many years ago. I think the Longwood Academy is a museum now."

"Richard Othello Albert Rickman, the Third, but please call me Rich."

"Ooh." Roger resisted the urge to laugh out loud at the initials. "It's a good thing your father never used his middle names. We would have given him even more grief!"

"Me? I love it. I can't wait for someone to tease me. I won't do it here with all of your guests, especially since this is the first time I've met many of these people, but I have a wickedly loud roar. It works great at the fraternity parties."

"After everyone's had a few?" Roger prompted.

"Oh, yeah…" Rich mused, then blushed. If Roger had been getting reacquainted with his father, there was a good chance he knew he was underage for drinking.

Seeing the telltale signs of chagrin, Roger thumped him on the back. "Just don't drink around my daughter. As a reminder," he cleared his throat, "my daughter is only sixteen. I was only recently made aware that her nanny had invited so many older young men to her soiree."

"That's pretty good, Mr. Thornwhistle: two oxymorons in one sentence."

"Excuse me?"

"This event is way beyond what I'd call a soiree…"

"And?"

"Older young men," Rich said, his smile barely contained.

"*Touché.* I guess I'd better warn you, though. My daughter is not only sharp, but she's also beautiful. Don't go falling in love with her, all right?"

"Sir, I can't promise that, but I will promise to treat her like a lady and not take advantage of her."

"And?"

"What do you mean, 'and'?"

Roger thumped him on the back. "Don't let her talk you into anything crazy like taking advantage of *you!*" He took one step back and looked at the now red-faced Rich.

"Great. Just what I wanted to see. At least you had the common sense to blush at my remark. Good move. Remember it one of these days if you have a daughter of your own. It's a scary business, having one who's both clever and beautiful. I'd like to keep her down on the farm, so to say, until she's a little – or rather, a lot – more savvy about the tricks and tropes of the world and the people in it, but I don't think that's going to happen."

"I can appreciate wanting that. I have a sister who's fifteen years older than me. I was the surprise baby. She got suckered into rotten marriage at an early age. I can't imagine having to deal with a carousing husband and a baby at any age, much less at twenty and in a country so far away from our mother. I promise you, I'll treat your daughter with respect."

Roger realized that during their discourse, they had wound up in the kitchen, away from the other guests, and were now in the way of the serving staff. "Either you're a good man, ROAR the Third, or you're an excellent bullshit artist. Let's hope it's the former and not the latter."

Now it was Rich's turn to offer a hand. He set it on Roger's shoulder. "I'll tell you right now, I'm a lousy liar. Never learned how and was told it was a skill a gentleman didn't need. I haven't even seen your daughter but with a father like you, she at least had the opportunity to learn how to be a lady."

"Bullshit?" Roger asked with a wink.

"I'd prefer to think of this one as I'm a man who's a good judge of character. You see, *my* father was a great teacher, too."

The two made their way back into the main room. Guests were practically elbow-to-elbow, the extra dinner tables taking up the milling around area that was necessary for social gatherings. Suddenly, Roger felt a tug at his elbow.

"There you are," Vickie whispered harshly. "Mom's been looking everywhere for you. I think she's having a meltdown."

Roger's eyes widened as he searched the room for her. "Where?" he asked.

"She went to her room. You'd better get to her before you-know-who sends her over the edge."

"Excuse me," Roger said, remembering he was escorting Rich. "This is my daughter, Vickie Lynn…"

"Go, go, go!" Rich said. "We got this."

The young duo watched Roger weave through the groups of three and four guests, standing with drinks in hand, carrying on small talk to pass the time.

"Damned Elsa!" Vickie hissed. "It's all her fault."

"The nanny?" Rich asked.

"You must have met her."

Rich nodded and opened his mouth, ready to share at least a little of his experience and rescue but closed it, continuing to nod. He suddenly realized he hadn't been introduced. "Oh, I'm Rich, by the way…"

Before he could say another word, Vickie cut him off. "Rich? Yeah, you and every other man who's introduced himself to me this evening."

"Excuse me?"

"I'm sorry. That was crass, but I've had no less than six men approach me in the last fifteen minutes, pawing at my hand, telling me all about their portfolios and athletic prowess. I could care less about how many letters a guy got in college or whether he's new money, old money, or no money. Geez!"

Rich pulled out each pants pocket, showing they were empty. "No money," he said and smirked. "I'd show you my elephant impersonation, but I told your father I'd behave."

"Your what? Oh, my…" Grace's hand flew to her mouth to cover her laugh. "Oh, please do not show that!"

"And just for the record, my name is Rich as in Richard. I'd tell you my whole name, but then I'd have to give you my lion impersonation, too."

"What does your name have to do with a lion? Are you a Leonard?"

"No, but I was born in the house of Leo."

"Capricorn," Vickie said, her hands up to mime goat horns.

"I knew that."

"How?"

"Duh? Isn't this your birthday party?" Rich asked.

"Duh is right. I'm sorry. We got off on the wrong foot. I'm extremely ticked because I thought this was just going to be family and a few friends. Next thing I know, I'm being fitted for a dress Nanny Elsa ordered one size too small so 'I' would fit the dress, not the other way around. I'm so hungry, I could eat the buttons off your jacket."

Rich looked down at his tux, found the button and was ready to pop it off when he felt her hand on his. *Zing! Oh, my God! That really does happen!*

"It was a joke," Vickie said, her voice soft and sincere, bringing him back to reality. Harshness overtook her tone as she continued, "Elsa claims to be Swedish, but I swear she's an escaped Nazi. She doesn't want me to eat tonight – she thinks I'm still too fat. She's intolerable when I disobey her, so how about I sit next to you? It's a buffet. If you double-load your plate, I can sneak bites from it."

"You're only sixteen?" Rich asked, verifying that he should squelch the tingles he was getting for a minor.

"Yup. Remember that. And if you see me in a desperate situation and one of my crew doesn't catch on first, please come to my rescue."

"Your crew?"

She nodded to the threesome watching the two of them talk. "The youngest one is my unofficial godfather, Dusty. You already met my father. The balding one shooting daggers with his eyes is my father's cousin, Hal. I don't know who that silver-haired guy is. He looks familiar, though. I think I saw him on the cover of a magazine or something."

"Yup. That's my father, Rick Rickman. He's been on the cover of Forbes, Wine World, and a few others. We own a few acres of vineyards in Oregon. It looks like they're looking out for you."

"Yeah, well, they can only look so far," Vickie said, thinking of Nanny Elsa's privileged access to her when a man wasn't allowed in the room.

Sensing her gloom, Rich touched her elbow, wanting to reconnect and see if that *zing* was still there. *Zing!* Yup. She may be the one, but if so, he had to wait at least two years for her. Damned gypsy fortune teller! 'Two years of torment until she is yours' was right!

"Come on. Let's go eat," he said. "Chances are, you're suffering from malnutrition or at least low blood sugar. I don't want you passing out. The way those guys are looking at us, they'd blame me if you fainted."

Comforted by his touch, Vickie looked up at him and smiled, feeling at ease for the first time all day. "How tall are you?"

"Six-three in my bare feet." He lifted one foot and checked the heel. "Probably six-five in these. Why?"

"Tall, compassionate, and Rich. Any other attributes?" she asked, trying to compose herself. *Dang! Why did you ask? The tingles are just because you're hungry!*

"I didn't earn the height, and my parents gave me the name. I learned compassion by example, and my mother picked out the tux. Nope. I really don't

147

have any attributes. I am the sum of my environment and genetics."

"Don't sell yourself short, tall boy. You could have resisted the clothing, chosen to go by a nickname, and ignored your parent's examples of compassion. I'd say your greatest attribute is making wise choices. Or at least good ones."

Rich chuckled then let go of her elbow and picked up a dinner plate. "I'll let you make the choices on food tonight. I'll eat just about anything." *I make wise choices? Yes, I choose you!*

***

The string quartet changed from dinner music to a waltz. "Care to dance with your old man?" Roger asked. "Or do you want to spend the whole evening with Rich?"

She looked down and blushed, then stood up. "Daddy…"

He led her to the dance area. "Sorry, I didn't mean to make you uncomfortable." He held one hand and placed the other on her waist, ready for the waltz. "Good Lord, girl! You're as skinny as a broom! Why haven't you been eating?"

Done protecting her, Vickie lifted her chin and declared with eyes squinted in barely contained rage, "Because Nanny Elsa says I'm too fat!"

"You are *not* fat," Roger hissed, returning the squint, then looking around the room for the tormentor. "That's it. I don't care what she has on us. She's getting fired."

"She has on us?" Vickie asked. "Has she been…"

Roger quickly put his hand on her mouth. "Don't say it, dear. Please, don't say a word. I shouldn't have lost my cool. You are the only thing in this world that matters to your mother and me. Truly. You have to know that we wouldn't have allowed her in this house for so long if it hadn't been for a good reason. Or at least a reason so profound that life itself wouldn't be worth living if we lost it. She threatened to have you removed. Poof. You would have been out of our lives if we didn't acquiesce to her demands."

"So, that's why you gave her your Maserati for Christmas last year?"

Roger nodded, his lips tight. "Please don't let your mother know I slipped. And please, for all the love you have for us, don't ask about what she's blackmailing us with."

"Daddy, I don't know and I don't care. All I want is for us to stay together as a family. Believe it or not, just knowing that she's using the 'B' word to keep her job makes me feel so much better. I thought it was because you and Mommy thought I needed correcting or changed or…"

"Sweetheart, you are and always have been perfect." He looked down at her bony shoulder. "Except for being too thin. I'll tell her I want you to start eating better, that I'm afraid you're suffering from bulimia or anorexia or whatever that disease is. If I ask her to make sure you overcome it, maybe she'll back off. At this point, all I can do is hope she tires of us. Or that she's extorted enough money and goods that she wants to start afresh in another country. Your Uncle Hal seems to think Costa Rica is a great place to send wayward women. Maybe I should get her a one-way ticket for Valentines' Day?"

Roger felt a tap on his shoulder. He turned and saw Papa Doc. "Care to let a party crasher butt in?"

"Party crasher?" Roger asked. "I asked specifically that you and Silas be invited." His face reddened as he realized he had told Elsa. Obviously, she wanted complete control over the guest list. "Yes, as far as I'm concerned, you're one of her grandpas. Hal told me that his invitation was a verbal from my wife. Damned Swedish tyrant!"

"Now, now, Daddy," Vickie soothed. "Go fume somewhere else and let me dance with Papa Doc."

Roger looked up and saw Silas had joined Rick, Dusty, and Hal near the bar, the group swapping stories as they watched the birthday girl dance. "Sounds like a plan," he said, ceding the dance to Papa Doc.

"Good evening, Silas," Roger said as he joined the crew. "I apologize for the invitations not reaching you and Doc." Hal raised his hand. "And Hal, too," he added. "My life would be so much simpler – and my blood pressure so much lower – if I could just get rid of that damned Elsa."

Silas leaned over and whispered in Roger's ear. "Don't worry about it. Hal has me in the loop." He stood up straight and looked at Rick Rickman, a face he recognized from the trade magazines. "We finally meet. I think we've done a little negotiating over the last few years. Silas Priest," he said, reaching out and offering his hand.

"Priest?" Rickman repeated, obviously unfamiliar with the name but shaking hands just the same. "Silas… Oh, yes! Silas! You helped me find out about that manager who was trying to steal me blind about three, four years ago! Ah, great going. I don't know if you ever heard the rest of the story. I was able to recover all my funds. Silly ass. He put all the cash in a safety deposit box then mailed the key to himself at the office. I was given a heads up and able to intercept it. Because it had the company name and his job title on it, I had full legal rights to take it. I kicked him to the curb and sent him on his way. No lawyers required."

"Yeah, I thought you'd like that. He thought I was doing him a favor, telling him to liquidate all his assets into cash, send them to a spot no one would suspect, and then grab it and hightail it out of the country," Silas said, laughing as he recalled the clueless embezzler.

"Excuse me, just a minute," Hal said, his hand on Roger to get his attention. "Did you tell Vickie Lynn to get her ears fixed?"

"Fixed?" Roger asked, then watched as his daughter danced with Papa Doc, waiting for her to turn so he could see.

"Shit! That tyrant! I'll bet Elsa is behind that. Vickie couldn't have had it done without an adult signing a consent form. I gave that bitch medical power of attorney when we first hired her. If something happened while they were at the park, I wanted to make sure she could receive medical treatment. Damn her eyes!"

Dusty and Hal both took a step forward, looking for Elsa. "Hold on there, guys," Silas said, physically restraining them. "Remember. This is Vickie Lynn's party. The deed has been done. No undoing it now. You don't want her to remember her sixteenth birthday party as the one…"

"Ah, crap!" Dusty said.

"Go ahead and say it, son," Hal said, seeing the same thing that had raised Dusty's ire.

"Ah, shit!" Dusty hissed, feeling better for losing his social filter.

The melody of Strauss's Blue Danube fell apart as two of the string quartet moved out of the way of the skinny crone who was backing into them, under verbal attack by a very irate Grace Rhodes.

"Her ears were perfect, you bitch! How dare you make her feel bad about her image. And I heard how you've browbeaten her into believing she's fat…"

Elsa picked her way around the violinist, standing behind his chair for protection from the angry godmother. "She'll never get a good husband with those Dumbo ears and pot belly!" Elsa hissed, then moved in front of the seat, no longer afraid. The crowd would be on her side. "I was doing her a favor."

Thunk!

Humph!

A quick punch to the gut and Elsa was bent over at the waist, the wind knocked out of her.

Grace looked around the room, suddenly aware that she had not only lost her temper but had struck out in anger. Dusty was standing next to Hal – her husband and father both wide-eyed. In a blink of an eye, they were grinning, transitioning from shock to glee at the same rate.

"Watch out!" a woman's voice called out.

Grace heard the whoosh of a punch being thrown and stepped back in reflex.

"You bitch," Elsa huffed with the missed blow. Still winded, the angry nanny held her hands up, ready for a boxing match, then realized the room was full of rich and influential guests. She looked up and saw that every one of them was slack-jawed in shock.

Fwap! Fwap!

"Never take your eyes off your opponent," Grace hissed. "And if you ever touch my daughter again, I'll gut you and use your liver for dog food."

"Your daughter?" Elsa asked, a glimmer of inspiration sparkling her otherwise glazed eyes.

Fwap!

The final blow – an open-handed slap – sent Elsa to the ground in a pile of sequins and snot, a trickle of blood mixing with the dribble of makeup sliding off her face. Hairpiece askew, her upper plate of false teeth had slid halfway out of her mouth. A perfect picture of retribution.

Grace looked up and saw Vickie clinging to the tall young man she had been eating dinner with. "Sorry, honey. Well… not really," she told her.

Vickie started giggling, a pensive nervous reaction at first, then winding up to the full laughter of absolute glee. "Well, you did say maybe someone would bash her for my birthday. Best sixteenth birthday present ever!"

Chapter 4: Birthday Bash

Rich grimaced at the emotional and physical spectacle but remained silent and supportive of the giddy teenager at his side, her boisterous laughs now settled down to intermittent chuckles. He didn't know the family dynamics but was uncomfortably acquainted with the tawdry and disgusting Nanny Elsa, now laid out on the parquet floor. She more than likely deserved the blows. Still, it was Vickie's birthday. "Shall we make the rounds and see if we can provide a little damage control?" he asked, urging the birthday girl away.

"Ooh, that was *rich*," she said with a giggle, indicating the rout but teasing him about his name. She quickly sobered up, realizing she didn't want to embarrass her parents with even more rowdy behavior. "Sorry about the tussle," she said sincerely. "That's been a long time coming."

"She probably deserved it," he said, nudging her upper arm-to-shoulder with body language that said, 'That's okay. I'm cool with it.'

She leaned into him and looked up. "Yes, that was very rich. No doubt the guests will remember this night for years."

"Yes, and now everyone will want to come to your parties. You can't hire that kind of excitement."

The young couple stood back and watched as Silas ushered in three valets to help lift the aging pugilist from the floor to her feet. As she regained consciousness, Nanny Elsa's arms flailed, resisting the assistance offered, her striking-out protests prolonging the performance. The hag was leaving the humiliation spotlight but not the partygoer's memories.

Silas drew out his handkerchief and made a quick swipe of the mess on the floor, dropped his improvised rag into a plastic bag he took from his pocket, then followed the group. *Now, who are you really, Nanny Elsa? A little DNA research might help. By the time I get the results back, you'll probably still be hanging around, your claws into someone else in this household or neighborhood. Six months is a long time to wait for lab results. Let's just hope I find out something from other sources sooner.*

On the other side of the room, Dusty and Hal came to Grace's side, chatting nonsense to keep her from watching the staff remove the fallen Elsa. "Dad, why don't you go see how Roger's holding up?" Dusty suggested, his quick eye movements letting him know he needed some private time with his wife.

"Don't worry, honey," Dusty said once they were alone. "Papa Doc made sure she didn't have any serious injuries. He called an ambulance just to cover our asses in case she decides to get litigious. I don't think the guests saw it as anything but self-defense. Actually, people seem to be having a good time now. At least they have something to talk about."

Young Rich stood off to the side, waiting silently for a break in their conversation. "I think Vickie wants to talk to you alone," he said when Grace noticed him. "She has something for you in the kitchen."

Grace looked back at Dusty. He shook his head and shrugged. "Don't look at me," he said. "You know that girl has a mind of her own."

An anxious Vickie waited at the breakfast bar for Grace. Starting to chew on her cuticle, she realized what she was doing and quickly brought her hand down and began twiddling her thumbs instead. When she heard Grace clear her throat, she stood up, making a concerted effort to keep her hands still.

"Hey, Grace," Vickie said, her arms crossed in front of her chest, hands tucked under her armpits. "Papa Doc said you should soak your hand in warm water and Epsom salts. I had the cook help me. I already had the Epsom salts. She just filled the big ceramic bowl with warm water. She said it's her favorite bread-making bowl; that it should keep the heat in longer than a stainless steel one. She said she'd do anything for you now. Everyone knows…"

"You're babbling, Vickie," Grace said, sitting down next to her. She put her right hand in the water, an unintentional 'Ooh' escaping at the comforting warmth.

Vickie leaned closer to the bowl and sniffed. "I don't think it makes a difference if they're scented salts or not. You'll smell like roses for a while, though." Vickie realized that now she was rubbing her thumb and forefinger together, another form of thumb-twiddling that she'd seen her godmother do hundreds of times over the years.

Grace watched her mimic her nervous habit, then looked up at her with one eyebrow raised. 'What did you want to talk about?' she asked without saying a word.

"I just wanted to thank you in private for the greatest birthday present ever," Vickie blurted out.

Grace chuckled. "We both got a gift with that one. Turn around and let me look at your ear."

Vickie carefully lifted her fall of curls, exposing the infected area that Elsa had smeared with a heavy application of cover-up, trying to hide the red inflammation.

"Oh, good Lord," Grace exclaimed just a little too loudly.

Dusty stepped in from the hallway. "Is everything all right in here?"

"Go get Papa Doc. He needs to clean this up. He has his medical kit in the car. He won't leave home without it."

Vickie waited until Dusty was out of earshot to speak. "Grace?" she asked, her voice soft and pensive. She waited until Grace was looking right at her to continue. "Why did you say I was your daughter?"

Grace blanched. Had she really said that? Out loud? "Oh? I said that?" she answered, her eyes blinking rapidly as she watched the doorway to see if anyone had heard.

"Yes, you did." Vickie reached up and pulled back Grace's hair, exposing one ear.

"Ooh, that's cold," Grace said and shook her hair back in place, feeling naked and exposed at being inspected, certain that Vickie had noticed that their ears were the same. Or were before the procedure.

"So, why did you say that?" Vickie persisted, not ready to let go of the suspicion she'd had since her thirteenth birthday.

"Well, you are my daughter," Grace said with a sudden surge of confidence. "You're my goddaughter, even if that's not a legal relationship."

"That must be why our ears look so much alike."

Grace chuckled, then – almost as an afterthought – said, "Yes, that's it."

"Funny. That's not what they told us in biology. Ear shape and pinnae are passed down from mother to daughter and father to son. That genetic trait is an even stronger and more direct indicator of relationship than hair or eye color."

The blood drained from Grace's face. "Really?" she asked, suddenly feeling as if she was going to faint.

Vickie laughed nervously, unsure if she wanted to continue talking about her suspicion or not. Her compassion got the best of her when she saw how upset Grace was. "Maybe it's true. I don't know. I just made that up. What I *do* want to know is why you looked like I just caught you in a lie when I said that…"

"Did someone call for a doctor?" Papa Doc called in from the hallway, Dusty standing behind him.

Dusty sat down beside Grace and looked at Papa Doc. *Do you feel it?*

Yes, I feel the tension in the room, too. That's why I was so bright and boisterous when I came in – to give the women a chance to recover their composure.

"I already had the bag with me. Looks like you're doing all you can for that hand, Grace." Papa Doc sniffed the air. "Tea or Damask roses?"

"Damask," Vickie said. The two women looked at each other and blinked, a visual agreement that they'd continue their conversation later – without anyone else around. Then Grace gave her a narrow-eyed maternal admonition and nodded, telling her to show Papa Doc her infected ear.

Turning around as directed, Vickie pivoted in her seat and pulled back her hair.

Papa Doc frowned, then looked at the back of her other ear. "Well, at least only one of them is botched. Sorry, that sounds crude. Who did this?"

"The surgeon at Silver Falls Dermatology," Vickie said. "Nanny Elsa insisted he was the best."

"He's a damned butcher!" Papa Doc hissed, then composed himself. "That's not what I'm talking about, though. Who put on all this makeup? This is still a new wound. It needs fresh air and to be kept clean in order to heal

154

properly. Don't worry. Your ear isn't going to fall off, but it may scar now. Well, first things first. I need to clean out this crud so it can heal right. Skin can't mend around foreign material. This is going to hurt, darling. Sorry, but I don't carry Lidocaine with me."

Papa Doc looked around the room. Grace was holding Vickie's hand and Dusty was standing in the doorway next to Ricky Rickman's kid – what was his name? – both frowning in concern. "Dusty, go get her a drink."

"Wine or champagne?"

"Neither. Whiskey. And make that two; one for her and one for me when I'm done. I sure hate to hurt my little girl, but it has to be done."

Papa Doc took out the jewel-encrusted comb from Vickie's hair and poked and scooted it, trying to find a way to keep his work area free from wayward curls.

"Here, let me help you," Grace said. With practiced skill, she inserted the comb with one-handed dexterity as he held the tress up, the two of them working as one. "You only had sons, so you probably never had to fix hair."

"Nothing more than a buzz cut in the summer when we were at the cabin."

"Thanks. And it may not be your birthday," Vickie said, then mouthed the word, 'Mom,' to Grace, "but it looks like you got a gift, too. I just hope she leaves and never comes back."

"That would be a gift to your whole family!" Papa Doc said, ending the remark with a snort of finality.

"Did I miss something?" Dusty asked, a drink in both hands.

"Nope," Grace said, all smiles at the prospect of the truth possibly coming out. "All's good here. Very good."

***

"All done," Papa Doc said. "Now, no hair product or spray perfumes or makeup or…"

"Got it. Keep the area free from anything but soap and water and this antiseptic."

"Yes, and just a dab. I'll be by in a day or two to check on you."

"Excuse me," Rich said, waiting in the doorway. "I have some good news. Or at least, I think it's pretty interesting."

"Shoot!" Dusty said.

"The party guests took a poll. Everyone here saw this fine woman," he nodded to Grace, "duck from a direct assault from Nanny Elsa. If said fine woman…"

"Her name is Grace," Hal said, now joining the group.

"Ah, the perfect name for her," Rich commented. "If Grace did throw the first punch, no one here tonight saw it. It would be the Swedish Serpent's word against everyone here."

"I'll say it again," Vickie held up her empty whiskey glass and toasted the

155

group, "best birthday ever!"

***

"Are you sure you're all right?" Roger asked his daughter for the tenth time. Or so it seemed.

"Yes, I'm fine. I have a little bit of a headache but getting a full night's sleep should help that. Are you sure they're keeping Nanny Elsa overnight for observation?"

"I insisted on it," Roger said. "Even if she wanted to come back, I have a little bit of say there at that hospital. Plus, Silas is hanging around, asking questions. He has his way of getting informationthe."

"Like maybe if she's on pain medication, she'll answer anything he asks?"

"I always knew you were a clever girl," Roger said.

"Just like my daddy," she answered automatically, just as she always did when he complimented her on anything. She gasped as she realized he probably wasn't her bio-dad. Then she smiled. Yes, but he was her daddy.

He gave her a kiss on the cheek. "Now, get some sleep. It's been a long and exciting day."

"That's for sure. You and Mom get some sleep, too. I worry about both of you."

"Don't. It's all under control. Probably now more than ever."

"Night, night."

Vickie waited until she heard his footfalls disappear, then stepped into the hallway to verify. *Yup. Gone to the other side of the house. Perfect. Now to do a little Silas-style snooping of my own.*

She had always been curious about what Nanny Elsa kept in her room. She had never been allowed in there. She had seen, though, where the not-as-clever-as-she-thought nanny kept her spare key. Vickie reached under the drawer on the vase table and felt around. *Yes!* The key was hers now.

The room wasn't dirty or messy, but it was crowded with neatly stacked boxes, all labeled with letters and numbers that meant nothing to her. The only area that was uncluttered was the bed and the desk. She ignored the bed. The thought of that woman in bedclothes – or less – turned her stomach. The desk was as intriguing as the box must have been to Pandora.

A pale-blue canvas journal with leather corners was set out, a ribbon trailing out the top as a bookmark. Vickie opened it and looked inside.

It wasn't a journal as in a diary, but a ledger. Columns of dates and commodities lined the one side, item numbers off to the right. Vickie glanced back at the cardboard boxes. Nanny Elsa had been accumulating goods not only from her parents – their names and dates were the most frequent on the listing – but from other people, too. She looked over the item names, printed out in a hand that was as clear as a computer font. The last journal entry was only two weeks ago:

12 December 2007. Thornwhistle Family hair comb: diamonds, rubies, sapphires. Under the column labeled value was marked: *est. $1,200,000*. The last column marked notes read: *Verify with jeweler*.

Item after item. Some were small such as *Merriweather Day Spa – the works – $800*. Others were obscure, like *15 January 1998 – New Bodyworks – Lap-Band – $40,000*. And some were just plain irritating. *5 December 2008 – 1992 Maserati Ghibli AM336 – est $75,000 – Note: intended 16th birthday gift VLT*.

"That bitch!" Vickie hissed. "Daddy was going to give me the Ghibli, but she blackmailed him for it."

Vickie thumbed through assorted papers – receipts and appraisals – that were in the back of the ledger and found what she was looking for: the title for her car. *"Voila!"* She rolled it into a tube and stuffed it down the back of her pajama bottoms. "Happy birthday to me all over again."

In the back of the ledger was an envelope with postal money orders in it. Uncashed ones from someone named Chuck Armstrong. "Papa Doc?" She thumbed through them. They were all made out to Gloria Thornwhistle and were from years past – some of them fifteen years ago. No, not Papa Doc. His name was A.B.C. Armstrong. Chuck was his son who'd been incommunicado for just about forever. But why was he sending money to her mother? And why did Nanny now have the checks? They had certainly expired by now. She looked at the post office stamp of where the latest one had been issued. Wolf Whistle, West Virginia in June 2005. At least it was a starting point.

Careful to cover any evidence of her snooping, Vickie set everything back in place including the spare room key taped to the drawer. Everything except the title to the Ghibli. She'd loved that car since the day her daddy first brought it home, all silver and shiny. *One day this is going to be yours*, he promised. And he was right.

Back in the privacy of her bedroom, she pulled out the paper and looked it over in brighter light. Her father had signed it over but hadn't written in the name of the new owner. His signature looked odd, though. It took a moment to realize what it was. He had dented the document from writing so hard. Stress. Duress. He hadn't wanted to do it.

Vickie looked at the bed. She wasn't the least bit tired. It was just the opposite. She was supercharged with a purpose. Exploratory energy was surging. Her suspicion that Grace was her biological mother just became more certain with her rock 'em, sock 'em, knock-down fight and the slip of the tongue at the party. She had also found out that her parents had been blackmailed for years. By whom was obvious: Nanny Elsa. The real question was 'why'? Daddy had said they didn't want to lose their little girl. Could Elsa have found out that Chuck Armstrong had proof she was adopted and she was tracking him? Did her parents actually think that she would choose *anyone* over them, even Dusty and

157

Grace? They all got along: why would she want to change her family dynamics? Well, except for Nanny Elsa, everything was perfect. Time to get rid of her.

Rummaging through her closet, Vickie found some comfortable workout clothes and a warm jacket. She hadn't found the key to the Ghibli in the desk. It had to be in the key box in the garage with the other cars. She grabbed her backpack, gloves, and a scarf. Time for a ride!

***

Vickie strode into the garage with confidence and walked smack into a big, muscular someone.

"Whoa! What are you doing here?" Rich asked, reaching out to steady her.

"I live here," she said, stumbling backward. "What are you still doing here?"

"You don't live in the garage. I'm here because I had a couple of drinks with Hal and the guys. They offered me a place to stay for the night, but my truck has a big back seat. Plus, they'd have to run me back here in the morning. Not that I didn't want to see you again, but I didn't want to be a burden to them." Rich looked at her attire and noticed she had a backpack, ready to hit the road. "Are you driving or hitching a ride?" he asked.

"Huh?"

He pointed to the bag. "Two in the morning, a packed bag, warm coat, sneaking into the garage... I'd say it looks like you're running away."

"I'm not running away. I left a note. Well, I was going to. Once I got out here," she added sheepishly.

"Which car are you taking?" Rich asked, looking over the eight assorted types of vehicles.

"I'm taking mine. The Ghibli," she said, chin stuck out in defiance. "And I don't have to tell you anything. I just told you that because you'd know when I drove it out anyhow."

"Can't let you do it," Rich said, arms crossed in front of his chest, a sly smile on his face.

"You can't stop me," she said, her voice controlled, attitude determined.

"Well, I am bigger and stronger than you. And I did tell your father I wouldn't let you get into trouble. Or something like that. Besides, if you just turned sixteen today, you probably don't have your driver's license."

"I have my learner's permit."

"Yeah, well, you have to have another driver in the car for that to work. I don't see one around."

"You'll do. Come on. Let's go."

"Whoa! Whoa!" Rich uncrossed his arms and took two long strides to stand in front of her. "I can't go anywhere with you."

"Why not?"

"You're underage. I'm not. I'd get busted for... Well, it's pretty much

158

illegal for anyone to take you anywhere without your parent's permission. Where are you headed at two in the morning? Why don't you wait until daylight and go with someone else? Lord knows you have enough people who care about you."

"How about you?"

"You're going to make me crazy, woman. I just told you…"

"Well, if you won't take me where I want to go, would you do me a favor?"

"Like what?"

"Take me to your place…"

"Nope. Still underage."

"Not that. What I want is to move my car off this property to somewhere Nanny Elsa won't find it. I'll bet my studded earrings that you have friends or family in the area where we can park the Ghibli."

Rich rolled his eyes. It was a *very* nice ride. He'd wanted one for years. With Maseratis, older was better, too. "Five miles down the road is my uncle's place. He has a big garage with lots of classics in it. We could probably slip another one in. But if you don't own this, you're stealing it. That's grand theft auto. That comes with more than a scowl and a slap on the hand."

Vickie opened up her backpack and pulled out the title. She had filled in her name as the buyer and backdated it to two days earlier. "See. I got it the day before my birthday."

"All right. Do you think you can follow me down the road? If you don't speed or weave all over the place, you shouldn't be pulled over and asked for your license. One question, though. Why do you want to move it? I'd be taking a big chance – or putting my uncle in a lurch – if your dad reports it stolen and it's found at his place."

Vickie didn't answer right away, her lips working back and forth as she thought of a good excuse.

"You know, I may be a lousy liar, but that doesn't mean I can't tell when someone else is lying to me," Rich said sarcastically.

"I didn't lie. I didn't say anything!"

"Yes, but you were thinking about what to say, and it wasn't the truth. Just tell me. What's the worst that can happen?"

"Nanny Elsa was trying to steal it from my father. Steal it through blackmail. He said it was my sixteenth birthday present and it is. I just can't keep it here until she's gone. She won't be back tonight, but they might – probably will – let her out of the hospital tomorrow. I don't want it here when she gets back. She wouldn't know it's missing for a long time anyhow because it's more of a summer car. It's usually stored in the garage all winter."

"Now see? Wasn't that easier? I can believe that's the truth. So, I see you have gloves. Leave a note and we can be on our way."

"You believe me?"

"Did you lie?"

"No."

"Okay, let's go."

Vickie grabbed the key out of the lockbox, scribbled, "I'll be back soon. Love ya, Dad & Mom!" on the dry erase board next to it, then got in the Ghibli. *As you always told me, Dad: soon is relative!*

Rich hit the button and waited for the garage door to open. "You go first. Wait until I get my truck out, and then follow me."

Haltingly at first, Vickie backed out. *Don't blow it, woman! Reverse is just like going forward, except exactly opposite.*

Rich rolled his eyes at her inexperience behind the wheel. Daddy probably always backed it out for her. She should make it down the road to Uncle Phil's house without a problem, though. The roads were dry and well-lit.

Rich added a scribbled postscript note to her quick 'See ya later' message and included his cellphone number, then backed his truck out. After making sure she was still following him, he pulled out his phone and dialed.

"Roger? Yeah, I know it's late. I'm glad you gave me your card. Vickie has the Maserati and is bringing it to my Uncle Phil's place up the road. Yeah, she said something about Nanny Elsa and making sure it was out of her clutches or something like that. Just don't go filing a stolen vehicle report. She has the title and it's signed over to her. I don't know your signature, but everything looked to be in order. I figure I'll let her do her thing, and then bring her back to your place in my truck. No, believe me, I know she's underage. I'd rather cut off my right arm than bother her! Yeah, well, if I didn't escort her, she'd be off on her own to parts unknown, ripe for trouble with whoever found her. She may be smart, but she's also good-looking and has an expensive car. She's a target for every flimflam man and Romeo on the east coast. I'll keep in touch. She doesn't know I'm contacting you, so let's keep it that way. And hey! Thanks for trusting me. That means a lot. See ya!"

Chapter 5: On the Road

January 4, 2008
3:30 AM

"Are you sure it's okay to leave it here? I'm sorta rethinking this. I still have to go someplace before Nanny Elsa gets out of the hospital and that's my only ride."

"How far? Can we be back before anyone knows you're missing?" Rich asked. "I'll drive."

Vickie took the map out of the console and opened it up. *Where in the hell is Wolf Whistle, West Virginia? I can already tell he's not going to let me go anywhere by myself. The key is in the locked dropbox now, so I can't get it back. Damn!* "Hmm. We're here and I want to go south."

"That's what you said. What I'm wondering is how far south. What's the name of the town?" *She's stalling. She doesn't know where she's headed. Fine. I have plenty of fuel. I'll play along for two hours, and then I'm hauling her back to Daddy. Hopefully, not kicking and screaming, but back to her parents, just the same.*

"Woodstock."

"New York? There's no way…"

"No, Woodstock, Connecticut."

"I know where that is, but it's east of here, not south."

"Oh, I must be holding the map upside down."

"All right, we'll go. But you try and get some rest. You get to drive us back home. Do you think you can handle this beast?"

"Um, what beast?" Vickie asked, blushing because she had been staring at the five o'clock shadow on his face. Or three A.M. shadow.

"This three-quarter-ton truck. Here. We'll find out soon enough. Use my coat as a pillow."

Rich reached behind the seat, grabbed his denim and sheered-wool jacket, and handed it to her. His spread-arm movement scented the air with male musk and fatigue, a faint hint of leftover cologne adding a spicy tang to the aromatherapy that made her lady parts tingle.

"Okay," she said, hoping she didn't sound as breathless as she felt, "I'll try to sleep. It's been a wild and crazy twenty-four hours."

Rich cranked up the fan on the heater. "Yeah, well, I certainly didn't see me taking an underage woman across state lines in the wee hours of the morning, either," he said, then realized that he had just said that aloud.

"Hmm?" she asked, snuggling into the soft, fleecy interior of his coat that smelled like her hero.

"Nothing. Just get some sleep."

Two hours later, the weary driver pulled into the all-night diner. The thunk-thunk of the truck passing over the curb and sudden absence of road noise awakened the damsel on her mission of discovery. "Wait. Where are we?" she asked, biting off the next question of, 'And who are you?' as she realized who he was: her gallant knight, escorting her on her quest.

Her smile of contentment widened. What he didn't know was that her final destination was West Virginia. Even if she couldn't find it on the printed road map, someone along the way was sure to have heard of Wolf Whistle!

"I have to stop for coffee and something to eat. You could use a big breakfast, too," Rich said, his voice rough and dry. He swallowed and tried to clear his throat, but the noise came out lusty – sounding more like an invitation to foreplay than a search for spittle. "And I need water, lots of water. The heater dried me out."

Click. Vickie unbuckled, leaning forward as she wiggled away from his coat. "You need this more than I do now."

Rich stared at her breasts bouncing around an arm's reach away… "No," he said, his voice now even lower and more guttural. Primal. "On second thought," he said, and pulled it onto his lap. "I'll meet you inside. Gotta get fuel." He shifted in his seat, moving aside his early morning discomfort, glad he had the jacket for cover in case she looked over.

"All right. Oh, and thanks. You're a great white knight. Well, all the white knights were the good guys but you're great. I guess they were all white, too – as in Caucasian – back in the feudal days of England. Oh, ignore me. I haven't had coffee yet and I'm rambling," Vickie said and opened the door, trying to leave the truck with at least a little dignity.

But, you're so cute when you babble! Rather than try and speak without a full voice again, Rich gave her a two-fingered wave of farewell. He paused before heading to the gas pumps and pretended to look for something in the console, waiting to make sure she entered the café. *Two years until you're eighteen… Two years from now, will you be even more intriguing? 'Two years of torment until she is yours.' Double-damn you, gypsy!*

"Hey, Roger! It's me, Rich. Sorry, my voice is shot. We're in Connecticut. I'm stopping for fuel and breakfast. I think this short trip will get her grounded to reality. Yeah, I know she's just a kid. She's on some quest for a unicorn or justice or something. Sorry. I need coffee. Just checking in. She's fine. Yeah, well, I'm hoping she calls you. Text me if she does. She's a good kid. Yes, yes, I know she's still a kid. Hey, the gas guy's here. Talk to you later. *Click.*

"How did I get myself into this?"

***

All fueled up and ready for coffee, Rich entered the small Mom and Pop restaurant. Momentary panic buckled his knees as he searched the room and didn't see her.

Vickie came out of the 'His and Hers' bathroom that was located right behind him and stood quietly, watching him search for her. When she realized that his level of concern wasn't irritation but terror, she decided to stop tormenting him.

"Looking for me?" she asked, a slight smile of mischief brightening her eyes.

He spun around, an audible gasp of relief escaping. "Who else would I be looking for?" he said, his voice raspy as a baseball fan after a double-header, his emotions mixed with frustration and joy. Seeing a table already set for the next customer, he took the glass of water and guzzled it down with a quick glug-glug. "Let's sit here," he said, his voice rehydrated and back to near normal. "I'll be right back."

The weary driver, still attired in formal dinner clothes less the tuxedo jacket, stopped at the checkout counter and souvenir shop. A pair of U Conn sweatpants and a long-sleeved tee that read 'Woodstock: Still a great place to be' would draw less attention to a man escorting a female minor. While waiting for the cashier to ring up his sale, he overheard an older man pause his walker at their table and address Vickie.

"Good morning, Ria. How's your dad doing?"

Knowing that he couldn't be talking to her, Vickie continued to read the 'Stuff you didn't know about Connecticut' advertisement and trivia flyer that was on the table.

"Hmph!" the senior muttered and continued to the cash register, frustrated that he had been ignored.

"Hey, Alice," he said when he got to the cashier. "What's Ria doing in here without Doc? Her old man never lets her go anywhere by herself. Plus, she ain't old enough to drive yet."

"Are you sure that's her?" Alice asked, looking around Rich to get a better view. "Nah. There's a definite similarity, but Ria's not that skinny. This one looks half-starved."

The old man nodded in agreement. "Yeah, plus she doesn't have those cute little elf ears like Ria. Damned if they don't look enough alike to be twins, though."

Rich took his change, headed into the restroom, then opened the door again quickly, looking back at their table to make sure she hadn't taken off in his truck. He shook his head, trying to clear the brain fog of fatigue. She couldn't do that. He still had the keys. He splashed water on his face. That helped a little, but what were those locals saying about her being a twin? They didn't know that she'd had her ears 'fixed.' He only knew because that was the reason why her godmother had pummeled Nanny Elsa.

That's a mother's defensive move, not a godmother's. And if I have this figured out right, Vickie is chasing down clues about what her nanny has been

163

blackmailing her parents with. Could it be that the Thornwhistles adopted a twin and this Ria is the other one? Grace does look enough like Vickie to be her mother. Crap. I gotta eat and get some sleep. Maybe if I could see this Ria, I'd know. Something is up if she really does look like Vickie's twin.

Rich approached the cashier after he came out, dressed as a tourist or local, not a hungover partier. "Excuse me," he said. "I have a little problem I wanted to see a doctor about before I got further down the road. Is there one around here?"

"Yup. Doc has a clinic a ways outside of town. Not that this is much of a town, but he likes being remote. He thinks city air isn't good for him and his daughter. That doesn't stop him from coming in and getting a nice stack of blueberry pancakes and a side of bacon once a month or so. Here. Let me draw you a map. He doesn't take appointments. 'Just show up when you're ailing,' he says."

"Sounds like my kind of man." Rich watched the gnarled hands draw a simple map on the back of a paper placemat. "Just tell him Alice sent you. Not that it'll get you a discount. He just asks folks to pay what they feel his time is worth. If they can't afford that, they usually work out something with jams and jellies or knit caps and afghans. He's pretty easy going."

"Thanks. I think I'll give him a little time, though. It's still pretty early. My cousin and I were just passing through on our way back from a big shindig in Massachusetts. Silly me. I totally forgot to bring a change of clothes. A plate of pancakes and side of bacon with a double-strength cup of coffee sounds great. She should know what she wants to eat by now, too."

"Be right there," she said.

"Hey, Cuz," Rich said as he slid into the booth.

"Cuz?" Vickie asked softly.

"Hey, cousins are fine to be traveling with," he whispered across the table. "Remember, I could get in a lot of trouble just being with you. Give me a little alibi or validation or something, okay? Now, what do you want to eat?"

"I'm not hungry."

"I don't know if you even know what hungry is anymore. You're shivering because you don't have a calorie to burn for heat. While you're with me, I want you to eat. And I don't mean just move your food around on your plate and pretend, either. I'll order for you."

"No, that's okay. I'll have an egg white and mushroom omelet, no cheese."

"Bullshit."

"Ew! That would taste terrible with eggs." Vickie sneered, then burst out laughing.

"Pancakes and bacon with coffee and an orange juice," Rich said.

"That's too much," Vickie started to protest.

"That's for me."

164

"Oh. Dang. That sounded pretty good."

Rich looked up and saw the cashier, now his waitress, marking on her notepad. "Double that order except you know how I want my coffee."

"Sure thing, Cuz," she said with a wink.

∗

"I can't believe I ate half of that pancake and three pieces of bacon."

"It was only one pancake, even if it did fill half the plate. So, on another subject, where are we going? I mean, why are we going?"

"I want to find out what Elsa's holding over my parents' heads. I know that comb she said was her family heirloom has been in my father's family for generations and was going to be mine. I guess she didn't know that I knew, or she wouldn't have tried to tell me such a bodacious lie. And the Ghibli! Dad bought that just after I was born. It was our summer touring vehicle. She knew that I knew, too, because she's been my nanny since before I was old enough to read. While she was gone, I snooped in her room. I found her ledger of ill-gotten gains. It lists everything she's taken, who she took it from and when, and its estimated value. That woman could probably buy a villa in France if she wanted. Why would she stick around?"

"Greed."

"Huh?"

"Greed. Plain and simple. She wants more. It's a sickness. I see a lot of it. Mr. A. has a home with ten bedrooms and twelve baths, so Mr. B. thinks he needs one with fourteen of each. Mrs. C. has a three-carat diamond ring, so Mrs. D. wants three-and-a-half carats. Truth is, one bedroom per person in the house is plenty, and it's only tradition that says a wedding ring is even necessary."

"Yeah, diamonds aren't for everyone," Vickie said with a snort. "They seem to get some people in trouble. Hence the hair comb Elsa extorted from my dad."

"Yes, but will you feel the same way when you find the man you want to marry? What would you do if he didn't offer you a great big chunk of ice to show off to your friends?"

Vickie looked up and sneered, her head shaking back and forth slowly. "You certainly don't know me. Just because I grew up entitled doesn't mean that I feel I deserve it all. I'll get my education, and then go out in the world and make a difference. Having the biggest house or more diamonds means nothing to me. Having parents who don't look like they're afraid of losing me or each other, is. I'm not on this quest for goods or money. I'm out to spare my parents."

"How are you going to do that?"

"The way I figure it, there's some sort of information Elsa is holding over them. If I find out what it is, then I can – how would you say? – deflate or devalue that tidbit. Blackmail is about words or pictures being withheld. I want to make that information worthless."

165

"You're pretty smart for your age, Cuz," Rich said, adding a wink.

"Must run in the family. Now, let's pay up and hit the road. We have a long way to go."

"About that," Rich said, adding a fake wince of pain. "Where is our final destination? You said Woodstock and we're here now."

"How far are you willing to go? I mean, it really is south of here."

"In for a penny, in for a pound."

"It's a little place called Wolf Whistle, West Virginia…"

Rich gasped in shock, then turned it into a groan. "I hate to cut this trip short, but I have to go see a doctor before we go too much further. I got a…a…"

Quick, think of a disease. She doesn't have a brother, so make up something male-related.

"I got a man-type problem. Something I need to talk to a doctor about. I asked about one when I came in, just in case. I was hoping it would get better if I ate, but it's still there. Come on. Let's go."

"But…"

"It won't take long. Just a little side trip. He probably has some medicine that will help. It's not something you can get over the counter, though."

Opening her mouth to protest again, Vickie realized that she was stuck. At his mercy. She couldn't go anywhere without him. Whether there really was such a thing as a 'man-type' problem that could be cured by a doctor's special potion or not, she'd have to give in just a little. At least he wasn't trying to hit on her. *Dang it!*

"Are you okay to drive? I mean, just tell me where we're going…"

"I'll drive. I got the directions before we ate, just in case. It won't take too long."

"But you don't have an appointment." Vickie suddenly paled. Was he going to take her into the woods and rape her? Had she really made such a rash decision? How stupid was she to be taking off with someone she'd just met, without letting her parents know where she was headed? Good looks and getting a *zing* when they touched was not a reason to be so reckless…

Under the glaring lights of the parking lot, Rich could see Vickie's fear about his sudden change in plans. He put a hand on her shoulder, startling her. "I'll never take advantage of you if that's what has you panicked. This is just a side trip. Trust me, all right?"

"Okay."

"And let me go in by myself first. It really is a guy thing."

***

It was only a few miles on the map but a lot longer on the twisting roads and one missed turn that resulted in backtracking. They finally pulled up to the long motor home with a magnetic sign on the side that read 'Doc's Clinic. C. R. M. Strong. Knock before entering.'

166

"Looks safe enough," Vickie said.

"I'll be back shortly." Rich started to leave the engine running to keep the heater going, then had second thoughts. "I'll take the keys. When you get cold, come on in. That should give me about five minutes of guy to doctor time."

Grrr.

"Hey, we don't have time for growling at each other. Besides, I'd win that one. Still, I don't completely trust you not to take off with my truck. I like you, but you did just sneak out with a hundred-thousand-dollar car a few hours ago."

Grrr.

"Later on that one, lady," he said, then left her in the warm truck. Fuming. Without tunes and nothing but his fleece-lined coat for extra warmth.

Knock. Knock. Knock.

The door opened right away. "Come on in," the good-looking bearded man in his mid-forties said.

The smell of coffee and bacon perfumed the air, the room bright with fluorescent lights and white walls, a desk and three chairs in the living room area rather than a couch. "I'm Chuck. Do you care for some coffee?"

"Rich. And yes, please."

"We're all rich in our own ways," Chuck said with a wink, then poured a cup for the obviously fatigued young man and handed it to him. "Have a seat. Sorry for the pun."

"At least it was a new one. Hey, I hate to bother you so early, but…" Rich sat down and rubbed a hand over his face, trying to figure out how to address the situation.

"So early or late?" Chuck asked while his visitor sought words.

"You called that one right," Rich said. He brought his hand down, looked up and noticed the picture on the desk.

Vickie.

Or her twin. Complete with the cutest ears that stuck out just a smidge.

"Is that your daughter?" Rich asked, picking up the five by seven acrylic frame of a teenage girl holding a twelve-inch long rainbow trout.

"Yes, that's Rhianna Lynn. I took that picture last year. She just turned sixteen yesterday."

Rich's hand went limp and dropped to the table, the photo slipping from his grasp.

"Whoa there, buddy. What's going on?"

Knock. Knock.

Vickie quickly opened the door, not waiting for anyone to answer, her hand covering her eyes. "I'm sorry, I'm sorry. I couldn't wait any longer. It's too cold out there. Are you decent?" she asked, babbling in frustration. Her head turned side to side. "Are you in here, Rich? I don't want to open my eyes in case the doctor's examining you."

"I'm right here, and you can open your eyes… No! Wait a second. Keep them closed."

Rich stood up and led her to a chair. "Sit," he told her, his eyes on Chuck. "I'm not a dog," she replied sarcastically.

Chuck's eyes widened at hearing her voice. Face obscured by her hand and head covered with a scarf, the curls that escaped were the same color as Ria's.

"Okay. Open your eyes."

"Tori Lynn?" Chuck asked.

"No. My name is Vickie Lynn Thornwhistle. Who are you?"

The man's face was ashen, his mouth gasping. Vickie could tell he was dumbstruck. "And are you okay? I mean, you're the doctor, right? It looks like *you're* the one who's sick."

"I think he is," Rich said.

"That bacon smells so good," a voice called from the hallway. "Oh, I'm sorry, Dad. I didn't know you had clients this early."

Vickie stood up and faced her doppelganger in gray sweats, her head wrapped in a towel. "*Who* are you?" she asked. *Am I having a dream? A nightmare?*

"Shit! I mean, shoot! Who are *you*?" Rhianna looked at her father, his eyes wide and mouth still agape. "Daddy? Do I have a twin?"

"Sorta," escaped softly, then he took a deep breath and shut his mouth. "And yes, saying shit is appropriate in this case."

"So, who's Ria?" Rich asked, watching Chuck for signs of lying.

"I am," the woman fresh from the shower answered. "Rhianna Lynn Strong."

Vickie noticed the hesitation when her twin said her last name. She was lying about it. Not the time to bring it up, though.

"So, if she's Rhianna Lynn, and I'm Vickie Lynn, who is Tori Lynn?"

Chuck took another deep breath and shook his head. "Me and my big mouth. Shoot."

"No, Daddy," Ria said. "Now's an appropriate time to say shit."

"Shit, shoot, either way, that's why I said sorta. You aren't twins – you're two of triplets. You were all adopted when you were just a few hours old to different parents."

Vickie and Ria stared at each other a moment, then both looked back at Chuck. "So, where's our sister?" Vickie asked.

"And who's our mother?" Ria echoed with the exact same tone and inflection.

"Eerie," Rich said.

"Yeah, right?" added Chuck.

"That's an evasive reply," Ria said. "I'm calling you out on that, as you so often say to me."

168

"Yeah, I guess I brought you up right."

"Yes, you did. And that's another evasive answer," she said, hands on hips.

"Are Grace and Dusty our parents?" Vickie asked.

"You know them?" Chuck asked.

"That's answering a question with a question," Vickie said. "Yes, Gloria and Roger brought me up right, too," she said, nudging her new-found sister with an elbow of camaraderie.

"Oh, Lord. I knew this day was coming…"

"Hey, Doc. That's more evasiveness. My parents brought me up right, too," Rich said. "Just don't tell me I'm related to them, okay?"

"Unless Dusty and Grace are your parents, no, you're not related." Doc ran his fingers through his long salt and pepper hair. "Why are you here?"

Vickie turned to Rich. "Yeah, why are *you* here? And you never did have a 'guy problem,' did you?"

"You're the only guy problem I have," Rich said. "While you three reconnect, can I go to my truck and get some sleep? I've been driving all night after a full day of family and birthday parties and rescuing damsels in distress and… I just need an hour or two. Please?"

"Ria, show him to the back bedroom and give him an extra blanket. I don't want him passing out. He's too big for me to move around."

"You've moved bigger," Ria said.

"Not without hurting for the next three days," he replied.

"Just saying…"

"Do you two always talk like that?" Vickie asked Chuck.

"Like what?"

"I don't know. Like she's your wife. You're not weird like that, I hope."

"Ew! No!" Chuck said in disgust. "She's my helper here at the clinic. This place isn't much, but it's all we can afford with how much we charge. We don't take insurance, don't have any foundations funding us, and part of my mission is to be mobile. I'm all over the place in this thing. I fix people up, and then I'm on my way."

"Like in Wolf Whistle?" Vickie asked.

"Do you know why they called it that?" Ria barely paused before answering her own question. "It's because the wind blows so hard, it sounds like it's whistling when it blows through the trees and rocks."

"And cracks in the door and window seals," Chuck added. "We left there years ago. How do you know about that?"

"I found an old money order made out to my mother," Vickie said. "What was that all about?"

"She loaned me money. I paid it back. I called that old motorhome we had The Whistler because it was so drafty. Her loan helped me buy this one. It was used but in much better shape and ten feet longer than the previous one. It's not as negotiable in the hills, but we manage to find a place big enough to park for a month. The little towns and hollows are happy to have us around to treat those who need it. We stay put until clients stop showing up."

"So, does that mean Rhianna's homeschooled?"

"You can call me Ria. Yes, I'm homeschooled. Can I ask you a question? Oh, I just did, didn't I? Oops. Another question. What I'm getting at is, are you sick?"

"No," Vickie replied, embarrassed at someone telling her she was inadequate.

"Hey, Dad. Let me take this one. Go finish your coffee and breakfast. I'm giving this beautiful young lady a check-up. Something's wrong with her and she doesn't even know it."

"But...but...we just met!"

"It's either me or Dad, but one of us is going to find out what's going on in that skinny pasty body. You forget: he and I both know what you *should* look like."

"She's got you there," Chuck said. "She sees herself in the mirror every morning. You may be beautiful, but I agree: you don't look right."

"We're not going back where Rich is, are we?"

"Nope." Ria ushered her to the tiny room on the other side of the office living room combination. "This is my bedroom." She pulled down a cabinet door and revealed a bin of personal belongings, including a pink stuffed unicorn.

Vickie reached up and touched it. "An ooni-corn! I had one almost like it. I was obsessed with them when I was little."

"Really? Me, too!" Ria pulled the animal out and gave it to her. "Hold onto her while I check you out. First, take off your shirt."

"Can I leave on my bra?"

"As long as I don't see anything suspicious, sure. This place is still chilly, even if it isn't as drafty."

Jacket and tee-shirt off, Vickie crossed her arms across her chest and shivered, her bony shoulder bones sharp and angular.

"Geez, woman! You're not much more than a skeleton! Don't your parents feed you?"

"Yeah, they noticed, if that's what you mean. My nanny says I'm too fat. She's bony and thinks I should be, too. If I eat, she makes my life miserable. I swear she has cameras hidden everywhere. If I so much as sneak an olive, she lectures me for an hour on how I'll never get a husband, that fat people have no self-control..."

"Have you told your parents about her?"

Vickie shook her head. "I can't."

"Or won't... So, let me approach this another way. What's the worst that can happen if they fire her?"

"She's already blackmailing them. I just found that out yesterday. Or was that earlier this morning? Anyhow, after my birthday party…" Vickie paused, her eyes glistening in recall of Grace punching Elsa.

"What's wrong? Or what's right?" Ria asked. "Now I know what Dad sees when something's going through my head. What you're feeling is showing on your face."

"Oh, it's right, very right." Vickie grabbed the rainbow afghan from the bed and wrapped it around her shoulders. "Okay, so here's the thing. I was about four when I first met my real mother – our birth mother – but I didn't know who she was. I was never told I was adopted. Everything led me to believe that I was just a late-in-life child. So, one day I kinda got rescued by a woman whose father is my father's – adopted father's – cousin. One thing leads to another, and we're in each other's lives. I sort of get a set of godparents.

"I started suspecting there might be more of a connection when I was thirteen. I confronted Grace – our mom – and she admitted a truth. Not the complete truth, but something she thought would satisfy me. She told me that her mother and my mom – the woman who brought me up – were sisters. None of them got along, so they just ignored each other. That was also her reason why we looked so much alike.

"I didn't get a clue that we were even more closely related until Grace – Mom – punched out Nanny Elsa at my birthday party. She got all wound up when she was slugging it out and referred to me as her daughter. Afterward, she said it was because I was her goddaughter. She tried throwing in a few other smoke and mirrors remarks, but I saw through them. Plus, I saw the shock in her face when she realized that she had claimed me out loud."

"Before I get all distracted with *Mom*…" Ria inhaled deeply with the word, savoring it, then licked her lips, determined not to get distracted. "Why did Mom punch your nanny? I assume Nanny Elsa is your nanny."

Vickie turned her head and showed her the ear that was still itching and burning. "Elsa talked me into getting my ears clipped. This one got infected."

"Ooh. That looks painful. I noticed the difference when I first saw you. I think I should have Dad check that out. So, lie back real quick and let me poke and prod. I think you look so pasty because you're malnourished and fighting an infection."

"Do you know how weird this is?" Vickie asked. "You look and sound just like me. You're not a phantom or a dream." She reached up and touched her arm. "So weird."

"Yeah, I do know, because I get the same feeling. Dad never told me, either." Ria's fingers deftly felt for an enlarged liver or other abnormalities, then satisfied she was in good health, offered her a hand to sit up.

"Yeah… And there's another one of us out there somewhere…" Vickie said dreamily.

171

"Yeah…" Ria echoed. "Really weird."

"Can I get dressed now?"

"Sure. Hey, let me give you a tank top to wear under everything else. Keeping clothing right next to your skin helps insulate your body heat. After you're dressed, I want Dad to look at that ear."

"Gotcha. Sis."

"Back at ya. Sis."

Both girls shivered in excitement with identical shoulder shrugs, then laughed the same short, "Hah!"

"This is going to be so much fun!" they said at the same time.

"Or not," Vickie groaned. "I still have to go home. I don't live that far away, but I have to go back and make things right for my parents."

"Get dressed, then we'll get Dad to fix you up."

***

Chuck inhaled deeply at seeing the infected wound, resisting the urge to comment on the sloppy work. He stood in front of her and asked, "Have you seen anyone else about this. Other than the person who did the deed?"

"Yeah, Papa Doc cleaned it up last night. He didn't have any lidocaine so let me have a drink of whisky to help numb the pain. How can anyone drink that stuff?"

"They drink it for effect, not flavor. Or so they tell me. Who is this Papa Doc fellow?"

"He's kind of like a grandpa to me. A. B. C. Armstrong is his name. Actually, I have lots of surrogate grandpas. Hal and Silas claim me, too."

Vickie paused her cheery rambling for a moment, then spoke sincerely. "Hey, Chuck. How come you just paled when I said his name?" Vickie looked at Ria and saw a similar reaction. "Okay, you two. Do you know Papa Doc?"

"He does, I never met him," Ria said. "He won't let me. Papa Doc is his father."

"Oh…" Vickie said, then giggled as realization hit. "You sign reads C. R. M. Strong. That's for Chuck Ar-m-strong, am I right?"

"Turn around and let me clean that ear again," Chuck grumbled, then smiled at her cleverness.

"Oh, my God!" Vickie squealed, bouncing up and down in place.

"Hold still," Chuck ordered, his hand on her shoulder. "Which epiphany did you just have?"

"Hal is my grandpa! My honest to goodness biological grandpa. And yours, too, Ria!"

"Took you long enough," Chuck said with a chuckle. "When I'm done, I need to put more topical antibiotics on that. I don't have any antibiotic pills left, so I want you to go back home and tell Papa Doc that your physician in Woodstock said he had confidence that he'll know which one to administer."

"I'm jealous," Ria said with a pout.

"Of what?" Chuck asked.

"She gets to know my grandpa and I don't."

"Both adopted and biological grandpas. And our father and mother…" Vickie said softly.

"Well, meeting them would be cool, too," Ria said. "I never felt shorted when it came to the parents' aspect of a relationship, but I knew about Papa Doc. I never had a grandfather. Dad, can we go there for a visit? I want to meet him."

"We'll see…"

Ria rolled her eyes at her sister and scowled. *That means no.* A grin bloomed and she raised an eyebrow. *But I have you now. Will you help?*

Face pinched in discomfort as the swab cleaned out the wound, Vickie cut her eyes to the side and gave a discreet thumbs-up. *I got your back, Sis!*

Chapter 6: Eighteenth Birthday

January 4, 2008
9:00 AM

"Hi, Dad. Yeah, I'm okay. I'm sorry I took off with just that lame note. Yes, I did! I wrote it on the whiteboard in the garage. Okay, well, it should still be there. I never thought about you not coming out there to find me. Yeah, well, I also moved the Ghibli. Hey, before you get too wound up, know that I love you and Mom, and the only reason I took off was to see if I could declaw Nanny Elsa. Yeah, well, you might think it's not my job, but she's not only declawed, I think I may have crippled her. No. Wait just a second. Are you sitting down? Okay, then sit down and put me on speakerphone so Mom can hear, too."

Vickie looked over at her audience. Rich had awakened and joined the trio at the table, contentedly gnawing on a piece of bacon between sips of coffee.

"Okay. Here goes. I met my sister. Just one of them, though. Dad? Dad? Is Mom okay? Oh, hi, Mom. Is Dad okay? Yeah, I know that Grace is my bio-Mom and Dusty's my bio-Dad. It doesn't change my love for anyone, though. But hey! I have Ria here. Her name's Rhianna Lynn Armstrong. Say hi, Ria."

Ria rolled her eyes in embarrassment, feeling like a four-year-old on Santa's lap being urged to tell him what she wanted for Christmas. "Hi, Vickie's mom and dad. It's cool to meet her. I didn't know about her, either. No, neither one of us fainted, but Dad got an earful. Yeah, well, say hi to my grandpa, Papa Doc, for me. I hope to meet everyone real soon."

Ria scowled, letting Vickie know she was done talking.

"Yes, Rich is here. He's tanking up on coffee and bacon, getting ready to hit the road back home. We're hoping to miss drivetime traffic. Okay, we'll be careful. Yes, Mom, I always wear my seatbelt. So, don't let Elsa back in the house. She has a ledger loaded with all the stuff she's extorted over the years and from whom. There's a key to her room stuck with tape to the bottom of the drawer in the vase table just outside her room. I don't know if you can legally take it, but at least take pictures of all the pages. I know you shouldn't blackmail her, but it would be so sweet to have her on the other end for a change. Why would you buy her a one-way ticket to Costa Rica? Okay, I'll ask Chuck. Love you! See you by dinner!"

Vickie hit end on the phone. "Wow. That went better than I thought," she said to the group.

Chuck picked up his cup and looked to see how much coffee was left. "They'll probably ground you for life when you get home."

"Only for two years. Or two years less one day. It was worth it! Now, Chuck, tell me about Costa Rica."

"Short answer – and all you ever need to know – is that's where Grace's mother was sent by Hal when he divorced her. You think Nanny Elsa is bad, this woman trumps her. Don't even bring up her name. Pure evil."

Ria glanced at Vickie who glanced back. Rich saw the tacit exchange, missed by the musing Chuck, and jumped in. "Do not ever think about messing with evil, either one of you. Think of it this way: no good can come from it. It will only hurt those you love if you disturb it. Someone else went through hell to get her sent away. Are you seriously wanting to hurt your mothers and Hal by connecting with her?"

"When you put it that way…" Vickie said.

"So, Dad," Ria interjected. "When do we get to meet Tori Lynn? And why do all of us have the same middle name."

"I have no idea why Lynn got stuck in the middle of all of you. Your name choices were by the parents, and none of us knew the other girls' names until later. Actually, nobody else knew Rhianna's middle name until today."

"That's question number two answered," Vickie said. "How about the first one: when do we get to meet Tori Lynn?"

Chuck looked up at Rich. *Help! I'm getting double-teamed!*

"Hey. They're your problems. I'm just the driver," Rich answered, all smiles as he sipped his coffee.

"No, you're not," Vickie said, sidling up to him.

Rich spat out his swallow, choking on it.

Chuck handed him a napkin and waited to make sure he could catch his breath before offering assistance.

"What do you mean?" Rich gasped.

Vickie tried to contain her grin, then gave up. "You're the Sherlock who figured this all out. I just got us headed in the right direction. Sort of."

"I've heard there's a twin thing that goes on," Ria said. "I wonder if there's a triplet thing, too."

"Yup. Gotta be that," Chuck said with a tone of finality. "And that's what you should trust to find Tori. I have to tell you right now, I do not know where she and her parents are."

Ria looked at Vickie and grinned. *Leave it to me. I'll find out her parents' names and let you know. We'll find her yet!*

***

January 3, 2010
18th birthday party

"I'm so nervous," Grace said, holding onto Dusty's arm. "Our little girl is eighteen today. She's going away, I know she is. She hasn't said anything, but I feel it in my bones. She's too young! Too naïve and vulnerable…"

"Like we were?" Dusty asked.

"Oh, Lord…"

"Hey! Don't worry about it. She has four sensible parents now. That's three more than you had. Plus, she has three grandpas. She would have had four if my dad had lived longer, but at least he got to love her as his great-goddaughter when she was four."

"Getting a little moist in here?" Chuck asked, surprising Grace with his first visit in eighteen years.

Grace – very emotional about Vickie turning eighteen and leaving – had been holding back her tears, but lost control when she saw him. She smacked him once on the arm. "Chuck? Why did you do that?" she hissed. "Why did you...you." Then she started blubbering, pounding on him, swinging uncontrollably, an emotional explosion of frustration, rage, and sorrow.

Chuck hadn't known what to expect after all these years and was prepared for anything. Keeping her at arm's length to stop more punches, he stared at how beautiful she still was, shaking his head at how her impetuousness hadn't faded. "I tried to talk you out of it dozens of times but you signed those papers. Twice. If it wasn't for me, you'd have lost contact with these girls forever."

Suddenly, she was helpless and remorseful, seeking comfort in his arms, rocking back and forth in his brotherly hug, still full of guilt at her poor decision but grateful that he had found a way to make it work for both of them.

Dusty looked at the handsome man holding his wife. "I don't think we've been introduced. I'm Dusty Rhodes, husband, father..."

"Counselor, comforter, and probably cook when needed," Chuck continued, then bent down and kissed Grace on the top of the head. "It's okay," he told her. "But I really *don't* know where the third one is..."

"Third one?" Grace and Dusty screeched, Grace pulling out of the embrace.

"Oops. You didn't tell her?" Chuck asked, looking into the hallway at Vickie.

"Nope. Mom and Dad – Gloria and Roger – and I decided not to. For a long time, Grace thought she'd lost twins. And then she found out that they were alive and adopted out and...

Vickie looked into the hallway and gave the hand signal to come in. "Well, surprise, Grace and Dusty!" She wrapped her arm around Ria's waist. "You'll have to be happy with just having the two of us around for a while. Even Chuck doesn't know where Tori is."

"Hi, I'm Rhianna Lynn Armstrong. I think you know my dad, Chuck, and grandpa, Papa Doc." She frowned at her father. "At least, the way you two were hugging, I hope you know him."

"I know Papa Doc," Dusty said, "but I just met Chuck. I heard about him, how he kept her alive and sane while pregnant." He took a deep breath. "Thank God she never said anything negative about him or *I* would have been the one punching him."

176

"Hey, girls!" Rich said, coming in with a fistful of gift bags in hand, oblivious of the excitement that had just transpired. "Long time, no see," he said to Vickie with an eye roll.

Vickie let go of her sister and nudged him, shoulder-to-shoulder, giving him a quick 'shush.'

"I'll pretend I didn't see that," Grace said, then did her own eye roll.

"Tori?" Dusty asked, trying to bring the conversation back to his being the father of triplets.

"Tori Lynn," Ria said. "Dad won't tell us her last name or the name of her parents. He's the best secret-keeper in the world." She pointed to herself. "I'm living proof of that. Don't worry, Dusty. We'll find Tori and let you and Grace know where she is."

"Yeah! We'll let you two know first!" Vickie said, her index finger held up to emphasize the number one priority.

Rich paled, Chuck and Ria gasped, and Grace and Dusty growled.

"What?" Vickie asked, bringing her hand down, looking around the room for the cause of the mixed emotions. When everyone's eyes followed her hand, she realized she had forgotten to take off her engagement ring.

"Oh, shoot!" she moaned.

"Nope," Ria said. "That one's worthy of an 'oh, shit!'"

"Rich…" Dusty said menacingly, his eyes narrowed as he tried to take his wife's restraining hand off him, ready to pummel the fiancé.

"Dusty! Don't hit him!" Vickie blurted out. "I just got it this morning. We haven't done anything stupid. We were going to announce it tonight. He wanted to give it to me in front of everyone. Come on, you and Grace were practically married when you were eighteen. At least, he's older and has a college degree, almost his masters."

Dusty relaxed and Grace started giggling, remembering their first night together, of innocence lost on the couch, the floor, the pool table... Then she remembered being caught by her mother the morning after. Suddenly, she sobered up, recalling the gut punches and threats of false charges that had robbed her of her daughters and precious time with Dusty, of being shot point-blank by the woman who had birthed her, thankfully now exiled to Costa Rica.

She took a deep breath to compose herself. "Are you two 'practically married'?" she asked, using her daughter's euphemism for sexually active.

"No," Vickie said. "I wish we were, but he said no."

Dusty clapped his hand on Rich's shoulder, a little harder than a friendship smack, a firm reminder that Vickie was still his little girl and not some floozy. "I guess I can thank you for that," he said, then whispered, "You have more restraint than I had. Three babies resulted. Remember that. Very fertile women. At least, the first time around."

"So, do I have your blessing? I mean, I've got another set of parents to ask, but it might go easier with Gloria and Roger if you've already given the go-ahead."

"Do you think we could stop them?" Dusty asked Grace.

"Not a chance in hell. Do you think he's worthy?" she asked him.

"He's been hanging around her like a dog at a butcher shop, not even stealing scraps, waiting for her to turn eighteen. He's got a career chosen thanks to Chuck's influence. Yup. I think the two of them will make a good team. Lord, I hope they don't have babies too soon."

"Why not?" she asked.

"I'm only thirty-seven! I'm too young to be a grandpa! However, a little IVF procedure and you could have another one."

Grace squeezed his arm and pulled him close. "Or two or three. I think I'm ready."

Chapter 7: Blue Collar Wedding

January 23, 2010

"I have a little information you might be interested in," Silas said, setting his laptop on the coffee table.

"Anything to distract me from thinking about my little girl getting married next week," Roger said. "Why is she in such a big hurry?"

Silas looked down his nose. "Well, if she really isn't saving herself for that young man, he's sure doing a good job of making it look like she is. That boy has got to have the bluest balls on the east coast. Not that I checked, but he sure looks frustrated to me!"

Roger shook his head, not wanting to think about the testicles of the man his daughter would be marrying. "What kind of info do you have?"

Knock! Knock!

Roger got up and answered the door. "Hal, Grace, Dusty! Come on in. Silas was just going to have a little chit chat with me. We can finish later. What's going on?"

"Actually," Silas said, "I wanted them here, too. We're going to have a little video conference call if you don't mind."

"Don't mind at all. Should I call Gloria?"

"He already did," Gloria said, coming in with a tray loaded with canapés. She set them on the counter of the wet bar. "The bar's always open here, so help yourselves or tell me what you want."

"I want to know what's going on," Roger said, his voice edged in frustration.

Silas opened his laptop and turned it around so everyone could see it. "Does anyone recognize her?"

"That's the bitch who ditched Grace just hours after she had the babies!" Dusty growled. "Dumped her incoherent and disoriented at that so-called recovery house, left her there to freeze. If Chuck hadn't told us where she'd be…" He grunted in a feral rage, too angry to continue.

The little inset window at the bottom corner of the computer screen suddenly became active as Chuck came into view. "That's Ellen, one of the two neo-natal nurses who were there when Grace delivered. I didn't know until just now that she was the one who moved Grace to recovery. I'm pretty sure she's the one who gave Dr. Buddy the heads up that the FBI was on its way, giving him the chance to escape. The other nurse came with me and stayed around for a few years, helping me with Ria and getting the mobile clinic started."

"Okay, Chuck – and only Chuck – do you know who this is?" Silas asked.

"Nope. Never saw her," he said, then leaned closer to the monitor to look at the angry faces on the gathering of family and friends on the other side.

"Should I know her?" he asked.

"That's Elsa," Roger hissed. "Vickie's nanny. For twelve years, she extorted thousands of dollars both in cash and goods from us. Two years ago, she slipped away from the hospital after she caught wind that she might have been found out."

"And," Silas said, keying in another picture on the monitor, "the same person known as Ellen Nyman; neo-natal specialist from Finland."

"Who are they?" Grace asked, looking at the side-by-side photos.

"One and the same person. These are her before and after pictures from the clinic where she got a nose job and a stomach staple. It seems she had a lot of dirt on quite a few people. She went around the country, working for black market baby doctors and white slavery mommy manipulators like Dr. Buddy. She'd collect information on the clients who adopted the infants, particularly those who claimed the children as their own biological babies, then blackmailed the parents for money to get a new body. Heck of a way to improve oneself," Silas said. "One blackmail after another; one tummy tuck or nose job, and then it's onto the next sucker."

"Until she couldn't get any skinnier," Roger said, "so then she started amassing material goods. Well, you've solved another one, Sherlock...er...Silas."

"I only have one dilemma left," Silas said. "I've contacted everyone in that ledger Elsa Ellen Nyman left behind. Some of the folks were happy to get the goods back, a few didn't want any part of them because they didn't want to remember that part of their lives, but most of the folks had filed with their insurance companies and already been compensated. They couldn't take the material goods back, so they said to just donate them to a good charity. That's where the dilemma comes in."

"You don't know which one to give it to?" Roger asked.

"Nope, I do. I was thinking about calling it Thrive," Silas said. "My dilemma is trying to figure out if I should have Chuck run it or give it to the girls."

"Heck ya, give it to the girls!" Chuck said via internet connection. "I have enough on my plate as it is."

"Which girls?" Hal asked.

"Don't know, don't care," Chuck said, "as long as it isn't me. Oh, were you asking me or Silas, Hal?"

"Anyone," Hal said, "but probably Silas since this is his idea."

"All of them," Silas said. "Gloria is already connected with lots of charities and knows the ins and outs of non-profits. Grace has been running back and forth between at least a dozen foundations, fighting white slavery and establishing recovery houses. And all the young girls – or both Vickie and Ria – have always had that nurturing, helping others bend. I just want to make sure that when we finally find Tori Lynn Whatever-Her-Last-Name is, she'll have a place to come if she has that same passion, too."

"All those in favor say, 'Aye.'" Roger asked.

Everyone said, "Aye."

"And then they all Thrived…" Chuck said. "I gotta scoot. I have someone waiting for me in the other room. I promise that Ria and I will be there next week for the wedding. We still haven't get a gift. Any suggestions?"

"Just yourselves. The young couple insists that it's a low-key event. For some reason, the groom and groomsmen are all wearing denim and fleece; the ladies, bright tees and flannels," Grace said.

"Except for the bride. Vickie said that wearing a white traditional gown was her gift to her mother," Dusty added.

"Probably the only bride in this family in generations who deserved it," Roger said. "Not that I'm complaining."

"Shush," Silas said. "Too much information."

"We'll figure something out for them," Chuck said. "Later!"

Silas closed the laptop and looked over at Roger. "Do you think he'd be so easy going if it was Ria getting married?"

"His day is coming, I'm sure," Roger said. "Maybe sooner than he thinks."

⋈∗∗

January 30, 2010

"I'm so nervous," Gloria said, her hands fidgeting with the corsage sitting in front of her. "I can't put this on myself!"

"No one's asking you, too," Grace said. "Let me help."

Grace picked up the single orchid surrounded with white violets; white on white flowers set on a gathered white lace background. She set her hand under Gloria's lapel and pinned the corsage on. "You know, I really think this is perfect. Yes, it's simple, yet elegant. Just like Vickie. She never needed all the bling. We both know it made her uncomfortable. She always rebelled, saying, 'Diamonds aren't for everyone.' But you know what? She's the diamond. Tough, simple, sharp…"

"Tough enough to cut through steel and determined enough to do it if needed. Yes, Grace, we brought up a great girl."

"I'm just glad you let me in her life!"

"And I'm glad you gave her life. My goodness, I don't know what we would have done if you had contested the adoption and tried to get her back. A simple DNA test would have proved you were her mother, and we didn't have any documentation. Do you know how much I feared she'd send off for one of those DNA kits and find out that Roger and I weren't her real parents?"

"But you *were* her real parents," Grace said. "Blood doesn't make a parent. Good grief, look at Victoria! She's my blood mother and horrid! She's your sister, but you two couldn't be more different. You may be my biological aunt,

181

but I feel like *you're* my sister. If I could 'un-mother' her, I would."

"Yes, and as soon as Vickie met you, she fell in love with you. She loved you for you, not because she was obligated by genetics. Blood meant nothing to her then and now. Love means everything and I know that."

"Yup, and that's why she's getting married today. I'm glad you and Roger are letting her. Those two just seem right together. I'm sure they'll have a wonderful life, pursuing their dream."

***

"Oh, my God! I thought Chuck was going to pass out when you punked him, coming out in my dress."

"He really did believe me for a minute there," Ria said, changing back into her casual maid of honor outfit – a denim skirt, leather boots, and white tank top with a red plaid shirt over it.

"Who was that guy you brought to play your intended?" Vickie asked. "He's kind of cute."

"No, he's an absolute doll! I thought you met him before, though. He was with me for a while at the rehearsal dinner."

"No, I was late, remember?" Vickie turned her back to Ria. "Can you zip this for me?"

Ria pushed the veil train aside and zipped her in. "Yeah, what was that all about? Late to your own wedding rehearsal dinner? I thought I was going to have to dash out and come back in and fake being you again."

"Again? You've done it before?" Vickie asked, turning around to give her the evil eye, then laughing at her own joke. "Yeah, I tried it three times but only got away with it once. It'd be easier if we lived closer. Now if the folks are suspicious, they look up to see if I'm wearing a hat or have my hair down. Kind of hard to fake the ears."

"Easier for you than me," Ria said. "You can stuff a wad of modeling clay behind each one to make them stick out. Taping mine back is a little more obvious." Ria held her ear back with one finger, checking the effect. "Do you think I should get my ears done?"

"Don't you dare! I know it's your body and all that, but you're perfect just the way you are. Don't let anyone else's idea of beauty make you change you, all right?"

"All right," Ria said. "Now, hair up or down?" she asked, lifting her loose curls.

"Let's go for the elegant country: hair up with denim and red flannel. Show off those angel ears!"

"So, why were you late to your own rehearsal. Were you and Rich finally getting it on?"

"Ria!"

"Ah, that's an evasive reply. I'll take that as a yes. Watch it. Grace said she got pregnant the first time."

Vickie blushed, lips pursed in frustration, wanting to deny what her sister suspected but knowing it was no use. She blew out her held breath. "Don't tell anyone, please."

"Duh! It's nobody's business, including mine. Two days early is close enough. You still deserve to wear white."

"What about you, Ria? The hunk? Are you two 'getting it on'?"

"Eet!" Ria made a noise like a penalty buzzer. "Not your business!"

"So, you're not blushing or mad at me for suggesting it which means you're not doing anything, but you'd like to be. I know I've never met him, but he looks familiar."

"Don't concern yourself with us. You're the one getting married in," Ria looked up at the clock, "fifteen minutes. Where are the moms?" she asked, walking through the doorway to look down the hall.

"Oooh! You said, 'Don't concern yourself with *us*,' not me. More serious than you want anyone but me to know about. Don't worry, my lips are sealed."

Ria quickly looked back at Vickie and said, "Shush!" then left.

A moment later, three women came in. "Oh, here you are!" Gloria said, following Ria back into the room, Grace beside her. "We were looking all over the place for you. I still think we should have had the wedding at the Club. At least, I wouldn't have gotten lost." Gloria fanned herself with the announcement. "I'm sorry, dear. Danged hot flashes make me moody. This is your day. Really, if this is where you want to have your wedding, it's fine with us. All of us."

"I hope so since it's almost time. Grace, would you help me with this makeup? I can't get this eyeliner straight and I know Mom can't see up close."

"Oh, I feel so inadequate," Gloria moaned.

"Why don't you help me with my hair?" Ria asked. "I can't see the back of my head and want to make sure I don't have a flat spot. Can you do that for me?"

"Oh, yes, dear. I'm so glad you and Chuck could come. Where is he?"

"I think he met a new old friend. They're getting reacquainted," Ria said.

"Man, I wish he'd get a boyfriend," Grace said. "He's been alone for way too long."

"A boyfriend?" Gloria gasped. "He's gay?"

"Well, duh!" Ria said. "Do you think Dusty would let a straight man hug on Grace like that?"

"Well, I don't know…" Gloria bent back to picking up the curls in Ria's hair and pinning them in place. "I guess it doesn't make any difference," she said.

"I know he goes on dates occasionally, claiming he's 'going out with the guys.' But I've seen the way some men check him out. Women, too, but he never returns their looks. He is the epitome of discretion. I don't think he knows

183

that I know. I tried to bring it up once and he got so flustered and embarrassed, I decided that it really wasn't any of my business. As soon as I'm ready to go out on my own, he can do his own thing, find his Mr. Right, or at least look around for him."

"Wow! That's pretty sensitive," Grace said, sitting back in the chair, overwhelmed with emotions.

"Brought up by a gay dad who is also a non-profit physician," Ria said. "Of course, I'm sensitive! Okay, are we about done here? I'm not wearing any makeup because as the sensitive person that I am, I'll be crying before Vickie takes her first step down the aisle. *Sniff, sniff.* See what I mean?"

Gloria opened her purse and handed Ria an embroidered handkerchief. "Here you go, honey. You can keep it. I packed at least a dozen of them."

"That's a good thing," Grace said, plucking one of them out of her friend's Coach bag, using it to dab under her nose. "I'm glad you planned ahead."

"Everyone decent?" Roger called into the room. "They're ready for us."

All eyes looked at Vickie and grinned.

"Last chance to back out," Roger teased. He suddenly became serious when he noticed his daughter was pale and blinking back tears. He moved in close and held her tight. "Because if you don't want to do this, it's not too late. Anything you decide is fine with us. No one will think less of you…"

Vickie reached up and stilled him with a soft hand to his chest. "I'm fine, Daddy. You're not losing me. You're gaining a son. I never heard you wish you had had one, but you're getting one anyhow. All right?"

Roger nodded and sniffed, then stepped back and took a handkerchief from the inside of his jacket to stifle his liquid emotions.

"Okay. I'm ready," Vickie said. She looked around the room. "All noses wiped and tears erased? I hope so because I'm ready to become Mrs. Richard Rickman the Third!"

Ria lined up the ladies in the order they were entering, making sure all the men were ready to escort the women. "Where's my dad?" she whispered to Grace.

"He dashed out of here before we came to see you. He said he had to go get Vickie's present. What did he get her?"

"Danged if I know. He's back to being Mr. Mysterious again."

Hal stood at the front of the line, waiting for the others to make last-minute adjustments, anxious at standing so close to his college sweetheart without her husband at her side. Finding a trickle of courage to make a joke, he whispered to Gloria, "I always knew I'd be escorting you down the aisle someday," and subconsciously added a flirtatious wink.

She lightly slapped his hand. "That was eons ago," she whispered harshly but with a tint of levity. She switched it to sincerity. "I'm not sorry Victoria messed everything up between us, though, because I wound up with Roger. But

I do regret her latching her claws into you."

"Yeah, well she was one vicious tigress. It took me years to get her off my back, but I managed it." He watched her face carefully and added, "At least I got Grace out of it."

She flushed suddenly, her gloved hand up to fan her face. "Damned hot flashes," she hissed.

Hal grabbed one of the flyers from the table next to them and offered it to her. "So, are my suspicions true?" he asked. "Victoria had others besides me?"

"As you have said many times, the only good you ever got out of my sister was Grace. Let's leave it at that. Blood isn't everything, right?" she asked, then fixed him with a stare that said, 'Drop it!'

Hal took a deep breath and groaned. "You're right."

The electronic keyboard in the hall started playing Mendelssohn's Wedding March, stopping any further discussion on the subject of Grace's paternity. Gloria looked over at Hal, moistness reddening his eyes. "Your granddaughter – my daughter – is getting married in a minute. Pull it together, Hal. You got this."

He looked at her and patted her hand again. "Yeah, *I do*. Come on, Mom. Let's go hear them share *their* I do's."

***

"I, Richard Othello Albert Rickman the Third, promise to love, cherish, and work through any disagreements with my spouse, through sickness and health, poverty and wealth, whether we're near or miles apart. You are and always will be my mate for life. Swans have nothing on us, Vickie Lynn Thornwhistle."

"I, Vickie Lynn Thornwhistle, promise to be your best friend, confidant, dedicated lover, mother to your children, helpmate, and coworker, and even cook and mend for you, wherever we may be, whatever our financial or health circumstances, forever and ever, amen."

"By the power invested in me by the Commonwealth of Massachusetts, I now pronounce you husband and wife," Silas said. He looked up to the audience, scanning for the one missing member of his adopted family – Chuck. He spotted him, grinning at the late arrival when he saw the three people he had brought with him. "Ladies and gentlemen, I present to you, Mr. and Mrs. Richard Rickman the Third!"

Rather than bend to kiss her, Rich stepped back, took a deep breath, then gave a graduate-level lion's roar. Loud and long, he embellished his performance with arms waving in the air before ending with a gasp and a huge smile.

The audience clapped, hooted, and whistled at his display of victory.

Vickie Lynn stepped forward and brought her hands up, then lowered them slowly, indicating she wanted everyone to calm down. "Now, as everyone knows, it's the lioness who actually does the hunting, making sure her mate is well-fed and safe from predators." She took a deep breath, looked around to make sure she had everyone's attention, then gave her own resounding roar, eliciting even more cheers, whistles, and foot stomps.

When she was finished with her loud feline claim, Rich pulled her close and looked her in the eye, letting her catch her breath for what was coming next. "Come here, wife. There's nothing in this world we can't conquer together."

The two embraced and kissed to more cheers and tears. Even Silas shed a few dribbles of liquid happiness before the couple finally broke apart. "To the banquet room, everyone!" he said. "Line up to kiss the bride, then it's cake and champagne!"

"Are you sure we should have come, Luther?" Leanne whispered from the back row, catching glimpses of the newlywed couple over and between the shoulders of the guests, trying to watch the proceedings without being seen. "I mean, we didn't even get an invitation."

"Are you kidding? We got a second-hand verbal and that's good enough for me. Plus, if Gloria would have known where to send the invite, I'm sure she would have. You've been wanting to see the other girls for over eighteen years, and now you're wanting to leave? Not a snowball's chance in the Sahara for that one. Look at Tori."

Tori Lynn Greene, huddled in-between coats and sweaters hanging from the hooks on the wall, was sneaking a glimpse of the guests, then pulling jacket sleeves back to disappear into the fabric and fur. *Why did we have to come here? Who are these people they want me to meet? I want to go home...*

The End of Diamonds Aren't for Everyone: Vickie's Story
Book Two of Triplets: Three Aren't One
Read on for THAT MAGIC TOUCH

That Magic Touch

Triplets: Three Aren't One

Book Three

Copyright

That Magic Touch

Brought up in the backwoods by a father dedicated to helping those less fortunate, Ria was a genius at healing but ignorant of life and relationships.

Would Evan be the one to show her what made life bright and enjoyable?

Dedicated

This story is dedicated to Diana Gabaldon. A long time ago, she shared that if writing is what you want to do, do it! Write, wr.te, write! I did and have found that just the thought of creating people, intense situations, and surprising solutions brings a smile to my face. Whether ycur passion is reading, writing, singing, teaching, healing or the arts, readers, follow it. Just don't forget to share the wisdom of following your dream with others.

Chapter 1: Previously

January 3, 1992

Gloria leaned forward, steadying herself on her husband's arm as she stood on tiptoes, trying for a better look. "Is that them?"

Roger gave his wife's hand a reassuring pat, then moved away from the group to check out the station wagon pulling up to the gas pumps. "I don't know. Did he tell you what he'd be driving?"

"Oh, yeah. He said he'd be driving a white van," she said. "Remember the password: Woodstock."

"Sounds like my kind of guy," Luther, the other father-in-waiting, remarked. He hugged his wife around the shoulders. "Remember when we were there?"

"How could I forget," Leanne giggled. "Over twenty years ago, and now our baby is finally here. That's a long gestation!"

"There he is! There's Chuck!" Gloria exclaimed, hopping up and down with joy at seeing her new friend driving into the convenience store parking lot.

"Settle down," Roger said. "You don't want to bring attention to us."

"Two middle-aged couples, snuggled up against the wind, looking like vultures ready to pounce... I'd say we were already suspicious," Luther said.

"Conspicuous," Leanne whispered.

"Whatever," Luther said with a shrug.

Chuck, driving the new-to-him white van conversion, looked beyond the gas pumps and saw the two couples standing by the bundled firewood, their smiles of anticipation marking them as the new parents. He waved briefly as he rolled past, coming to a stop near the alley at the end of the building. He felt safer in the dark, out of sight of everything but owls searching for dinner. "Tranquility base: Stork One and Stork Two have landed," Chuck said to his female cohort.

The neo-natal nurse, snuggled up to the gym bag full of newborn baby girls on top of the foldout bed behind him, grunted that she'd heard him, but didn't comment.

A mixture of fear and excitement washed over Chuck as he got out and approached the huddled foursome of wannabe parents. "Anyone for a game of golf? Is there a good course around here?"

"How about Woodstock?" Gloria said, then ran up to Chuck and gave him a big hug. "Are the babies inside? Are they okay? I thought I was going to have a total meltdown when Dr. Buddy called and said the mother had died, and that they couldn't get the babies out in time. Chuck, he said that Grace and all three babies had passed."

Chuck's eyes widened. "Grace was alive when I left." He opened the side door, exposing his new traveling nursemaid and the bundle of babies.

"I'm still alive," Grace Two said indignantly, then groaned softly as she realized it was a misunderstanding about the name she shared with the babies' birth mother. "I think you'd better call me Nanny." She looked at the eager parents crowded around the open door, the women squeezed in front of their husbands to keep away from the chill. "Why don't you ladies come inside?"

Gloria led the way, Leanne right behind her. The younger of the two peered into the unzipped bag. "Which one is ours?"

"It's between you two who gets Aqua and who gets Pinkie. The yellow-wrapped sweetheart is mine," Chuck said, watching the allocation of babies from the front seat.

"Oh, my God!" the silver-haired Leanne exclaimed. "They're identical! I can't believe it. How will we know whose is whose?"

Little Pinkie opened her eyes, started to squall, then caught sight of Gloria and smiled. "I don't care if she's the biggest or not; this one's mine."

"Then that must mean she's ours. Oh, I can't believe it. I swear I feel a tingling in my breasts. I'm as barren as a moon rock, but I swear she's kicked in a bucket load of estrogen." Leanne looked up. "Can I take her home now?"

"That's the plan," the nurse said. "Oh, and don't even try to get in touch with Dr. Buddy. Either of you. If they haven't caught him yet, they will. You're lucky Chuck and I got in the middle of this or you wouldn't be celebrating motherhood tonight."

"Thank you," Gloria said to the nurse. "Truly. Chuck has my number. If you two run into any trouble or need a few bucks, just give me a call." She unzipped her jacket and put the swaddled baby inside. "Come on Vickie. You're coming home."

Leanne copied Gloria's tactic of coat kangaroo-pouching her baby. "And you, too, Tori Lynn. Daddy's waiting outside."

Leanne stepped out of the van, then suddenly yipped. "She latched on! Oh, my Lord! I'm going to see if Luther can set me up with some of those plant estrogens. I may be able to nurse my baby still! Sing hallelujah!"

***

"That went well," Chuck said after the two couples had left. "Are you ready to hit the road, Nanny? Hmm. I really do like that name. It fits you. No nonsense, but nurturing."

Grace Two, now renamed Nanny, couldn't help but smile. "New name, new beginning. Works for me. Did you remember to pick up distilled water for mixing the formula? I didn't see any in here."

"Oh, shoot! I'm glad you noticed. No, I forgot. I'll run in and get some

191

right now. Do you want a soda or coffee or anything?"

"Coffee, black, would be great."

"I'll get you something else, too. Stress eats up calories and we have a long way to go," Chuck said, then mumbled under his breath, "Wherever it is we're heading."

Chuck walked in the convenience store and looked around. "Where do you keep the water?" he asked the clerk.

"What is this? There's a real run on bottled water tonight. Back there. See that kid with the ball cap? Yeah, right next to him."

"Thanks. And is the coffee fresh?"

"Just made a pot. Don't tell me; you want a giant chocolate bar, too," the clerk said, adding a chuckle.

"Hey, that does sound good."

"Just follow the kid. He's after the same stuff."

Chuck went to the back of the store where the young man was and found the water. "Dang!" he said, checking the label, then noticed the kid had picked out a bottle with a different colored cap. "You got the last distilled water, didn't you?"

Dusty lifted up his jug of water. "Shoot. I don't want this kind. Here, I'll swap you. I was after spring water for drinking."

"Thanks," Chuck said, then headed to the coffee kiosk. "What did we do before convenience store coffees?" he commented.

"Shoot. I don't know," Dusty answered. "I don't think I was born yet. For me, they've always been around. I didn't even know what a rotary phone was until I was clearing out my dad's attic. I can't imagine having to stay in one room while talking, tethered to a six-foot curly cord."

Chuck blew out a breath, stopping short of a full laugh, and shook his head. "Yeah, our folks really had to rough it. Have a good night, what's left of it," he said and saluted the young man in farewell.

"Yeah, you, too," Dusty said. "I know it's going to get better because I just found my woman. Thank you, Lord!"

Chuck paid for the water, coffee, and candy then walked to the side of the building and rapped on the side door of the van. "What's the name of Snoopy's bird?" he asked.

Click.

The young nurse opened the door and let him in. "Do we have to keep doing that?" she asked.

"No, probably not. I'm just trying to bring a little levity to this harrowing evening. I know my emotions are all over the place. Elation at getting out of there with all three babies alive; fear of either being caught by Buddy's crew or being charged as an accomplice by the FBI; excitement with being able to help two couples get the daughters they were told were dead; and absolute sadness and loss at having to walk away from Grace. Lord, I hope the guys got her. Oh, shit!" he said, his voice loud as if he'd just been pinched. "I can text them!"

Chuck pulled his cellphone out of his front pocket and tap, tap, tapped the quick message to his father. 'Did U get her?'

***

Dusty handed the jug of water and chocolate milk to Hal, his girlfriend's father. He may have just lost their twins in a tragic birth, but at least he still had her. And a great support network of family who cared for her.

Beep! Beep!

"What was that?" Dusty asked, looking around.

"My cellphone," Papa Doc said. "I got what they call a personalized alert tone for my incoming texts." Chuck's father took the blocky gray cellphone out of his shirt pocket, tapped a few buttons, and then put it back in his pocket. "Someone just checking to make sure all went well on our end," nodding to Grace.

"It's going to take time for my daughter – hell, all of us – to heal," Hal said. "Some losses take longer to get over. Let's hope you haven't lost Chuck because of all of this."

"Only for a little time. My son has a nurturing soul and is a gentleman. I think he's just stepping back so Dusty can help her heal."

"What do you mean? He didn't know Dusty was coming with us or that we even found him," Hal said. "That was last minute, remember?"

"Yeah, I wouldn't know your son if I sat on him," Dusty said. "Hey, does anyone want some chocolate?"

Grace listened to the men banter back and forth, their voices rising and lowering with their emotions and concerns. She hadn't heard her father and two surrogate uncles in a month and didn't realize until now how much she had missed them. She looked out the window. The world was getting better, itty bit by itty bit. Dusty was here. Would he accept her as she was? The way he had held her – sobbing uncontrollably with joy – when he rescued her after she had been abandoned by Nurse Ellen, she knew he'd do anything for her. He seemed to be sharing her feeling of loss for the babies, too. All her men could mourn with her. And they would heal together, too.

All but Chuck. Where was he? She closed her eyes tight and tried to find a thread of recent memory, struggling to recall the last words he had said to her. There it was. An echo of his words. He was leaving her, he said – leaving so she wouldn't associate him with her loss.

Which would have been worse, the loss of the babies to adoption or death? Definitely death. With adoption, they would still have been happy little people with families who cared for and cherished them. Now with death, they were just little corpses. Was it her fault they had died? Did she do something wrong?

Grace looked at Dusty, blinking back the tears that had returned. A familiar movement out of the corner of her eye caught her attention. She leaned over him to watch the man coming out of the convenience store. "Who's that?" she asked, pointing out the window.

Dusty recognized him as the man he had swapped jugs of water with. "Just some guy from the store. He got coffee and water, too. Why? Do you know him?"

She sighed then leaned back into his arm. "I thought I did…"

"Grace, I know it's not exactly romantic – my timing and all – but I want to make a new life with you as my wife. I have a lot going on now. I have my own business and everything. I still want to marry you and always will. We can start again with a family as soon as you say the word. I kinda know what went on with the other guy, and it doesn't matter to me. I mean, I know you have been hurt in about a million different ways, but I want to help you heal. Would you let me? I mean, I'd do it however you want, but I'd rather do it as your husband than as your best friend."

Grace leaned into Dusty and inhaled his unique scent of boy and man. She felt the first smile in ages come to her face. She looked up. "Yeah, I think I'd like you better as a husband. Let me get healed up, and then let's get married. But if you don't mind, I'd still like to live with Papa Doc and Silas for a while. And hang out with my dad, too."

"And me?"

"Duh! You'd be living with us, too. One great big dysfunctional family."

Chapter 2: His Girl Friday

Rrrr. Rrrr. Click. Click.

"Crap!" Chuck groaned. He smacked the steering wheel in frustration, then looked back at the stunned nurse, holding the baby close, bouncing her gently to settle her down.

Little mews of discontent seemed to be working up to a full roar. "This isn't going to work," she said. "This baby's hungry. Come back and feed your daughter."

"But the water's cold. Won't that upset her stomach?"

"Just get back here and I'll see what I can do about the engine," she said indignantly, shifting toward the end of the bed, making room for him.

Chuck made his way between the front two seats into the back, then flicked on the overhead light so he could see. Nothing.

"Just what I thought," his frustrated cohort said. "Here, I took a few bottles of the pre-mixed formula from the clinic before we left. I stuffed one down my bra so it'd stay warm. I suggest you do the same."

"Huh?" Chuck asked, shuffling around her so he could sit down.

"Not stuffed down your bra, doofus!" she said. "If you always keep one stashed next to your chest or belly, it'll be at body temperature, ready to feed her when she's hungry."

Tingles of anticipation and appreciation ran up Chuck's arms and down his shoulders into his gut, settling into a warm glow of nurturing comfort. His daughter. He sat down and snuggled the child close. Yes, she was his. Rockets couldn't blast her away from him now. Nor could a piece of paper. Grace may have known about the first two, but this third one – this bonus baby – had been his spirit child since the day he first heard her heartbeat.

The nurse's hand bumped his, offering him the bottle in the dim glow of the convenience store parking lot. "Helluva a way to start life, eh? Let me go see what I can find out," she said, then scooted out the door.

Scores of times over the past eight months he had tried to talk Grace into keeping the babies. He'd spent hours trying to convince her that with all of the loving people she had in her life, they would certainly be able to keep her 'twins' out of reach of her evil mother. Would she have willingly given him the third child if she had known about her? Since she had already refused to keep the first two, it really didn't make a difference.

"Quit beating yourself up, Chuck," he said softly as he fed his baby her first meal. "You presented every possible argument for her to keep them so many times, it pissed her off. Her fears could not be abated by logic or tempered by hope, no matter how much you tried. Twice she signed papers giving them up. She was one determined woman."

He should feel bad that she had been left with nothing, but that wasn't the

195

way it was. She was left with a loving father and two surrogate uncles who'd reshape the world for her, one of them his own father. Plus, Dusty, the man she had sacrificed it all for – saving him from her mother's vendetta – just might come back into her life now. Maybe she'd catch up to him after her body had healed. She could share or withhold the information about losing 'twins.' That was her decision. Only he and a very limited few others knew that she – Grace Stillwater – had birthed triplets. This little gem was his. Rhianna Lynn Armstrong. The shadow. The echo behind her sisters' heartbeats.

The side door opened. "Got any tools around here?" the former neo-natal nurse now acting as mechanic asked.

"Yeah, some came with it when I bought it. They're stashed under the passenger seat in a box."

That door shut and the front one opened, bringing the temperature of the conversion van down to near outside temperature: below freezing. Chuck unzipped his coat and snuggled his daughter close, one hand next to her cheek keeping the nipple in her eager mouth. "There, there, Ria. Daddy has you."

Is this a sign of things to come? Everything falling apart around us? Am I being punished? By doing something I thought was right – giving these three girls families who could not have children any other way – was I playing God? Did I make Him angry? Lord, I did what I thought was right. Yes, it was a bit selfish to take one of them for me, but I really felt as if she was meant to be mine. Really. Truly.

Vroom!

Chuck was startled out of his introspection and prayer of contrition by the sound of the engine roaring to life. The hood closed with a clunk, then his female companion opened the door and put the toolbox away. She looked back and saw his wide-eyed, slack-jawed expression. "What? I can do more than stuff a bottle in a baby's mouth or wipe her ass. I have skills. Now, what direction are we going? I think I'll take the first shift. Looks to me like you have your hands full."

"South," Chuck said. "But can you drive a manual transmission?"

"Give me a break. I can fix 'em, drive 'em, or steal 'em if I have to. I've been on the streets since I was just a bit bigger than your little nugget there."

"Okay. Oh, and just for the record, I think Nanny is a poor choice for a new name for you. You're more of a Friday."

"Friday. I like that much better," she said. She settled into the driver's seat and buckled up. "Come on, Miss Daisy. We're headed south, leaving the ice and snow to the crazy Yankees."

***

Three days later

"How far south did you want to go, Chuck?"

"Until it doesn't freeze at night or we run out of money," he said. He

196

rubbed his sleep-deprived eyes. "Where are we now?"

"Florida. Would you believe they have a Woodstock here, too?"

"I'm beginning to think every state has one. Just like every town has a Main Street. Do you feel like splurging on restaurant food? I'm getting tired of canned food and crackers."

"As long as you're buying. I only managed to get a few bucks together. I pretty much was a slave to Dr. Buddy and his outfit. I don't like to think of myself as a thief. I was just taking what I thought I earned. I'll never get back what I deserved, though."

Chuck rubbed his hand over his face, confused and disoriented. "I don't think I'll ever be able to make up to you what you've meant to me, and it's only been a day or two since we met. I can start with pancakes and real coffee, though."

"It's been three days, Chuck. You're sleep-deprived. You have mommy brain. Watch out that you don't get the baby blues, too."

"Huh?"

"Let's eat," she said. "Mom and Pop Pancake House sounds like a winner to me. Look there: 'Try our bottomless cup of coffee.'"

"Yeah, too bad you can't buy a good night's sleep as easily."

"Since you don't have a final destination picked out, how about we get something to eat, and then find a wide spot off the side of some back road to park for a few days? You need to get caught up on rest before I leave."

"Leave? Friday, where and how are you going?" Chuck asked, his voice pitched high in panic. He groaned softly as he realized how desperate he sounded. "I'm sorry, but I really didn't know that taking care of an infant was going to be so labor-intensive. How in the heck am I going to see patients and take care of a newborn at the same time? And wherever you're going, do you think they'll need an on-call doctor? Could we work together for a while? All I need is enough for food, gas, and formula."

"I don't know where I'm going, so I guess to keep you from losing it completely, I can stick around for a while. At least until Little Bit gets on a schedule."

"She's already on one. One ounce of formula every hour. It takes fifteen minutes to get that in her, and then she's out again. How do mothers do this?"

"Most mothers' babies are bigger than four pounds. Her tummy's too small to hold much but she still digests it at the same rate. Her feeding intervals will get longer as she grows. And most mothers either nurse the baby and or they have a partner to help take care of it. I really don't have a destination, so I'll hang around until I do, I suppose. Come on. Run a comb through your hair and throw on a clean shirt. I'm hungry and I swear I can smell that coffee from the parking lot."

"Well, I know I can smell the bacon," Chuck said, hastily taking off his shirt. He rummaged through his backpack, coming up short, then felt a nudge. "Wear this. It's mine but doesn't look girlie."

"Thanks," he said and pulled it on over his head. "Nothing girlie about you, Friday." He looked up and noticed her scowl. "And that's a compliment, not an insult. Just in case I offended you...which I didn't mean to."

"Yup, you're sleep-deprived, malnourished, in need of coffee and could use a partner, Mr. Mom."

"I agree to all but the last one. A girl Friday will work just fine for me. You're not the kind of *partner* for me in that respect."

"Good to hear," Friday said, setting Ria in the car seat-carrier. "Hand me that little receiving blanket. I'm going to tent the car seat. It may not be cold here, but I don't want restaurant germs settling on her. And make sure you wash your hands before touching her after we leave. She doesn't have an immune system yet."

"How about you go in without me and I'll stay here with her?" Chuck asked. "You have me scared now. Just order something to go for me. How about bacon, pancakes, and coffee?"

"Nope. You're coming in with me. You're not going to become a germophobic hermit, trying to keep your child from experiencing life. Yes, she's not getting anything out of this excursion, but you need it. Remember, if you're going to have a mobile clinic, you're going to need to learn the area. Listen to conversations, ask about local medical care, pop in at the library and do some research on their computers about median income and family size. Find those areas where there aren't any services."

"Maybe you're right about needing a partner. I may have the medical skills, but it seems like you have the social and promotional talents required to find my niche."

"Niches. We don't want to settle into one area for too long. At least, as long as I'm with you. I'm breaking my own rules committing to hanging out with you two for more than a week or two."

"So, you'll stay?" Chuck asked, hoping he didn't sound like he was begging.

"As long as you don't piss me off too much, fuzz face. You're either going to have to buy a razor or grow a beard. You look like a homeless druggy."

Chuck stepped into the front of the van and pulled the rearview mirror down. "Jeez! Why didn't you say something?"

"I just did. Don't worry about it. When we go in with the baby, they'll know you're the dad. You look more like a new father than an addict."

"I guess it's going to get better. At least, I know not all parents look this rough."

"Wouldn't know for sure. I never had one around long enough to find out."

He glanced sideways at her, not wanting to address the remark but wanting to see her reaction to sharing a small part of her past. Yes, she regretted it. She was looking away, her lips pulled tight in a scowl. "Let me get my wallet. I'm buying," he said, wondering if it was her child or parent who wasn't around long enough. Or both.

Chuck popped open the dash and looked for his wallet, noticing something that wasn't there before. He didn't unwrap the red handkerchief but nudged it with the side of his hand as he grabbed the billfold. A gun. Yes, she was being cautious. Very cautious. He would need to be, too.

***

"Well, that was extremely satisfying on two levels," Chuck said, bounding into the back of the van, Ria still asleep.

"I take it you're still cool with me driving?" Friday asked.

"Hey, you heard the directions just as clearly as I did. I never took you for the chauffeur-type, but I'm notorious at getting lost."

"I'm going to fuel up, pop into the store, and grab more distilled water. Do you want to take a nap in the parking lot? Ria seems to sleep better in the car seat than even snuggled up to you. You'll get better rest if she's not right next to you, waking you up with every little movement."

"Yeah, let's give that a shot. That is if you don't mind."

"Would you stop saying that?" Friday said, a low guttural growl escaping. "You sound so needy."

Chuck laughed. "I am needy. But thanks for telling me. If we're going to get along, we have to be honest with each other."

"I agree. That being said, while I'm in the store and before you fall asleep, would you use some of those baby wipes and give yourself a sponge bath? You're getting ripe."

"Okay... I guess a once a week visit to a truck stop would be in order."

"Huh?" Friday asked.

"They have public showers. You know, pay to suds and rinse."

"So do lots of laundromats. I'll ask around about that while I'm in the store. Wash up, then go to sleep. She isn't going to stay zonked out for much longer."

Chuck yawned. "Don't have to tell me twice," he said, then pulled a blanket under his chin. His neck slumped to the side, and he was out.

"Sweet dreams, Dad."

After getting fuel, Friday pulled over to the less-traveled side of the store which was also closer to the pawn shop. She reached in the glove box, took out the handgun she had taken from the clinic and shoved the bandana-wrapped package inside her flannel shirt. She closed the van door behind her. "Thanks for helping Chuck start his clinic."

Friday walked out of the pawn shop with a mere four-hundred dollars, a lot less than what she thought the ivory-handled pistol would fetch but a lot more than his initial offering of one-hundred. It wasn't until she took it back, ready to walk out of the store, did he slip and let the gun lust sparkle in his eyes. It wasn't the most valuable handgun around, but it was unique. No receipt requested also helped the transaction. Yes, the gun was going underground and would never be recovered by Dr. Buddy. She snorted as she pushed the bills deeper into her jeans pocket. Back to where it had come from.

***

Tap. Tap.

Chuck looked up from giving Ria her bottle to the rapping on the window. He started to get up to open the door but was stilled by a familiar voice.

"I got this," said Friday. "I just wanted to make sure I didn't catch you in the middle of your bath."

The back door opened and a whoosh of cold air entered the van. Chuck brought the blanket up around Ria. "What'd you get besides water?"

"Not now. Let me unload so I can shut the door. I have a full tank of gas, but I don't want to burn it up running the heater if I don't have to."

"Ria's fed and should fall asleep as soon as we're moving again, so do you want me to drive this time?"

"Nope. I asked around when I was shopping. I think I've found our destination. I'll drive until we get there. If there's an available spot to stay for more than a night, you can unload and set us up." Friday climbed in the driver's seat and cranked up the ignition. "Then I'll get some sleep."

Ria and Chuck slept for the next three hours until the van stopped. The crunch of gravel roused the dozing father, a smile spread wide. *I don't know how long I slept but I feel great!*

Tap. Tap.

Chuck pulled back the curtain, verified it was Friday, then stepped out and looked around. "So this is it?"

"Looks decent enough to me. There's a campground down the trail, outhouses are walking distance and downwind, and there's a creek that's supposed to be full of fish. Oh, and lots of folks living rough who could use a healing hand."

"Sounds like this crazy man's Eden," Chuck said. "Give me a sec and I'll be out."

Verifying Ria was still sleeping, Chuck grabbed the white and red cotton baby-carrier sling he had bought on his shopping trip with Gloria weeks ago. After a few adjustments for his larger-than-a-typical woman's size, he slipped Ria into it. "Ah, my little *bambina*, all ready for Papa to work."

The refreshed new father, having enjoyed another nap, reached his arms out and around to check his range of motion with the baby cradled next to his body.

"Looks like you're pregnant," Friday said with a chuckle.

"That's the first time I've heard you laugh," Chuck said, finishing his stretch.

"First time anything's been funny in the last four days," she replied coldly.

"Ouch. Too true," he replied with a grin of irony rather than respond with her same snarkiness. He opened the back door of the van to reveal her generous load of supplies. "So, boss lady, what do you need for me to do here?"

"The rest of the stuff can be dealt with later but for now, how about setting these tarps up? I got some rope and bungees, too. I figure you needed one to keep the rain out and a few others to keep the privacy factor up for your patients. Oh, and the camp chairs are for us to share with them as needed." Friday reached into her back pocket, pulled out a packet, and tossed it to him.

"What's this for?" he asked, checking out the multipurpose knife, still in its original packaging. "And did you steal it?"

"It's a Leatherman. Other than a hatchet which is already in the tool kit under the front seat, it's all you should need out here. And I spent enough money at their store that I figured they shouldn't mind that I gave myself a thank you gift."

"Yeah, speaking of that, where'd you get the money for all this? I still have my cash on me."

"I got skills," Friday said. "And since it's been almost two days since I've had any sleep, I'm taking my break. Set this place up as you'd want it. Just a hint, though. People might not like being seen approaching. Leave a subtle entrance from the back for the bashful folks who don't want others to know they need help."

"One outdoor clinic with public and discretionary accesses, coming up." Chuck nodded to the side door. "The bed's all yours. Sweet dreams, and once again, thanks."

"Yeah, well thank you, too. I needed a way out of that nightmare. I only hope that they did catch up with Dr. Buddy. Someone has to shut down guys like that. He's hurting too many people on both ends. Taking babies from the girls by claiming to help childless couples – which would be all right if he'd let them go back to their old lives and families afterward, not kidnapping them and keeping them as birthing vessels. And the new parents – taking their money, getting them all worked up with a baby on the way then telling them the baby died. He's making himself rich and breaking hearts all over the place in the process. Sorry. I'm tired and rambling. If you find something you can't handle, leave it until I wake up on my own. I'm going to bed."

Chuck brought up his hand to give her a reassuring pat on the back that he had it handled, then realized she wasn't the touchy-feely compassionate person he was and would take offense. "Night-night."

Readjusting his daughter in the sling so she was out of the way, Chuck pulled out all the supplies he thought he'd need and the camp chairs. "Come on, darling. You're going to help Daddy build his first mobile clinic. How about calling it 'Doc's Clinic'? Do you like the sound of that?"

Ria's hand reached out then settled under her chin, a sweet smile on her face, her eyelids fluttering as she dreamt. "What do babies dream about?" he asked softly. "Well, I hope they're happy thoughts and hopes. I know mine are. And they all settle around you."

An hour into his set up, Chuck came to a point where he couldn't progress without a second set of hands. "Sorry, darling. Your little hands aren't strong enough to help yet. But they will be one day. You just sleep and grow for now." He set up the red camp chair and kicked out his legs, visualizing how he could make this work. "One of these days, we'll have a real motorhome with office space and an exam room and even a kitchen and bathroom with running water. How am I going to potty train you on a five-gallon bucket?"

"Need a hand there?" a friendly male voice called out.

Startled, Chuck sat up quickly, instinctively covering Ria from any potential harm. He stood up and turned to face a tall and handsome man, broad-shouldered and with a grin that could melt the heart of any man or woman. "Oh, hi. Yes, as a matter of fact, I could use an extra pair of hands, if you don't mind."

"Looks like your arm's broke and you don't care to use your sling. I know I don't."

"This?" Chuck asked. He held out the edge of Ria's sling and glanced into it to make sure she was still sleeping, a smile broadening his face. "Oh, this isn't for a broken arm. Come here and look."

The whiskered man in his thirties approached, looking side to side to make sure this wasn't an ambush. A squirrel ran across the ground behind him and up the tree, startling him. He looked down as he walked, back in defensive mode, searching for IEDs. The ground was cleared. He was safe. No insurgents.

Chuck noticed the signs of PTSD. The man was probably one of the people 'living rough' that Friday had mentioned. The noises and pace of city life weren't comfortable for many who had it. Post-Traumatic Stress Disorder wasn't necessarily treatable but he knew not to make any sudden movements.

"Oh, my goodness!" the man said in a hushed whisper. "That's the smallest baby I ever saw! Is it yours?"

"One hundred percent mine," Chuck said.

"And your wife?" the man asked, suddenly glum. "What does she say when you say that?"

Tentatively putting his hand on the other man's shoulder, Chuck looked him in the eye and said, "Don't have one. Never did. She's adopted by me alone."

"Oh," the man said.

The sparkle in the man's eyes let Chuck know that he was interested in him in more than just a 'setting up camp' way. Playing house together might come in later!

"Oh, where are my manners?" the man said, his hand thrust out to shake Chuck's. "I'm Harvey. This area has been my home for…for a while." He shrugged in embarrassment.

Chuck took the strong hand in his, unconsciously sighing at the touch of another man who might be willing to be more than friends, then realized they had been holding hands a little too long and let go. "Oh, and I'm Chuck. Here's what I have to work with," he said, pointing to the opened tarps strung through with ropes. "I'm trying to build an enclosed structure. I'd like two entrances. You know, so folks won't see who's coming and going?"

"Ooh. You're building a privacy shelter so you can play doctor. Sounds like fun to me," Harvey said, eyebrows raised suggestively.

Chuck blushed and Ria squirmed at the same time, his sudden warmth disturbing her rest. He leaned forward just a bit to let air get between their bodies, then waited while she settled back to sleep. "First things first: privacy. And yes, I will be playing doctor, but I really am one. This is my mobile clinic."

"Not too mobile if you're attached to a couple of trees."

"Hey, it's a starting point. Rome wasn't built in a day and all that. I had a clinic in a building in the past, but life changed. I'd rather bring up my daughter in fresh air and sunshine than smog and fluorescents."

"So that's a girl?" Harvey asked, nodding to the sling.

"Yup. So," Chuck said, changing the subject. "If we get this done before she wakes up, we might have a little time for a cup of coffee. At least, I'm pretty sure I have some left."

Harvey brought his arm up around Chuck's shoulder and gave him an affectionate squeeze. He bent close to his ear and whisper, "Coffee not required."

Chuck blushed again but moved Ria away from his body before she got too hot. "Then let's get on it!"

"Words I thought I'd never hear again," Harvey drolled, then picked up the tarp half-hanging from the tree. "Hold this here and I'll secure it. I can put this up by myself, but I'm rather enjoying the company."

"Me, too," Chuck said. "Me, too."

Twenty minutes into their set up, Ria awoke. No slow announcement of her hunger this time, she went from sound asleep to squawling within two seconds.

"Oops. 'Scuse me for a few minutes here," Chuck said, sitting down in the camp chair. He pulled out the warmed bottle of formula from his tee-shirt pocket under the sling, stuck the nipple in his mouth and quickly licked any lint from it, then offered her the bottle.

Harvey picked up the other camp chair and set it up across from Chuck. He leaned forward to watch, his jaw dropped open in awe. "Wow. A guy can do that?"

"I hope so because that's my plan," Chuck said, leaning back in the chair, his legs kicked out.

Harvey sat back and copied Chuck's pose, bringing his boots up next to his, playfully rubbing them back and forth.

"Bootsies?" Chuck asked.

"Huh?"

"Well, I've heard of playing footsies, but bootsies?"

"Feed your daughter and let's see what else we can come up with, all right?"

"Oh, very all right," Chuck sighed, his boot rubbing Harvey's.

"What's going on out here?" Friday's voice boomed.

Startled, Harvey tumbled out of his chair and rolled to the ground, coming up in a crouch in a fighting position, the knife he pulled from his belt held at the ready.

Chuck pulled his legs back and sat up as straight as he could in the saggy-bottomed cloth chair, trying to regain composure.

Ria screamed at the sudden tension in the air, letting everyone know she needed to be seen to first.

"Well?" Friday echoed, lifting her chin at the stranger in her camp. "Who are you and why are you here?"

"Damn it, Friday!" Chuck said. He stood up awkwardly, using both hands to hold Ria close. He bounced her gently and tried to calm her. "This is a public clinic. Or will be. You have to get used to strangers coming in."

"You said you didn't have a wife," Harvey said. "So, does this mean she's *just* your girlfriend?"

"Hell, no!" Friday and Chuck said at the same time.

Friday glared at Chuck at his reply even though she had given the same one. "I'm his assistant," Friday said. She inhaled deeply as she realized that these were just two guys wanting some alone time together. How would she feel if he had intruded on some hoped-for intimacy for herself the same way?

"Sorry," she said, genuinely humbled, her hand out in greeting. "We've all been a little short on sleep for the past few days. If you two are okay, give me the baby. I'll see if I can settle her down inside the van with me."

Harvey stood up and quickly sheathed the knife. "Friday?" he asked, shaking her hand firmly, looking deep into her eyes.

She returned the greeting with the same brisk social posturing. "It's not the name I was born with, but I answer to it."

"Fair enough. I'm Harvey. No one uses last names around this place. So," he nodded to Chuck, "he tells me he's a doctor. What's your story?"

"I just work with the guy. Broken people come to us and we patch them up as best as we can with what we have."

"Nobody 'round here has any money," Harvey said, his eyes narrowed as he looked at the two of them as if they were con artists.

"Did you hear her say anything about fees?" Chuck asked. "I only charge what a person feels my time is worth or what they can afford. I accept all forms of payment. As far as I'm concerned, you just paid in advance by helping me out. Do you need anything fixed?"

Harvey snorted in derision. "You saw the way I jump at sudden noises. I don't think you have anything that'll fix that."

"Nothing I sell or can get my hands on," Chuck said. "If you would, spread the word around the area. I don't have much to start with, but I do want to help others. I've got skills and training. People get sick or injured and have pains. I just want to make people feel better. That's it. Plain and simple like me."

"Well, there's nothing plain and simple with lofty goals like that, Chuck." Harvey reached out and shook Chuck's hand in farewell, his hand settling on top of Chuck's for an extra moment. "I'll see you around." He opened up the pleat in the red and white sling and looked down at the sleeping baby. "She sure is pretty. Congratulations, Dad."

And then he was gone, silent in his trek through the forest floor, an expert at being quiet, quick at disappearing into the trees.

Friday and Chuck watched the silent exodus until Harvey was out of sight. Ria lay content, snuggled in Daddy's warmth, her fist in front of her mouth, comforted by its nearness.

Friday finally spoke up. "It looks good," she said. She pulled on the tarp and saw it could easily be pulled open, riding on the roped-laced eyelets like a shower curtain on a rod. "Nice touch. Come on. Give me a hand with organizing what I picked up at the store. You're the one who needs to know what we have on hand and where it is."

The two worked together for twenty minutes, combining the scant supplies Chuck had already purchased with the ones Friday had just picked up. "Where'd you get the money?" he asked again.

"I got skills," she replied, using the same answer.

"I know that. I just want to make sure you're not stealing folks blind and I'm going to get in trouble for it. Or even worse, lose you."

"You don't need me," Friday said.

"I need you a hell of a lot more than you need me! Ria and I both need you. You may not like the idea of family, but if we're going to live together, we're family. And family needs to be honest with each other."

"Okay. I stole a gun from Dr. Buddy's office. It was a fancy one with ivory handles and gold inlays. I took it to the pawnshop in the shopping center and got four-hundred bucks for it. I managed to stash a few bucks in the lining of my gym bag over the years but keeping us poor is one way he kept us on hand. I want to keep that as my seed money."

"You're not very old. Are you a registered nurse?"

"Nope. Ellen taught me what Dr. Buddy wanted me to know about babies. Neither one of them wanted me to know more than what I needed for pregnancies, deliveries, and neonatal care. If I had a degree, I would have found a way out earlier. So, yes. I want to learn everything you can teach me while I'm here."

"No problem," Chuck said. "But that won't help you on the outside. I mean, the real outside – the legitimate world – not off the grid, working in campgrounds and parks."

"We'll see where life takes me. Who knows? A few years down the road, maybe I'll break off and start my own rural clinic."

"I'll see if I can find some medical books at the local libraries while we're on our healing mission. I don't plan on staying anywhere for too long, though."

"I'd ask you why, but I really don't care. Your reason is yours alone. Not mine."

"No," he replied, setting his hand on top of hers for emphasis. "My reason is mine *and* my daughter's."

Chapter 3: Adjustment Period

Six months later

"Did you know it was going to get this hot?" Chuck asked.

Friday chuckled as she twisted up the bottom of her tank top and pushed it into her cleavage, creating a sort of bra. "It is summer in the south, you know." She took a long pull from her water glass. "Damn! I wish folks would pay you for work with ice cream instead of ratty blankets and wilted veggies. I'm sick of soup and we have enough blankets to make a mattress!"

"Even ice cubes would be appreciated. I did get some beer from one old guy. Do you know how bad it tastes warm?"

"Got any left?" Friday asked, head tilted, a sly grin growing.

"Five out of a six-pack, why?"

She reached out for it. "Because I can stash it in my secret spot. That's where I haul the spring water from. Creek water is tainted most of the time, but I found where it bubbles out of the ground, cold and clear..."

"Grab the kid and a bottle, and I'll put up the closed sign," Chuck said. "And bring that map. Let's go research our next location. It has to be somewhere higher, though. I wasn't cut out for the heat. At least, without an air conditioner."

"Pussy!" Friday said, laughing with abandon.

"Meow," Chuck replied.

The three hiked up the hill to an overgrown area, so verdant that it seemed to create a mountain out of the vines and brambles. "Here," Friday said.

Chuck took the long branch she offered him and turned it over in his hands, noticing it was well-worn from being handled. He looked at her, eyebrow raised. "And..."

"Your arms are longer than mine. No matter how far I reach, I always seem to get scratched. Since you're about a foot taller than I am, your reach should be a lot longer, too." She took back the stick for a moment and inserted it into the brambles. "Right here. Pull back with the crook end and discover my little heaven on earth."

Friday took the baby and carrier off Chuck and slipped it over her shoulder. She bent forward and held Ria close while Chuck held back the thorny branches and twisty vines, providing a prickle-free passage for them.

"Wow! Why didn't you tell me about this? Good grief, this place has to be at least ten degrees cooler than our campsite."

"If we both were hiking up here on a regular basis, folks might get the wrong idea," she said. Chuck answered her with a scowl. "All right, all right. The truth. I've never had anything of my own. I was the youngest of eight kids and got everyone else's hand-me-downs. It wouldn't have been so bad except the next three oldest were boys. I never even had a second or third-hand dress until I was ten, and that was because a neighbor lady felt sorry for me. It was at least a generation out of date, but I felt so pretty, twirling around, the skirt spinning out away from me…"

"You know, you really are a pretty woman, Friday," he said, not looking at her, instead marveling at the little pool fed by the spring. He squatted down and gently set the cans of beer in it.

"Yeah, a whole hell of a lot of good that did me in life. When I got knocked up, my parents sent me away, and then I had the baby literally torn away from my arms. I know she was alive when they took her. She was only sleeping. I know it!" she hissed, trying not to scream and upset Ria but finally letting it out after all these years.

"Did you look for her?" Chuck asked.

"How could I? I had nowhere to go. I was healthy, young, and gullible. They could pretty much do whatever they wanted with me."

"So, you were locked up?"

"More or less. They kept me around to help the other girls who were pregnant. They offered me good money. 'What else are you going to do? Become a hooker? We'll give you a decent wage plus room and board to help the other young women here. But if you don't want that, go ahead. You'll be scorned. You're already a fallen woman to your family.' They messed with my mind, Chuck! I was a child. Shit, in some ways I still am. I'm only twenty-two!"

"Well, if it makes you feel better, only your frown makes you look older. When you were laughing a few minutes ago, you looked like a teenager. Free from the cares of the world."

"But I'm not free. I'm trapped again. No skills, no family I can talk to or go back to. We're two paupers, trying to help others, out on some sort of fantasy quest. Shit, we don't even have enough money to pack up and go somewhere where people pay real dollars for your skills. You'll be working for scraps and someone to haul firewood for the rest of your life if we hang out here. We – rather, you – need to find an angel who'll fund you at least enough for a halfway decent motorhome. Something with running water and a solid roof, not a tarp and water hauled from a spring or creek in gallon jugs."

"We'll leave here and I'll find the money. Mark my words, we'll go pack up camp and leave at the crack of dawn. However, for right now, I'm willing to see if this beer is cooler than warm." He picked up one out of the chilly water and handed it to her. "Cheers?" he asked.

She took it and saluted him with it. "Okay, but one thing…"

"Hmm?" he asked tipping back the brew. "Ah, close enough to cool. What else do you want?"

"I want that third beer. Equal partners in the goods we take, at least the stuff worth a darn."

"Sounds good to me because, hey, if you weren't here, I wouldn't be able to do much more than see one or two people a day. Babies really are labor-intensive."

"So I'm just finding out." Friday grabbed a beer and popped the top. "Maybe one of these days, I'll get to find out for myself," she said and tried to gulp away the start of another bout of depression. "Maybe."

***

An hour later – all the beers and the baby's bottle finished – Chuck held Ria over his shoulder, trying to urge a burp out of her. "Well, are you ready to head back, Friday? And since we've both had a few, make sure we don't forget to get more bottles fixed for my little angel."

Friday gently touched Ria's cheek. "You know, it's a good thing she's fair and not dark-haired like my little girl. I would have run like the wind with her the first time your back was turned."

Chuck's mouth gaped in shock, then quickly shut as he realized it was the beer talking. Maybe. "Well, as you've found out, being a single parent isn't easy. Even though I've never heard you say it, I'm sure you love her. Maybe not as much as me…"

"Chuck, the more I get to know you, the more I like you. I'd pretty much given up on…" Friday opened both hands and looked around. "Given up on everything. Then I see the love and devotion you have to your ideal and your little family. I guess all I need is my own ideal and family."

Reaching out with his free arm, Chuck gave Friday a quick hug. "You *are* family. Our family."

Friday looked up into Chuck's bright blue eyes and swooned. She hadn't had a man since she was five months pregnant with the baby she'd lost. Even then, it was rough and without pleasure. There had to be more to sex than grunting and sharing body fluids. Surely, Chuck would be a gentle lover, one who saw that she was satisfied before he achieved completion. She closed her eyes, puckering up as she imagined gentle caresses and kisses…

Chuck pulled back, releasing Friday from the hug, turning away from her lips that were suddenly a mere inch from his. "The sooner we head out, the quicker we'll be done with breaking camp. We need to catch a few hours of sleep before leaving. Daylight comes pretty early in the summer. Actually," he babbled, standing up awkwardly and grabbing the grotto-entry stick, "our business at this site has pretty much come to a standstill. I think folks come by just because they're bored and want someone to talk to."

A slight groan escaped Friday as she realized she had just hit on Chuck. Yes, he was physically appealing and probably the nicest man she'd ever met. Scratch that – he was the nicest *person* she'd ever met. Why did he have to be gay? "Sorry," she mumbled as she moved past him while he held the briars and vines back.

"Hey," he said softly, coming close to her. "It could have just as easily been me except I think I have more tolerance for beer. We're both in need of someone. Let's hope our next site has more to keep us busy and focused."

"And maybe an available guy for both of us," she added with a nervous chuckle.

"I'll second that one," Chuck said, following her as she led the way down the slope.

A few minutes later, they arrived at camp and saw a client waiting. Or at least a person kicked back in the red camp chair.

"Where you been?" Harvey asked with a tinge of jealousy. He looked Friday up and down, his eyes narrowed, then smiled flirtatiously at Chuck.

"I should ask the same about you," Chuck said, his hand reached out in greeting. "I haven't seen you in months. Actually, since the day we met."

"Oh, I had to leave to take care of some stuff. I was just wondering if your little friend there could watch your daughter for a while. Maybe you could come up to my place for a drink or two. You know, spend some man-to-man time together," adding a wink.

Chuck felt his loins tingle and his gut knot. He'd just promised Friday he'd tear down their site tonight so they could bug out at dawn. It wouldn't be right to ask her to do all the work plus watch Ria. Especially since it was just so he could get laid!

"Dang," Chuck groaned and shook his head. "I'm going to have to say no for tonight. Actually, probably forever. We're leaving and we don't even know where."

Harvey's chest puffed up in indignation, the tattoos on his lower arms twitching as his muscles flexed. "What? You just come back from getting a little with your baby mama tart and don't want a little of this?" he asked, grinding his hips seductively.

Friday's eyes widened at the bulge in the man's pants. Everything about him was physically perfect but his package was so huge, it was practically obscene!

Chuck saw how red Harvey's face was getting and turned toward Friday. He slipped out from under the baby's sling, offering it to her with a nod that said, 'Watch her and take care of yourself. This might get bad.'

"I've made a commitment," Chuck said calmly once his ladies had left the area, "and I intend to stick to it. As far as what goes on between Friday and me, that's our business. Now, if you didn't come here to have me see to a medical condition, I'll have to ask you to leave."

"You owe me!" Harvey growled. He reached out and yanked on the rope that secured one side of the strung-up tarp, pulling it to the ground. "I helped you set this place up, so you owe me!"

"Well, it looks like you're undoing what you did, so I'll consider that a wash."

"Why you pantywaist little cock…"

Chuck threw a short blow just below Harvey's left ribcage, dropping the big man to his knees with the quick but efficient hit. "Please leave now. And as far as the kidney injury goes, there's nothing I can do for it. Only time and rest will mend it. Get out of here and never darken my life again."

Harvey stumbled to his feet, clutching his side, a dribble of saliva hanging from the corner of his mouth. "It's not over, Doc."

"Actually," Chuck said, "it is."

An unintentional groan escaped Harvey as he moved to get up. He had to struggle to stand up straight but made it. He took his first step forward, then stumbled as the pain overwhelmed him. One hand shot out and stopped him from biting dirt as he fell. He tried to resume his cock-of-the-walk strut that had worked so well in prison, then relinquished himself to the fact that he'd have to stay hunched over to move. "It's not over," he repeated softly, then shuffled into the brush, branches breaking, his mumbled cuss words eventually fading into nothingness.

"Wow! That was intense," Friday said, coming out from behind the van once she was sure Harvey was gone.

"How's Ria?" Chuck asked. He looked close to search her face for signs of being traumatized, then up at Friday. "And how are you?"

"She's fine. I'm scared shitless," Friday admitted. "How's your hand?"

Chuck turned it over and looked, then brought it up to his lips to check for small contusions or ligament tears that weren't yet visible. "Hurts like I smashed it into a rock. I guess knowing the human body's weak spots comes in handy. That and being a Golden Gloves boxer when I was a teenager. I about killed one older brother with a blow like that. Not literally, but it did keep him off my back for quite a while."

"So, what do we do first? Soak your hand in a little Epsom salts solution?"

"Yeah, you're a quick learner. Here, I'll take Ria if you'd be so kind as to set me up."

Friday slipped out of the sling and transferred it to Chuck. "Think of it this way. If we weren't already leaving, having a goon like him after you would be a good reason to get out of Dodge. He's spooky."

"Yeah, we have our guardian angels looking over us today, that's for sure."

***

The next morning was chilly and clear and full of promise. "Wake up, Sunshine," Chuck said, nudging her with a cup of instant coffee.

Friday groaned, started to roll back over, then popped up, frantic. "Is he here? Did Harvey come back?"

"No. Relax. We're loaded up and ready to go. Here's some coffee to get you started. We'll splurge on bacon and egg breakfast sandwiches and a fast-

211

food bathroom washup."

"You're so generous," she said, taking the cup from him. "Give me a few and I'll be ready to pilot or co-pilot; your choice."

"No, it's you who's so generous, Friday. I hope you stick around a lot longer. You really are family."

***

The next day, further on down the road

"Good news," Chuck said, handing Friday a cup of convenience store coffee.

"You mean other than not having instant coffee for breakfast?" she asked.

"Yup. While I was paying for gas and getting Ria's water, I met a guy who asked if this was my van conversion. Seems like he has a motorhome that's too big for him and his wife, and he'd like to downsize. We're going to meet him at his place and do some straight across trading. I hope."

"If it has running water and a roof that doesn't leak, I'm all in."

"I didn't say the same thing, but I sure thought it hard enough. I don't want to play hardball, but if we can get a little cash or something else we can use, I'll see if I can work that into the deal. Oh, and when I saw he was wearing a cross, I sort of lied..."

Friday scowled. "You mean, you lied. There is no such thing as 'sort of lied.'"

Chuck rolled his eyes. "I told him we were married and Ria was our daughter. She's fair like I am, so it's not a big stretch. How about we were married two years ago? January third sounds good."

"Ria's birthday. And where are we from?"

Chuck downshifted and pulled up in front of a large home overloaded with aging trees. "Everywhere, I guess. We'll have to wing it. We're here."

"Wait!" Friday said, reaching out to stop him. "Don't you think we might want to use another last name in case Harvey's still on the prowl?"

"You're right. Let's drop the first part, just in case he's smart enough to tail us. That's the other reason I want to swap vehicles. I don't think he'll be looking for us in this older middle-class neighborhood. It doesn't fit my job description."

"Mrs. Chuck Strong," Friday said, then brought up her bare left hand. "I must have lost my wedding ring."

"Or we used it to trade in for this. A little sympathy may go a long way. Just in case, would you see if you could tidy up a little while I'm inside talking?"

"Yas-suh, master," Friday said in a deep southern accent. "Anythin' you say, boss."

"Grr," Chuck growled, then opened the door, reaching back to pat her on the shoulder. "Thanks."

"Go, go! Before he changes his mind!"

Five minutes later, Chuck and the RV owner were back. "Mr. Baker, this is my reason for getting up each day...unless the baby gets me up first. My girl Friday and the woman who makes me smile, Grace."

Friday was all smiles at the clever introduction, but her face fell momentarily when Chuck used the name she had used at Dr. Buddy's. She quickly regained her composure and smiled, reaching out to shake his hand. "Nice meeting you, sir."

"Oh, just call me Pastor. Everyone else in town does. So, do you mind if I look around?"

"No problem." Friday picked up Ria and the car seat carrier, handed it all to Chuck, then got out. "How about we wait under the tree?" she asked.

Chuck looked back and forth, then sighed. Hopefully, Friday had put the magnetic sign with his real name on it under the mattress or some other out of sight place. The last thing he needed was to lose the deal because he had given a false name.

"Did you tell him you were a doctor?" Friday whispered to Chuck as she settled down next to him on a grassy spot in the shade.

"No, why?"

"Duh! You have pharmaceutical drugs in there!"

"Shit!"

"Yeah, shit. Go explain," she said, shooing him away. Friday looked back down at Ria, now wide awake and reaching for her. She took her out of the carrier. "Come here, Little Bit. Daddy's going to get us a bigger home, one with running water and room enough for you to crawl in. No? You don't want to crawl? You want to go right from rolling over to walking?"

"She's adorable," a voice from above them said.

"Huh?" Friday looked up and saw an older woman, probably the pastor's wife. "Oh, yes, she is. I'm Friday. Well, Chuck refers to me as his gal Friday."

"You two been on the road long?" she asked.

"Ever since Ria was born," Friday answered with a shrug, glad she didn't have to lie.

"Yes, Pastor and I were traveling ministers. We'd go from one hardship area to the next, ministering to the poor and needy. Then the church would send us down the road again. We had our first son in a little van just about like yours until he was two. When I was ready to have my daughter, we told the church board that we really needed bigger accommodations. They had us set up over in West Virginia just after Mary Catherine was born. She only lived with us in that little thing for two months."

"And then you got a bigger home?" Friday asked.

"Nope. She caught pneumonia and died. Pastor put his foot down after that. He said I'm not sacrificing any more of my children. Either get me a solid

213

roof and indoor plumbing or I'm changing affiliations. Well, they got us this big house and we've been doing the Lord's work in this area ever since."

Friday's hand was on Mrs. Baker's at the word died and stayed there until she finished her story. "Do you want to hold Ria?" she asked.

She nodded and sat down next to them. "You're so lucky. I never got to see my daughter get this big. This one's tiny but she seems to have great motor coordination. How old is she?"

"Six months," Friday said, handing her over. "She was a month early."

The pastor walked up to the trio. "Looks like you have a babysitter at the ready, Mrs. Strong, if you want to come and check out our old motorized Conestoga."

Friday smiled at the man as he spoke, but couldn't help flinching at the name Mrs. Strong. "Please, call me Friday," she said. "It's not the name I was born with but is the one I'm comfortable with."

"Amen to that. The Lord works in mysterious ways," the Pastor's wife said. "Catherine never felt right. You can call me Kitty."

"Yes, Kitty. She's already fed and should be dry. If not, let me know and I'll take care of it."

"Oh, I know my way around diapers. I even have a few in the house. We have a closet full of goodies if you're running short." Kitty double-checked the snugness of Ria's onesie tee-shirt, too small to be buttoned at the bottom, and saw it was a cloth diaper on her, not disposable. "On second thought, you go ahead and check out the ride with the men. Little One and I are going shopping."

"Oh, no…" Friday started, not wanting to be obligated.

"Nope. Let an old lady play dress up for the daughter she never got a chance to raise. Whether you trade or not, the clothes are yours to keep."

"Thank you. Truly," Friday said, tears filling her eyes at the generosity of strangers.

***

"Well, that was a great haul," Chuck said. "Since we didn't have much, it didn't take long to swap everything over. A whole new wardrobe and disposable diapers for the kid, and a case of assorted home-canned goods. What more could anyone ask?"

"How about a destination?"

"Wolf Whistle, West Virginia," Chuck replied snappily, a grin wide on his face. "Hey, Pastor Baker was all over the place before settling down in Georgia.

"What's the holdup?" Friday asked from the back.

"Looks like a roadblock. Go ahead and strap her in, then sit up here with me. I don't know what the law is about babies and car seats around here."

Friday anchored Ria's car seat to the floor brackets and climbed up front. "Yup, it's a roadblock. That's the good thing about not doing anything wrong: you can't get busted."

Chuck pulled to a stop and the officer stepped up to his window. "Good morning, sir, miss," he said. "There's a fugitive in the area. A convicted murderer escaped from prison six months ago but was spotted nearby last night." He handed the flyer to Chuck. "Have you seen him?"

Friday leaned closer to see and they both gasped, "Harvey," at the same time.

"Yes, that's one of the names he uses. So, I take it you saw him?" he asked, pen and notebook in hand, ready to take notes.

"You might want to look at hospitals and clinics," Chuck said. "He sort of had a kidney injury – left side. I told him there was nothing he could do about it, but I don't think he's the kind of guy to listen to anyone."

"What? Are you a doctor or something?" the cop asked.

"Yes," Chuck said, then pursed his lips, not comfortable about elaborating.

"So, did you examine him?"

"Nope, but I am the one who punched him. He came to our site and started tearing things up, threatening us. He was limping pretty bad when he left but was able to walk. You said he was a murderer?" Chuck asked.

"Serial murderer," the officer said, flipping through his notebook. "He was severely homophobic. He'd ask a guy out on a date and then, wham!"

"Wham?" Friday asked and looked over at Chuck.

"Tortured his victims until they died. That guy was sick. I won't go into details – the lady being here and all – but let's just say he was a technicality away from getting the death penalty. He has the rest of his life sentence to serve in Florida. Knowing about the injury will definitely help. Anything else?"

"He was dressed in tight denim jeans and a white tank top," Chuck added. "Oh, and was wearing Wellington boots and was walking."

Friday put her hand up, recalling the stumbling adversary. "Or trying to. In other words, he was on foot. We never saw a vehicle."

"Yes, I think that's about it, Officer," Chuck said. "If you have a card, I'll call if I see him again. I certainly don't want his kind walking the streets or cruising the parks."

"You and me both," the cop said, giving Chuck a sly wink, handing him his official card with his cell phone number and nickname scribbled on the back. "Give me a call, even if you don't think it's important."

"Hey, Pete!" an officer called out from ahead. "They caught him! We're shutting down the roadblock."

Chuck started to hand back the card then changed the gesture to put it in his shirt pocket. "Just in case something else pops up," he said, giving Pete a wink. He stepped on the clutch and shifted into first.

Thump. Thump. Pete tapped the side of the van, giving Chuck a personal farewell. "Take care out there," he called.

"Oh, we will," Chuck said. "We will."

Chapter 4: Wolf Whistle

Four years later
Wolf Whistle, West Virginia

"I can't believe she's only four and a half years old and can read like a third-grader," Friday said.

"Or an adult from this neck of the woods," Chuck said.

"Yeah, it's sad that the education system can't be more stringent on school attendance. The teachers try, but if they can't get a kid's butt in the seat, it doesn't make a difference."

"Yup, an endless circle of poverty. These folks are so far off the government's radar, we can't even get welfare or disability insurance for those who qualify!" Chuck picked up his spiral-bound journal with names and clients, dates and procedures. "I've tried and tried, but they don't want to get a social security number. 'My daddy and grandpappy never had one and they did just fine. What do I need one for? Just to pay taxes?' If I've heard that once – or a variation of the same – I've heard it a hundred times."

Friday looked down her nose at him.

"Well, I hear it at least a couple of times a month," Chuck amended. "So, what do you have for me today?"

"No clients yet. In case you haven't noticed, we're running out of canned food. However, we still have that hen that hasn't laid an egg in a month or more. Sounds like chicken and dumplings for dinner," Friday said, brandishing the hatchet, checking the cutting edge for nicks.

"Damn! I wish I'd never asked you to show me how to butcher a chicken," Chuck said and took it from her.

"Hey, I'll do it if you want to gut it, pluck it, and cook it."

Chuck turned around and started walking to the hen house "Which one is she?" he asked, certain that she was following him. "I don't want to get the queen of four-egg omelets by mistake."

"This is the one, Daddy," Ria said, holding the chicken upside down by the legs. "I caught her for you. Can I kill her?"

"Uh, no. Sorry, honey, but I don't trust your aim. I know you can hit a target on the tree with this thing," Chuck twirled the hatchet in his hand, "but since I'm the one who'd be holding down her head, I'm going to have to pass on that until you're a little older."

"You won't have to hold her; I can do it by myself. Watch this, Daddy." Ria put the chicken on the chopping block breast first, then pulled the legs back to get full body contact with the stump. With one hand, she held it down securely until it completely settled down. She then drew an imaginary line from the tip of the hen's beak forward – four inches long – then repeated it, a smooth rhythmic stroking movement. The hen was transfixed. Frozen. Dumb cluck hypnotized. "Can I do it, please," Ria begged.

"All right. Friday, get ready to chase it if she doesn't get a clean shot," Chuck said, handing his daughter the hatchet.

Thwack!

The chicken's head flew off with a well-placed blow. "I did it! I did it!" Ria squealed, jumping up and down, clutching the hatchet close as if it was her favorite toy.

"Whoa! Wait! Give me that hatchet. Our dinner escaped!" Chuck screamed. "Quick! The job's not done until you bring it to the table."

Not wanting to relinquish her prize tool, Ria scowled at him as if he was teasing her. Friday turned her around by the shoulders and pointed her in the direction the headless hen was running. "Go get it!" she said, patting Ria on the bottom to push start her.

Chuck took the hatchet from her and forty pounds of female vanished through the bush, chasing the headless chicken.

"Does that happen often?" he asked Friday as they stood back, watching the braided blonde grasp air, trying to catch the hen, then disappear around a clump of greenery.

"No, but it isn't that uncommon. Come on, let's help her. I don't want her to chase it into the blackberry bushes. I'd rather eat bullion and biscuits than climb through thorny brambles to get our chicken and dumplings."

"Ria! Ria!" they called out but didn't get an answer.

"How'd she disappear so quickly?" Friday asked.

"She's Ria," Chuck replied. "I refuse to worry until five minutes have passed." He looked at his watch. "I started counting two minutes ago. Ria! Ria! Come out, come out, wherever you are!"

"I'm over here, Daddy. Come help me."

"Oh, shit!" Chuck said.

"You're not supposed to say that," Ria called out.

"Are you okay?" Friday asked, ignoring her comment.

"I am, but he's not." Ria stepped out of the tumble of brush and onto the deer trail, dead chicken in hand.

"That's a she," Chuck said.

"Not the chicken," Ria said. "Him. He's hurt." She handed Friday the chicken and crawled back into the bushes. "Don't worry, sir. My daddy's a doctor and he can fix you up, good as new."

Chuck got on his hands and knees and followed her into the temporary shelter. There lay a beautiful specimen of man, handsome in just about every way except the grimace on his face, his five o'clock shadow more of a five-day shadow, his cheeks hollow from dehydration.

"I won't trouble you with asking if you're okay because I can see that

217

you're not. I will ask if you can walk, though."

The man shook his head biting his chapped bottom lip in defeat.

"Friday, go back to the clinic and grab the cot. We'll use it as a gurney. Ria, go with her. Put that chicken up high where that stray dog can't get it, then bring me a bottle of water – a small bottle, not a jug." He turned to the man. "Save your breath. Don't even try to talk until we get you a drink. We'll have you fixed up in no time."

The man nodded again, his eyes squeezed tight as if to cry. But there were no tears. He was too dehydrated.

A minute later, they were back. "Here's the cot," Friday said, lifting up the aluminum-framed camp bed. "Do you need a hand getting him onto it?"

"We'll see." Chuck maneuvered the cot into the shelter the man had been living in, covered in leaves to keep warm. "Now, I'm going to roll you onto this. Are there any open sores or broken bones I need to watch out for?"

The man shrugged, nodded to his kilt-covered crotch, then shook his head.

"Hernia? Sore balls or groin?" Chuck asked.

The man's eyes widened as he nodded in affirmation.

"Lots of pain?"

He kept nodding.

"I think I can help with that. As my daughter said, I'm a doctor."

"Here you go, Daddy," Ria said, reaching in with a bottle of water. "And I made sure the dog couldn't get the chicken."

"Thanks, dear." Chuck turned to his patient and said, "Just a dribble on the lips. I don't want you to sit up. That'll cause more pain. I can only give you a little at a time or you'll just throw it up. That's more pain for the hernia and more dehydration for the body."

Chuck wiped a few drops onto the man's full lips, moistening them so they wouldn't crack further. His mouth parted, ready for more. "Just a little…" He dropped in about a tablespoonful, then put the cap back on the bottle and handed it to Ria.

"Let's do this. It's going to be uncomfortable for a bit, but we're just a hundred yards or so away."

Chuck rolled his patient onto his side to make more room, settled the cot close to him, then rolled him back onto it. "Easy peasy," he said, noticing the man's grimace but lack of audible complaint. "Ready for this, Friday?" he called out to his waiting assistant.

"I can take this end without having to crawl in," she said. "Just say the word."

"Just a sec. Ria, crawl out and hold back the brush. Now, sir, are you ready?"

The patient nodded. His prayers had been answered.

"On two," Chuck said. "One, two!"

With a practiced coordinated effort, the four-footed ambulance exited the overgrown shelter, Ria doing her best to protect the man from the one stringer of blackberries that seemed to be everywhere.

"See, I told you I'd get help," she told the man as she walked beside him, doing her other job: distracting the patient from his discomfort.

"Ria, go get the door. We're taking him inside right away," Chuck said. His mind tumbled over whether he still had any sutures and where they'd keep the handsome Scottish stranger once they fixed him up. He wouldn't be able to hike home – wherever that was – for at least a few days. It looked like one more person would have to be fed with their meager rations.

An audible groan escaped from Chuck as he realized his last thought was a selfish one. At least one more person would live to see tomorrow because Ria's first chicken kill had escaped, causing her to find an injured man on the brink of death. A few ounces of food versus a man's life. No contest. "Thank you, Lord," he said audibly.

Chuck felt the man's hand on his. He couldn't speak, but the man could now smile in gratitude. "You're welcome," Chuck told him. "But you might not be too happy with me pretty soon. If you have what I think you have, surgery is needed. I have everything I need except a pain killer. Well, I have Ibuprofen but I'm not going to put that in your empty stomach. Are you ready for me to examine you?"

The man nodded and took his hand away, then stared up at the ceiling in the aging motorhome living room.

"Ria, go wet a washcloth with drinking water and let him suck on it, then stay up by his head. Friday, grab that prep kit we got last month. Team, we have ourselves our first major surgery."

"Lucky me," the man groaned, then passed out.

Chuck checked his carotid pulse and lifted the man's eyelids, making sure he was just unconscious and not dead. "Yes, I'd say you're lucky if you stay konked out for the whole surgery. I am going to assume he gave me permission to operate. Ria," he said, his daughter already back from her first task, "go grab a couple of drapes. Friday, it's time for this man to get his life back."

"Can I watch?" Ria asked.

Friday looked at Chuck, one eyebrow raised.

"She's not afraid of blood and knows anatomy better than most adults. I guess if she can't handle it, she can go outside," he said, then flipped the man's kilt up. "Ouch."

"Is that what a man's testicles are supposed to look like?" Ria asked.

"Nope," Friday said, then moved the kilt out of the way and unbuckled his belt. "This needs to come off. I'd say we have us a West Virginia Highlander."

"With a major inguinal hernia in his low lands region," Chuck added.

"I never saw a grown man's penis before," Ria said innocently, staring.

"It's a lot bigger than little boys' penises."

"So is a man's nose," Friday said, her face pinched in concern. "Look at them someday. Little button noses on boys, big honkers on men."

"Let's get on with this before he wakes up. Now, no talking, Ria. I have to concentrate. I haven't done this in a while. And if someone comes to the door, you take care of it, all right?"

"Yes, sir," Ria said, her chest puffed in pride. "I'm you're best number two helper."

***

An hour later

"That went well," Friday said, wiping down the surgery implements, getting them ready for their alcohol bath. "How long do you think he'll stay out?"

"Not long. When you get done there, would you offer him that wet washcloth again? I didn't want him to suck on it while operating, just in case it revived him. Oh, and if it wasn't obvious to you, it looks like there will be four for your chicken and dumplings dinner. And for a few more meals after that. He won't be able to go anywhere for a while."

Friday looked back at the man, the most handsome man she'd seen in years. Rough-looking with his scruffy beard but with coal-black hair that she'd always found appealing. Her nether regions tingled, a feeling she hadn't experienced with the sight of a man in a long time. *Have my prayers been answered? Is it time for me to leave and my escort has just arrived?*

"Ria, where's that chicken?" Chuck asked, interrupting Friday's reverie.

"I hung her on the clothesline." Ria pointed out the kitchen window. "See?"

"Clever kid," Friday said, sealing the lid on the alcohol bath. "Since she butchered and caught it – in that order – I guess that means you get to clean it and I'll cook it, Dad. Ria, why don't you go see if you can find a stalk of wild celery for me? And when you get back, pick out some of the better-looking carrots and onions. We'll dress up the first dinner you supplied meat for extra nice."

Chuck held up his hands, inspecting the digits that had just held and reinserted a man's protruding bowels, repairing the tear in the scrotum they had intruded into. Then he looked out the window at the dead chicken, hanging on the clothesline, its feet secured together with one of his clean white socks. "A man for all seasons and hands for all reasons," he said, taking the filet knife from the butcher block. "Believe it or not, sometimes I miss fast-food restaurants."

As soon as he was out the door, Angus opened his eyes and looked around. An unexpected throat tickle startled him. He tried to hold his breath – he didn't want to cough – but that made it worse.

220

"Just breathe in to the count of four and exhale the same way," Friday said, quickly at his side, her hand firm on the bandaging, applying gentle pressure on his scrotum in case he did start coughing. "In, two, three, four. Out, two, three, four. Again, two, three, four. Out, two, three, four."

Concentrating on his breathing did the trick and the cough never materialized. Still afraid to speak lest it start again, he looked up and smiled weakly.

"Are you all right now?"

He nodded, then glanced at her hand, cradling his balls.

"Oh, I guess I can let go now," she said, blushing.

His grin widened and head canted to the side. 'If you have to,' he seemed to be saying.

"Here, let me get you some water." She started to set down the damp washcloth but handed it to him instead. While she was at the sink, she noticed him swipe the cloth across his face, then bring it to his mouth and suckle on it.

"Here, you'll get more from this," she said and brought the drink to his mouth, letting him sip the scant half cup of water. "I'm sorry we don't have any straws. We reused the ones we had until they split and were useless. We don't treat ourselves to a soda unless we go into town and that's not very often. It's not just because it's a lot of trouble to break up camp with all the ropes and tarps that make this place a clinic. We also need money for gas. Most of our patients pay for services with food or critters. We have enough fuel left to get to town but not enough for the return trip."

Angus reached for where his sporran should be – willing to pay for the services – then looked around nervously, realizing it and his money was gone. His kilt was, too, and in its place, a white bed sheet covered his loins.

"Oh, we didn't want to get blood on your plaid." She looked down at his dark brown boots, ornate with crossed leather straps and metal buckles, the soles thick with tire tread that had been cut to size to replace the original leather. "I'm sure glad you weren't wearing jeans. I don't think we would have been able to get them off over those boots."

He looked back to the water cup, one eyebrow raised.

Friday answered his unspoken question. "Give it a few minutes. If that little bit stays down, I'll give you more. Oh, and we're having chicken and dumplings for dinner. You're invited."

His mouth opened to speak then closed quickly and morphed into a scowl.

"Well, I hope you didn't plan on popping in and leaving right away after surgery. How long were you out there?"

Angus put up three fingers.

"Three days? Good Lord, man. It's amazing you're still alive!"

"I'm a Scot," he said, his voice rough, low, and heavily accented.

"Well, I sort of guessed that by your dress." She saw his glare and tried again. "Dress as in attire, not dress as in skirt. So, is there a Scottish settlement around here?"

He looked to the water cup again and grinned.

"So, you'll talk if I give you more water?"

His grin continued, his eyes now bright as he nodded.

"You're behaving more like a wily Leprechaun. And before you ask, no, we don't have any marshmallow bits." She gave him another half cup of water, enjoying the view of his strong frame as he shifted beneath the sheet. Now she was even more intrigued with him. *Don't get emotionally involved. A good-looking body is what got you in trouble the first time around!*

"Angus McDermott, at your service," he said, his accent thick and sultry. "And yes, my grandsire was Irish. Yer not the first to notice the wily trait. Our wee settlement is a two-hour hike over the hill if a person's in fair health. I heard of yer husband's healing clinic from some travelers coming through. My sister insisted I come see if he could cure my problem."

Friday's hands waved in front of her face, trying to erase some of what he had said. "First off, he's not my husband. And second, in a few days, you should be healed up enough to go back but not until then. And third, what about your wife? Why did your sister send you?"

"I havena a wife! Although my sister did say as to bring one back if I found a strong and capable lass. She's getting ready to drop her fourth child and could use a hand around the house and garden. So, that bein' said, does that mean you and the healer are betrothed?"

"No, we'll never be married," she said, blushing with a mixture of excitement and anger. The first man who's thrilled her in over five years, and he'd take any strong woman for a wife! But he *was* looking for one. Would he be better than sharing a double bed with a gay man? For a day or two, she'd like to give him a try just to get rid of four and a half years of sexual frustration. She looked back at his wonderous body, the ample balls and more than adequate cock that was sure to please once he had regained his health. Three or four days with him might be better.

Would he treat her as respectfully as Chuck, though? Not a certainty by any stretch, especially if he was old school. By his speech and attire, he was more than old school; he was Old World! And looking for a wife like he was considering what kind of milk cow to get! Get out of that fantasy, woman!

Stomp. Stomp.

The familiar sound of Chuck's footfalls on the steps brought her back to her senses. She'd stick with the commitment to Chuck that she'd made four and a half years ago, even if it had expired three years earlier. Safer. Plus, they wouldn't stay in this windy hollow forever. One of these days, folks would stop coming or he'd feel the call of exploring the next settlement down the road.

"Did I interrupt something?" asked Chuck.

"Ach, I'm too frail to be doin' anythin' worth interruptin'," the slightly flushed patient replied. "My apologies on my rude approach to yer homestead, me bein' so infirm that ye had to portage my frail carcass the rest of the way to yer clinic. I'd stand to greet ye, but I dinna think this lass wants me to be up and movin' around yet."

"She's a smart young medico and I trained her well. She's not a doctor or a nurse, but if I was sick or injured, I'd want her nearby," Chuck said, his hand out to shake his patient's.

"Angus McDermott, at yer service," he said, "although I seem to be more of a liability than an asset at this moment."

"We all have our weak moments," Chuck said. "It seems my daughter found you just in time. Another few hours and you would have died from dehydration. Speaking of that, would you like more water?"

"He's had a full cup and kept it down," Friday said, refilling his water glass. "I do think that keeping his intake to clear liquids for another couple hours would best. By the time I have our chicken dinner done, he should be able to have a Ria-sized portion."

"What's a Ria?" Angus asked, his eyes shifting back and forth suspiciously.

"I am!" Ria said, popping up at his elbow. "I'm the best chicken rancher in West Virginia," she bragged.

Angus started to debate her claim with stories of his nephew, then suddenly felt weak and wobbly despite the fact that he was barely sitting up. "Ye certainly are," he said and scooted his elbows back to his sides and lay down all the way. "If ye dinna mind, I think I'll take a little nap while dinner's cooking."

Friday and Chuck shared a 'look,' recognizing the post-surgery fatigue that comes after the initial elation of finding out the procedure was a success. "That would be a good idea," Chuck said and lay his hand on the man's forehead, checking for fever. None. "A body needs sleep to heal."

"Aye, then I'll do my best to follow the doctor's orders," Angus said, then shut his eyes and was out.

***

Two hours later

Angus's eyes fluttered open and he inhaled deeply. "Did I die and go to heaven?" he asked.

"Nope," Chuck said. "You're still in Wolf Whistle. How are you doing there?"

"My sniffer's still working. I never thought much about it, but if angels cooked, I'm certain it would smell like this."

Thunk! Clatter! Thunk! Thunk!

"What's that?" Angus asked.

233

"Stay here with Angus," Chuck told Ria. "And don't let him get up or leave." He turned to the big Scot. "It's the wind. I have to take the tarps down or they'll rip to shreds."

"I'll give you a hand," Friday said. "Ria, set the table with bowls and spoons. Leave the glasses in the cupboard." She set the lid back on the pot. "Dinner will be delayed."

Chuck and Friday quickly and efficiently untied the ropes and bungees, dropping them to the ground so they could concentrate on folding the blue plastic tarps, holding them tight under their arms as they moved on to the next one.

A gust hit and knocked a branch from a tree, at the same time, blowing the tin from the top of the chicken coop. "Grab that!" Friday said. "It's our last piece!"

Chuck handed her his two tarps and wrestled the partially attached aluminum siding from the structure, cutting his hand in the process. "Damn!"

Friday rushed to his side to help and saw blood dribbling past his wrist. "Double damn! Give that to me and you take these and get inside. I'll be right there."

"What are you going to do with that?" he asked, ceding the metal to her and grasping his wound.

"Not let it blow away. Get inside. Now! That's an order!"

Chuck looked at her wide-eyed at her commanding tone. Never the meek one, he hadn't seen this side of her since they first met at Dr. Buddy's clinic. She was definitely taking charge right now. "Got it," he said, taking the last tarp and heading back to the motorhome.

Holding onto the three-foot-wide by eight-foot-long siding was like holding onto a heavy-duty kite in a mega-storm. Like a sail, the wind caught it and tried to carry Friday away. She wasn't going to let it go, though. Metal siding was a prized commodity in this region, and she and Chuck had worked hard to secure this piece. She wasn't going to let someone downwind get it for free. Finally, she got it under control then realized why. She was at the abandoned building at the end of their site, the one that used to be a smokehouse but had been condemned by the county. Shelter! She kicked at the lock at the door to no avail. Then she realized the hinges were older than the lock and hasp and kicked at them. Success. She wrangled the siding inside, then threw the door in there, too. They could deal with these hours or days later; whenever the blow was over.

Crap! Chuck's hand. I gotta get back!

Eyes squeezed shut as she headed into the wind, Friday didn't notice the huge branch flying right towards her. She didn't see it when it hit her, either.

Blindsided. Out cold on the ground and where Chuck wouldn't expect to find her.

***

"Let me help," Ria said, her hand hovering above her father's as he tried to wrap a temporary bandage across the cut in his palm.

"I got this," he said, then the gauze slipped again. "Okay. You win. Go for it."

Ria bit her bottom lip as she made sure the sterile strip didn't twist as she wound it around his hand. Finally done, she picked up the scissors. "Hold it tight," she told her father and cut the end. "Still got it?"

"Yes, Doc," he said, trying not to worry about Friday.

Ria snipped the trailing edge down the middle, then wrapped and tied the two pieces, securing the bandage. "Done!"

"I couldn't have done better myself," he said. "It looks to me like you have that magic touch. You're a natural healer. Now, I'll be back in a minute. I have to go find the cook!"

"Can I be of help?" Angus asked, uncomfortable at feeling useless.

"Yes. Stay here. Ria, same job. Make sure he doesn't go anywhere. One lost person is one too many."

Chuck opened the door and nearly had it ripped out of his good hand. He reflexively reached for it with his injured right hand, then stopped before following through. Stepping outside, he shoved the door closed but was unable to turn the handle to secure it.

"I got it," Ria said while he held it shut.

Chuck ducked low to keep from being blown about like that panel of siding, his eyes squeezed nearly shut to keep out pine needles and blowing debris. He traced the path from the chicken coop back to the RV. Nothing. Then he walked around their home to the back of their lot. Still nothing. He was headed up to the old brick smokehouse, his range of vision still limited, when he nearly stepped on her, hidden beneath a long-needle pine branch.

"Friday?" He bent forward to move the camouflage aside, then winced in sudden pain as he grasped it. *Damn! I'm going to have to put this hand in a sling. I can't stop reaching with it.*

Between using his foot and good hand, Chuck managed to uncover Friday, but he couldn't lift her.

The cot. If he could roll her onto it like he had Angus, he could haul it like a travois.

Back to the RV. The door was locked, though. He pounded on it. "Open up, Ria!"

The door opened with a whoosh, Ria catching it at the last second. She looked at him, alone and empty-handed, then looked behind him. "Where is she?"

"Let me in first." Chuck stepped inside and held the door with his good hand. "She's on the path. I need the cot you're on, Angus. Do you think you can get onto the couch by yourself or do you need help?"

"I can help him," Ria said, quickly at the recovering man's side.

Angus grimaced as he sat up, then rolled off, using Ria's shoulder as support. He didn't say a word, focusing all his attention on transferring himself. He managed to get situated on the couch, the sheet clutched in one hand at his side, the other grabbing the back of the sofa. "Done!" he proclaimed breathlessly.

"Ria, bring me the cot. I don't think I can do it by myself, so you'll have to help me. Angus, you'll have to live with the door open for a bit."

"Take the lass with you now," Angus said. "I'll bide."

Chuck held the handle as the wind blew the door open, his firm grip keeping it from slamming and breaking the window. Young Ria turned the aluminum frame cot on its side and dragged it to the doorway, leading it down the steps as her father grabbed the end, holding it tight against the gusts.

The father-daughter duo headed into the wind to find Friday, still unconscious, where the storm wreckage had knocked her down. Grabbing Friday by the hip, Ria pulled her best and only friend towards her as Chuck positioned the cot beneath her. "Let her go now," he shouted against the wind.

Chuck watched as Ria released her gently, her grimace of fear making her look more like her mother, Grace, than ever. A few minor adjustments and they had her settled. He stepped to the head end of the cot. "Come up here and help me pull," he said. "We're not going to carry her like we did Angus."

A tailwind assisted the two on their return to the RV, storm debris gratefully blowing out of their faces instead of into it. They stopped where their awning had been. The door was still open, thumping and banging it against the RV's siding as gusts relented then slammed it anew. Angus was upright, standing in the doorway, his kilt now belted on. "Just in case ye needed some lightweight help."

Chuck grunted then bent to the task of getting an unconscious woman up two steps with only one good hand.

Friday's head and shoulders suddenly lifted. "What happened?" she asked, her weight shifting as she tried to sit up.

"Hold on!" Chuck ordered. "Ria, set it down."

Chuck rushed to Friday's side, his eyes wide with fear. "Can you climb the steps?"

"Of course, I can," she said. She started to sit up, then swooned. "Oh, shit!"

"You're not supposed to say shit," Ria said, looking back and forth between her two parental figures, making sure she wasn't going to get in trouble for repeating the forbidden word.

"You're right, sweetheart," Friday said. "It's okay in an extreme circumstance, though." She turned back to Chuck. "Let me try this again."

This time, Friday moved slowly, one hand on Chuck's shoulder to steady herself as she sat up. "I got this."

Another concerted effort and she was standing mostly upright, hunched over to stay on her feet as the wind gusted to near hurricane force. Holding onto Ria's shoulder, she climbed the steps. Chuck stood behind her, holding tight to the cot, so it didn't fly away. He didn't want Friday to try and chase it down, too!

"Angus, I think you can handle this much weight. Pull this inside, would you?" Chuck asked, pushing the cot upright through the doorway, grateful for the momentary lull in the wind.

Once inside, Chuck pulled the door closed and secured it with the deadbolt, the only other way to keep the wind from grabbing it open. He turned to Friday. "Well, did you save the tinware?" he asked sarcastically.

"Yes," she answered in the same tone. "As a matter of fact, I did. I also got that old brick smokehouse door opened. It's empty. Now we have a storm shelter in case we ever need one."

Angus and Chuck both snickered at the same time. "Like now?" Chuck asked.

"Maybe. How's your hand?"

Chuck held up the bandage. "Ria's a natural. Fixed it up just fine."

"Did she put stitches in it, too?"

"I didn't have time," Ria said. "Besides, he wouldn't let me. He missed you and went out to find you, almost before I even had it tied off."

Friday looked up at Chuck, his everpresent small flashlight in hand, ready to check her pupils. "Why?"

"Duh! Because I care. Now, chin up."

Chuck flashed the light in both eyes then repeated the gesture to verify his first conclusion. "Hmm. I don't like that, but there's nothing I can do. You have a concussion. I don't want you sleeping for more than an hour at a time. You'll probably be cursing me by morning for waking you up all night."

"No more than you'll be cursing me for making you."

"I can do that," Angus said. "I'm a light sleeper when need be."

Chuck frowned – ready to tell him no – then thought of how he'd feel if there was chaos all around and he wasn't allowed to help. "I don't think you'll pull on your stitches with nudging her shoulder. Looks like you get my spot in bed. Ria, I'm sleeping with you."

Ria tried to temper her excitement. She hadn't slept with him in ages, and he'd never slept with her on the pullout bench that served as dinner table seats ever! "All right," she said, swishing her smile into a serious look. "Just make sure you don't drink a lot of water before bedtime. I don't want you peeing the bed."

Friday and Chuck laughed, then Angus realized it was a joke and joined. "I promise," Chuck said. "Now, is the stew hot enough to add the dumpling dough yet?"

"Can I do it?" asked Ria.

"Might as well," Friday said. "You've proven your worth as a meat provider, search and rescuer, medic, and ambulance driver. We might as well add chef to your resume."

***

"So, this is where you two sleep and yer not..." Angus was stilled from completing his comment by a sharp elbow.

"My personal life is none of your business. Now, shut up and let me sleep." Friday pulled one of the many afghans they had acquired as payment for services over her head, trying to shut out both the noise of the storm still raging and the queries from the hot guy nestled inches away from her.

"Yer shiverin'. Here, let me..." Angus scooted closer, snuggling up to her back, and wrapped his arm over her waist.

"Knock it off," she hissed. "Don't you know a woman means it when she says no."

"But I dinna ask ye a question."

"And I didn't ask for you to cuddle, either. How would you like it if a big old black bear just walked up and laid its paws on you?"

"What are ye talkin' about, woman? That blow to the heid scrambled yer brains."

"Just because I'm a woman and lying near you doesn't mean I'm up for grabs to you or any other male who happens by. An unwanted hand is just as uncomfortable as a bear paw and potentially just as disastrous."

"I was jest tryin' to keep you warm. I wasna trying to compromise yer virtue."

"Just let me sleep."

"All right...Say, what is yer name?"

"Just call me Friday."

"Like the day of the week?"

Rather than explain the relationship of Robinson Crusoe and his helper, Friday, to a man who probably had never read the story, Friday grunted, "Yeah," and hunkered down, asleep before she thought again about how close he was to her.

"Friday," Angus said, pushing her shoulder even harder. "Wake up!"

"Huh?" she asked sluggishly, drool slipping out of the corner of her mouth. She brought her hand up to wipe it and missed, hitting herself in the eye instead. "Crap."

"Are you all right?" he asked.

"I don't know," she slurred. "No," she amended after hearing herself. "Get Chuck."

228

"I'm here," Chuck said, laying his hand on her forehead. He looked up at Angus. "Sort of hard not to hear everything when you're just a few feet away, despite the noise outside. No fever. I think you might be dehydrated. You're skin's too dry. When was the last time you had anything to drink?"

"Just whatever was in the chicken and dumplings. Before that, I don't remember. But you're right," she said, smacking her lips. "The salt in the soup would have sucked out water from my cells. If you don't mind, would you get me a drink of water?"

"Got it," Ria said, handing her an oft-reused water bottle.

The three watched as Friday chugged the whole bottle down, then handed it back to Ria. "Now, let me get some sleep. And if you don't mind, Chuck, let's try that new theory about letting the concussion patient get plenty of rest. I don't think I'm going to slip into a coma. I'm simply exhausted."

Chuck looked over Friday at Angus who shrugged one shoulder. "Should I let ye have yer place back?"

"Nah. I'd rather you sleep with her than on the floor or cot. Let's all get some sleep. Maybe the blow will be over by morning."

"Not likely," Friday mumbled, then snuggled back into the afghan.

The next morning, Angus gently nudged Friday's shoulder, testing for life and alertness. She responded with a quick snort, then rolled over, hands tucked under her chin, her face in his chest. Her nose twitched as she unconsciously sniffed a new smell. "What the…" she hissed, bounding out of bed in one swift movement.

"I dinna mean to startle ye," Angus said. "I jest needed to get out to use the privy. I dinna think it would do Chuck's surgery any good to climb over ye."

Friday looked over Angus and saw Chuck was in bed with them, fast asleep, snuggled next to him. "What's he doing there?"

Chuck awoke at the sound of Friday's voice. "Oh, sorry. Ria was kicking so much that I wasn't getting any sleep. You and Angus were only using half the bed, so I didn't think you'd mind. Sorry. I thought I'd be up before anyone noticed."

"Well, you two wait there. I get the bathroom first," Friday said, trying to keep her grin contained.

In bed with two gorgeous men. So what if one is gay? Chuck needs someone, too. Oh, crap! What if Angus is gay? Would he stick around? Would Chuck decide it was time for me to hit the road? Shut up! No thinking until at least one cup of coffee has been consumed.

Friday came out of the tiny bathroom to Ria waiting, her knees held close together in bladder urgency. "My turn," she said. "The guys went outside."

"Good for them. I'll get breakfast started."

Stomp! Stomp! Stomp! Stomp!

"I guess the wind did die down some," Friday said once both men were

229

inside.

"Minimal damage since we got our tarps down in time. I took a look at the old smokehouse. Definitely usable space. You look better. How's your speech?"

"If Peter Piper picked a peck of pickled porcupines, how many prickles would he get?"

"That's not how it goes," Ria said, giggling.

"Okay, how's it supposed to go?" she asked.

"If Patsy Perkins poached a pool of purple poodles, how many puppies would she get?" Ria replied. "Beat that one, Daddy."

Chuck took a deep breath, searching for words with the letter P to swap around into a nonsense riddle, then blew it out. All he could think about was how great it felt being close to another man. A fairly healthy man who aroused desires in him that he had hoped were dead. Nope. Although he loved Friday, she didn't arouse him. He didn't love Angus any more than any other person who happened upon his clinic in search of medical assistance. But he certainly reawakened his desires. *Damn!*

Angus looked back and forth between the couple who weren't a couple. Suddenly it was clear as a freshly washed window. Chuck was like his Uncle Fergus: he liked other men. He sighed in relief. No competition for the lovely lady who was also a fine healer and decent cook.

Waiting until Chuck had left outside with Ria, Angus asked, "So, Ria isn't yer biological daughter?"

"Nope. My daughter is gone. I've been helping Chuck with Ria since she was born." Friday looked at Angus and saw he was intense, studying her as if he had more questions. "She's his, not mine, but we both love her. Any other questions?"

"Only one. It probably isna the last time I'll ask, but this is the first time. Will you marry me?"

"What?"

"All right, the second time, then," Angus said, his smile wide and infectious as he started to repeat himself.

"No, no. Don't bother. Are you serious? You just met me! How could you ask a life-changing question like that? Am I just some prime breed of cow you want to bring home to help with your sister's kids and garden? If you're looking for a slave, you're in the wrong place. I've been one before and won't go back."

"Wait. What? You were a slave?"

"Pretty much. When you can't come and go at will and are expected to work at specific tasks for no more than room and board, then you're a slave."

"Or you live in the hills of West Virginia," Angus said. "So, I take it you'll give me yer answer sometime before I leave?"

Friday was surprised by the grin she felt on her face. "Yeah, sure. But not today."

"All right then. It may take me longer to heal than Chuck thought if yer not leanin' toward an aye answer. I may not be stubborn, but I am determined. And jest to keep you from wonderin' about my motives, it isna yer skills as a cook and healer that interest me. It's the wily woman who's trapped inside; the one who's been livin' with a girly man for four and a half years out of a sense of honor and duty to help him rear his bairn. She's been deprivin' herself of the joys of her own life; of findin' and bein' with a man who wants to make her feel like she was glad she was born with breasts and a womb."

Her grin disappeared into a slack-jawed gape of awe. She realized her mouth was hanging open and shut it. She swallowed, trying to compose herself at hearing such an honest and heartfelt evaluation of her situation, one that had escaped her even. "Then I guess it will be four for dinner again," she said, a timid smile now in place.

"Aye," Angus said, moving in close, one large hand held up. "And I'll keep my bear claws off of you until you ask for them."

Stomp! Stomp! Shuffle! Shuffle!

Angus and Friday moved apart, allowing room for Chuck and Ria to enter the compact quarters.

"Let me check your cut," Friday said when Chuck came in, glad for the distraction.

The two sat down at the kitchen table across from each other. Friday focused on his hand, carefully unwrapping the gauze bandage, aware without looking up that the men were checking each other out. Not a word was being spoken but with that realization alone, she knew they were 'chatting' with eye movements. She longed to watch them, to see what was transpiring, but she knew it would stop if she did. Evidently, Ria was too young to understand that unspoken universal language that came after being around men for years and having life experiences.

"She did a great job," Friday said, her head still down. "You're right about the stitches. We'll have to see if we can get more butterfly bandages next time we're in town. I'll clean it again and rebandage it."

"Can I do it?" Ria asked.

Friday looked up at Chuck. He pulled his gaze from Angus. "Excuse me?" he asked.

"Ria wants to do the doctoring on your hand again. It's up to you," she said.

Chuck finally looked down at the work she had done. "Looks good to me. Ria, why don't you clean it up again then rewrap it?"

Ria looked at Friday and grinned. *Dad's being silly. He wasn't listening, huh?*

Friday nodded. "If you need help, honey, let me know. You got this. You're a natural. Just don't go treating anyone other than family and always get permission, all right?"

"All right. Now, Daddy, this might feel cold…" Ria looked up at her father and saw he was staring at Angus again. His eyes dropped to Friday and he sighed deeply, as if he had just lost her.

Even a four-year-old could understand at least a little of the silent language of men. She looked at Friday and saw her look at Angus. She'd never seen her look at anyone else like that. Was that why Daddy was sad? Was Friday going to leave with Angus? Ria felt her eyes get misty, tears starting. *Focus on what you're doing! That's what Daddy and Friday always said. It may be hard, but if you focus on the procedure and don't think about how difficult it is, you'll get through it faster and better.*

Ria picked up the roll of gauze from the tray Friday had set beside her. She wrapped her father's hand gently. He would still be with her. He'd stay with her forever…

Focus! Another three wraps and she was done. Handing her the scissors, Ria looked up and saw her father was looking at her now, not Angus. *Yes, he'll stay with me my whole life, even after I'm grown up. I'm his helper now. I'm his Friday.*

***

"Friday, why don't you check Angus and make sure there isn't an infection starting," Chuck said, not expecting her to refuse. "I'm going fishing with Ria."

"You're what?"

He chuckled softly at her surprise. "Hey," he said, coming up close so only she could hear, "I'm sure he'd rather have you check his balls than me. He likes you. You'll be safe without me. Besides, I really don't think he's the type to take advantage of you. He's a big man in many ways, a gentleman being one of them."

"How do you know that?"

"We *talked* while you were checking out my hand."

"Yeah, well, I was wondering what you two were chatting about. I had the feeling it was about me."

"Ria asked me about it later. Even she picked up on his attraction to you. She asked if the right woman came along, would I leave with her or could she come with me."

"Oh, Lord…"

"Yeah, well, she did say she was positive I'd never leave her. She was also just as sure you were going. Whatever you decide to do is fine with both of us. Has he asked you to marry him yet?"

"How'd you know?"

"Like I said, we 'talked.'"

"Go ahead and go fishing," Friday said, a pink blush rising. "I'll check his incision, then putter around here, cleaning up some of this storm mess. If he's up

232

to it, we might string up the tarps again."

"Well, don't let him get too carried away. You can tell him I said not to do anything that hurts or strains. Remember, he's probably still weak from dehydration and lack of food for three days. Don't make him work too hard."

"No worries there."

Chuck looked at Friday and shook his head. "So, did you answer him?"

"What? About getting married? Come on. Get real. I haven't even known him for twenty-four hours and you expect me to make a lifetime commitment?"

"You made a four-and-a-half-year one to me and Ria with less. If I had been – shall we say, wired differently – we'd probably still be together."

"I haven't even left yet and you're already writing me off," she said, scowling in embarrassment.

"Did you hear what you just said?"

"I haven't even left and..."

Chuck raised his injured hand, stopping her. "You said *yet*. You've already made up your mind but don't realize it. Yet."

He looked up. Angus was standing in the doorway, listening to their exchange. "Turn around, Friday," Chuck said. "You have a patient to attend to and Ria and I have fish to catch."

Ria ran up and hugged Friday around the middle. "I love you, Friday," she said, then ran to her dad, sniffing back tears. "Come on, Daddy. We have fish to catch."

Friday looked up at Angus, his face unreadable. "Well, that was awkward," she said. "Go inside and lie down. I want to check your stitches."

Angus sat on the edge of the bed he had shared with her the night before, his hands in his lap. Trying to calm his excitement before she examined him, his mind went over all the gory scenes he'd seen in life: the slaughter of farm animals, the sight of his sister giving birth, and then he found his dick-softening image.

Overwhelming grief overtook him, the memory of his wife and child lying together in a coffin, blue-toned skin, grim-faced, their skin hard to the touch.

"Are you all right?" Friday asked. "You look like death warmed over."

He took a deep breath, trying to calm the tears that were coming, but it was no use – two had already escaped.

"It's okay," she said, putting a calming hand on his shoulder. "You don't have to be bashful. It's nothing I haven't seen before."

He chuckled, coming out of the misery and ugliness that was his past into the beauty of the present and hope of his future. Friday.

"Well, *this* is different," Angus said, not even trying to soften his thick accent. "Before, you were a healer. Now, yer the woman I asked to marry me. I'm havin' some trouble keepin' my excitement down." He looked down at the bulge that had started again at her touch, covered by his large hands but still obvious.

Friday swallowed audibly. They were alone for at least an hour. Was she afraid of him? No, he had told her he wouldn't lay a hand on her unless she asked. That was what she was afraid of. She was afraid of herself.

"Let me check out the incision first," she said, trying to keep the breathlessness she felt out of her voice.

Angus lay back on the bed, keeping his cock covered with his tartan, exposing the area that had been repaired with stitches. Her touch was soft and gentle, her hands warm and caring. Blood surged, causing his shaft to pulse and harden even more. "Christ, woman! Yer drivin' me mad. Is it or isn't it healin' properly?"

Friday pulled the tartan over her exam area, inadvertently creating an obscene tent. "How are you feeling?"

"Horny as a stallion in a corral full of fillies." He put his hands under his hips, keeping them under control but also creating an even larger presentation of manly prowess. "If I dinna sit on my hands, they'd be all over you. I've never felt such a draw to a lass. Do you want me to ask again or will you jest answer aye and we can get on with it? We can find a priest or parson or justice of the peace later. I promise I'll provide fer you, never let you go hungry or cold. I'll give you as many bairns as you want, too. I see the way you look at wee Ria. You do want yer own, aye?"

"Aye," Friday said, then lay down beside him, looking into his dark blue eyes. "I think I told you I had a daughter before. I'd like at least two or three more. A son here and there might be nice, too."

"Well, we can start on it right now," he said. "I did overhear Doc tellin' you not to let me do too much. If I start to ailin', I'll have you here by me, ready to fix me again."

"Oh, I don't think you'll need fixing. Here, let me take off your plaid. We have at least a while before they get back. Oh, and if you change your mind after being with me right now, it's okay. I won't be offended."

"Oh? Well, I'll be mightily offended if you change yer mind! I may be a bit fast the first time, me not havin' had a woman since my wife died three years ago, but the second and third time should serve you well."

"Well, if that's the case, let's get started. But be gentle. It's been over six years for me. I may have reverted back to being a virgin!"

***

Two hours later

"Hold on there, Ria," Chuck said. "Let's stay out here for a while. I want to cook these over a campfire. They taste better."

"But can I go in and tell Friday I caught six fish?"

"Nope. We'll surprise her. She'll come out when she's ready. She might be seeing to Angus's needs. Why don't you sing the periodic table of elements for

234

me while I get it started?"

"Again?" she asked. Seeing his scowl, she began, "There's hydrogen and helium, then lithium, beryllium…"

"You know, you're lucky, Ria. Not many kids have the opportunity for a great education. Their parents may be smart, but too often they don't take the time to share their knowledge. One of these days, you'll thank me for being such a tough taskmaster."

"Hey, there," Friday said, standing in the doorway, Angus close behind her.

Chuck looked up and noticed the difference immediately. He sighed with a mix of frustration and loss at the change in his best friend. She was definitely committed to the man who had come to him in need of medical repair. If the nearness of the two – inside each other's personal zones – wasn't enough to say they had just enjoyed each other's bodies, their identical grins of satisfaction would have. Angus had convinced her, body and soul, to be his.

"Are you all right, Friday?" Ria asked. "You look kind of funny. Actually, you both do."

"I'm fine," Friday said. "I'll get a frying pan. Looks like we're cooking fish outside today. God, I'm glad it's summer. I can't stand the lingering smell of frying fish inside."

She turned around and Angus smiled at her, letting her pass. He resisted the urge to pat her bottom. It didn't make a difference, though. She was his and they both knew it.

Ria's narrowed look of distrust at Angus hadn't faded. Angus saw it and explained, "Ria, I've asked Friday to marry me and she said yes. We'll be leaving soon."

Ria took a deep breath, ready to protest, but knew it wouldn't do any good. She'd learned a long time ago – at least last week – that you couldn't win an argument with an adult. They always won. "Well, you be good to her," she said, then bent down to add more sticks to the fire her father had started, hiding her face so the others wouldn't see her tears.

"I promise to be good to her. Thanks for taking good care of her for all these years. Now, it's my turn. I promise you, I'll cherish her." Angus walked over and lay a gentle hand on Ria's head. "Truly."

***

"That was a fine dinner, Chuck," Angus said, his arm around a blushing Friday.

"That wasn't just dinner," Chuck said, "so, don't try and fool us. Ria and I both know it was our last supper with Friday."

Friday reached out and put her hand on Chuck's arm, trying to soften his scowl. "What would you have us do, Chuck? What if it had been you who had found that perfect someone? I would have understood."

Chuck patted her hand, then picked it up and kissed it. "You're right. I guess it's sour grapes. I had my chance…"

Friday snickered, then changed it into a cough. "Wind's blowing the wrong way," she said, looking back at Angus who was rolling his eyes. Evidently, he had figured out Chuck's preferences in lovers.

Angus spoke up. "Friday said she didn't have much to take with her. She doesn't need any household goods because I have everything we need. She can tote everything in her James bag."

"That's gym, as in gymnasium, not Jim as in James," Friday said, then leaned in and kissed him on the cheek.

"Ew…"

"Knock it off, Ria," Chuck said. "Just because we don't do that doesn't mean others don't display affection in a physical manner."

Ria fought back her tears. She was hurting on the inside – like her intestines were tearing apart –frustrated with discomfort at this new emotion and unsure of how to handle it. "Will you come back and visit us, Friday?"

Friday took a deep breath but Chuck cut in. "We're leaving, too, darling. Tomorrow we'll pack up and head on down the road."

"But...but…" Ria protested.

"But what?" Chuck said. "Other than Angus, no one has come to see us in three days. Last week, it was only two old guys and I think they were just here to ogle Friday. We've fixed up everyone who needs it. I'm not going to stick around in this heat waiting for someone to get a fishing hook buried in a finger. Let's move north. At least as far as the gas in this ancient and ailing RV will take us."

"Speakin' of patients," Angus said, reaching into his sporran. "I never did give you payment for yer services. I ken it isna much, but I think it will help ye get a head start." He handed him a packet of folded bills. "A little extra as a dowry fer takin' yer helpmate and the surrogate mother of yer child."

Chuck glanced at the tidy bundle of bucks – a five-dollar bill on the outside – and put it in his front pocket without counting it. "Thanks. Every little bit helps. As far as your stitches go, they're the dissolving kind. If they start to bother you, Friday can take them out if you're healed. Friday, make sure you take a first aid kit with you. From what Angus alluded to, there are a few other people living in your new neck of the woods. They might need a hand, and other than myself, I can't think of anyone else more suited to working in these rough conditions."

"Can I go to bed now," Ria asked, her eyes skirting past Friday and Angus, focusing on her hero, Daddy.

"Why don't you help me clean up, and then we'll both turn in early," he said.

"I got this," Friday said. "You cooked, we'll take care of the dishes."

"I didn't come to break up yer family," Angus said, standing up gingerly. "And I may have jested about my sister tellin' me to bring home a wife, but it was jest that: a joke. I dinna plan on findin' such a fine person," he placed his hand on Friday's shoulder. Then he looked at Ria and nodded. "Or bein' felled by pain or rescued by such a courageous young lass."

Ria rolled her eyes in embarrassment then allowed a grin to escape. "Just don't take my daddy from me, too!" she exclaimed.

"No worries there," Chuck said. "No one on this earth could tear me from you. You'll have to be the one to leave, not me."

"I'll never leave you!" Ria declared, her bottom lip stuck out in defiance.

Chuck grinned at her devotion. "Not until you're eighteen you won't," he said, pulling her shoulders close to him for a hug. "You were too much trouble to get!"

Friday looked over at him, recalling their hasty exodus from the birthing clinic, Ria with both her triplet sisters smuggled away in her gym bag. "And you've been worth every frantic moment we spent," she said, piling the last of the dishes into her hands. "We'll keep in touch, I promise. I don't know how, but we will."

Chuck reached into his pocket and pulled out a plastic business card. "There's only one person I keep in contact with. Silas will know where I am and how to find me. Here's his phone number and address."

Friday turned around, her arms laden with plates. "Put it in my back pocket. I won't forget it."

Angus stepped between them, intercepting Chuck's move to put his hand on his fiancée's fanny. "I'll take charge of this, if you don't mind," he said, taking the card and putting it in his sporran. "No one will get into this without me bein' awares."

Just don't keep it from Friday or there'll be hell to pay! Chuck choked back the verbal threat but knew it showed in his eyes.

Angus nodded. *Dinna worry. She'll have access to it. I willna keep her from you. If she wants to come back, she can. I'll make sure her life is so grand and full of children, though, she willna want to leave.*

Still facing Angus, Chuck shut his eyes briefly then opened them to stare. *You do that.*

"Are you all right, Daddy?"

"Just a little tired, dear." Chuck called to Friday inside the RV. "Just put the dishes in the sink. We're going to bed early."

The clatter of dishes on porcelain answered his request. Friday came to the doorway. "Then Angus and I'll go for a walk so we don't disturb you. Sleep well. We'll see you in the morning."

Yeah, right. You'll be gone before daylight. I know I would.

***

237

The next morning, Ria woke up and looked around. "They're gone!" she exclaimed, then turned to see her father come up the steps. "Daddy, did they sleep outside? They didn't even say goodbye!"

"They said goodbye last night. At least, I believe they thought they did. Don't worry. I made sure I gave Friday the card for Silas. She's not out of our life. She never will be. She's part of both of us. She's the closest thing you'll ever have to a mother and knows it. I don't know when, but I do know she'll be back. Maybe not to live with us, but we'll see her again. Who knows, maybe she'll have more children by then."

"More children? I'm her only child."

"No, she had one before I ever met her. Her daughter was taken away from her. I doubt she'll ever get her back, but Angus wants to give her more babies."

"Why wouldn't you give her more?"

"It's complicated," Chuck said, then held her close. "Come on. Let's eat something, then pack up everything we want to keep. I'll put a 'free' sign on what we're leaving. Next time someone comes by to chit chat or have me check on a rash, they'll find it. They'll know it was our time to move to greener pastures."

"Greener pastures?"

"That's a phrase. When the cows or goats or sheep have eaten all they could in their area, the shepherds move them to greener pastures. That means more grass to eat so they'll grow bigger and stronger. That's what we need."

"All right, but I think it would be better to say we're going where there are folks we can make stronger and healthier, not cows or goats."

"You're right. Oatmeal or cold cereal?" Chuck asked.

"Cold cereal, no milk. I don't want to wash more dishes."

Chuck looked at the sink. "Just like life, there's always a dirty dish to be washed. Let's get started."

He took off his watch and put it in his pocket, then felt the wadded bills Angus had given him as payment for services and dowry money for Friday. He pulled it out and unfolded it. The five-dollar bill had been wrapped around five one-hundred-dollar bills. "Whoa!"

"What's wrong?"

"We have money enough to go wherever we want and also buy food! Angus gave me dowry money..."

"Dowry money and what's wrong, Daddy?"

"I just realized something. The bride's family is supposed to be giving the groom the money, not the other way around. What I did for him wasn't worth five-hundred and five dollars!"

"Maybe the stitches weren't, but Friday's worth a lot more than that."

"Amen to that!"

238

Chapter 5: School Days

September 3, 1997

"Hello, Dr. Armstrong. My name is Thelma Ritter. I'm the schoolteacher in this district. Part of my job is to make sure all school-age children attend our classroom at least one day a week."

Chuck looked at the thin crone and shivers went up his spine. She looked as if she hadn't smiled in ten years, at least. A grin arose unexpectedly on his face. *So, that's where the phrase sour puss came from!*

"Did something I say amuse you?" she asked with a scowl.

"Nope. Just wondering how high your elementary school goes. As in, which grade level, not the ceiling height."

"Sixth grade," she replied, her chest puffed out in pride. "And I teach them all."

"Well, I appreciate the offer, but my daughter is homeschooled."

"Does your wife do the teaching?"

"No, I do," Chuck said, not wanting to disclose his marital status and have every single woman in the hollow chasing him.

"Are you a certified instructor?"

"No, but I am a medical doctor with more hours in college than any elementary school teacher I've ever met or heard of."

"Well, just because your fanny was in the classroom more than mine doesn't make you a better teacher."

"I agree, but just because you have a teaching certificate doesn't mean you're a better teacher, either. Tell me, do you have any sixth graders in your class right now?"

"Yes, I have one very bright young man."

"I'll tell you what, you create a standardized test and we'll give it to him and my daughter at the same time. If she beats his score, you'll leave us alone."

"But he's twelve! Your daughter is what, seven?"

"She'll be six in January – four months from today."

"No, no. That will never work." She glared at him, her doubts of success as plain as her pointy features.

"Of course, we'll both be in the classroom supervising. I wouldn't expect you to send the test home with her," Chuck said, his chin up with self-confidence.

"All right. I'll give them both the same test I give students before they can attend middle school. Shall we meet at the school at, let's say, ten o'clock?"

"That sounds good except for one thing," Chuck said.

"Yes…"

"Where's the school?"

239

The next day, Chuck and Ria hiked the half-mile to the school, leaving their home on wheels attached to the tarps and trees. "Is that it?" Ria asked, pointing to the small ramshackle building.

"Must be. There's nothing else around here, plus there's an old tire swing on that tree. The playground equipment, I suspect."

"Oh, there! If you look carefully, you can see that beat-up old sign. Butcher Hollow Academy." She got the giggles. "Academy?"

"Hey, be nice. Being smart won't get you near as far in life as good manners."

"Yes, sir. See, I can use my manners on you, too."

"I don't think she'll appreciate your sense of humor," Chuck said, trying to suppress his grin.

"Or understand irony," Ria said.

"That, too."

"Good morning, Mr. Armstrong. Ria," Ms. Ritter said, a tall tow-headed boy at her side.

"Excuse me," Ria said. "He's *Doctor* Armstrong."

The teacher glared at her, then softened the scowl into a fake smile. "Yes, yes, so he is. Welcome to our humble academy. This is Jim Bob Johnson, the sharpest young man I've ever had the pleasure to teach."

"You're only twelve?" Chuck asked the gangly youth with the blond peach fuzz mustache.

"I just turned thirteen on the Fourth of July," Jim Bob said, then looked at the teacher as if to ask if it was okay to tell the truth.

Ms. Ritter blushed at getting caught in the deception. "A month or two either way…" she said, then stepped back to let Chuck and Ria enter the classroom.

"Where are the other students?" Chuck asked.

"The whole lot of them is down with influenza," she said. "I told them to stay home if they were sick. We didn't need them to be spreading their germs around."

"Sound advice," Chuck said. He looked around the room and only saw six desks. "Where do you want Ria to sit?"

"Jim Bob sits up here next to me in front. She can pick any of the others as long as it isn't too close to him. We don't want eyes straying from their papers," she said, a sneer rising on one side of her face as she looked at Ria.

Chuck bit back his ire, his lower lip sucked in to keep from commenting.

"Don't worry," Ria deadpanned. "I'll keep my paper covered so he's not tempted," then allowed a self-righteous smirk to show.

Pride swelled in Chuck at her cleverness and ability to resist intimidation. "Here, Ria. Wipe the desk before you sit down. This year's influenza strain is particularly virulent."

Ria took the disposable wipe from him. "Yes, sir," she said, then bent to work, scrubbing the desk, hiding her wide grin

Ms. Ritter ignored the jabs and handed out the papers. When offered a pencil, though, Ria politely refused it. "No, thanks. I brought my own." She held up a four-inch-long paisley-printed pencil. It was her lucky pencil, one of the last items she still had from Friday.

"I'd prefer..." Ms. Ritter began, then realized she was being petty, insisting that she use one of her standard yellow pencils. She looked up at the clock. "This is five pages of work pertaining to everything a student should know by the time he or she graduates from the sixth grade. You have one hour to complete the test. No bathroom breaks until you're finished."

"Isn't this the same one I took last June?" Jim Bob asked.

The teacher blushed crimson this time. "No, this is a different one," she lied, her eyes blinking rapidly trying to regain composure.

"Oh, okay," he said, then looked over at Chuck and shrugged one shoulder.

An awkward silence filled the room as both students stared at Ms. Ritter. Chuck finally said, "They're waiting for you to tell them they can start."

"All right, class," she said. "Begin. One hour is all you have. Wrong answers will count against you, so no guessing."

Ria bent to the task, whizzing through the math problems, double-checking the instructions. She raised her hand in the air.

"No questions," Ms. Ritter said.

"I think she's allowed one," Chuck countered. "She's never taken one of your tests. If it isn't appropriate, you don't have to answer it. Ria, what's your question?"

"Am I supposed to show my work on the math problems? It doesn't say?"

"Either way," Ms. Ritter said, then looked at Jim Bob, still working on the first question. "You know, there's a song we used to sing in our classroom to help us remember," she said, then looked at Jim Bob again, trying to get his attention.

The boy was intent, though, and didn't have time for her.

She started humming a tune, totally out of character for the prim woman, then Chuck realized what she was doing. "Hold on a minute," he said when he saw Jim Bob's eyes brighten. At hearing the tune, he quickly ran through the page, marking off numbers of the multiple-choice questions without even reading them.

"What's wrong?" Ms. Ritter asked.

"I'll tell you what's wrong," Chuck said, taking the paper off Jim Bob's desk. He looked at the boy and read the second question. "Jim Bob, what's seven times six plus two?"

The boy's eyes squinted tight as he tried to visualize the problem.

Chuck turned the paper face down and said, "Go ahead and write it out if you need to."

Jim Bob did, but came up with an answer of forty-five.

"Okay, next question. If you had five cars and all had four wheels and two cars had six wheels, how many tires would you need? Go ahead and write it down. I can repeat it if you'd like."

Jim Bob tried, but couldn't figure it out. Chuck turned the paper over. "So, how come you got these answers so quickly?"

"Because this is an ABBACDCD test," he said.

"And how did you know that?"

"Because of the song Ms. Ritter was humming. It's a tool, she told us."

"Yeah, well, she's the real tool," Chuck said. "Ms. Ritter, how about giving me two other tests? One that doesn't have a song attributed to it."

"Done!" Ria said.

"But that was less than ten minutes," Ms. Ritter said. "How'd you get done so fast? Did you guess?"

"Nope. You said I didn't have to show my work. These were easy. Daddy gives me tougher tests. Do you want to check them or should he?"

"Here," the teacher said, snatching it from Ria's hand.

Ms. Ritter went down the page, chanting ABBACDCD as she went, verifying the coded answers. "She must have cheated."

"You're the only one who cheated," Chuck said. "And you're certainly not doing Jim Bob or anyone else any favors by giving them answer keys. Do you think life is going to give them cheats on how to survive in the real world? Or maybe you don't have faith that they deserve anything but a second-grade education? Nope, you're not getting my daughter into this school. As a matter of fact, I think you should be reported to the school district."

"No, no, don't do that. They can't get any teachers to come out here. I'm all they have."

"Well, then teach! I see books on the shelf. Teach them skills they can use in life. That was a great question about tires and wheels. Keep up with real-life situations and how to fix them. Tell them how to halve or double a recipe, how to balance a checkbook or fill out a job application. For God's sake, teach them to read!"

"Are we done now, Daddy?"

"Yes, we are. Jim Bob, nice meeting you. If you're ever in our neck of the woods, drop by and say hi. I have a few books you might want to borrow."

"Thank you, sir."

"Come on, Ria. Let's go see if we can catch a frog. It's time for a biology lesson."

***

Five years later – Lakeview, Pennsylvania

"Hello, Dr. Armstrong. I'm Harvey Taylor, the school teacher in this area. I'd like to invite your daughter to attend our school. It's a state law, by the way."

"Ria's homeschooled," Chuck explained, knowing this was going to be the same scenario it always was when they changed locations.

"Are you a certified teacher?" he asked.

"No, but let's make this quick for both of us. How about setting up an appointment for my daughter to take a grade placement test. Do your elementary schools graduate at the sixth or eighth-grade level?"

"Eighth grade around here."

"Fine. Let's meet at your school tomorrow at ten o'clock. If Ria passes your eighth-grade placement tests, you'll give her a certificate and leave us alone."

"But, sir, she's only ten, maybe eleven years old."

"Ten, but that doesn't matter. Are you willing?"

"Yes, sir. I'll see you tomorrow."

The next day, eleven o'clock

"Well, that one was easy," Ria said, brandishing her diploma. "Do you think they'll let me take the high school test?"

"Don't get cocky. You're not even a woman yet. We'll keep up with your studies. At least, the libraries around here are better than the ones in the backwoods. I'd love for you to attend at least one semester of real high school for the science labs they can provide. Plus, it wouldn't hurt for you to learn how to get along with kids your own age."

"But they're so boring," Ria said.

"Cluck, cluck, cluck," Chuck replied.

"Yeah, yeah, yeah. I'm getting cocky again."

"But so perceptive. Let's go grab our tackle and go fishing to celebrate."

"Ah, Daddy. You're so perceptive, too."

"Well, I can't think of any time you don't want to go fishing, but you're right. You get that from me."

Ria turned away and grimaced. He was a wonderful man – probably the most perfect one in the world – but he'd never talk about her mother. One of these days, though, she'd find out about her. Until then, she'd claim all the good things she had were from him. Her doubts and insecurities must come from her mother because he certainly didn't seem to have any.

Chapter 6: Thirteen

June 2005
Wolf Whistle, West Virginia (again)

Ria picked her way through the woods, following the deer path to the wide spot in the stream that historically had the best trout fishing. She had broken her fishing pole on her last expedition but had the reclaimed brass eyelet screws and line in one pocket, her Leatherman tool in the other, ready to construct a new willow pole. She always had a mint tin filled with fishing lures in her hip pocket, ready to tie on at dusk, the best time of day for catching trout.

She had taken to the trail early today, though. Something was going on. Daddy seldom asked her to 'make herself scarce' unless he felt the person coming to the clinic was a bad influence or was foul-mouth and without restraint. Or was a scummy lowlife who he feared might try to hit on her or make a pass.

She knew all about the facts of life – both the physical aspects and the social ones. Over the years, many battered women had come to them for help. They were usually distraught, totally without a filter on their explanations of how they had got so messed up, blathering on and on about what their man had done – or tried to do – to them sexually. Her father had explained to her early on that in a perfect world, the assaults would never happen. Almost every time, there was alcohol involved. A few times, they had packed up their home and clinic on a minute's notice, spiriting away a woman and her children to a relative in a different town, one time their trek taking them two states away.

It really was providence, Divine intervention, he explained. It was better to be fluid in their lives and help others than let the abuses continue. If they had remained where they were and simply sent the woman on her way, the man would probably figure out who had done the sheltering or relocating – the new guy in the area. Twice Daddy had been attacked by the angry spouse-type person. The couples weren't always married, but the man always felt as if the woman was his to do with as he pleased. It didn't help that the children saw this and carried it on into their lives as adults. 'Daddy had to knock some sense into Mama' made sense to the boys. And the girls thought that was the way life was supposed to be, too.

"We have to help break the cycle, Ria. We fix bodies, but if we can fix spirits and lives, too, then we should. We're blessed to be so mobile."

And that was part of their problem today. The RV they had been living in since she was six-months-old was finally giving up. Metal fatigue was literally making it fall apart at the seams. The wind blew through every crack and crevice, bringing moisture with it when it rained or snowed. It was summer now, but they knew they had to do something before the freezing nights began in late

September. The structure was too feeble to drive to another spot. The universal joint had fallen apart again, and this time, the driveline was so rotted out, a complete one would be needed to make it go again. The cost of one was more than the vehicle was worth.

And that's why Daddy had called Silas.

"If anything ever happens to me, you call this number," he said, showing her the plastic business card stuck to the refrigerator that was now just an icebox. It, like just about everything else, had failed. "I'm hoping he can find us out here. I've made arrangements for another home for us."

"Please tell me we're leaving this vacuum."

"Vacuum?" he asked.

"Yes, I swear it sucks the life right out of me. You know, when you blow hard over an object, it creates a vacuum? Well, the wind blows so hard here, it may not suck the life out of me, but it sure zaps the joy out of everything. Well, except for the fishing, and that's only in one spot."

Chuck looked at his watch, verifying the time of his inner clock. "Head on down and do some fishing. Give me an hour or two. Better yet, I'll come and join you later. He should be gone before dark."

"No worries," Ria said. She grabbed an apple from the counter, noticed it had a wormhole in it, then grabbed another one, just as marginal. "I'll make sure I cut it before eating it."

"The only thing worse than finding a worm in your apple..." Chuck began.

"Is finding half a worm," she finished. "I am so ready to leave!"

"Catch dinner first," Chuck said, then kissed her on the top of her head, his eyes open, checking for ticks. "And keep away from the bushes. Deer ticks are rampant this year."

Five minutes down the trail, the sound of a man crying brought Ria out of her introspection about life and where it would take her and her father this time. No matter what, it would be different. They would have a new home. She trusted him to figure out how they would leave this desolate valley and find a motorhome.

It was a young man, maybe eighteen but certainly no more than twenty, and he definitely wasn't from around here. He was wearing clean, unripped denim jeans, not frayed and work-worn overalls. His dark hair was short and appearance overall was well-groomed. She looked down and saw he was wearing bright white and red sports shoes, not muddy boots. Yes, he was a transplant, probably lost and that was why he was crying.

Ergh! Don't assume! Daddy said to get the facts first, then deal with the situation. Assuming makes you the first part of that word: an ass.

"Excuse me," Ria said. "Is there something wrong?"

Evan wiped his nose with the back of his hand, wishing he had long sleeves instead. He looked up and stared. "Stillwater?"

Ria looked over at the pool where she loved to fish. "Yes, it's still water. That makes for the best fishing. Watch," she said, hoping to distract him and get him out of his funk. She bent down and grabbed a fistful of sandy soil and tossed it into the water. *Plop, plop, plop.* "See? Nothing."

"No, that's not what I meant, but what are you doing?"

"When the time is right for the fish to feed, they'll be all over the place, jumping out of the water to catch the mayflies. You see, that's what they think that surface disturbance is: hatchlings. They come up to feed. At least, the trout do. Catching catfish is a whole different method."

"Okay. That's logical. But are you a Stillwater? You look just like our friend's daughter. I can't remember her name. I haven't seen her for a few years, but if you aren't her, you could be her twin."

"Nope. I'm not a Stillwater. And if I have a twin, my daddy never told me about her. So, is whatever was bothering you over?" Ria reached in her hip pocket and took out a red handkerchief and handed it to him. "Here, take this one. I have dozens at home."

"Thanks," he said and turned away to blow his nose. He turned back, started to offer it back to her, then realized how crude that was. "If you don't mind, may I keep this? I can pay you for it," he said, fumbling in his hip pocket for his wallet.

"No, I don't mind if you keep it, but I do mind if you try to pay for a gift. Lots of folks who come to our clinic pay in goods. We wind up with dozens of afghans and handkerchiefs, chickens and canned foods. We don't have money, but we keep fairly warm and well-fed. At least, we eat a lot of eggs. When the hens quit laying, then we get fried chicken or chicken and dumplings."

"And fish," Evan said, nodding to the long bare stick she held.

"Were you trying to fish here?" she asked, then sat down on the boulder next to him, not wanting to whittle her pole while standing. Besides, this was her favorite spot in the whole world. So far. She'd share it but didn't want to give it up.

"Well, sort of. I got mad a few minutes ago and threw the pole upstream as far as I could. I felt better for about ten seconds. Then I tried to retrieve it and got soaked." He stepped down on the ground and his shoe squished.

"Take off your shoes and turn them upside down. Loosen the laces first and pull the tongue and insole out so air can get inside. They won't dry completely, but by the time we get done fishing, your feet will be dry and the shoes won't be sopping wet."

"Sounds like the voice of experience," he said. "Oh, and I'm Evan, by the way."

"Evan by-the-way, I'm Ria Armstrong. My dad's the doctor around here. I'm his helper."

"Armstrong? Are you any relation to Papa Doc Armstrong?"

"I don't know. I never heard the name. The only relative I have is my father, Charles Darwin Armstrong. Folks who know him well call him Chuck. I only know his real name because that's what's on his driver's license."

"That's why we're here – to see a guy named Chuck. We drove a big ol' RV in here. I guess Silas is going to drive all of us out of here in it, back to the car I drove in. We caravanned into a little town about half an hour away. The roads were too rough to tow anything, even a compact car. I guess we're all going to leave via the RV. When we get back to the Bug, Silas and I will go back to hell. I mean, Massachusetts."

"Why did you say hell? And get back to what bug? That sounds more ominous than going back to hell!"

"Bug is the nickname of a car: a small Volkswagen car. Hell is because I don't want to face life anymore. My father died. Everywhere I go at home, I'm reminded of him, of all the fun he and Dad and I used to have. I literally hurt right here," Evan said, touching his breastbone.

"Are you sure you don't have a bruised sternum?" Ria asked, then sucked back her embarrassment. "Sorry. It's the doctor in me, always looking for a physiological answer to pain. I remember that pain now, though. I guess at one point, I really had a mother, but I don't remember her. I had someone in my life who was a mother figure, though. Friday and Daddy took care of me since the minute I was born. She left when I was almost five. They say you don't remember anything before that age, but I do. I barely remember her face, but I remember the pain of loss. You're right. It's smack dab in the middle of the chest."

"How did you get over it?"

"Time. Oh, and distracting myself with doing positive stuff. I mean, it may sound weird, but I work hard at learning everything I can. Daddy had been training her to be a medic and I was right alongside her, learning everything. I bugged him after she left to continue teaching me as if she was right there next to me. She was sort of my invisible friend. I knew she wasn't dead, and he promised me that I'd see her again someday, but I took what I could. Do you think you could do that for your father?"

"Yeah, I think so. At least, I know he'd be proud of me. Shoot, he was always proud of me. Both dads were, but Father was so sure I'd wind up a doctor, too. 'You're so much like me at your age,' he'd say. It was definitely encouraging."

"Evan, if he was alive right now, he'd be saying the same thing, I'm sure. You seem like a decent guy. Does that mean you're all alone now? What about your mother?"

"As I said, I had two dads. I'm down to one. Like you, I never knew my mother. My two dads adopted me when I was a few days old. They said I was their fifty-grand present to themselves."

"They bought you?"

"Yup. Hey, not many people start life having their worth practically pasted on their ass. I mean, butt."

"Ass is right in this situation. But, how can you have two dads? Isn't that illegal or something?"

"No, it's not illegal. Two people of the same gender can get married in most states in the union although it's still a capital offense in many countries. Where have you been all your life? You didn't know about this?"

"We've been in the backwoods since the day I was born, I think. If my dad didn't tell me or I didn't read it in a book, I didn't believe it. You'd be surprised at some of the nonsense these folks believe. Did you know that some of these women still believe that babies won't be conceived unless they're married? They're all sorts of confused to find out they're pregnant before the preacher comes around."

Evan chuckled. "Yeah, and it was probably the guys who told them that, too."

Ria laughed and pointed at him, "You're right! How long have you been around here?"

Evan looked down at his Rolex. "About an hour. You know, you're a great distraction. How old are you?"

Ria sighed, not wanting to let the sharp, handsome young man know she was so young. "I'm a high school graduate. I'm taking some correspondence college classes, but I probably won't graduate with a BS unless I go to a brick and mortar facility. That's one reason Daddy wants us out of here. He says this area is holding me back."

"Well, it looks like we're going to be around each other for a few more hours, at least. Why don't you show me how to fish with a stick?"

"Well, unless you're going to spear them, you need a hook and line, and preferably, a fly."

Evan looked up and focused on an imaginary house fly, then reached up and snatched the air. "Here," he said, offering it to her.

Ria took the pretend fly and put it in her mouth. "I'll keep it in here until I'm ready with the line," she mumbled as if her mouth was full.

"Ria," Evan said, laughing, "you make life worth living. I hate to say how miserable I was, but that all seems like a bad dream now."

Ria gulped, then laughed. "I accidentally swallowed it," she said, feigning a frown. "Don't catch another one until I'm ready."

Two hours went by, the young couple laughing and bumping shoulders at their jokes and silliness. When the sun got lower in the sky, Evan bent down and grabbed a fistful of sandy soil, then threw it where Ria had earlier. Suddenly the pool was alive with little fish mouths poking up, an occasional trout leaping completely out of the water. "Look at that!" he exclaimed.

"Shush," Ria said. "They're dumb but not deaf. Now, watch me." She whipped the pole with the string and bird-feather fly tied to it overhead, then let the lure settle on the surface. *Zap!*

"You got one," Evan whispered excitedly, "and on the first try, too."

"They're hungry tonight," she said, bringing the line in, hand over hand. "Normally, I let the first ones go, but it looks like it's going to be four for supper, so we'll keep them. Do you want to try?" she asked, setting the flopping fish into the shallow holding pool she had excavated years ago.

"I thought you'd never ask." Evan took the pole from her and tried to copy her smooth movement. "Don't laugh. This is my first time. I've fished before, but it was off the back of a boat in the ocean. Swordfish are tough to reel in, but this looks like more of a challenge."

"Only if you don't know what you're doing or fishing in the wrong spot."

Evan caught a twelve-inch trout on his second try. "Oh, my God! I can't believe it!" he hissed, screaming in a whisper.

Ria removed it from the hook and added it to hers. "Go for at least two more. They'll be biting for just a few more minutes, and then they're done for the day."

The fourth fish was a whopper: fifteen inches long, at least. Evan pointed the tip of the pole toward Ria for her to take off the fish and add it to the holding pool. Instead, she took a device out of her pocket, clicked it over his tail fin, then released it back into the main pool.

"Why'd you do that?" he asked.

"He's the old man of the pond. He stays here. I guess I should have let you punch his tail fin. When I release a fish back into the water, I mark him. It's just a hole puncher and I don't make a complete hole, just a little arc. I want to track how many times I've caught the same fish." She bent down to the holding pool and picked up a twelve-inch fish by the gills. "See his tail? I've caught and released him at least six times. A few times, I've forgotten the hole punch, but you get the idea. I kept all these today because from what it sounds like, this is my last time fishing here. Still, the old man needs to stick around."

"Wow, that's cool," Evan said. "So, do you think we should be heading back? The sun is getting low and I don't know my way around here. I guess I should have stayed where I was. Silas won't know to look for me here. Then again, Silas is known for his tracking skills. He can find anyone or anything with the slightest of clues."

"Silas Priest or Holmes?" Ria asked, chuckling.

"Priest, but he's a sort of Sherlock Holmes. So, I guess you've heard of him?"

"Slightly. I just know that if something happens to my dad, there's a card on the fridge with his name and number. I guess he's my escape from hell ticket."

249

"Funny, that's what my father told me, too. It's weird that we're connected that way."

"Yeah, weird," Ria echoed. She took out her Leatherman and gutted the fish, throwing the remains into the water.

"Isn't that polluting the water?"

"Nope, that's feeding the catfish and crawdads." She picked up a stick and ran it through the gills of the four large trout. "Here, you caught 'em, I cleaned 'em, and you can tote them back. I'll let Dad cook them. I want to meet this guy, Silas. I gotta know who he is and why I was kicked out of the clinic because he was coming. Something's fishy and it isn't the trout."

"You're right," Evan said. "I'm almost always within earshot of him when we go anywhere. Then again, maybe he thought the woods would cure my moodiness."

Ria looked up at him. Tall, dark-haired, intelligent. A tingle swept over her body, settling in her groin, a warm feeling she'd never had before. Her eyes opened wide. So that's what all the chatter is about! My first crush! *Makes sense. Two months after my first period and now I'm getting urges. Crap! I don't want to wind up like these other women, at the mercy of hormones. But dang! It feels so good!*

"Are you all right, Ria?"

Ria looked up and grinned. "Yeah, I'm fine. Just a flush. I'm sure it will go away." *But do you want it to go away? Dang, dang, double dang!*

"Here they are," Chuck said when he saw them approach. "So, you're Gregory's grandson."

"And Keith and John's son," Evan said, his hand out to shake Chuck's. "But I guess Silas told you that John died two months ago."

"Yes, he did. That was unfortunate." Chuck winced at his choice of words. "Shoot, I'm sorry, losing a parent is so much more than that. I'm sure it was devastating. How's Keith doing?"

"He's grieving. We all are. Even Grandpa Gregory, the ironman of composure, lost it. John wasn't his biological son, but he loved him just as much, maybe even more since he had chosen to be a part of the family, not obligated to be."

"That's a wonderful way to put it," Chuck said. "So, it looks like you and Ria found each other."

Ria blushed unexpectedly at the words 'each other.' Chuck noticed it but didn't react. Instead, he nodded to the stick in Evan's hand. "Looks like I have four fish to fry. I'm glad you caught big ones. It's our last night here and we might as well feast. Too bad you didn't catch the old man."

"I did, but Ria put him back. It was nice seeing him, though. After she told me about him, I sort of felt bad about these," Evan said.

"Don't," Ria said, coming up to touch his elbow in reassurance. "Just think

250

of these fish as carrots in the garden, put there for us to harvest. We just left the old man in his element so he could get bigger. His day will come, but it wasn't today."

"Sounds like you've brought up a philosopher," Silas said. He put out his hand. "I don't think we've ever met," he said, studying her face, so much like Vickie's.

"She looks a lot like the Stillwater's girl, doesn't she?" Evan asked.

"That girl's a Thornwhistle," Silas corrected. "Hal Stillwater and Roger are cousins. They're close, very close." *No need to share the girl's name or tell anyone that they're sisters! Chuck already knows it and Evan doesn't need to.*

Chuck felt the awkwardness in the air and decided a distraction was needed. "Silas, while I get this fish going, would you show Ria around the new RV? You're more familiar with it than I am, anyhow."

"It would be my pleasure." Silas turned sideways, arm stretched out to grandstand the introduction to their new residence and clinic. "Your new castle, Miss."

"It's not new, Ria," Chuck called after them. "It's gently used, but definitely much better than what we've had for the last thirteen years."

"Wow!" Ria went to the sink and marveled at the faucet, touching the spray head appreciably. "And this range! Three burners and an oven, too? What's this?"

"That's a microwave. It runs on electricity, not gas. There's a built-in generator by the back wheel well. It runs on gas, so I guess in a way, the microwave does, too," Silas explained, then looked away, resisting the urge to stare and try to find differences between the two girls. He knew there weren't any, though. They were definitely identical. Two of three.

Ria stepped into the back. "Two bedrooms!" she exclaimed. "You mean, I get my own room? I won't have to sleep on the kitchen bench?"

"That's right," Silas said. "That's one of the requirements your father asked for: privacy for you. As you can see, it's still small, but any bigger and it would be too big to drive into the spots you two seem to be so fond of finding to set up shop."

"Clinic," Ria corrected mindlessly as she looked around the living room. "These chairs will have to go. We can put our old exam table right here, maybe a small desk and two chairs there in the corner. Yes, get rid of the couch and this could be the perfect office and exam room combination." She looked up at Silas. "Did you know I've never been in a traditional doctor's office? One of these days, I'd like to check one out just to see how the rest of the world works."

"When I get my own place, I'll make sure you're one of the first to see it," Evan said.

Silas looked at the youth, then grinned. These were the first words of hope for his future Evan had spoken since his father had fallen ill to cancer. The long ordeal had taken its toll on him, but evidently, there was more than one kind of healing in these backwoods. He noticed the look on Evan's face as he watched for Ria's answer. Oops! He'd have to make sure the boy – young man, he reminded himself – knew that Ria was only thirteen. There was definitely an attraction between the two.

***

"Daddy, I have a question for you," Ria said, pensive but curious. She'd never felt this hesitation before and didn't want to be intimidated by her new emotion.

"You know you can ask me anything," he said, suddenly uneasy at her wariness.

"Did you know that two men could be a couple?"

"Yes, and two women can be, too. Why do you ask?"

"Because Evan said he had two dads but one of them died."

"Yes, I knew both of them before you were born. They were very happily married."

"How come I never knew about it?"

"I never saw a reason to bring it up. You were never going to meet them, as far as I knew. John and Keith, that is. There are loads of same-sex couples, but in these backwoods, most of the people are ultra-conservative. They don't believe that it's possible for two people of the same gender to be compatible, to want to live their lives together as a couple." He looked deep into her eyes. "Every one of us is different. One of these days, you'll start to get urges. I don't know if you'll get them for another woman or a man. It doesn't matter which. As long as you are responsible and don't have sex before you're married, all will be fine."

"So, if I fell in love and wanted to marry another woman, you'd let me?"

"Ria, you can pretty much do anything you want after you're eighteen. I'd prefer that you decided on who you wanted to spend the rest of your life with after you were in your twenties or thirties, though. Before that, urges are mostly hormonal. Strictly chemical with a tad of physical appeal thrown in."

"You mean most people don't fall in love with ugly people?"

"Skin ugly is usually what people see first. After getting to know a person, you'll see the inner beauty. The same goes for someone who is handsome on the outside. They can be horribly ugly inside: mean, vicious, or cruel. Just get to know people before deciding how close you want to be to them. Be nice to others. If they don't treat you the same way, then move on. They don't belong in your life."

"So, you and Friday…" she prompted, hoping he would answer her inferred question.

"I loved Friday very much, but we didn't have that physical attraction. She and Angus did. Now, are we done with this? I need to finish taking what I want from this place. We're heading out early in the morning."

"Yes, sir," she said, using her 'be polite to new people' voice. "I'll be ready in the morning, too."

* * *

Later that evening

"So, Silas, did you happen to see Vickie when you went to pick up my loan from the Thornwhistles?"

"Yes, I did. We didn't interact, though. She was on her way out the door with her nanny. It's eerie, seeing both girls. They truly are identical. They move alike, have the same sway when they walk, even flip their hair out of their faces in the same manner."

"Have you ever seen the other one, Tori?"

"Nope. Luther and Leanne evidently sold everything they had and headed west. Not that they had much. They were botanists but the patents Luther should have been credited for went to his boss. I would have been bitter about the loss, but he said it had to be a sign that corporate life wasn't for them. I'm not sure where they are, but I can find out if you'd like."

"No, don't bother. I'm sure they'll pop up sometime in the future," Chuck said, an empty spot in his gut screaming for closure. *Just tell him you'd like to see all the girls together one more time. Chicken!* Chuck shook off his insecurities and looked back at Silas. "What about Keith? How's he doing?"

"I'm sure he'd love to see you again, but I think he still has a lot of grieving left to work through. It's been hard on him and Evan. Tonight was the first time I've heard anything positive out of the boy. I know they're not related biologically, but they're similar in so many ways. Keith may be more of a numbers sort of man, but he's also passionate about life and making the most out of it. I see the same trait in Evan. It wouldn't hurt for you to pop into their lives and do a little mentoring for his son."

"Silas, I don't have to hide anything from you. The truth is, I still have feelings for Keith. It's been twenty years since we were together. Whether it was puppy love or not doesn't make a difference. He's like a twenty-dollar chocolate truffle. I know I can't indulge, but the desire is still there."

"Chuck, give it time. Evan was supposed to start pre-med this fall. When John started going downhill fast, both he and Keith put their lives on hold to be with him every minute possible. When he died, Evan spent a lot of time alone. The isolation was tough on Keith, but he knew his son had to grieve in his own way. Seeing you make something out of nothing in this poor section of the world gives the boy a sparkle in his eye I thought wasn't possible."

"Are you sure the sparkle wasn't for Ria?"

Silas chuckled. "Yeah, well there is that attraction. Don't worry. I'll make sure he knows her age. He has a lot of school left before he can go out on his own."

"You said he was starting pre-med in the fall. He couldn't be more than nineteen. How'd he do that?"

"He's eighteen. Like Ria, he's bright. Very bright. He graduated from high school at fourteen, then did five years of college in four. He has a passion for healing that I've only seen twice before."

Chuck grinned. "Don't tell me; Dad and me."

"Okay, I won't tell you, but you're right. By the way, the old man says you owe him about thirteen birthday and Christmas cards. Don't keep away too long. He may be out of the woods when it comes to cancer, but you and I know that it could come back at any time. Even if not, he's not a spring chicken."

"Yeah, he's an old cock and sent you here to give me a heavy dose of guilt for staying away."

"He doesn't need to give you any and neither do I. Anyone with any acuity at all could see you've been beating yourself up for the last decade or so. When are you going to come back and see Grace? You know, don't you, that she doesn't know she had triplets. It was four years before she knew that her 'twins' were even possibly alive. That so-and-so doctor who delivered her told her they died."

"He did? I knew he had told the other two sets of parents that she had died in childbirth and the babies with her, but I didn't know he told Grace they were dead, too. Good God, man. That's horrible! Grace must have thought she was responsible somehow. Shit! I don't need this kind of guilt!"

"You don't need any kind of guilt. You saved the girls and from what I've heard, you also saved that young woman you call Friday. Whatever happened to her?"

"A big, dark-haired Scot came out of the woods and spirited her away. Took her to Scots Dale or someplace in these woods and married her. He said he wanted to give her lots of babies, so I hope that's what happened. If you ever hear from her, let me know, would you?"

"Why would I hear from her?" Silas asked.

"Because I gave her one of your cards. I gave one to her husband, too. Angus McDermott is his name. I didn't know I was going to miss her so much. It's been eight years, but it hurts like it was last week."

"Chuck, I love you like a son," he said, his hand heavy and comforting on his shoulder, "so I'm telling you this. Find someone. Even if it's just dating and casual groping, go out and interact. Make sure the next place you set up your clinic is near enough to civilization that you can go out and have a beer with the guys. At least then if you do come in and reconnect with Keith, you'll know whether it's an old infatuation or the real thing."

Chuck reached up and patted Silas's hand, grateful for the advice. "Thanks, I needed that. I mean, I really didn't need permission, but I did if you know what I mean."

254

"Absolutely. Come on. Let's go check out the accommodations."

"And chaperone the youngsters," Chuck added.

"Yup," Silas said. "I never reared a daughter, but when they get to this age, it has to be scary."

Chuck looked back at Silas with eyes narrowed. *He didn't say he'd never fathered a daughter. Maybe the rumors were true. Could he really be Grace's sire?* His face relaxed into a smile. *Sire, possibly. But Hal was one-hundred percent Grace's daddy.*

***

"Thanks for showing me how to fish," Evan said, his hand out to shake Ria's.

Instead, she came in and gave him a big hug like she'd seen her father give Silas. *Tingle!* She pulled back and half-smiled, half-grimaced at the new sensation. "I'll find another good fishing spot near wherever it is we're going next. Maybe you can come back."

"I'd like that. How about we have a standing fishing date? As they say, same time next year?"

Ria shrugged, hoping her blush wasn't as red as it felt. "I never heard that phrase, but sure. Silas and Dad keep in contact. I'm sure he'd like to come with you. Maybe your dad would like to come fishing, too? If he hasn't experienced it in a while, it might make him feel better."

Evan nodded, then looked away, the tears starting again. *Dammit!*

"Look, we all have to die. Your father is at peace right now. It's those he left behind who are hurting. I don't know if that makes you feel better or not, but I'm sure he'd want you to move on. Don't forget him, for sure, but find the joy in life. Remember the little things he taught you and share those with others. Did he teach you how to draw or tie fancy knots? How about baking or wood carving? That's what I'm talking about. You're his legacy. Don't let what he taught you in love be lost by not sharing."

"How old are you again?" Evan asked. "I mean, you don't look that old, but you sure have an adult spirit. You're smarter than the counselors I've been talking to for the last three months."

Ria punched him in the upper arm. "Age is just a number. Yup, I'm an old soul. That's what happens when you don't interact with kids your own age when you're growing up."

"Well, kudos to your dad for raising you right."

"I'm not a carrot or a tomato," Ria said with a smirk. "I'm a person. He reared me or brought me up."

"Gotcha," Evan said. He picked up her hand and kissed it gently. "Lady Ria."

She inhaled deeply at the sensation. "Rhianna," she sighed.

"All right then," he said, still holding her hand. He brought it up to his lips again and said, "Farewell, Lady Rhianna. I hope to see you next summer. Next time, I'll bring you a handkerchief."

"Come on, kids," Chuck said. "Break it up. Silas has stuff he needs to do back in the real world, I'm sure."

"Yes, I have 'stuff' to do," Silas said, "but I think *this* is the real world. Where we live is more synthetic. If I had to do it all over again, I'd be rural like you two."

A wide grin spread across Evan's face. "I like that idea. Being a country doctor sounds like a very good plan."

Chuck reached out to shake Evan's hand. "Just make sure you finish school first. You could do it without a degree but having that doctor's certificate will keep you out of trouble if it ever comes calling. Think of it as having a vaccine. Painful at first, but worth it in the long run to keep the really bad buggers away."

"See you next year, Dr. Armstrong," Evan said, shaking Chuck's hand heartily.

"And say hi to your dad for me," Chuck said. *And thanks for giving me hope, too.*

Chapter 7: Fifteen and Sixteen

Summer, 2006

"I hope you don't think of me as a bad penny that keeps showing up," Evan said.

Ria took the pole out of his hand and unwound the knot that had formed around one of the eyelets. "Bad penny? Nope. I can't even say you're an annoyance. Actually, other than you and Silas, we don't have anyone who keeps popping into our lives. Shoot, we're so mobile, I think that if I've known anyone for more than a year, they're an old acquaintance."

"So, you don't have any family at all?" Evan asked, taking back the pole.

"Just Dad and me."

"Me, too. Sorta," Evan said. His face skewed up, wondering if he should say something or not.

"Okay, what's on your mind," Ria said. "You have that look again..."

"Well, if you're Rhianna Armstrong and your dad is Chuck Armstrong, that means that Papa Doc is your grandfather."

"Who?"

"Papa Doc."

"Papa Doc Duvalier? The Haitian dictator?"

"Ugh! No, Papa Doc Armstrong. He lives up the road from us. I see him at barbecues and get-togethers every once in a while. My dad's been getting out more and more and taking me with him."

"Why do you think we're related?"

"Duh! Come on, Ria. Same last name, same friends, same occupation..."

"Could be a coincidence."

"They look alike, too. I mean, Chuck's a younger version of Papa Doc. I could ask if you'd like."

"Nah, I'll ask my dad when the time is right. He's kind of sensitive about our isolation and the reasons behind it. I mean, his mission is to take care of people in rural areas without access to health care, but sometimes I think it's just an excuse to stay hidden."

"Do you think he's on the lam or something?"

"Lamb?"

"Lam. It's a term that means he's lying low to keep away from the law."

"Nope. If he was, he wouldn't be using his real name."

"True. Not that you advertise or anything."

"Word of mouth has been working for fifteen years. Why spend money on it?"

"Hey," Evan said, suddenly changing the subject and his attitude. He set the fishing pole on the ground next to the blanket. "I want to take a picture of

257

you. I got this new phone and the camera in it is fantastic."

"A camera in a phone?" Ria strode through the shallow water to where he stood digging into his front pocket.

"Yeah, it's the latest cellphone. It won't work out here for making calls because there aren't any cell towers, but I can still take pictures and notes or do computations on it. It has a calculator and even some games to play if I'm really bored. Actually, the only game I ever play is Solitaire."

"I understood two things: calculator and Solitaire. I have a calculator at home and a deck of cards to play Solitaire. How does that relate to a phone?"

"Haven't you ever seen digital or electronic games?"

"I've seen pinball machines. Is that what you mean?"

"Come over here and let me show you," Evan said, guiding her back to the bank where their blanket was spread out. "One of these days, I'm going to have to get your father to take you to where real civilization is." Seeing the frown on her face, he changed his approach. "There is a whole different world once you get on the grid."

Ria's scowl grew, indignation close and anger only one wrong word away.

"The electrical grid is what folks generally mean, but ninety-five percent of America – or thereabouts – are connected by computers and electronics. One day, there will be free wi-fi for everyone, everywhere, mark my words."

"I know what hi-fi is. Is wi-fi just another form of high fidelity?"

"Actually, it's a trademark name referring to wireless networking connections. Do you have a telephone?"

"No, but I know what one is. If we need one, we go to the library or a market. They almost always have a payphone."

"And those phones are connected to wires which are connected to more wires, right?"

"Yes…"

"Well, this IEEE 802.11x technology uses radio waves to communicate from a base to the unit receiving the waves. In a home network, the router moves the signal from a cell tower or cable to a device such as a computer or a cellphone. This cellphone has little bars that show how strong the signal is."

Ria took the phone and turned it over, checking out the bright blue and white cover and small built-in monitor screen. "I don't see any bars on this."

Evan scooted close to her and leaned in to shade the sun from the device. "Here, it was sleeping." He clicked the button and the screen brightened up to show a river scene with a young Evan and two men, one at either side, all of them smiling. The image was peppered with small icons.

"That's me and my dads when I was thirteen. I'm not very old, but those were the good old days. Those little pictures are shortcut icons to apps."

"I'd say you were speaking Greek, but since I know some Greek, that has to be a whole new language."

"You're close. I was speaking Geek. There are new words coming into the English language every day. Apps is short for applications, but everyone says apps. Technology has become a universal language. People are connected to the internet all over the world. It's unstoppable. Revolutions can be won or lost with information or the lack of it. These little devices are the key. Did you know they even have phones that don't need cell towers – the repeaters? They bounce the signals off of satellites." He pointed to the sky. "Scary, huh?"

"Does that mean those satellites can look down on the user, too?"

"Probably. They have imaging that can read the text on the book a man's reading from its orbit miles above the earth." He thought about what he had just said. "Well, if they don't have that ability today, they will in the next few years. The learning curve of man and artificial intelligence devices is phenomenal. Just think of it as how much faster you started accumulating data after you started reading."

"Accumulating data? That's a weird way to say learn." Ria ran her tongue over her teeth as she realized how ignorant she was of the world. She knew more about the human body and healing than most people, but a simple word such as 'app' was foreign to her. Four-year-olds in ninety-five percent of the world probably knew what it meant!

"Do you think my dad knows about cellphones?"

Evan's face fell. He had said too much. He knew Chuck had a cellphone. It was old technology but still worked. Silas had sent him texts on it in the past. The texts wouldn't show up unless Chuck moved into an area with cell reception, but the two of them had agreed years ago to do that at least once a month. "You'll have to ask Chuck about that," he said, skirting the answer that wasn't his to share.

Ria sighed deeply. The conflict on Evan's face was as plain as the freckles across the bridge of his nose. She wouldn't push it. "So, where's the camera in this thing?" she asked, leaning as close as she dared. She'd like to think she had control over her own body, but it took more effort not to reach out and touch him when he was seated close and without a shirt.

Pushing arrow and enter buttons on the bottom half of the device, Evan opened up several apps and finally the camera. "Would you let me take a picture of you?"

"Yeah, why not?"

"How about going over there and holding up a couple of those fish we caught? You can hold up mine, too, if you'd like."

"Nah. I'll just hold up my big one. Can you make a print copy for my dad? As far as I know, he doesn't have any pictures of me."

Evan's eyes widened but he remained mum. Talk about a private man! He was positively obsessive with his desire to keep himself and his daughter in hiding.

Ria held up the twelve-inch-long trout up and smiled.

Snap! Snap!

"Now, make a silly face. This one's for me."

Holding the fish so she was face-to-face with it, Rhianna pretended to kiss it.

"Perfect! Now, put it back with the others then step away. I want your whole body in this shot."

"Why?"

"Because when I come back next year, I want you to see how much you've changed. I wish I had taken a picture of you the first day we met. You were a cutie then, but nothing like you are now. I can't wait to see what you look like when you're fully grown."

"Well, I have to say that sounds sexist and condescending and a few other negative adjectives!" said in a harsh tone.

"No, no! That's not what I meant," Evan answered. "Do you want to take a picture of me? I'm sure I've changed a lot since we first met, too."

"Stand up and turn around," Ria said, her tone still chilly.

"I really didn't mean to offend you," he said softly, obeying her instructions, slowly turning in place. "I'd never intentionally say or do anything to upset you or embarrass you or…"

"Hold it right there," Ria said, cutting off his groveling. "You look like you've added more muscle mass. Have you been working out?"

His back to her, he looked over his shoulder and said, "I'm on the rowing team in school. I know I had to buy larger shirts. I also grew an inch and a half in the last year. I guess I'm a late bloomer."

"Yeah, well, as my daddy always says, perfection takes time."

Evan's face reddened. He cleared his throat and turned to face her. "So, do you think I'm perfect?"

"Nope, but you're getting there."

"My turn," Evan said. "Let me check you out. I mean, I just finished a class in whole body diagnostics. Let me see if I can spot something wrong that even you don't know about."

"Okay…" Ria said hesitantly. "What do you want me to do?"

"Turn away from me."

"Shirt on or off?" she asked.

"Off. I mean, it has to be off so I can see your spine."

Ria yanked her tee-shirt off over her head and tossed it onto the blanket. Last year's bathing suit top barely covered her perky breasts that had grown two sizes in the last year, but she knew she was still decent. "What now?"

You're a doctor, you're a doctor. Look at her with the eyes of an old man looking for defects. Evan touched the tops of both her shoulders at the same time, checking for similarity in muscle tone and height. Then he gently prodded her spine, causing her to giggle and squirm when he got near her waist and above her cutoff jeans. "Arms out straight like you're making a tee."

Ria obeyed, then waited patiently as he tried to lower her arms. "Resist me," he said.

"Every chance I get," she said, then laughed.

"Bend over at the waist," he directed, still standing behind her.

Ria formed a perfect right angle.

"All right. Stand up straight and look at me."

Ria gracefully pivoted in place and looked at him, then changed her focus from his dreamy blue eyes to the end of his nose. "Like this?"

"Shut your eyes, then arms out again and touch your right index finger to your nose. All right, left index finger to nose."

"How much longer? I want to go swimming. It's getting hot."

"Just a couple more. Stand on one foot. Now the other. Shoot! I can't remember the rest of the poses. Yes, Ria, you're pretty much perfect. At least, you're coordinated and perfectly symmetrical."

"Done then?"

"Yeah, sure."

Her back still to him, she picked her way to the edge of the deep pool. "Too early for fishing," she said over her shoulder, then dove in, hiding her embarrassment at being intimately examined beneath the chilly water.

Evan set the phone down, kicked off his tennis shoes, and followed suit, coming up out of the water right next to her. "I don't ever want to fight with you or offend you. I know we're too young for anything serious, but you really are my best friend. I mean, I have lots of acquaintances in school and through the country club, but I never share anything deep with them. Like how I felt about the loss of my dad and such. You're the only one who knows the real me."

"But we only write letters and see each other once a year for a few days."

"Ria, do you realize how special you are? I have to respect the fact that you've been isolated and kept from the world as I know it. When I show you parts of it, though, you pick up on everything so quickly. You're bright and kind and everything a man could want as a partner or best friend."

"Except I'm too young..."

"Yeah, well, I'm definitely going to respect that! I don't know who would castrate me first if I did anything to compromise your virtue: Silas or your dad. I'm not going to find out, though. I never knew I was a patient man, but I'm finding out that I am. But, we both have a lot of growing to do and knowing that helps with restraint."

"How's school going?" Ria asked, her head bowed, very uncomfortable with the direction their conversation was going, especially since he was standing in the pool so close to her, his bare chest next to her barely covered one.

Evan reached over and brought her chin up so she was looking at him. She

261

was only a scant foot away, definitely in the danger zone if he couldn't control his urges. "I'm doing everything I can to graduate early. Everything, that is, except take summer classes that would interfere with the little bit of time we have together. Silas's excuse for bringing me along on his annual checkups is that he's grooming me to take over for him when he dies. He says he's not that old, but death can snatch a person away in his prime. That happened to my dad and almost happened to Papa Doc. He wants to make sure there's someone he trusts to keep the secrets."

"What kind of secrets?" Ria asked, a mischievous grin on her once dour face.

"Ahh… If I told you that, what kind of secret keeper would I be?" he answered. "The one secret I will share with you is one of my own. I want to move away from traditional healing. I only have a year to go for my MD degree, but I plan on taking classes on holistic medicine."

"Whole-body healing?" Ria asked, although she already knew the answer.

"You say that as if you know all about it."

"I do. That's pretty much what Daddy does. He never calls it that, though. I found out when I was doing my own studying. We don't accumulate much, but I don't think he's ever thrown away a medical book. It might be a hassle finding the right one since a lot of the older ones are in boxes that we use to support the mattresses, but unless it's an old PDR, he keeps it."

"PDR?"

"You mean I know something you don't? It's Physicians' Desk Reference."

"I know what you mean, but I have mine on my phone. I'll show you when we get out."

"I never thought about having books on an electronic device. I know the library has a computer, but I never really investigated how to use one. I just check out as many books as I can carry and leave."

"Just like learning to read, once you master computers and the internet, a whole new world opens up to you. I'll see what I can do for you. I might be back before next year. After all, isn't your sweet sixteen birthday coming up?"

"I don't know how sweet it will be, but yes, nine days after Christmas I'll be sixteen."

Evan closed his eyes, trying to think of how he could put together a computer and a receiver for internet that would work in this area. "What are the chances you two will be moving in the next six months?"

"Actually, pretty good. Clients have been slowing down. I think we've fixed up pre-existing conditions – or at least provided long term care plans – for those who have decided to give us a shot. The other ailments are taken care of by the volunteer fire department. They hold their own clinic on Sundays in the back room of the post office. It's quaint, but they'll actually come out to the folks if stitches are needed."

"I take it that service wasn't available before you and your dad came here."

"Yeah, it was my suggestion. They ate it up. Sometimes folks can't see that they have their own solutions to problems because they're too close to them. It takes an outsider to point them out."

"And that's another thing I love about you," Evan said, then blushed scarlet at his admission of attraction.

Ria grinned at his discomfort. "I think it's time to get out of the water. We're going to be all pruney."

"I'll let you get out first," Evan said. "I think I'll take a lap." *Take a lap or three and try to hope the excitement goes down! Damned body won't listen to reason or the fact that you're only fifteen!*

Ria swam to the edge of the deep pool then stepped out, being careful of the slippery rocks. She had built a series of steps this spring, as soon as the water was warm enough, but they were already grown over with moss. She teetered on one and reached out, trying to stay upright. Grabbing air and losing her balance, she gave up her awkward struggle and fell backward, into the cushion of the water.

Seeing her distress, Evan had rushed forward, ready to catch her if she fell, waiting for her with open arms. "Watch your head!" he shouted as she dropped.

Splash!

Turning sideways to avoid clunking heads, Evan brought his hand up and lifted her shoulders out of the water. "Are you all right?" he asked.

"Just about three shades of embarrassed is all."

"Don't worry. I got your back. Always."

"I know you do. Come on. Help me out. I won't look. I'll even throw you a towel."

Now it was Evan's turn to blush. "I guess you're not as young as I thought."

"I am, but remember, I've been in the rough and tumble world of folks who don't hold back on their explanations of life and what's going on. I've never watched a soap opera, but I'm sure I've seen the storyline of most of them."

Gently touching her back in reassurance as they both walked up the slippery steps together, Evan looked down to make sure things had calmed down with fear. They had, but with touching her, he was getting hard again. He pulled his hand away and a chilly breeze came up at the same time. *Phew! A natural remedy!*

"Here. I think we should head back. My body thinks it's older than it is. If I hang out here too much longer, my brain will lose its veto vote."

"Gotcha," Evan said, taking the towel from her. "As long as one of us keeps a cool head, we'll be okay. Heaven help us if we both lose control."

***

December 27th, 2007
One week before Ria's 16th birthday

"You got another letter from Evan," Chuck said, handing her an oversized card envelope. "This one feels like it's another picture. You did tell him thanks for this one, didn't you?" he asked, nodding to the five-by-seven acrylic framed photo of her holding a big trout that graced his desk.

"Yes, I did," she said absent-mindedly, rushing to open the first letter she'd had in a month.

Dear Ria,

I'm sorry I haven't written as much lately. I'm in clinicals now and have been running on four to five hours of sleep a night. I wish I could be there for your sixteenth birthday but I can't seem to squeeze even eight hours to myself much less the two days of travel it would take to just see you for a few moments.

I was downloading everything off my old phone onto my new one when I found this. It was saved to the wrong folder. Actually, it popped up just when I needed it most, so I guess it wasn't the 'wrong' folder after all. I printed it out and have it on my desk and in my wallet. It even pops up on my screensaver. You're always just a smile away from me.

Ask your father to give you a big hug from me. If all goes well, I should be able to come out at spring break.

Warmest regards,

Evan

"What did you get?" Chuck asked.

"Looks like a picture," Ria said, tearing off the paper toweling wrapped around the acrylic frame.

"Oh, my God! I totally forgot about this! Look!"

Ria handed her father the photo of her 'kissing' the trout.

"Oh, is there any way you'll let me put this on my desk?" he asked.

"Nope. This is coming into my room. I don't need any smart-aleck remarks coming from our clients. These folks don't know it was a joke. They already think I'm weird. They might believe I really was kissing the fish! Besides, if this is what brightens his day, just seeing it and knowing he's looking at the same image, maybe at the same time, means a lot to me."

"You are such a romantic, Ria. Where'd you get that from?" Chuck asked, then realized what he had said.

"Must come from that woman who birthed me, eh?" she replied. "Don't worry about it. Good or evil, if there's a trait I have that I don't share with you, I'll always credit or blame it on her. Believe it or not, I never felt deprived. You've done a great job, Mama Daddy."

"You haven't called me that since you were six."

"At least, not out loud or to your face. I'm sorry if I haven't said it enough, but you really are the greatest."

"Yeah, well, Lord knows I tried. But I've often wondered if I didn't do you a disservice by helping you achieve so much of your potential. I've never heard of a sixteen-year-old doctor, but you really do have that magic touch. Plus, you have more skills than many who are out there practicing."

"And that's the reason: practice. I've been practicing for at least ten years."

"I'll never forget you begging me to let you put stitches in that puppy the boar had gored. I thought that old man was going to flip when I said yes. I told him someone had to hold the dog down. I mean, yes, he was a puppy, but he was still at least twenty pounds. Since he wasn't willing..."

"Yup. I really wanted to keep that dog, too."

"That's another thing I regret: never letting you have pets."

"Don't worry about it. We had chickens, didn't we? Besides, I still have a lot of years left to own a dog or cat. However, next time someone offers a nanny goat, I'd appreciate it if you said yes. Goat milk is so much better than canned milk."

"Deal," Chuck said, his hand out.

"Deal!" Ria said, then gave him a big hug. "Now, I have to go find the right place for this. Why I never thought of taking a picture of Evan, I'll never know."

"Because you don't think technology, you think biology."

"Now *that* I get from you!"

***

January 4, 2008 (a week later)

Ria stepped out of the hot shower and dried off quickly. She hastily threw on her sweats and wrapped her hair in a towel. The winter chill in Connecticut was almost impossible to get rid of, but she'd try. She sniffed the air. Breakfast!

"That bacon smells so good," she called out from the hallway. She stepped into the combination exam room and office and saw her father had company. "Oh, I'm sorry, Dad. I didn't know you had clients this early."

"*Who* are you?" the young woman asked

"Shit! I mean, shoot! Who are *you*?" Rhianna looked at her father. *Who is this person who looks so much like me?* His eyes were wide and mouth still agape. "Daddy? Do I have a twin?"

"Sorta," he said softly, then took a deep breath and shut his mouth. "And yes, saying shit is appropriate in this case."

"So, who's Ria?" the young man asked, intently watching her father for sgns of lying.

"I am," Ria answered. "Rhianna Lynn Strong."

Ria flushed as she stammered the last name she and her father had decided to use this far north. She was lying but hoped neither of these two strangers noticed her flub or cared what her last name was.

265

"So, if she's Rhianna Lynn, and I'm Vickie Lynn, who is Tori Lynn?" the thin young woman who looked so much like her asked.

Chuck took another deep breath and shook his head. "Me and my big mouth. Shoot."

"No, Daddy," Ria said. "Now's an appropriate time to say shit."

"Shit, shoot, either way, that's why I said sorta. You aren't twins – you're two of triplets. You were all adopted when you were just a few hours old to different parents."

Ria and Vickie stared at each other for a moment, then both looked at Chuck. "So, where's our sister?" the one named Vickie asked.

"And who's our mother?" Ria echoed with the exact same tone and inflection.

"Eerie," the young man said.

"Yeah, right?" added Chuck.

"That's an evasive reply," Ria said. "I'm calling you out on that, as you so often say to me."

"Yeah, I guess I brought you up right."

"Yes, you did. And that's another evasive answer," Ria said, hands on hips.

"Are Grace and Dusty our parents?" Vickie asked.

"You know them?" Chuck asked.

"That's answering a question with a question," Vickie said. "Yes, Gloria and Roger brought me up right, too," she said, nudging her new-found sister with an elbow of camaraderie.

"Oh, Lord. I knew this day was coming…"

"Hey, Doc. That's more evasiveness. My parents brought me up right, too," the young man said. "Just don't tell me I'm related to them, okay?"

"Unless Dusty and Grace are your parents, no, you're not related." Doc ran his fingers through his long salt and pepper hair. "Why are you here?"

Vickie turned to the man. "Yeah, why are *you* here, Rich? And you never did have a 'guy problem,' did you?"

"You're the only guy problem I have," he said. "While you three reconnect, can I go to my truck and get some sleep? I've been driving all night after a full day of family and birthday parties and rescuing damsels in distress and… I just need an hour or two. Please?"

"Ria, show Rich to the back bedroom and give him an extra blanket. I don't want him passing out. He's too big for me to move around."

"You've moved bigger," Ria said.

"Not without hurting for the next three days," he replied.

"Just saying…"

"Do you two always talk like that?" Vickie asked Chuck.

"Like what?"

"I don't know. Like she's your wife. You're not weird like that, I hope."

"Ew! No!" Chuck said in disgust. "She's my helper here at the clinic. This place isn't much, but it's all we can afford with how much we charge. We don't take insurance, don't have any foundations funding us, and part of my mission is to be mobile. I'm all over the place in this thing. I fix people up, and then I'm on my way."

"Like in Wolf Whistle?" Vickie asked.

"Do you know why they called it that?" Ria barely paused before answering her own question. "It's because the wind blows so hard, it sounds like it's whistling when it blows through the trees and rocks."

"And cracks in the door and window seals," Chuck added. "We left there years ago. How do you know about that?"

"I found an old money order made out to my mother," Vickie said. "What was that all about?"

"She loaned me money. I paid it back. I called that old motorhome we had The Whistler because it was so drafty. Her loan helped me buy this one. It was used but in much better shape and ten feet longer than the previous one. It's not as negotiable in the hills, but we manage to find a place big enough to park for a month. The little towns and hollows are happy to have us around to treat those who need it. We stay put until clients stop showing up."

"So, does that mean Rhianna's homeschooled?"

"You can call me Ria. Yes, I'm homeschooled. Can I ask you a question? Oh, I just did, didn't I? Oops. Another question. What I'm getting at is, are you sick?"

"No," Vickie replied, embarrassed at someone telling her she was inadequate.

"Hey, Dad. Let me take this one. Go finish your coffee and breakfast. I'm giving this beautiful young lady a check-up. Something's wrong with her and she doesn't even know it."

"But...but...we just met!"

"It's either me or Dad, but one of us is going to find out what's going on in that skinny pasty body. You forget: he and I both know what you *should* look like."

"She's got you there," Chuck said. "She sees herself in the mirror every morning. You may be beautiful, but I agree: you don't look right."

"We're not going back where Rich is, are we?"

"Nope." Ria ushered her to the tiny room on the other side of the office living room combination. "This is my bedroom." She pulled down a cabinet door and revealed a bin of personal belongings, including a pink stuffed unicorn.

Vickie reached up and touched it. "An ooni-corn! I had one almost like it. I was obsessed with them when I was little."

"Really? Me, too!" Ria pulled the animal out and gave it to her. "Hold onto her while I check you out. First, take off your shirt."

"Can I leave on my bra?"

"As long as I don't see anything suspicious, sure. This place is still chilly, even if it isn't as drafty."

Jacket and tee-shirt off, Vickie crossed her arms across her chest and shivered, her bony shoulder bones sharp and angular.

"Geez, woman! You're not much more than a skeleton! Don't your parents feed you?"

"Yeah, they noticed, if that's what you mean. My nanny says I'm too fat. She's bony and thinks I should be, too. If I eat, she makes my life miserable. I swear she has cameras hidden everywhere. If I so much as sneak an olive, she lectures me for an hour on how I'll never get a husband, that fat people have no self-control..."

"Have you told your parents about her?"

Vickie shook her head. "I can't."

"Or won't... So, let me approach this another way. What's the worst that can happen if they fire her?"

"She's already blackmailing them. I just found that out yesterday. Or was that earlier this morning? Anyhow, after my birthday party..." Vickie paused, her eyes glistening in recall of Grace punching Elsa.

"What's wrong? Or what's right?" Ria asked. "Now I know what Dad sees when something's going through my head. What you're feeling is showing on your face."

"Oh, it's right, very right." Vickie grabbed the rainbow afghan from the bed and wrapped it around her shoulders. "Okay, so here's the thing. I was about four when I first met my real mother – our birth mother – but I didn't know who she was. I was never told I was adopted. Everything led me to believe that I was just a late-in-life child. So, one day I kinda got rescued by a woman whose father is my father's – adopted father's – cousin. One thing leads to another, and we're in each other's lives. I sort of get a set of godparents.

"I started suspecting there might be more of a connection when I was thirteen. I confronted Grace – our mom – and she admitted a truth. Not the complete truth, but something she thought would satisfy me. She told me that her mother and my mom – the woman who brought me up – were sisters. None of them got along, so they just ignored each other. That was also her reason why we looked so much alike.

"I didn't get a clue that we were even more closely related until Grace – Mom – punched out Nanny Elsa at my birthday party. She got all wound up when she was slugging it out and referred to me as her daughter. Afterward, she said it was because I was her goddaughter. She tried throwing in a few other smoke and mirrors remarks, but I saw through them. Plus, I saw the shock in her face when she realized that she had claimed me out loud."

"Before I get all distracted with *Mom*…" Ria inhaled deeply with the word, savoring it, then licked her lips, determined not to get distracted. "Why did Mom punch your nanny? I assume Nanny Elsa is your nanny."

Vickie turned her head and showed her the ear that was still itching and burning. "Elsa talked me into getting my ears clipped. This one got infected."

"Ooh. That looks painful. I noticed the difference when I first saw you. I think I should have Dad check that out. So, lie back real quick and let me poke and prod. I think you look so pasty because you're malnourished and fighting an infection."

"Do you know how weird this is?" Vickie asked. "You look and sound just like me. You're not a phantom or a dream." She reached up and touched her arm. "So weird."

"Yeah, I do know, because I get the same feeling. Dad never told me, either." Ria's fingers deftly felt for an enlarged liver or other abnormalities, then satisfied she was in good health, offered her a hand to sit up.

"Yeah… And there's another one of us out there somewhere…" Vickie said dreamily.

"Yeah…" Ria echoed. "Really weird."

"Can I get dressed now?"

"Sure. Hey, let me give you a tank top to wear under everything else. Keeping clothing right next to your skin helps insulate your body heat. After you're dressed, I want Dad to look at that ear."

"Gotcha. Sis."

"Back at ya. Sis."

Both girls shivered in excitement with identical shoulder shrugs, then laughed the same short, "Hah!"

"This is going to be so much fun!" they said at the same time.

I have a sister and a mother and another father! And another sister! So alone in family one minute, and then overloaded with them the next! Sing hallelujah!

Chuck inhaled deeply at seeing the infected wound, resisting the urge to comment on the sloppy work. He stood in front of her and asked, "Have you seen anyone else about this. Other than the person who did the deed?"

"Yeah, Papa Doc cleaned it up last night. He didn't have any lidocaine so let me have a drink of whisky to help numb the pain. How can anyone drink that stuff?"

"They drink it for effect, not flavor. Or so they tell me. Who is this Papa Doc fellow?"

"He's kind of like a grandpa to me. A. B. C. Armstrong is his name. Actually, I have lots of surrogate grandpas. Hal and Silas claim me, too."

So, Silas knows about me having a twin – or rather, two triplet sisters? Does Evan know? Shit! That's what he was talking about the first time he ever saw me. That's why he thought I knew him.

Ria watched and listened rather than join the conversation. Her sister paused her cheery rambling for a moment, then spoke sincerely. "Hey, Chuck. How come you just paled when I said his name?" Vickie looked at her and saw a similar reaction. "Okay, you two. Do you know Papa Doc?"

"He does, I never met him," Ria said. "He won't let me. Papa Doc is his father."

"Oh…" Vickie said, then giggled as realization hit. "Your sign reads C. R. M. Strong. That's for Chuck Ar-m-strong, am I right?"

"Turn around and let me clean that ear again," Chuck grumbled, then smiled at her cleverness.

"Oh, my God!" Vickie squealed, bouncing up and down in place.

"Hold still," Chuck ordered, his hand firm on her shoulder. "Which epiphany did you just have?"

"Hal is my grandpa! My honest to goodness biological grandpa. And yours, too, Ria!"

"Took you long enough," Chuck said with a chuckle. "When I'm done, I need to put more topical antibiotics on that. I don't have any antibiotic pills left, so I want you to go back home and tell Papa Doc that your physician in Woodstock said he had confidence that he'll know which one to administer."

"I'm jealous," Ria said with a pout.

"Of what?" Chuck asked.

"She gets to know my grandpa and I don't."

"Both adopted and biological grandpas. And our father and mother…" Vickie said softly.

"Well, meeting them would be cool, too," Ria said. "I never felt shorted when it came to the parents' aspect of a relationship, but I knew about Papa Doc. I never had a grandfather. Dad, can we go there for a visit? I want to meet him."

"We'll see…"

Ria rolled her eyes at her sister and scowled. *That means no.* A grin bloomed and she raised an eyebrow. *But I have you now. Will you help?*

Face pinched in discomfort as the swab cleaned out the wound, Vickie cut her eyes to the side and gave a discreet thumbs-up. *I got your back, Sis!*

Chapter 8: Eighteen and Legal

January 28, 2010

"I had to call in a lot of favors," Evan said, "but I have forty-eight hours off. I couldn't swing the wedding, though. Can you text me the address of the rehearsal dinner? I should be able to make it by seven."

"Sure. Hey, would you help me play a trick on my dad?"

"You name it! He's been making me squirm for the past five years. Just make it a good one. I'll probably only get one shot."

"Okay. I have Vickie's wedding dress with me. We can't do it at the rehearsal tonight, but we can do it tomorrow. We'll have to build up to it at dinner, though, dropping subtle hints that should drive him nuts."

"What are you talking about?"

"I'm going to come out wearing Vickie's wedding dress! I think tomorrow at noon ought to do it. We can make sure everyone but him knows about it, making him think he's being left out of our wedding on purpose."

"Isn't that a little too mean?" Evan asked. "I don't mind making him feel uncomfortable, but I don't want to gut the poor guy."

"Nah, he'll be fine. Maybe I won't tell anyone else. That way he won't feel too singled out."

"Speaking of single, what's going on between our two dads? They sure have been in close contact for the last few months. Not that I'm complaining. Dad is finally through the miserable part of grieving. I know he still misses Father, but at least he isn't crying anymore. Well, not that I've seen. Actually, he has a spring to his step that I don't remember *ever* seeing."

"Oh, my God! Do you think they're dating?" Ria asked, her hands under her chin with excitement.

A series of emotions raced across Evan's face as he considered the implications. He shook his head, trying not to think of them. "Ria, I have to ask you something right now. It's actually pretty time-sensitive."

"Sure, what gives?" she asked, not giving him her complete attention, thinking instead of all the hints and suggestions she'd drop to make her father squirm at the thought of her getting married.

"You didn't hear me, did you?" Evan asked.

"I'm sorry," Ria said. "You're right. My mind is all over the place right now. Go ahead. I know you said it was time-sensitive and here I go, fantasizing about a make-believe wedding."

"Would you marry me? We don't have to do it right away, the wedding that is, or anything else. I mean," he stammered. "I'm not asking just to keep up with your sister and Rich. I do want you to be my wife – or at least my fiancée – before my dad and your dad get too serious, though. I don't want to marry my stepsister, but do want to marry you. Actually, I've wanted to marry you since…"

"Yes! Yes! Yes!" Ria exclaimed, jumping up into his arms. She smothered him with excited kisses, then bent down for a long and thorough smooch that sent tingles throughout. She finally pulled back. "You've wanted to marry me since when?"

"Since you were fifteen and a half, I think. That sounds so perverted, especially since I was twenty, but it was only your body that was young."

"No, my body and my social skills were both juvenile. Intellectually, I was an adult, but I had to have a lot of life experiences in a short time to get to where I am today. Spending weekends with Vickie and Gloria, Papa Doc and Silas helped. It was good for my dad, too, having time away from me. But I often felt like something was missing in my life. Even finally meeting Grace and Dusty and acknowledging them as my bio-parents didn't fill that void. No, I never felt complete until we were together for our few days every summer. When you were gone, it was as if I was pinging a signal and no one was there to acknowledge it. You stepped back into my life and –voila! – the signals and circuits were completed."

"So, you'll wear the dress for a preview? It won't be just to punk him?"

"Let's just say we're going to prepare him. I'm sure Vickie will let me borrow her dress when she's done with it. I do want to wait until you're done with internships or residencies or whatever comes next before getting married. From what I've heard, they run you ragged those last few months. You don't need to worry about taking care of your wife at the same time."

"Honey, taking care of you is going to be a pleasure." Evan reached down and readjusted himself through his slacks. "And if part of me had its way, it'd be pleasuring you right now!"

"Well, we are betrothed…" Ria cooed.

Knock! Knock! Knock!

"Hey! Are you in there, Ria?" Vickie called.

"Damn!" Ria hissed. "Yeah, I'll be right out!" she hollered.

"To be continued?" Evan asked.

"I certainly hope so. But remember, dress up nice tomorrow so you'll be ready for the show at noon."

Vickie paced the hall in front of the room her sister had sneaked into, waiting impatiently for her to answer. The door opened a crack, then Ria slipped out, a tall dark-haired man following very close behind her. Both had flushed faces tinged with embarrassment. No need to call them out on what they'd been doing!

"Hey, Sis," Vickie said. "I sort of need a favor. Could you cover for me for an hour or so at dinner?"

"What? You're going to miss your own rehearsal dinner?" Ria asked, then felt the loss of Evan. She turned and watched as he ducked into the men's room.

"No, I'm just going to be late," Vickie said, her face reddening.

"You know, you're a lousy liar," Ria said. "Tell me what's going on, or at least enough that I can give a believable excuse. You do know I'm supposed to be there, too."

"Yeah, I know. This gets a little sticky. I don't want anyone to get in trouble, but Rich is in a bind. I have to sort of bail him out. Not bail as in he got arrested, but as in a predicament. Just be me for a few minutes, make an excuse for Rich, then duck out and come back in as yourself. It'll be believable if your hair's down."

"Okay, but I want to ask a favor. Can I borrow your dress tomorrow? You won't need it until Saturday. I want to wear it to shock the stuffing out of my dad."

"Why?"

"Why not? I'm sorry. That sounded cruel. I think it's because I have eighteen years of childish pranks backed up in me. I never got to do this kind of stuff when I was young. I don't know if it's stress or excitement or jealousy or whatever because you're getting married first, but I suppose just once I want to see my 'always mellow and in control' dad wound up about something!"

"Sure. It's at the house hanging outside my closet. You know the access code to get in. If that makes you feel uncomfortable, just ring the bell. You know you're always welcome. Of course, if you need to get rid of some more of that mischief, go ahead and pretend you're me. Just let me know what you're doing and when, so I don't meet myself coming or going!"

"Thanks," Ria said and gave Vickie a quick kiss on the cheek. "You're the best."

"Back at ya," Vickie said, then left to rescue Rich from his fraternity brothers' bachelor party.

Ria waited until she was sure her sister was gone, then knocked on the men's room door. "Coast is clear," she said.

Evan came out, his face and hair damp.

"What happened to you?" she asked.

"I couldn't take a cold shower, so I did the next best thing: stuck my head in the sink under cold running water. Are you sure you want to wait until I'm done with my internship?"

"Come on. I have to play Vickie's role at her own wedding rehearsal dinner. You'll have to wait in the wings until I leave. Then we can come back in as ourselves. It's a small price to pay for borrowing the wedding dress. I'm sure she would lend it to me anyway, but this is going to be my grandest performance. All the parents and grandparents will be there."

"You didn't answer my question," Evan said, nudging her shoulder.

"I have a plan about that," Ria said, a twinkle in her eye. "I've been

273

reading books that aren't on my dad's approved reading list. I have a plan for your – shall we say? – discomfort? Don't ask. Let me surprise you after we get pretend married tomorrow. I hear it's the next best thing and won't get me pregnant."

"Man, I'm glad you're eighteen now!" Evan exclaimed in a hushed voice. "Just tell me where you want me and when. I'm yours to command, fiancée!"

***

"I can't do it," Ria said. "I can't go out there and fool everyone who loves her. It's not fair to them."

"Then don't do it," Evan said. "Teasing someone is one thing, but truly pretending to be someone you're not isn't right."

"Okay. I got a plan. Hang back in the foyer until I call for you, all right?"

"Your wish is my command," Evan said. He looked at his watch. "At least for the next eighteen hours or so."

Ria waited until the wedding party had settled down at their tables and were looking everywhere for the bride and groom to be. "It's time," she whispered to herself.

Entering the room to an audience of friends and family, all standing up and cheering the person they thought was Vickie, Ria waved to the group and threw kisses. "Thank you, thank you, thank you," she said, then walked up to her place at the center of the long table of honor. She stood next to the empty chair where Rich should have been and put her hand on the back, waiting for the crowd to settle down.

"I'm sure many of you also came here to see Rich." She nodded to Rick Rickman, Rich's father, then the woman at his side, Mrs. Rickman. "Well, unfortunately, young Mr. Rickman has been detained. And if you haven't figured it out already, his dear fiancée has rushed to his side to take care of his dilemma."

The low rumble of whispers covered the room like a soft blanket. "Yup, it's me: Rhianna. Vickie asks your indulgence in not being able to be here, but I can understand her choice. Great food and good company over the health and security of her fiancé. Here, here, to Vickie Lynn Thornwhistle and Rich Rickman!" she said, lifting her glass of sparkling cider.

After the cheers and applause died down, Ria moved toward the mic again. "I'd like to take this opportunity to say a few kind words about my sister, and then invite others to do the same. It's a little unconventional, but so are they." She paused at the silence that followed, then added, "But in a good way," then scurried over to sit next to Gloria, Vickie's mother.

More applause followed, along with the clanging on his glass by Rick Rickman. "I love this family!" he declared, causing more applause. "Has anyone ever seen such flexibility when it comes to unexpected or adverse situations?" More applause.

Gloria leaned over and whispered, "You did great, dear. If your father was here, I'm sure he'd be just as proud of you as we are."

Ria looked up and saw Evan waiting for her signal. She motioned to him, then looked everywhere. No father. What in the heck was this? No bride or groom? Hopefully, the food was good and Vickie and Rich were safe.

Evan sneaked in, hunched over as he approached her side. She nodded to Rich's empty chair beside her. "Might as well be the groom-in-waiting for a while," she whispered. "This is going to be a long night."

* * *

"Hey, Dad," Ria called out from her bedroom. "How flexible is your schedule today?"

"I don't have any clients lined up, if that's what you mean. No paperwork or chores. No dirty dishes to wash since we ate out, and no dinner to cook, either, because they loaded me up with leftovers. Why? What's on your mind."

Knock! Knock! Knock!

Sweat poured off Evan's forehead despite the winter chill and his lack of warm coat. The tuxedo provided minimal warmth but nerves took care of the rest.

"Evan?" Chuck asked, seeing him dressed up. "Why the tux? The wedding's not until tomorrow."

"Vickie's wedding is tomorrow," Ria said, coming out of her bedroom wearing Vickie's gown, her hair piled in curls atop her head, her eyes blinking at the irritation of wearing mascara for the first time. "I figured today was a good time for ours. Silas is nearby, just waiting to do the honors. What do you say, Daddy? Are you ready to give me away?"

Chuck plopped down on the exam table, his legs as limp as maple syrup dripping off a pancake. "Whoa! When did this happen? You don't *have* to get married, do you?"

"Well, I figured one of us should get married. You didn't and still had a child."

"That's different."

"Daddy, you didn't raise an idiot. I know that babies and marriage don't necessarily go hand in hand. I just thought it would be fun to wear a wedding dress. Did I scare you?"

"Yes," Chuck said, then turned around and looked at the back of his pants. "Oh, thank God." He picked up the cleaning cloth he had left on the exam table and tossed it to the kitchen sink. "I thought I'd shit myself."

"Oh, Daddy," Ria said, rushing up to hug him, her eyes streaming with black mascara. "I thought this would be funny." She paused and allowed herself to chuckle, then looked at Evan to see his reaction. He was ghostly white in fear.

"I guess it wasn't as funny as I thought it'd be. But you do know I'm

275

going to get married one of these days."

"Yeah, well, let me get used to it gradually. Vickie and Rick have been going together for two years. It really wasn't too unexpected."

"Begging your pardon," Evan said, his color returning. "But even if it wasn't dating or 'going together,' Rhianna and I have been fond of each other for five years. I guess what I'm saying is, I've asked Ria to marry me."

"And…" Chuck said, his eyes wide as he looked to Ria.

"And I said, 'Yes!'" Ria exclaimed, jumping up and down. "Oops," she said, then grabbed a tissue from the box on the desk and wiped her eyes. "I can't get the dress dirty. Vickie needs it tomorrow."

"Well, as long as you don't 'need' it tomorrow or anytime soon, that's fine with me. Evan, you're a fine young man, and I appreciate your devotion to my daughter, but don't you think she's a little young to get married?"

"No, I don't or I wouldn't have asked her. I did ask that we wait until I'm done with my internship, but right now, that hasn't been decided."

"How much longer?" Chuck asked. He looked at Ria and saw her blanch. "And would they let you intern at a rural clinic?"

"Oh, Daddy!" Ria exclaimed, her tears sprouting again. "Excuse me, guys. I really have to change out of this dress. I'm so excited, I could pop!"

"Six months, sir. That would make it early summer completion."

"Well, if it makes a difference, put my name down. You might want to ask Papa Doc, too. He has an inner-city clinic that could always use a hand. Between the two of us, we should have your options covered."

***

January 30, the next evening

"So, why were you late to your own rehearsal. Were you and Rich finally getting it on?"

"Ria!" Vickie exclaimed.

"Ah, that's an evasive reply. I'll take that as a yes. Watch it. Grace said she got pregnant the first time."

Vickie blushed, lips pursed in frustration, wanting to deny what her sister suspected but knowing it was no use. She blew out her held breath. "Don't tell anyone, please."

"Duh! It's nobody's business, including mine. Two days early is close enough. You still deserve to wear white."

"What about you, Ria? The hunk? Are you two 'getting it on'?"

"Eet!" Ria made a noise like a penalty buzzer. "Not your business!"

"So, you're not blushing or mad at me for suggesting it which means you're not doing anything, but you'd like to be. I know I've never met him, but he looks familiar."

"Don't concern yourself with us. You're the one getting married in," Ria looked up at the clock, "fifteen minutes. Where are the moms?" she asked, walking to the doorway to look down the hall.

"Oooh! You said, 'Don't concern yourself with *us*,' not me. More serious than you want anyone but me to know about. Don't worry, my lips are sealed."

Ria quickly looked back at Vickie and said, "Shush!" then left the room, hunting for the missing mothers.

A moment later, three women came in – Gloria following Ria, Grace right beside her. "Oh, here you are!" Gloria said. "We were looking all over the place for you. I still think we should have had the wedding at the Club. At least, I wouldn't have gotten lost." She fanned herself with the paper announcement. "I'm sorry, dear. Danged hot flashes make me moody. This is your day. Really, if this is where you want to have your wedding, it's fine with us. All of us."

"I hope so since it's almost time. Grace, would you help me with this makeup? I can't get this eyeliner straight and I know Mom can't see up close."

"Oh, I feel so inadequate," Gloria moaned.

"Why don't you help me with my hair?" Ria asked. "I can't see the back of my head and want to make sure I don't have a flat spot. Can you do that for me?"

"Oh, yes, dear. I'm so glad you and Chuck could come. Where is he?"

"I think he met a new old friend. They're getting reacquainted," Ria said.

"Man, I wish he'd get a boyfriend," Grace said. "He's been alone for way too long."

"A boyfriend?" Gloria gasped. "He's gay?"

"Well, duh!" Ria said. "Do you think Dusty would let a straight man hug on Grace like that?"

"Well, I don't know…" Gloria bent back to picking up the curls in Ria's hair and pinning them in place. "I guess it doesn't make any difference," she said.

"I know he goes on dates occasionally, claiming he's 'going out with the guys.' But I've seen the way some men check him out. Women, too, but he never returns their looks. He is the epitome of discretion. I don't think he knows that I know. I tried to bring it up once and he got so flustered and embarrassed, I decided that it really wasn't any of my business. As soon as I'm ready to go out on my own, he can do his own thing, find his Mr. Right, or at least look around for him."

"Wow! That's pretty sensitive," Grace said, sitting back in the chair, overwhelmed with emotions.

"Brought up by a gay dad who is also a non-profit physician," Ria said. "Of course, I'm sensitive! Okay, are we about done here? I'm not wearing any makeup because as the sensitive person that I am, I'll be crying before Vickie takes her first step down the aisle. *Sniff, sniff.* See what I mean?"

Gloria opened her purse and handed Ria an embroidered handkerchief. "Here you go, honey. You can keep it. I packed at least a dozen of them."

"That's a good thing," Grace said, plucking one of them out of her friend's Coach bag, using it to dab under her nose. "I'm glad you planned ahead."

Ria only paid half attention to the banter that was going on as the ladies primped and finalized makeup and hair. "Where's my dad?" she whispered to Grace.

"He dashed out of here before we came to see you. He said he had to go get Vickie's present. What did he get her?"

"Danged if I know. He's back to being Mr. Mysterious again."

***

Chuck sneaked into the back of the wedding hall with his three guests. "Go ahead and sit here in the last row. If anyone asks, you were invited by the family of the bride. The Thornwhistles don't know you're coming, though. Just act like you belong, because you do!" he said, patting the insecure Leanne on her shoulder.

He turned around and saw that Tori had disappeared again. "She won't go far, will she?" he asked Leanne.

"No, she's bashful but not a runner." She looked over at the cluttered coat rack and saw movement. "Two to one she's in there. Don't worry. She didn't want to come but can't go anywhere without us. She may be eighteen, but she doesn't know how to drive on anything other than farm roads."

"Shush!" Luther hissed. "Dang! It's over. That's about the quickest wedding I've ever been to."

"It's the only wedding – other than our own – you've ever been to," Leanne said. "Now come on. I want to meet the bride and groom…and that beautiful young bridesmaid!"

The newlywed couple walked down the aisle in reverse, following the strewn rose petals to the reception hall. Luther, Leanne, and Chuck stepped back, marveling at the beautiful women, waiting until the happy couple and their families had passed before following.

"Grab your daughter, Luther," Leanne said. "She won't come otherwise."

Luther reached into the coats and jackets, his experienced grasp finding her upper arm. "Come on, sweetheart. No one here's going to bite you."

"Can we go home now?" Tori whispered.

"There's nothing but rain and gloom in out there now. If you come out willing and behave, I promise you a surprise like nothing you've ever seen or expected."

"Well, she may have seen," Leanne said, "but she certainly isn't expecting this. At least, in this format."

"What are you two babbling about?" Tori asked, her curiosity piqued. "You know I can't resist a mystery."

"Ah, you're right there. Come on. And take off that silly hat!"

Tori pulled off her knit cap, her blonde hair flying everywhere with static

278

electricity. She pushed the blond strands behind her ears and stuck out her chin. "Now, show me something I didn't expect," she said. "Because you know I have a pretty vivid imagination."

Luther held out his arm, waiting for her to join him. "This way, darling. I have a few people I'd like you to meet."

Tori followed, her head down so she didn't have to face the crowd. She was more comfortable with plants and animals than people, and her parents knew it. They were right, though. Western Oregon was nothing but rain and gloom in January. It had started in September and probably wouldn't end until May. It was great for plants but bad for people's humor. She wasn't too fond of knitting and crocheting but spent a lot of time doing both. It was an excuse to keep her head down and away from interacting with people. She sucked it up, curious again about the mystery of seeing something familiar in a new way. A grin grew at the adventure. It couldn't be, could it?

Tori looked around the room, her smile of anticipation as warm and bright as the mood of the people. It was a wedding. She loved weddings. At least, reading about them. This was the first one she'd ever been to. Or almost been to. She grunted with disgust at herself, her shyness stealing her joy again. When would she ever outgrow it? 'One of these days' her parents always said. Well, she'd just have to choose a day. And today – with all these positive vibes, happy voices, and joyous music, the smell of fragrant food and warmth of bodies moving around – this was a good day to claim moodiness was dead. Long live joy and hope.

Clink! Clink! Clink!

All eyes went to the noise of a knife hitting the side of a crystal glass. "Here's to Mr. and Mrs. Richard Rickman," the father of the bride announced. "Health and happiness – and a bit of prosperity – to our very own Rich and Vickie Rickman!"

Tori's eyes widened as she looked at the bride and groom. They had been at the front of the hall when she came in, but their backs were to them. Then she watched as a young woman went up to the bride and gave her a big hug. It looked like the bride was hugging the bride! This version was wearing jeans and flannel, though, just like she was. And she looked just like her except her hair was piled on top of her head in curls instead of down on her shoulders. They were identical twins! Or two of triplets. Both of them looked just like her!

"Mama? What's going on?" Tori asked, her face pale.

"Is this a surprise or what?"

"Do I have sisters you didn't tell me about?"

"Well, yes. Sort of…"

"Papa, did you know about this?"

"Yes, well, sort of…"

Tori glared at them then walked away, right up to the front where the two sisters were still standing close to each other, holding one another's hands.

"Hi," Tori said, her hand thrust out between the two. "I think I'm your sister, Tori. I mean, I'm Tori, and I think I'm your sister."

"Tori!" Ria and Vickie exclaimed, reaching out as two halves of a Siamese twin to grab her close. "We heard there was a third but didn't know where to find you or even your last name. How did you know where to find us?"

Chuck stepped up to the stunned trio. "Vickie, this is your wedding gift: meeting your other sister. Well, I guess it's an engagement gift to you, Ria, and just a surprise to you, Tori."

"But why did you wait so long?" Vickie asked.

"I couldn't do or say anything without permission from Luther and Leanne." Chuck held his hand above his eyebrows and scanned the room, finally finding the elderly couple who had reared Tori as their own, pretending she was their biological daughter. He waved them up. "It took a long time to find them. We thought they were still on the east coast. I think Silas found about two thousand places they *weren't* before starting on the west coast."

"Oregon," Tori said simply. "Eventually." She turned to her sisters. "So, I'm not crazy, right?"

"Why would you think that?" Ria asked.

"Because, well, you know how you can look in the mirror and see your other self? Didn't it ever seem weird, like you should be able to just reach in and grab that other person and pull her out to stand beside you instead of in front of you?"

"Well, kinda," Vickie said, "but I thought everyone felt like that."

"Maybe they do, but I felt something was still missing. Then we moved into a place that had a double mirror in the bathroom. I could move it just so, and then there'd be three of me: me and the two images. It felt so right. I used to get in trouble because I'd take so long in the bathroom. I'd be in there, carrying on conversations in a low voice so no one else would hear. Or rather, my parents wouldn't.

"I always wondered if Mama and Papa were my real parents, too, because I didn't look like either one of them. Plus, they were a little old. Mama even showed me a picture Papa had taken of her nursing me. I'm not quite sure how that was possible, but since Papa can make hair grow on a turnip with the right herbal concoction, then I guess he could have put something together so Mama could get milk."

Tori hooked an arm into each sister's, glad all over again that she wasn't crazy, that there really were two on this earthly plane who looked like her. "So, yes or no: are our biological parents here?"

"Yes," Ria and Vickie answered, then looked at each other with raised eyebrows. *Tori looks like us, but she sure is different!*

Tori scanned the room and spotted Grace and Dusty, staring at them, misty-eyed, hugging each other. She nodded to them, acknowledging them. "That was a no-brainer," Tori whispered to her sisters. "Even if we didn't look like them, the reaction on their faces proves it. So, I guess I'll hear the whole story about why they gave us up later. Let me see if I can pick out a grandma or grandpa..."

"We don't have a grandma here," Vickie said. "She's sorta *persona non grata* and also out of the country."

"Fair enough. Everyone has a skeleton or two in the closet. Best to leave them alone, I say." Tori kept looking, bypassing the one older gentleman who looked as interested as her biological parents, but not alike physically. She spotted Silas and noticed his ears, broad shoulders and regal stance. "Him!" she said with complete confidence.

"Nope," Vickie said. "Him," and pointed to Hal. "He's our mother Grace's dad. It's kind of hard not to notice Grace is our mother. She's almost like an older triplet. Or would that be quadruplet?"

Tori shook off the discussion on the mother. "Nope. I'll bet three DNA tests to a donut that he," she said, this time pointing right to Silas, "is Grace's biological father. The other guy definitely has an emotional investment in all of us, but *he's* her father and our grandfather."

Silas watched as the latest triplet to come into his life pointed at him as she carried on an intense conversation with her sisters. Thirty-seven years after Victoria had gotten him drunk and had her way with him, he'd been busted. He looked over the room, pretending to scout out the crowd in general but really looking at Hal's expression. He was looking right at him, crestfallen. He knew.

Hal walked over to him. "I always wondered if I was her bio-dad," Hal said. "It was rumored that Victoria was sowing her last wild oats the week before the wedding, but I always hoped it was just a rumor she started so I'd think she was in demand by others. I didn't want to believe there was any chance another man was Grace's father. It's kind of hard to ignore the family resemblance between you two, but I convinced myself that you were either some long, lost cousin or her ears were a result of a recessive gene popping in. Well, if it was to be anyone, I'm glad it was you."

"Did you ever wonder why I never have more than one drink?" Silas asked.

"And did you ever wonder why I did?" Hal asked, answering his question with his own.

"Do you forgive me?" Silas asked.

"For what? Getting tricked by Victoria? Shit! I'm jealous. You got off easy. I had to live with the bitch for nearly nineteen years!"

Silas tried to hold back his laugh, then saw that Hal was giving into his, so joined him. "We weren't the only two. It's not my place to name names, but she was pretty loose there for a week or two. But you're right. It had to be me. I never realized it, though, until Grace came into the Armstrong family. When she showed up with Victoria, crashing Papa Doc's party, I knew she had to be my issue. Actually, when she started dating Alex, I was glad she was mine."

"So, Papa Doc really was one of the others, then?" Hal asked, tight-lipped.

Silas shrugged. "Yes, we both had a butt-pucker moment when we saw Grace and Alex hanging all over each other. We didn't want half-siblings getting carried away. We never said anything directly to each other, but when I saw Papa Doc do a double-take, looking at her ears and then mine, I knew he knew. It was kind of funny, both of us exhaling at the same moment as realization hit." Silas noticed Hal was still grim-faced.

"You are and always have been Grace's daddy. I'm just happy to be one of the guest grandpas to the girls. And now there's one more. By the looks she was giving me, she figured it out within two minutes of being here."

"Well, she is your granddaughter. It looks like she got more than the ears from you. She's pretty damned perceptive."

Silas sighed then grinned. "Never a daddy, but now an acknowledged granddaddy. I'm sure glad no one in this family gives two flips about whose blood flows through who."

"Back at ya," Hal said.

Chapter 9: Grand Reception

January 30, 6:00 PM, on the highway

Evan pulled into the gas station to fill up. He checked his phone for messages. *Go ahead and stay a couple more days. I got you covered. Bob*

"What the hell? You couldn't have let me know earlier?" Evan looked at the clock on the dash. Six o'clock. There was no way he'd make it back in time for the wedding, but he could be there for the reception. And maybe more one-on-one time with Ria and her 'I can't get pregnant this way' solution to his pre-wedding excitement. He shifted in the seat, not wanting to remember their stolen half-hour together before he got out to fuel the van.

Stepping into the cold blast of late January pre-blizzard took care of any residual stiffness. "Just grab a couple of granola bars and the biggest cup of coffee that will fit in the cupholder, and then it's back to Massachusetts."

Evan picked through the snack section, finding the meal bars with the least amount of sugar, then waited for the man in the kilt to finish filling his coffee mug. "Nice cup," he said to the man.

"Thank you. My son made this." The Scot held up the artisan cup with 'Da' inscribed in the side. "He's quite the artisan."

"He certainly is," Evan said, reaching up to touch the colorful glaze. He turned to the counter, unable to look away from the confrontation. "Looks like someone is having a bad day."

"Aye, that's my wife givin' the owner a fit. We had a flat tire and no spare. He's sayin' we'll have to wait a day or two fer another to get here. She's unwillin' to wait and insists he take one from his own vehicle and sell it to us so we can be on our way." The man took a pocket watch out of his sporran and checked the time. "I think we already missed the weddin' but if we were able to get out of here now, we'd be able to get to the reception."

"Strange. That's my story, too, except for the flat tire part," Evan said. "You wouldn't be going to Vickie and Rich Rickman's wedding, would you?"

"Aye! We would! Are you sayin' that's where yer headin'?"

"Aye, I mean, yes! As soon as I pay for the gas I just bought and this, I'm heading that way. I have room for you in my van. You and your wife are welcome to join me."

"I hope it's a big van. I have a few bairns to bring along, too."

"I may not have enough seatbelts for everyone, but unless you have a dozen in your tribe, we'll make it."

"Ach, I only have seven plus the one in the oven. Come on. Let's tell her the great news."

"Excuse me, Wife," Angus said. "I have a solution to our dilemma. Sir," Angus said, addressing the frazzled store owner, "is it all right with you if we leave our vehicle here fer a bit? I've acquired a ride to our destination. Go ahead, if you don't mind, and order the tire fer us. We'll be back to pay fer yer time and trouble after the celebration."

The harried man looked from the big Scot to Evan and back again. Seeing the grins on both faces, he felt it grow on his own. "Anything to keep her from asking me again," he said.

Evan handed him a hundred-dollar bill. "This is for the gas, coffee, and these snacks." He put up his hand, asking him to wait, then hustled back to the meal bars, grabbing ten more. "And these. If there's anything left, apply it to their bill. Come on, folks. We have a wedding reception to attend!"

By the time Evan had the windows washed and mirrors readjusted, the tribe of Scots had piled in and settled on the bed, captain's chair, or floor with a minimum of discussion and no arguments. "You have a well-behaved family... I'm sorry," Evan said, as he settled into his seat and buckled up. "We never exchanged names. I'm Evan Fraser."

"Ach, another Scot! I'm Angus McDermott. The name's Irish for that was my grandsire's name, but we're Scots."

"Or have taken up with them. Just call me 'Ma,'" Friday said. "I'd tell you the name of all our sons, but since you can't see their faces yet, it wouldn't make a difference. I just holler, 'Son,' and they all come running."

"Are you friends or family of the bride or groom?" Evan asked.

"We were invited by a friend of the bride," Friday answered, then looked back at her husband, scowling. *Let me do the talking, please.*

"What she said," Angus echoed. "I'm jest here as the backup sitter fer the bairns."

Evan looked over at Ma's swollen belly. "Is it time for a daughter?"

"After having seven sons in thirteen years, I certainly hope so!"

"Now, dinna I tell you I'd give you all the bairns you'd want? I never said anythin' about whether they'd be sons or daughters. That's up to the Almighty, not me."

Evan took a snack bar out of the sack, then handed the plastic bag to Ma. "Take one, then send the rest back. I don't know when you ate last, but it's been a long day for me. We have at least another hour and a half. That is, if I drive the speed limit."

"Don't hold back on our account," Friday said, then used her teeth to rip the corner of the plastic wrapper. "Speed limits are for those who don't have a deadline." She took a big bite of the nut and grain concoction and chewed the first food she had eaten in the last thirteen years that wasn't prepared by her. She bent over and used the glow of the dash lights to read the ingredients. Half of them she'd never heard of, all with -ite or -ose at the end. Garbage chemicals. She gulped the mass down, then handed the rest of the snack bar back to her husband. "Let the boys share these. I'm not as hungry as I thought."

Evan's mind was awhirl, concentrating on his speed – keeping it nine miles over the limit – calculating his rate in miles per hour and the distance to the wedding venue, trying to estimate their time of arrival.

Friday was anxious to find out who this generous young man was but leery of engaging him in conversation. She had stayed off everyone's radar for years and it was only curiosity that brought her out today. Chuck had told her via Silas that it was Vickie's wedding. So, if Chuck had a relationship with Vickie, was it be possible that Ria knew she had another sister? She shook her head, trying to stifle the question she'd asked herself dozens of times a day since she'd first got the invitation. And what about the third one? Tori Lynn, the one who was adopted by that aging hippie couple? Had they stayed connected with Vickie's family?

"If you don't mind, I'm going to take a nap," she said to Evan. Emotionally, she was exhausted. Being eight months pregnant had also zapped a great deal of her energy. She sighed, happy to have a homecoming of sorts, but also glad she had made the decision to stay with Angus. Legally, they weren't married, but that was only because she wasn't ready to share her legal name with anyone, bring herself back into the real world or onto any agency's database. It didn't matter. As far as she was concerned, she was Mrs. Angus McDermott or Ma, forever and ever. Amen!

"We're here, Ma," Evan said, gently touching her shoulder. "We made good time. We're only fifteen minutes late."

"Huh? Oh, yeah. Just in time to make a grand entrance, I'm sure. Come on, sons. Let's find a bathroom and clean up a bit first."

Angus carried his youngest son over his shoulder, the other ones holding each other's hands in pairs as they followed behind him. "I got this," Angus said. "Jest go see to yer own needs."

"This way," Evan said, leading the way to the back entrance. The bathrooms are to your left."

Evan left the Scots and headed to the noisy banquet hall. Endless chatter and clanking plates and glasses verified the ceremony was over and the dinner and toasting had begun. He looked up at the long table in front of the hall and gasped. "Three? There really is another one?"

The three identical women – two dressed in flannel and denim, the other the bride in white – were in an intense discussion. He couldn't be certain, but one of the flannel-clad ladies looked a little bit different. Ah, that's what it was. Her hair was wild. Ria wouldn't attend her sister's wedding with hair that looked like it had been kept under a knit cap for the last two years! Yes, his Ria was perfectly coifed with curls piled atop her head. He looked at two of the other women dressed in flannel. Only Ms. Wild Hair was wearing blue, a brilliant azure plaid that accentuated the color of her eyes. And those of her sisters, too.

They had to be triplets! There was no other explanation.

"Amazing, right?" Ma asked.

"Did you know there were three of them?" Evan asked.

"Yup, but I haven't seen the other two since they were a couple of hours old."

"Which other two? I mean, which sister are you here for?"

"Ria."

"Hey! Are you Friday?" Evan asked, suddenly remembering the story of Ria's early years.

"How'd you guess."

"I suppose it's your nurturing spirit. Besides, Ria told me you ran off and married a Scot. No denying him. Looks like you two still get along famously."

Friday patted her belly. "Is it that obvious?"

"Let's wait for a break in their conversation. May I present you? Oh, and you know I'm Evan Fraser, but what you don't know is that I'm Ria's fiancé."

"Hmm. I always knew that girl made wise choices. Oh, lookie there…" Friday nodded to Chuck. "My old bed mate."

"But I thought he was gay," Evan whispered.

"He is. I didn't say we ever had sex. Did you see that little RV we lived in? It was not much bigger than your van."

"Actually, I did. For about a minute. I was with Silas when we delivered their new one. Or their gently used one. Ria said it was the first time she'd had her own room. By the way, she's an RN now. Got her degree and is working on getting further certification. She may not be the youngest certified nurse in the state, but by the time she takes her finals, she may be the youngest Advanced Nurse Practioner on the east coast."

"Good for her. Hey, look. I think now's our chance." Friday looked back at Angus and the boys and waved. "Give me a moment, and then I'll introduce you."

"Go aheid. We'll await yer signal," Angus said, bouncing the two-year-old toddler on his shoulder.

"Congratulations, Vickie, Rich," Evan said, his hand out to shake Rich's. "I get to kiss the bride, right?" he asked the groom.

"Just don't get carried away," Rich said.

"Or start comparing us," Ria said, laughing.

Evan gave Vickie a gentle kiss on the cheek. "I'm sorry I missed the wedding. I was halfway back to school and got a text from my roommate, telling me he'd cover my shifts for the next forty-eight hours. I figured I could at least come and toast to your good health and happiness."

"Well, being married assures the second one, but not necessarily the first, so I appreciate the blessings," Vickie said. "Who's your friend?" she asked, noticing the stares and sly smile on the pregnant woman he'd brought with him.

"Oh, her?" Evan said, grinning. "Just someone who came along for the ride. Actually, you haven't seen Vickie in how long?" he asked Friday.

"Eighteen years and twenty-seven days," she answered.

"Friday?" Ria asked, then shouted, "Friday! It's you! Oh, my God! You're huge! I guess you and Angus are still together. Oh, my God! I knew I'd recognize you if I ever saw you again. I mean, you look a lot different being pregnant and all..." Ria paused to take a breath and try to rein in her babbling, then burst out crying.

"I've missed you," she wept, hugging her surrogate mother.

"I've missed you, too," Friday said, crying just as much.

"Here," Gloria said, coming up to hand both of them a handkerchief. "I brought lots of them."

"Who's she?" Vickie whispered to Chuck.

"She's the woman who helped me smuggle you and your sisters away from the crook who told Grace you were dead."

"She what?" Vickie screeched.

"Hey, long story that I thought you knew. I'll tell you all about it someday. But not today. Just know that she's a great person, so be nice."

"So, is she one of my presents, too?" Vickie asked.

"Nah, you're one of hers. I knew she's wanted to see all three of you again. As far as I know, this is the first time all three of you have been together since the day you were born. Meeting Tori is a present to both you and Ria."

Ria moved over to Chuck, pulling on Friday's hand to join them. "Dad, are you responsible for Friday coming tonight?"

"Guilty," he said. "Oh, and I think you remember Angus." Chuck turned around and motioned for the big man surrounded by young males of stair-stepping sizes to join him.

"Oh, my God! Are all these your sons, Friday?" Ria asked.

"Hers and mine," Angus answered.

"Why does she call you Friday, Ma?" the red-haired boy who looked to be four years old asked.

"Because before I was Ma, I was called Friday. But you still call me Ma, all right?"

"Yes, Ma," he said, then sniggered into his hands.

"These are my sons," Friday said, her face beaming with pride. She began at the oldest and started naming them. "This is Young Angus, Brian, the twins Colum and Dougal, Ethan, Fergus, and Gavin. We're hoping this one is our Hannah, but we'll have to wait about six or seven weeks to find out if she sneaked in or we're getting a Hamish or Hector."

"You never had a daughter?" Vickie asked.

Friday skirted the answer by saying, "Ria is the only daughter I ever brought up, and that was for a little less than five years. It seems that Chuck did a fine job by himself." She looked over at Chuck, now standing close to Evan's father, their hands at their sides, barely touching. "Or did he find someone?"

"Not that I know of, but I'm not privy to his private life," Vickie said, a sly smirk arising. The two men were discreet, but anyone who saw the two men in the same room couldn't help but see their longing gazes and coy smiles.

Vickie stood on her tiptoes and looked over the crowd. "I don't know how many people my parents invited. I swear I don't know half of them."

"Almost half of them are *my* family," Friday joked, then looked over the crowd. Standing next to the bride, she felt amazingly comfortable in the presence of someone she'd just met. Suddenly, she reached out and grabbed Vickie's hand. "Who's that woman?" she asked.

"I don't know. Mom, Ria, do you know who she is?" Vickie asked.

"No, dear," Gloria answered. "She must be one of the dozen 'extras' Chuck asked me to make accommodations for. I'm pretty sure I've never seen her before."

"Ditto," Ria said. "She kind of looks familiar, though."

Chuck had been eavesdropping, his all-knowing smile wide.

Ria and Friday both noticed it and looked to each other as they had in the past, their silent agreement acknowledged. "Go for it," Ria said.

Friday opened her mouth to ask, then looked again at the woman. She was smiling at her. A loving smile that brought tears to Friday's eyes.

"Is she?" she asked Chuck.

"Yup. Took Silas nearly fifteen years to find her..." he began.

Friday didn't wait for the rest of his answer. She 'excuse me'd' through the standing and seated crowd to the young woman she recognized as her daughter.

"It's you! It's really you, isn't it?" Friday asked, tears streaming down her face.

"Yes, I'm pretty sure," the woman answered, her tears just as numerous. "I mean, we can do another DNA test, but according to Mr. Silas, it's a sure thing." Not waiting for an invitation, she reached around and did her best to hug her very pregnant mother.

"Sorry," she said. "It looks like we're both expecting. This is my first. Are those my brothers over there?"

"Seven brothers," Friday said, then patted her belly. "We don't know about this one yet. She's not due for another six weeks."

"She? Does this mean you're claiming a daughter?"

"The only daughter I'm claiming is you. Did you have a good life? I mean, did you get loving parents and a decent place to live?"

The woman nodded, then turned to an empty place setting on the table beside her and took a cloth napkin to wipe her nose. "Excuse me," she said.

"I'm sorry," Friday said. "I don't even know your new name."

"Rhianna. My parents said it was written on the label of the little gown I was wearing when they got me. They liked it, so it stayed. Is that the name you gave me?"

"Yes, it is." Friday felt a hand on her shoulder and turned aside.

"For your daughter," Gloria said, her eyes red-rimmed from crying. "Congratulations!"

Clink! Clink! Clink!

Roger waited for everyone to stop talking. "As the father of the bride, I'd like to thank all of you for coming. I see we have a few surprise guests tonight, too. It looks more like a family reunion than a wedding, but the bottom line is, we're family. Whether we were born into a family, legally adopted, or 'claimed,' I think everyone here is connected one way or another to each other. Here's to family!" he said, raising his champagne flute in toast. "Forever may we remember and love one another!"

"Here! Here!" and cheers answered his toast.

"Now, Chuck, you seem to be the instigator of about half of these reunions…"

"Or maybe all of them…" Chuck said with a sly smile.

"So, are there any more surprises you'd like to share?"

Chuck looked at Keith and grinned. "Well, I guess one more to share with family won't break the scales. Ladies and gentlemen, I'd like to introduce my fiancé, Keith Fraser."

Evan's father eased himself out of his chair, red-faced and chagrined. "I guess there's no better way for Chuck to come out than among friends. For those of you who don't know, I was widowed a few years back. I didn't think anyone could fill that void, but Chuck did. We've known each other since college, but with one thing or another – including children for both of us and my marriage to John – we drifted apart. We'll wait for our children to be married first, but in the meantime, here's to love and family, and happy ever afters!"

"Mama, what's he talking about, marrying another man," Tori asked.

"Hush," Leanne said. "I'll let your father explain it to you later."

Tori looked over at her newly discovered sisters. Their faces were bright with happiness, clapping, whistling and cheering for Chuck and Keith and their announcement. "I guess that's another part of the world that's been kept from me for eighteen years. Looks like I have a lot of living to catch up on."

Conclusion of Ria's story. Read on to check out HOW LOVE GROWS, the next book in TRIPLETS: THREE AREN'T ONE series.

How Love Grows

Triplets: Three Aren't One

Book Four

Copyright

How Love Grows

Weed and wine grapes were all around her, but all Tori was interested in was the young man who had come to take care of the marijuana plants.

Would he think she's crazy, too?

Chapter 1: Commitment

Mid-December 1991

"There you are, Dr. Buddy," the exuberant botanist declared, his hand outstretched in greeting. He looked around the desolate, snowy city park, making sure the two of them were alone. He continued, his voice now soft in case someone was eavesdropping. "Fifty-thousand dollars cash, just like you asked. I hope you don't mind that it's in an old valise. It's the only thing I had big enough to hold that much. Now, when are we going to get our baby?"

"Mr. Greene..." the obstetrician began, hoping his grimace of distaste at touching the cracked and sun-faded leather suitcase wasn't visible.

"Please, just call me Luther," the balding man said. "As in Luther Burbank."

"Ah, I see your parents had aspirations for you the moment you were born," the bootleg-baby doctor said, able to be more personable now that he felt the weight of the cash in his hand. "Your child is due in February but since it is one of a multiple-birth, I believe he or she will arrive early; say in a month or so. I have your contact information. I'll call as soon as the baby is ready to be picked up."

"So, you still don't know if we're getting a boy or girl?" Luther asked. "I thought you could detect the gender at five or six months gestation with ultrasounds."

"We can but since this is, shall we say, a private adoption, we prefer to remain out of and off the medical information system. We'd have to create a profile for the mother, record her personal information and more. We hold the privacy of our patients – both the unborn and the pregnant – in the highest regard."

"And the other baby is already spoken for by Gloria and Roger Thornwhistle, correct?"

"Please, please, Mr. Greene," the doctor began, then noticing the distressed man's scowl, corrected himself. "Please, Luther, let's not use names. I'd prefer that you and the other adoptive parents never interacted. I'm not sure if these babies are identical, but if they are, there would be red flags raised about the adoption process."

"Huh?"

"If you were at a party with the other parents and you both had your children with you, don't you think there'd be questions about the relationship between the two youths if they were identical? Many of my clients prefer to claim the offspring as their biological children to avoid questions about how the adoption was transacted. I assure you, the mother has given her consent, but just in case she changes her mind later in life, don't you think she might want to see or reclaim her child, her children?"

"Oh, I never thought of that," Luther said, his face as pale as the leafless birch trees that surrounded them. "I guess it's time to move west."

"West, south, to Timbuktu, Africa – it really doesn't matter. I suggest you keep away from the northeastern portion of the United States, though. The other parents are prominent members of society. They'll certainly want their child to accompany them to many of the events they sponsor."

"Yeah," Luther said softly, still stunned at the idea of having to pull up roots. "My wife did say her old college roommate…" He took a deep breath to compose himself. "Her former sorority sister – who shall remain nameless – was quite active socially."

Dr. Buddy patted him on the shoulder, trying to calm the distressed man while keeping a tight banker's grip on the battered briefcase of cash. "Just make whatever arrangements you need to soon. You and your wife will be able to make a prosperous new start wherever you go, I'm sure." He lifted the money bag. "Who knows? Maybe you can find a way to make this grow on trees."

"Yeah, sure," Luther said glumly, then lifted his hands to blow warm air onto them. "Hey, I've taken enough of your time. I have to go. I forgot my gloves and don't want to get frostbitten."

Dr. Buddy patted his shoulder one more time before pulling his hand away. "You'll be getting a call from me in a month or two. Here's hoping for a safe delivery for mother and babies."

"Huh?"

"There's always a risk with childbirth," Dr. Buddy explained, biting back the smirk that was rising. "Whether the baby and mother survive or not, there are still costs involved. Didn't your wife tell you that this," he lifted the case of money, "is non-refundable?"

A chill ran up Luther's back. He tried to ignore the shiver of suspicion wrapped around his gut-clenching sense of evil foreboding, but the ominous pair of negative emotions were as palatable as his rising bile. "No, she didn't."

"I'm sure I mentioned it to the missus. I can't give out paper contracts for transactions of this personal nature, but I always make it a point to confirm my no refunds policy. If giving birth to a live baby was easy and one hundred percent assured, we wouldn't be meeting right now, would we?"

Jaws clenched to molar-grinding tightness so the rebuke he felt roiling didn't escape, Luther nodded that he had heard the doctor, then turned and walked away. Empty-handed and potentially empty-hearted in a month or two. How could the world be so full of promise one day, then teetering on the edge of disaster the next, knocked out of whack by greedy and manipulative monsters?

Yesterday, he had been burned and betrayed by his research partner. The unscrupulous over-educated monkey of a man rushed to D.C. as soon as they reran the test numbers, saying he was going out for lunch. He didn't waste even a moment to file for a patent. On the application, he claimed the innovative method and unique chemical elixir combination was the result of an epiphany and that he had performed the tests by himself and verified them with an independent lab. He left out that it was Luther's idea and they had done the experiments and research together over a course of months.

Now, the overgrown ape in a white jacket was sure to be the sole recipient of the millions of dollars the largest horticultural corporation in the western hemisphere had promised for the cloning technology.

As a result, he was one hundred percent clinically depressed. But, no matter how bummed he was, he had to roll out of bed and solve his monetary dilemma. A last-minute find of an adoptable infant had been brought to his wife's attention. Leanne's college roommate had called and said that for a *mere* $50,000, they could adopt a newborn from a woman who was clean, healthy, and never used drugs. She was only a few hours drive away. No dealing with airplanes, passports or government restrictions.

By the end of the afternoon, he'd pawned everything he could lay his hands on and cleaned out both their savings and retirement accounts. Yes, they were destitute. He'd even let go of his piano and first editions of Hemingway to get the cash to 'buy' the child that he'd been unable to create with his loving wife.

Now after meeting the doctor, he realized that this arrangement had all the markings of a scam. Whether the man was a licensed physician or not, he had the aura of a perpetually greedy devil, his eyes blazing with dollar lust.

All he had left in life were Leanne and hope. Hope that it wouldn't be the end of their love if the adoption fell through, too. He hadn't been able to give her the baby she'd wanted for twenty years. It didn't make a difference that she was the barren one, not him. Both of them had agreed to gamble on a backstreet adoption. They'd take the last of their money and cash in as much of their assets as was needed to start their family. Everything else was just stuff.

He ran his hand over the top of his bald head, wiping off the melted snow before he got back in the car. "I just hope my gut is wrong this time," he said, then put the key in the ignition. "Sometimes I hate it when I'm right."

***

"I know it's not much," Leanne said, bringing the platter out from the kitchen, "but I couldn't see spending all that money on a turkey when it's just the two of us. At least for a while. Just think… Any day now."

Luther watched his distracted wife set the dish too close to the edge of the plastic work table they'd been using to eat dinner on since they sold their oak drop-leaf table to invest in Dr. Buddy and the baby. "Watch what you're doing and stop gazing at the calendar," he said, pushing the plate closer to the center. "I promise, no matter how hard or long you stare at that numbered grid, it won't make time go faster. It's a constant."

"Hey, I have a degree, too," she snapped, then immediately became remorseful. "I'm sorry. I know I'm not pregnant, but sometimes I feel like I am. I mean, my moods are all over the place. The only thing worse is hearing myself apologize all the time because I've been bitching at you."

Luther picked up her hand and kissed it. "You may not be pregnant, dear wife, but you are expecting. Or as they say now, '*We* are expecting.'"

Leanne giggled at his grand gesture. "Yes, *we* are," she said. "Let me get the rest of the food. It may just be chicken, but it's a big one. I figure we should run out of meat about the same time that you're tired of chicken enchiladas or chicken soup."

"Or chicken salad or chicken and dumplings."

Leanne left the room and came back with a divided dish of mashed potatoes and peas and saw that Luther was now down in the dumps. He was mood-swinging again, too. She sat next to him, took his hand, and prayed. "Lord, I know you have great things planned for our new family. Thank You for helping us see that we don't need physical *stuff*, but only You and each other. Please guide us to where You want us. And thanks so much for our health and for keeping us together. Amen."

Luther squeezed her hand tight in response. "Thanks. I needed that. I sometimes lose focus. You're right, though. I'd give up every material object I own and the value of all my intellectual property to keep us together. I may not have a job, but I do have prospects. I was waiting to tell you until I had the final word on it, but I think I've lined up a position out west."

"West? How far?" Leanne said excitedly. "I'm ready to get away from all this ice and snow."

"How about Oregon?"

Her face fell. "Which part? I know it gets cold there, too."

"Willamette Valley – it's considered a Mediterranean climate. It's not much for winter chill but has long and dry summers. There are opportunities for growing dozens of different herbs, too. Lavender, mint, rosemary… Growing grapes would be fantastic but take a major financial investment. We'd have to work for someone else until we saved enough capital for our own venture."

"Our own vineyard…" Leanne mused. "A little bit of Italy on the west coast of America…"

"Or mint and lavender fields," Luther added. "The return on those would be sooner. We'll see. We may have to start in California. First things first: Christmas dinner!"

***

Ring! Ring!

"I got it! I got it!" Leanne shouted as she pushed the laundry basket out of her way.

Biting his lip, trying to keep the stomach-churning feeling of dread from turning into tears, Luther hugged the back of the door, staying partially hidden from his eager wife.

"Yes, this is she," she said, her face aglow. "Yes, I recognized your voice. Well, is it a boy or a girl? And when can we come to get her?"

The phone dropped from her hands and Luther rushed to catch her as her legs gave way. He verified she hadn't injured herself, then looked in her face, ready to ask what had happened. No words were needed, though. She couldn't have spoken even if he had asked. He picked up the phone as if it was radioactive, barely touching the hard plastic as he held it near his ear.

"Hello?" he asked. "Yes, this is Luther Greene. Oh, no; the mother, too? All three of them? There were four? Oh, three babies and the mother. Hey, thanks for calling, but I have to see to my wife. She's not doing too well right now. Bye."

"She's dead," Leanne babbled. "Dr. Buddy said our daughter was dead..."

"I know, I know, sweetheart. I talked to him, too." Luther sighed deeply, then decided to tell her his suspicions. "She might not be, though. I mean..."

Before he could finish the thought, Leanne had sprung back to life at the word *not*. "What do you mean?"

"I think Dr. Buddy's a con artist. I know he has a pregnant woman at his birthing center. He showed me a picture that he had snapped when she was sleeping. He even made sure the TV was on in the background so I could see the weather forecast on the news program. He wasn't lying about that. And she was huge! Yes, he probably wasn't lying about her having triplets, either. However, she didn't look sickly. He is a licensed obstetrician in New Hampshire – I verified that as soon as you told me Gloria was going to adopt a baby through a doctor's office. But when he took that money out of my hand last month... I swear, it was as if the devil's own was taking it. I guess I should have told you about my fears, but just in case it wasn't a scam, I decided to keep it to myself."

"So, what do we do?" Leanne asked, focused on picking up the laundry she had knocked over, concentrating on something she was in control of.

"Call Gloria and see if she got the same call," he said. "Do you want to or do you want me to?"

"I got this," she said, setting down the basket. "I may not have my baby, but I do have hope."

Leanne dialed her friend's number, then hung up and retried. "It's busy. Maybe she's talking to that bastard, Buddy."

Luther chuckled, glad that rage had overtaken her grief. If it had to be one of the two strong emotions, he'd take the rage. Nothing was sadder than a wife who couldn't get up off the couch because of depression.

"There she is!" she finally said, then closed her eyes to concentrate on the call that was going through. "Hi, Gloria? Yes, did you get a call... No, wait! Don't fret or fall apart or whatever you want to call it. At least, not yet. Luther seems to think that Dr. Buddy is scamming us. Yes, there's a good chance the babies are fine. Shoot! I don't know. Maybe he has a dozen people he's promising those babies to. Yes, I know. I saw the same pictures. Don't you think that he could just as well have shown them to twelve people as two? Okay. Well, right now, I'm going to pray and I suggest you do, too. Don't you have a friend who's a private detective or something? Okay, so he does it as a hobby. Maybe this guy Silas can help us out. Yes, keep in touch. Those first words literally knocked me off my feet, but Luther caught me. I'm sure we'll get our babies eventually. Okay. I love you, too."

"Well?" Luther asked.

"You make phone calls if you need to, I'm going to find every candle in this house, then get down on my hands and knees and pray for a miracle."

"Frankly, dear, I don't care which one of us gets an answer first as long as it's that we have a daughter, waiting for Mama and Papa to come to get her."

"Amen to that!"

***

"Gloria, this is Chuck. Hey, I have great news. I just helped deliver three small but beautiful and healthy baby girls. I know we should wait a few hours, but I thought you might want to come and get yours early. What? No, she didn't die. No! Nobody died. All three babies are fine and so is the mother. Who told you that? Oh, he's in so much trouble already and why I wanted you to come early, but this is worthy of an expedited ticket to hell. No, do not call him back and give him a piece of your mind or contact him about anything else ever again. He's about an hour away from getting busted for white slavery, kidnapping, racketeering, and probably a whole bucketload of other charges. You have to get here fast, though. Remember that gas station mini-market where you dropped me off last month after our shopping trip at the mall? Right, that's it. Get there, stat. Do not stop for anything other than to call the other parents. I don't have your friend's number but if Buddy told you the girls died, I'm pretty sure he told that to everyone else he'd contracted with for delivery of a newborn. I don't know what to say to them because I don't know who they are. I do know you, though. Hey, I gotta go. Oh, and the password is Woodstock. I'll be driving my new old white work van. *Ciao*!"

Gloria set the phone down, tears streaming from her eyes.

"Are you all right?" Roger asked, holding her tight. "Don't worry, I know it deep down in my bones that we'll get a child one of these days. Hopefully soon, but I know…"

Holding her hand up to ask him to stop his babbling, Gloria nodded. "Hold that thought." She picked up the phone again and dialed Leanne.

"Hey, sweetheart. It's me, Gloria. Yes, I got the same phone call from Dr. Buddy, but don't you believe a word he said! You and Luther put on a coat and drive to that little gas station convenience store at Hemingway and Sherlock.

Our daughters will be there! Yes, they're alive! Now get going! We don't want to be late!"

"Wha... What's that all about?"

"Roger, grab your keys and I'll explain on the way." Gloria looked around the huge foyer with a renewed vision. Yes, it was a grand mansion by anyone's standards, but in a few minutes, it would be their daughter's home.

***

"Leanne!" Gloria squealed as she ran into her friend's open arms. "Dr. Buddy lied to us. They're all fine. Nobody died and we still get the babies. Are you ready for this?"

"I've been ready for this since I was three and playing with rag dolls," Leanne said with a feigned frown. She shrugged both shoulders to her earlobes in excitement and started hopping up and down, her joy uncontainable.

Luther moved around the ladies and shook Roger's hand. "Can you believe this?"

"Not yet," Roger answered, his tone reserved. He shook his head, trying to remain the calm and sensible person of the group. Suddenly his smile popped free, his anticipation overriding doubt. "Oh, I am so ready!" he said with unrestrained excitement.

A silver vehicle pulled up to the fuel island on the opposite side of the station from them and all heads turned.

"Is that them?" Gloria asked, clinging to her husband's arm as she stood on tiptoes, trying for a better look.

Roger gave her hand a comforting pat, then moved away from the group so he could see who it was. "I don't know. Did he tell you what he'd be driving?"

"Oh, yeah. He said he'd be driving a white van," Gloria said. "Remember the password, 'Woodstock.'"

"Sounds like my kind of guy," Luther remarked. He hugged his wife around the shoulders. "Remember when we were there?"

"How could I forget," Leanne said, then giggled. "Over twenty years ago, and now our baby is finally here. That's a long gestation!"

"There's Chuck!" Gloria exclaimed, hopping up and down with joy, her hands tucked under her chin at seeing his familiar face behind the steering wheel.

"Settle down," Roger said. "You don't want to bring attention to us."

"Two middle-aged couples, snuggled up against the wind, looking like vultures ready to pounce... I'd say we were already suspicious," Luther said.

The driver of the van looked beyond the gas pumps and saw the two couples standing by the stack of bundled firewood, their smiles of anticipation marking them as the new parents. Chuck rolled past them and came to a stop at the side of the mini-store, out of sight of anything but owls searching for dinner. "Tranquility base: Stork One and Stork Two have landed," he said to his new companion, then opened the door and got out.

"Hey, there," the perky young doctor said as he approached the huddled foursome. "Anyone for a game of golf? Know a good course around here?"

"How about Woodstock?" Gloria said, then ran up to Chuck and gave him a big hug. "Are they inside? Are they okay? I thought I was going to have a total meltdown when Dr. Buddy called and said that Grace had died and they couldn't get the babies out in time. That they had all passed."

Chuck's eyes widened. "Grace was alive when I left." He opened the side door, exposing his new traveling nursemaid and the gym bag full of babies.

"I'm still alive," Grace Two said indignantly, then groaned softly as she realized it was a misunderstanding about the shared name. "I think you'd better call me Nanny." She looked at the eager parents crowded around the open door, the women squeezed in front of their husbands to keep away from the chill. "Why don't you ladies come inside?"

Gloria led the way. "Which one is ours?" she asked once inside, peering into the unzipped bag.

"It's up to you two who gets Aqua and who gets Pinkie," Chuck said, watching the allocation of babies from the front seat. "The yellow-wrapped sweetheart is mine."

"Oh, my God!" Leanne exclaimed. "They *are* identical! I can't believe it. How will we know whose is whose?"

Little Pinkie opened her eyes, started to squall, then caught sight of Gloria and smiled. "I don't care if she's the biggest or not; this one's mine."

"Then that must mean she's ours. Oh, I can't believe it. I swear I feel a tingling in my breasts. I'm as barren as a moon rock, but I swear she's kicked in a bucket load of estrogen." Leanne looked at the dark-haired young woman who'd been taking care of the babies. "Can I take her home now?"

"That's the plan. Oh, and don't even try to get in touch with Dr. Buddy. Either of you. If they didn't catch him, they will. You're lucky Chuck and I got in the middle of this or you wouldn't be celebrating motherhood tonight."

"Thank you, Nanny?" Gloria said, unsure of her name. "Chuck has my number. If you two run into any trouble or need a few bucks, just give me a call." She unzipped her jacket and put the swaddled baby inside. "Come on Vickie. You're coming home."

Leanne copied Gloria's tactic of kangaroo-pouch carrying the baby in the coat. "And you, too, Tori Lynn. Daddy's waiting outside."

Leanne stepped out of the van, then suddenly yipped. "She latched on! Oh, my Lord! I'm going to see if Luther can set me up with some of those plant estrogens. I may be able to nurse my baby still! Sing hallelujah!"

Chapter 2: New Beginnings

January 3, 1992

The young mother, now devoid of the babies she'd carried for eight months, was distraught at her loss. She'd made a decision, though, and for eight long months had believed it was right. Her best friend in the world had tried the whole time she'd known she was pregnant to talk her into keeping her babies, knowing that between him and their extended family, they could keep her evil mother out of the babies' lives, but she wouldn't believe him.

Now it was too late. The babies were dead and it was all her fault. If she'd chosen a traditional hospital, they might have detected the problem sooner and been able to take the babies in time. They'd all be alive. Even if she had signed away her parental rights and couldn't get them back, they'd be living – loving and being loved by parents somewhere.

What was it that Dr. Buddy said was the problem? Grace shook her head, all her memories a jumble of random words and technical mumbo jumbo, twisted and skewed by the residual sedatives still in her system. His explanation still didn't make sense. Would it ever?

Chuck? Where had he been during these last hours? She blinked back her tears of loss. She had sent him away, using harsh words she could never take back. The man had stood by her for months. Pretended to be her lover if needed, given up his family and his medical career to protect her away from her vile and vindictive mother. And she'd returned his caring with curses and scorn. What kind of scum was she to treat a generous and caring man like that?

Grace's shoulder twinged in discomfort. The subconscious pain always came when she thought of her. What kind of mother would shoot her own daughter? It couldn't even be considered a crime of passion since she had done it in cold blood. Thank God her reflexes were quick and she ducked in time to save herself from death at the close-range firing. Still, she'd need to watch out for the woman's sudden reappearance.

"Gracie, do you want something to eat or drink?" Dusty asked.

But I'm safe now. Dusty's back in my life. Mother wasn't able to scare him away.

"Something to drink," Grace said. "Maybe water?"

"Get her some chocolate milk and pick up a gallon of water, too. She needs some calories and we all could use the water," Papa Doc said.

And I have Papa Doc, Daddy, and Silas, too. Between those four men who love me so much, maybe I'll be safe...

Grace snuggled into her father's jacket, inhaling his familiar scent. *How could I ever believe he wouldn't protect me. I've been such a fool.*

A gush of cold air came into the cab of the truck. She looked up. They were at a gas station and Dusty had his hands full. When had that happened? Time was skewed – as shattered and scattered as a thousand-piece jigsaw puzzle thrown across a rock garden.

"Here you go, Mr. Stillwater."

She looked up to the voice. Dusty was handing a jug of drinking water and a carton of chocolate milk to her father. *Yes, Dusty still wanted her. Did he know what she'd done? What she'd been through? About the other man she'd been with? If he didn't know and found out, would it change his mind?*

Her father speaking to Dusty brought her back to reality. "Seeing as you've been through so much hell and still seem pretty set on marrying my daughter, you can go ahead and call me Dad or Hal, whichever feels more comfortable."

Beep! Beep!

Confused and afraid that she might be hallucinating, Grace sat up and looked for the source of the roadrunner's chirp.

"What was that?" Dusty asked, looking around.

"My cell phone," Papa Doc said. "I got what they call a personalized alert tone for my incoming texts." He took the phone out of his shirt pocket, tapped a few buttons, and then put it back. He looked at Hal and grimaced. "Someone just checking to make sure all went well on our end," and nodded at Grace.

"It's going to take time for all of us to heal," she heard her father say. "Some losses take longer to get over. Let's hope you haven't lost Chuck because of all of this."

Chuck! Where is he? Did she send him away forever? What had she said?

"Only for a little time," Papa Doc said. "My son has a nurturing soul and is a gentleman. I think he's just stepping back so Dusty can help her heal."

"What do you mean?" Hal asked.

Daddy sounds confused. He's not the only one!

"Chuck didn't know Dusty was coming with us or that we even found him. That was last minute, remember?"

Does Chuck even know Dusty by sight? No, they've never met; although I did mention him a few million times in the last eight months.

"Yeah, I wouldn't know your son if I sat on him," Dusty said. "Hey, does anyone want some chocolate?"

Grace tried to quiet her persistent doubts and focused on the sounds of her men bantering back and forth, their voices rising and lowering with their emotions and concerns. She hadn't heard her father and two surrogate uncles in a month and didn't realize until now how much she had missed them.

And Dusty. He was here now, safe from her mother's false accusations.

She looked out the window. The world was getting better, itty bit by itty bit. The man she had gone through hell for was here. Would Dusty accept her as she was? The way he had held her – and sobbed uncontrollably with joy – when he rescued her after she had been abandoned by Nurse Ellen, she knew he'd do

301

anything for her. He seemed to be sharing her feeling of loss for the babies, too. All her men could mourn with her. And they would heal together, too.

Everyone is here but Chuck. Where is he? She closed her eyes tight and tried to find a thread of recent memory, struggling to recall the last words he had said to her. There it was. An echo of his voice. He was leaving her, he said – leaving so she wouldn't associate him with her loss.

Which would have been worse, the loss of the babies to adoption or death? Definitely death. With adoption, they would still have been happy little people with families who cared for and cherished them. Now with death, they were just little corpses. Was it her fault they had died? Did she do something wrong?

Grace looked at Dusty, blinking back the tears that had returned. A familiar movement out of the corner of her eye caught her attention. She leaned over him to watch the man coming out of the convenience store. "Who's that?" she asked, pointing out the window.

Dusty recognized him as the man he had swapped jugs of water with earlier. "Just some guy from the store. He got coffee and water, too. Why? Do you know him?"

She sighed then leaned back into his arm. "I thought I did…"

He's alive and moving on with his life. I should, too.

"Grace, I know it's not exactly romantic – my timing and all," Dusty said.

She turned to him, warmed by his presence. She felt a smile rise, the first one in ages.

"But I want to make a new life with you as my wife," he said and put his arm around her to snuggle her close. "I have a lot going on now. I have my own business and everything. I still want to marry you and always will. We can start again with a family as soon as you say the word. I kinda know what went on with the other guy, and it doesn't matter to me. I mean, I know you have been hurt in about a million different ways, but I want to help you heal. Would you let me? I mean, I'll do it however you want, but I'd rather do it as your husband than as your best friend."

Grace leaned into him further and inhaled his unique scent of boy and man. She felt his nearness light up her face. She looked up. "Yeah, I think I'd like you better as a husband. Let me get healed up, and then let's get married. But if you don't mind, I'd still like to live with Papa Doc and Silas for a while. And hang out with my dad, too."

"And me?"

"Duh! You'd be living with us, too. One great big dysfunctional family."

***

"Leanne, are you sure you want to try this tea? I mean, it won't hurt you but it might make you a bit moody." Luther lifted the teapot with his concoction of fenugreek, fennel, and half a dozen other herbs. "And it might taste nasty, too, but should help amplify your body's own trace amounts of oxytocin and help with milk production."

"I'll try anything, even though I think I could probably do it with only the stimulation of her suckling or whatever those fancy words are for making milk." Leanne poured out a cup of the pale brew and guzzled it down. "Do I taste ginger in that?"

"Just a few slivers in the whole pot. I didn't think it would hurt, plus if the other herbs upset your tummy, it would help."

Luther looked into the dresser drawer he had lined with towels and scarves and saw that his little five-pound blessing was awake and squirming. "Ready to try again?"

Leanne sat down in the rocker – one of the few pieces of furniture they hadn't sold – and bared a breast. "Yes, I am. She's tiny and doesn't need much to start. I'm glad I read up on how much babies need to eat. We may not have formula, but Lord willing, we'll be successful right out of the chute and never have to buy any."

"And Mama-made will be easier when we're on the road," Luther added.

Leanne winced at the sudden contact. "Man, she can suck!" she whispered emphatically, keeping her volume down so she didn't startle the blonde baby.

"Our little Tori Lynn Greene," Luther said, tears coming to his eyes. "I've never seen anything so beautiful as my wife nursing our child."

Sniff. Sniff. "Now you got me going, too," Leanne said, then paused. "Oh, my God! That's what they're talking about! I swear, my milk just let down. Whoosh! The sensation is indescribable but real. Oh, we are so doing this, little one." She looked up at her husband and added. "Papa."

"I used to think I wanted to be called Dad or Daddy, but when you say it, Papa sounds so right. Yup, Papa it is."

⋉✳✳

Two months later

"Are you sure it isn't too early in the year to be heading west?" Leanne asked for the third time since breakfast

Rather than answer, Luther looked her way and scowled.

"I'm sorry. I know it's the right choice. I'm just scared to death of snowstorms and flat tires and…"

"Leanne, where's your faith? We've seen so many miracles in our lives, overcome so many obstacles, and you still doubt?"

"I know, I know," she said, then looked down at the map again. "Are you sure you want to go all the way to California? Wouldn't Texas be closer?"

"Maybe, but there are more diverse horticultural opportunities available in California. Besides, I hear they're thinking of making marijuana legal there soon. I'd love to get in on the ground floor of that industry."

"That'll happen when pigs fly," Leanne said. "And no, don't even think of doing any underground or black market growing or selling or…"

Luther put his hand on his wife's arm. "I'd never do anything illegal or risky. I got out of growing that when I married you. What makes you think I'd risk arrest or imprisonment with you two depending on me?"

Leanne put her hand on top of his. "I never thought you would. It's just you have such a gift of making plants thrive. Not many men can just look at a plant and see what it needs. I'm sure we'll find the right employer for you once we get to California. If you can do that for annuals, I'm sure you can do it for grapes and other perennials, too."

"And if I don't care for all the rules and restrictions they have in the Golden State, we can always venture north a bit. Lots of green in Oregon!"

"A lavender farm. Now that sounds interesting…" Leanne mused, sniffing the hand lotion on the back of her hand. "A cottage industry of creating handmade soaps and lotions…"

"Sounds like a lot of work," Luther said. "Let me try to use more brains and less brawn to make a living. I'm not getting any younger. Let's save your passion for sweet-smelling botanicals to crafting, not selling retail or wholesale."

"At least until Tori's older and doesn't take so much of my time." She noticed Luther's look of confusion. "Not that I'm complaining. I've had twenty years to cook, craft, and sew. I'll be back to doing more of those in a flash, wondering what I should do with so much time on my hands."

"Yup, these are the good old days," Luther said. "Enjoy them."

***

April 1994

"That's it – we're moving!" Luther announced as he walked in the front door of the ramshackle converted chicken coop he and his family had lived in for two years.

"How soon?" Leanne asked, looking around to see how much trouble it would be to pack up. When she realized there was nothing she cared about other than her family and a plastic tote of their 'treasures,' she smiled broadly and added, "Do we want to go tonight or wait until morning?"

"I do love you so, wife," he said and held her close. He looked around the room as she had with the same 'what do I need to pack' attitude and wondered why he had waited for two years to see if life growing mint as a sharecropper would ever get better.

"I'm sorry I kept us here so long," he said. "I really did think that everything would turn around. If only I hadn't been robbed of my patents…"

"The toilets of the world are overflowing with the crap that 'if only,' regrets, and looking back are made of. Knock it off. Face forward!"

"Crap! Face Forward!" two-year-old Tori said, looking up from her favorite toy: an interactive four-sided rotating plastic cube.

"Sometimes I wish she hadn't started talking," Luther said.

Leanne chuckled. "Yup, she's a genius at picking out the key points in a conversation, that's for sure."

"She has all she needs for toys with that thing," Luther said, bending down to play with her. He picked up the cube and looked at the mirror side. "Where's Tori?"

"Babies!" she said, grabbing for it, bouncing in place with glee.

"Do you think she remembers that she had two sisters?" Luther asked, trying not to frown.

Leanne stared at her child, visualizing two babies who looked just like her sitting next to her. She blinked and the image was gone. "I don't know. Maybe I'll ask her when she's old enough to understand. I know that every once in awhile, I see all three."

"No, don't ask her. It will only complicate her life. Let's keep everything simple. How about you make some sandwiches and we take off tonight? We can sleep in the back of the station wagon."

"Blankets, bologna, our box, and our baby. Yup, moving day is simple. Are you going to leave a note or call?"

"Call who? No one's checked on us in six months. Nah, we don't owe anyone and I'm not going to harvest anything, so there's no income lost or due. Let's head south. Even if I have to take a job as an itinerant fruit picker, we'll be fine. We may have to live on nectarines and strawberries for a while, but we'll be fine, I know it."

"I know it, too."

"Strawberries!" Tori said.

***

January 3, 1997

"She's five years old today," Leanne said. "So big compared to when she was born…"

"And old enough for public school next year," Luther said. "They probably would have made an exemption for her and let her enroll early because she could read already."

"I know, but I'm not ready for her to leave me. I mean, if I thought they could teach her something I couldn't, I'd let her go."

"No, you wouldn't," Luther said, one eyebrow raised.

Leanne looked up and saw the gesture that meant 'I won't let you win this one, no matter how much you want to argue. Go ahead and give up now because you know I'm right.'

"What can they teach her that I can't?" she asked, unwilling to admit defeat without at least a discussion on the subject.

"School will teach her how to get along with others, how to interact and carry on a conversation with someone her age who isn't imaginary. Good grief; how to play team sports, turn somersaults and cartwheels…"

"You're probably right," Leanne agreed, frowning in defeat.

"Don't be sad, Mama," Tori said. She walked over and stood next to her mother's chair. She put her arm around her mother's neck and snuggled her close. "You're doing a great job teaching me. Knowing how to turn somersaults and cartwheels won't help me develop a more efficient energy source or create a cleaner environment."

"Good Lord, Tori!" Luther exclaimed. "What have you been reading?"

Tori picked up the latest scientific trade magazine her mother had brought home from the recycling center. It was a year old but new to her. "This."

He rolled his eyes and shook his head in amazement.

"Okay, I see what you mean. School doesn't start for a few days, though," Leanne said.

"Winter break ended today. Tori, do you want to go to school with other kids? They might be a bit boring at first, but I'm sure you'll find things to do with them that your mother and I can't."

"Like turn somersaults and cartwheels?" she asked.

"Among other things. Going to school will be a brand new universe for you to explore, interacting with people who have different perspectives and interests in life..."

Tori set her hand on her father's and, paraphrasing Renée Zellweger's classic line, said, "You had me at brand new."

***

The next day was brisk, even for a California winter day. "Ready for school?" Luther asked.

"Her or me?" replied Leanne.

"Both. Either."

"She's fine. I'm a mess," Leanne said. She ran the brush through her hair one more time, noting that it was now more salt than pepper. "Do you think I should color it?"

"Absolutely not," Luther replied, then kissed the top of her head. "I love your silver highlights. Mark my words; platinum locks will be the new golden tresses in a few years. I don't want you changing your looks for anyone, even you. You're perfect. You're the best you that can possibly be."

Leanne giggled, remembering the night before. They were in their fifties but were as frisky and passionately in love as they had been in their twenties.

"Is this what kids wear to school?" Tori asked, walking into their room.

Luther swallowed the laugh, but Leanne couldn't help herself and chuckled at the comical combination of styles. "No, honey. I don't think they wear jeans and a tutu at the same time."

"Why not? It's almost freezing today. You make me wear pants when it's cold," she said, rubbing her hand down the side of her denims, "but it's also my first day of school and I want to look pretty." She spun around and showed off the handmade skirt of pink nylon net.

"Yes, dear," Leanne explained as gently as she could. "But wearing a fairy princess dress might be a little too much. Let's just stay with blue jeans and a flannel shirt."

"Fine! But don't blame me if they can't tell if I'm a boy or a girl."

"What?" Leanne and Luther asked at the same time.

"Because my hair is short," Tori said, her head hung down in shame.

"Oh, sweetheart," Luther said, holding her close. "You're beautiful whether your hair is long or short. I thought you liked it short so it didn't tangle."

Tori's glower would have been comical if she hadn't been so distraught.

"How about I put a ribbon in it?" Leanne asked. "Boys never wear those."

Nodding as she thought about it, Tori said with a sincerity beyond her tender years, "Let's make it a pink ribbon, just to be sure."

"Pink it is."

⋈

Luther and Leanne drove up to the front of the elementary school, chilly from both anticipation and the cold north wind. "This is such a big step in our little girl's life."

"Our life, too," Luther added. "Next thing you know, we'll be helping her pick out a wedding dress."

Unbidden tears suddenly burst forth from Leanne, but she caught them with a hankie. "Danged allergies," she said as she wiped them away.

"It's the wrong time of year for hay fever," Tori said. "And it's okay to cry. Don't fear the unknown: embrace it!" she added, sniffing back her own tears of apprehension.

"Oh, my!" Leanne said. She looked at Luther. "What have we done?"

Luther had been thinking the same thing. Their daughter's philosophy on life was at least ten years beyond that of others her age. Is this why nature didn't give older people children? Did they teach them too much too soon?

"Sweetheart," Luther said, holding Tori by her shoulders, looking deep into her eyes. "These other children might not have had parents who shared as much with them as we do with you. Try to use smaller words."

"You mean monosyllabic not a lesser-sized font, right?" she asked, ending her question with a wink.

"Just give them a chance, and whatever you do, don't try to make someone feel dumb. That's cruel and we're not mean people."

"Yeah, mean people suck. Can we go in now? People are staring at us."

Luther and Leanne looked up and saw little faces peering out the window, two adult women behind them, watching the pensive family having their last chit chat before coming in. "The start of a new year and a new phase in your life."

"Our lives," Leanne whispered. "My days are going to be so empty."

Chapter 3: Adjustment Period

"Mr. and Mrs. Greene and Tori Lynn," the school secretary read, looking over the application. "So, you adopted her or are you her guardians?"

"Excuse me?" Leanne asked indignantly, not even trying to hide her anger.

"Oh, I'm sorry. I thought you had legal custody of her in some way." She looked up at Leanne's gray hair, then ran her fingers through her own silvery locks. "We're a little old to be biological parents of kindergartners."

"Speak for yourself," Leanne hissed, her eyes narrowed and fists clenched at her side.

"What my wife is saying is what difference does it make to you or the school or anyone else? If there's a medical emergency and she needs a blood transfusion or a kidney, we'll let the medical professionals take care of that. My concern is that *my* daughter won't languish in the classrooms; that the teachers will be able to offer her intellectual stimulation and challenges."

"Oh, don't worry about that, Mr. Greene. Some of our kinder-kids can already read."

"That's *Dr.* Greene," Luther said. "I'm a botanist. And Tori can already read and perform basic math computations."

Leanne cleared her throat and nudged Luther. He clarified his remark. "Tori can read way beyond the first-grade level and perform advanced mathematical computations."

"You know, it's not always good to teach a child beyond her age," the secretary admonished, making sure she kept her eyes focused on her paperwork, not engaged with the elderly couple who were so proud of their prodigy.

Luther grabbed Leanne's clenched fist. "At least one day," he whispered. "Let's give it at least one day…"

Her hand relaxed into his. "Okay."

"Now, if Tori is ready," the secretary said, standing up and facing the trio, "let's go introduce all of you to her teacher and the aide."

"Excuse me," Tori said. She pointed to the woman's enamel lapel pin. "Are you from Latvia?"

"What? Why yes! How'd you know?" She looked down at the colorful pin with a single rhinestone and verified what she already knew: the country name wasn't on it. "Do you know what this little jewel signifies?"

"First, I knew because the shape of the pin looks like Latvia. Second, I'm not sure, but that jewel looks like it's where Riga would be. It might be a suburb, though. I don't know the names of all the cities."

Leanne beamed with parental pride. There was no reason to tell the self-righteous secretary that Latvia was her native country nor that they had a stylized map of it in their living room.

The group entered the small and tidy classroom, the walls lined with plastic and wicker baskets filled with assorted toys and shelves of colorful picture books. The floors were covered with patchwork mats and rugs decorated with pictures of farms and roads. The whole area gave off a warm, homey vibe, assuring the hesitant parents that they had made the right decision. There was so much to offer their daughter in this room. Outdoor activities, crafts, and the library would certainly enhance Tori's life experience way beyond what the two of them and their limited resources could offer.

The introductions to the teacher, aide, and the class as a whole went well, so Luther and Leanne bade Tori farewell, comfortable that no harm would come to their little girl.

"Do you think they'll let us come back and have lunch with her?" Leanne asked Luther on the way back to the car.

"You're going to have to cut the cord sometime, dear. Let her try this out her own way. She'll never be able to stand on her own two feet if you keep clutching her so close to you."

She looked at her watch. "All right. But I want to get here fifteen minutes before school's out to pick her up just in case there's a crowd."

"Come on, wife," Luther said, his arm around her shoulder. "I think I have something that will take your mind off of her. It's been a while since we had alone time in the middle of the day. I took the whole day off work, so the next five hours are just for you and me."

"Well, maybe you will and maybe you won't distract me, but it will be fun trying!"

***

"You can hang your backpack on the hook at the number fifteen," Mrs. Johnson said. "That's one and five. Do you know your numbers?"

Tori grinned, remembering that she wasn't supposed to make anyone feel dumb. Papa had said the kids, but he probably meant the teacher, too. "Yes, ma'am."

And then she couldn't help herself. "It's the digit one and the digit five – both prime numbers – not the sum of one and five which would be six, which is not a prime number. And neither is fifteen. A prime number, that is. It is the product of two primes, though: three and five."

The teacher looked around the room to see if the other students were paying attention to their conversation. They weren't. They were gathered around the terrarium, intent on watching the tarantula consume its meal of young crickets. "I like numbers, too," she said. "They're kind of like a foreign language to most five-year-old students, though. Maybe you'd better only chat about prime numbers with me."

Tori nodded, glad that she had already made a friend. Maybe Mrs. Johnson could teach her how to turn somersaults. Nah. She was as old as Mama. She'd probably have to learn that from another kid.

"What are they doing?" she asked before hanging up her backpack.

"We have a classroom pet. It's a big hairy spider. It's lunchtime for Mr. Tarantula. Do you want to watch him eat?"

"Spiders don't have hair, they have setae which look like hair but aren't made of protein," Tori said, then noticed the wide-eyed stare that always meant she'd shared too much. "But they sure look like hairs, huh?"

"Yes, they do. Why don't you use your first day here just to observe? Just like if you were researching in the field, you'd want to watch your subjects in their natural habitat before coming to any conclusions about what they're doing or why." Mrs. Johnson lifted up the backpack to put it on the hook. "This is terribly heavy. Is there something breakable in here?"

"Only if you drop it," Tori said, then took the bag and finished setting it on the hook carefully.

The rest of the morning went smoothly, Tori watching her peers as they stacked blocks, strung colored beads, and cut out paper circles. Rather than create her own intricate patterns and designs, she intentionally scaled back her talents, mimicking the others so she didn't stand out. *Now I know how Jane Goodall felt when she interacted with gorillas! You don't have to be smarter or stronger or prove anything! This is fun.*

Finally, it was lunchtime. She took out her colorful cloth lunch bag and the wax-paper wrapped sandwich and apple and sat down at a table by herself, waiting to see if someone would join her. A minute later, the freckle-faced red-haired boy who had been staring at her all morning sat down beside her. He set his action hero lunch box down and opened it up, displaying his plastic packets of sugary snacks and a juice box.

"What do you have for lunch? If it's good, we can trade," he said, peering past her boring homemade-bread sandwich see what was in her cloth bag.

"Oh, that's not to eat," she said. She stood up so she could use both hands and lifted out the canning jar filled with water and a goldfish.

"Ew! Is that what you're eating for lunch?" he asked.

"Ew!" echoed the other kids at the adjoining table.

"Sushi!" someone said and laughed.

"No, her name is Suzy, not Sushi," Tori said. "She's my pet, not my lunch." She looked at the plastic-wrapped processed food the redhead had wanted to swap and shook her head. "And thanks but no thanks. I don't eat that kind of junk. Do you know how long it takes for that plastic to decompose in the landfill?"

"Huh?" he asked.

"Never mind. Let's just eat our own food." Tori leaned close to the jar and looked at the fish. "I think you'd better stay home tomorrow, Suzy. This isn't as much fun as I thought it'd be."

After they finished lunch, the other students started disappearing. Tori put her fish back in the bag and went to Mrs. Johnson. "Where did they go?"

"Oh, I'm sorry, Tori. I forgot to tell you. After lunch, you're free to go outside and play on the playground until twelve-fifteen. There's the clock. I'll bet you already know how to tell time, don't you?"

"Yes, ma'am. But would you watch Suzy for me? I'm afraid she might get kicked over if I take her outside."

"Sure thing, sweetheart." She took the quart jar and verified there were air holes in the top. Of course, there were. She held it close, protecting the little girl's treasured pet. She'd have to talk to her parents. Tori was a precious jewel. If she hung out with traditional kids full time, though, she'd lose her shine. One day a week would probably be enough to keep up with her social skills. Any more than that and she'd become dull and common or pick up bad habits. She definitely wanted to keep up with this little one.

After recess, Mrs. Johnson gave the drill as the children began to come in from outside. "Okay, line up. If you have to use the bathroom, do it now. If you don't, still go in and wash your hands," she said.

"It's this way," a little dark-haired girl said, taking Tori by the elbow.

Tori walked into the restroom and was stunned. So many mirrors! Bypassing the toilets and sinks, she went into the corner where two mirrors intersected, providing an infinity perspective. "Wow!"

"Pretty awesome, huh?" Melinda said. "It's like there's a whole bunch of you."

Tori reached out with both hands and touched each mirror, her eyes staring as if in a trance.

"Are you going to be okay?" Melinda asked. "You look kind of spooky."

"It's like there's more than three of me. It's like there are hundreds and hundreds…"

"Come on," Melinda said, "they're not going anywhere. You can go potty first and I'll wait for you. We don't want to be late for storytime."

"Bye, bye," Tori said softly to the images. "Nice seeing you again."

***

"There she is," Leanne said, pointing her out at the end of the line of youngsters.

"Our little girl looks so grown up with her backpack…and is she frowning?" Luther asked.

"If you can't tell, then you need glasses, Papa. Don't say anything. Let her talk to us first."

"Be careful," Tori said, handing her mother the pack. "I brought Suzy to school today, so don't spill her."

"You brought your goldfish to school?" Luther asked. "I'm sorry. That's what you just said, isn't it?"

"I thought she'd like it, but she didn't. Can she stay home with you

312

tomorrow?"

"Yes, dear. We'll take good care of her," Leanne said.

"And can I stay home with her?"

"What? Don't you like school?" Luther asked. He felt his wife's glare of disapproval but ignored it. "You know, sometimes first impressions aren't right. I figured it would take you up to a week to like school."

"Oh, I like the school and the teacher and some of the kids, but they called me crazy. I'm not crazy, though. I saw my sisters today, and maybe I shouldn't have told Melinda, but I thought she could keep a secret."

Luther slammed on the brakes at the revelation, thrusting all of them forward. "Sorry. My foot slipped," he said, then quickly glanced at Leanne to see her reaction.

Yes, she was just as stunned. They both looked at Tori, waiting for her to elaborate.

"They were both there, wearing the same hair ribbon and everything. Both of them!" she said, not even trying to contain her elation.

"Whoa, wait!" Luther said. "You said you have two sisters and you saw them today? Where?"

"See, you didn't say I didn't have two sisters. You asked where."

"Tori Lynn..." Leanne said, her voice low with her no-nonsense intonation.

"They were in the back of the mirror. Both of them!"

Luther and Leanne both exhaled in relief at the same time. "You were looking at your own reflection, sweetheart. You don't have a sister hiding in the back of a mirror."

"Sisters," she said in an authoritative voice. "There were two of them and they looked just like me. I promise."

"And I promise to teach you about mirrors and the principle of light refraction and reflection this afternoon as soon as we get home."

"Mama can come into the girls' bathroom with me tomorrow and see. I'll prove it."

"Or we can use a hand mirror in our bathroom mirror and show you the same thing at home. Just because you see more than one image doesn't mean there is more than one person. Can you imagine if there was a flesh and blood person behind every reflective image? There wouldn't be enough food in the world to feed everyone."

"Okay, I'll let you show me your side of the story, but I know I have two sisters."

Tori watched as her parents shared a guilty look then turned back to watching the road in silence. Maybe they were right about reflective surfaces and images and the world getting too crowded if there were real people on the other side, but she knew as sure as she was breathing air and not water that she

313

had sisters.

But she also knew she'd never mention it again. She didn't like her parents pretending they didn't know. Or being called crazy.

Chapter 4: The Compassionate Use Act

July 3, 1997

"Happy birthday, sweetheart!" Luther and Leanne sang out.

Tori rubbed the sleep out of her eyes, then did a double-take at the colorful bicycle sitting in the middle of the living room. "It's not my birthday."

"Well, it sort of is," Leanne said. "It's your half birthday."

"It's exactly halfway between your fifth and sixth birthdays," Luther said. "Actually, I was looking for any excuse to fix up this bike and give it to you."

"But where am I going to ride it?"

"Oh, that's the other surprise. We're moving to Oregon. Papa's going to grow grapes."

"Does this mean I won't be going to school again?"

"No, but you wouldn't be going to school until late August or September anyhow. I'm sure you and Mama will find plenty to do this summer at our new home."

Another season, another reason to move. Apricots, cotton, lavender, and mint. When will we ever settle down? Papa loves green. As soon as he wins the battle of the blight or whatever else is bothering the orchard owner or farmer, we're moving again.

"Are you sure you want to do this, Luther," Leanne asked while Tori was in her room, changing out of her pajamas.

"I know it's hard on her, but all she really needs is consistency. It's not the configuration of the clapboard shack or trailer we're living in, it's us and her routine. We're her home. You can be her teacher again if it would make you feel better."

"It's not what would make *me* feel better, but what's good for her. I don't care if she's the smartest child in the whole school. I want her to be the happiest, most well-adjusted."

"Yes, me, too." Luther sighed and shook his head. "But how can she be happy and well-adjusted if we're miserable? I'm sorry, but I have to have a challenge. Anyone can earn a few bucks by pulling fruit off a tree."

"What makes you think that's all you do? Except for that mint-growing venture five years ago, every field you've touched has thrived. The only reason you're not making a decent wage is because you don't go blowing your own horn and let them know you have a doctorate. Or tell them about how you fine-tuned their fertilizer and irrigation schedules and that's why they have record-breaking harvests. I know no one is willing to pay for a horticulturist but mark my words, you let these landowners know that when you're on board, they're making a hell of a lot more with you than without you. They've been getting your college-level skills, even if you're job title is field supervisor."

Luther chuckled. "Yeah, who would have thought that my two years of high school Spanish would come in so handy, earning me my living where eight years of college couldn't."

"You're more than a translator who knows how to read labels and set up pest strips. Please, whatever you do in this next job, let them know who you really are. And for heavens sakes, ask for a decent wage! We need another vehicle. Our station wagon was worn out years ago!"

"Well, I'll see how it goes. I will ask them for a company truck, though. No more hauling fertilizers in the family rig!"

***

"Wow! It's so green!" Tori said. She rolled down the window and stuck her face into the wind. "And it smells so happy!"

"So, you really are your father's daughter," Leanne said with a chuckle.

"Of course, I am," Tori said. "Who else's would I be?"

"I mean, you take after him, not me, where it comes to plants and such. Who else would say that plants smell happy?"

"Well, they do. And marshes smell sad because they're rotting, but composts piles smell young because they're transmuting from waste into energy, eager to help more plants grow."

"Now that poet aspect – weaving words not usually associated with each other, creating unusual but picturesque descriptions – that you get from me," Leanne said.

Tori kept facing out the window. This trip was taking forever! The roads went on and on and on, up and down, more twists than a bag of pretzels. And the hills were more like oversized gopher mounds.

"Do they have mountains in Oregon?"

Leanne turned around in her seat to face her. "Of course, they do. We've seen lots of them yesterday and today. These here are more like foothills but we saw lots of mountains around Redding."

"But they didn't shoot straight up and there was barely any snow."

"After we get settled, I'll take us for a day trip to Mount Hood. That's covered with snow all year round. Did you know you can even ski in the summer there?"

"But Hood's only one big bump, not a whole range like we saw when I was a baby."

"What? You couldn't possibly remember that!" Leanne said. "You were only two months old."

"Uh-huh," Tori said. "I remember it was really cold but you wanted me to see how tall the summits were. You bundled me up and held me close and told me that maybe one day, I could climb to the top of a mountain that high."

"You must have seen a photograph," Luther countered.

"Nuh-uh. I don't remember seeing any baby pictures of me. Ever!"

"She's right," Leanne said. "You had to sell our camera so we'd have enough money for gas to come across country. The first photos we had of her were spoiled when the water heater flooded."

"Well…well…I think you must have seen pictures of those mountains in a book or magazine. There's no way a baby can remember what was going on when she's only two months old!"

"Yeah-huh," Tori said, then sat back in her seat, not wanting to try to convince him. *I remember everything!*

An hour later, Tori awoke from a nap, flinching at the realness of her dream.

Her two sisters were next to her but she could see them now, not just feel them bump and tumble over her. They had just been born, pulled out of their wet and warm world. She missed their touch but knew they were near. That had to be them squalling. They sounded just like her: angry that they were apart. She remembered the bright light and a new sensation: fabric. Then it was dark and they were all snuggled together again. Suddenly, wham! They were gone again and people were talking. It was cold, very cold, and then she was warm again. Mama had her but her sisters never came back.

Tori inhaled, recalling the first time she'd smelled her mother's scent. She'd figure out where her sisters were one of these days. She'd have to keep it to herself that she remembered them, though. Nobody understood or even wanted to try. Not Melinda, Mrs. Johnson, or even her parents.

She was certain that they had all been together once. She really did remember everything about being born. She wasn't imagining them, either. They were as real as she was.

"Oh, you're awake now. Did you have a good nap?" Leanne asked.

"Uh-huh. Hey, where we're going, do you think they'll have sidewalks so I can ride my bike?"

"No, but I'll show you what they do have when we get there. It'll be even better. Leanne, how much further do we have?"

Leanne looked at the odometer and then her note. "We just passed milepost 90. Our turnoff is just ahead. Oh, I'm so excited! Our very own vineyard to maintain."

"Why are there so many Christmas trees and why are they so small?"

"They're small because they're baby trees," Luther said, " and there are so many because this is where they grow them for people all over the United States. Or one of the places they grow them."

"Wow… It'd take a lot of popcorn to make strings to decorate all of those!"

"Oh, right here!" Leanne said. "Take this road until it ends."

"If You Can Imagine Vineyards," Tori read. "That sounds like a fun place to work."

317

"I hope so. Let's go in and meet some new people."

The crew of three stepped out of the aging station wagon and stretched, taking in the vastness of the rolling hills that surrounded them and the newness of the modular office, so unlike the buildings or trailers Luther had worked before.

"I think I'm going to like it here," Tori said. "It looks like this place is just beginning, just getting started like we are. We can grow together, huh?"

"Like I said," Leanne bragged. "My little girl."

"Hey, there! You must be the Greene family," the tall handsome man walking toward them said, his hand held out in greeting.

Luther shook it heartily. "You don't look like a Julio Mendosa..."

"Julio had a family emergency and had to leave. If you're Luther Greene and are willing to take on extra responsibility right away, you have two sections of fertile Willamette Valley to turn into a vineyard. Oh, I'm Rick Rickman, by the way. I bought this property as an investment last year. I didn't think I'd wind up working it hands-on, though. Julio's a great guy, came highly recommended, but when your family needs you, you see to them first, right?"

"Yes, sir. I brought mine with me. This is my wife, Leanne, and our daughter, Tori Lynn."

"Beautiful women. Now, let's go inside and talk a little business first, then hop on the Gator and take a tour."

The vineyard owner noticed the look of terror on the young girl's face. "It's not an alligator, Tori Lynn," he explained. "It's like a mini car that goes up and down the rows. That way your daddy and I don't have to walk so much."

"You can call me Tori," she said, reaching out to shake his hand like she'd seen her father do. "And I think these paths are what Papa was talking about for my bicycle. Yes, he's right. These are much nicer than sidewalks. And softer to land on if I fall."

"Well, next week you might have a couple of young men here to ride with you. My son and nephew will be here for a few days before we leave for Europe. I planned to go there for pleasure, but now it looks like I'll be doing some research."

"*Vignobles et vignetos*? Luther asked.

"Yes, vineyards in France and Italy. If the weather is good, we'll also sail to Greece. They grow a *cabernet sauvignon* there that's supposed to be exquisite."

"If it's possible to bring back cuttings, I'd be interested in getting a few. I'm not sure what varieties you're growing, but I'd like to see about bringing in some heirlooms and hybridizing some new ones. The world can always use a few new fruits."

"Like pluots?" Tori asked.

"Yes, dear, like pluots."

"Looks like the next generation hybridizer is already taken an interest in your work," Rick said.

"She'd rather work with me than just about anything."

"Except read," Leanne said.

Luther nodded in agreement. "I'd say it's going to be tough to find a school for her, but I think we've already decided to try hybrid homeschooling. One or two days a week with a traditional school so she keeps up with her social skills and activities, then the rest of the time my wife will work with her. I'm afraid we taught her too much too soon."

"I had the same situation with my son, Rich. He's a bright boy. If he's anything like your daughter, there's no keeping them back. He's only eleven and doing college calculus for fun."

***

"Do I have to go to school," Tori asked, trying not to beg but willing to if that's what it took to stay home.

"Yes, you do. We agreed that you'd go at least one day a week; more if you want to."

"Who's we?" Tori asked, scowling. "I don't remember talking about it."

"Your papa and I had the discussion. You were miserable half the time in kindergarten but the other half, you enjoyed yourself. You have to learn to get along with people your own age."

"But they're so boring."

"Then find something you and the others are both interested in. Maybe sports or crafts. Life isn't just about words and numbers. Not everyone in the world can read, you know."

"Why not? I could teach them instead of going to school…" Tori saw her mother's frown and realized she was trying to make a point, not looking for help with ending illiteracy. "Okay, fine. One day a week. But that doesn't mean I have to like it."

"Well, it sort of does. If you go into it expecting to be miserable, you probably will be. Look at it as a challenge. You don't have to make everyone your friend. How about you just try not to fall down or wet your pants on the first day of school."

"Mama! I haven't wet my pants since I was a year old!"

"You were ten months old," Leanne corrected.

"I know. I was there, remember? I just rounded up for convenience. All right, I'll try."

Chapter 5: The Teen Years

June 2009

"Mama, do you remember those boys we met the first year we moved here?"

"The ones who taught you had to ride your bike?"

"Yeah, whatever happened to them?"

"Oscar and Rich? I don't know. Your papa might know. He's the one who handles all the emails with Mr. Rickman. I wouldn't doubt that one of these days, Rich will take over his dad's businesses. I don't know about the younger one, the nephew. Oscar was always so quiet. I don't think I ever heard that boy say a word. Nice enough and had the sweetest smile, but it seemed like he always had something on his mind."

"Yeah, I know."

"Why did you ask? I haven't thought about them in years."

"Oh, nothing really. I just found this old sticker in one of my books. Oscar gave it to me." Tori held up a decal that looked like it had come out of a vending machine.

"Oh, that's cute. A pink unicorn."

"Yeah, he kind of grunted and handed it to me. He had football stickers all over his bike. I think he got this one by mistake and it was too girly for him."

"Oh, speaking of the Rickmans, Mr. Rickman is coming out today. Maybe he'll have his family with him."

"Tell them I said, 'Hi.' I have some stuff to do."

"Tori Lynn..."

"Really! I do. I um... I have to um..."

"I'm glad you're a lousy liar but very unhappy that you don't want to at least say hi. You're seventeen years old now. One of these days, you're going to have to go out in the real world and get a job. You'll have to talk to other people, make real conversations, and eventually get your own home. Who knows, you might even wind up getting married and having your own family."

"Ew! Mama! That's gross."

"What's gross? Working or having a family?"

"I'm not afraid of work. I'll just keep helping Papa and take over his job when he's ready to retire. But I don't want a boyfriend and I certainly don't want to make babies."

"We already had this talk. It may sound complicated, but when the time comes – and if you've found the right man – I can pretty much guarantee you're going to like it. Having a baby? Oh, I would so love to be a grandmother..."

"Maybe you can borrow one. That would be simpler for both of us."

Leanne huffed in defeat. "I'm sure glad I only have one of you."

Tori's eyes widened in surprise, a grin of providence growing into a devilish smirk. Mama had just given her the perfect opening to an adult discussion on what really happened to those sisters she knew she had, and why they were a secret. Just as she had gathered the courage to jump in on the subject, she noticed the window. A cloud of dust was rising among the otherwise green and beige striped landscaped. A groan escaped. Someone was coming up the road. The Rickmans were here.

"Are you okay?" Mama asked.

Tori clutched her lower belly and said, "I gotta go. I think it's that time of the month a little early." Before any more discussion could be held, she rushed out the side door, leaving her mother to deal with the big boss and any male kin he may have brought with him.

Two minutes later, two men walked in the front door of the office. "Looks like we got here just a little too late," Rick said. "Was that Tori that I saw leaving?"

"Oh, hi, Mr. Rickman. Yes, she had a minor emergency to attend to. This isn't Rich, is it?" Leanne asked, nodding to the scruffy-faced young man with hunched shoulders wearing a knit cap.

"Oh, no, no. This is Oscar. Rich is back east, attending university. Oscar here doesn't have the desire to go to brick and mortar schools. He's more of a hands-on kind of guy. Is your husband here? I need to talk to him about some business opportunities I think he might be interested in."

"I'll call him," Leanne said. She picked up the radio. "Luther, you have company in the office. Don't dawdle. Over."

"Got it. Roger and out," Luther said.

Before Leanne could offer the men a drink, Luther was in the office. "I was on my way here when I got the call. Oh, hello, Rick. This is Oscar, right?"

Oscar looked up briefly and grinned, then nodded in greeting.

Luther shook both men's hands. "What can I do for you gentlemen?"

Oscar's grin grew into a full smile. He was being included in the conversation. He might like working here. He wasn't invisible or worse – in the way.

Rick looked around the room to be sure, although he already knew it was just the four of them. "Everything's great with the numbers and photos you've been sharing. The wine from those new mega-producing grapes will be the rage once it ages for a while, plus everyone will be wanting the plants. So, let's get down to the reason for my visit. I have a business proposition for you."

"It doesn't entail moving, does it?" Luther asked, looking at Leanne to make sure she felt the same way. Her anxious frown confirmed that she did.

"No, no. Everything can be done from here. The laws are changing in a hurry. I know I was going to expand into those eighty acres I bought next door that used to be Christmas trees, but rather than grapes, I want to put up some greenhouses."

Luther's eyes flitted from Rick's to the young man beside him. Rick nodded that it was all right to speak freely. "If you're talking about getting into the cannabis game, I'm a few steps ahead of you. Actually, almost forty years ahead of you. Come on. I have something I want to show you. Leanne, we'll be right back."

The three men rode in the Gator to a massive greenhouse that was not visible from the road. "When did that go up?" Rick asked.

"This is the research station you authorized four years ago. I didn't think you'd mind if I used a few feet of it for my own personal use."

Luther opened the door and waited for their reaction. "Wow!" Oscar and Rick both exclaimed.

Rick looked at Oscar, surprised that the very reserved and timid young man had spoken. He grinned with contentment. Yes, his nephew would love working here.

Impossible to miss were the twelve massive custom-built wooden barrels hosting a small forest of marijuana plants at the back of the greenhouse. The three men passed between the long, wire-topped tables loaded with containers of grape cuttings, an orderly array reminiscent of a log-cabin quilt, the leaves of the merlot and chardonnay grapes separated onto their own tables, further defined by the ages of the plants.

Rick was a vintner and interested in them, but he'd come back and see them later. "Those are the biggest marijuana plants I've ever seen," he said.

"Really?" Luther asked as he stood next to one of them, showing off that it was already six feet tall. "Because it's barely half-grown. It won't mature until September or October when the days get shorter. If this was a full-on greenhouse with the right kind of lights and in-floor heating, I could have these girls growing all winter long. Oh, and just for the record, these are legal plants. My wife and I both have medical marijuana cards."

Luther watched as young Oscar pulled a bottle of hand sanitizer out of his pocket and cleaned his hands. He barely heard what Rick was saying as he watched Oscar inspect the plants, lifting leaves, looking for problems.

"I'm sorry, Rick. I'm a little distracted. Is Oscar a botanist? He looks like he knows what he's doing."

"We were talking about kids being prodigies? Well, this kid loves to grow. He's positively obsessed with plants and what makes them sick or thrive. He was taking peanuts out of the bird feeder and growing them in pillow stuffing when he was four. His obsession was driving my sister nuts, but I saw him for what he is: a genius."

Luther followed Oscar, shadowing him as the young man took a pinch of soil and tasted it. "Not too salty, is it?" he asked.

Oscar shook his head, flicked off the dirt, then gave him a soil-stained thumbs up, grinning.

"So, how much did you plan on putting under cover? And do you have someone to take care of the paperwork? That's a whole other business, fitting into the government's guidelines, making sure we have the right documents and aren't growing too much."

"Got two former NORML lawyers setting it up right now. It's too late in the season to start only because we don't have enough greenhouses set up. That's one reason I have Oscar here. If you don't mind, I'd like him to be your go-to guy on the layout."

"It's not too late," Oscar said, his sultry voice startling the two men.

"Because…" Rick prompted.

"I can hire a crew and have the greenhouses up in a week. The NORML guys have licensed clone vendors ready to sell to us with a phone call. They told me if they got the go-ahead, they could have us licensed to grow in a week."

"A week to set up the buildings and a week to get the paperwork in place. Both could happen at the same time. Okay, Oscar, I'll make the call. Luther, I know you're the man in charge of this whole operation, but if you don't mind working with Oscar, I'd like him to take on the burden of getting the tents and plants in place." He spread his arms out, indicating the hundreds of young grape plants. "You already have quite a bit on your plate. Last year's crop was fantastic. The vineyards are thriving under your care. I don't doubt this year will exceed last's. As always, if there's anything you need, just ask."

Oscar raised up his hand.

"Yes, son?" Rick asked.

"I'll need a place to stay, preferably on-site I'm going to be putting in a lot of hours."

"Is it all right if he pulls in a travel trailer back here? I'm sure you already have all the hookups."

"Go for it," Luther said, his eyes bright at the idea of having a huge grow operation and an eager young man to help make it come together.

Rick reached in his pocket and took out his gold card. "This one's yours. Use it for everything you need, including a home on wheels. I have the feeling that this will just be the first phase of our new venture."

"I never thought I'd see the day," Luther said.

Rick chuckled. "Forty years ago at Woodstock – smoking weed in the open, too many of us to fear getting busted – and now running a legal grow operation."

"You were there, too?" Luther asked, eyes wide as he took in the youthful appearance of the handsome billionaire.

"I was only fifteen at the time but fiercely determined and not easily deterred. Even back then if I wanted something, I went for it. I was in New York visiting my granny and sneaked away that August night. She about had a heart attack when no one could find me for four days. When she did, she didn't stop scolding me until I was back on the plane to my parents in England, escorting me right to my seat. Phew! That woman could sear the hairs off my ears with her creative brow-beatings."

"I have to admit," Luther said, "I feel a lot better about it since it is legal. I have a daughter now. Once she came into our lives, a lot of things changed. Of course, we missed it, but when the laws changed and medical options popped up, we were right there. Old age isn't as painful with a little canna-relief."

Rick looked at the size of the plants and shook his head. "By the hearty growth of the plants you grow, I'd say you're getting a lot of canna-relief."

"No leaf for us," Luther said. "Only the buds. Yup, these are the good old days now."

Rick smacked him on the back in familiar agreement. "Amen to that."

Thunk-thunk!

Both men turned at the sound of the fans shutting off and then coming back on. "What's that?" Rick asked.

"Sounds to me like Oscar's checking out the electrical panel. I think we're going to need to buy a bigger generator, too. We won't need lights for a while, but we will need constant ventilation and water pumps. Before I go see if he needs some help, is there anything else you need from me?"

"How about a handshake. I cover all the costs and you get 10% of the net profits as your bonus. Even with Oscar here, you're going to be putting in more hours. I want to make it right."

"As long as you and your guys are taking care of all the reselling and all I have to do is grow and harvest, I'm down with that."

Rick reached out and the two shook hands traditionally, then did a fist-on-top-of fist exchange like the two inner hippies they both were.

A handshake agreement and the billionaire and the botanist both walked away happy, both of them getting a great deal.

***

Oscar glanced at the movement behind the corner of the greenhouse then continued with his calculations, not concerned about the noise. There weren't any large wild animals in this region that concerned him. Moles and skunks were more of a problem than coyotes and deer. At least with doors on the buildings, the larger mammals were less likely to gain access to the plants than the vermin. Cougars might be a problem if they were spooked. His mind tumbled over and over, potential problems and what he could do about preventing them distracted him from his primary task: finding out what was needed to get four mammoth greenhouses erected and operational in seven days.

He took out his phone and checked for a signal. Damn! No service.

"It'll work down by the office," a shy female voice called out from the area he'd seen the disturbance.

324

He nodded and grunted, not verbalizing the word, "Thanks," but letting it be known he'd heard.

Oh, yeah! When I came out here ten, maybe twelve years ago, Luther had a little tow-headed daughter. She might be the one attached to that voice. Cute but crazy, jabbering on about how she was going to be the best bike rider in the world when she grew up. Shoot! She couldn't even stay on the path without me running along behind her, holding the bike seat to keep her upright.

Musing as he walked, his face down to watch for the bars to pop up on his phone indicating he was in a service area, Oscar almost walked into his uncle's SUV. He heard the tittering of someone laughing at his near collision.

Silly kid. He hit the icon and redialed his last call, then spun around suddenly to see if he could catch sight of her.

Not a kid! She's a grown woman now, or pretty darned close. Curvy in the right places, too.

Oscar watched as she sprinted through the opening between the rows of vines, graceful as a gazelle, disappearing over the rise. "Hello! Is anyone there?" asked the voice on the other end of his phone call.

"Huh? Oh, yes. Samson? Yes, yes, sorry about that. I got distracted. You know that big pie-in-the-sky quote you and I were talking about yesterday? How soon until you can have it ready to ship? You did? Really? Great! Here's the address. You can either bill Rickman Vineyards LLC or I'll give you a credit card. Okay, send the invoice to the usual address. Yes, it's great to have a rich uncle but even better to have one who trusts your instincts. I don't think I forgot anything but one thing I'll need out here is a bigger generator. Do you think you can hook me up? Really? You're sure it's in good shape? Yup, 100KW would be just fine. Can you arrange delivery and payment on that, too? Fantastic. I gotta jet. It looks like I need to rent a few pieces of equipment to level and compact the foundations. The ground isn't as flat up close as it looks in photos. No, I won't be able to send you any of the harvest. If you want any, you'll have to come and get it yourself. And bring your medical marijuana card! We're not doing anything illegal here. It's all on the up and up. All right. I'll let you know if I need anything else. Oh, and text me the carrier and BOL number. Bye!"

Leanne heard an unfamiliar voice. She listened at the opened window. It had to be Oscar. For someone who didn't talk much face-to-face, the young man was sure chatty on the phone. She sat back at her desk and watched through the front window as he went to his uncle's Hummer to get something. He moved differently now, too. Just half an hour ago, he was shrunken down, timid as a scared dog. Now he was standing tall. Broad-shouldered and handsome despite that tacky knit cap and two-week-old beard. Better not let him get too near Tori when he was strutting like this! She may say she didn't want anything to do with guys, but this one was spewing appeal!

"Pfft! Less than an hour ago we were chatting about men and babies. How could I have been so eager for a grandchild? I'm not ready for my little girl to grow up! I'll have to make sure I keep those two apart."

Chapter 6: Forbidden Fruit

Later that day

"Tori, would you put together a salad for dinner? We have some leftover chicken. That chopped up with lettuce, tomatoes, cucumbers, and red onions should be enough. Oh, and you can split that loaf of French bread and spread garlic butter over it. If we use the toaster oven, it won't heat up the house."

"I thought we were having spaghetti for dinner."

"Too hot to boil noodles. Remind me and I'll have your father change out the propane tank on the grill. We can start cooking outside again. I didn't think it was going to get warm so early."

"Just wait a few days. The weather is sure to turn back to cool." Tori paused, her curiosity stronger than her timidness about men. "Hey, Mama, how come that one guy didn't go back with Mr. Rickman?" She although already knew the reason – she'd been eavesdropping while the men discussed their new business venture – but wanted to hear her mother's version.

"Your papa has a new partner of sorts. At least, young Oscar is going to take over the cannabis growing."

"There are only a dozen plants and they don't need much attention."

Leanne came up to Tori and stood a foot from her face. She knew Tori was just seeing if she'd tell her what she already knew. "You know more than I do about what's going on with the new venture. You were there, listening. I had to depend on your papa's memory to tell me everything. So, since that's the case, how long do they think it'll take to get this up and going?"

"A week," Tori said. She opened the refrigerator and started pulling out the components of the salad. "At least that's what Oscar said. I think that's nearly impossible, though. They plan on setting up greenhouses on that parcel over the hill that had all those Christmas trees on it. That ground is as lumpy as an old straw mattress: stumps and half-rotted trees, high spots and dried-up puddle ponds."

"Well, you can either work beside them and give them pertinent information, or you can work beside them and keep it to yourself, helping no one. Either way, you're working. Your papa did say he was a vested partner is this. Maybe this project will earn enough to send you to college."

"Ew! Why would I want to go to college? Anything I want to know, I can look up on the internet."

"Yeah, right. And those sources are so reliable. Darling, nothing will replace interaction and discussions with professors and like-minded people. Until you experience it, there's no way I can convince you, so I won't try."

Tori rolled her eyes, hearing the same lecture on learning. She took the knife out of the block and checked the blade for sharpness. Just to be sure it would cut through the tomato, she ran it across the steel a couple of times. "What we really need is some clearing equipment out here – like a brush or root rake or…" she said as she set to work on deboning and chopping the remains of the roasted chicken.

Tori felt her mother's hand between her shoulder blades. "Let the guys take care of it. If you see that there's an easier way to do it or a shortcut to save time, let them know. Until that happens, wait and see. Mr. Rickman seems to believe that Oscar can handle it."

"Okay," Tori said, ending the word on a high note, the doubt in her voice unmistakable. "But if they need help, I hope Papa asks me. I don't want them to think I'm a butt-insky know-it-all."

"There are only a few people involved in this project. If you approach them with a positive suggestion, they'll appreciate it." Leanne paused, thinking about the dynamic and often defiant attitude Tori approached every situation with. "Or at least they'll listen to you. Be gentle, though. Sometimes you have to sneak up on a puppy to give him a pill, not sit on him and cram it down his throat."

"Wouldn't know. I never had more than a goldfish," she said with a pout.

"Well, I am sorry about that. With your father's allergies, that's the best we could do."

Her knife held high so it was out of the way, Tori reached out and gave her mother a one-armed hug. "I know, Mama. And Papa also told me that it was you with the allergies, not him. He only claimed them so you wouldn't feel so bad about it. He'd rather have me angry at him than you. It's just part of life. I have so much freedom that not having a needy pet was probably the best for me."

Leanne smiled weakly and returned the hug. *But not giving you a pet to be responsible for was a huge mistake on our part. You would have been better off caring for a critter – learning to be responsible – while I dealt with cases of tissues and buckets of antihistamines!*

Twenty minutes later, Luther had arrived home, as chipper as if he'd just won five-hundred dollars on a lottery ticket. He set his broad-rimmed hat on the hook on the wall. "Well, this might work out great – having an extra set of hands and a young, strong back. It's going to take a while for that truck and trailer to get here. In the meantime, what's for dinner?"

"Chicken salad and as soon as you swap out propane tanks on the grill, garlic bread," Leanne said, setting the last plate on the table. "It's too hot for the toaster over, too."

"Consider it done," Luther said and put his hat back on. "Oh, and you might want to put some of that salad in a container and take it out to Oscar in the greenhouse. I guess I'll start calling that Number One since we're going to have at least five of them this year and more in the future. I doubt that he wants to take the time to go to town to eat. That young man's going to lose his voice if he's not careful. He's been on that phone of his non-stop since he got here."

"Oh, that's so sweet," Leanne said. "A young version of you: hardworking and dedicated."

Tori rolled her eyes at her mother's reminiscing. "I'll chop up a couple of carrots and apples to add to the mix and maybe throw in some raisins, too. Stretch it out a little."

"Sounds good to me," Luther said and was out the door.

***

"Ah, fresh bread and salad, the perfect summertime meal," Luther said, patting his belly as he sat back. "Tori, why don't you ride your bike up the hill and take that dinner out to Oscar? You haven't seen him in years, but he might remember you."

Tori looked back and forth between her parents. They had that dreamy-eyed look that they always got just before asking her to take a long ride. Yes, they wanted some of their 'quality alone-time' together. She'd rather be far away than hear the giggles behind their bedroom door, even worse when they tried to suppress them with a 'Shush, Tori will hear us' admonishment.

She wanted to face Oscar again as much as she wanted to smash her thumb with a hammer, but she'd figure a way to deliver the salad and bread without actually meeting him again. "How about if I take a long ride after? I can check on the pest traps while I'm out there?"

"Yes, I'd appreciate that. There's a high wind forecast for tomorrow. I want to make sure whatever insects were caught aren't blown out," Luther said, Leanne's hand on his, her smile growing at the promise of a late afternoon liaison.

"Don't worry about the dishes, dear," Leanne said. "I'll get them. Go ahead and pack up the rest of the garlic bread to go with that bowl of salad. Oh, and make sure you take a fork and a few napkins for him. I doubt he has any utensils."

"How about a tablecloth, candle, and bottle of wine, too?" Tori said, ending with a huff of sarcasm.

"Actually, that's a good idea," Luther said. "Maybe not the candles and wine, but all he has to eat on are the tables in the greenhouse. A dropcloth would be nice, as would a bottle of water. I don't think there are any cups out there."

"He can drink out of the hose like I do," Tori said, dropping the salad into the cloth shopping bag.

"Tori Lynn Greene!" Leanne scolded. "Why are you so mean?"

"I'm sorry. I'm not used to having anyone around..."

"Well, get used to it. You're not going to live life as a hermit. You have too much to offer the world to be hiding in the garden or between rows of grapes."

"But I like plants more than people!"

"And how many people do you know? We made a big mistake,

329

homeschooling you for most of the last eleven years. Starting this next semester, you're going back to public school."

"But Mama! I don't want to go!"

"Enjoy this summer and your solitude because come September, you'll be thrown into a pond of people, learning to swim in social circles, and get along with people with both the same and dissimilar interests," Leanne said.

Luther looked at his wife, shocked at her insistence but glad she finally was agreeing with him.

"Papa?" Tori asked, hoping he'd come to her defense as he always did.

"You're seventeen, Tori. You have to learn to interact with others one of these days. Consider this the big bandage you've put off removing for the last eleven years. You have to do it. We can't shelter you forever. What's going to happen when we're gone?"

"But...but...where are you going?"

Leanne scowled. "We're starting our sixties now, dear. When you're my age, I'll be over a hundred. Do you know what the odds are that anyone will live to be that old?"

Tori remained mute, frowning. She knew.

"Less than ten percent that I'll still be alive which means over ninety percent that I'll be dead. The statistics are even worse for your father since he's male and already older than I am. We don't want to leave you alone in this world, unable to interact with others. We know you're a bright, charming woman, but others don't. And they won't know because you freeze up or hide as soon as you see them!"

"Fine. I'll take this to Oscar. But I'm going to check all the bug traps, so don't expect me back for a long time."

"I expect you back home before dark," Luther said. "There's no way you can check them in the dark."

"I'll take a flashlight."

"You can take a flashlight, a candle or fifteen boxes of matches, but I still want you back before dark. Understand?"

"Yes, Papa."

Luther stood next to her and gave her a big hug. "Sweetheart, we love you. If we didn't, we wouldn't want to see you grow. Just consider meeting new people as hardening off a plant before putting it in the garden. By going to school for a year, you can get used to people gradually. Spend a few hours with them as you all work together on projects, and then come home to us. I'll have Oscar here to help me if it's something your mother and I can't handle."

Tori huffed but didn't reply.

"And as far as staying gone too long this evening, if something happens to you, I want to be able to find you. I know you're young and strong but life sometimes throws us a fastball."

"That's a curveball, but I know what you mean. All right."

Tori tossed the bread, utensils, large dish towel, and an empty cup in the bag and looked back at her parents, holding back the tears. They were kicking her out.

Luther saw her sniffing and knew it for what it was. "Sweetheart, you have nearly three months before school. Maybe you can start working with Oscar. You two got along great when you were little. From what I see, you both have the same interests, too. Just one year of high school is all we're asking. Who knows? Maybe you'll find something else that interests you and you'll want to go to college to pursue them."

"And leave you and Mama?"

"Live one moment at a time. Just take the dinner to Oscar. You can figure out the rest of life later."

"Okay. I'll try."

* * *

The door to the greenhouse was open. *Ergh! Doesn't he know that's just an invitation for whiteflies, aphids, and beetles to come in?*

Tori stepped in and looked around. If she had her druthers, she'd just drop the bag of food and split. But only five minutes earlier, she'd committed to trying to interact with people. A devilish grin sneaked in. *And if by interacting that means I get to chew out Oscar for leaving all the plants in the greenhouse vulnerable...*

She set the dinner on the table just inside and closed the door behind her. Then she saw it...or them. Two feet were sticking out under the table. She walked over slowly. Was he asleep?

A moan of discomfort came from his unconscious body followed by coughing as he awakened.

Tori squatted down near his feet and whispered, "Are you okay?"

His frustrated grunt as he shifted positions scared her upright. He sounded like a wild animal! She rushed back to the door, hand on the latch and ready to leave, then paused. What would she tell her parents? Shoot! She couldn't tell them anything. They were spending 'quality time' together and she didn't want to barge in on them during *that*!

"What happened?" he asked, his voice still low but no longer menacing.

"You turned into a werewolf," Tori said, then started giggling nervously. "Huh?"

"Sorry. I say stupid stuff when I'm scared."

"Tori?"

"Uh-huh."

"You got big."

Tori glanced from his feet up toward his head, and then back at his very large sneakers. "So did you."

331

Oscar started to sit up, then collapsed back to the floor.

"You'd better stay put for a minute," she advised. "Let me get you something."

Quick! Think! What in the world could you get him that would help? Here you thought you were so smart, watching all those videos and reading all those books on emergency preparedness and you freeze up! Freeze, that's it. Give him a cool cloth to reduce swelling.

Tori grabbed the dishcloth from the food bag and quickly doused it with the hose, waiting just long enough for the water to run cool. She squeezed it out then dashed back to Oscar to try out her self-taught first aid skills.

He hadn't moved but was now flipped over, staring up at the bottom on the table above him, frowning.

"Here, put this wherever you clunked your head," she said and handed it to him.

He didn't take it from her or react to her presence. He was mesmerized, absorbed in whatever it was he was studying. Rather than ask, she leaned down and looked up at what he was focused on.

She stared up at what she thought was the same spot. "I don't get it," she said. "What's so interesting?"

He reached up and pointed to the intersection where the bottom of the table was welded to the top. "If they had attached it here instead, not only would it be stronger and have more clearance, but I wouldn't have hit my head."

"Okay, but what were you doing under the table?" Tori asked, staring at the same poor design.

"Picking up this," he said. He held out his fist and waited for her to hold out her hand.

Curious about what it was and surprised that she wasn't the least bit afraid of him, she opened her hand and accepted the token.

"My charm! I thought I'd lost it. Oh, thank you, thank you."

She heard him grunt and realized she was in his way and he couldn't get up. She scooted back. "Don't move too fast now..." she said, offering him help.

He looked at her offered hand, then rolled over onto his knees. "I'm too big for you," he grumbled and grasped the edge of the table to pull himself up.

Tori watched to make sure he wasn't going to fall over and when he was upright, she said, "The reason I'm here is I brought you dinner. We couldn't see that you had a way to get any for yourself since your uncle just dropped you off and left. I guess he figures you're going to sleep in the greenhouse, too."

A slight smile of irony tried to emerge, but the pain its movement caused stilled it. "Don't worry; I have a plan." He looked at her and saw she was intent on the metallic trinket in her hand and may or may not have heard him. "What is it – a comma?" he asked.

"It's a goldfish." She moved next to him and held it up so he didn't have to bend over to see it. "I've had a pet goldfish ever since I can remember. I'm trying to talk Papa into letting me have a whole bunch of them. If I could dig a big hole, I could make a pond. Papa says a pond would draw too many mosquitoes, though."

"Why not get a big container and set it in here? If mosquitoes come in, the goldfish would eat them. And the water would.. "

"Be great for fertilizer, right?" Tori said, finishing his thought.

This time, Oscar worked through the discomfort and smiled. Someone who thought like he did!

"'Great minds think alike,' my papa says," Tori said. "I want a big container, though. I was thinking maybe an empty drum. But not one that once had oil or antifreeze or anything toxic like that in it."

"Why not get a watering tank – a trough – like the ones they use for livestock? It'd have to be plastic, though," Oscar said, his voice no longer soft, louder now that he had someone to share ideas with. "The zinc from the galvanized ones leach into the water. It'd kill the fish."

"And we can put a pump in it and use the fish poop water on the cannabis plants!" Tori said, hopping up and down, bouncing on the balls of her feet with excitement. "Better than that starting all over with hydroculture because we already have the plants half-grown. The fish will feed on the mosquito larvae, too. It's a win-win-win situation!"

"I can order the tank to be brought in with the other supplies." Oscar stood tall and looked around the greenhouse, calculating how much water would be needed for the twelve planters. "We won't be using the tank water exclusively for the pot plants. I mean, they need just regular water, too, so we don't burn the roots."

"Well, yeah! Duh!" Tori said. "But we'll have to ask Papa if he wants to use any on the grapes. Those are his babies."

"What kind are they?"

"They're some heirloom varieties he got started from cuttings your uncle brought back from Italy. They found some old, grown-over vineyards back in the hills somewhere on one of the islands. He sorta, kind of smuggled some canes and root cuttings out of the country. Don't tell anyone, though. I think it might be illegal."

"Nah, it's not illegal. He's on at least a dozen different boards in as many countries. They swap and trade all the time. I know about that one. Rumor is that the vines are from the days of Nero."

"Really?" Tori squeaked, fascinated. At hearing a new tone – giddiness – in her own voice, Tori suddenly shut down. "Oh, I brought you dinner," she said in a business-like manner, the spell of their planning for a future and reminiscing about the history of grapes broken by the sound of her own excitement.

Oscar looked around to see if someone else had come in and distracted her, then realized what it was. He felt it himself and reddened in embarrassment. They were attracted to each other. Maybe not on a major level, but the warmth and brightness of the mood was suddenly doused by the chilliness of their own fears at the emotional change. Better to focus on the project.

"Dinner?" Tori said.

"I'm sorry," Oscar replied, realizing he was off in his own world again and hadn't heard her. "Thanks. I think I'll start with two one-hundred-gallon tanks. Do you think you can find the goldfish or do you want me to look?"

"I can do that. I just buy feeder goldfish from the wholesale pet store. You have enough to do to get the greenhouses started. Oh, and by the way, I'm supposed to help you with that. The ground is dry now, but I know where all the low spots are on the old Christmas tree lot. And how are you going to put in a foundation and set up the structures in a week?"

"A construction crew and their equipment should be in here at daybreak," Oscar said with confidence.

"You'd better put your stakes up tonight then. They'll lose at least an hour of work time because of the morning fog. It gets so thick out here, they won't be able to see the corners."

"Dang! I knew I forgot something." Oscar bent to his phone, ready to call in and have them added to his order, then remembered he didn't have cell service.

"I can help with that," Tori said. "We have lots of marker stakes in the shed. Go ahead and eat. I'll be back before you finish the garlic bread."

Without waiting for his reply, Tori was out the door, eager to get out of his presence.

Or so she thought.

She had never felt lonely. Ever. At least since kindergarten. Her parents were always a bike ride away. Why did she suddenly feel so empty? She looked down at the front fender of her bicycle. Earlier today she had put on the unicorn sticker he had given her years ago, even before she knew he was coming. Was it some kind of omen?

"Stop being so dreamy, woman! You should never have picked up another one of Mama's novels. Stick to non-fiction! It's safer."

Tori dropped her bike at the front of the storage shed, punched in the keycode, and went inside, flipping on the light to scare away any spiders. There. The Gator was already empty. She backed it up to the shelf loaded with wooden supplies and pulled out four bundles of stakes with fluorescent-orange painted tops. After Oscar was done with them, she could put them back. Besides, since Papa was a partner in this venture, he wouldn't mind sharing these. She momentarily thought of asking him for permission, then grimaced, thinking of what he and Mama were doing.

"Mama said I'd enjoy it if the right man came along. Maybe she's right…"

She shook her head, trying to get out of that untapped emotional area. "Just take him the stakes and help him set them up."

Oscar was outside of the greenhouse waiting for her, munching on the last bit of garlic bread, when she drove up. "Since you know where we're going, why don't you drive."

He hopped in and sat next to her, his eyes forward. Suddenly self-conscious, he swiped the crumbs off his two-week-old beard. *Why are you worried about your appearance? You've never tried to impress anyone before. Ever!*

"Right over here is the low spot. It's hard to see because the ground is completely dry. You don't want water running into the greenhouse or undercutting the foundation," Tori said.

Oscar nodded in agreement. "If you were in charge of this, where would you set up?"

"Since this is going to eventually be a year-round operation, I'd set it up so the long side is going to be facing south. The prevailing wind is from the west but it's not too gusty because of the mountain effect. This way you can have the doors open and cool it off quicker in the summer. I'd go uphill as far as possible to catch as much winter sun and avoid puddling. See those rises? I'd work with them, not against them. But I'm not the boss."

"Neither am I, but you know this area better than I do. All right. Let's walk it out and then put up the stakes."

Oscar watched Tori as she walked in front of him, dawdling intentionally to catch the view of her bubble butt as she half-sprinted ahead of him, excited about the new project.

"And we really need to keep this spot open. I come out here sometimes to watch the sunset. At Spring equinox, is sets between those two hills and at the autumn one, between those two."

"Then I'll make sure I save this area. One of these days, you might want a home here," he said softly, then wondered why he had said that.

Tori had been intent on showing him the view and turned back to scowl at him at his words. "I'm not moving away," she said. "I have a home."

"You're not going to live with your parents forever, are you?"

"Why not?"

Oscar shook his head and sighed. "I'm sorry. I don't even know why we're talking about that kind of stuff. I'm just here to set up and help run the cannabis operation. I don't mean to get in anyone's way."

"I'm sorry, too. I'm a little sensitive. My parents are older. We were just having a talk about them not living forever. Do you know how hard that is for an only child to hear?"

"Even tougher to deal with," Oscar said under his breath, then looked up and said boldly, "You set the corners and if I don't agree after I start with the crew out here, I'll ask you about it. Do you have the time to help me?"

"I'm a millionaire when it comes to having time," Tori said, then remembered her parent's earlier admonishment. "At least until the bills come due in September."

"Bills in September?"

"I have to go to school."

Oscar raised his eyebrows. He never thought about it but just realized she was probably underage.

"But only until January third. After I'm eighteen, I don't think they can make me do *anything*!"

He shook his head and grinned.

"What's so funny?"

"There's always someone, somewhere, who will make – or try to make – you do something they want you to do that you don't. Age doesn't make a difference. Come on. Let's see if we can get this done before sunset. I'll bet it goes down right about there, right?"

Tori walked over and stood under his pointing arm to see where he was pointing to. "If not right there, pretty darned close," she said. She suddenly realized how near she was to someone who wasn't her parent and ducked away.

Oscar stayed focused on the outside, not moving a muscle as she darted away from his side. It wasn't until she was gone that he realized that the warmth of her nearness – the same that he had felt in the greenhouse – had come and left again. Why her? Other people – even women he had crushed on and dated – never pulsed his personal space like she did, causing it to fill and empty so drastically she could be a pool of warm water.

He shivered. Or a hot springs. Was he trying to sabotage the major project ahead of him, fantasizing about someone who could never be his, to distract himself so he'd fail? Was this too much for him to undertake and his uncle had made a big mistake trusting him?

The thunk, thunk of Tori hammering in the stakes brought him out of his trance. She wasn't a vixen after his money or an adversary looking to take him or his family down. She was a hardworking young woman who loved her family. She was also a silly girl who loved goldfish, riding her bike, and exploring new ways to grow plants. *Enjoy having a friend. Listen to her. Do not get involved on a romantic level. Better to have her as an ally than an ex.*

Chapter 7: School Days

August 2009

The summer of Tori's seventeenth year went by quickly. Oscar followed her suggestions about orientation and where to set up the greenhouses, letting her help him every step of the way. Luther was very flattered that someone – besides himself – paid attention to his daughter's advice. Leanne was equally tickled that their bashful little girl was carrying on conversations with a real human being – not her imaginary friends. Tori was still timid around the subcontractors and inspectors, though, and mysteriously disappeared when they came to the site.

The attraction between the young couple was obvious but neither parent spoke of it, afraid to jinx it. Even after their workday was done, Tori spent time with the young cannabis specialist. Her parents could have set their clock by her after dinner disappearance. As the days got shorter, her vanishing act got earlier. Tori had a standing date, although they didn't dare refer to it as such. She'd help clean up the kitchen or putter around the house until a half-hour before sunset. "I'm going for a ride," she'd say, then be gone. They didn't worry. They knew where she was.

Oscar's travel trailer arrived the third day after he was on the job. He parked it on the ridge next to the greenhouses, right where Tori had said the perfect viewing spot for sunsets was. They worked elbow-to-elbow, or at least within six feet of each other, for ten hours a day. After work was done and she had spent dinner at home, she was still eager to go 'sundowning' with him. The two watched the sun set, discussing what they'd be working on the next day, or just sitting silently. Content.

In late August, the perfect melody hit a sour note. Oscar felt bad that he was the cause of it, but he couldn't help it.

"Luther, after the harvest, I need to go back and spend some time with my mother. I really think we need to do a little reverse construction on the greenhouses, too. We, meaning I, need to have in-floor heaters installed in the spring. I want to wait until the winter rains come and see the flow down the mountains first, though. Not that I don't trust Tori's layout for the buildings, but if we're going to pour concrete and invest in all the plumbing, hardware, and labor to get it in place, I want to make sure there isn't a natural wash she didn't remember."

"That might make her feel a little insulted," Luther said, "but I agree with you, one hundred percent. Just having buildings where there weren't any before could make a difference. It's better to skip a planting and not make money than invest in one and lose double the amount."

"All right. I'll draw up the plans and figure the bill of materials, but I won't order anything until February. As soon as the harvest is over, I'll move the tables out of three of the greenhouses and into one. We can finish the last one off until later. I've never spent a winter here, but I understand it's pretty wet."

"I've seen it go six months straight without a sunny day, every one rainy or misting. Great for growing trees, but it can take its toll on human emotions. Yes, definitely take a break and spend time with your mother. I'm sure she'll appreciate it. Remember Oscar, no matter how old you get, you're still her baby."

"I guess that's how you feel about Tori, too," Oscar said, then inhaled quickly, afraid that he was out of line.

Luther chuckled as his discomfort. He put his hand on the young man's shoulder. "She's our one and only. If we could have had more, we would have. I'm afraid we kept her too close, though. You're the only person she works with or even talks to. I don't know if she said anything to you or not, but we're insisting she go to school for at least a semester. Hopefully, she'll attend a full year, but I doubt it. She doesn't need the classes. She's already graduated high school, or rather, passed the tests." Luther laughed. "She did that right before her thirteen birthday just for kicks. Nah, she needs to be able to get along with other people."

"Oh, she'll be fine," Oscar said.

"Did you know she still talks to her imaginary friends?" Luther whispered. "She'd clobber me if she heard me tell you."

"I knew she did when she was a lot younger. If it gives her comfort, what difference does it make? She's great at what she does here. She says she wants to take over for you when you retire. Of course, she doesn't really want you to retire. She insists she's going to live with you for the rest of her life."

Luther canted his head toward his shoulder, looking at Oscar quizzically. "She talks that much to you?"

"We talk about everything. I even teased her about saving that little unicorn sticker I gave her when I was here that first summer."

"She said she found it in an old book."

"She said the same thing to me and I believe her. She said it was like an omen that her friend was coming back." Oscar beamed at sharing the story, glad to have someone to brag to; someone who really understood Tori. "Having her claim me as a friend is one of the greatest honors I could ever have."

Luther nodded, a smile of gratification rising. "Oh, you don't know how happy I am to hear that. Not that she's claimed you, but that you've claimed her."

"I didn't say that," Oscar said, blushing. "I said it was an honor to…" He sighed in resignation. "I guess it's no use denying it. Yes, I really like her. A lot. I'm almost afraid to leave after harvest. I'm afraid the magic will be gone. That

338

when I come back, I'll just be the guy who works here."

"No more sunsetting?" Luther asked, one eyebrow up.

"Yeah, no more sunsetting," Oscar said with a full frown.

"I'll tell you a secret. If the magic is gone, it was never really there. It was only an illusion. If the magic was real, it will still be there, sunset or not. Time – especially just a few months – won't make a difference. You were gone the first time for what, ten or eleven years, and you still have a connection?"

"Yeah, but we were just kids."

"And as far as this old hippie goes, you're still just kids. Leanne and I have been together for over forty years and still have that zing. When it's there, it's there. That is, unless you intentionally try to kill it. All I ask is that you never be mean to her. Treat her as you would want someone to treat your daughter, and we'll all get along great."

"Wow! Words of wisdom I wish I had heard from my father," Oscar said.

Luther patted him on the back. "I guess that's why I'm in your life: to give them to you because your father couldn't."

Or wouldn't. Oscar patted Luther's back in the same friendly manner. "I guess I'll close up shop for the day." He looked up at the sky. "Sunset's coming in about twenty minutes. I don't want to miss it."

"Wouldn't think of keeping you from it. See you tomorrow. Oh, and if I were you, I wouldn't mention needing to leave until a day or two before you're gone. It's going to crush her. I'd rather have your last few weeks or days here with her in a good mood. You don't want to be around her in a sour one."

"Thanks for the heads up. No reason to upset her early."

***

Early-September 2009

"These harvest machines are so fast," Luther said after watching the demonstration video. "For our own use, we always do it all by hand."

"Twelve plants versus twelve hundred plants?" Oscar said, pointing to the forest of marijuana plants over ten feet tall in front of him. "I don't think we could hire enough people to process that much bud."

"Still, Leanne and I will trim our own plants, thank you very much. There's a certain joy in preparing it yourself."

"Understood," Oscar said. "I'll make sure when the crew shows up that they keep away from your greenhouse. I'm glad Rick subcontracted this out and neither of us has to deal with the harvest, packing, or distribution end of the operation. Growing is the fun part. It's so hard to believe that they can go from little four-inch clones to ten-foot monsters in only four months."

"Yeah, and I'm glad we kept them all in greenhouses! I was talking to old Mike Cooper down the road. He was growing his plants outside. Lo and behold, a mile away, some farmer decides to grow hemp plants. You know, for rope and fabric and stuff? Anyhow, they seeded it, of course; they didn't use clones. Over half the acreage came up male plants. And you know what happens when the males get older – poof! All their little hemp pollen went sailing off in the wind, makin' love to his female plants. Seeds! Oh, he was pissed! Ruined his whole crop. He made back some money but not all of it. Yes, planting under cover does more than protect the grapes from the taint of marijuana stink. It keeps the girls making bigger buds, sterile, and pure to variety."

"Oh, and speaking of girls, how did Tori do with her first day of school?" Oscar asked.

"I'll let you ask her," Luther replied, looking down at his watch. "It's getting close to sundown. She'll probably tell you anyhow, but she had a rough time. Not only was she the new kid, but she's so quiet, the other kids took it as she was stuck up. You and I both know she's not, but she does have a little attitude. Still, the teasing's already started. I'd like to go in and throttle those bullies. All that would do, though, is get me thrown in jail." He rolled his eyes and smiled, adding, "But it might be worth it."

"No, it wouldn't just be sending you to jail. It would kick you even higher up on Tori's hero chart. You're already her idol."

Luther blushed, then looked at his watch again. "You'd better get going. This is the highlight of her day."

Oscar chuckled. "Yeah, mine, too. You brought up a stellar daughter." He turned off the lights in the office. "I'll see you in the morning."

"No, sooner," Luther said. "We told her to bring you back to the house for dinner tonight."

"Got it. And thanks."

***

When Oscar got to his trailer, Tori was already sitting on their blanket, straightening out the wrinkles so it looked perfect. "Nice day for sunset viewing," Oscar said as he approached so he didn't startle her.

She looked up and smiled, her eyes twinkling with excitement. "Every day is a good day for it."

"Okay," Oscar said. "Spill. Why is every day a good day for watching a sunset?"

"Well, for one thing, it means school's out."

"Oh, a bad day, huh?"

"Every day is going to be a bad day there. I feel like I'm serving a prison term. Only ninety-nine days and I'm done with my sentence."

Oscar frowned as he did some quick calculations. "I thought you had to go to school until you were eighteen."

"I do, but I'm not going to start a new semester. I'm only going until December 23rd, the day the semester ends. My birthday isn't until January third, so I get an eleven-day reprieve."

"Get out of jail early, eh?" Oscar asked with a chuckle. He turned away from watching the pending sunset and saw she was frowning at his remark. "What? School's rough for everyone."

"Really? Even you?"

"Duh! Especially me!"

"Why? You have it all."

"Me?" he asked, chuckling. "Okay, promise you won't laugh if I tell you about what I went through?" Tori's shrug of non-commitment was enough for him to continue. After his short talk with Luther, he didn't want to be right. He'd rather help her build up her own wall of protection from those creeps at school who teased or bullied her.

"I don't know how much you know about boys, but when they hit puberty, their voices change. It was just starting to change when I was here years ago. That's why I didn't talk much then."

Tori nodded but didn't comment, waiting for him to give a valid reason for why his school years could possibly be as bad as hers.

"It took years for the squeaks and croaks to stop. Maybe if I had talked more it wouldn't have taken forever, but it was a miserable five years."

"Five years?"

He nodded. "Finally, I was a sophomore in high school. I'd grown a foot over the summer and let my hair grow out. I kind of sort of, used to hide behind it. My mother always went on and on about how beautiful my eyes were. Her flattery flipped on me, though. The compliment became the reason to keep others from seeing their color."

"Emerald green," Tori said with an impish smirk. "I looked."

Oscar turned to her. "I'm not keeping anything from you, Tori," he said with sincerity, then amended his statement. "Except anything that might get me in trouble legally."

She canted her head to the side, wondering what he meant, then dropped the question before it came out when he began speaking again.

"Do you know how hard it is not to talk when you have to give an oral report? It's impossible. I either had to fail a class or speak up. Failure wasn't an option, so I spoke. My five-minute report on methods of cloning tender perennials became the subject of everyone's gossip."

"I think you sound like Gregory Peck. Dreamy."

"Yeah, that was the problem. They'd tease and taunt me until I talked, just so they'd hear my voice. The girls would giggle and the guys – most of them – would laugh.

"The other guys?"

"They'd giggle, too," he said.

"I don't understand."

Oscar rolled his eyes. "You don't need to. What about you? Do they tease you about anything or are they just obnoxious jerks in general?"

"'You won't talk because you're so pretty,' the girls say, practically snarling and hissing with their claws out. Shoot! Me? Pretty?"

"You are. I mean, it's genetics mostly: your bright sky-blue eyes, glistening blonde hair, flawless skin, fit body. Whether you sabotaged what you were born with by eating junk food and being a couch potato; or ate right and stayed active, you'd still have the foundation of perfection. I'm sorry. I'm rambling. It's true, though. You're inherently beautiful.

"However," Oscar continued, sitting up straight for his declaration, "I sincerely believe that true beauty shines from within. You could have been as bald as a cantaloupe, with close-set squinty eyes, and a hook nose that went to Jersey and back, and I'd still think you were pretty. It's that caring, sharing person inside who's so radiant. You could have messed up this – my first solo operation – by giving me incorrect intel, telling me the wrong location for the greenhouses, feeding me contacts for lousy subcontractors or withholding information. But you didn't. You brought me dinner, helped me feed, trim, and prune the plants, and even shared your plans for a modified aquaculture with me. Your inexpensive idea helped these plants thrive at a low cost while still maintaining their organic certification."

"Yeah, well, Mama always said 'Do unto others' and Papa said 'Karma's a bitch,' so I figured no matter which one of them was right, I'd better invest in at least a little of both philosophies."

"Works for me," Oscar said, venturing an arm around her shoulders.

Elated that she didn't flinch, he snuggled closer. "It's getting cold. Let's watch our sundown, and then go have dinner."

He felt her shoulders tense. "Your dad and I were talking before I got here; he invited me then. Hey, lookie there." He pulled her closer and pointed to a hawk circling the vineyard below. "Rodent control."

Tori relaxed at his switch in topics. "Yeah," she said, burrowing as close as she could into his warm, solid frame, barely noticing the bird. *I could stay here forever!*

***

The next morning

"Do I have to go to school, Mama?"

Leanne held up two different color flannel shirts for her to choose from. "What do you think I'm going to say?"

Tori scowled in reply.

"You told us you'd give it at least a semester. The semester ends December twenty-third and so you have…" Mama paused, trying to remember how long she had.

"Too long," Tori answered and swung her legs out of bed. "I don't think I'll ever agree to anything ever again."

"Never say never," Leanne said, setting both shirts on the dresser. "Hurry up or you'll be eating cold oatmeal in the truck on the way into school."

Tori growled as she set about her morning routine, rebraiding her two-foot-long braids that were fuzzy from sleeping in them. Even if she didn't want to go, she didn't want to look like a slob. She looked down at her feet, wiggling her sock-covered toes. "Easy decision. If I'm going to be miserable everywhere else, at least my feet can be comfortable." She put away the new mary janes her mother had set out for her and put on her well-worn cross-trainers.

"Easier to walk home in these if things don't work out," she huffed, then started day two of her sentence.

No one had paid much attention to her or her rural appearance on the first day of school. The chatter and jeers were directed at others, friends and classmates they hadn't seen all summer, catching up on brags and gossip. She waded through the nonsense, finding her way to the lab and art classes her parents insisted would benefit her the most.

The only reason she made it through that first day without leaving was she knew that Oscar would be upset if she left. She knew he was proud of her for working through her discomfort, glad that she was at least giving it a try. After dinner, he had given her a quick squeeze of reassurance across the shoulders. Oh, how she wished he was brave enough for a face-to-face hug. Her shoulders hunched up in anticipation. Or maybe even a kiss.

"I promise you'll survive this," he said.

"And then what? Surviving isn't living."

"Well, it certainly isn't dying, either." Oscar saw she was near tears. She had hoped for reassurance, not her friend agreeing with her parents.

"Look, consider this a storm you have to get through. You're young and able to bend with the gusts of rudeness and adversity. You may not realize it now, but this is making you a stronger person," he said, "giving you deeper roots."

Sniff. Sniff.

Oscar knew she was too upset to speak. "Hey, I'll help you in every way I can. Deal?"

"Deal."

***

"Another day, another drama," Tori said to her image in the mirror. "At least I have sundowns with Oscar to look forward to."

She walked into the kitchen, her chin out rather than hanging down in depression.

"Well, you seem like you're in a better mood today," Mama said.

"We have a lab this morning that interests me," Tori said casually, using that as an excuse. The last thing she wanted to admit to anyone was that she had been hugged by Oscar yesterday and was looking for more of the same. Or maybe something even better.

Tori picked up a piece of toast and set it on her plate, then grabbed the jar of apple butter. "I know the principle behind growing crystals, but the lab has more raw materials than we ever had when we did it when I was homeschooled."

"I'm glad you could find a bright spot to focus on," Papa said, setting down the newspaper. He suspected the real reason was just to pass the hours until she could spend time with Oscar. Now that the professional crew was taking care of harvesting the plants, there wasn't much – other than paperwork – to do.

***

The teacher explained in detail what the project was: growing crystals. She held up a bottle of bluing. "Many of you may have grown crystals on coal or charcoal with bluing, ammonia, and salt. We're going to start a project using bismuth, a heavy metal, today."

Tori tried to hear the teacher, but the three others at her table were chattering about their plans for the weekend. "Shush," Tori said.

All three at her table plus the students nearby immediately quieted and stared at her.

And then started laughing.

Tori wanted to cry but didn't. "How can you hear what the teacher's saying if you're talking about who's buying the booze for the punch?" she hissed, staring at the broad-shouldered boy in the football jersey in front of her.

He paled as he looked up at the teacher. "It wasn't me," he said.

"It better not be," the teacher said, her eyes narrowed. "One more mess up, mister, and you're off the team."

"Ooh-ooh!" The class chanted, laughing at him.

He turned and scowled at Tori. "You're dead meat, Blondie."

Tori flipped her braid over her shoulder and looked at the teacher. "As you were saying?"

The teacher grinned at the precocious new student, then began anew, speaking louder, taking courage from the girl who had dared put down the star quarterback. "We're doing two trays of crystals per table. One dish will be fast-growing, the other slow. The instructions are on your worksheets. Make sure you don't get the bluing on your clothes or body. It won't scrub off."

The students began their work, shuffling papers and measuring. Tori was intent on arranging the bismuth in the pan and didn't feel Jackson the quarterback lift up her braid. Nor was she aware of him squirting bluing on it. It wasn't until she heard the stifled giggles of those around her that she looked up and felt the resistance on her head, his hand still holding her hair.

"Your braids are so beautiful," Jackson crooned, then laughed out loud, waving the end of her plait in front of her face, showing off its new intense blue color that ran halfway to her head, then he dropped it.

Tori glared at him, her teeth set, holding back the urge to bite the smirk off his face. Instead, she caught sight of the scissors on the middle of the table. "Really?" she asked, her narrowed eyebrows separating, one lifted up with impending mischief. "You really like my hair?"

"Yeah. It's such a gorgeous shade of blue," he said, laughing even louder.

Tori grabbed the scissors like a knife and pointed them at him menacingly.

Jackson took pensive steps backward, his shoes squeaking on the hard tile floor. He stumbled into a stool and kicked it aside, nearly falling down, catching himself at the last moment with one blue hand grasping the windowsill. He was cornered by the crazy new kid, pinned down by the scissors in her hand.

Tori reached up and made a show of putting her fingers through the handles, grandstanding as she tested them, snipping the air. The whole class gasped as one.

Jackson clutched both hands in front of his crotch protectively. *She wouldn't, would she?*

Turning the shears toward herself, Tori grasped her blue braid with her free hand, and with three angry snips, cut it off just below her ear lobe. She dropped the scissors on the table with a clang, then took one step toward Jackson, paralyzing him. Emboldened by his fear, she slapped the bluing end of her plait across his face, letting go of it at the last moment, dropping it in disgust.

The plait now rested on his shoulder, limp, staining his team jersey, his face painted with a long blue splash.

"There! If you like it so much, you can have it!"

Tori snapped up her backpack from the floor and walked up to the teacher. "I don't think I'll be coming back. The conditions here aren't conducive to learning. And yes, he volunteered to bring vodka to the party. He already bought it and it's in the trunk of his Volvo."

"Wuh...wuh... Well, bye," the teacher said, stunned. Her wide-eyed stare quickly turned into a grin of delight. She looked over at Jackson. Three young women and his male minion were tending to him, trying to wipe the Prussian blue dye from his face. "You are so busted, mister," the teacher said.

Tori listened outside the door, out of sight but within earshot. It was a miserable but memorable day. She strutted out the front door of the high school, glad that she had worn her walking shoes. It would take over an hour to walk home but she'd do it. No matter what she had promised, she wouldn't be coming back to *this* school!

She got to the head of the road just after noon. Hoping no one was watching, she walked through the vineyard, keeping on the service roads, bypassing the main road to the office, heading right to the greenhouses. Sooner or later, though, she'd have to let her parents know they didn't need to pick her up after school, today or any day.

"You're back early," her mother said.

345

"What are you doing here?" Tori asked, startled that her mother was in her sanctuary, not the office.

"I should ask you the same thing," Leanne said, then stepped closer, checking out her daughter's lopsided hairdo. "What happened?"

Tori sniffed, hoping to find some backbone, but it was futile. She was tired from the long walk, weak from missing lunch. Five miles was a long trek when you're used to biking everywhere. "I was attacked," Tori said, glad that she had found a dynamic word.

"Someone cut your hair?"

"Duh!" Tori said, not wanting to explain that she had done it.

"I'm going to call that school right now," Leanne said, her face brilliant red with anger.

"They already called me," Luther said, walking in on the pair.

"Why didn't you tell me!" she asked, her rage redirected at her husband.

"And where is your radio, wife?"

"Oh, shoot!" Leanne patted her pockets. "Sorry. Again."

Luther let the perpetual argument about keeping in communication drop and instead focused on his daughter. "Are you all right?" he asked Tori, pushing the wayward hair from her unbound partial braid out of her face. "Looks like Mama needs to even things up a bit."

Tori started giggling at his reaction but it soon turned into tears. "It was horrible!" she said. "They hate me! I didn't do anything, but they still hate me! How do they get away with it? Why?"

"Their parents don't care," her father explained. "I know that's not fair to the other students, but that's pretty much what it boils down to. Their folks shove them out the door, put dollars in their pockets, and ignore them so they can get on with their own lives. Years ago, folks needed their family. They worked together, ate together, helped each other with everything. Nowadays, Mom and Dad – if there are two parents – go to work, drop the kid off at school, and expect the teachers to take care of manners, respect, reading, math, everything."

"Yeah," Tori said. "And the students outnumber the teachers by so many, it's ridiculous."

"Hold on a minute," Leanne said. "I think I'm missing something in this discussion. What went on?"

"Oops!" Oscar said, walking in on what was obviously a serious family discussion. "I just need to pop in here a minute. I forgot my gloves."

"Go ahead and take a break," Luther said. "You might want to sit in on this. You're practically family. It's better if you hear it now so Tori doesn't have to tell the story more than once."

"Did the school call you?" Tori asked.

Luther looked down his nose at her, not even bothering with words.

"Oh, yeah. I guess they would need to call you if I left campus, huh?"

"Go ahead, sweetheart," Leanne said to Tori, nudging Luther at the same time to urge him to let up on 'the look.'

Tori closed her eyes and recited the story without emotion – as if she was reading a list of names from a telephone book. At least it was drama-free until she got to the conclusion.

"But at the end, it was the neatest thing!" she exclaimed, her face now radiant with elation. "When I got to that class, the teacher was so cowed by the students, it was pathetic. After I scared that full-of-himself jock to the point that he almost peed himself, the teacher found her voice. She wasn't going to take his snarky attitude anymore. I'll bet the same's going to happen for everyone else in that class, too. So, you know what? I made a difference. It felt so great!"

"Well, that's what we were hoping for," Luther said proudly, then took his tone down to humility level. "Sort of. We were hoping you would feel empowered in some way, but if you feel better about yourself for helping another person feel self-assured, that's just as good."

"Even better," Leanne said. "Two for one."

"And in only two days," Oscar added, grinning in pride at the girl he was so fond of. "Oops. Sorry. Not my place."

Luther said, "Nah, speak freely." He clapped the blushing young man on the shoulder. "Yup, that's my girl. What would take anyone else a year, she can figure out in two days."

Leanne spoke up, breaking the spell. "All right, everyone. Lunch might be a little late. I have to give my baby her first major haircut. When you decided to grow your hair out forever in kindergarten, I was wondering how long that would last. Well, at least, I have one long braid to keep in my treasure box."

"Yeah, you don't want that other one," Tori said with a devilish smile. "Dyed blue and covered with brat cooties."

* * *

Leanne used the step stool to reach the old wooden box, taking it down from the top shelf in her closet. "I haven't looked in this thing since before we moved here. I always meant to, but with moving and starting a new job, I either never had the time or I didn't remember. Come on, sit down with me. Who knows what treasures we'll find."

Tori sat beside her mother at the kitchen table, offering her a dishtowel to wipe off the layer of dirt and grime that had accumulated over the years with vineyard dust that seemed to sneak in through every window and door.

She watched her mother wordlessly, wishing they could get on with the exploring so she could get her haircut and dash back to Oscar. Even if there was nothing to do, there were always garden pots to wash and sanitize.

"There it is!" Mama screeched in joy. "Your father's old wallet. We used to hide a fifty-dollar bill in it. It was our emergency money. We came across the

347

country when you were so little, poor as church crickets."

"Church mice," Tori corrected.

"Mice, crickets: what difference does it make? None of them have money. We always found a way to earn enough to get us further on down the road."

"How come you were so poor? Papa got his doctorate years ago."

"I guess you're old enough to know. We don't like to bad mouth people, but your father was a partner in a research company. He developed a new formula to treat clones so they'd root within in hours, not days. He was going to file for the patent in the morning, assured of millions of dollars from the horticulture industry. However, his partner printed out the research data and deleted all references to the project on their computers, saving it on his own laptop, then took the first train to the patent office. He filed for it under his own name, leaving your father out of all potential earnings. When your papa protested, the man got a lawyer and, long story short, we were left with nothing but our savings. If we had continued the fight, we may or may not have won."

Leanne glanced up at Tori, wanting to tell her that rather than hire a lawyer, they used all their savings and sold or pawned everything of value to buy her adoption. Their daughter was worth it, but there was no way she could share that secret.

"You and Papa really did go to Woodstock?" she asked, holding up the creased and faded tickets that looked genuine.

"Oh, my! It's still in there," Leanne said, glad to be distracted from her guilt. "Yes, we went when we were practically teenagers. I mean, I was, your father's older. Yup, we're serious when we say we're just a couple of old pot-growing hippies."

"Here's your same fifty-bucks," Tori said. "Money looked different back then."

"Yes, it did. What else is in there?"

Tori took the old-style fifty out to show her mother and found something behind it.

A laminated photo. Tori stared at it. Speechless.

"What is it, honey? You looked like you just saw a ghost."

She handed it to her mother, still stunned.

"Oh, that's so fantastic!" Leanne gushed. "And here we thought we didn't have any baby pictures left of you after the flood ruined everything. This was your father's favorite picture and it's even more priceless now."

Tori took the picture from her mother and studied it, making sure it wasn't modified or a mock-up. Nope. It was the genuine article. Her mother was nursing her. She didn't know much about babies, but she didn't look very old. She was round and chubby-cheeked, not gaunt and lanky like a newborn. Definitely too small to walk, too. *I really am their child. Then who are those other two girls I see? I could have sworn I had sisters!*

Tori felt her mother gently replait her remaining braid. "Are you all right, sweetheart?"

"Yeah, Mama. I'm just having a very emotional day."

Her mother kissed the top of her head, reassuring her. "It'll be all right. Trust me."

"Sure," she sighed. *The other kids were right. I really am crazy!*

Chapter 8: Hat for a haircut

Tori picked up the hand mirror, verifying both sides of her hair were even in length. She huffed in frustration. She'd worn braids ever since her hair was long enough to plait. Suddenly, she looked older. Was it the empowerment she had earned at school today or simply the change of hairstyle?

"I said, do you like it? I can cut off more if you want?"

"No, Mama. This is fine. If you don't mind, can I skip lunch with everyone? I'm tired after the long walk."

"And all the excitement?" Leanne prompted.

"Yeah, that, too," Tori agreed. She set down the looking glass. She wasn't even curious if she'd still see her two sisters if she looked into the bathroom mirror with it. Were they really just her imagination?

"Honey, this is part of growing up. You experienced at least one new and intense emotion today. Rage wasn't new, I know, but rage in defense of self is different than being mad at a person or situation. You also helped someone find her own power. That's a joy not everyone gets to feel, at least until you watch your child grow up and stand on her own two feet."

"Like you today with me?"

"Yes, I got that same joy today. Your father did, too," Leanne said dreamily.

Tori looked up and saw the sly smile Mama always got when she was feeling frisky about Papa. A nap now would definitely be a good idea. She'd need to take another long walk tonight so she was out of the house this evening. Or maybe she'd stay longer with Oscar after sunsetting.

"I'm going to take a shower before my nap, so please don't do dishes or laundry until I'm done."

"Got it. No hot or cold water surprises," Leanne said.

Tori stepped into the warm shower, the silkiness of the water on her skin different now that her hair wasn't interrupting the sensation. No covering over her neck or back. Or her breasts. She squirted a big blob of shampoo into her hand, realized she probably didn't need as much, then went ahead and used the full amount. It produced way too many suds; tiny dense bubbles that meant she definitely didn't need to wash it twice. She grabbed her washcloth and hurriedly soaped it up, not wanting to indulge in giving herself a shower smile. Frustrated with herself and life in general, she scrubbed hard, trying to wash away anger and humiliation, rushing through her usual routine, eager for the oblivion that sleep offered.

She dried off quickly, wrapped the towel around her head, then slipped into bed, naked and exhausted. Why was growing up so hard? Couldn't she stay a kid forever? "Silly ass! Nobody wants to deal with negative emotions! Stop thinking you're so special that you can skip over the pain and humiliation of growing up!"

Tori's last thoughts before she fell asleep were of watching a sunset with Oscar. No, she really didn't want to stay a child. She wanted to grow up and be a wife. But that didn't mean she didn't wish she could just skip through the rough times.

The sound of a gentle rapping at her door awoke Tori. "Are you all right, sweetheart?" her mother asked.

"Huh? What time is it?"

"Almost six. You've been asleep for almost three hours."

"Oh, shoot! Thanks, Mama. I'll be out in a few minutes. I guess I was more tired than I thought."

Tori shook her towel the rest of the way off her head, slipped on her sports bra and tank top, stepped into her sweatpants, and grabbed a flannel shirt to ward off the evening chill, tying it around her waist.

"What happened to you?" her father asked when she came into the living room.

"What do you mean?"

"You look like Medusa."

Tori stepped in front of the decorative mirror above the fireplace and groaned. "I forgot about my hair. I guess I'll have to do something with it."

"At least comb it," Luther said. He saw her frustration and added, "Don't worry. It'll come back. I promise."

"Just like everything else that's been happening to me, I want it to just hurry up and be over!" Tori took another look at herself, grunted, then went back to the bathroom to try to tame her hair.

It was impossible. The blonde tresses, so used to being contained in braids and weighted by length, were free and flyaway; clean, carefree, and full of static. She ran her comb under the faucet, wetting it repeatedly before swiping it through her slept-in kinks and curves, wild from being wrapped in a towel for three hours. She considered wetting it completely again but decided against it. She'd have to settle for the tamed-down mess rather than spend the evening with a chilled, wet head.

By the time she was done with dinner, she had forgotten about her new hairdo. Mama was still making googly eyes at Papa. Were they getting younger as she got older? Nah. Mama had shared the contents of Papa's old wallet with him before they sat down to eat. They were thinking of Woodstock and nursing babies. Ugh! A quick assist with washing dishes and she was ready to leave.

"I guess I don't have to ask where you're going," Papa said.

"Yes, we're going to watch the sunset. After that," Tori glanced at the shelf of DVDs and pulled one out without looking at it, "we're going to watch a movie."

"Sleepless in Seattle?" Mama asked.

351

"Sure, why not? It's one of your favorites, right? I guess I'll finally find out what all the hoopla's about."

Luther started to ask her not to stay out too late, then changed his mind. He glanced at the clock and did some quick calculations. An hour until sundown and then a two-hour movie. Tonight he'd bring out a bottle of wine, too.

Leanne walked over to Luther at the screen door, standing beside him as he watched Tori set the movie in the basket, ready to pedal up the hill to Oscar's spot. Oscar and Tori's spot. "It's a good thing I trust him," Luther said.

"She may not have been interested in boys before he came along, but she sure is now," Leanne added.

"He's a man," Luther said. "On the one hand, that's scarier. On the other, not so much. She's almost eighteen. One of these days, she's going to want to move away and start her own family."

"True, but she'll always be our baby. Come on, I hear that bottle of wine you've been saving for a special day calling us."

"You read my mind, wife," Luther said and kissed her on the temple.

***

Tori arrived at Oscar's trailer, excited for the sunset to begin. She rapped on the door then heard him holler at her. He was already up the hill, their blanket spread out, two glasses of lemonade set on the small side table they used for picnics.

"The low clouds and smoke from slash burns should make for spectacular colors tonight," he said, doing his best not to stare at her wild hair.

Too late. His gaze had lingered a moment too long. Tori's hand went up to her head. "Oh, man! I totally forgot about it!" she said, her eyes red as tears began.

"Here," Oscar said, taking off his knit cap. "This will keep it out of your eyes. It'll grow back. I promise."

"You sound like my father."

"I hope that's a good thing for you because I consider it a compliment. He's a cool guy."

Tori swiped the back of her hand under her nose, checking for nasal leakage. Assured that only a dribble of tears had made it out, she tucked her wayward locks under his hat. "Hey, this feels good. It's like my head is getting a hug."

"Yeah. Now you know why I wear it all the time."

"And here I thought you had premature balding," Tori teased. She looked up. "Hey, look. It's starting early. Let's time it."

Oscar started to offer her a drink then saw she was settling in. Yes, he'd rather cuddle up to her and watch a long sunset than sip on lemonade and munch on veggies. After a few minutes, he reached up and pulled up an edge of the knit cap.

"Don't. I have Dumbo ears," she said, her shoulder shrinking away from him, breaking their magic bubble of contact.

"No, you have magic elfin ears."

"You mean like I'm a magic elf or the ears themselves are elfin?" she asked, then laughed, knowing which one he meant.

Oscar leaned forward and held her face, turning her head gently to kiss each bared ear. "Lovely ears on a beautiful woman who is magical."

"Huh? I mean, I heard you but how am I magical?"

"You make my heart sing. Every muscle in my body and breath I take is charged with happy tingles when you're near me. The mere thought of you excites the cells in my body."

"Cells can't be happy," she protested.

He kissed her on the mouth without warning, quickly before he lost his nerve. "Did that make your mouth happy?" he asked. "Because if it didn't, I'll never do it again."

Tori replied by leaning into him, knocking him back onto the picnic blanket, returning his tentative buss with a full body contact kiss, breastbone to breastbone, her hands on his shoulders pinning him down. Absorbed in the moment and driven by instincts, her mouth explored his with abandon and he responded the same way.

Hormone-enhanced emotional reactions took over as their bodies ground against each other passionately, seeking more physical joining, stymied by cotton and zippers.

Tori shifted, trying to get closer to him. "Whoa, whoa, whoa," Oscar pled breathlessly, breaking away as she changed positions. "I mean, I'd like to keep going, but if we do, I'm afraid I won't be able to stop."

"Stop? Am I doing something wrong?"

"No, you're doing everything right. Too right…"

Ring! Ring! Ring!

"What's that?" Tori asked, embarrassed as she realized how brazen she had been. She felt her face redden and was glad that something had interrupted them. Hopefully, she would have time to think of an excuse for her bold response to his gentle kiss.

Oscar stared at his phone, the obvious source of the alert. "Danged if I know why it's ringing. We don't have cell service out here." He picked it up and saw his cousin's face on the screen.

"Hold that thought," he said to Tori with a grin of chagrin, then clicked answer on the phone.

"Hey, there, Oscar," Rich said. "I hope I'm not interrupting anything. I've been trying to call you all day. I remembered you said you didn't have cell towers out there, but I was hoping you had internet. Cool, eh? A long-distance call over wi-fi."

"Yeah," Oscar replied, answering the second question and also the first one about interrupting at the same time. "So, what's so important? I haven't heard from you in ages."

"Dad wanted me to get in touch with you. He's on a trip to Antarctica and in and out of service. He asked me to contact you about your mother. Have you heard from her lately?"

"Um, no. That's not unusual, though. We only talk around the holidays, and even then it's iffy."

Before Rich could reply, he held up his hand, asking Oscar to hold on. "I'm on the phone, sweetie. I'll be there in a few."

Oscar's eyes widened. It was Tori! Tori was standing behind his cousin, chatting about a dinner or something. He looked back and saw Tori was still on the blanket, sipping on a lemonade, letting him finish his phone call without interruption. "Who's that?" he asked.

"Oh, that's my girlfriend. I'm pretty sure we'll get married," Rich whispered into the phone when her back was turned. "I can't make it official until she's eighteen, though. She's a cutie, huh?"

"Yeah, huh."

"Oh, and about your mother… Dad said he talked to her just before he went into that dead zone. She's acting, how should I say…"

"Squirrelly?" Oscar offered.

"Yeah, that's it. Anyhow, it's that time of year again and he's worried she might do something stupid. He said damn the crops and harvest; would you go help her? She's his only sister and he can't get to her soon enough or he'd go. I'm sure he doesn't want you to mess everything up this first season, though. Are you at a point where you can break away and spend some time with her? I know things are a little uncomfortable with the two of you, but give her a week or two of your time. Autumn in Paris is awesome."

"You don't have to say anymore. I'll give her a call in the morning and see how she's doing. Oh, and congratulations on the engagement."

"Shush," Rich said, his smile growing. "Not yet. I'll tell you a secret, though. When you find the right one, it feels so perfect. It's like putting on your favorite shoes: comfortable and ready for a long journey."

"I'm not a pair of old tennis shoes," Vickie called from the background. "Hope to meet you one of these days," she said, walking up close to cuddle into Rich, both of them waving goodbye.

"Yeah, you, too," Oscar said, leaning closer, wishing he had a way to capture a screenshot and show Luther that Tori had a doppelganger.

The screen went blank but not before Oscar had noticed that there was a difference between Rich's girl and Tori: the ears. His gals ears didn't stick out. *Still, almost twins.*

"After the sun goes down, do you want to watch a movie with me?" Tori asked, letting him know that she knew he was done with the call.

"Yeah, sure." He looked at her and smiled. Worn but comfortable shoes. Nah, she was more like a worn and comfortable flannel shirt, ready for him to wear as they tackled the world together. He felt his excitement return and rolled sideways so it wasn't so noticeable. "Um, one thing, though. Normally I wouldn't mind, but I think we'd better stay away from romances and chick flicks tonight. I'd hate to get carried away and do something your father would have me arrested for. You're still only seventeen."

She looked away from him, hiding her scarlet blush. The sun was still a minute or two away from setting completely. "All right. But can we at least snuggle until the color is gone from the sky?"

"Hmm. How about until the first star comes out," he said, wanting a moment or two longer.

"Real star, not a planet," Tori amended, setting her lemonade back on the table. "Come on. The show's still on."

* * *

Oscar was waiting in the office when Luther and Leanne showed up at eight the next morning.

"Where's Tori?" Luther asked. "I thought she left early to help you in the greenhouses."

"I haven't been there yet," Oscar said. "I wanted to talk to you two first. I know that Tori doesn't want to go back to school. It sort of isn't my business but it sort of is, too. I mean, your family is your business but she's my unofficial assistant. I want to give her a portion of my shares."

"Oh, no, no," Luther said, then halted when Oscar raised his hand. "That's not what I wanted to talk about. I have a family dilemma. I have to fly back to Paris to see my mother." He shrugged and frowned, not wanting to explain further.

"Understood," Luther said. "Family first. I hadn't made the official phone call to the school about her attendance, but this makes it easier for me, too. I'll just say she has to stay home and help with the family business. Plain and simple. No further explanation required for anyone. I will tell you, though…" Luther got comfortable in his office chair and grabbed a pencil, twirling it between his fingers to help him concentrate. "The parents of that boy who dyed her braid called the school. They wanted to press assault charges."

"What?" Oscar asked.

"Yeah, I wish I'd been there when that happened," Leanne said. "Luther told them that their big football player son attacked her first. All she did was defend herself. With a lock of her own hair!"

"Well, it was a little more than a lock," Luther said, "but not much more. I guess the principal is on our side. There's always been a zero-tolerance for bullying but no way to enforce it. The teachers are too afraid of the students."

"So, how's that going to change?" Oscar asked.

"They were afraid of losing their funding. It turns out that the teacher in that class had submitted a grant request. The school no longer has to depend on endowments from rich parents for sports."

"That doesn't make sense," Oscar said.

"It had something to do with matching funds for academics and sports. Her grant is not tied to any athletic program. But their problems with finances aren't ours. Tori was only attending school so she'd get some people skills and maybe a little exposure to what life was like outside of just the two of us."

"Three of us," Leanne amended.

"Or more," Oscar said. "She's not ducking into dark corners when the trim crew comes in."

Luther chuckled. "Kind of hard to do that in a greenhouse," he said.

"So, since she's got some people skills going and knows what's needed to bring the crops to harvest, I wanted to ask you if she could take over. That's why I wanted to share my cut. We can work the numbers out later or do it right now." Oscar looked around the office. "As soon as we figure out where she went."

"Probably looking for you," Luther said.

"Luther!" Leanne hissed, smacking his arm.

"Oh, and do you think you can give me a ride to the Portland Airport tomorrow? We'd have to leave at," Oscar looked at his watch, "at about ten-thirty."

"AM or PM?"

"AM. I know it's short notice but…"

"Family first," Luther said. "Come on. Let's walk around and see if there are any loose ends that need to be tied up. I think you have more confidence in her than I do."

"Don't tell me: you still think of her as your baby, right?"

"Kind of hard not to."

***

An hour passed and Tori still wasn't around.

Or at least, she was trying to be invisible. After they had done a cursory check on the four dedicated cannabis greenhouses, the men returned to the office. Luther reached into the pile of jackets and coveralls hanging on the wall and pulled Tori out by the upper arm.

"This stops now, young lady," he said. "You're embarrassing me and yourself. And probably Oscar, too. We need you to step up to the plate."

"What does that mean anyhow?" she asked, indignant at being caught.

"It's your turn at bat," Oscar said. "I have to leave tomorrow morning. I need you to take over while I'm gone."

"But…but…why?"

"I have to go take care of my mother. It's not something I necessarily *want*

356

to do but what I *need* to do."

Tori looked at Oscar, then her father, and back at Oscar. "Is she going to die or something?"

"That could happen. Do you want to help me help her? I know you've never met her, but she is a mother. We tend to think of moms as tough and able to take care of the world. But many times, they're not. Often they're as vulnerable as babies."

"Just a lot older," Tori said, frowning.

Luther took his hand off her arm and lifted her face to his. "If your mother needed help, what would you do? Would you drop everything and be there for her or just hope someone else would come by and take care of her?"

Tori paused, thinking about what he had asked. "You're the only one who could take care of Mama as well as I could," she said, then glanced up at him. "And I'm not too sure about that. Yes. I understand. I'll behave and step up to the plate. But I don't have to like it!"

Oscar looked at her. Her bottom lip was stuck out defiantly, her head still covered with the knit cap he had given her the day before. "Look for the good part in any job you do. I know you already like all aspects of growing and harvesting. You'll be doing all the same work we do every day but without me."

Tori sucked back her scowl and lifted her chin. Determined. "I can handle it. Just don't get too used to being gone."

"Now *that* I'll promise."

Chapter 9: The Ultimate Embarrassment

Oscar spent the day making phone calls and scribbling notes in a journal so Tori had a guidebook with names and numbers in case she needed them. But he knew she wouldn't. If she could overcome her aversion to talking on the phone, she'd have the job mastered.

"Go ahead and schedule a harvest crew for greenhouse one for October seventh," Oscar said. "I'll be right here in case you freeze up."

Tori took his kid-glove approach at helping her as a challenge to succeed on her own. She picked up the phone and dialed from memory, then felt her chest tighten. Yup, freeze up.

Oscar reached for the phone but she turned around, denying him access. She coughed once, forcing air into her lungs, then spoke, her voice thin and just above a whisper.

"Sorry 'bout that," she said. She cleared her throat again, her voice now stronger and confident. "I had something stuck. Let me start again. This is Tori Greene at Chill Out Growers. Yes, we're the new grow site right behind If You Can Imagine Vineyards. My partner and I…" She paused, looking over at Oscar to give him a wink, "My partner and I are looking to schedule a crew to come out and harvest three hundred plants. Yes, I know this is the busy time of year and that's why I'm calling early. Really? You booked up that long ago? I was hoping that four-weeks' notice would be enough. Do you have a smaller crew that could come out or can you recommend someone else? Oh, we're not afraid of startups as long as they have good recommendations. All right, put the Dragonfly crew down for the week of the thirtieth. Nah, if you say they're good, I'll believe you. No need to put us on a cancellation list. That's Tori. T-O-R-I. Like Victoria but without the start and finish. Just the good stuff in the middle. Right. Thanks!"

Tori handed the phone back to Oscar and sat down hard in the chair. She leaned forward and covered her face, emotionally spent. "Did I sound like a rambling idiot to you or was that just to me?"

"Tori, you had more confidence than a five-hundred-pound Sumo wrestler coming up against a five-pound Pekinese! I'm so proud of you that I might give you all the phone work."

"Oh, no you don't," she said. "That scared the pee out of me." She sat up quickly and looked at the chair. "Nah. No pee," she said and laughed.

"You're so cute when you're strong," Oscar said, giving her a kiss on the forehead.

"You missed."

He sighed deeply. "When's your birthday again?" he asked although he already knew it was three months away.

"Don't worry. I'm sure if you asked them nicely, my folks would let you take me out on a date. Not that I can think of anywhere I want to go. I mean, I'd rather watch sunsets and DVDs with you – munching on microwave popcorn – than go to a theater."

Tori finished her declaration, then stuck her face up and shut her eyes, waiting for another kiss.

"I'm not sure if I can make sunset tonight," Oscar said, one hand on her shoulders, the other pushing stray hairs behind her ear. "I have to go into town and take care of some business in person." He rolled his eyes. "Lawyers and bankers," he said. "I'll try to be back but you know how traffic is."

"There they are!" Luther said, popping into the office.

Oscar's hands dropped to his side as if the boss had just caught him with his fingers in the till.

Luther looked aside, letting the guilt-ridden young man compose himself. "We'd like you to join us for dinner tonight, Oscar. I know it's your last night but you still have to eat, right?"

"I'm sorry. I have to take care of some legal mumbo jumbo in Portland before I leave the country. Looks like I'll have to eat my first drive-through food since I came to work here."

"Better take some antacids with you," Luther warned. "You never seem to have them when you need them. And there's no worse place to have an upset stomach than when you're stuck in I-5 traffic."

"I'll pick some up when I head into town for fuel. There's no problem taking the work truck, is there?"

"It's your uncle's truck, not mine. I'm not going anywhere, so help yourself."

***

Tori sat at her window, headphones on as she watched for headlights coming up the hill. It was already nine o'clock and he still hadn't returned. Sunsets weren't the same without him. "You're smitten, woman," she said aloud. "Just like a romance novel, hung up on the hero. Hopelessly infatuated with him, yearning for his hands on you…"

She picked up the book she'd been reading. "I gotta stop reading this stuff. Just because every bit of it's true doesn't make it easier to handle. Dang! If you'd asked me a year ago, I'd say these romance stories were as real as Cinderella versus the Vampire! Pure sensationalism!" She took out the bookmark, ready to read again, then looked out the window. Someone had just turned onto their road. It had to be him. No one came out this far who didn't belong.

Tori stood up, grabbed for her flannel shirt, and was stopped short by her corded headphones. "Dang it!" She took them off and threw them on the bed, slipped on her shoes, and opened the door and listened.

359

"Sing me another song, Luther," her mother cooed.

Ew! I don't know which is worse: the lovemaking or the parts that come before and after it. At least, they're busy and won't know I'm gone.

Tori hopped on her bike and sped to Oscar's trailer, ready to spend some 'quality time' with him. How far would he let her go tonight? Tingles ran up her body as she recalled their passionate make-out session on the picnic blanket, 'not' watching the sun go down. What would have happened if they hadn't been interrupted by that call from his cousin? She reached up and fastened the top button on her flannel against the chill, knowing that the shiver was from thinking about him, not the evening air.

What was the worst that could happen? She knew. She could get pregnant. Would that be so bad? It would mean he'd be in her life forever. Did she want that? Absolutely! Scenarios of possibilities and different love scenes from Mama's romance novels played over in her head, sending shivers up her chest and spine, warming her lady parts as she pedaled furiously to get to his place before he did.

Fwap!

Just as Tori pulled up to Oscar's trailer, the bike chain flew off, sending her skidding into his gravel front yard. As she was kicking the wrecked bike away, the headlights of the truck shone on her.

The engine shut off but the lights stayed on as Oscar jumped out to help her. "Are you all right?"

She looked up at his face. Not a sign of a laugh or a giggle at her pratfall, only concern for her. "I don't know yet. It just happened."

"Here, let me help you get up."

Oscar put his arm under hers and led her up the steps and onto his bed. "Let me shut off the truck lights. Don't try to do anything. I'll be right back and take care of you."

Tears burst out, caused by embarrassment, not pain. That would come later when the stun of the crash wore off and the tenderness of knees and elbows skinned raw took over.

"Oh, man," Oscar said, bringing the flashlight close to her knee. "That looks painful. What happened?"

"Chain broke," she said, sniffing back tears.

"Do you want me to clean it up for you or should I take you home and let your mom deal with it?

"She's busy."

"Okay. How about your dad?"

"They're busy together," she said and rolled her eyes, unable to keep the giggle out of her voice.

"Oh, I see. Or I don't see. I mean..."

"Yeah, best not to think about it. Could you do it for me? I'm not too good

360

at the sight of blood. I'd hate to add barf and make it the ultimate embarrassment."

"No problem. Let me get a basin and squirt bottle."

Oscar gently and compassionately tended to her injuries, enjoying the feel of her skin beneath his hands, her willingness to let him do what he would to her. "Why did you come out so late?" he asked when he was done with the first aid.

"I wanted to spend more time with you." She shrugged, looking through his window toward her house and noticed that from his bed, he could look into her bedroom window if her blinds were open. A sly grin grew. He was smitten with her, too. She wouldn't tell him what she'd discovered, though.

"Helluva last night together," he said, adding a nervous chuckle.

"What do you mean? We're together on your bed, aren't we?"

"Tori Lynn Greene!" he exclaimed, then laughed.

"I didn't know you knew my middle name."

"I've heard both your parents call you out with all three names. I guess it isn't Victoria, is it?"

"I used to make jokes that there were really three of me. All together, I was one named Vickie-Tori-Ria. I had heard the name Victoria somewhere and thought that's what it was. Mama said no, my name was just Tori, not Victoria. 'We didn't need the extra at the beginning and the end,' she said."

"Well, Vickie-Tori-Ria, do you want me to drive you back tonight or do you think you can drive yourself? I still have to pack."

"I'm just Tori," she said, remembering the photo of Mama nursing her. *So much for being one of three...*

"So..." Oscar prompted her when they were standing next to the truck. "Drive yourself or I'll drive?"

"I got this," she said, her hand out for the keys.

"Yeah, well you may have been in my bed tonight, but know this, you'll be in my heart every night while I'm gone. I'll set up that app that Rich used so we can talk. There's a nine-hour time difference so you'll have to call me before noon."

"I don't have a smartphone," she said, trying not to start crying again.

"No worries. That's one thing I stopped off for when I was in town. I'll get it set up for you in the morning. For right now, though, I really need to pack and then get some sleep. I'm wiped out."

Tori twirled the keyring around her finger. "Yeah, me, too. Wiped out after wiping out. Either Papa or I will pick you up tomorrow at seven. Is that too early?"

"It's never too early to see you," he said, then kissed her on the top of the head.

"Yeah," she said, then carefully stepped into the truck. *I'll give you an hour or so to pack, and then I'll be back!*

Tori pulled up to the house, turned off the headlights, then sat, wondering if she should go in. Mama and Papa's bedroom was dark. They were asleep. Not even the gentle glow of the candles Mama lit for their time together was visible. She pulled her shirt together, glad that she had worn one of her heavier ones. It was still summer by the calendar, but early September evenings were cool, especially after ten o'clock at night. She looked over at Oscar's trailer. His lights were off now, too.

Hoping her parents wouldn't hear the sound of the truck starting, she drove up the hill slowly, looking back at her house to make sure the lights stayed off. Great. Her parents were still asleep.

The only sound she heard as she stopped a hundred feet from Oscar's place was the chirping of frogs. *Great! Cover noise for the crunch of gravel.*

She walked to the house. Still in the front yard was the mangled mess of the bike she'd ridden since she was eight years old. Definitely time for some new wheels. The sparkle of the pink unicorn sticker reflected in the brightness of the full moon. She'd get some goop and transfer it to her new ride, though. She paused at the top of the three steps into the trailer, the frogs stilled by her presence. She listened for sounds from Oscar. Nothing. Cool. He didn't snore like Papa.

Glad that he never locked his door, Tori slipped inside, soundlessly closing it behind her.

Neat and tidy as always, Oscar had cleaned up the mess from doctoring her, tossing the bandage packaging into the garbage. The basin had been washed and dried, ready for cut-up watermelon, chips, or salads. His home would be clean and ready when he returned.

Tori carefully set the keys on the hook on the wall, slipped off her shoes, and tiptoed over to his bed. He slept on the side of the double bed closest to the window, a gentle breeze blowing across his bare-chested body. She inhaled deeply, memorizing the scent that was already familiar to her. Unclothed, it was stronger, more enticing. She noticed one of his shirts tossed on top of a laundry basket, the denim one he'd been wearing when he performed first aid. There was a smear of her blood on it. It was too soiled to wear without pretreating and washing, but in much better shape than the ripped and dirty flannel she was wearing. She put on his shirt and tossed hers in the basket. She'd take it with her when she left. Right now, her shoulders were cold.

As quietly as if she was sneaking an acorn from a sleeping squirrel, Tori pulled back the lightweight thermal blanket and crawled beneath it. Oscar made a small noise of discomfort, then readjusted his shoulders into the pillow and fell back into his deep sleep.

All she wanted to do was see him one more time. Be close to him. They didn't even have to talk. She took in all she could of his appearance with just the

362

moonlight from the window. His hair was short but just a little wild. She still had his hat. He hadn't asked for it back. Hopefully, he never would. If he asked, she'd tell him she wanted to wash it first. She definitely didn't want to do that but that's what she'd say. It smelled of him. She inhaled again, his bare shoulders so close to her. Why was a man's scent so attractive? Why would women spend hundreds of dollars on perfumes when a person's natural aroma was nature's way of pointing mates in the right direction.

Mates. She shuddered. They had all the time in the world to get to know each other. He didn't know when he'd be back but they were partners. Mates of the clothing-required type…

She hadn't meant to fall asleep and didn't realize she had until a fly landed on her lip. She sputtered, hoping she didn't swallow it.

"What the hell?" Oscar jumped out of bed and grabbed his pillow to cover his nakedness. "What are you doing here?"

"You were naked?" she asked.

"Yeah, I always sleep without clothes on. You didn't answer my question. What are you doing here?"

Tori stood up and turned away from him, the pain of her bruises and abrasions zipping through her body, embarrassed all over again that she had done something stupid. "I…I…" she looked down and realized she was wearing his shirt. "I came to get your shirt. I'll get the bloodstain out of it for you."

"You have to go home. Now. Tori, you don't understand what a big deal this is. I could get arrested and sent to prison for this. I know we didn't do anything…" He paused, trying to remember what happened before he went to bed. "I'm sure we didn't do anything, but just being in the same room could land me in jail, especially with me naked, for God's sake!"

"I'm sorry, I'm sorry," Tori kept repeating, stumbling over the laundry basket as she tried to pull her shirt out of it.

"Just go. And don't tell anyone you were here. I'm serious. Your dad could not only have me arrested, he might also shoot me!"

Tori stumbled down the steps in tears, disoriented. She spotted her crashed bike, confused about how she had arrived, then spotted the truck.

And her father.

Luther was pulling up in the Gator, his broad-brimmed hat shadowing his angry face. "What's going on here, young lady. Or should I say, young woman?"

"It's all my fault. Don't shoot him. Don't have him arrested. He didn't do anything. We didn't do anything. I promise. I'm so stupid!" Tori blurted out between heavy sobs and tears.

Luther looked up and saw Oscar at the open door in sweatpants and no shirt. "What's going on here?"

"I told you, Papa, nothing!" Tori screamed. "It's all me! I'm so stupid…"

363

"Go home, Tori. Your mother's worried sick about you. I'm going to have a talk with Oscar."

"But Papa..."

"Go! Now!" he growled.

Oscar stepped back out of the doorway, letting Luther come in. He didn't make a sound. Nothing he could say would help the situation.

Luther sat down at the small kitchenette table, snorting in rage, taking deep breaths to contain his rage. He looked up at Oscar and saw a total lack of emotion and felt compassion.

"She came in and you didn't even know it, right?"

Oscar nodded but remained mute.

"You didn't do anything to her, right?"

He nodded again, then reached over to flip on the coffee pot.

"What am I going to do with that girl?"

Oscar opened his mouth to speak, then paused. He looked at the distraught parent. "Keep loving her and don't alienate her."

He saw Luther's shoulders relax and added, "And maybe put a lock on her bedroom door and window."

"Lord Almighty, I'm glad it was you and not some young buck out for thrills," Luther huffed.

"She came over to see me after I got back from Portland. She said the chain came off her bike. I'm pretty sure that's what happened because she skidded across the yard and really did a number on her knees and elbows. I doctored her up and sent her home in the truck. I guess I should have escorted her."

"Hindsight's twenty-twenty," Luther said. "How about if I hang out here while that coffee's brewing. It's still early yet. I'll let her stew a bit, let her mama chew on her and soften her up so she doesn't repeat the same mistake for a while."

"Well, you won't have to worry about me for a few months. It looks like my mother's losing her mind. Again. They want to commit her to an institution. I want to spend some time with her and see if I can pull her head out of her southern realm. She didn't take it well when my dad left."

"Take as much time as you want. We'll still be here when you get back. At least, I hope you come back. Tori may have made a big mistake, but there's no use in cutting out her heart. She's mighty fond of you, you know."

"That goes both ways. I have to tell you, though, when I woke up, buck naked and with her by my side..."

"What? You were naked in bed with my daughter?" Luther screeched, riled up anew.

"That's how I went to sleep!" Oscar hollered back with nearly as much vigor. "I always do! I didn't expect anyone to join me!"

Luther settled down slightly, then started laughing. "I can't imagine how you felt, going to sleep a single man, then waking up with a seventeen-year-old in bed next to you. Damn! I'll bet you were confused."

"Yeah, you may think it's funny, but put yourself in my place!"

Luther's face fell. "Yeah, I guess that's right. I suppose that would either mean a prison sentence or a shotgun wedding."

"The first terrifies me, the second..." Oscar thought about it for a brief moment. "Well, at least it was Tori and not some woman I didn't know or care for."

"You got that right. Go ahead and get showered and dressed or whatever you need to do. I'll wait for the coffee to finish and give Leanne time to chastise that wayward daughter of ours. Still going to the airport at ten-thirty?"

"As long as she hasn't crashed the truck, too. I don't think that Gator would make the minimum speed limit on the freeway."

Chapter 10: Emotional Hangover

Honk! Honk!

Luther waited a minute for Oscar then got out of the truck when he didn't come out of his trailer. He looked at his watch again. They were running late. The ten minutes he'd spent trying to convince Tori to join them hadn't helped.

When Luther walked in, Oscar looked up, startled. "Sorry. I guess I was off in my own little world. I didn't hear you pull up. I couldn't find my paperwork. Here it is!" He pulled out a bulging shipping envelope from the shelf above his bed. "I knew I put it in a safe place, but you know how that goes. By the time I put it away last night, I was exhausted. I'm glad I found it." He glanced around, unplugged the coffee pot, then patted himself down, checking his pockets. "Passport, ticket, power of attorney… Yeah, I'm set."

Luther climbed in the truck and watched in sympathy as the anxious young man stood at the top of the steps, searching for Tori. "She's not here," he sighed in frustration.

"What? She didn't want to come with us?" Oscar asked.

"Would you want to be stuck in the front of a truck with someone who'd just witnessed your most humiliating and embarrassing moment ever?"

"I guess not. I didn't even get to show her the phone I bought her. Would you give it to her? I left it on the kitchen counter with a bow and a note on it, telling her we can video chat with it."

"You could have saved yourself a lot of money. We can do that with our old desktop computer, too."

"I know but it's a lot more personal when you don't have to be at work to talk..." Oscar chopped off the end of his sentence before he got to 'with your boyfriend.'

Luther noticed the awkward halt but didn't comment on it. "She's still wounded. It's her own damned fault, though!"

"Think of it as she's hit a growth spurt. It's an emotional one, but she's still adjusting to new feelings. She never had any power over anything or anyone. Suddenly, she's in charge. Or at least she thinks she is."

"What are you talking about?"

"Okay, try to back away from the fact that she's your daughter, and embrace the part where I'm your co-worker explaining my dilemma. Just for grins, let's call her Suzy."

"That was the name she gave all her goldfishes, but okay. Go ahead."

"So, I have a girlfriend, mostly platonic. She wants to do more, but I know she's both too young and vulnerable."

"And inexperienced," Luther added with a throaty huff.

Oscar ignored the man's protective growl. "So, Suzy and I kissed one day. That's all. Both fully clothed, nothing below the belt or anything like that."

366

Another guttural growl but Oscar saw that the possessive papa was still holding it together.

"Suzy wants more. Oscar does, too, but absolutely, positively won't give in."

"Good man. He'll live longer that way."

"Exactly. But what's he supposed to do about Suzy? While he was asleep, she sneaked in and crawled into his bed. She could have put him in prison for life if her father had been the unreasonable sort."

Luther sighed, stroking the steering wheel as if it was a cat he was trying to calm down, but it was his own nerves he was working on. "Evidently the man knew his daughter very well. Yes, sounds like Suzy needs to take a time out. Hmm. How long did you say you were going to be gone?"

"I didn't because I don't know."

"I understand what you're saying about Suzy, so listen to my story about Tori. She's different. She lives in her own magical world. I'd love to see her have a normal life. You know that I care for you, right? Don't get me wrong, I'm not trying to thrust her on you, but I don't want to see her hurt either. I don't think she'd ever recover. She's already reeling from just this morning."

Luther signaled a lane change and switched topics, too. "I don't think you're aware that it wasn't until you arrived in our lives that she stopped spending so much time in her imaginary world."

"You mean the one where she talks to *the others*?" Oscar asked hesitantly.

"You know about that, I mean, *them*?"

"Yeah, when we were little, I overheard her talking to her reflection in a stock tank. She seemed to think there really was someone there. I don't think she ever knew I heard her conversation. At least, I never said anything about it to anyone until now. Even then I knew how vulnerable she was. Like a little fairy princess who – if I said the wrong words – would flit away and never come back. I didn't want that. I mean, I wasn't going to be responsible for crushing someone's spirit or essence, that's for sure."

"Thanks. I appreciate that. Yes, she has two imaginary friends. She never talks about them to us. She tried when she was small but hasn't brought them up since she went to kindergarten. I guess she told her little friend and the teacher about them. The teacher told us about it at our conference. She said not to worry, that she'd outgrow it. I don't know whether she has or hasn't. Like I said, it's something we don't talk about."

"I see she put my hat in the truck. Here, give it back to her, please. Tell her I said I want her to keep it so her ears will stay warm until her hair grows out. I'll be back. I promise. I don't know when but make sure she knows that I will."

Luther sighed but didn't say a word.

"I understand her like not many others possibly could, Luther. Other than my mother, Tori is the most important woman in my world. I have to take care of Mom, though. You see, she's another fairy princess. I don't want to hurt her, either."

***

"She still won't take the phone?" Oscar asked, video calling from France.

"Won't even look at it," Luther said into the desktop monitor, shaking his head in frustration.

"Same thing on the cards and letters?"

"They're in a pile at the corner of her desk, untouched. She still comes to work but now that the harvest and trimming are done, she just mopes around, sweeping floors, watching the goldfish swim in the tank, dusting empty shelves. I really don't have anything for her to do. I'd love to take her and the missus on a vacation. Since the vineyards are done for the winter and we're not planting more cannabis until spring, I could hire a caretaker to watch the place. Tori's here but she's empty, like a pillowcase without the pillow."

"Blowing in the wind without any substance or purpose," Oscar said. "Dang. On the upside, my mother is responding to the new shrink. He's weaned her off almost all of her meds, making sure she exercises daily, gets fresh air and sunshine, and keeps away from all alcohol and sugar. The sugar is the hardest part for her, being in France and all. She never cared for wine, so that's not a real problem. Whiskey and tequila aren't easy for her to find, especially since I made sure she didn't get a drivers' license."

"Well, keep checking in. If something changes, I'll call."

"Do me a favor, Luther. Go ahead and set up her new phone with this app we're talking on. Set it in her room where it's not too obvious. If she's having a good day, let me know. I'll pop in. I know from dealing with my mother that timing is everything. You have to smile when they're looking."

"I hear you there. Thanks for checking in, Oscar. Roger, over and out."

Leanne stepped into the office. "Did I just hear Oscar?"

Luther chuckled and pointed to the computer. "Right there. He said to set up that new phone he got Tori. Don't tell her. We're hoping to catch her on a good day. He's either a saint or an idiot the way he chases after her."

"Hmph!" Leanne snorted. "Wouldn't you have chased me this long if it was us and not them."

"Yeah, I suppose I would."

"You suppose!" she said indignantly, then laughed. "Don't worry about it. I'm the one you chased until I caught you, remember?"

"Very much so," he said, holding her in a full-body embrace. "How about we take a vacation?"

Leanne grinned. "Sounds like perfect timing. Remember Chuck?"

"Chuck who?" Luther asked with a scowl of suspicion.

"I never knew his last name. Let's just say remember the angel who delivered our child?"

"Oh, yeah! Gloria and Roger's friend. Hell ya, I remember him! If he hadn't jumped in the middle of our," Luther whispered the word, "adoption," then shook his head, leaving off the rest of the story she already knew.

"Yes. You're right. He's the sole reason we're a family of three today," Leanne said. "He never asked us for anything. Not that we had anything to give him, but he's asking a favor now. It seems that Gloria's daughter is getting married at the end of the month. Somehow or another, the birth mother and Tori's two sisters are all in each other's lives. Everyone is cool, no contested you-know-whats," she said, then whispered, "custody disputes."

She took a deep breath and smiled, recalling their early years. "Chuck just wants to give Vickie the gift of meeting the other sister she's known about for two years. Actually, Ria – that's Chuck's daughter – is the maid of honor and will be there, too. He never said anything about us to anyone earlier because he had promised discretion. He's certainly given it!"

"Do you think Tori will agree to go on a vacation? And are you sure she's strong enough to know about the others?" Luther asked.

"Pbbt! On the first one. I'm not giving her a choice. She's coming! Plus, that girl's so mad at us now, what's the worst that could happen when she finds out she was adopted? I don't want to say anything beforehand, just let the girls meet each other. Tori will figure it out."

"But I thought we weren't ever going to tell her," Luther said, frowning in disappointment. He paused, remembering that she was a woman now and could probably handle the truth. "Ah, what the hell. Maybe it will shock her into reality. This depression or anger – or whatever the hell it is – has been going on for almost three months. It's time for it to end."

"Oh, and this just came in the mail," Leanne said, handing him an official-looking plastic envelope.

Luther used his knife to open the overpack that read 'Damaged in processing equipment.' He opened the second and third envelopes. "Well, lookie there." He held up the torn inner card. "It's a wedding invitation from Rick Rickman. His son, Rich, is getting married. Hey, Gloria's daughter's name is Vickie, right?"

"Yes, Vickie Lynn Thornwhistle."

"Looks like the young lady is marrying well. She's the one marrying Rick's kid. You do remember Oscar's cousin Rich, right? I guess we got our unofficial invitation to the wedding before the real deal. We can sit on either the bride or the groom's side!"

"Ah, I'd say going to the wedding was meant to be," Leanne said. "That makes me feel better about the revelation already." She scowled at Luther. "But I still don't want to be the one to tell her!"

"You and me, both," Luther said. "Maybe we made a mistake and maybe we didn't by leading her on. Either way, she's going to be mad that we didn't tell her sooner. Mum's still the word for now, though. I don't want her to blow up while we're driving cross country. I don't think that truck could contain her rage!"

***

January 30, 2010

"I think this is the place," Luther said, verifying the address on the invitation.

"It's about time," Tori grumbled. "You didn't tell me it was going to take four days to get here!"

"It was only three and a half. How long did you think it would take to cross the whole United States in a truck? In winter!"

"Hmph!"

Leanne looked at the clock in the dash for the hundredth time in the last two hours. "We made it in plenty of time, but it looks like everyone else is already here."

Luther had an aha moment. "Did you remember to take into consideration the last time zone change?"

"Oh, shoot!"

Luther didn't say a word. What good would it have done? Instead, he drove around to the back of the reception hall, looking for an open parking place. He saw a man waving at him. "Is that Chuck?" he asked.

"Oh, my! It is. Look, he saved us a spot."

Leanne unbuckled and was ready to get out before Luther even had the engine turned off. "Oh, it is you!" she squealed, rushing into Chuck's open arms. "Are we too late?"

"It's just getting ready to start." He looked up and saw Luther standing beside the truck, talking to the other occupant, apparently discussing whether or not she would be leaving the vehicle. "Is everything okay?" he asked Leanne.

"He can handle her. At least, he can do it better than I can. She's stubborn. Just give him a minute..."

The two stood close, sharing each other's warmth, and watched silently as the insistent father tried reasoning with his reluctant daughter. A moment later, Luther was escorting her by the elbow. Chuck tried not to stare at the angry young woman as she approached, so alike in physical features to his own daughter and her sister. He'd seen that glare of defiance many times over the past eighteen years, but she had something else showing through. He couldn't put a finger on it, but she was different.

The four walked into the back of the wedding hall. "Go ahead and sit here in the last row. If anyone asks, you were invited by the family of the bride. The Thornwhistles don't know you're coming, though. I asked them to make sure they left room for a few spares. Just act like you belong, because you do!" he said, patting the insecure Leanne on her shoulder.

370

He turned around and saw that Tori had disappeared again. "She won't go far, will she?" he asked Leanne.

"No, she's bashful but not a runner." She looked over at the cluttered coat rack and saw movement. "Two to one she's in there. Don't worry. She didn't want to come but can't go anywhere without us. She may be eighteen, but she doesn't know how to drive on anything but farm roads."

"Shush!" Luther hissed. "Dang! It's over. That's about the quickest wedding I've ever been to."

"It's the only wedding – other than our own – you've ever been to," Leanne said. "Now come on and let's get our daughter. I want to meet the bride and groom…and that beautiful young bridesmaid!"

Luther, Leanne, and Chuck stepped back and applauded, marveling at the beautiful women and their handsome escorts as they walked down the center aisle in reverse, following the strewn rose petals into the reception hall. "Oh, and we did have an invitation," Luther said, pulling out the rumpled card and showing it to Chuck. "I work for the groom's father. We're here for Rich, too!"

***

Tori remained hidden behind plain and fur-trimmed coats, her back pressed close to the wall as she tried to make herself invisible. She moved a jacket sleeve out of the way, still curious enough about what was going on to peek out and investigate. This wasn't a church but was just as busy with people all dressed up and milling around, babbling – talking to each other without saying anything significant. She let the sleeve fall back in place and stepped back, shoulder blades to the wall.

She heard her mother's voice call to her softly. "Come out and meet my friends."

Rats! She found me.

"I can see you plain as day," Leanne said, then whispered, "Come on, sweetheart. You're embarrassing your papa and me." She looked to her husband. "Grab your daughter, Luther. She won't come otherwise."

Tori squirmed in the confines of the musty woolen and polyester outerwear hanging on the bar above her. She didn't want to leave, but she didn't want to make a scene, either. *It's going to be okay. It's going to be okay. Just smile and nod. They promised it would be just a few minutes, and then we could go home.*

Suddenly, she felt her father's grasp on her upper arm. "Come on, sweetheart. No one here's going to bite you."

"Can't we go home now, Papa?" she mumbled.

"Give us a few minutes. We drove for three and a half days to get here. Let your mama and me have at least a little time to chat with our old friends. Come meet a few of them. Not all of them. Just a few special ones."

"But I really, really want to go home now," Tori whispered.

"There's nothing but rain and gloom out there now. If you come out willing and behave, I promise you a surprise like nothing you've ever seen or expected."

"Well, she may have seen," Leanne said, "but she certainly isn't expecting this. At least, in this format."

"What are you two babbling about?" Tori asked, her curiosity piqued. "You know I can't resist a mystery."

"Ah, you're right there. Come on. And take off that silly hat!"

Tori pulled off Oscar's knit cap, her blonde hair flying everywhere with static electricity. "Now, show me something I didn't expect," she said. "Because you know I have a pretty vivid imagination."

Suppressing her urge to bolt, Tori sucked it up and followed, curious again about the mystery of seeing something familiar in a new way. A grin grew at the adventure. It couldn't be them, could it?

Tori looked around the room, her smile of anticipation as warm and bright as the mood of the people. It was a wedding. She loved weddings. At least, reading about them. This was the first one she'd ever been to. Or almost been to. She grunted with disgust at herself. Her shyness had stolen her joy again. When would she ever outgrow it? 'One of these days' her parents always said. Well, she'd just have to choose a day. And today – with all these positive vibes, happy voices, and joyous music, the smell of fragrant food and warmth of bodies moving around stress and anger-free – this was a good day to claim moodiness was dead. Long live joy and hope!

Tori looked up. They had stopped. "This is my former college roommate, Gloria," Leanne said, pulling her daughter forward. "And this is Tori Lynn Greene."

Suddenly close to a stranger, Tori panicked and popped back into the security of her shyness shell, wishing she could run home all by herself. She hung her head and pressed her chin tight to her chest so she didn't have to look into the beautiful woman's eyes. Maybe today wasn't the right day to try and stomp out moodiness after all.

The stunned mother of the bride blinked several times at seeing the terrified young woman. Moments ago when Leanne had come up to say hi, she half-expected to see Tori with her. The two women hadn't seen each other in over eighteen years – since the night they picked out their babies from Chuck's smuggled gym bag. But the triplet sister was here now. She was so similar to the others but at the same time, so different. *Definitely assembled from the same genetic code. But unlike Vickie and Ria, this one apparently didn't even get a smidgen of the generous dose of confidence the other two had.*

Gloria quickly recognized the girl's shyness as anxiety and decided she might be the only one who could help her. Ignoring her own daughter and the rest of the wedding party for the moment, she reached over and put her hand on the frightened young girl's shoulder. "Let's go into the cloakroom, shall we?

There are so many people in here, it has to be overwhelming for a small-town girl."

Leanne and Tori silently followed Gloria into the calmness of the small annex, the loft of the coats and jackets acting as soundproofing from the tumultuous din of the wedding guests in the main hall. Already feeling more comfortable back in her old hideout, Tori reached up and touched a mink coat, marveling at its softness. "Why did they kill them? Don't people know that these creatures need their fur, too? Wool can be just as warm or warmer and it's a renewable resource. You don't have to kill the sheep to get it."

"Tori Lynn!" Leanne scolded. "It is not your place to tell people what they should or shouldn't wear. Now, you've barely been introduced and you're criticizing? I swear, sometimes it's better when you don't talk."

"She might be right, you know," Gloria said to Leanne. "These aren't mine, so I don't know if they're real or synthetic. Either way, I prefer wool in the winter, cotton in the summer. How about you, Tori?"

"Same here," Tori said, her shyness evaporating like mist on a campfire at having the stranger agree with her. "See," she opened up her gray woolen jacket to reveal a blue plaid flannel shirt and white cotton tank top. "I like cotton, too."

"My goodness," Gloria said, excited at the girl's rapid recovery. "If you had arrived half an hour earlier, you could have been in the wedding! The bridesmaids were wearing flannel, too!"

"In a wedding... I don't know," Leanne said. "She's not too keen on strangers."

"Strangers? Well, Tori, my name is Gloria Thornwhistle and I don't want to be a stranger. I have a daughter the same age as you. When things settle down, I'd like you to meet her. As far as meeting new people, you're just going to have to trust your parents to have good friends."

"Trust those trusted by those I trust?" Tori asked, then answered her own question. "Yes, ma'am. I can try that, at least for today. Mama and Papa said I was going to meet some very special people here. They promised me it would be a short trip, though." She looked down at her watch, the black faux leather band similar to everything else about her: simple and uncomplicated. "There's three hours difference between here and Oregon, you know," she said, a mischievous grin on her face.

"Tori Lynn Greene!" Leanne hissed. "It's rude to watch the clock when you're in a social setting."

"But that's the truth. Plus, you're the one who said they're friends. Gloria understands me, I'm sure."

"You are a little minx, aren't you?" Gloria said, impulsively hugging her as if she was Vickie or Ria.

"Yes, I suppose I am. But do you think that's a good characteristic?"

Gloria nodded emphatically, holding back the tears of joy. "I definitely want you to meet my daughter and her sister. You'll see that you three have a lot in common."

Leanne looked up at Gloria and paled. "But…but…I think I changed my mind. It might be better if they don't meet."

"Too late. I got this," Gloria said. "Let's go find them."

Clink! Clink! Clink!

The women stepped out of the cloakroom and looked to see who was trying to get everyone's attention. It was Luther's boss, Rick Rickman. "It's about time he showed up," Tori whispered.

"Hush!" Leanne hissed.

All eyes went to the father of the bride, rapping his knife on the side of a crystal glass. "Here's to Mr. and Mrs. Richard Rickman," he announced when the chatter had stopped. "Health and happiness – and a bit of prosperity – to our very own Rich and Vickie Rickman!"

Tori sneaked a glimpse at the bride. She'd been so intent on hiding that she hadn't been curious about who Rich was marrying or what she looked like. She looked oddly familiar, though. Her young blonde bridesmaid – wearing jeans and flannel just like she was – was giving her a big hug now. It looked like the bride was hugging the bride! That's what was odd. They were twins. Identical twins.

Those two aren't identical twins! They're two of triplets. Except for the hair, we all look alike! I'm a triplet and they're my sisters!

Blood drained from her face and her knees felt weak. She leaned into her mother, clutching her arm for support. "Mom? What's going on?"

"Is this a surprise or what?" Leanne asked. She was definitely caught up in the moment, giddy with excitement, happy that she hadn't protested too much about letting Tori know their secret.

"Do I have sisters you didn't tell me about?"

"Well, yes. Sort of…"

Tori realized that her father was now standing next to her.

"Papa, did you know about this?"

"Yes, well, sort of…"

Tori glared at them. Adrenaline surged and she felt the blood rush back to her muscles. She walked away from parents. Radiating a fierce determination that parted the crowd in front of her like Moses marching through the Red Sea, Tori strode up to the pair of women at the podium.

Chin up, Tori stood in front of them and thrust her hand out in greeting. "Hi," she said boldly. "I think I'm your sister, Tori. I mean, I'm Tori, and I think I'm your sister."

"Tori!" Ria and Vickie exclaimed, then reached out to grab her close. "We heard there was a third but didn't know where to find you or even your last name. How did you know where to find us?"

Chuck stepped up to the exuberant trio. "Vickie, this is your wedding gift: meeting your other sister. Well, I guess it's an engagement gift to you, Ria, and just a surprise to you, Tori."

"But why did you wait so long?" the bride asked Chuck.

"I couldn't do or say anything without permission from Luther and Leanne." Chuck held his hand above his eyebrows and scanned the room, finally spotting the elderly couple. He waved them up. "It took a long time to find them. We thought they were still on the east coast. I think Silas found about two thousand places they *weren't* before starting on the west coast."

"Oregon," Tori said simply. "Eventually." She turned to her sisters. "So, I'm not crazy, right?"

"Why would you think that?" Ria asked.

"Because, well, you know how you can look in the mirror and see your other self? Didn't it ever seem weird, like you should be able to just reach in and grab that other person and pull her out to stand beside you instead of in front of you?"

"Well, kinda," Vickie said, "but I thought everyone felt like that."

"Maybe they do, but I felt something was still missing. Then we moved into a place that had a double mirror in the bathroom. I could move it just so, and then there'd be three of me: me and the two images. It felt so right. I used to get in trouble because I'd take so long in the bathroom. I'd be in there, carrying on conversations in a low voice so no one else would hear. Or rather, my parents wouldn't.

"I always wondered if Mama and Papa were my real parents, too, because I didn't look like either one of them. Plus, they were a little old. Mama even showed me a picture Papa had taken of her nursing me. I'm not quite sure how that was possible, but since Papa can make hair grow on a turnip with the right herbal concoction, then I guess he could have put something together so Mom could get milk."

Tori hooked an arm into each sister's, glad all over again that she wasn't crazy, that there really were two on this earthly plane who looked like her. "So, yes or no: are our biological parents here?"

"Yes," Ria and Vickie answered, then locked at each other with raised eyebrows. *Tori looks like us, but she sure is different!*

Tori scanned the room and spotted Grace and Dusty. The couple was staring at the three of them, misty-eyed, hugging each other. She nodded, acknowledging them. "That was a no-brainer," she said softly. "Even if we didn't look like them, the reaction on their faces proves it. So, I guess I'll hear the whole story about why they gave us up later. Let me see if I can pick out a grandma or grandpa..."

"We don't have a grandma here," Vickie said. "She's sorta *persona non grata* and also out of the country."

"Fair enough. Everyone has a skeleton or two in the closet. Best to leave them alone, I say." Tori kept looking, bypassing the one older gentleman who looked as interested as her biological parents but not alike physically. She spotted Silas and noticed his ears, broad shoulders and regal stance. "Him!" she said with complete confidence.

"Nope," Vickie said. "Him," and pointed to Hal. "He's our mother Grace's dad. It's kind of hard not to notice Grace is our mother. She's almost like an older triplet. Or would that be quadruplet?"

Tori shook off the discussion on the mother. "Nope. I'll bet three DNA tests to a donut that he," she said, this time pointing right to Silas, "is Grace's biological father. The other guy definitely has an emotional investment in all of us, but *he's* her father and our grandfather."

Silas watched as the latest triplet to come into his life pointed at him as she carried on an intense conversation with her sisters. Thirty-seven years after Victoria had gotten him drunk and had her way with him, he'd been busted. He looked over the room, pretending to scout out the crowd in general but really looking at Hal's expression. Grace's father was looking right at him, crestfallen. He knew.

Hal walked over to him. "I always wondered if I was her bio-dad," he said. "It was rumored that Victoria was sowing her last wild oats the week before the wedding, but I always hoped it was just a rumor she started so I'd think she was in demand by others. I didn't want to believe there was any chance another man was Grace's father. It's kind of hard to ignore the family resemblance between you two, but I convinced myself that you were either some long, lost cousin or her ears were a result of a recessive gene popping in. Well, if it was to be anyone, I'm glad it was you."

"Did you ever wonder why I never have more than one drink?" Silas asked.

"And did you ever wonder why I did?" Hal asked, answering his question with his own.

"Do you forgive me?" Silas asked.

"For what? Getting tricked by Victoria? Shit! I'm jealous. You got off easy. I had to live with the bitch for nearly nineteen years!"

Silas tried to hold back his laugh, then saw that Hal was giving into his, so joined him. "We weren't the only two. It's not my place to name names, but she was pretty loose there for a week or two. But you're right. It had to be me. I never realized it, though, until Grace came into the Armstrong family. When she showed up with Victoria, crashing Papa Doc's party, I knew she had to be my issue. Actually, when she started dating Alex, I was glad she was mine."

"So, Papa Doc really was one of the others, then?" Hal asked, tight-lipped.

Silas shrugged one shoulder. "Yes, we both had a butt-pucker moment when we saw Grace and Alex hanging all over each other. We didn't want half-siblings getting carried away. We never said anything directly to each other, but when I saw Papa Doc do a double-take, looking at her ears and then mine, I knew he knew. It was kind of funny, both of us exhaling at the same moment as realization hit." Silas noticed Hal was still grim-faced.

"You are and always have been Grace's daddy. I'm just happy to be one of the honorary grandpas to the girls. And now there's one more. By the looks she was giving me, she figured it out within two minutes of being here."

"Well, she is your granddaughter. It looks like she got more than the ears from you. She's pretty damned perceptive."

Silas sighed then grinned. "Never a daddy, but now an acknowledged granddaddy. I'm sure glad no one in this family gives two flips about whose blood flows through who."

"Back at ya," Hal said.

"Excuse me, excuse me," a young man said, pushing past the two men, rushing toward the three sisters as if he was a doctor and one of them was having a heart attack.

"Who's that?" Silas asked. "I thought I knew everyone here."

"That's Rich's cousin, Oscar. He and his mother were able to come at the last moment."

"Oh, yeah. She's the one who's been spending time at that French resort."

"Resort, clinic, rehab," Hal said, shrugging his shoulder. "She's Rick Rickman's sister and he'd do anything for her."

Silas looked back to see what was going on in the other direction. Often the excitement wasn't where the person was headed but where he had come from. The tall African American woman was watching Oscar, a sly smile of pride on her face. *She obviously has an emotional investment in the man. Her son, maybe?*

"Tori?" Oscar asked, pulling her shoulder toward him so he could look into her face. "You came!"

"Why are *you* here?" she asked indignantly. She looked back at her sisters and their beaus. "And did you know about them? That I had sisters?"

"Not until a few minutes ago..."

"I thought you were in France, taking care of your mother," Tori said harshly, not giving him a chance to explain.

"I was! We – Mom and I – just got here! I didn't see the bride and bridesmaid until the wedding started. I knew that Rich's fiancée looked a lot like you because I saw her in the background of a video chat I had with him a few months ago. You're not identical, though. I mean, there is a definite similarity," Oscar said, looking at the two women he now knew were Tori's sisters.

"I don't look like her?" Tori asked, looking at the bride. She snorted in derision.

"Well, you look more like her," Oscar said, nodding to Ria the bridesmaid, moving his ear forward like hers. "Rich's wife, not so much. Let's just say you may look a lot alike on the outside, but your vibes are very different."

"And so's our hair," Tori said, frustrated that she was so plain.

The groom spotted Oscar and Tori. "Hey, Tori! Long time, no see," Rich said. "I didn't know you were a triplet! Good Lord, I only knew you as a kid, blonde and frisky as a cat with a bell on its tail. I had no idea you'd grow up to be such a beauty. I mean, I guess I'd better tell you right now in case you haven't figure it out. I'm married to your sister."

"Only one of them, I hope," Tori said, scowling.

The conversation between them suddenly stopped. All three watched as a very pregnant woman came up to Ria. Words were said, then the two were involved in an extremely emotional reunion, full of hugs and tears. Their excitement was spilling over but not making any sense to Rich, Tori, or Oscar.

Tori punched Rick in the upper arm and said, "I'm joking," breaking the tension between them. "Geez!"

The two men both breathed a sigh of relief. Rich turned to Oscar and gave him a hearty smack on the shoulder, happy to see the cousin he hadn't seen in five years. "Hey, cuz, glad you could make it. Did you say your mom came, too?"

Grateful that Rich had diverted the conversation and rescued him from the rest of Tori's scolding, Oscar nodded in his mother's direction. "Yup. Look at her. Healthy and radiant..."

"I don't know what went on there and don't need to," Rich said. "She's always looked beautiful to me."

"Trust me. It was touch and go there for a while," Oscar said. "Come on, Tori. I think it's time you met my mother."

"I'm still mad at you," Tori said, resisting his proffered hand.

He put his arm around her shoulder and kissed her on the top of her flyaway hair, sputtering as it tickled his nose. "Don't you think I'm the one who should be mad at you for what you did? Your little stunt could have landed me in jail or got me shot. But I'm not. Life's too short for anger." He bent close to her ear. "Just think of how many kisses we could have shared."

She pulled away a little bit, not willing to break away completely – he still felt wonderful – and said, "But you were in another country, on another continent."

"True, but we're here together now. Can we be friends again?"

Tori bumped into his chest with the side of her head, closing the gap between them with a gentle, physical exclamation point. "Maybe more. I'm eighteen now."

Oscar barely heard her last declaration over the noise of the gathering and was just introducing her to his mother when it registered what she had said. "Ma...Mom," he sputtered. "This is Tori, the young woman I was telling you about. Tori, this is my mother, Julianna."

"Nice to meet you, Tori," the woman said.

Tori's neck craned back as she looked up at the woman. "You're sure tall," she said, then shook her head in embarrassment. "Sorry. You two don't look alike at all!"

"I'm adopted," Oscar said, glad that Tori had focused on the height difference, not her color.

"Really?" Tori asked. "Me, too. I mean, I just found out. How long have you known?"

"Pretty much forever. My parents bragged about it. 'Most parents are stuck with what they get. You were the pick of the litter' or 'We bought you off the top shelf' or 'You were the puppy with the cutest eyes.' Pretty much whatever hit them to say at the time. I think I must have heard a hundred reasons why they wanted me."

"Wow. I never thought of it that way," Tori said.

Oscar was distracted by a minor fracas at the front of the room. "Hey, Mom, could you hang on a minute? I need to scoot and see what all the excitement's about. Rich looks a little stressed."

"Sure. Tori and I'll be fine, won't we?"

Tori looked from the tall woman to where she thought her parents should be. Zip. They were gone. She sighed. She was mad at them for lying about who she was her all her life, denying her the sisters she knew were real. It was better to stay away from them right now. She probably wouldn't be able to hold back her rage.

She turned back to Oscar, "We'll be fine. She can tell me about France. I've never been there."

Julianna's smile slipped slightly. "Let's go over here where it's quieter," she said and headed to the table farthest from the commotion.

Tori followed. She'd never seen a woman so dark or so beautiful. She'd seen pictures of African Americans but had never met or seen one in person.

"You're going to hear about it sooner or later," Julianna began, skipping over the pleasantries and nonsense in case they were interrupted. "I was in a fancy nut house."

"Like Brazil nuts or Macadamias?" Tori asked, confused.

"No, like an insane asylum. People think I'm crazy. I'm not but all the medications they fed me had some pretty nasty side effects."

"Why would they think you're crazy? I mean, not to be presumptuous or anything, but people thought I was crazy, too." Tori said, then paused and leaned forward, eager to tell someone who might understand.

Julianna saw her excitement. "Go ahead. You first."

"You see, I *knew* there were two others just like me, that I had two sisters. No one had to tell me. I remembered them from before we were born. I remember everything. I didn't have proof until just a few minutes ago. My parents never mentioned it even though they must have known. I guess I should be glad they didn't feed *me* medications! I told a teacher and a friend about my sisters when I was in kindergarten. The teacher told my parents I would grow out of seeing and remembering others who weren't there. After that conference, I didn't tell anyone. But still, my parents could have told me about them! Do you have sisters you see who the doctors tell you are just your imaginary friends, too?"

Julianna smiled at the innocent young woman her son was so fond of. Yes, she might understand. "No, not sisters. I was born in another time…"

Tori nodded but remained mute. Curious.

"Let me ask you a question first. Do you believe in time travel?"

"You mean like with the right equipment or starting from the right place, I could go backward or forward to another date?"

Julianna nodded, her bottom lip sucked in with apprehension.

"Duh!" Tori exclaimed. "Why not? I mean, just because we don't know how to do it today doesn't mean it isn't possible. Do you know people used to think the world was flat and the sun was the center of the universe? People were burned at the stake for believing stuff that we now know is true. Just because people hadn't figured out how to transmit sounds or knowledge through the air two hundred years ago didn't mean it wasn't possible. They just didn't have the right tools!"

Tori took the smartphone Oscar had given her out of her pocket. "Right now, I could just push a couple of buttons and talk to someone halfway around the world. How is time travel any different? If I had the right device, I could push a couple of buttons and be in 1776."

"Oh, my Lord! You are precious. You're not just saying this to humor me, are you?"

"No. I wouldn't do that," Tori said. She looked up and saw her mother approach. She stood up and waved, ready to forgive. "I'm over here."

Leanne bit off her admonishment about taking off and sat down next to her. What Oscar had told Luther was right. Tori was experiencing emotional growth spurts, this one right before her eyes. The once timid girl was interacting with strangers, not hiding in a coat rack.

Clink! Clink! Clink!

All three women looked at the podium. Roger Thornwhistle was trying to get everyone's attention, waiting for them to stop talking. "As the father of the bride, I'd like to thank all of you for coming. I see we have a few surprise guests tonight, too. It looks more like a family reunion than a wedding, but the bottom line is, we're family. Whether we were born into a family, legally adopted, or 'claimed,' I think everyone here is connected one way or another to each other. Here's to family!" he said, raising his champagne flute in toast. "Forever may we remember and love one another!"

"Here! Here!" and cheers answered his toast.

"Now, Chuck, you seem to be the instigator of about half of these reunions…"

"Or maybe all of them…" Chuck said with a sly smile.

"So, are there any more surprises you'd like to share?"

Chuck looked at the handsome man at his side and grinned. "Well, I guess one more to share with family won't break the scales. Ladies and gentlemen, I'd like to introduce my fiancé, Keith Fraser."

A handsome and slightly graying man eased himself out of his chair, red-faced and chagrined. "I guess there's no better way for Chuck to come out than among friends. For those of you who don't know, I was widowed a few years back. I didn't think anyone could fill that void, but Chuck did. We've known each other since college, but with one thing or another – including children for both of us and my marriage to John – we drifted apart. We'll wait for our children to be married first, but in the meantime, here's to love and family, and happy ever afters!"

"Mama, what's he talking about, marrying another man," Tori asked.

"Hush," Leanne said. "I'll let your father explain it to you later."

Tori looked over at her newly discovered sisters. Their faces were bright with happiness, clapping, whistling and cheering for Chuck and Keith and their announcement. "I guess that's another part of the world that's been kept from me for eighteen years. Looks like I have a lot of living to catch up on."

***

"So, are you going to stay mad at me forever?" Oscar asked Tori, keeping a cautious two feet away from her.

"Are *you* going to stay mad at me forever?" she replied and took a step toward him, closing the gap by half.

"I asked you first," Oscar said, grinning but not moving.

"I guess that depends on when you're coming home." She stepped forward, set her face into his chest, and inhaled deeply, hoping he'd hug her close. When he didn't, she looked up at him. "It was easier to be mad at you when you were far away, but right now…"

Oscar bent his knees and picked her up. He held her close, up high so her head was above his. "You have to tell me what's going on, what you want. I'm not a mind reader and you aren't either. I'm scared to death to hold you, kiss you, want you. Afraid that you'll shut me out again. Is that what you want?" He set her down and took a step back. "Because if you do…"

Tori jumped up and grabbed him around the neck, awkwardly placing a hard kiss that missed its target, the two of them clunking noses.

"Let's try that again," Oscar said. "I wasn't ready."

Tori's eyes lit up with a smile as bright as the bride's. "Prepare to be ready for me for the rest of your life!" She leaned in again, this time tilting her head to find her mark. When she finally pulled away from the kiss, she whispered, "Did I do that right?"

"I don't know. Let's try it again," he said and winked.

"That's enough, granddaughter," Silas said.

Tori pulled away quickly and Oscar released his hold, letting her slide to the floor in a controlled drop.

"I didn't mean to startle you," Silas said with a sly grin.

"Yes, you did," Tori said, then rolled her eyes and added, "Grandpa."

"Actually, it was my idea to come over to talk to you," Julianna said, smiling at Tori, then patting her on the back with reassurance. "It looked like you two were having a serious discussion. We were going to wait, but then again, I didn't want you to get too carried away when you started using body language instead of words."

Oscar looked back and forth between his two favorite females. "I take it you and Tori found something in common? I mean, she generally isn't a very social person."

"Oh, we get along famously," Julianna said. She reached out and pulled Silas close by the elbow to join the family circle. "I wanted to talk to you before you two made too many plans for your future." She winked at Tori with the word 'future' and continued. "Silas and I have been chatting, too. It seems like we have a lot in common. He's a bit of a sleuth. He and I are going to North Carolina to do a little exploring in a month or two. In the meantime, we're going to be doing some research. In other words, you won't need to come back to France with me, Oscar."

"But...but...you just met him!" Oscar said.

"Actually, we knew each other a long, long time ago. We didn't recognize each other at first, but I think you two know how that is, right?"

"Mom..." Oscar asked, the concern in his voice evident. *Are you talking about that time travel nonsense again?*

Julianna saw the concern and said, "Don't worry about me. I'll keep in contact."

"Just make sure you have the right device," Tori said with a big smile and a wink.

"Absolutely!" Silas and Julianna said at the same time, looking at each other.

"That's my granddaughter," Silas said. "She's already got the hard stuff figured out."

Conclusion of HOW LOVE GROWS

Note: This may be the end of Tori's story of finding her sisters and her true love, but it's just the beginning for Julianna and Silas. Read more in THEY CALL ME SHERLOCK, up next.

They Call Me Sherlock

Triplets: Three Aren't One Book Five

Copyright

They Call Me Sherlock

Life gets exciting for the rich and clever 'butler' when his sweetheart from the 1969's Woodstock Event shows up looking younger than possible.

What was her secret?

And did she still care about him as much as he did her?

Chapter 1: Woodstock

Thursday, August 14, 1969
near Middletown, New York

"I'm sure this is the way," Silas said to himself, clutching the straps of his backpack. He pulled out the map he'd picked up at the gas station before he left home in Plymouth, Massachusetts. Yup, walking away from the sun in the morning and towards it in the afternoon would keep him on the right heading.

"An Aquarian Exposition." He looked at his ticket for the hundredth time since waking at dawn. "Ugh. It'll never catch on. They should call it Woodstock like the deejays do. Easy to remember. Solid and earthy but still groovy."

The sput-sputter of a vehicle with a hole in its muffler caught his attention. He tucked the map under his arm and stuck out his thumb.

The VW microbus covered in brilliantly colored peace signs and flowers slowed to a stop a couple hundred feet in front of him. A ginger-haired male with a picked-out afro hairdo stuck his head out the window. "Headed to Woodstock?"

"Yes, I am!" Silas hollered as he ran toward him.

The side door opened and marijuana smoke roiled out. He coughed and waved it aside, then saw the inside of the van was packed with at least a dozen people. He bit off the question, 'Are you sure you have room?' and stepped in. He grabbed the window frame as the van lurched onto the highway while he stood, looking for an open spot.

"You can sit on my lap," a young man with pouty lips said, his eyes blinking in unabashed flirtation.

"Or mine," an ebony young woman offered. "I don't bite." She nodded to pretty boy. "He might."

"No contest." Silas twisted in place, trying to find a way to sit down without putting his body parts in someone else's face.

"Take off the pack first," the friendly female said. "Then hold it in your lap. We're less than an hour away. I'm sure we'll manage for that long."

He did as told and lowered himself as gracefully as he could. The cramped quarters were packed with knees, heads, and elbows, a reefer being passed back and forth between them. Pretty Boy reached out and greeted Silas with a heavily costume-jeweled hand. "Pleased to meet you. I'm Eros. And you are?"

"Arrows?" Silas asked, the last syllable ending as a squeak, surprised by the young woman grasping him by the hips to pull him the rest of the way onto her lap. "Like bows and arrows?" he added, stifling a laugh.

"Eros! You know, like the Greek god of love? It's the name I chose. So, who are you?"

Silas chewed back his chuckle, then realized that although he'd been in the van less than a minute, the marijuana-charged atmosphere was getting to him. Or it was simply the lack of oxygen. "Me?"

Eros scoffed but didn't take his eyes from him.

Silas could feel the young woman sink her face into his back, the tremors of her laugh stifled by his body, hidden from Eros. He cleared his throat and said, "They call me Sherlock."

"Oh," Eros responded dryly. "That's John F. driving, and that's Buttercup from Boston – you can tell when she talks – Sunshine the blonde, Raven with the black hair, Levi in the ripped denims, Luther the botanist, Rapunzel with the long hair, Angel from L.A., Semen from Hard Rock…"

Silas felt a new wave of giggles get buried in his back, then heard nothing else Eros said. That is until the angry young man's voice raised loud enough that everyone in the van stopped talking. "You have to have a name, woman, so spill. It's the cost of the trip."

"No, it's not," John. F. from the driver's seat called back brightly. "It's right on the bumper sticker: Ass, Grass, or Gas – Nobody rides for Free."

"I got a few bucks," Silas whispered to her over his shoulder.

"Dorothy from Oz is in the house… I mean, in the van!" she called out boldly.

Cheers erupted from everyone but Eros who had sunk back into his cramped corner and was sulking. He looked up at 'Sherlock' one more time with his best doe-eyed pout of innocence, but it was futile. The tall Adonis with long dark hair was now half-turned around on the Amazon's lap, his face radiant with enchantment and flirtation. Definitely hetero. Not even a chance he was curious.

"Wow!" John F. said, slowing down to pull over to the side of the road. "Come on out, everyone. You gotta see this."

The dozen dazed youths rolled out of the van, backs arching, arms and legs stretching at reclaiming the ability to move freely, clearing their smoke-filled lungs with fresh air.

"Wow, is right," Silas said, staring at how long the line of vehicles was ahead of them. "And we're a day early. I wonder what it's going to be like tomorrow."

"Worse," his warm-bodied chair replied tersely.

He turned around and saw her again for the first time. She was huge! Not fat but a giantess. She was half a head taller than he was, with broad shoulders and a commanding presence that made him want to shelter in place with her for a lifetime.

"Dorothy?" he squeaked.

She chuckled. She was used to people's first reaction to her height and used humor to deal with it. "Not my real name," she said dryly. "Do you want to go through the gate or try and sneak in with the others?"

Silas patted his backpack. "I already bought my ticket. I don't think it's right to steal. There are costs involved with renting the venue, providing electricity…"

'Dorothy' rolled her eyes. "I'll catch you later then," she said. "I'm short of cash. At least what they're using here. This was sort of last-minute deal for me."

"What? You got a pocket full of pesos or something?"

She smiled broadly. "Yeah, something like that. *Adios!"*

And then she was gone, her long-legged stride catching up to the others before he realized the two of them hadn't decided on a hookup spot. He turned around and saw the hundreds of cars already slowing down to join the queue. There would be thousands, maybe even hundreds of thousands, of visitors to this event. How would he find her? "Shit!"

***

The agent at the gate was polite even if a bit harried. "Yeah, if you can find a flat spot, go ahead and set up your tent for tonight. Don't get carried away, though. Make sure you can strike it in a hurry. Once the music starts, folks will stomp over everything to get to the stage. Next!"

Silas took off for the side of the hayfield his microbus group had been headed toward when they had parted company. He grinned to himself. He didn't know much – actually knew nothing – about her. But, she was very, very tall. As long as she was upright and not standing in a hole, he'd find her, her stunning smile beaming bright above the crowds.

After four hours, he still hadn't found her. He went back to the site he had chosen for his tent and picked up the official-looking 'Keep Back: Unexploded Grenade' sign he had made before leaving home and returned it to his backpack.

Click!

Silas looked up and saw Rapunzel, Luther at her side. "Cool trick," Luther said, then looked away, scanning the area through his camera lens for more shots of interest.

Noticing the stares from the crowd around him, Silas suppressed his smirk and waved a two-fingered peace sign to those who were either scowling and flipping him off, or grinning and giving him a thumbs-up reaction.

"That was clever, Sherlock," she said.

"Oh, hi." He dropped the bag and some of its contents spilled out. "You found me!" His smile of happiness was even more brilliant with the added shine of sweat, both from the heat of the August afternoon and the exertion of looking for her.

She nodded to his backpack and the tent pieces sticking out. "Looks like you came prepared."

He picked up a tent peg and hammer, shrugging with a mixture of embarrassment and modesty. "I do my research and try to anticipate any situation."

"Even rain?"

Looking up, he saw the dark clouds gathering, just like the forecast had predicted. "Yes, ma'am," then bent to work.

"Ma'am! I'm not anyone's ma'am. I'm not even seventeen."

Thwack!

Silas gasped at the pain, his thumb throbbing from the missed strike. "Sixteen?" he squeaked, his injured hand now stuck under his armpit.

"Here, let me," she said, picking up the dropped hammer. "I'm pretty good at this sort of thing. I grew up on a farm. My da was always building something, and I'd do anything to keep out of the kitchen."

"So, are you from around here then?" Silas asked, letting her take the lead on the shelter project.

She paused to think of a clever answer but went back to her initial reply. "Oz."

"All right, *Dorothy*. Did you come on a tornado?"

She snickered and shook her head. "Why do you ask so many questions?"

He inspected his injured thumb, thought about putting it in his mouth to ease the fiery pain, then realized it was filthy. He blew on it briefly. "Questions? Me? It's just who I am, I guess. Inquiring minds want to know… Hey, that's kind of catchy."

"Yeah. Right. Here, use your good hand to hold this. I want it taut to make sure I have the pegs in the right spot."

Silas did as told, letting his smile of appreciation bloom free as he watched her work, tight milk-chocolate brown curls pulled back at the nape of her neck with a leather thong.

"So, since I'm doing all the work, or at least most of it, are you going to share your spot with me, *sir?*" she asked sassily, looking up to feel the first drops of rain on her face.

"Sir? I'm not even eighteen yet," he said.

She laughed out loud. "Gee, I knew there was something else about you I liked."

"Else?"

She wiped her hand on her skirt, looked at it to make sure it was relatively clean, then ran her fingers through one side of his long hair, bringing a wayward strand back behind his ear. "You have very nice hair."

"Thank you. And yes, I'd be honored to share my meager accommodations. Who knows? You might have other valuable skills."

"I might…"

***

"It's too early to go to sleep," he said, looking up at the drab olive-green nylon ceiling.

"And there's not enough room for *some* of us to sit up, even if we had a deck of cards." She paused a moment, then asked, "Don't tell me you brought cards…"

"Yes, I did but that's only because they were already in my bag from my last trip. Do you want to build a castle?"

"Do you mean a house of cards?" she asked.

"I don't aim low," he said wryly and leaned close to look her in the eyes. "A castle."

"Is that a tall person joke," she asked, a shiver of attraction running up her arms despite the sultry temperature.

"No. I aspire." He wiped his upper lip with the side of his hand. "And perspire. Dang. I didn't bring a razor."

"Really? All this craziness that's going to happen, and you worry about being clean-shaven?"

"Going to happen?" he asked, one eyebrow raised. "Do you know something I don't know?"

She gulped, coughed slightly to buy some time, then replied, "With half a million people, of course, it's going to be crazy."

"Where did you hear half a million? Last I heard, the high estimate was two hundred thousand?"

Tempted to cough again, this time she went with the catch-all lame excuse that always worked at home. "Really? I guess I got confused."

"You know, if it wasn't so cloudy, it would be a perfect night for watching the stars." Silas pointed up. "See, there's the Big Dipper, Orion's Belt…"

She scooted head-to-head and pointed out an imaginary constellation. "That's Leo, right. Oh," she pointed through the tent opening to the east. "And we should be able to see Venus and Mars in the morning. Last bright lights in the sky."

"No," Silas said and turned to face her.

"No?" she shifted to her side and lifted onto her elbow, scowling.

He copied her movement and neared her, as close as he could get without his eyes crossing. "No."

"Yes!" she said, a frown of playfulness almost breaking into a laugh.

"No, because by morning, the sun – the last bright light – will be out."

"No. The sun will be the first bright light out."

Silas sighed in defeat and leaned closer. "First and last in a continuing cycle. It's all relative."

"I don't know about relative but it's not important."

"The argument of the ages: which came first," he said and paused, waiting for her to finish the thought.

"The dinosaur or the egg?" she said.

"You're so funny." Then he leaned in three inches and kissed her gently on the mouth, paused to appreciate the softness, then pulled back. "Umm."

"That one, we can agree on," she said, then leaned to meet his mouth again. "Umm."

***

They awoke the next morning to the sounds of shouts and footsteps. "Over here's a good spot!" and "No, someone's claimed it already."

"Day One begins," she whispered. "Are you ready?"

Silas smiled broadly, then shifted the front of his jeans as inconspicuously as possible. "I will be. Let's take this down and find the porta-potties. They should still be clean."

"Let's go together, though. I don't think I could find you again. At least with the *great number* of attendees that are supposed to show up," she said, teasing him.

He felt so complete. Fulfilled. The empty spots in his emotions were now warm and cuddly. They hadn't got carried away last night but they had perfected kissing. Three more days and nights with her. And she didn't want to get separated again, either!

The two quickly struck the tent, packed it, and spotted the johns in the distance. "Over there," he said.

She nodded but didn't speak, preoccupied. *She has to be here. Mali always said she wanted to come.*

Silas watched as she searched the grounds as if she was looking for someone. *Maybe she's trying to spot one of the headliners. Don't say anything to make her feel self-conscious.*

They both used the facilities then came out, pinched-faced and scowling.

"If this is the first day, I don't think I want to eat or drink the rest of the time I'm here. Yuck!" Silas said.

"What do you mean? At least you're a guy. Then again, why do you think I wore a full skirt?" she said, bowing her knees and bending into a half-squat.

"What? I mean, you'd do that?"

"Hey, that's what the women did in the old days and still do in some areas of the world."

Silas gulped as he realized that meant she probably wasn't wearing underwear. A thrill went down his belly then crept lower, thoughts bubbling of lying with her for three more nights sans undergarments. He glanced back at the portable bathrooms, the grossest thing he could think of on such short notice to turn his stomach and stifle his surging stiffy. *She's sixteen, she's sixteen. Even if you're only seventeen, she's only sixteen!*

Chapter 2: The Wedding Party

January 30, 2010
After Vickie's Wedding
Near Plymouth, Massachusetts

Silas noticed the tall dark woman sitting alone, isolated from the rest of the rambunctious wedding party. It couldn't be her, could it? She looked too young. Without thinking, he found himself walking toward her, holding his breath in anticipation. In hope.

He paused at her table, but before he could get the nerve for an introduction, she spoke. "It's you, it really is you...isn't it?" she asked.

With a smile so wide, his cheeks hurt and his eyes teared, Silas sputtered, "I was going to ask you the same thing. Woodstock '69?"

"Ah, a very good year."

"Good and wet," he agreed with a chuckle. "But the music was fantastic. May I join you?"

"Might as well. You never did tell me your real name. It really isn't Sherlock, is it?"

He shook his head, his grin still wide. "My name is Silas Priest, but yes, they call me Sherlock. You're truly not Dorothy from Oz, though..."

Silas watched her twinkle of delight fade into embarrassment. "I was trying to find a clever name, too. Actually, I did feel like I was in the land of Oz. Everything was so strange there. So primitive."

"Yes, positively the most unsanitary place I've ever seen. A hut in equatorial Africa would be the Hilton compared to that mess of mud and ponchos. Where did you go? As I recall, it was Monday morning and Jimi Hendrix was supposed to come out for the finale. I went to get our milk bottles refilled with water. When I returned, you were gone. You'll have to forgive me for not getting back to you, but without so much as a real name or even a hint of where you were from, I wasn't able to track you down."

"You looked for me?"

Silas nodded, his smile now a smirk of irony. "For two long years."

Her wide-eyed reaction was worth the search, questioning stoned hippies and frustrated farmers in the neighborhood, following false leads, and hoped-for fantasies. Maybe she hadn't been trying to hide from him.

"Don't worry about it. I may not have found you, but I did stumble into a great career and made some fabulous connections. Now, please tell me your real name before, *poof,* you disappear again," he said, his hands tickling the air to emphasize his statement.

"I shouldn't be too hard to find now. At least, I'll be in the states. It looks like my son has found the girl he's been pining over since last summer. I doubt he'll want to return to France with me. He's over there with her now, trying to make things right." She nodded at Oscar, the handsome young man with fair skin and dark hair who was awash with emotions, frustrated at trying to get his point across to the fireball with short blond hair who was dressed for shoveling snow rather than a wedding.

"He's had girlfriends before," she continued, "but this is the first time he's been infatuated. He and Tori had a spat before he came to see me. I thought he'd have a meltdown not being able to see or talk to her for months. It looks like they're communicating now, though."

She sighed, watching their courting from afar, Oscar stepping in, then backing away. The girl doing the same, both of them uncertain of what to do next. "I sure hope she doesn't break his heart."

Silas turned to watch, too. The young couple's initial confrontation had been chilly but was quickly warming up to a pensive touch, then a hug, and now an awkward nose-crunching kiss. "You do know she – Tori – is my granddaughter, right?"

The woman's jaw dropped open then shut with a *hmph* of realization. "I knew there was something else I liked about that girl. She's so perceptive and open-minded…must be a family trait."

Silas put his hand on the table, then catching her eye to watch her reaction, moved it on top of hers. "If it is, it's a recessive gene. She and her triplet sisters may look alike, but those three are not one. Definitely. Actually, I think the one trait they all have in common is they're all dynamic – forces to be reckoned with – but all in different fields. Now, what do you mean by something *else* you liked about her? What was the first thing?"

She rolled her eyes, trying to think of what to say that wouldn't be a lie nor would be telling him too much about her. She didn't want to scare him away.

Lifting her chin, she decided to invest it all. "She's quite brilliant, you know. She and I were discussing time travel. She offered a few very interesting observations on it."

"Oh, okay," he said, nodding, waiting for the rest of her comment. When she didn't say more, Silas picked up the thread, hoping to erase the awkward pause. "I take it you both believe in it. I mean, most people don't, so if you two were of one accord, it must be because she's not closed-minded."

"No. I mean, yes. I mean…" She took a deep breath to search for the words.

Seeing that he had made her uncomfortable, Silas changed the subject. Sort of.

"You know, if I'm not being too bold, I'd rather have the answer to another question or two. First, how do you stay so young? I mean, it was forty-one years ago that we were together. We were only a year apart. Sixteen, you said. So, did you have a drop or two of Fountain of Youth water or did you…" Silas bent forward across the table, waiting for her to lean closer.

She saw the glimmer in his eye and fell for his charm again. "Yes," she drawled as she bent near his lips, those full, soft portals to pleasure that had given her her first tantalizing kiss so many, many years ago.

He blinked twice at her nearness, then realized she was waiting for him to speak. "Or did you slip forward through time twenty-five years," he whispered with a wink.

Still focused on his mouth, she felt rather than saw his playfulness. Instead of making a joke out of his words, she took the teasing torch and ran with it. "The latter," she said dryly, then added, "but it was only twenty. A woman still needs to take care of herself, you know. I moisturize, eat my greens, and try to find something positive about every sour situation."

"Really?" Silas said, pulling back to examine her expression. Faces didn't lie.

"Oh, yes. You'd be amazed at how stress, hate, anger – all those negative emotions – not only age you but also tear your body apart. They literally eat up your immune system, so it attacks itself."

Julianna watched as he closed his mouth and swallowed. Emboldened by his shock, she leaned forward again, waving at him minimally for him to come back. "I don't believe there's such a thing as a Fountain of Youth, though" she whispered, intentionally avoiding the topic of time travel. "I think it's just a fairy tale."

Silas's head shook back and forth slowly as he realized who she was. Or rather, what her age secret had to be. "No, there really is a Fountain of Youth. Or there was. At least, I know there are a few little blue vials of its water scattered around the world." He took a deep breath, hoping to inhale two day's worth of confidence so he could share his secret with her. "I know it's real because I actually held a bottle of it once."

Julianna scoffed but didn't say a word. He was making fun of her. So much for having a happy ever after.

Silas reached out and held her hand. She tried to pull it away, but he grasped it harder, hoping he wasn't hurting her but eager to keep her in his life.

"I know it's real because I really did have it in my hands. It was years ago. I was tracking it down with an old – very old – acquaintance. Have you ever heard of a man called Master Simon?"

She blinked, fluttering her eyes as if she was trying to rid herself of a wayward lash, wondering where she had heard that name. She remembered and her eyes widened. "The time traveler?"

"He calls himself Simon, the master of dimensional transportation with an emphasis on acquiring rare and exotic specimens of nature and man for the benefit of furthering our understanding of life on earth," Silas said in one breath, then inhaled deeply and huffed to recuperate.

"That's a mouthful," she said, laughing. "My dad used to call us fairies. I mean, call them fairies," she stammered. "I mean, he called time travelers fairies. Not the ones with lacy wings that were killed by disbelief like Tinkerball or…or…"

"Tinkerbell," Silas corrected. He picked up her hand and kissed it. "I guess I should have asked Simon for a drop or two when I had the opportunity. When you and I first met, we were only months apart. Now you look young enough to be my daughter."

"Huh? Wait! You mean, there really is a liquid you can drink that will make you younger?"

He grinned and answered, "You mean, you really can go back – or forward – in time?" one eyebrow lifted, his sincerity obvious.

She sighed and brought their joined hands to her face and kissed the ball of his thumb, noticing the faint scent of bay rum.

"Wow," he whispered. "It takes a lot to shock me, but I think a minor earthquake just rumbled through this old man's body. I still have one question, though."

"Anything. You already know my biggest secret."

"What's your name?"

"Julianna. So, do you think we can pick up where we left off? I'm over eighteen now?"

He chuckled. "I'm *well* over eighteen and although I didn't skip a couple of decades or drink a magic elixir, I'm not ready for a pine box, either. Remember how we spoke of exploring North Carolina?" he asked.

Julianna's eyes dimmed then brightened, the whole gamut of emotions zipping through her body in a moment. "Call it a leap of faith, but I think I'd follow you to the ends of the earth… Unless you're some sort of creeper that just got out of prison or…"

"No, not a creeper or miscreant of any kind," he said. "And I'd follow you to the end of *time*. Even if you are a creeper!"

"Deal!" she said, then leaned forward and gave him a gentle kiss, the first sincere one in decades. She pulled back minimally. "And I'm not a creeper, either. But I think we'd better not get started kissing or we'll make a scene."

He moved in for one more, then pulled back. "I hate to say it, but I think you're right. To be continued elsewhere."

"Absolutely!"

Chapter 3: Eighteen and Legal

"Speaking of eighteen now," Silas said, sitting tall in the chair. He looked over at the boisterous young couple – her son and his granddaughter – becoming the center of attention at the wedding party. He stood up to make sure trouble wasn't brewing. "It's hard to believe we were younger than they are now when we first got involved."

"Hmm. Speaking of involved…" Julianna mused, watching the physical interaction between the two. "Looks like they're getting a little *too* carried away. I think it's time for me to step in."

"Eighteen long years. That's how long it took me to find Tori and her adoptive parents. I only met her less than an hour ago, yet I feel as if I've known her all my life. Oh, I'm sorry. You said you wanted to check on them? I'm sure they'll be fine, but if that's what you want."

"Well, one thing is obvious, she's very fond of Oscar. Do you want to have some fun? Let's shake up the kids. You know, mess with them a little."

"Okay, and then let's find someplace private that's warm and dry…and with indoor plumbing," Silas said, then whispered, "This hound dog's getting too old for pup tents."

As they weaved their way through the tables and chairs. Silas placed his hand gently on Julianna's upper back. He knew she didn't need guiding but couldn't resist touching her. Tingles of his adolescent crush echoed through his body as he held onto her, making sure he didn't lose her again.

"That's enough, granddaughter," he said in a mock stern voice.

Tori quickly pulled out of the elevated hug and kiss as the red-faced Oscar released his embrace, letting her slide to the floor in a controlled drop.

"I didn't mean to startle you," Silas said with a sly grin.

"Yes, you did," Tori replied sassily, then rolled her eyes and added, "Grandpa."

"Actually, it was my idea to come over to talk to you," Julianna said, smiling at Tori, patting her shoulder with reassurance. "At first, it looked like you two were having a serious but angry discussion. We were going to wait until you had it sorted, but then your method of conversation changed in a hurry. I didn't want you to get too carried away using body language instead of words."

Oscar looked back and forth between his two favorite females. "You and Tori? You're buddies now? I mean, Tori has never been a very social person. So, that must mean you two found something in common."

"Oh, she and I get along famously," Julianna said. She reached out and pulled Silas close. "I wanted to talk to you, Oscar, before you and your lady friend made too many plans for your future." She winked at Tori with the word 'future' and continued. "Silas and I have been chatting, too. It seems we have a lot in common. I have a mystery and he's a bit of a sleuth. I think we're going to North Carolina to do a little exploring and research soon, very soon."

Julianna furtively grabbed Silas by the hand and looked at him, sending him a silent 'Just trust me' with her fervent clutch and deep gaze. He winked and squeezed back in reply. 'Message received.'

She swallowed hard and turned back to the young couple. "In other words, you won't need to come back to France with me, son."

"You're leaving? With him? But...but...you just met!"

"Actually, we knew each other a long time ago. I recognized him right away, but I think you two understand taking advantage of a situation when the *time* is right, yes?"

"Mom..." Oscar asked, his concern obvious with the tone of that single word. His eyes narrowed, *"Are you talking about that time travel nonsense again?"*

Julianna saw his inferred question and said, "Don't worry about me. I'll be in good hands. I'll make sure to keep in contact." She held up her phone and grinned.

"Just make sure you have the right *device* for the job," Tori said with an exaggerated wink, referring to their initial conversation about with the right mechanism, time travel would be possible.

"Absolutely!" Silas and Julianna said at the same time. On saying the same word at the same time, they smiled at each other, hands clutching in adolescent excitement.

"That's my granddaughter," Silas said. "She figured it out before I did."

"Mom..." Oscar grumbled, his voice just a half-tone above a growl.

"I'm okay, son," she said. "Really, I am. You have the keys to the car and the hotel. I'm going to make up for lost time with Silas."

"Whoa. Wait," Tori said, her face pinched as she tried to figure out what was going on. She turned to Oscar. "You mean my grandpa and your mother are dating?"

"Yeah, it looks like it," Oscar said, not even trying to hide his frown.

"Yes, we are!" Julianna crowed. "Wasn't it just a few hours ago, Oscar, that you told me to get a life? Maybe I'd meet someone here in the US?"

"Yeah, but..." Oscar looked Silas up, down, and back up again to stare at his gray hair. "But..."

"Don't worry about it..." Silas bit off the term of endearment 'son.' "We're taking our time with getting reacquainted," he said primly, adding a nod.

"Doubling up on relatives?" Tori said dryly. "That should make sending out Christmas cards easier. Oh, and Grandpa..."

"Yes, dear..."

"Don't lose her again, alright?" Tori said with a wink.

"I promise."

***

Julianna and Silas headed toward the cloakroom, eager to leave the wedding venue. They stopped and gave farewells to Julianna's nephew Rich and his new bride, Vickie – another one of Silas's newly acknowledged triplet granddaughters; Ria the third triplet and her beau, Evan; and the rush of others they encountered on their way to what turned out to be a not-too-discreet exit.

The pair stepped into the parking lot and the brisk winter night's air. "So, where to now…?" Julianna asked, then faltered, suddenly ill at ease.

"Are you okay? You look gray…I mean…you don't look like you feel too good." Silas put his hand on her arm as she pulled her cashmere jacket close.

She chuckled at his discomfort. "A black woman gray? Is that a racist joke?"

"No, it's an 'I care about your health' question."

Julianna closed her eyes and shook her head, refusing to give in to insecurity. Her stomach relaxed with the conscious effort. "Don't take this wrong, but we have to be brutally honest from the get-go. Because if not, I'll go right back in and leave with my son."

"Good Lord, yes! By all means, be honest. However, I don't think either one of us needs to be brutal. I mean, we've both just shared deep secrets that anyone else would take as proof that we belonged in a nuthouse."

"Silas, I've been in a nuthouse," she said, her eyes half-closed with the pain of recalling the shame and humiliation.

"It wasn't like Bedlam, was it?" he asked gently. "I meant no disrespect. And for the record, just from what I know of you this evening and of our weekend in August of '69, I'd say your committal to an institution was an accident. You're not crazy. Just…how about we say you're *overly experienced*?"

Julianna's discomfort and anxiety evaporated, and hope and joy replaced it. "I never thought of it like that! How could I possibly explain a concept if the psychiatrist had no reference point? I'm sorry I doubted the veracity of you and your experience with the Fountain of Youth. I had no reference point, so treated you just like those overpriced shrinks my husband sicced on me." She rolled her eyes and said, "God rest Hugh's soul wherever he is."

"I thought you were divorced," Silas said. "I'm sorry. I guess it doesn't make a difference whether you're a widow or divorcee." He squeezed her close. "You're mine now."

Julianna let him hold her tight, glad that between their position and the darkness, he couldn't see the fear in her face. *I don't know which I am either.*

Chapter 4: Rude Awakening

"Where to now?" Silas asked, opening the door to his classic Cadillac for her. "Do you have a preference? Find a hotel or head to my place?"

She waited for him to get comfortable then laid her head on his shoulder. "Which is closest?" she asked then giggled. Before he could answer, she suddenly sat up. "Crap."

"Excuse me?"

"I forgot my wallet. It has my ID. I don't know if they let you rent a room without it."

"I'll tell you what," Silas said, patting her leg in reassurance. "Since I don't know this town, and don't want to chance having an issue checking in without the proper identification, how about a twenty-minute drive to my place? I'm pretty sure my roommates will still be busy with the wedding fête for at least a couple more hours."

"You have roommates? At your age?" Julianna asked, her voice rising at the end. She scoffed. "You're messing with me, right?"

"Nope. Two of the other grandpas to the triplets and I share Doc Armstrong's place. It's a convenient arrangement for all of us. However, if you don't mind waiting for an extra five minutes, I can guarantee complete solitude. No need to hang a sock on the doorknob."

"A sock on the doorknob? What does that mean?"

Silas chuckled. "It was an old college trick. If a roommate had a girl in the room and didn't want to be disturbed, he hung a sock on the door. The guys and I haven't had to resort to that old ploy, though."

"No socks or no girls?" Julianna asked, not sure whether he was teasing or not.

"Lots of socks, but none of us ever met a woman worthy of bringing back. We're pretty much three confirmed old bachelors."

"Twenty-five minutes," she said, squirming with a coy chuckle.

"Beats the hell out of forty years."

She put her head back on his shoulder and sighed as he pulled out of the parking lot. "I agree. However, if I sit still for very long, the meds I'm on make me drowsy." She yawned and covered her mouth. "Excuse me! I think I'll take a nap now so I'm perky later…"

And then she was out, emitting soft little snores between sighs of 'mmm…'

Twenty minutes later – the speed limit severely bent but not too badly broken – Silas pulled in front of his twenty-acre estate. He pushed in his security code, the chain and gear mechanism groaning and screeching as the front gate swung open.

The unfamiliar noise startled Julianna, rousing her from deep sleep to a half-lucid panic, her arms flailing, batting at Silas. She clutched at the seatbelt as if fighting off unseen assailants, her head thrashed back and forth.

"Whoa! It's okay, Julianna," Silas said, foot on the brake. He tried to restrain her hands – both to protect her from herself and to avoid another blow to his face, but that enraged her even more. Cowered beneath his elbow, he put the Cadillac in park, grabbed the key, and got out.

He rushed to the passenger side and opened her door. She lurched out, enraged. "You're fine, sweetheart," he said soothingly, standing out of reach, his hands behind his back. "No one's going to hurt you. You can wake up now."

As quickly as she'd erupted into a Class Five tizzy, Julianna snapped out of it. Her eyes wide, she looked around at the unfamiliar terrain and gated yard, at the mansion at the end of the long driveway. She blanched, trying to orient herself. Swallowing hard, she closed her mouth, and turned around in place, taking it in, hoping something would be familiar.

And then she saw him.

"Silas?" she asked. "It is you, isn't it?"

"Yes, it is." He bit off the question, 'Are you okay,' not wanting her to be more flustered than she already was. "I guess arriving early threw you off a little."

"Where are we?"

"At the bottom of my driveway. If you'd like to get back in the car, I'll take you to my home."

Julianna gawked at the brightly lit mansion, a mini-version of the White House. "That…that's your house? No, I'm sorry. Of course, it's not. Are you the caretaker?"

"Oh, it's my home, all right. Lock, block, and cellar stocked with wine barrels. Don't tell anyone, though. A lot of folks still think I'm the butler. I get fewer requests for charity donations that way."

Dazed, Julianna walked to the car, Silas's hand gently touching her back. She let him guide her into the front seat, then saw his face. A long scratch shone bright red with fresh blood. "Did I…?"

Silas could feel the burn of the fresh wound but didn't reach up or acknowledge its presence. "Let's get inside. It's cold out here."

A long, eerily quiet minute later, he pulled into the below ground level garage. He started humming Janice Joplin's 'Take another piece of my heart' as he pulled in beside an orange and white restored VW microbus –1959 Westfalia camper special – accented with colorful vinyl decals of pop art flowers and peace signs.

"That's not the same version we rode in," Julianna began.

"No…" he agreed and waited.

"I think it's better." Julianna let herself out of the Cadillac and moved to the classic camper special, her hand hovering above the window as she looked inside. "Oh, my…"

"That's what I thought, too. It's too cold to take you for a spin, but as soon as the roads are clear and dry – or at least all the ice and snow are gone – we can take this baby over the mountains and plains, to all the rivers, lakes and oceans, campgrounds and wide spots from here to the ends of the earth."

She turned and looked at him, embarrassed. "I'm sorry I…" She stared at the fresh scratch and started to cry.

"Sorry for falling asleep? Or for being confused when you woke up with an old man you didn't recognize driving a car you'd never been in before? Either one would have been a good reason to be startled. Now, this is just the basement. It's a bit chilly in here, so let's go in the house. How about a hot toddy or a cup of cocoa?"

"Cocoa," she said, a smile rising. "With marshmallows, if you have them."

"I think I can make that happen."

Silas led the way into the kitchen, grabbed the remote from the wall, and with three taps, the mood was set in the den: lights on dim, gas fireplace lit, and the stereo playing sitar music by Ravi Shankar.

"What's that?" Julianna asked, nodding to the device he was returning to its home on the wall.

"*My* butler," he said, chuckling. He turned the kitchen light to bright and investigated the contents of the cupboard and the refrigerator. "Hmm. Only half and half – no milk. That ought to do. Would you like Mexican or American cocoa?"

"What's the difference? Is Mexican made out of *jumping* cocoa beans?"

The unexpected joke almost made Silas drop the carton. "No, the Mexican kind has cinnamon and a dash of cayenne. You can still have marshmallows, though."

"I'll try the Mexican," she said, then sidled up to him while he pulled the ingredients from the cabinet. Her hand hovered above the scrape, then moved behind his ear as if pushing long hair back.

"I cut it right after Woodstock," he said to her unspoken question. "This is about as long as it ever gets."

"Why?" she asked and tucked her hand under her arm.

"My father said it was time to get a job, pay my way in the world. Long hair wasn't conducive to high-paying employment. I worked my way through three years of college. I couldn't afford the luxury of being the hippie stoner war protester who was the inner me."

"You? A stoner? While everyone else at Woodstock was getting high, you were holding your breath!" Julianna laughed in recall. "I remember how you got ticked when some of the others were blowing smoke up that little dog's nose."

"And I'd still get riled about that." Silas took his set of measuring spoons out of the drawer and measured out the cocoa and sugar and added them to the small saucepan. "That poor pup had about one-fiftieth of a person's body mass. Who knew what it would do to him?"

Julianna's laughter stopped. "I never thought of that... I guess you do that a lot though, huh?"

"What?"

"Think," she said softly. "Sometimes I don't do that enough." She pointed to his scratch. "I react."

"You were sixteen when I met you and from what I could tell, living on your own, right?"

"Well, yeah..."

"You weren't done growing emotionally or intellectually. I don't know anything about your parent or parents, but whether they were saints or serving life sentences on Alcatraz, they never had a chance to finish your education in life. Or whatever you want to call it."

"Oh, I had both parents. They were more in the saint category, but you're right. I left before I completed the finishing school of life." She sighed deeply. "That's why I made sure no matter how much I wanted to take off and find..." Julianna gulped, stopping herself from telling too much. "Take off and find the meaning of life," she said and rolled her eyes, hoping he thought that's what she had meant to say.

Silas's eyes narrowed as he inspected her for signs of fibbing. Most definitely hiding but no overt lies. "So, you weren't necessarily happily married to Oscar's father, but you stayed with him for the boy's sake, correct?"

"Spot on, Sherlock. I'd ask how you knew, but it doesn't matter. When a situation like that happens, the kids are the ones who suffer. Suffer from mountains of guilt because they see how miserable their parents are. Guilty because if they weren't around, the parents could be living separate lives, either with or without a new partner. Either way, Mom and Dad would be free from their imprisoned lives of co-parenting."

"And people wonder why I never married..."

"Hugh wasn't a bad man. He couldn't sire a child, though. We liked each other enough – we both volunteered at the shelter where I used to live. One day, a lady came in off the streets very pregnant. She made me promise that if something happened to her, I'd take care of the baby. Well, five days after Oscar was born, she was gone. *Pfft!*

"So, there I was with a baby and an heir-craving co-worker who'd been helping take care of Oscar since the day he was born. Well, getting married was the easiest way to legalize the adoption of a child with no mother available to sign away her rights. So, we made it work. Mostly. I mean, Oscar's a good kid, never been in trouble, and I think he turned out just fine."

Julianna beamed with classic maternal pride. "He finished college early. He's a talented botanist who has a major crush on your granddaughter."

401

"And Tori was adopted by one of the most gifted botanists in the world and his loving wife. A fine match, for sure. But you're wrong on one point."

"What?" she asked, then stuck her finger into the powdery concoction of cocoa, sugar, and spices, then licked it. "Yum!"

"He's not a kid; he's a young man. I can see it in his eyes. He's wise beyond his years; skeptical and analytical, yet passionate. I like him," he said with a broad smile and nod of endorsement.

Julianna laughed, then bent to kiss Silas on the cheek close to the scratch. "It sounds as if you just described yourself. Let's get the cocoa started, then I want to clean up that long-nailed sleepwalker's mishap."

Silas scooted the saucepan of dry ingredients to the back of the counter. "How about a little first aid then cocoa? I have a medicine cabinet in my room."

"Just make sure you have everything you need in there. I am still fertile, you know…"

Silas looked at the clock and groaned softly, his eyes half-closed in frustration. There wasn't a market or pharmacy open within an hour's drive. "Maybe a Band-Aid, and then a few hours of foreplay?"

"Ah, every woman's dream. Except for the Band-Aid part."

He grabbed her hand and brought it to his lips. "Maybe this time you'll let me bring out my stethoscope…"

Julianna stepped into his arms. "Lead the way, Doc!"

Chapter 5: The Red Room

"Which one is your room?" Julianna asked, her hand softly touching the polished carved oak handrail as they ascended the broad swirling staircase to the second floor.

"All of them," he said.

"But you said you had roommates .."

"I do, but not here. I usually live with my friends. Life changed for them. They were used to having family around. I wasn't, but I did enjoy their company. I was the best cook of the three, so they bribed me, and I moved in with them. We became a happily unmarried trio."

"Bribed you? With what?"

"I'll tell you later."

"If I'm a good girl?" she asked coyly, her eyes shining with mischief.

Now at the top of the stairs, Silas slipped his arm around her waist and spun her around to look down at the view of the entryway and sitting rooms, polished marble floors gleaming, classic antique furniture upholstered in deep roses and burgundies accented with lamps and sconces of polished brass.

"Maybe being a bad girl would be better. ." he cooed as he kissed her below the ear.

"And all this is yours?" she squeaked at his tickle, taking in the magnificence.

He pulled back and grinned. "Does it make a difference? Let's just say none of this is stolen nor is it in danger of being repossessed."

Julianna pursed her lips and squinted, trying to figure him out. "I thought you were a butler."

"I was." He stepped closer and rubbed his nose on hers. "Great retirement plan and benefits program. Oh, and dental, too."

"You're silly," she said and gave him a quick kiss.

"And you're out of practice. I remember kisses that lasted for hours…"

"And made you squirm," she said, squatting down a little so she was rubbing up against him, belly to belly.

"Damn! I should have taken Hal's advice to keep a box of condoms on hand 'just in case.'"

"Hal? Who's he? Your butler?"

"No, one of my roomies at the other house."

"You own two homes like this?"

"No." Silas brought her fingers to his mouth again and kissed them gently, glad to have the opportunity to divert her attention so he could rearrange himself with his other hand. "Do you want to pick a room or should I?"

"Which was the last room you used for a liaison?" she asked.

"What? I mean, really? What kind of question is that?"

"I don't want you to be thinking of another woman while we're – how should I say – getting reacquainted?"

"Julianna, you can take your pick of any or every room in this house and not rouse any romantic memories or leftover vibes from another female. Or male. At least, as it pertains to me. Over the years, there have been other residents here, and I can't speak for them or the ghosts they may have left behind. There are twelve bedrooms plus assorted offices, parlors, game rooms, and a library, not to mention the bathrooms, kitchens, and the guest house. All are, shall we say, chaste, devoid of any sexual experiences of mine."

"Any?" she asked, one eyebrow raised.

"Well, solo doesn't count," he replied, quickly kissing her again to hide his blush. "Come on. If you don't pick a room, I will."

"Which is the room you slept in last?"

"This way," he said, arm around her waist. "The red room as I call it." He opened the door to a large suite with a huge dark European oak desk as the focal point. A picture window at the far right of the room provided a view for the king-sized bed, smothered in oversized red pillows.

"A guy's room…with pillows?" she asked, a giggle in her voice.

"Pillows aren't just for decorations, you know. They're great for propping up in bed to read or for back support after a rough day of…of whatever."

"Ditch digging or tennis?" Julianna teased.

Silas bent his head and answered, "Gardening. I'm a closet farmer, I suppose. You should see the tomatoes I get at Hal's place. We have a competition every year – Doc, Hal, and me."

"Hmm," Julianna mused, feigning interest as she slowly started unbuttoning his shirt.

"Hmm?" he replied as a question.

"I want to see that farmer's tan."

Goose pimples raced up his arms at her touch, her long delicate fingers pulling off the shirt across his shoulders. "Danged undershirt," she whispered, tugging it out of his slacks.

"Let me help," he said softly and unfastened his belt and the top closure of his trousers.

She tugged again, freeing the tee. He crossed his arms and pulled it off over his head.

"My silver Adonis," she said, her fingers stroking his shimmering chest hair. "Oh, my!" She lightly brushed his abs. "Not an ounce of fat on you."

"It's dark in here," he said, nuzzling her hair, still bashful about touching the rest of her. "I have more than a bit of…ahem…insulation, but if you don't see it, I won't point it out to you."

She stroked the front of his slacks familiarly, ending at his waistband. "Looks like you're trying to point something out to me."

404

"He remembers you."

"Oh, does my puppy want to come out and play?" she asked coyly, tugging at the zipper tab.

"I may be an old dog, but the spirit is still there."

"And the muscle," she said, unzipping his pants. "Oh, and the question is answered..."

Silas pulled her chin up to look at him. "What question?"

She giggled and kissed him. "Boxers, briefs, or commando. I guess you gave up freestyling, eh?"

"Knit boxers definitely have their benefits. Comfortable and discreet. Now, how about you?" he asked.

"Nope, neither boxers nor briefs."

"Commando?"

She lifted the side of her skirt and guided his hand up her thigh. "Thong underwear, a late-twentieth-century creation that, although not necessarily comfortable, does help establish a sleek line under today's form-fitting garments."

Silas gasped as she led his hand to her bared fanny. He cupped her ass cheek and sighed deeply, hoping it didn't sound like the desperate groan it was. "Would you allow me?"

"Go for it," she cooed into his ear. "I've been yearning for you for decades." She looked up at the ceiling. "And zero chance of precipitation in here."

"Lath and plaster interspersed with drywall," he replied, fumbling with the zipper at the back of her dress with his free hand. "Much better than a Yellow Front emergency shelter."

She shoved his pants past his hips. "Still, these are easier to take off than button-fly 501s."

He laughed at the memory as he stepped out of his loafers and kicked them aside. "They were hard for everyone unless they were so old, they'd become flannel-soft and pliable."

She stroked him again. "Still hard, not flannel-soft," she said and giggled. "If you take too much longer getting me out of this dress, though, I'm going to rip it off!"

Zip!

"Got it. I'll say one thing about me, I am tenacious."

"And determined," she said, then wriggled out of her dress. "And they're not the same thing." She let go of him, then bent to tug his slacks off the rest of the way, pulling them away as he stepped out. She hastily folded them and threw them on the chair beside the bed, then tossed her dress on top. "Phew! I guess we're out of practice. Hopefully, next time it won't take so long."

"Gawd, you're gorgeous. Still. No, wait. Even more so. I never saw so much of you at once."

Julianna stuck her thumbs under the straps of her lacy push-up bra. "And there's even more to see."

Silas stepped backward, almost tripping on his shoes before he regained his balance. He threw all but two of the pillows off to the side of the bed, then pulled back the bedspread and covers, exposing vibrant red satin sheets. "Join me?"

Julianna kicked off her shoes one at a time, her eyes fixed on his as she moved toward him seductively, her hands rising to her breasts with an unspoken invitation. "All night foreplay?" she asked.

Feeling himself throb in anticipation, Silas winced, remembering the trick he'd learned from an old Elvis Presley movie. *Just recite your multiplication tables.*

She kissed him softly, then pulled away. "Can we get under the covers first? My feet are cold."

"Whatever the lady desires." He held back the covers for her, then picked up the remote from his side of the bed and clicked a few buttons. The sound of ocean waves crashing on the surf resounded from the hidden speakers in the ceiling, the lights dimmed to moonlight brightness, and the foot portion of the warming as the heating pad kicked in. Ideal.

Bra and panties still on, Julianna climbed into bed, a sudden flare of uncertainty searing hot as Hugh's last hurtful words screamed at her. *You're nothing but a slut!* She did as the last psychiatrist had told her and ordered her demons to leave her alone. "Shut up! You're a liar!" she mouthed, barely breathing as she spoke. No sound came out, but the emotional rebuff worked.

Silas watched the long-legged beauty ease onto the silky sheets, her milk-chocolate hued body as perfect as any man – or woman - could ever want. He glanced up just in time to see her lips move in a silent admonition. Uncertainty. Conflict.

He slid in, pulled the blankets up, and rearranged the pillows, opening one arm out to her. "Come over here and let me hold you. I'm not going anywhere, and I hope you aren't either. We don't need to rush things. It's been a long time. Let's get to know a little about each other. I mean, even if we could erase the last forty years and skip to the day after Woodstock, we probably wouldn't have wound up in bed with each other. We were still minors, after all."

"Why are you so smart?" she asked and sidled over to him. She lay her head on his shoulder and rearranged her hair so it wasn't in his face.

He kissed her forehead. "I read a lot. Plus I watch and listen to what's going on around me. It's not intelligence, per se – although I hope I have at least an average amount – but it's what you do with what's out there that solves problems or gets answers."

"Observe and interpret?" she suggested.

"See, you have it, too. Like right now. We were so wrapped up with each other, the past we lost and the present we were suddenly gifted, that we were about to head full speed into… Well, I don't know, but I was ready to go all the way, as we used to say."

"Me, too."

"Yes, and I'm pretty sure it would have felt fantastic, but it's the aftereffects, the residual emotions, that are left with us forever. It's better to prepare ourselves, like a garden. We can't go slinging seeds before we clear out the stones and weeds, break down the clumps, and level the ground so it – we – will thrive."

Silas shifted sideways so he could look at her, see her eyes. "Julianna, I've been a single man my whole life. I've never met a woman I wanted to share…" He waved his hand around the room, stopping at the huge picture window. "I never met a woman I wanted to share my world with. Except you. I had to wonder if my infatuation with you was all a fantasy. I could have had others. I've met a few worthy women who would have been quite satisfied to have me as an escort, a partner in business or travel, but they didn't give me that zing.

"When we met at the wedding, rather when you recognized me there – and I realized you were real and still gave me that zing – I knew I'd been right to hold off on settling for second best."

"That's a lot to live up to," Julianna said, frowning.

"Yes, and that's why we're talking and not eh hem…"

"Well, that and you don't have any condoms…"

Silas rolled his eyes and sighed. "True. I think if I had a drawerful of them, we'd be after-glowing instead of lying here, semi-clothed, introspecting, frustrated. Damn it."

"How about a little hybrid farming? We can toss out a few rocks and weeds, but do a little prodding and kneading, too."

Silas reached over and grabbed her bare bottom, his thumb under the hip of her thong. "Just don't leave me again. I don't think my heart could stand it."

She closed her eyes and came in close. "You're my everything," she whispered, and kissed him, ignoring his comment. "My everything," she repeated and rolled over on top of him, holding him tight between her legs, ready to be in charge of the wildest dry hump ever.

***

Silas reached over, terrified she was gone.

Something was wrong. Julianna was still here, asleep next to him, her soft snores the same as they were when they shared a tent forty years ago. He relaxed back onto his pillow, then realized what was odd and sat up straight. He looked around the room and saw he was right. The power was off. The soft music had stopped, the hum of the heater was silent, and the only light was the glow of the moon, reflecting off low clouds through the curtainless window.

Kerthunk!

And there it was. The backup generator kicked in. The music and lights were still off, but the heater and battery-operated light in the hall were on now.

Julianna startled at the mechanical noise, her snores now whimpers of fretful sleep.

He patted the side of her hip. "It's all right. I'm here with you," he said softly.

She moaned sweetly in reply. "Silas?" and rolled over to face him. "It is you, isn't it? I wasn't dreaming."

"Well, I don't know what you were dreaming, but yes, it's really me. I don't ever want to lose you again."

"Now, isn't that sweet," a woman's gruff voice called from the doorway.

Silas started to reach for the gun in the top drawer of his nightstand, then changed his mind and grabbed his discarded undershirt. He pulled it on over his head, using the time to try and figure out who could have bypassed his security systems.

"Who's she?" Julianna asked harshly, pulling the sheet over her bare bosom.

"I have no idea," he growled, then reached over and patted her leg in reassurance, then left it there. "But she certainly doesn't belong here."

Julianna squeezed his hand in a silent response of trust.

"Oh, sweet, sweet Silas. How soon you forget," the woman said as she walked into the room, stopping in front of the desk. "I'm the woman who gave you a child. You must have figured that out by now, surely. I mean, isn't that why they call you Sherlock?"

A deep breath, almost a growl, came from Silas. He wanted to speak but decided to give Victoria the Viper, his buddy Hal's ex-wife, the rope she would certainly give him to bind her with.

"Who's the floozie?" Victoria asked, nodding to Julianna. "Aren't you going to introduce us? No, wait. She's just an escort and you never remembered her name if you even bothered to ask it. As if she'd give you a real one."

"Can I deck her?" Julianna asked Silas coolly. "She did break and enter, right?"

"No and yes. I mean, wait. Yes, you're correct – she did not have permission to enter. But no, don't hit her. I don't think she's worth the legal hassle if you hurt her."

"*When* I hurt her," Julianna corrected.

"Oh, she's such a cute little tart. And obedient, too. Are you into chocolate now, Silas dear?"

"Oh, go ahead," Silas said. "She's in the country illegally, I'm sure. ICE won't care if she's bruised up a bit."

Julianna jumped out of bed, even though Victoria had a gun pointed at her.

Whoosh!

The pillow Silas had thrown when Julianna leaped out took the viper off guard, her pistol firing harmlessly into the ceiling.

Julianna's elbow flew up in an offensive move, sending the intruder stumbling against the desk.

One-two, one-two, right cross, uppercut!

Bare-assed Julianna stepped back, letting the pummeled female drop to the floor.

"Have I told you lately how hot you are?" Silas asked, standing beside the bed. "There's nothing sexier than a naked woman taking down a thief and blackmailer except…"

Julianna wiped the hair off her forehead and looked back at him. "Except?" she asked.

"Except when that sexy naked woman is mine," he said and came to stand next to her.

Julianna stared down at the front of him and giggled. "That shirt doesn't quite come low enough for decency, but it does prove you're telling the truth. You look pretty sexy yourself."

Silas followed her gaze then reacted quickly, his hands automatically covering his aroused privates in embarrassment.

"Still got it, eh?" the awakening voice mumbled from the floor.

Julianna picked up the tossed pillow and covered the woman's face, securing it with her foot. "You get dressed first. It's time to take out the trash."

***

"Now what?" Julianna asked.

Silas finished tying Victoria to the snowboard, verifying the shop-rag gag was secured and he wouldn't have to hear any more of her curses.

"I'll make a call and let Hal decide what to do."

"No! No!" Victoria protested through the gag, twisting and turning so hard to escape that she knocked her improvised fiberglass stockade sideways.

Clunk!

Now on the concrete floor, face down, her pleas continued.

Silas touched Julianna's arm. "Let's go upstairs. It's too noisy here in the garage."

She nodded and followed, turning around at the last minute to stick her tongue out at her nemesis.

"Grrr! Bitch!" Victoria mumbled, then kicked furiously.

"Hello, Hal? Yeah, sorry to wake you so early after the wedding and all, but we have a major problem. She's back. Yeah, *her!* She broke into my place an hour ago. She's neutralized, but I don't know what to do with her. Are you sure? I was just joking when I said I'd drop her off at the immigration office. All right. I'm pretty sure it's still in the federal complex. Well, here's hoping she doesn't bullshit them and get right back out. Really? I didn't know she had outstanding warrants. Oh, that's right. I forgot about the assault with a deadly weapon. I was just glad Grace was okay. Shooting her only child ought to impress a judge enough that he keeps her locked up without bail. Okay, I'll keep you informed. Hush! Tell Doc I never kiss and tell. Bye."

Silas clicked end on the phone call and smiled at Julianna. "I take it you got the gist of what's going on?"

"I got the chapter headings, but you can fill me in on the details while we're in transit. Or for the next week, if needed. She shot her daughter – your daughter?"

"Thanks for not alluding that she and I ever were a couple, because we weren't. Short version, she got me drunk and I woke up cuffed to a bed in a seedy sex hotel, bare-assed naked and with the hangover from hell."

"That sounds awful!"

"The worst part was waiting for someone to come get me. Those maids were used to all sorts of strange stuff, so my situation wasn't anything out of the ordinary for them."

Julianna stifled a giggle. "Oh, I'm so sorry." She suddenly sobered up, thinking of how she'd feel if it had been her instead of him. "That bitch! She should be tarred and feathered for that. She...she..."

Silas put his hand on her shoulder. "I got over it. No one even knew for sure that I had sired a child that roofie-hazed night until Tori pointed it out at the wedding. Hal and I suspected it for a long time, especially since he could never sire another child and tested sterile, but we never spoke of it. I've been close to Grace through him. Although I missed the day-to-day events of her life, I was around for many of the major events. Plus, now I have three granddaughters I can acknowledge. That's how Hal bribed me into moving in with him and Doc. Full access to the daughter and granddaughters I couldn't acknowledge without raising a ruckus."

"Triplets?"

"Super fertility runs in the family," Silas said. "Now you know why I was extra careful last night." He kissed her softly, then moved in and finished with a sigh-inducing finale. "Don't ever think I don't want you because I do." He looked in her eyes and saw fear begin, so didn't add the, 'And always will,' he'd been thinking.

Julianna put her head on his shoulder, tears starting to well at those unsaid words she was glad he hadn't spoken. She'd never wanted anyone so much in her life. Would he be her undoing, though? Her desires always seemed to attract disasters. "I'm sorry, you were saying?"

"It's cold outside. All I can offer you are some of my gym clothes. I don't have women's clothing here."

"Well, that makes me feel better," Julianna said. "I can't imagine you in a

Dior gown." She squinted and tried to visualize him in a strapless, white floor-length dress. "Nah."

"What? Why not? I may be missing the bust, but I do have decent legs. Put me in something split up to here," he said, touching the outside of his thigh, "and I'd be a real head-turner."

"Come on, Sweet Meat," Julianna said, laughing. "You're going to get me all turned on and we still don't have any condoms."

"Really?"

She shrugged and frowned. "I don't know. If we run out of things to do, we'll try it. But first, let's take out the trash."

"Oh, yeah…" Silas feigned gagging. "You take one end of the snowboard, and I'll take the other. She should fit in the backseat of the Caddie."

"If not, we can force her a little, maybe stick her in upside down and sideways."

"Or cut her in half…" Silas said. "Nah, too messy. I like that old car. I've had other Cadillacs but that '89 DeVille has a special place in my heart."

"Your first?"

"Yup. Come on, partner. Work first, then I'll make us a fantastic breakfast."

"Good, because I never got my cocoa last night." Julianna saw him smile at her remark. "Yes, I know, but you got yours, right?"

"Just like you, I'm still waiting for the cream to be added," he said with a wink.

Chapter 6: Disappearing Act

"Where'd she go?" Julianna asked, tugging at the crotch of the borrowed sweatpants which were too short for her long legs. She bent down and looked under the Cadillac while Silas did the same, looking under all of the other vehicles.

"Damned if I know." He turned around and winked at Julianna. "All right. She'll either show up or is gone for good. In the meantime, let's go play around a little."

Julianna squinted at him dubiously. "Sounds like a great idea to me, my Adonis. Come send me to paradise with your majestic member!"

Silas's hand flew to his mouth just in time to stifle his laugh.

Julianna saw that she had probably gone too far with her joke and he couldn't reply. When she realized her words would probably be wrapped in giggles, too, she hummed loudly and grabbed onto him as they beat a hasty exit.

As soon as they were out of the garage, Silas opened the electrical panel on the wall, flipped a switch, and secured the area. "Come on," he whispered. "If she hasn't already left, she won't get out. Let's go check the security footage."

Silas led her to the annex just off the kitchen. He noticed the saucepan with cocoa ingredients was right where they left it and sighed.

"Work first," Julianna said, noticing his focus. "If she's truly vicious and unpredictable, I don't want her on the loose." She paused and added, "Even if I can kick her butt."

"That's my woman." He pulled up a stool and offered her the desk chair in front of the monitor. Cordless keyboard in hand, he tapped and swiped, bringing up the last half hour of the garage footage. "There she is," he said, pointing.

"And there she goes. What is that? A garbage chute?"

"Yes. Too bad I never use it. It's clean. I guess I could set off that old pest exterminator bomb that's been on the shelf for at least a decade, but if she's still inside, I don't want to kill her."

Julianna turned to him with an eyebrow raised.

"Just because I hate her and want her out of my life doesn't mean I want to kill her."

"And she is the mother of your daughter and grandmother to your granddaughters?" she said as a question, shaking her head in disbelief.

"Giving birth doesn't make you a mother any more than having similar DNA makes you a grandparent. Hal and the nanny are the reasons Grace survived that bitch. As far as I know, Victoria doesn't know anything about the triplets. We did a pretty good job of isolating Grace from her. I'm sure she knew she was pregnant, but not that she had a multiple birth. She'd have to be pretty clever to find out who the adoptive parents were, so the girls are safe."

"Unless Victoria found out Hal was going to a wedding and she showed up, saw all those young women who looked like Grace, and sorted it out herself? It wouldn't take a genius. The girls look more like quadruplets than triplets and a mother."

"Shit! So much for me being a Sherlock. Now what, Miss Marple?"

"Hey! I get that one! If you pay me a nickel, I won't be an amateur sleuth anymore."

Silas reached in his pocket and pulled out a coin. "No, not that one," he said, holding it up to the light, then put it back.

"Wait! Let me see that," Julianna said, suddenly panicked.

"That's just my lucky coin," Silas said, leaving it in his pocket. "Let's not get distracted." He rewound the video and saw Victoria had managed to get into the trash chute with the snowboard still attached to her back. He tapped on the keyboard and brought up an exterior camera.

"And there she goes…" Julianna said, then looked back at Silas.

"She either has an accomplice who's going to pick her up or she's going to get stopped by the locked gate. I doubt she can make it through there, even as skinny as she is, but if she does, the community watch group will grab her."

"So, you're saying let nature take its course?" Julianna asked.

"Yes, I am. However…" Silas tapped a few keys and hit enter. "Now the fence is electrified. It has enough juice going through it to stun a buck."

"Or a doe," Julianna said wryly, fidgeting in the chair. "Are we done here then?"

"Don't you want to watch her do the spaz dance when she gets zapped?"

"I'll catch it on reruns."

Silas set the keyboard back on the counter. "Are you all right?"

She winced at the familiar words she'd heard for years, the phrase that meant she was acting squirrelly and an increase in medication was on the way.

By her reaction, Silas realized he had just used negative trigger words. "I'm sorry," he said, ignoring what he had just asked. "You have to be ravenous. A big breakfast always makes the world brighter. Especially after kicking a major witch's butt."

Despite her insecurity, Julianna giggled. "Witch with a capital B. Did anyone ever tell you that you were a sweetheart?"

"Yes, but I told him that I was saving myself." He stood up and offered his hand. "Would you like to come with me? I'd ask if you'd like to supervise, but I know the way around my kitchen. However, I have no idea what kind of food you prefer. Sorry, I don't have any Twinkies, Oreos, or any of the other junk food we used to eat. I gave it up for Lent…" He squinted and tipped his head back and pretended to calculate, his fingers writing numbers, mumbling, "Carry the one, take away five…" before looking back at her. "Lent 1970. And since the computer's in the other room and my mental calculator doesn't work before breakfast, 'a long time' will have to be the accepted answer."

413

Julianna shook her head and moved close to him, holding his expressive hands in hers. "Are you for real? I feel as if I'm still asleep or in a drug-induced dream. Why hasn't someone come along and grabbed you up."

Silas looked down at their intertwined hands. "She just did."

Her tears were back. What would he do if he saw them? She took a deep breath and sighed. Probably nothing but try to make her feel better. "Breakfast. Eggs with any kind of cheese and or vegetables you have on hand. Skip the bread but coffee and some of that half and half would be very much appreciated. I think you're right. I have low blood sugar."

Silas kissed her on the cheek. "Some of us are more susceptible to it than others. Don't let anyone make you feel bad about it. We *all* have frailties. It's just some of them are more noticeable than others."

That did it. The tears started pouring out, followed by shoulder heaves and hiccups. "Why are you so nice?" she wept.

He grabbed a double-fistful of tissues and handed them to her, then gave her the whole box. "Did you ever hear the phrase, 'Treat others as you would like to be treated?'"

"The Golden Rule? Yes... But..."

"Did you know that pretty much all the major religions of the world have a variation of that same quote as a mantra or standard or law or whatever you want to call it?"

"Credo?"

"Yes, that, too. If I was shaky from hunger, in a strange house, had just battled an attempted murderess before she struck again, and was trying to make sure I didn't look..." Silas stalled, looking for a word that didn't mean crazy. "Trying to make sure I wasn't *unappealing*, good Lord, woman. That's enough stress to cause a major zit."

Julianna's sobs had been drying up with his consoling, but at his last remark, she started laughing. "Oh, my God! I forgot about that. Right before a big dance or photo day, I'd always get a huge pimple."

"Stress just takes different forms as we age. From what you told me last night, I have about twenty more years of life experience than you have. Would you let me help solve some of your problems? I mean, the easy ones for sure. Like making breakfast. We'll tackle clothes next, and then..." He shrugged.

"Finding condoms?"

"That's not what I was going to say. We need to get 'close' before we get 'close.' I don't care what you've done, I'll always want you. That's not going to change. But I don't want you for a one-night stand. I know it makes you uncomfortable when I get all sappy, so I won't."

Julianna's face skewed up and she snorted.

"I'll *try* not to get all sappy..." He sighed. "Let's just get through breakfast. I think I'm a bit hypoglycemic, too."

"Battling an attempted murderess rapist before six will do that to you," Julianna said. "Point me to the coffee and coffee maker. That much I should be able to handle."

***

"That was probably the best mushroom omelet I've ever had! What's your secret?" Julianna asked.

"The company I keep."

Julianna scoffed before drinking the last of her coffee. Her face scrunched up in distaste. "Maybe I was wrong. I think I'll let you make coffee next time, too."

"I like your positive attitude."

"Huh?"

"You're already looking forward to another morning with me. See, all we needed was food and to be rid of The Viper." Silas looked at the clock. "Oh, shoot! I should have called Hal right away to let him know she's on the loose again. Dang! Where is my brain?"

Julianna pointed to herself with her thumb. "Somewhere between ground zero and six-four," she said.

He smiled back at her and picked up his phone. "I thought you grew. I did, too. Back in '69, I was only five-ten. By the time I was twenty, I'd squeezed out another couple inches." He pushed and held a button, speed-dialing Hal.

"From what I recall, both horizontal and vertical."

His eyes widened and he sputtered into the phone just as the call connected. "Sorry about that, Hal. Something got to me. Hey, I'm sorry I didn't call right away; I got distracted. The Viper escaped. *Poof!* We had her all tied up to my old snowboard, but she managed to wiggle her way over to the garbage chute. No, dang it. It was clean. It hadn't been used in twenty years, at least. Yeah, well we can hope a raccoon was living in there. It'd serve her right, coming out covered in vermin turds. I'll run back and review the surveillance videos and see if she has an accomplice. Well, you know how it is. Or maybe you don't remember. Yes, I got distracted. Hush. Be nice. I can't commit to dinner because we have some shopping to do plus anything I do, I'd like to get her okay on, too. Well, if this is what having a ball and chain feels like, you can keep the key. I haven't smiled so much in years. Okay. I'll keep you posted on any news. Oh, and make sure Doc eats his banana every day. It doesn't count if he gives it to the dog. Bye."

"Ball and chain, eh?" Julianna asked.

"I was bragging, not complaining," Silas said. "Doc's been a widower for years, and Hal was miserable, married to Victoria until about eighteen years ago. We have a video of her making whoopie with her porn star gigolo. She'd do anything to get her hands on that. She ripped off all Hal's and Grace's bank accounts before he caught her. She's *persona non grata* from here to Costa

415

Rico. Their prenup said infidelity would negate any alimony or settlement. He made sure it ran both ways. The screwing she got was the screwing she deserved."

"And you had sex with her when she was married? Couldn't he get out of the marriage with you testifying or whatever?"

"That happened a week before they were married. Plus, I wasn't the only one. She was a sneaky slut. But that doesn't make a difference now. Let's go look at the security footage and see if she has a sidekick."

"Or if she got zapped," Julianna said, eyes bright with anticipation.

"It would be worth the nickel cost of admission to see that," Silas said, watching Julianna's reaction closely.

Her smile dimmed into a frown of deep thought, then popped back but without the shine. "And since it's on tape, we can watch it over and over again," she said with forced enthusiasm.

"Come on. We'll pass on the popcorn this time."

Silas sat down with the keyboard. He punched keys and played with the mouse, rewinding and fast-forwarding, until he found it. "Look at that!"

"Who is that brute?" Julianna asked, remarking on body-builder hulk who was trying to pull Victoria off the charged fence. "Don't touch her, don't touch her, you idiot! Oh, man! Talk about getting knocked on your butt!"

The clueless muscleman with the thinning hair managed to loosen his hold from Victoria's shoulder and stumbled backward. He shook off the stunned aftereffect, then planted his feet firmly, and karate kicked the now frizzy-haired intruder off the fence and into the bushes.

"That's electrician's safety 101. When there's a live wire – or person with electricity running through her – use a stick or broom handle or anything that's non-conductive to break the contact."

"Fast forward a bit. Can you tell what kind of vehicle they're driving?"

Silas sped through the next ten minutes but nothing showed. "He must have parked in the blind spot. My neighbor doesn't believe in security cameras or I'd ask to see his footage."

"So, does that mean we lock up the place, go shopping for some *condom-ments*," she said, adding a wink, "and maybe drop by the hotel to pick up some clothes for me?"

"How about just locking up and then go shopping? If we go back and find Oscar and Tori, they might want to hang out with us."

Julianna shook her head emphatically. "You're right. Let's hurry up and go so we can hurry up and get back to make up for lost time. As far as shopping goes, I don't know this part of the world, but you might want to see if there are any Big and Tall Women's clothing stores around. It's either that or I'm back to wearing men's sweats and tees."

"Gotcha," Silas said, opening a browser. Three clicks later, he'd found the store. "Ten minutes away. Whole Lotta Ladywear, coming up."

Chapter 7: The Card Game

"I don't have any experience shopping with women, but from the horror stories I've heard from men who were brave enough to go – or were blackmailed into going – shopping with the fairer sex was supposed to be miserable. This wasn't bad at all."

"First off, I think I'm not in any way the fairer sex," Julianna said, holding up her dark-skinned arm and smirking.

"I meant in a dainty way…"

She stood tall, shoulders back, her sly grin now wide.

Silas shook his head. "And you can handle yourself in a bare-knuckle boxing match better than any man I've ever seen. So, were all those men lying, or are you just that magnificent?"

"The latter. And you already know about the other stereotype I've been shattering my whole life."

"That is…"

"I can't cook. I can't even brew a cup of tea with a teabag and pot of boiling water much less a cup of coffee or espresso. I'm still waiting on my Mexican cocoa, by the way."

Silas pulled up to the gate, rolled the window down to punch in his security code, and stilled. "Oh, jeez…"

"What?" Julianna asked and leaned in front of him to look.

"Oh, jeez is right. Do you think they did it before or after she broke in the first time?" The panel looked like a bomb had been thrown at it, jagged tears through the metal shield, the plastic keypad melted into a Dali-surrealistic blob.

Silas put the car in park and got out to get a closer look. Although it was still the middle of winter, it was a sunny day and the driveway was clear. It hadn't snowed in two weeks, but he noticed the fresh breaks in the frozen hillocks along the fence line. The icecaps were too old and brittle to hold a footprint, but they had been stepped on. The tracks were on the side opposite of Victoria and her gigolo's earlier spaz dance.

"New tracks?" Julianna asked, now standing beside him, watching his narrow-eyed gaze.

"I doubt they were here last night. Looks like they came back."

"Or they never left," she said.

He looked at her, curious. "True. We never heard or saw a vehicle leave."

"Your neighbor who doesn't believe in security cameras, is he here, or does he leave for the winter?"

"Gone until spring. You're right – they might have holed up there. Maybe I should call you Sherlock."

"Nah. The name isn't big enough for both of us. I'm just picking up stuff you'd probably see if you could take your eyes off of what's really intriguing

418

you," she said, grinning and squeezing her breasts together.

"I hate to admit it, but that's very possible. Still, that's no excuse. It's our safety I have to consider."

"Do you know what she wants?"

Silas cleared his throat. "That, my dear, is the real mystery. Come on. Let's go inside. I'll call the cops and report a break-in next door, then make some cocoa. I'm not going to let her dictate my life."

"How are we going to get inside?"

Silas reached around the access panel to the other side of the brick and concrete pillar, moved his fingers about for a moment, then felt the notch and pushed hard. The gate swung open. "I try to always have a plan B."

"Good idea."

Once in the garage, Julianna grabbed the shopping bag and got out. "I'm going to put on some girly clothes while you make your phone calls," she said and dashed upstairs.

The little tingle that meant something was wrong raced up Silas's back. He shifted in his shirt, trying to rid himself of it, but he knew it was futile. That fifth sense was there to protect him. Once again, he felt that Julianna was hiding something. Part of him was glad they hadn't gotten closer. She had that same 'It's not you, it's me' aura that meant she was going to bolt soon. 'Let's enjoy each other while we can. I'm not worthy.'

"Damn it!" he said aloud, knowing she couldn't hear him. "You are worthy, woman! If you just wash away that stigma, you could enjoy life." He sighed. "And me," he added softly.

He took his phone out of his pocket and quickly dialed the police station, bypassing 9-1-1. "Hey, Sarge. This is Silas Priest. Well, just in case you didn't recognize my voice I thought I'd better identify myself. Hey, my neighbor John Rathmore is out of town for another couple of months but it appears someone's camping out over there. Yeah, I figured you'd want to check it out. Right. You, too. And give the missus a hug from me. Bye."

Silas stared at the phone. No need to tell anyone about the break-in at his place. He didn't want or need cops snooping around. If there were any clues here, he'd find them.

By the time Silas was done with the call, Julianna had changed clothes and was already in the kitchen, her head in the refrigerator. "Look what I found," she said, shaking the pint-sized container of half and half. "I'm still waiting on my cream…"

He walked over and kissed her gently. "Cocoa first?" he asked, taking it out of her hand and setting it on the counter.

"Or maybe *condom-ments*?" she asked, holding up the box of twelve condoms.

He gently nudged her hand down and kissed her more thoroughly. "I don't want to go too fast," he whispered.

"I don't care how fast you go the first time. I'm sure the second and third time you'll last longer."

Silas pulled out of the embrace and cleared his throat. "You insult me, woman. Only a dozen?"

"No, I bought three boxes of twelve. I figure they should last us for a day or two."

"Now you're flattering me," he said with a chuckle. He suddenly sobered. "But I was serious about my garden analogy. Clearing out our problems before jumping in and sowing seeds."

"Or deep plowing?" Julianna asked with a grin.

"Or deep plowing. I know it's going to be good. Even if we have a bit of awkwardness at first, we'll soon find perfection."

"At least sixty-nine forms of perfection," she joked.

"And if we run out of ideas, there's always the Kama Sutra. I'm sure I have a copy of it around here somewhere," Silas said, looking around the room as if searching. "But I want to know more about you and want you to know about me. What if you're a Democrat and I'm a Tea Party Republican? What then?"

"We won't discuss politics."

"What if I want children and you don't?" he asked, one eyebrow raised.

"Really? At your age? I mean, I know I'm young enough, but you? You're what, fifty-eight?"

"Good memory, woman. Don't worry about the number. Remember, I have a contact who has a little blue bottle of Fountain of Youth water. I might decide to ring him up and ask for a drop or two. You know, I could sire a child now, but I'd like to be around long enough to watch him or her grow into adulthood."

"How could you? I mean, with the way this world is going to hell..." Julianna saw his slight smile. "You did that on purpose, didn't you? You don't really want a child? Would you want to rejuvenate just to watch a child grow up in this mess?"

"We need to talk, Julianna. It doesn't have to be an interrogation. Let's make a game out of it. Loser has to answer a question. Honestly. No dancing around the truth or redirects, okay?"

Silas pulled open a drawer in the kitchen, rummaged through it, and found what he was looking for. "Remember these?" He took them out of the plastic bag and handed them to her.

"Oh, my God, Silas. Are these the same cards we played with at Woodstock?" She held them to her nose, sniffed, then wrinkled it.

"Yes, they are. That *eau de* marijuana and rain aroma stays as long as I keep them bagged up. I take a sniff every once in a while, just for the heck of it. I remind myself that I wasn't always a lonely old man. I had to bring them here because the guys accused me of snorting something illegal when I had them there."

"You keep them in the kitchen?"

"Nobody but me messes around in here. Can you imagine a thief ransacking pantry shelves for valuables? No, they'd look for a safe or would look in the desk. I believe in hide in plain sight."

"But those cards aren't valuable to anyone but you or me."

"Who says that's the only thing around here in plain sight?" he asked, watching for her reaction.

Fast blinking. Guilt. Or planning, conniving. *Crap! Start the honesty game. Now.*

"Isn't it too early or too late for cocoa?' he asked. "How about a wine cooler or mulled wine instead?" *Lower the resistance with alcohol…*

"How about a throwback to the sixties and seventies: sangria! I saw you have fresh oranges," she replied, eyes bright.

"Ah, a feast. How about a big bowl of crinkle-cut potato chips, French onion dip, and a pitcher of shortcut sangria: orange juice and Boone's Farm?"

"Now you're making me hungry."

"I won't shortcut on the sangria, and we'll have to use sliced cucumbers or baby carrots for the dip. I haven't had potato chips in years. I have to watch my figure, you know."

"Say, how come you have fresh food in the house? I thought you didn't live here?"

"I don't, but I do know how to text my personal shopper and have him bring over a few of the necessities for me while I'm out shopping with my lady friend."

"Well, 'him' must not have been Hal or he would have stocked you with another necessity."

Silas winked, kissed her on the cheek, and whispered, "Give me five minutes to slice, dice, and combine. In the meantime, take a look around the place. Pick a room to play cards in."

Julianna strolled through the house, her fingertips gliding across the polished surfaces. Nothing was dusty or out of place. It was ideal. She'd lived that life before, but this one didn't feel restricted. If she smudged a mirror or left a coat on a chair rather than hang it up, Silas wouldn't care. He'd never make her feel bad about a misspoken word or a few dollars spent on frivolities. She inhaled deeply. The scent of freedom. True, there was wealth here, too, but she'd rather be free of guilt or insecurities than have billions of dollars to share, spend, or burn.

"I have the sangria in the refrigerator chilling. We can drink a little now, but it is much better after letting the flavors blend for an hour or so." He handed her a wine glass with a slice of orange on the side, little triangles of various citrus and strawberries floating inside.

She took a cautious sip. "Ah, it's already the best I've ever had. Come on back to the kitchen. I think it's my favorite room so far. Except for 'the red room.' I'm pretty sure you don't want to go in there yet."

"Operative word there is yet. Let's see if we can cram forty years of life into a few hours of cards."

"It was only twenty for me, remember?" she asked.

"And that, dear women," he said, toasting her and clinking glasses, "is one of the more fascinating subjects I want to find out about."

Julianna smiled weakly, then realized it was a conditioned reflex. He wasn't a prying psychiatrist trying to figure out her psyche, or an angry husband who wanted to force her into his mold of the ideal woman. Silas really cared about her. *'Damn it!'*

Silas watched as a palette of emotions colored her face, ending with an ashen pallor at her silent lip-synched curse.

"Let's use the breakfast nook, then," he said, breaking her out of her last glazed-eyed mood. "The sun's still there. We can play cats and bask in the natural light."

He took her hand and led her to the bright yellow corner with a window seat. "You can't be sad when bathed in sunlight and buttercups, right?"

"And have a gentleman's gentleman at hand to see to my every need?"

"*Every* need," he stressed. "But in time. That's because I *truly* do care."

"So, what do you want to know?"

He handed her the cards. "Poker? Winner of each hand gets to ask a question."

She shuffled, then held them to her nose again, inhaling deeply. "They really do bring you back with the aroma, don't they? Okay. Five-card stud. Penny ante?" she asked, recalling the coin he had in his pocket.

"Sorry, not enough coins in this mostly cashless house. We'll have to do with toothpicks." He grabbed the little dispenser from the lazy susan and dumped out two piles. "No dollar value; these are just to make it fun."

"When you hear some of what I have to say, it's going to get very interesting, even without coins, cards, or toothpicks," she said. "Since I have the deck, I'll deal first."

"Yes, I was a gentleman's gentleman – a butler – for a few years. My employer was the former owner of this house. I, shall we say, saved his bacon and proved my worth as both a friend and an employee, and he gave me half interest in his estate, willing me the balance of everything on his death."

"So, you were partners?" Julianna asked.

"Yes, but that still isn't well known, so I'd appreciate it if you kept that confidential. Now, deal again. I have a few burning questions of my own."

Silas lost the next hand, too. "So, by partners, were you financial partners or lovers or both?"

"Really? I'll tell you what, let's say right now that we share any or all secrets *except* our sex lives."

"Why? Are you afraid you'll have a dirty little secret that will make me not want you? Because if that's the case, nothing you can say will change how I feel about you. It might get me a little turned on if you had a male lover, but I wouldn't think less of you."

Silas sighed and shook his head. "Right now, any sex partners we may have had or not had are not here to give their permission to share stories about intimacies. It just isn't right. Agreed?"

"Okay. Taboo subject."

"We were financial partners and friends. It wasn't well known because he did have a family. Giving away half a fortune to a butler who didn't have so much as a college degree would have had the dear man committed by his family. He would have lost it all, and they would have squandered it before a year was out."

"All this? They'd spend or lose all this in less than a year?"

Silas nodded. "Some people, right?" He reached for the cards. "Let me deal a few."

Julianna lost the next hand. "How did you do it?" he asked. "I mean, Tori alluded to having the right device for time travel. What do you need?"

"There are several ways to travel," she began then looked up.

Silas was scowling at her. "I can see an evasive answer brewing," he said. "I asked 'What do *you* need?"

"I needed a coin. A special one. Plus you have to be in the right place."

"Does it have to be at the right time, too, like in those *Lost* novels?"

"You've read them?" she asked, wide-eyed and sitting up straight.

Taken aback by her concern, Silas nodded. "Yes, I told you I read a lot. Are they true? I mean, real?"

"You wouldn't believe me if I told you, so I'd better just wait until I lose another hand. Can I try some of that mellowed sangria now? If you could, add an extra splash of wine."

Two more hands went by before Julianna lost again.

"You never answered, does it have to be at a special time?"

"To travel, no. You do have to focus on where you're going, though. Otherwise, you could wind up in the middle of a tree."

"A tree?"

"You go through trees, like between them," she said, her eyes half-closed. She poured more wine in her cup, sloshing a little over the edge with her unsteady hand. "The trees are the markers to magnetic portals. You know, like the Bermuda Triangle and The House of Mystery? There are lots of places like that all over the world – magnetic vortexes. Some folks are more sensitive to finding them, but anyone can go through the portals with the right coin and focus. *Poof!* That's the easy way to go."

She lifted her glass to him in toast, tears filling her eyes. "But if you get stuck in a wrong time, without a coin, you're screwed. Or you'll have to do unsavory things to live."

"Like marry someone for convenience?" Silas offered, his hand gentle on her arm.

"No sex stories, remember?" she said, a gleam of disgust in her eye.

"How about some of those veggies and dip?" Silas asked. "The flavors and the sour cream should have blended by now. I think your tummy is a bit too empty to handle that much wine."

"But you did that on purpose, right? Got me drunk so I'd tell you more. Take away my inhibitions?"

"You didn't win a hand of cards, but I'll answer. Yes. I wanted to know why you were so interested in that coin I pulled out of my pocket earlier. It's the right one, isn't it?" He took the ancient Greek drachma out of his pocket and set it on the table in front of her.

She didn't have to say a word. The glow on her face answered for her. "Yes, it is. Do you know how long I've looked for one of these?" she asked, holding the silver coin up to the daylight to peer through the holes.

"Oh, I'd say about twenty years. You disappeared from Woodstock on that Monday morning in 1969 and jumped to 1989, right? That's where you lost your twenty years."

"Uh-huh." She set the coin down and looked up at him, tears now rolling down her cheeks. "And now that I have one, or at least know where one is, I don't want to use it."

"Why?" Silas asked, his face devoid of emotion.

"Because I don't want to screw up again and leave you."

"Oh, shit, woman!" he said, scooping her up from the breakfast nook, holding her in his arms like a lost child he'd just found. "It would take a lot of work to get rid of me. I've been looking for you for forty years."

She suddenly pulled back from the embrace. "Say! Where did you get it? And I don't think we need to play cards for answers anymore. We're beyond that."

"Amen on that. Oh, and that guy Simon I told you about? That master time traveler with the yard-long title?"

"The fairy king?"

Silas chuckled. "Yeah, something like that. He gave me that in exchange for the bottle of Fountain of Youth water I found for him. I'm sort of serious about getting younger, though. I mean, I'm not infirm or anything. I think you saw last night that all my parts work just fine…"

"Like I said, finer than when you were seventeen!"

"Yeah, well, my desire is greater, too."

"Does that mean we can go upstairs and use at least one of those condoms?" Julianna asked.

"At least two or three," Silas said and kissed her again.

Chapter 8: Like Riding a Bike

"Phew! You may be an old man, but you wore me out."

"Please tell me we can eat before going for fourths," Silas said, panting and grinning at the same time.

Julianna took the robe from the back of the chair and threw it at him. "Hide that thing from me for a while. It's addicting!"

"There's another robe in the closet on the left side. Oh, and back at you about covering up." He looked down at his belly. "Again? You have to be kidding. No, I'm cutting you off from Jules for at least an hour."

She looked and saw his excitement returning. "Really?"

"No, not really," he said. "I mean, *it* thinks so, but I don't. Hurry up and put on some clothes. It's all your fault."

Julianna faced him, one hand in front of her crotch, the other across her breasts. "This side?" She turned around and ran her hands up her fanny, bending over slightly and giving him an encouraging smile.

"Both, either, any part of you!" Silas covered his eyes with one hand, his cock with the other. "Don't look, either of you."

"Your dick doesn't have eyes," she chuckled.

"You and I know that but it doesn't. Down boy. Don't give me a heart attack. I have a lot of time to make up for, but I don't have to do it all today. Or even this week."

Julianna slipped the robe on and wrapped it closed, then knelt on the bed and gave Silas a long kiss. "How could I ever think of leaving you? Even if it wasn't the best loving I've ever had, it's you, the man with the sense of humor and compassion that I…"

She took a deep breath, then changed positions and cuddled up beside him. "I almost said it again, didn't I?"

"Is that why you left before?" he asked gently.

"Yes, and no. I mean, when I almost said it before, I realized I was falling for you. I had a mission. I couldn't let others get in my way."

"Mission?" he asked.

Her stomach grumbled in reply.

"Wait! Hold that answer," he said. "We're not doing that low blood sugar thing again. Come on. Help this old man up."

She looked at the terrycloth tent on his belly.

"Not him. Me. He really does have a mind of his own." He picked up the robe covering his cock. "Sorry I've neglected you for so long, dude. She's here to stay. I hope. Either way, if you don't pace yourself, you might break off. And unlike a gecko tail, you won't grow back."

He looked over at Julianna. "I think he'll listen now." He patted himself, already softer. "I scared him."

"Don't worry. I'm sure he'll come out of it. Yes, let's have at least a light dinner. Then I'll tell you about the mission. I promise."

Silas's tummy grumbled in reply. "Ah, the other hungry beast awakens."

***

Julianna swiped the cucumber slice through the French onion dip. "Um. It's even better than with potato chips." She put it in her mouth and chewed.

"And better for us, too." He copied her gesture with a carrot stick. "Eh, what's up, Doc?" he joked, then crunched it comically.

"Are you always like this? Lighthearted, whimsical…you know?"

"With whom? I have to be inspired. True, the guys and I kid around a lot. That's one reason for our odd little family over there. No drama or grumbling allowed. I'd like to think that's how we'll be, too."

"As long as you don't bitch about my housekeeping, cooking, what books I read, or how I spend my money," Julianna said, her forehead wrinkled with memories. She picked up a carrot and ate it without dip, realizing he hadn't said anything. "You're not even going to comment about my known shortcomings?"

"Maybe I will if you bring up any. So far, you haven't mentioned drunken orgies with strangers, stealing me blind, arson, or serial murders. Cooking and cleaning can either be done by me or hired out, and what you read and spend your own money on isn't for me to dictate. You wouldn't do that to me, would you?"

"No… We're back to that Golden Rule, aren't we?"

"It never left, sweetheart," he said and put his hand on hers. "Now, don't fill up on veggies and dip because I have a light dessert. I was able to get fresh figs."

"Really? You are a wonder, aren't you?"

He shrugged then grinned. "They're *Mission* figs," he said dryly, one eyebrow raised.

"Oh, yeah. I was supposed to tell you about my mission after I had a bite to eat. Well, in a manner consistent with full disclosure, here goes. My elder sister ran away. I was trying to find her. Pretty simple, huh?"

"I take it she knows how to travel through time, too?"

"Yes, she does. It's a family tradition." She leaned forward, invigorated by his attention, glad there wasn't any skepticism in his voice. "Do you want to know more or go play?"

Silas wriggled in place, cleared his throat, and gave her a half-grin. "I think we ought to let our dinner settle. Hold on and I'll get those figs."

He brought out a china platter lined with golden-green fruit, ruby-red grapes, and slices of white cheese.

"Hey, you tricked me! Those aren't Missions or they'd be purple-black. Those are Kadotas. I may not know much, but I do know my figs."

"Yes, you're right, but you have to admit, it was a decent segue."

427

"True." Julianna leaned over the dish, inspecting the array. "We had both varieties at our place in North Carolina. It was years before we had enough to dry for winter. We kids would eat them as they ripened." She picked one off the platter, pulled off the stem, and bit into it. "Oh, man. The only way this could be better is if it was still sun-warmed." She sniffed it. "I miss the smell of green things growing. Some people think fig trees stink, but I don't. They remind me of stability, continuity, the sweetness of things to come."

"Maybe I should call you Shakespeare." He picked up one of the fruits, looked at it, then smelled it and copied her style of eating, pulling off the stem, biting into it like an apple. "You're right. Sweetness worthy of an Elizabethan ode."

She took another one and chose a slice of cheese. "Havarti?"

"My favorite."

"Mine, too! Oh, and I guess you want to know about the mission and the family tradition. Which first?"

"Your choice. I'm not going anywhere."

"Okay. So, my da was born in North Carolina of an American mother and a Scottish father." She paused and smirked devilishly. "In 1771."

"Really? I mean, go on. I'm intrigued."

"They came back to the twentieth century when he was about five or six. They moved to Scotland and that's where he picked up the accent. And attitude, but I digress. When he grew up, he decided he wanted to go back and see his grandparents."

"In the eighteenth century?" Silas asked.

"Yup. He made it with minor difficulties but wound up buying a slave."

Silas nodded, taking another fig and piece of cheese.

"He did it to spare her another flogging but fell in love with her."

"Your mother?"

"You got it, Sherlock. He couldn't marry her in eighteenth-century North Carolina, so brought her back here. They married, had lots of kids – biological, adopted, and foster – and lived happily ever after until my seventeen-year-old sister ran away with a psychotic Swede."

Silas coughed, nearly choking. "A minor? Gone? I bet they were horrified."

"You don't know the half of it. The world then is not what it is now. It's going to get crazy in about ten years. You're right to be a gardener. You might want to plow a few more acres or at least stockpile shelf-stable food, meds, and paper products. Oh, and cleaners and sanitizers. But I'm getting off topic again.

"Because there were so many kids involved, plus travel restrictions and the need to keep our farm going – and Da being held under a microscope by some government creepers – he couldn't go anywhere. I overheard him and Mom talking about it one night. He was going to risk it all, pretty much put the family farm and all he owned in jeopardy, and leave to find my sister. So, I took one for the team, so to speak. I left a note, told them to stay put, I'd find her, and that if they truly loved us, Da would let me do it. I sort of hinted I'd jumped forward in time and saw it all turned out okay if I left and he stayed."

"You lied."

"I assumed heavily. Or predicted with prejudice..."

Silas squinted at her and shook his head.

"Okay. I lied. I did it to save everyone and everything. Even if I never got her back, the rest of the family would be safe and not homeless. That wasn't too much of an assumption."

"But you never found her, did you?"

"Nope. Almost, though. Her name is Mali, like the country where our mother was born. You see, Mali and I were close. Very close. We'd bicker like any other sisters eighteen months apart, but we'd also finish each other's sentences, anticipate what we wanted to do next. Or where to go. She had a kind heart for hard-luck cases. I guess we both got that from our parents. At one point, there were fifteen kids in our family counting all the foster kids and strays.

"I knew she'd been researching the Valdez oil spill for her class report. We were homeschooled via distance learning – the internet – but still had projects to do. She was passionate about ecology. She used to fantasize that if someone could have been there and made sure that wreck didn't occur, all those birds and animals – the thousands of fish and seals – and the economy of the whole area would have been spared."

Silas offered her another fig and she accepted it, eating it eagerly. She swallowed and continued.

"We shared everything, including secrets. I knew she'd been hanging out after basketball practice at the community center with this tall, redheaded guy. I never saw him, but she said he reminded her of Da. That's why I knew he had red hair and was about six-foot-seven."

"Wow! Is that why you're so tall?"

"Mom was the same height as I am now: six-four. I don't think there was a chance any of us could have been short unless dwarfism showed up. So, Mali had a major crush on the guy. She said his name was Storm and he was a Viking descendent."

Julianna leaned close to the table and Silas followed. "He told her Erik the Red was his grandfather and he was a time traveler. He wanted her to be his consort."

Silas sputtered. "But how? I mean, I don't want to interrupt you, but why did your father believe you could go on a time travel rescue mission? Did you have a coin?"

"Nope, but he did. I took it. Actually, it was the only one. He and Mom

429

were able to share it. He couldn't follow me because I had the coin."

"Oh, crap. That poor man. He lost both his daughters and had no way to chase them down."

"Yeah, well, I didn't think about that until much later. That's a whole 'nother kind of guilt I have to deal with. And that's why I was so interested in your coin. I want to go back and tell him I'm sorry. I'm not sure when to go and make sure I catch him, though. Plus, now there's that other thing."

"What? What other thing?"

"You. I don't want to go anywhere without you. Mom and Da managed with one coin, but I don't want to take that chance. Do you think you could find another one?"

"Wow. I don't know how to get in touch with Simon. When he compensated me for my detective work with this, I thought he was being cheap. I didn't know what it was, but he said I'd find out when the time was right. Meanwhile, I should never let it out of my sight. 'Just consider it a good luck charm,' he said."

Silas handed her the coin. "I guess there are other ancient Greek drachmas in the world. I'm sure I can find one. Somewhere."

"With this as a pattern, you can drill holes the right size and in the right spot. I think that's been a problem in the past; holes in the wrong places." She handed it back to him. "Care for a little time traveling holiday, dear?"

"I'll grab my hat and sunblock whenever you say go, but I think I'd like to do a little research first. It might be there's a coin available at one of the antiquities shops. We can still travel wherever you'd like, though."

"How about whenever? I think I just figured out the date."

Chapter 9: Dropping In

"When?" Silas shook his head minimally, his lips pulled tight as he reflected on his one-word question. "I guess I mean that both ways. When do you want to leave and what time?"

"Well, there's no rush to leave. I want to go to the summer of 2015. It's a short hop forward – only five years. We don't have to worry about learning new idioms or slang, and we won't need new driver's licenses if we time it right."

"So you can mess with the year but not the day of the year or season, right?"

"Yup. Unless you're Simon. I guess he can slip in and out of any era. No one's figured a way to pop into different locations, though. You still have to be at the portal closest to your destination. No starting in Oregon and winding up in Orlando."

"So, where do you want to go?"

"Back to the old MacKay Manse in North Carolina. I know the date my folks bought the property and a little about what went on soon thereafter. I'm pretty sure they'll be there. And since that's where I was born and spent my first sixteen years, I could probably find the place blindfolded."

"Whoa, whoa, wait a second," Silas said, shifting in his chair. "You want to go to the future but to a time and place *before* you were born?"

She nodded and took another fig.

"But won't that scare the dickens out of your parents? I mean, will they even know who you are? Shoot! Would they even believe you if you told them?"

"Well, since both Mali and I look like paler versions of Mom, I'm pretty sure at least Da will believe me. Plus, Mom's only been through time once that I know of, but Da's popped back and forth a few times. He's more likely to accept me. They didn't talk about time travel much. It only came up once and we had to swear not to mention it to anyone outside the family. Still, they wanted us to know our heritage. That was the only way to explain Mom being born as a slave in 18th century Africa."

"Hush and keep it in the family? I don't blame them. They probably regret saying anything." Silas shook his head. "Do you realize your parents lost two daughters because they shared their history with you? If they had never said a word, you'd never have taken that coin. And Mali would never have believed there was such a thing as time travel and wouldn't have left with that slimy Swede."

"Actually, he's Norwegian," Julianna said sniffing, tears welling. "But psychotic Swede sounds better."

Silas looked up and saw her eyes getting red and realized he'd blown it. It was too late to take back his words, though. "I'm sorry. I should have kept my big mouth shut. I mean, I'm sure you came to the same conclusion a long time ago. It's just a lot for me to process and sometimes I think out loud." He reached over and held her hand. "I can't believe you've had to live with this for twenty years…and with someone who wouldn't believe you. I don't know how you survived."

"I had a son to bring up." She sighed and wiped her nose on her napkin. "I guess the more he needed me, the easier it was to ignore my past screw-ups. When he got older and had his own interests, I tried to find a way back home. I never mentioned time travel around Hugh, but he tracked my internet searches, and the books and articles I read. He knew what I was up to. I had confided in him right after we took on the responsibility of rearing Oscar together. I told him I thought Ciara – Oscar's birth mother – was a time traveler and that she either went 'sometime' else or she was kidnapped by the baby's father.

"Hugh ignored my first suggestion of what had happened to her and told me, 'Well, if she was kidnapped, she can be found.' I didn't pursue either option any further. The next day, he told me he hired a private detective to find her. Neither of us wanted to report it to the officials because we wanted to keep Oscar. I didn't think he'd harm Ciara if he found her. Offer her a million bucks to stay out of our lives, maybe, but he wouldn't hurt her."

"So, he knew but doubted you."

Julianna scoffed. "Being told and knowing are not the same thing. He trusted his detective to find any trace of her. Of course, all he had was her first name. Not even a photo. If she cut and dyed her hair, she could be anyone, especially after losing her baby belly. After two weeks of looking, he gave up. Or so he told me. It didn't make a difference. By then, neither of us wanted to find her."

"What about the baby's father? I mean, the man who got Ciara pregnant? Wouldn't he want the child if he knew about him?"

"Pbbt. No. Can we talk about something else?" She looked at the fig still in her hand and set it back on the plate. "Content with a full belly," she said with a wry smile. "Isn't it time for a nap?"

Silas took a deep breath and pushed the platter aside. "Do you always have such great ideas?"

"Hey, I'm bound to stumble on a good one now and then. I'd say race you to bed, but I don't have that much energy. Plus, I don't want to leave a mess here." She stood up and reached for his empty plate.

The two cleared the table together. "This much I can do," she joked, rinsing the glasses and setting them in the dishwasher as he finished putting the fruit and cheese away.

When they were done, they went upstairs to the red room, the mussed sheets and pillows blissfully reminding them how the bed got in such disarray. "The two spooned together on the big mattress, her belly to his bottom, a new sensation for Silas. A woman not only caring for him but protecting him, too. He could get used to it. He looked forward to it. A whole new volume of emotions had just been unsealed. And she was the perfect partner to share it with.

***

Silas awoke to the sound of Lionel Richie singing the refrain, 'You are my everything.' He reached over and no one was there. Startled, he threw back the covers, looked under the bed and in the closet, and even checked behind the curtains.

"Julianna? Julianna? Don't scare me like this…" He grabbed his robe and started to run to the kitchen, then realized how stupid he must look. He turned back, found his slippers, and made his way down the stairs as if he had all the time in the world. At least, he hoped he looked that way on the outside. His gut felt like he'd dined on broken glass and sulfuric acid. "Julianna?" he called again, forcing his voice to sound calm.

You told her to check out the other rooms in the house earlier. She probably couldn't sleep and now she's taking you up on the offer. Chill out, nervous Norman. Where would she go? Or how?

Silas checked everywhere, alternately calling out and whimsically singing 'Oh, where, oh where has my little girl gone,' making certain she would hear him one way or the other.

Twenty minutes of searching the house, plus a thorough inspection of the garage later, she still was missing.

'You are my everything…'

Silas was back in the bedroom changing into his street clothes when he heard it again. He hadn't been dreaming when he heard it the first time. On the bedstand was her cell phone. He picked it up and a picture of Julianna and Oscar making silly faces flashed, then disappeared. "Hello, hello?" he called into the phone. "Damn!"

He quickly hit call back and Oscar answered. "Mom? Where are you? Why…" Oscar stopped. "Who's this?"

"It's me, Silas Priest," he said. "You called and your mother didn't pick up, so I answered it."

"Duh! I called fifteen times, at least! What have you done to her, Silas? She always answers my calls on the first ring. Well, maybe two…"

"Um, she's not available right now. Would you like me to take a message?"

"No. I want to talk to her."

"As I said…"

"I know what you said and I don't trust you. Were you two having sex?"

"Wha…What? I mean, that's none of your business."

"That means you were. She hasn't had anyone *pay attention* to her in a long time. You did something to upset her, I know you did."

433

"I promise you, I did not."

"Then let me talk to her."

"Oscar, how can I make it any clearer, she is not available right now. Here, let me try again. Julianna!" he called out, holding the phone to his chest so he didn't blast the young man's eardrums. "It's Oscar and he wants to talk to you." He put the phone back to his ear. "See? She didn't reply. She's busy."

"No, she's not there. I can hear the fear in your voice. You did something to upset her. Were you two talking about that time travel nonsense? You may not know it, but that's what got her sent to the in-sanitarium. Twice. They messed her up with drugs. It took me months to get her out of there and off those psychotropic pills and herbs."

"Whoa. Wait. You got her out? Wasn't your father the one who put her in?"

"That's family business and you're not family." Oscar paused and snorted. "Yes, but he disappeared, I was the one they contacted when the automatic payments were canceled."

"So, your father is missing and now your mother is, too?"

"Aha! So, you don't know where she is, do you?"

"Actually, we were…um…resting when you called the first time. I awoke to music and she was gone. However, I didn't know the song was her ring tone. I thought I had been dreaming. I didn't hear your other calls because I was checking every room in this house plus the garage for her. Nothing. Zip."

"You must have a lot of rooms for it to take that long to look."

"Nineteen plus the garage."

"What? Couldn't afford twenty?" Oscar asked snidely.

"You can be rude, or if you'd like, you can help me look. I just realized I didn't check the guest house."

"Ring me in, then," Oscar said. "I'm at the front gate. By the way, it looks like someone was having target practice on this thing. I hope it still works."

"Target practice? Not a cherry bomb?"

"I'm no cop," Oscar said, "but these sure look like bullet holes to me."

"Hold on." Silas took his spare remote from the bedside table and pressed a button. "Is it opening?"

"It's trying… Nope."

"Okay. Back up. I'll see if I can get it to swing the other way."

Silas tried a different series of numbers, then heard, "You got it. Where do I go now?"

"I'll meet you out front," Silas said, the phone on speaker as he hurriedly dressed. He tucked his snowboots under his arm and rushed barefoot down the stairs.

He heard the thumping at the door as he leaned against it, slipping his feet into the boots. "Impatient kid!" he huffed, then took a calming breath. One excited male was one too many when looking for a missing person, especially a loved one.

The door swung open as soon as he unbolted it. "Grandpa!" Tori shouted, rushing into his unsuspecting arms. "Do you know how long I've been waiting for a grandparent? Either one, a grandma or a grandpa. Hey, are you going to marry Julianna? Because if you do, then Oscar will be my stepbrother. Ew. That'd be weird, huh, Oscar?"

"Grr! Tori, you promised you'd help look but not get in the way."

Tori pulled her dark knit cap over her short, flyaway blonde hair and huffed, pouting precociously, her eyes sparkling with mischief.

Silas reached out and pulled her inside, letting Oscar follow. "Let me grab my coat. And please, let me lead the way. There was a ruckus earlier. I want to take point in case there are any footprints or clues."

"A ruckus? Was my mom hurt? Why didn't you protect her? What kind of man are you?" Oscar's face turned red as he blurted out his questions, and it wasn't just the winter cold that caused it.

Tori opened her mouth, ready to tell him to chill out, but her boyfriend gave her the look. She brought her hand up and rubbed underneath her nose. She ignored her gut. She'd speak up when and if she saw something they didn't. Oscar wasn't the most observant person and she wasn't sure about her grandfather, but she saw and remembered everything. She'd wait.

Silas groaned and shook his head, knowing there was no calming the young man with words. The only solution was to find his mother. "This way," he said and took off toward the guest house.

"Is this place yours?" Oscar asked as they walked around the mansion. He gazed up at the second story and all the windows. "Nah, couldn't be. You're just the butler, right?"

"What difference does it make," Silas said, jaw clenched as he bent down to pick up a ponytail elastic. He brought it to his nose, sniffed, then held it away, frowning.

"Do you recognize the smell?" Tori asked. "Although by the face you made, I'd say you do."

"Here," he said, offering it to her.

She took a tentative whiff, then made the same sneer of disgust. "Ugh!"

"Let me," Oscar said, reaching for it.

Tori looked at Silas, smirking but staying silent.

"Ugh, is right! That is definitely *not* my mother's. Besides, she uses the fat ones. These skinny bands wouldn't hold her hair."

"That's Eau de Tigress," Silas said. "Some people find it appealing, others - meh. You're right, though. It isn't your mother's scent."

"Oh, God," Oscar said. "You've been sniffing my mother."

Tori whispered to him, "By his concern, I think they've been doing a lot

435

more than sniffing."

"Not now, Tori," Oscar grumbled.

"What? You'd rather some icky man have the hots for her? Someone who wouldn't care if she *poof*, just disappeared? Hey, at least he cares for her and he's helping find her, so cut him some slack, all right?"

"Hey, if it wasn't for him, she wouldn't be missing. She'd be safe and…"

"Hush!" Silas said, then held his arms out to make sure they stopped. "There's someone up ahead."

Tori and Oscar moved around Silas, trying for a better vantage spot.

As soon as he saw what it was, Oscar jumped in front of Tori and pulled her to his chest. He covered her eyes, not saying a word. He looked back at the entanglement, stunned at what he was shielding her from. He looked over at Silas and shook his head. "What the hell?' he mimed.

Silas stepped forward, saw the action, then turned around and herded the young couple into the bushes. He put his finger to his lips, admonishing them to be still.

"Ahh…ahh…oh…" a husky male voice groaned.

Silas and Oscar snickered as Tori huffed, frustrated that they knew what was going on and she didn't. She opened her mouth but caught the look from both men and pursed her lips in anger.

Rustling and footsteps came from the site of activity. "Now can we leave?" a woman hissed.

Silas peeked out then popped back into the bushes. "Victoria," he whispered to himself.

Oscar's eyebrow raised in confusion as Tori's eyes widened in surprise.

Groaning softly, Silas fixed his granddaughter with a glare, shaking his head. "Not now," he whispered. *Not ever, I hope.*

Two people slushed through the yard, stomping on crunchy patches of crystallized snow, heedless of being seen. Atlas and Victoria made their way to the fence. The three watched as the man pulled back an evergreen cedar, allowing the skinny woman clad in a form-fitting black catsuit access to the outside world through a break in the wall.

"So, is anyone going to tell me what they were doing?" Tori huffed.

Oscar looked at Silas, more than happy to cede that explanation to him.

As Silas was trying to figure out how to explain fellatio to his innocent heir, she popped off another question.

"And who was that man? He looked like a wrestler or bodybuilder or something."

Grinning at being given a pass at answering her first question, Silas quickly replied. "That's André the Giant, and no, as far as the research I've done, he was never a wrestler and was only a bodybuilder for his own…ahem…diversion. He's an actor in a specialty movie genre and the…ahem…boyfriend of your grandmother."

"That was her grandmother?" Oscar asked, his voice squeaking out the designation.

Silas rolled his eyes in embarrassment. "Need I say there was a lot of alcohol and other factors involved in the procreation process."

"I know big words, too," Tori said. "Does that mean she drugged you then got you drunk and that's how Grace was conceived?"

Now it was time for Oscar to do the eye roll. Silas noticed and explained. "You might want to get used to Tori being brighter than you think." He cleared his throat. "That is, if you plan on keeping her in your life."

"He doesn't have a choice," Tori said, grabbing Oscar's arm. "And was Victoria giving him a blew job?"

Oscar and Silas both coughed and laughed at the same time, each one clinging onto delayed recovery so the other would have to offer Tori the correction. Eventually, it was Silas who explained. "That's blow, not blew. And thank you for calling her by her given name and not her genetic designation."

"Well, that's out of courtesy to you but from what I hear, she's a real piece of work…and not a good kind, either."

"So, she decided to come back," Julianna said, startling the trio.

"Mom! You're here! You scared the pee-waddles out of me. Don't do that!" Oscar screeched, hugging her tight.

Silas stood back and held the shivering Tori – now deprived of her boyfriend's warmth – and waited for his turn to speak.

"Oscar, I told you where I'd be. I'm fine." She looked up at Silas and smiled. "We're fine."

Relieved, Silas grinned back, holding in his fear-infused scolding, very similar to Oscar's. "You were here?" he asked calmly.

"I couldn't find a pen or paper to leave you a note. I…um…get insomnia, even if I'm bone-tired, content, and with a full belly. I decided to take you up on a tour of the house. It's beautiful. I was on the balcony – wondering if I should get dressed and check out the guest house – when I saw Victoria had returned. It looked like she brought her pet ape with her, too.

"I went inside to let you know, but you were gone. I figured you might be looking for me…" She looked at Silas and caught his half-smile and shrug.

"So, I went after you. I was upstairs when Oscar and Tori came to the door. I um…had to change clothes and get some shoes, and then I followed you out here."

"Can we find someplace warmer?" Tori asked. "I mean, if we're going to investigate, that's fine. Let's do it. I'm freezing my eyelashes off just standing here, though."

"Let's see what *else* they were up to," Silas said with a soft grunt of disgust as he tried to dislodge the mental image.

437

Silas punched in the code and opened the door. "This is your guest house?" Oscar asked, looking at the expansive living and dining room combination. He nodded to the other side of the room. "And that's the fanciest kitchen I ever saw."

"You haven't seen the one in the main house," Julianna said.

Oscar snorted. "All you'd ever need is a big microwave, Mom."

"Or..." she said, threading her arm through Silas's, "a huge kitchen with a man who knows his way around it. Silas likes to cook."

"Me, too!" Tori popped in. She saw Oscar's scowl. "At least, I want to learn how."

"Stick around and we'll work on it," Silas said, arm out to welcome her to his other side.

"Are you taking all my women?" Oscar grumbled.

"She's my granddaughter and your mother is my girlfriend from many years ago. Are you wanting to deny either of them family or friendship? You know, the heart's capacity for love is limitless."

"Shakespeare," Julianna whispered, then giggled.

"No, it's not..." Tori said, then looked over and saw her smirk. "Oh, yeah. You're saying he puts words together well, huh?"

Julianna nodded then looked around the room. "Well, Silas, does it look like they got in?"

He pulled away from the women and checked the doors and windows for the short pieces of thread he left dangling. All were still in place except for the one that had fallen when he opened the back door to get in. "Let me check the bedrooms."

Oscar trailed behind him, Tori at his elbow. When they reached it, they all stopped and stared.

"They really tore this place up," Tori said. "And you better get a piece of plywood for that window or it's gonna freeze in here."

Julianna stood behind the shocked trio. "Oh, my," she gasped, observing the broken lamps, scattered bedding, and knifed pillows. Glass and down feathers covered the floor like ice and giant snowflakes "What were they looking for?" Oscar asked.

Silas shook his head back and forth, dazed. "Those stupid, stupid people. Did they really think I'd hide it in a pillow?"

"What is *it*?" Oscar asked.

"And why did they only look in one room?" Julianna added.

"And stop here? I mean, either they found it or they left without it," Tori said. "And if they didn't find it, why did they leave?"

Silas gave Tori a quick hug across the shoulders. "If I didn't know it already, I'd swear we were related. That's a great question. And the answer is, they found a decoy. However, I think they trashed the room and tore apart the pillows out of sheer orneriness. They broke the windows to get in but must have bypassed my alarms somehow."

Tori looked in the window track. "Bubblegum and tin foil," she said. "They messed with the electrical signal. Crude but clever."

"Just like them," Oscar said. "What now?"

"As Tori said, get some plywood and secure the room from the elements. And devise a new alarm system. They'll soon find out that videotape isn't the one they were after."

Chapter 10: The Insurance Policy

"What videotape were they after?" Julianna asked.

Silas cut his eyes over to Oscar and Tori, checking out the window frame. "Insurance," he said.

"What kind of insurance?" Tori asked, turning back to join them.

"Hey, we're all adults here," Oscar said, his arm now around Tori's shoulder. "You might as well let us know what we're getting into."

"Who said *we're* getting into anything?" Silas asked.

"You did. We're family now, right?" Oscar said, looking to his mother.

"So, you're all right with me dating Silas?"

"Yeah, well, he's going to be in my life one way or another with Tori. I might as well accept him. I might learn something. I saw he has a garden going fallow out there. He might be able to learn something from me, too."

"I wish there was a way I could do a mind meld or something so I could bypass any discussion, but since there isn't a way to do that…"

"Yet," Julianna whispered, then cleared her throat.

"Tori, that woman who was here earlier today made life miserable for Hal, my friend and your other grandfather."

"The man who brought up Grace, my biological mother. Right. Got it," Tori said, chin out. "I was told Victoria was a horrid person and don't ask about her, so I won't. No details necessary."

"Thank you. Hal had set a prenuptial agreement in place before he married her, so a divorce would have cost him everything. He was willing to do that, but we…ahem…found a way around it. You see, if she was unfaithful to him *while married*," Silas said. He stressed those two words to remind Julianna that he hadn't been intimate with Victoria when she was wed, whether he was drugged or sober, and to drop a hint to the other two that that's what had happened.

"If she was *caught* being unfaithful, he could divorce her and not owe a nickel of alimony, nor any share of their joint property. The prenup went both ways, but Hal wasn't – isn't – the cheating kind."

"So, you or someone else found her a boyfriend or caught her, right?" Tori asked. "Although if it had been me, I would have dangled a footlong carrot in front of her – set her up with cameras in place so I could film her when I was ready – rather than chase her all over town, trying to catch her in the act."

Oscar and Julianna looked at Tori with wide eyes, then at Silas, who had the same awed expression. He closed his mouth and swallowed. "Yes, one way is easier than the other, for sure. Anyhow, we – Hal and I – got the damning evidence, the divorce was rushed through, and the tape was to be held by me. It wasn't needed for the decree. Theirs was a no-contest dissolution so no embarrassment for her or loss of money for Hal. He shipped her off to Costa Rica with the admonition that if she came back, he'd share the video with the world. Her reputation would be ruined."

"But maybe now she wants the notoriety," Oscar said.

All eyes turned to him. "Hey, she'd be an instant celebrity, right? Vintage porn is the rage in some circles. Or so I've heard. But even if she didn't have a great backstory to go with it, she could put it out there to smear Grace and her granddaughters – you, Hal. Shoot, she could probably bring the American flag into the mix if she was clever enough."

"Talk about backfiring on you," Tori said, shaking her head. "Hey, could she just make another one and say it was the original?"

"Are you kidding?" Oscar asked. "There are so many amateur debunkers out there – no offense, Silas – who'd have it taken down in no time. If it was the real deal, though, it'd be as good as the Zapruder film."

"Huh?"

"The one that shows John Kennedy being assassinated, dear," Silas said, his hand on her shoulder. "Maybe they didn't talk about that in school."

"Yeah, huh. I would have remembered."

"I'd ask where the tape was, but I don't want to know," Julianna said. "Not that I'm curious, because I'm not. I just don't want to be asked and subconsciously glance at where it was or be tricked into telling."

"Or maybe someone could kidnap us," Tori said excitedly, "and demand the information or they'd kill us!"

"You've been watching too many movies," Julianna said.

"No, reading a lot of books," Tori replied, her rapid-fire supposition now slowed down to dejection. "But you're right. Sorry. Overactive imagination, I guess."

"No worries. The insurance is safe. Oscar, are you and Tori going to be all right? I mean, do you have a place to stay?" Silas asked, then suddenly paled. "Did your parents let you go with Oscar? By yourself? You'd better check in with them."

"Oh, they're cool," Tori said. "I guess they decided to do a little reminiscing while on the east coast. They haven't been here since I was born. Oscar promised to be respectful," she added with a giggle.

"You didn't hear what your dad told me," Oscar said, then gulped. "But you're right. I have an alert set on my watch to remind me to check in every evening."

Silas nodded, then frowned at the broken window. "Julianna, would you help me secure this? I have some hurricane season plywood we can use in the garage. I'd ask your son, but I think you have him bested in the height department."

Oscar stood next to her and stretched comically, tiptoeing in his boots and still four inches shy. "Yeah, she's every bit as strong as I am, too. Point us to the broom closet and Tori and I'll clean up the glass and feathers for you."

"Right over there," Silas said, nodding to the far side of the kitchen. "I don't know what I did to get such a great family, but I'm grateful."

"And if you need more help for anything, I have two sisters and their men to help. Plus a bonus mom and dad," Tori said.

"Sorry. It's just Mom and me," Oscar said with a shrug.

Silas clapped him on the shoulder. "And that's enough." He looked up at Julianna, smiling in pride at her son's acceptance of her boyfriend. "I take that back – that's plenty."

***

"I want to see it," André said. He grabbed for the videotape and caused Victoria to swerve on the road, barely missing a parked cop car.

"Not yet," she said, tucking it under her arm. She winced at the discomfort and handed it to him. "Just hold it. It's not like film. You can't hold it up to the light and see little images. We'll have to get a VHS player."

"But we don't have any money," André groused. "I could be making some big bucks on the beach as an escort if you hadn't talked me into coming to Boston in the winter."

"We're not in Boston…" Victoria said, biting off the word 'idiot.' "We're just a few miles from where the Pilgrims landed hundreds of years ago."

"Yeah, well, didn't they all freeze to death or something?"

Rather than agree with him, she said, "I didn't say we'd *buy* a tape player. There are other ways, you know."

André looked down at his crotch and rearranged himself. "I just hope it's a warm place. I don't like stripping in cold clubs."

"Not that!"

"Oh, I guess I could stand on the corner like the old days. I gotta watch it, though. Half the johns are gay."

"Not that, either," Victoria said, not even trying to hide her exasperation. "I told you, hooking is no longer allowed. I'm your one and only. Dancing doesn't count. You're not letting those old bitches do anything but stuff money down your G-string."

André swallowed hard and tried to keep his face stoic, but couldn't stop thinking of the sorority party where he'd been the featured attraction. He was fond of Victoria – and put up with a lot of her nonsense about becoming instant millionaires because of that – but having his whole body stroked and oiled by a dozen unwrinkled women in one night was enough to keep him happy for a month. And what those six perky coeds had done for him…

He shifted in his seat and set the videotape on his lap, trying to calm his excitement. He looked out the window and stared at the icy gray sidewalks, people in heavy coats hurrying to parked cabs or building entrances of glass and concrete. He looked down again, the tape settled back on his lap. Yes, living that kind of life was enough to wilt any man's dick. Better to stick with the old woman who'd do anything for him. Even if she was as wrinkled and sour as a hundred-year-old lemon.

"We're here. I'll go in and talk us into a room," Victoria said.

André looked in the lobby. "You'd better let me. He may be a guy, but I'll bet you dinner he's not into women."

"All right," she said. "Just make sure you let him know we want a room with a VHS player. We brought our own movies, got it?"

André patted the back of her head like an old dog's, then got out of the stolen Chrysler, tugging his pants to give himself the best presentation.

The clerk watched as the most gorgeous hunk of man meat he'd ever seen climbed out of the silver-toned sedan, rearranging man parts that seemed to belong to a horse. "Oh, my…" he crooned, squirming as his fantasies began.

"Don't forget," Victoria called out, stepping out of the car to make sure the hotel clerk knew André was checking in with a woman.

"Good day, sir," the clerk said, his eyes blinking with excitement. "Do you need a suite for you and your mother?"

André couldn't help but laugh. "Yes, and if you would, make sure it has a VSH player in it. I'll put in an old movie and hopefully, she'll be asleep in minutes. I…um…like to play by myself to my own kind of movies. That is unless there's someone around to stimulate me."

"VSH? Oh, VHS players. Yes, yes. We have a few in back. Just fill this out and I'll go grab one. Or two. Sometimes it's fun to have two different *shows* going at the same time while…um…playing around."

The clerk went through the curtain. Thuds and thunks of boxes and shelves being moved around drifted out. "Just give me a minute or two. I know they're in here somewhere," he hollered.

André walked around the counter, looked down, and saw the cashbox. Unlocked. He popped it open, grabbed the large bills and left the ones and coins, then closed it and came back around.

"I found them!" the clerk sang out, then set two dusty boxes on the counter. "What time does your mother go to sleep?" he whispered.

André pursed his lips and nodded. "I have to feed her first so she'll be good and drowsy. You'd better give me at least an hour. Knock three times and if I don't answer, give it another five minutes. Just in case. Oh," André reached in his pocket and took out five twenties. "I'd rather keep this off the books if you don't mind. If I'm a little short, maybe we can make up the difference some other way."

The clerk glanced down at the bulge in André's pants. "Oh, this will be fine," he said, tucking it in his front pocket without counting it. "I'm sure you're not…ahem, short."

André kissed the tip of his index finger then placed it on the clerk's nose and winked at him. Mesmerized, the clerk handed him the room key. André accepted it and picked up the two boxes, letting his new friend open the door for him. "Later," he whispered.

"Um..." the man whimpered like a sad puppy, then walked back to the desk, sighing.

André opened the car door and set the tape players on the back seat. He looked at the number on the key and nodded to the end of the complex. "I got us a suite where we won't be disturbed. Oh, and two VSH players just in case one isn't working right. They look new. Maybe we can make a few bucks selling them."

"I'm not a fence," Victoria said. "And that's VHS and that technology is so old, I'm surprised the players are even around."

When they pulled in front of the room, Victoria took the key from his overloaded hands and opened the room. "Pee-ew! This place smells of stale cigarettes, stinky feet, and B.O."

"Yeah, well, what did you expect?" André asked, setting their backpacks and the boxes on the bed. "It's not this easy to sneak into the Ritz."

"Ritz, Schmitz. Once we get this uploaded and advertised, we'll be rolling in it! That battering ram of yours and my squeals are sure to be the next rage of pay-for-porn."

"Only because of the story behind it, right? I mean, you and I could make a new one but it's not the same, huh?"

"Well, we did make this almost twenty years ago. I've aged a little bit..." Victoria saw André roll his eyes and changed her wording. "We've *both* aged a little bit. You're softer in the middle...but not where it counts."

"And you've lost a few pounds but you know what they say..."

Victoria giggled like a schoolgirl at a tickle-fest. "The closer the bone, the sweeter the meat. Oh, you big lunk. You are such a romantic!" She unzipped her jacket and threw it on the back of the chair. "Let me take a quick shower while you set up the player. I'll be right out."

André opened the box and took out the packing material and black and silver-toned machine. He turned it over, then heard a soft knock at the door just as the shower turned on.

Knock, knock, knock.

He set the box down and opened the door a crack. "She's in the shower. You're early."

"I know, but I thought you might need these cords. Just match the colors on the ends to the TV and tape player, then turn the TV to channel three. If you can't figure it out, we can wait until she's asleep..."

"André, would you bring me my conditioner, sweetheart."

"Sweetheart?" the clerk asked.

"Mothers," André huffed, then laughed. "Yeah, I'll ring you up as soon as the coast is clear." He repeated his coy fingertip kiss on the eager man's nose, then shut the door.

"Oh, yeah – conditioner." André dumped the contents of Victoria's backpack onto the bed and found the little purple bottle of thickening hair cream. He glanced at the label. 'For thinning hair or baldness.' "Maybe she'll share," he said, running one hand through his sparse locks.

"Was there someone at the door?" she asked when he handed it to her.

"Yeah, the manager or whatever he is brought me the cords to hook everything up. I'll see if I can get it going." He looked down at her body. Bonier than he remembered. Then up at her face. More wrinkled and spotted than ever without makeup.

"You like?" she asked seductively, her tongue covering the gap where her partial plate – now in a cup on the sink – would be.

"Oh, yeah," he said, his hand rubbing across his mouth to hide his lie. *That clerk just might be the diversion I need tonight. Give her a few snorts of wine and she'll be out until dawn.*

* * *

Fifteen minutes later, Victoria was still working on her 'quick' shower. André had all the cords routed and plugged into the holes on the TV and was studying the trash news magazine he had heisted from the convenience market earlier in the day. "Those can't be real," he said.

"What can't be?" Victoria asked, stepping out of the bathroom, fully painted with make-up, false tooth in place, hair styled, but only a hand towel held over her middle for clothing.

"Her boobs," he said, then looked up. "Wow! You look good, woman," he added, almost believing himself. She did look a whole hell of a lot better than she had in the shower. At least she had teeth and her hair didn't look like wet seaweed heaped on top of an ancient pier piling.

"Are you ready for a blast to the past? I know I was there when we made it, but I've never been the star of my own porn video. Would you like a little warmup or should we go straight to the main event?"

"There's nothing little about this warmup," André said, cupping his genitals. "But let's go check out the wayback machine. I've been in plenty of pornos, but never one with you. Plus, I've seen my classics so many times, they're boring. I'd like some new excitement."

"Oh, I like that. Maybe we'll see something we haven't done in a lo-ong time," she said, stroking him familiarly. "Let's get it on."

Already reclined and with his boots off, André unbuttoned his pants and started shoving them down his hips.

"I meant the movie. I mean, turn on the TV and tape player first. I want to make sure everything is working right "

"Well, we already know this is in fine shape…"

"André, please, just for once. Everything in this world isn't about your

445

cock. Yes, it's big and beautiful but…" Victoria stopped. She'd lost him once before when she tried to stop him from being so self-centered, and it had taken her years to get him back. Imperfect or no, she needed him. "I'm sorry. Go ahead and get undressed. I'm sure you have it set up right already. I have the tape right here."

"She's just a bit out of sorts, Buddy," he said to his dick. "She said she was sorry, so don't hold it against her. Well, hold it against her maybe later, but for now, let's go back in time twenty years before either one of us had even one gray hair."

Victoria stifled a groan. He was talking to 'Buddy' again, having a conversation with his dick. Maybe he really was crazy. But whether he was or wasn't, he was manageable. She slid the VCR out and looked at the cords in the back. "He must be colorblind," she mumbled and plugged in the wires correctly. "Here we go."

She turned the TV and VCR on, stuck in the tape marked 'V and the Giant,' and slid next to André on the bed.

Black and gray crinkles came on the screen, then horizontal lines settled into a test pattern. "Is everybody ready?" a voice called out.

"Huh?" André asked.

"It's Dick and Dandy Doodle Time!"

"What the hell?" Victoria screeched.

Knock, knock, knock!

"Not now," André yelled at the door, then grabbed the remote from Victoria.

He fasted forwarded through grainy black and white images of marionette puppets and actors in gaudy costumes. He stopped and watched. "Who are you going to make happy with that big club?" the woman in Marie Antoinette garb asked the pasty-faced clown holding an oversized baseball bat. "It's not the size but how well you swing it that counts," she taunted.

Victoria reached for the remote but André pulled it close, knees on elbows as he bent forward to watch the underground parody of a kid's show from the fifties. "Was she talking about the guy's dick?" he asked.

She tossed her small towel at his head, hopped out of bed, and ejected the cassette. Grumbling in frustration, she held the tape up toward the lamp and looked at it.

"You can't see anything that way," André told her, repeating her earlier warning. "It's not like it's on real film or anything."

"Ergh!" She set it down and grabbed her backpack, pulling out her twice-worn but least filthy black jumpsuit. "I don't know which one I'll castrate, but I'll get either Hal or Silas." She paused, snorting in barely controlled rage. "Hell, I'll get them both. And I'll throw in Doc for free."

"Who's Doc? Oh, he's that other roommate, huh. Hey, are they gay?"

446

"What? No. Hell, who cares? I've spent every dollar I could steal on getting here just to get this tape, and then some idiot goes and switches it out on me!"

"Hey, Victoria. Sweetie. Isn't whoever did that like a genius or something? I mean, not to sound rude or nothing, but if the trick hadn't been on us, it would have been pretty funny. Hey, can I watch the rest of that show? I mean, we can't go anywhere or do anything anyhow. I mean, unless you want to get kinky. I think I know someone who might be interested in a three-way."

"What? Who? And how did you hook up with someone so fast? I've been with you twenty-four-seven for six weeks now. No, never mind. And no, I don't want to hook up with anyone right now. I'm too pissed to see straight. I need a drink. Damn! We don't have any money."

"If you leave me the remote, I'll give you some money so you can go out. Unless you need me to drive."

Victoria looked at André, his eyes cutting back to the TV as if by staring at it, the show would return. "Trade ya," she said, overthrowing the remote to the door. "Now, where's my drinking money."

André fumbled in his jeans pocket, pushing down a few bills so he wasn't giving her everything he had taken from the till. "Here. And take one of those menus with you. It has the hotel's name and address on it. If you're too drunk to drive back, at least you know where to tell the taxi to bring you." He looked at the TV. "You know what I'll be doing."

She took the money and was ready to put it in her pocket when she realized she was still naked. She picked up her outfit, sniffed it, and made a face. She took the bar of soap from the sink and rubbed it under the armpits, then put on her refreshened catsuit. Finally ready, she stepped into her boots, reached across André for the keys, and gave him a quick dispassionate kiss goodbye. "Don't laugh so hard you give yourself a hernia."

"Oh, I won't. Maybe after a wine cooler or two, you'll figure out where they could have hidden the real tape. And don't forget your coat," he said, handing it to her from the back of the chair.

"Thanks. Sometimes I don't know what I'd do without you."

And then she was gone, engine revving and tires squealing as she sped out of the parking lot, a loud long blast on someone's horn indicating she hadn't looked before pulling into traffic.

Knock, knock, knock.

"Come in. Oh, wait…" André said, still naked.

Click. "Don't worry. I brought my key," the clerk said, his hair slicked back and smile bright.

"Before you lie down," André said, offering him the cassette, "bring me that remote. You gotta see this movie."

"Okay, but just so you know, I can do two things at once."

447

André grinned broadly and patted the bed beside him. "Go for it."

Chapter 11: Clumsy

"When Tori gets back, you two finish up here," Julianna said, pulling off the work gloves Silas had offered her. "And don't forget to vacuum after you've swept twice..."

"And use the mop with the disposable cloths so there won't be any shards or tiny bits left behind," Oscar recited dispassionately. "I know, Mom. This isn't the first broken glass mess I've cleaned up."

"Well," she answered with a grin, "it's probably the first one you didn't create, though."

"Okay, that's it. I'm not protecting him anymore." Oscar set the broom against the wall and put his hands on his hips. "You know all those 'clumsy' messes I made? It wasn't me. Or at least, they weren't my fault. Dad may have been a great guy in many ways, but he had some major faults and one of them was his temper when it came to perfection. If I couldn't get a chess combination memorized or learn to throw a curve ball right away, he'd push me around. He wouldn't out and out slug me, but he'd shove me up against a wall or cabinet or door or whatever else was near. 'Oops!' he'd say. 'You sure are clumsy, kid.' Frankly, when he disappeared, I was glad."

"Wha...what?" Julianna gasped. "He struck you?"

"Yeah, well if by *struck me* you mean used the force of his body against mine, causing me to lose my balance, then yes, he struck me."

"Oh, Oscar... I had no idea! I mean, I knew he brow-beat the hell out of me, but I had no idea he'd harmed you. I'm so, so sorry. How can I ever make it up to you?"

"Mom, you don't have to make anything up to me. I realize now he's the reason you were in that nuthouse, strung out on that psycho-bullshit drug therapy. I mean, whether or not I agree with your belief in that time travel nonsense..."

Julianna interrupted, "And every time you call it nonsense, you're reinforcing your disbelief in it. Sorry, go on."

Oscar rolled his eyes. "Yeah, I'm sorry, too. The point is, he was manipulative. I can't tell you how many times I wanted to run away. I couldn't though. I had to protect you."

"Protect me?" Julianna gasped.

"Mom, did you ever notice how sometimes your research books would go missing, or your hard drive would suddenly crash? That was me. Didn't you think it was a bit odd, especially since it was always when you believed you were really onto something?"

"Yes, but I thought Hugh was the one sabotaging me. I figured he would do anything to stop me from finding a way..." Julianna took a deep breath and decided not to hide the truth from him any longer. "He wanted to stop me from finding a way home or to my sister…whenever she was."

She paused, reflecting on what he had just said. "Wait. How would you know when I was 'really onto something'?"

Oscar chuckled. "You'd glow. Not like a light bulb, but you were radiantly happy. He saw it, too. He'd start snooping into your reading material. I caught him once." He held up his left arm. "That's when I had my 'clumsy fall' and broke my arm."

Julianna's jaw clenched and her eyes widened in rage. "If he wasn't already dead, I'd kill him!"

"Yeah, well, that might not be the case, right? I mean, that suspicious note was all they had to declare him legally dead. A hastily written suicide note left before he took off to parts unknown. No body or data trail found. *Poof!* Just gone."

Julianna wobbled and put her hand on the counter to steady herself.

Oscar took a fresh cloth and wiped it across a bar stool. "Mom, come sit down a minute. It's 'fess up time on something else, too."

"I'm not sure if I'm proud you're telling me this or pissed that you took so long."

He shrugged off the comment. "It doesn't make a difference. No matter what you say, we can't change the past. Or at least, we can't change what we've already done."

"Now that I'll agree with, the operative words being 'we've done.' Go on."

"I left that note. Or rather, those notes. I planted lots of them over the last two years. I hoped he wouldn't find any of them, but I took a chance. I figured I'd deal with his wrath if he discovered it was me who had written them. Besides, I knew I was going to Oregon and figured I'd be out of striking range if he did find one. The only person he could hurt would be you. I knew you'd kick his butt if he laid a hand on you, so I wasn't worried there."

"Yeah, well, there are other ways of hurting a big person without using fists. So, he vanished on his own, or did you help him along there?"

"I had nothing to do with that part. I kind of hope he got himself a mean girlfriend in Timbuktu who won't let him communicate with the outside world. I don't wish him dead, but there's an uncomfortable portion of my brain that worries I have some superpowers and 'wished' him gone. You know, sent into an unknown portion of the universe."

"Purgatory?"

"Yeah, that's what it'd be. I just want him away and out of our lives. Is that wrong?"

"Nope," Julianna said tersely. "Me, too. So, you wrote that note…"

"Notes," Oscar interjected.

"Notes, so if he did disappear, at least one would be found. Then the police would think he committed suicide even if they couldn't find the body?"

"Yup. And when the cops called and said he was gone and you were *indisposed*," he grinned and shook his head at the word then proceeded, "I rushed back to the house, destroyed all the notes they hadn't found, then came and rescued my damsel in distress."

"I'm your mother and too old to be a damsel, but I was definitely in distress at that institution."

"So, you said you were wandering around the property earlier today? Still dealing with the insomnia the meds caused?"

"It was just the house but unfortunately, yes. However – and this is very important for you to believe – I am very happy with Silas. He was my true love when we were teenagers and we're picking up where we left off. Of course, it's a lot easier since we don't have to worry about college or money or …ahem… missions."

"I'll ignore the last part for now, Mom. Yes, he seems like a decent guy. I asked around about him and tried a little online research. Everyone who knows him, likes him. The last part came up nil, though, which means he's either a cyber genius who can manipulate data, or he's never done anything wrong. I mean, no matter how good a person is, if he's screwed up, there's going to be a record of it somewhere."

Julianna smiled nervously, not wanting to bring up that Hugh's public record probably portrayed him as a saint. An ideal man on paper wasn't necessarily one in practice.

The door burst open and Tori popped in, stomping her boots. "It's starting to snow again. Hey, do you want to build a snowman?"

"Let's finish up here first," Oscar said. "Maybe by then, there'll be enough to build a big one."

"Yeah, huh? There probably isn't enough for my Barbie doll. Well, when I get one."

Julianna smiled at her boisterous innocence then realized it would probably never leave. Silas had that same ability to find the good in any situation, and he'd lived forty years more than she had. "Didn't you ever have a Barbie doll?"

"Nope. I had stuffed animals and rag dolls that my mother made me. Except for a few weeks when I was in kindergarten, my parents homeschooled me. We lived off the grid. Well, sort of. We had electricity, but my life was pretty much just the three of us and books. No television or movies. They said there was too much garbage in the world. Still, I probably found out more about life than they wanted me to. Like about Barbie dolls."

"Gee, even my folks got me *action figures*," Oscar said. "My dad wouldn't call them dolls, but Mom wanted to stimulate my imagination."

"Yeah, well when I get a job and have my own money," Tori said, "I'm going to buy at least one. Or maybe three, so they can be sisters."

"Having sisters is good," Julianna said, giving Oscar a sidelong glance, reminding him they needed to continue their conversation.

"We'll talk more later," he told her softly then turned his attention back to Tori. "We can go shopping after we clean up this mess. That'll give it time for the snow to accumulate. Plus, we're going to be hanging out together for a few days. Using our imagination with *action figures* sounds like fun."

Tori giggled into her hand. "I know something else that sounds like fun," she said, blushing as she looked at Oscar with dreamy eyes.

"Granddaughter…" Silas said in a mock stern voice.

"Jeez! I didn't hear you come in," she squeaked.

"Yes, and you remember that. Just when you two think you're alone, getting ready to do something you shouldn't, be aware. I'm quiet and I'm sneaky." Silas looked at Oscar. "And I was a young man once, too."

"Yes…yes, sir," Oscar said, then caught Silas's wink and relaxed. Sort of.

"I'm taking your mother back to the house. We'll fix a big breakfast for us."

"And by 'we,' he means he'll cook and I'll hand him stuff," Julianna said, grinning at Oscar.

"That's a relief because I'm hungry and I'd like some real food."

* * *

"Damned cops," Victoria hissed at the patrol car parked in front of the house she and André had crashed in the day before. "So much for having a warm place for me to stay."

She came out from the bushes and looked up, pulling her jacket tight against the fresh onslaught of snow. "I'll be damned if I'll go back to that hotel until I have the real tape in hand. André will probably sleep all day anyhow."

She watched as a second cruiser pulled up to the first. She couldn't hear them, but suddenly the lights on both vehicles shone bright, rotating patriotic colors as they sped away. "Well, that's fortunate."

Threading her way back through the bushes, she retrieved the poorly hidden house key from the planter of plastic mums and let herself in. After cranking up the stove to warm up the kitchen, she rummaged through the pantry, coming out with a snack pack of tuna and crackers. She devoured the pungent feast, then realized it was the first solid food she'd had in almost a week. Wine coolers and bar mix didn't count.

Warmed and sated, she headed back outside to her portal through the properties. She sneaked through the gap and kept close to the bushes – and away from the fence. "What in the hell is he doing, having a party?" she asked. "And who are they? No, that can't be Grace…"

She watched as a woman with blonde flyaway hair tucked into a dark knit cap playfully threw a hastily formed snowball at a young man who couldn't be much more than twenty. The two tossed a few more, then gave up when he shouted out, "Let's do this later. There'll be a lot more snow after we get back

452

from shopping."

"That can't be Grace. She's too young." Victoria realized she was talking to herself and stopped. Then she saw Silas and her jaw clenched.

"Come on, Tori," he said to the young blonde. "You don't want to get cold and wet now."

"Yeah!" the young dark-haired man with the Gregory Peck-deep voice hollered. "Save that for when we have enough snow to make it worth my while. I'll give you a pummeling you'll never forget."

And then the dark giantess came over, her hand settling on the young man's shoulder. "Now, Oscar, you be nice. You don't want to scare her away, do you?"

"No, Mom, I wasn't going to." He laughed then bent down, grabbed a fistful of snow, and made a hasty ball. "I was just going to terrorize her a little."

He threw the ball and the girl ducked, racing to the house as the group followed her to what looked like a family date.

"That has to be Grace's daughter, the one who just got married. No…Silas called her Tori. The invitation said the girl who got married was Vickie." A snarly grin split Victoria's craggy face. "Ah, Grace had twins…"

***

Julianna set the table while Silas prepared a huge breakfast casserole, stretching the meager amount of eggs, half-and-half, and ham with some of the vegetables he was going to use for dinner. "Looks like I'll have to do a little shopping," he said.

"*We* can do that," she said, looking up to give him a wink. "And speaking of we, do you have that itchy, crawly feeling like you're being watched?"

"Yes, I do. I was hoping it wasn't just suddenly having kids in the house after being alone with you and being…so…"

"So uninhibited?" she asked.

"That's a good way to put it. Why? I'm sorry. You wouldn't have brought it up if you felt uncomfortable. For what it's worth, I did send a text to my friend at the precinct. No one was at the neighbor's, but there were signs it had been recently occupied. They said they'd keep an eye on it. Does that make you feel better?"

He came to her side and gave her a peck on the cheek as she leaned over to set out the silverware.

She stood up, pulled him close, and gave him a lingering kiss, ending with a sigh.

"Ew, Mom," Oscar said.

"Ew, Grandpa," Tori followed, adding a giggle behind her hand.

"Yeah, how would you like it if you caught me kissing?" Oscar asked.

"No problem," Julianna answered. "As long as it was someone you cared for."

"Like me," Tori popped in.

"And it was *only* kissing," Silas said.

"Yeah, well, that goes right back at ya, *Grandpa,*" Oscar said, his sarcasm heavy.

"We're adults," Julianna said.

"And so are we," Oscar answered, shoulders back.

"Well, as far as that goes," Silas said, "your mother and I are at least double, if not triple, adults. But don't worry. We'll be discreet. By the way, where are you two staying?"

"Oh, that's kind of complicated. I moved us out of the hotel, packed up everything, and put it in the car. Tori's folks said we could take a sightseeing tour if we wanted, too. They just wanted us to call in every night."

"Yeah," Tori added. "I don't know what got into them, but I'm not complaining. I guess they trust Oscar a *lot.*"

Julianna and Silas looked at each other. No words were spoken, but he nodded in silent assent. "You two can stay in the guest house," he said. "No reason to run up a hotel bill."

"Plus, you can keep an eye on us, right?" Tori asked, giggling.

"Duh," Oscar mumbled.

"And you won't have to eat restaurant food," Julianna said, sniffing the savory aroma of the breakfast baking in the oven.

Oscar inhaled and grinned. "Well, what do you think, Tori?"

"I'm all for it."

"Brunch won't be ready for another half hour, so you can unpack now if you'd like," Silas said, handing Oscar the key.

"You know, it would be pretty hard *not* to like you," Oscar said, taking the key with his left hand, reaching out to shake Silas's with his right.

"Thanks. Back at ya."

Julianna put her arm around Silas as they watched the young couple chase each other out the door, boisterous with teenage enthusiasm. "Yes, it's not hard to imagine us at that same age."

"So, while they're gone, I have a few questions. After we get the second coin, what then?"

"We can't go anywhere for a few months. It has to be the time of year my folks got their property. I know where the time portal near Woodstock is, but we'll have to drive from New York to North Carolina afterward."

"But we're leaving from 2010 to 2015. How are we going to get around? Do we pack a bunch of cash and buy a car? Or rent one? Or rely on public transportation?"

"Shoot, I just showed up. I forgot what a pain that was. Of course, being young and in the sixties and eighties, I didn't have too much trouble. I just held out my thumb."

"Weren't you afraid someone was going to attack you?"

Julianna snorted. "Me? As big as I am? Nope. I could give the 'I got separated from the rest of the basketball team' story and even claimed to be a New York model once, but no one ever tried to assault me."

She saw Silas raise an eyebrow and grin. "If you think I'm good looking, you should see my mother."

"I could easily believe you were a model," Silas said, his smile now wide and mischievous. "Do you want to come upstairs and pose for me?"

She looked around. "The kids might pop in," she whispered.

"We'll lock the door." Silas followed her gaze. "Not the back door, the bedroom door. Even better, how about the shower?"

"Only if we don't turn on the water. It takes a long time for this much hair to dry. Race you up there?"

"I'll hurry, but remember, you still have twenty years on me," Silas said, then winked and pushed his chair aside, scrambling toward the staircase.

"Cheater," she hollered and followed after him.

***

"I was sure it would be ready by now," Silas said as he put his sweatpants back on, "but I didn't hear the timer."

Knock, knock, knock.

Julianna looked to make sure Silas was finished dressing, then opened the door.

"Breakfast is served," Tori said, her eyes dancing with a smirk. "I saw it counting down to zero, so I shut it off and got the pan out of the oven. And I didn't even burn myself."

"Where's Oscar?" Julianna asked.

"Oh, he didn't think I could handle it and tried to help me."

"And he got burned?" Silas asked.

"Yup. One of these days, he's gonna learn he has to trust me."

Julianna leaned down and whispered, "Sometimes you have to let them help. A man needs to be needed."

"Oh," Tori said softly.

"We all need to be needed," Silas told her. "It doesn't make a difference if you're a man or a woman, young or old."

"And that's what being an adult times two or three means – picking up on life's lessons through experience," Julianna said. "Stick around. You might learn something."

Tori looked behind Julianna and saw Silas looking for his other shoe. "Does he believe you? I mean, about time travel?" she whispered.

Julianna nodded. "Very much so. We're going to take off, but it won't be for a few months. I'd really like it if you knew what was going on. I mean, I'm pretty sure you and Oscar will still be together. I don't think he could handle me

455

just disappearing. That's what happened to his father, too."

"Was he a time traveler, too?" Tori asked.

Rather than reply that Oscar's biological father truly had been one, Julianna danced around the truth. "Hugh was Oscar's stepfather. We don't know what happened to him but according to the police report, he committed suicide. They found a note, but his body was never found. Please, don't ever bring it up to Oscar, though. He's very sensitive about it."

"Yeah," Tori answered, then whispered, "suicide sucks."

"Found it," Silas said, holding up his lost slipper. "Sometimes I think those darned things can walk on their own."

The trio joined Oscar at the breakfast nook, his hand wrapped in a damp paper towel. "No, I'm not *clumsy*," he said, looking at Silas with a scowl.

"I didn't say anything, but if I did, I'd say it was kind of you to help Tori." He opened the refrigerator and brought out a bowl. "How about some fresh salsa? I chopped up some tomatoes, onions, and peppers when I was prepping the casserole. The flavors should be blended by now."

Julianna took the container from him and set it on the lazy susan in the middle of the table. "Ah, home-cooked beats take-out anytime."

"No, it all depends on the chef," Oscar said, nodding to Silas with a half-smile of apology. "I tasted it. It's delicious. Sorry I've been such a sourpuss."

"We may not be related by DNA, but we both have the same low blood sugar issue," Julianna said, then set a big slice of casserole on her plate. "I don't know why I'm so hungry..." she began, then stopped.

"Yeah, waiting for breakfast to cook burned up a lot of calories, huh?" Oscar said, looking at her with a big grin.

Silas bent his head and blushed, rearranging the napkin on his lap.

"It's okay if you're tired and need a nap," Tori said. "We'll wash dishes for you."

"Nah, we got this," Silas said. "You two better hustle and get your shopping done after we eat. The main part of the storm is supposed to hit this afternoon. This little fluff coming down is just a warning."

***

"Damned snowflakes. Whoever said they were romantic?" Victoria bent over at the waist and shook them out of her sparse hair, then pulled the jacket's hood over her head. "And when are they going to leave? I have to get that tape. This is taking a lot longer than I thought. If I don't get some income generated soon, André is going back to making money with his super salami some other way...and without me. Damn it."

It was an hour before Victoria saw activity at the main house. The boy – Oscar, they'd called him – and her granddaughter were leaving. "Ugh, I'm too young to be a grandmother. Well, at least to an adult. This Tori has to be nearly twenty years old by now. Has it really been that long?"

Victoria tried to count backward, remembering how old Grace was when she got pregnant and how many years she'd spent in Costa Rica, locked out of the United States by her ex-husband and the immigration service. Who cared if the attempted murder charges against her were true or not? She was still an American citizen and they should let her back.

The kids had left and the curtains to the room she'd found Silas and his iron-fisted girlfriend in earlier were closing. "Yeah, well, so what if you're still able to get it up, Silas? You keep popping those little blue pills and keep her away from me while I get that tape. It's a big place, but I'll find it."

She slumped back against the shrubbery, chilled and desperate, the canned tuna and cracker breakfast roiling in her gut, leaving a foul taste in her mouth. "I have to have a backup plan. He has to have some sort of valuables or jewelry in that house. He's too clever to fall for blackmail, and there's no way I could take his Amazon down, even with André's help." She rubbed her jaw and noticed the swelling from their first encounter had gone down with the winter chill.

"He'd have to have a lot of Rolexes to finance the kind of lifestyle I want, but maybe..."

"Boo!"

Victoria jumped at the shout and turned around to see André's grinning face.

"You were gone for a long time," he said. "I figured you'd be back here. I mean, you did say you were gonna find the right tape."

Still trying to slow her heart rate, she nodded her answer. After a moment, she asked, "How'd you get here?"

"Oh, that clerk fellow at the hotel's a real nice guy. He said anything we need, just let him know."

Victoria's stomach lurched but she held her food down. She knew that twinkle in André's eye and it wasn't from a free ride. Or maybe it was.

"Are you okay, Victoria? You look a little green around the jills."

"That's gills, and yes, I'll be fine. Fine as soon as I get that tape or figure out how to make money off Silas some other way."

"Hey, I got a good idea. Anyone who owns a house this big has to have lots of bucks."

"He doesn't own it. He's just the butler," she said. "That doesn't mean he doesn't have lots of stuff in there to steal, though." She looked down and saw André had brought both backpacks with him. "Dump out one of those. We're going shopping."

"I thought you didn't want to fence."

"Life changes and you have to be willing to make adjustments when it does."

André squatted down to unzip the bags. "Do you want me to throw your clothes in mine or mine in with yours?" he asked, looking up.

Victoria's eyes got huge. Four love bites colored his neck. And she never gave hickeys. "I. Don't. Care," she hissed, then turned aside and puked.

Chapter 12: The Photo Album

"Do you think she'll come back?" Julianna asked.

"I'm pretty sure she will. That is if she's not here already."

"Wait. What? I mean, we just can't sit around and wait for her, can we?"

"Have you ever hunted?" Silas asked, sitting down next to her. "It's not necessarily *hunting* as much as waiting. You have to wait for the prey to come to you."

"Then what? Shoot her? Throw a net over her?" Julianna pulled her robe closer as a chill of uncertainty covered her in goosebumps.

"I'm not sure, but I do know one thing. I won't let her out of our sight this time." He adjusted the pillows, kicked back, then patted the bed next to him. "Time to talk."

"Yeah, I hate to say it, but I agree. So, we wait?"

Silas nodded, his arm opened to cuddle her close.

"Didn't you tell me she tried to kill her daughter? Was it a gun? I mean, if she tried to shoot her own child, what would she do to the woman who not only stole her man but beat the stuffing out of her?"

Silas chuckled. "You didn't steal her man because I was never hers to begin with. As far as you proving you are the better woman, I figure if you don't want to take her on again, I'll have a go at her. I wouldn't hit a lady, but she's no lady. As soon as I – or we," he said, adding a wink, "have her incapacitated, I'll call the cops. She probably left prints if she was hanging out next door. Breaking and entering, plus the outstanding warrants ought to keep her busy with the legal system for a long time."

"Plus breaking in here and the guest house."

Silas shook his head. "Nope. I'm leaving the trespassing here off the books. They'll want to know why, where's the home's owner, all sorts of stuff. I'd rather clean up messes and board up windows and be able to maintain my very low profile: Silas the butler and caretaker who never gets in trouble."

"What about that goon of a boyfriend? Won't he be a problem?"

"He's a porno poster boy – a body without a brain. If she's not there to tell him what to do step by step, he'll find someone else. You see, he doesn't need a woman, he just needs a host, a warm body to sponsor his existence."

"Man, that's too bad."

Silas laughed.

"No, I'm serious. I kind of needed Hugh so we could adopt Oscar. Besides the fact we both loved the child, he wanted an heir, and I had made a promise to the birth mother. He was a decent guy and we worked well together, so we married. We did have a few good years at the beginning, but then he got so controlling." Julianna shuddered. "No, I was *stuck* with Hugh, but I didn't *need* him. My parents taught us better than that."

"So, about your parents and visiting them. I think we got distracted last time." Silas brought her hand to his mouth and kissed it. He noticed the faint narrowing of flesh on her third finger where a wedding ring had been worn for years, now bare. He'd have to fix that.

"You're getting distracted again," Julianna said, pulling her hand back.

"Rough draft of a plan – do you have one? I'm new at this."

"You don't know how good it feels to talk about this with someone who believes me. The only other one I feel comfortable with is Tori. To her, it's so logical."

"It is logical," Silas said, scooting up so he could talk with body language, too. "With the right device, challenges are simplified. Think big mountain, pickaxe, and dynamite. Do you realize how long it would take to move a mountain with a hand tool versus dynamite?"

"Can you imagine how many…everythings… there are in twenty years? How much food and sleep I skipped over? How many bills I didn't have to pay, and movies I missed?"

"How many emotions and life experiences?"

Julianna grunted. "Yes, I know. You truly are twenty years wiser than I am."

"No, you're twenty years younger and less seasoned. Let's just say you missed twenty years of hay fever."

"Okay, so before the kids come home…" Julianna paused, smiling as she savored what she had just said. "That sounds so wonderful."

"Kids or coming home?"

"Both. Anyhow, I really think we need to bring Tori into this. I kinda, sorta let her in on this."

"What?"

"Hey, someone has to be our anchor. Plus, she outright asked if I had told you – and if I had, did you believe me – about time travel. I wasn't going to lie to her. You know, her parents may have isolated her from a lot of the world, but she has her head on straight with telling the truth and knowing right from wrong."

Silas inhaled sharply, holding back the pain of not knowing two of his three granddaughters because they had been adopted to strangers. He relaxed and breathed out. They were in his life now. Even if they moved to different parts of the planet, he'd be able to communicate with them. "Whoa. What's an anchor?"

"It's a focus point. If we left and wanted to come back to this time, we'd have to have someone here who we had a strong emotional bond with. Plus, I don't ever want to go a time where I don't have someone to connect to again. I must have been nuts to hop from '69 to '89 with nothing but historical data and a photograph to go to. Going back to my parents before I'm born is a gamble, but one I'm willing to take."

"A gamble?"

She smiled. "Remember I told you how much I look like my mother? Arriving as a stranger and trying to interact with family is chancey. But since my da is a veteran traveler, I think I can convince him who I am. He told us he and his grandfather looked to be the same age when he visited him as an adult. He knows the disparity is possible, so because he has experience with scrambled timelines, I think he'll accept me.

"However, on this end, I want Tori as an anchor. Then there's the other thing to consider. What are you going to do with this place? Just lock it up and be gone for five years without a trace? I'd suggest you put it in Tori's name or have her acknowledged as the caretaker. That way, if we go to the portal near Woodstock, jump forward to 2015, and hitch a ride back here, we'll have access to whatever goodies we need at this location."

"Like wheels?"

"You got it, Sherlock."

"Well, you're right except for one thing."

"What's that?"

"It's not *if* we go, but *when* we go. I'm more than happy to kick back with you here – in this time – getting to know you and my family better for as long as you'd like."

"Even if we have to watch out for the wicked witch of the west wall?"

Silas sat forward and lifted the edge of the pillow, exposing a gun.

"You'd shoot her?"

He whispered, "It's a paintball pistol. Looks like a real Walther PPQ. It'll sting and mark her – or him – but isn't lethal. I'm counting on the fear factor. But if I do have to shoot, the shock should be enough that I can back up the assault with a tackle."

Julianna bent down to look closer at the non-lethal weapon, then put the pillow back on it, tears brightening her eyes. "I don't know if I'm crying because I'm scared or because I'm so happy you wouldn't kill someone, even in self-defense."

"I'd duke it out first, even if I knew I'd break and bloody a few knuckles. Still, I'd rather fight with words and wits than bullets and blades. With the former, the only thing to get hurt would be feelings."

"And I don't even want to think about the latter," Julianna sighed and snuggled close.

***

"Are we going back to the little house or check out the big one?" André asked. "Because if you ask me, there's gotta be a whole lot more loot in that mansion."

Victoria glared at him, enraged at both his infidelity and stupidity.

Suddenly, her ire subsided as the glimmer of a plan came into focus and her glower became a grin.

"Are you feeling better now?" André asked. "Because you're looking better. Hey, now that your stomach's settled down, do you wanna go over to that little house and pretend it was yesterday? That's was fun, sneaking around and having sex outside where we might get caught."

"Nah," she said with a fake smile, "we'll wait. How about we go check out the big house? That was a good idea you had. Maybe the front door's unlocked. Grab that empty backpack and you can play reverse Santa."

"Huh?"

"You take an empty bag inside and fill it with goodies for all the good boys and girls. Oh, and you and I are the only good boys and girls."

"Yeah, that'd be fun. Upstairs or down, first? 'Cause you know I always like going down…"

Victoria picked up the empty backpack and shoved it into his midsection with more force than necessary. "We're doing it my way. We'll start at the top and work our way down," she said, glaring at his hickeys.

André wrestled his way out of the shrubbery and onto the driveway, strutting toward the front door.

"What are you doing?" Victoria hissed.

"You said we were starting at the top. Isn't this the way?"

"Maybe for them, but we don't want to be seen. Look up there," she said, pointing to the flagpole in the middle of the roundabout driveway. "Those are security cameras up there. Silas is sure to see us if we go through the front. We'll go through the garage. Come on. You can give me a boost through my secret exit, then I'll unlock the side door from the inside."

"Why can't I go the same way as you?"

"Because you're too big."

André looked down at the front of his slacks, grinning. "Yeah, I am…"

"No, your shoulders are too broad for the chute. Besides, I couldn't lift you. Come this way. I'm getting cold out here."

***

Silas put his hand out for Julianna to pause her story. "Someone's here," he said. "Get dressed."

She slipped off the robe and picked up the sweatsuit she had bought earlier. By the time she pulled the hoodie over her head, Silas was already dressed. "That was fast," she whispered.

He grimaced, his intended grin skewed by knowing a confrontation was imminent. He reached under the pillow, grabbed the pistol, then stuck it in the back of his waistband, leaving it exposed and accessible. "Take a deep breath."

"I did," Julianna replied.

"I was talking to myself," he said and chuckled weakly. "We've got this."

462

From the second-story window overlooking the driveway, Silas saw an older pickup truck approach.

"Anyone you know?" Julianna asked.

"Nope. Just a sec. The door is opening. Someone's getting out."

Julianna clutched Silas's arm as they waited. Finally, a man – older by his cautious posture – made it out. He walked slowly, clutching the side of the truck bed as he moved gloved-hand over gloved-hand to the passenger door, wary of the new-fallen snow.

"I think those are Tori's parents," Julianna said. "Didn't she say they were checking out the east coast and that Massachusetts was their old stomping ground?"

"Something like that," Silas agreed. "Let's go say hi. Two to one, though, they're checking on the kids. I know that's what I'd be doing if one of them was mine, that young and essentially by themselves."

"One of them is mine, and believe me, I'm glad they're staying here. As you said, we were their age once. I sure hope they had 'the talk' with Tori about getting pregnant."

"What about Oscar? It takes two, you know," Silas said, nodding to the stairs.

"Just bring it up to him if you want to see the brightest blush in the world." They walked side by side down to the front door. "Every time he'd even mention a girl around his father, Hugh would give him a lecture about respecting women and safe sex. I think he was eleven when he heard the talk the first time."

Ding, dong, ding.

"And here they are." Silas opened the door, Julianna at his side, both of them smiling wide. "Come in and warm up and dry off," he said.

"Here, let me take your coats, Leanne," Julianna offered. "You remember Silas Priest, I'm sure."

"Yes, yes," Luther said. "Tori's surprise grandfather. Looks like she got one of her wishes granted. She always wanted a grandparent. Both our folks passed a long time ago."

Julianna took the damp coats and hats and Silas hung them up. She glanced over to the parlor on the right. "In here?" she asked.

"Yes, that's a good idea. If you'd like, Luther, I can take your truck into the garage before it gets covered in snow. This is only the beginning of the storm. It's supposed to be a big one."

"Oh, we didn't want to impose," Luther said. "We just wanted to drop in and see how Tori was doing."

"The truth is," Leanne explained, looking down and then back up, trying to hide her guilt "I was missing my little girl so much, I pestered him until he said he was either going to tape my mouth shut, or he'd drive out here to make sure

463

they were really with you and not out… Well, out and about."

"They're shopping right now," Silas said. "From what I see, they're very responsible. And they are both of age. Now, whether that means they're adults…"

Luther laughed and turned to Leanne who was scowling.

"It's hard for me to imagine she's on her own," she said. "I mean, that we're not with her, under the same roof. She led such a sheltered life, but that's our fault. We wanted *some* control over her environment, but when she was old enough to interact with others, she didn't want real friends. She was always talking into mirrors." Leanne saw Silas and Julianna's confused looks and explained. "We had no idea she remembered them. She was only hours old when we got her, but she recalled having two sisters and would play with her imaginary versions of them.

"Anyway, she's always been a loner. She worked with Oscar last summer, but other than him, it wasn't until she met you, Julianna, that she spoke with a stranger. She," Leanne's clenched fist quickly opened and her arm moved out, indicating the vastness of the enormous sitting room and parlor, "suddenly blossomed."

"Sometimes it's fast and other times, you don't even notice they've changed until they're off to college or getting married."

"Married? Is that where they are?" she asked, tears and sniffles starting.

"No, I'm sure they're not," Silas said. "Actually, I believe they're buying Barbies and action figures to keep them entertained when they're not building snowmen and having snowball fights. They're not in any hurry to grow up from what I can see. They just enjoy each other's company."

"Oh, thank God!" Leanne said, wiping her nose, her eyes bright with relief.

Luther looked out the window and saw the truck already had a heavy white dusting. "Maybe I will take you up on that indoor parking. But I think I'd better drive. That ignition's a little finicky."

Silas handed Luther his coat and hat, then grabbed his own. "Ladies, we shall return," he said. "Make yourselves comfortable."

"It's an older truck," Luther said, apologizing, "but it's paid for and made it across the country without any problems." He paused then added. "At least, any problems I couldn't fix with duct tape or spray grease."

Silas took out his smartphone and clicked on the remote garage door opener. "I still have a few spots open. Why don't you take that one? Oscar and Tori can park at the other end. We old folks need to save our steps."

Luther paused to take off his fogged-up glasses, then drove in next to the Volkswagen microbus, blinking to keep his focus on parking and not staring at the vintage ride beside him. As soon as he stopped, he was out of the truck, eager as a teenager to investigate the VW.

"Is that yours?" he asked, his hand gliding over the curtained windows.

"I'm sorry, of course, it is…isn't it?"

"Yes, it is. Reminds me of my youth, hitching a ride to Woodstock in one."

"Really?" Luther asked, wide-eyed. "That's how I got there, too. Only it wasn't like this. It was older and had brightly colored posies and peace signs all over it."

Silas chuckled. "Yeah, mine did, too. I think about half the vans there did."

"Oh, wait," Luther said. He opened the truck, reached behind the front seat, and brought out a tattered cardboard box. "When I was at my buddy's place this morning, his widow gave me this. I was trying to catch up with some old friends, and he was one of the few names I remembered. Anyhow, he died two years ago, God rest his soul. His wife said she wasn't at Woodstock and since I was, that she was sure John F. would want me to have it. Would you like to look through these together and see if we can find anyone we know? I'm pretty sure I'm in a few of them. I borrowed his thirty-five millimeter and shot a few rolls of film while he was… Well, he got pretty stoned. I figured if he wasn't going to remember the event, I'd show him what he missed."

Little flashes of recall popped like sparks from a grinder. That name – John F. Silas nodded his head minimally and grinned. "You know, I can't think of anything I'd rather do. Let's go show the ladies."

***

"What's that?" André asked.

"Shush!" Victoria hissed. She looked around and saw the quilt covering the bed in the van. "Lie down and hold still. I'll cover you."

"But…"

"That's the garage door opening, dummy! Someone's here."

"Don't call me dummy."

"Sorry. Now hush!"

Victoria tossed the quilt over André, then climbed under the tiny table, hugging the wall under the window of the VW as close as she could. She looked up and saw André move, then settle in. She stifled her urge to tell him to hold still and exhaled in frustration. Just a few more hours and they'd be in the clear. A vision of the hickeys on his neck popped into her mind. Just a few more hours and *she'd* be in the clear and he'd be framed.

***

"Guess what, Leanne?" Luther called out, toting the cardboard box, Silas following behind him with their coats and hats.

"What?"

"Silas was at Woodstock, too! We're going to look through these old photos and see if we can find him."

Julianna looked at Silas, mute but wide-eyed.

He grinned at her, then looked to Leanne and said, "Well, I hear there were five hundred thousand people at the event. What are the chances?"

Julianna's fear evaporated with the odds, then turned into excitement. Visions of the sea of people – all muddy but content – enveloped her as she recalled her first four days of teenage freedom. Then the sting of anxiety with not finding her sister popped in. "Five hundred thousand," she repeated softly, forgiving herself one more time for not being able to locate Mali in a crowd that huge.

"Oh, and get this," Luther said, still as excited as a cat chasing a dragonfly. "He has a VW microbus down in the garage!"

"Like the one John F. had?" Leanne asked.

Julianna's face turned to Silas, her big brown eyes refilled with worry.

Silas winked at her and grinned, showing his confidence. "Luther says it's not the same as the one you rode in…Rapunzel."

"What? Where'd you hear that name?" Leanne asked. "Nobody but Luther's called me that in over forty years."

Silas looked at the bun on top of her head. "I'd say if you let those pinned-up locks down, they'd be to the back of your knees, at least."

"Oh, yes, I guess that's a logical deduction," she said. "I never thought anyone else would pick up on that."

"I guess that's why they call me Sherlock."

Julianna sat down with a thunk, unable to keep her emotions and fears from stealing the strength in her legs.

Leanne squinted at him as Luther put his glasses back on. "Nah, it couldn't be, could it?" she asked softly.

"Well, Luther," Silas said, clapping the still-stunned man on the shoulder, "how about we break open that book and go down memory lane."

Julianna watched them interact, the past forty years evaporating, the gray-haired crew suddenly young hippies again. Barely taking a breath, she kept mouth and body still – trying to be invisible but knowing it was impossible – while the three decided on the best place to look at the photo album.

"We can put it on the coffee table," Leanne suggested.

"But then Julianna couldn't see it," Luther protested. "Oh, maybe she's not interested. She's too young to have been there, right?" he asked, looking over at her.

Julianna blinked rapidly, coming out of her trance. "How about some drinks?" she asked, ignoring his question. "Hot or cold, soft or hard. Silas has everything from soda to liquor to sangrias and has been known to make a mean cup of cocoa." She looked at each person in turn, quickly bypassing Leanne who was studying her – unsure but still curious. "Or hot cider? All I have to do is heat it and pour it in a cup with a cinnamon stick. I think I can do that. You three get started and I'll join you in a few."

Leanne watched Julianna leave, then looked to Luther, trying to catch his eye. "Ahem…ahem…"

However, her husband was now absorbed in the big denim-covered photo album, faded denim fabric painted with peace signs and marijuana leaves. "Here we are getting ready to leave," he said, pointing to a group photo in front of the microbus. "When we started, there were only four of us."

In the kitchen, Julianna spilled the hot cider as she poured it into the last cup. "Damned fumble-fingered female," she said softly as she set the pan on the burner. She suddenly went weak-kneed. "Those were Hugh's words. Forget them. He's not here. And even if he was, Silas would escort him off the property. Stop beating yourself up, Jules. What's the worst..."

Standing behind her, Silas cleared his throat, rescuing her from her more self-flagellation. "Sweetheart, don't fuss over spilled cider. And don't ever feel guilty for looking young. You wouldn't feel bad for any of your other millions of assets, would you?"

"Millions of assets?" she asked, setting down the potholder and turning into his arms.

"How do I love thee, let me count the ways. Your eyes that sparkle when you see me in the morning, your softly curled cocoa-brown hair that springs to the touch, those long legs that reach from the floor all the way to heaven. Shall I continue or have you figured out what I mean?"

"I get the idea, but you're wrong. My eyes sparkle *every* time I see you."

"Come on," Silas said, setting aside the dishcloth. "I'll clean up the mess later. We have guests."

"Do you think they'll find out it was us?" she asked.

"If they don't, I'll tell them. In case I've never told you before, I'm proud of you. Every part of you, including our past, our right now, and what we'll have together when we're old and gray. Or rather, you're old and gray and I'm older and grayer." He ran his fingers through his short gray curls. "Or maybe bald. Who knows?"

Julianna moved in close and kissed him briefly, paused, then came back for a more thorough smooch. "Where is a tray, dear. I can carry them all at the same time, but I want to seem at least a little classy."

"Well, you're in trouble there. I can let you choose a tray, but you'll always be *a lot* classy. There's no little about you. And yes, that's a tall person joke."

"Gray-ate to know," she said, ruffling his hair. "Come on. They have to be wondering what happened to us by now."

Silas opened a cabinet, exposing a dozen serving trays. "*She* may be wondering, but he's absorbed in the pictures."

Julianna snorted as she arranged the cups and a bundle of napkins on the silver platter.

"What's the problem? All she can do is be jealous you aged so well. Be proud of yourself for eating all those greens and exercising regularly," he said

467

and winked. "No one needs to know you managed to skip twenty years of life."

She chuckled and picked up the platter. "Care to bet who figures it out first?"

"Oh, hands down, she will."

"You're on."

Leanne was seated close to Luther when they walked in. Seeing them, she stood up. "I can look at this later. Why don't you two get on either side?" She paused and inhaled deeply. "That smells divine."

Julianna held out the tray and Leanne took a cup and a napkin. "I love hot cider," she said, then sipped it cautiously. "Oh, I'll bet that was pressed from local orchards. It tastes just that much different from Oregon apples."

"I've never been to Oregon," Julianna said, then walked over to Luther and bent down to offer him a drink.

Luther took one, then pointed to a picture of three glassy-eyed guys and a girl in a cloud of smoke, passing a marijuana joint between them. "Those were the days. Who would have thought it would be legal one day. At least, we grow medical marijuana in Oregon now. Mark my words, pretty soon, you'll be able to buy it anywhere in the US."

"I'm pretty sure you could do that in 1969," Silas said with a chuckle.

"Oh, I mean legally. If we can get every state in the union to follow Colorado's suit and legalize it for both medical and recreational, eventually they'll have to make it good to go on the federal level, too." Luther held out one arthritic hand. "My body is literally eating up the cartilage in my hands and feet. The only relief I can get is with a homemade cannabis cream and maybe a toke or two before I go to bed if it's been a rough day. I couldn't get the same effect with liquor without pickling my whole body."

"Or at least your liver," Leanne said. "I'm glad we have options."

Luther took an appreciative sip of the cider and was back into the album. He looked up at Silas and Julianna. "Come on and sit down. We might as well get used to each other. Looks like our kids are going to be friends – or more – for a long time."

"Yeah, it's the 'or more' part that terrifies me," Leanne said, then sat in the chair across the coffee table from the other three.

"Hey, look at that…" Luther pointed to a picture. "Unexploded grenade, huh?" he asked then stared deep into Silas's eyes, squinting to merge the image of the youth with long, dark hair in the photo with the gray-haired man beside him. His grin widened. Then he looked at Julianna and back at the young woman in the photo. He frowned, then slightly bent the edge of the picture and removed it from the album. He held it beside Julianna's face. "Dorothy?"

Julianna smiled with confidence. "I win!" she said, then reached around Luther to give Silas a playful pat on the back.

"Dorothy from Oz?" Leanne gasped. "Oh, my Lord. It is you! I want to know what moisturizer you use. You look great."

"Well, hooking up again after forty years was what, one in a million chance?" Luther asked.

"One in five-hundred-thousand," Julianna said, "but who's counting?"

Chapter 13: Proof Positive

"I never saw Silas again until the wedding," Julianna said, now confident and wanting to control the direction of the conversation.

"She recognized me first," Silas said. "Without a doubt, that was the happiest hour of my life. I found her and was able to acknowledge my daughter and granddaughters, all within a timeframe of less than sixty minutes."

"I wonder what your astrological chart looks like for that date and time," Leanne said. "I'm a little out of practice, but if you tell me your birthday – and Julianna's, too – I can work up a chart for you."

Julianna sputtered, conveniently choking on her cider to end the conversation. Her feigned health issue worked to awaken Leanne's maternal healing instincts, deflecting her attention and sending her plot to create supernatural astral charts to the trash bin. "Thanks, I'm fine," Julianna said a moment later. "And no, I don't want to cheat destiny or get a glimpse of the future with determining how much impact a planet will have when it's in whichever house or whatever."

Silas caught her gaze and rolled his eyes. *You already know too much about the future. How many times have you tried to mess with timelines already?*

Julianna frowned quickly in response, then looked up and smiled at the sound of someone coming in the front door. "The kids are home," she said brightly.

"Oh, I so want to show these photos to Tori," Leanne said. She turned to Silas and clutched his hand in hers. "When she was just an infant, we had a flood. We lost everything. Woosh! All gone. She's never seen me without gray hair or wrinkles. She's going to be so thrilled." She looked down and saw that in her excitement, she had brought Silas's hand to her bosom. "Oops. Sorry," she said and patted it, giving it back to him with a soft chuckle.

"And she's never seen her grandfather as a young man, either," Luther said. "And, Oscar," he shook his head in disbelief, "he's going to be amazed at how little you've changed, Julianna. He could only hope to have inherited those genes."

Julianna laughed. "He'd have to get them through genetic splicing. He's adopted, in case you didn't notice."

"Don't mind him," Leanne said. "He's special that way. He only sees the inner person. You could walk out of this room and he wouldn't be able to tell anyone what you looked like, whether you're short or tall, black or white."

"Yes, but I would remember if she was rude or polite," he said.

"The important stuff, right, Luther?" Silas asked.

"Amen to that." Luther stood up to greet the kids who had just walked in. "Tori, take off your boots and come see what your papa and mama looked like before you were born."

470

"Oscar, you come over here, too," Leanne said. "Did you know Silas and your mother were at Woodstock with us? Who could have guessed?"

Oscar stared at his mother, eyebrows pinched together. He opened his mouth to speak, then let it shut and closed his eyes, trying to remember the year. The media had made a big deal last summer about the fortieth anniversary of Woodstock. His eyes popped open and he stared at her.

"Doesn't seem possible, does it?" Julianna said and winked at her stunned son.

He stumbled backward against the door, smacking the door handle into his lower back. "I…I'm okay," he said.

"You'd better hold onto me while you take off those wet boots," Tori said aloud, then rushed up to help him. "Told ya," she whispered, then bent to work as his boot jack. She looked at the group, gathered around the big home-crafted photo album. "And it looks like they have proof, too."

Oscar emitted a low growl as Tori finished helping him. He took a deep calming breath, then patted her shoulder, letting her know to stand up so he could kick off the last one.

"Are you going to be okay?" she whispered.

"Hold me close, just in case. I have a lot to process already, and I haven't even seen the pictures yet."

Julianna stood up and offered Oscar her place next to Luther, sitting on his other side and taking over Tori's job as caregiver.

"I've heard you and Mama talk about Woodstock," Tori told her father, keeping her eyes on Oscar, "but why didn't you show me these pictures before?"

"These were given to us by the widow of a friend we visited earlier today. I thought you'd get a bang out of these. Look, that's me. See how long my hair was."

"Wow, you were good-looking, Papa. Where's Mama?"

"That's me. Back then, I went by Rapunzel."

"Because of your long hair?" Tori asked.

"Duh," Oscar said, then immediately apologized. "Sorry. That was rude." He bent over the album and asked, "Where's my mom?"

Silas turned a few pages and showed the picture of a handsome young man with long hair standing next to a sign that said 'Keep Back: Unexploded Grenade.' A tall dark-skinned woman stood at the edge of the shot, definitely Julianna. "There she is. And that's me with the sign," Silas said, bringing his hand up to his head. "Hard to believe I ever messed with having that much hair…" He looked at Oscar and winked.

Julianna was radiant as Oscar stared at her, his mouth agape. "It was such a wet, muddy mess, but the vibes were awesome," she said. "I want to see some of the other pictures. John Sebastian was wandering through the crowds. Did you get any of him?" she asked Luther.

The adults hovered over the book while Oscar leaned back into the couch, stunned. He stared at his mother, remembering how many times he'd crashed hard drives or hid her books on time travel, not just to protect her from his father's wrath if he discovered she was 'at it again,' but to stop her nonsense. Luther and Silas were of a similar age both then and now, although Silas was more fit and still handsome. Then he looked from is mother to Leanne, both the same age at Woodstock. Huge difference. Mom looked at least twenty years younger. The twenty years she had told him once, she'd 'lost' when time traveling to find her sister.

Silas brought out a magnifying glass and was sharing it back and forth, checking for celebrity faces. "Hey, I think I know him," Luther said. "Last I heard, he worked in the NYU Ag Department. Who could forget that nose? I bet he'd like to see these photos, too."

"Give him a call and see if he's still there," Leanne said. "We can go see him and you two can compare notes on your plant research."

"It's okay to say cannabis cultures, dear. We're all adults."

"Just some of us more so than others," Julianna whispered to Silas.

Luther thumped the photo album. "Other than The Nose from NYU, John F. was the only person I knew. I guess that guy who called himself Eros wound up a billionaire or something," Luther said. "I wish I had written down some of the names even a year later. How soon we forget."

"It probably wouldn't have made a difference," Silas said. "If you recall, I think you and John F. were the only ones using real names. If that *was* his name. Oh, and Eros wound up making his millions on inflated government contracts. You know, the million-dollar screwdrivers? He was one of them. A sly little sh...stinker."

"You can say it. We're all adults," Julianna said, "He was a sly little shit."

Silas looked up and saw the white glow of heavy snowfall through the window. "Well, Tori, it looks like you and Oscar will get to build your snowman today." He turned to Leanne and Luther. "Care to camp out here tonight?" He nodded toward the second floor. "We have plenty of room."

"Yeah, Papa," Tori said. "They even have a guest house. That's where Oscar and I are staying."

"A guest house?" Leanne asked, her smile rising quickly. "Well, then, I think we'll just share that with you two." She looked at Luther, her head down like a bull ready to charge. "Right, Papa?"

Recognizing the tone, Luther set the magnifying glass down to give her his full attention. He noticed the smile of relief on Julianna's face. There would be two chaperones for the child-adults tonight. "Sounds like a good idea to me. Thanks for the offer. We'd be happy to accept."

***

"No, we have to stay hidden," Victoria said. "There's no telling when those two old fossils will be back to get their truck and leave."

"But I have to go pee real bad," André said, still lying in the van's bed, the quilt kicked off, his knees rocking back and forth in discomfort.

"Oh, all right. But make it quick."

André rushed out of the cramped van into the vast and immaculate garage, breathing in the fresh air. He and his very friendly clerk had showered together, but Victoria still stank of old-lady body odor and cheap hotel soap. He looked around for a bathroom but didn't see one, so he hustled to the outside door. He pushed it halfway open and saw it was snowing heavily. "Don't close the door. Don't close the door," he chanted to himself, remembering how many times he'd been locked out when an outside door shut.

A long minute later, he finished whizzing, spelling his name in the snow. "Well done, Buddy." He looked down to shake his member. "Oh, shit!" he said, seeing the hickeys. "That little asshole bit me." He sighed. "Well, I guess it was fun at the time, though, wasn't it big fella? I guess there won't be any blowjobs from her until the marks go away."

"Gotcha!" a playful young woman's voice sang from across the yard. A young man's laugh followed.

André quickly stepped back into the garage. He looked back at the van and saw Victoria leaned against it, puffing a cigarette. "Hey! I thought you gave those up."

"I did," she said.

He gasped. The ice in her voice was colder than the snowflakes on his exposed skin had been. "Um, I don't know if you heard, but there are people outside. I think we'd better lay low again."

"Who?" she asked, throwing the half-smoked butt to the polished concrete floor, grinding it out.

"I don't know. I didn't look. It sounded like a girl and a guy laughing. It's snowing, too. I think she just hit him with a snowball."

"My granddaughter," Victoria said, then huffed at the designation. "Tori," she said softly, rolling it around in her mind, tickled at her having the same name. Well, almost the same name.

"Are you okay?" André asked. "You got that funny look again."

"Yeah, I'm as fine as I can be, imprisoned in an old hippie van with a…a…man child."

"Hey, is that an insult? Because if it is, I'll just get up and leave. You can stay here by yourself. I'll slip into the big house tonight and haul out the loot without you. I'm just being nice to you, you know."

"Sorry," Victoria said sarcastically.

"Hey, say it like you mean it."

She took a rage-squelching breath, wishing she was anywhere but here, then remembered that if she played nice, she'd get everything she came for, and

André would get the blame. "André, I'm sorry. I truly am. There, is that better?" she asked, giving him an ounce of sincerity.

"Yeah, I guess so."

"Fine, then. Why don't you take a nap? It'll make the time go faster."

"Yeah, okay." He lay down on the bed then turned to face her. "It's my second favorite thing to do in bed. Hey, do you want to guess what my first favorite is?"

"No, thanks. My brain is fried. Go ahead and sleep. I'll wake you when it's time to rob the place."

André rolled over and tried to get comfortable. Victoria stood up and adjusted the quilt over his shoulders. "Sweet dreams, ya big lug," she said under her breath.

***

"Let's see," Silas said, moving aside packages in his walk-in freezer. "This has been in here a while, but not too long. I only have a limited amount of fresh vegetables but do have a lot of frozen ones. Do you think they'd rather have surf or turf?"

"I don't know about anyone else, but I'd rather have both," Julianna said. "I'm sure Oscar feels the same. Go ahead and fix them all. I never have leftovers with Oscar."

"Are you sure they'll be okay in the guest house with the kids?"

"Absolutely. I know I'll feel a lot better with them just one bedroom away from a parent or two rather than fifty yards away from us."

"Ditto for them, I'm sure."

"If by them, you mean Leanne and Luther, I agree. Then again, there's a lot of pressure off the kids, too. Nobody wants to be the one to be bashful about saying no to the first time."

"Just in case, I tossed a three-pack of condoms in the bedside table. If they get carried away, believe me, a guy's going to look everywhere for one."

***

"That's it, I'm done," Oscar said, knocking the remains of the last snowball from his cheek. "Let's go to the little house and change into dry clothes. If I know my mom, she'll have food waiting for us. Now that Silas is in her life, though, I hope he takes over *all* the cooking. Having anything warm after a snow battle is appreciated, but packaged toaster pastries and instant cocoa from the microwave are pushing the limits of a hot snack."

"Let's go in through the garage," Tori said. "I don't want to make a mess in the front room like last time. That was kind of rude."

"Yeah, I didn't even think about it to tell you the truth. Did Silas give you the access code?"

"My *grandpa* didn't," she said the name with pride, "but I'll bet you your dessert tonight I can guess it. Come on, I'll race you."

474

First to the door was Oscar. "I just won back my dessert, but if you can't figure it out, I'll get yours, too."

Tori pulled her glove off with her teeth and punched in her birthdate. *Click.* "Told ya."

Oscar held the door open for her then stepped inside. "Ew, it stinks in here," Tori said. "Someone's been smoking."

"That's for sure," Oscar agreed. He sniffed again, then coughed. "Tobacco. I've never seen Silas smoke, but maybe he can't kick the habit and comes out here."

"Nope. I'd be able to smell it on his clothes or hair when I hug him. He just smells like a man."

"Okay," Oscar said tersely, then looked around. He heard something move then saw the VW bus shudder as if someone inside was moving around. He looked at Tori and put his finger to his lips and shook his head. "I guess it was just my imagination," he said a few decibels above normal. "Come on, we're done in here."

"But…" Tori started to protest but stopped when he put his hand on her mouth gently. She huffed, then quickly bent over and took off her boots, leaving her coat, hat, and scarf on.

Oscar took the boots and pushed her ahead of him into the house, not caring that he was trailing melted snow behind him.

As soon as they were inside, Tori opened her mouth to give him the dickens. "Not now, Tori. You can rip me a new one in two minutes. I have to talk to Silas first."

Once in the kitchen, he pulled Silas aside. "Someone broke into the garage. You can smell cigarette smoke and I saw the microbus bouncing around. Either you have a visitor or a very big rat."

"Both, I suspect," Silas said. He looked at Tori, now wide-eyed with a mix of fear and excitement. "No, you don't get to investigate, young lady. If it's who I think it is, she's attempted murder in the past. I don't want you in harm's way."

"Is it the person who has a line on my genealogy chart?"

"What? Oh, yes, I assume so. She and her…her…"

"Paramour?" Oscar asked with a strained laugh.

"Do you two make a game out of finding novel descriptions for common nouns?"

"Sure. You just did, too," Tori said. "See. It's a genetic tendency."

Julianna ignored the light banter, a scowl wrinkling her forehead. "Did you put it back under the pillow or hide it someplace else?"

"My Walther PPPQ?" Silas pulled open a kitchen drawer and shoved aside the spare dishtowels, exposing the pistol. "Its twin is back under our pillow."

"PPPQ? Is that for paintball PPQ?"

Silas kissed her on the cheek. "Yup. Now, if you'll set the table, I'll fire up the grill." He nodded to the large burner on the stovetop. "Flame-broiled lobster tail and prime rib aren't quite as good with propane as charcoal, but grilling inside is infinitely more convenient."

"I guess this means we're still playing the waiting version of hunting, right?" Julianna asked.

"You got it, Sherlock," he said and pulled her close to give her a real kiss.

"Ew! Are you two doing that again?" Tori asked, then giggled into her hand.

"Still," Julianna said and leaned over and whispered in Tori's ear. "And one of these days, you'll understand."

"I already do," Tori said back in the same soft voice. "It's just Oscar and I are more discreet. Especially since my parents are here. They still think I'm a six-year-old."

"And they probably always will." Julianna nodded to Oscar, searching the contents of the refrigerator for something to drink. "He's been through a lot in the last six months. I used to look at him as a child. Now I see him as my hero."

"Yeah, he told me how he rescued you from that in-sanitarium," she continued in the same hushed tone.

Julianna stood up and took a deep breath. She looked around the room, so different than the ten by ten room she'd been kept in while in France. Her voice returned to normal volume. "I know you know it's not called an in-sanitarium, but it should be. For years, everyone thought I was nuts. Now, the three people I care about most are comfortable enough with my past and my present to make jokes about it with me. I think that's complete healing."

"Cheers, Mom, on your well-deserved emancipation," Oscar said, toasting her with a can of tomato juice. He came and stood next to her. "I'm just sorry I didn't understand sooner. Shoot, I still don't understand. But you know, I don't have to know how a car drives to know that it can. To accept it can go from point A to point B. I guess it's the same for you." He shook his head. "Actually, I think my brain would explode if I tried to figure it out, so no explanation is necessary, okay? Just don't go taking off anywhere – or any-when – without telling me, all right?"

Julianna pulled him close and kissed him on the top of his head, hiding her tears. "Deal."

***

"This meal makes me grateful I gave up being a vegan eighteen years ago," Leanne said.

"I've always been grateful for that," Luther commented. "This was the best steak and lobster I ever had."

"I'd ask if I could move in with you two just for the eats," Oscar said, "but I think I'll only be around for a day or two more. Tori and I are going on a tour."

476

"What?" Leanne gasped.

Julianna put her hand on top of hers and patted it gently, urging her to wait.

"Yup. We joined the Youth Advocates Council. We'll be traveling with an evangelical group reaching out to street kids and the homeless in need of guidance, job counseling, medical, you name it."

"Yup, we're the point people," Tori bragged. "You know, like if we were astronauts, we'd be the ones making first contact with the aliens."

"Now, that sounds pretty interesting," Luther said, nodding. He turned to Leanne who was dabbing her tears with a napkin. "Do a little time-tripping, sweetheart..."

Silas, Julianna, Oscar, and Tori all gasped and looked back and forth between each other, tight-lipped.

"Huh?" Leanne asked.

Luther continued. "If you and I had that opportunity when we were eighteen and nineteen, do you think we'd want to go on a project like that, or stay at home with our parents and go to college?"

"Already graduated," Oscar popped in, then sat back and grinned.

Leanne looked at him, eyebrow raised.

"Yes, he did," Julianna said, beaming with pride. "Top of his class, too. Go on, Luther."

"Leanne, I think this is great. Plus, they'll be supervised with some level-headed folks. I've heard about the group. Mark my words, these kids out there, giving up their comfort and video games to bring others out of despair and poverty, will be tomorrow's leaders. There's no way I'd want to deprive Tori of this opportunity."

"Well, when you say it like that. I mean, it's not as if they're getting in an old bus filled with pot-smoking hippies out to make love... I mean, out to make music and protest against war..." Leanne paused. "What were our parents thinking, letting us go..."

"They knew we had to grow up, too. I know my folks were more into the protest for peace part of the movement. Looks like our daughter will be going into the world to make a difference with others in a new way. See how much has changed in forty years? Shoot, who would have thought we'd be growing marijuana legally now?"

Julianna fought the urge to raise her hand and stifled a chuckle.

Oscar caught the reaction and smiled. *My mother, the time traveler.*

Chapter 14: The Shootout

"It's a good thing you held still when I told you to," Victoria scolded.

"You know, I don't like the way you're treating me. I think I'm going to leave. Right now. I can pull this job on my own."

"André, you don't know how to get into the house."

"Yes, I do. I just follow those wet footprints left by that kid. Easy." André opened the door of the van and stepped into the garage. "Damn! It does smell like cigarettes out here. You know, you really should quit smoking."

"Wait, where are you going?"

André walked boldly to the door the young couple had left through, then looked back at Victoria. "Those prints won't stay wet forever. I'm going to see where they go first, then I'll come back and wait until night when everyone's asleep before I do the upside-down Santa. See, I'm no dummy."

"That's reverse Santa," Victoria said under her breath. She waited for him to return, thought about it twice, then gave in to the urge. "Screw it. I only have one left. I might as well smoke it and be done with it."

She dug into her backpack, found the lighter, then went to the door André went through for his piss break. "He won't smell it if I smoke out here."

She stepped outside and took three long, deep drags on the filtered smoke then tossed the butt into the bush. "Oh, crap," she said, twisting the doorknob. "Crap, shit, double damn…" She pulled and pulled, rattling the door, hoping.

"What's the matter?" André asked through the slightly opened door, a self-satisfied grin splitting his face. "Did the *dummy* lock herself out?"

"Shut up," she hissed, then ducked under his arm and pushed inside.

The two didn't speak to each other for hours. André passed the time twiddling his thumbs, humming the same tune over and over. Finally, Victoria blew up. "Would you stop singing that alphabet song?"

"It's Twinkle, Twinkle Little Star, and I'm not singing it. I'm humming it in all the languages of the world. Hmph! So there."

"If I ever get out of here…" Victoria mumbled then gritted her teeth until she felt a pop.

"Son of a bitch!" she screamed.

"Hey, Victoria, you'd better keep your voice down," André whispered. "Someone's gonna hear you. Hey, are you all right?"

"No…" she hissed, remembering not to call him a dummy. "I juth broke the wire on my parthial plate, damn it." She pulled it out of her mouth and threw it across the van, bouncing it off two cabinet doors before it landed in the mini sink.

André swallowed his chuckle and went back to humming his song, this time in Australian.

***

"Two-to-one they're waiting until they think everyone's asleep," Julianna whispered into the collar of Silas's t-shirt.

The two were lying down, cuddled together under a big synthetic fur spread. They had agreed to pass on the lovemaking for the night and to sleep in clothing they wouldn't be ashamed to face Luther and Leanne in.

"I think you're right. If they're in the VW bus like Oscar suspects, it shouldn't be too much longer until they come in."

"Do you think we should have told Luther and Leanne what's going on?"

"Nah. Tori and Oscar know. I doubt Victoria and the great ape will go back to the guest house. Thanks for telling them it was hurricane damage on the window and not a break-in."

"That was Oscar's idea." Julianna got up on her elbow. "He's really fond of you. It didn't take too long."

"I think it's because of Tori."

"Maybe a little bit, but he knows how I feel about you. He told me tonight he's never seen me so happy."

Clunk!

"And there they are…" Silas whispered. He pulled out his smartphone and swiped across the screen, opening the security camera app. "They're coming from the garage through the kitchen. Look at that."

"Oh, good grief. He's looking in the refrigerator?"

"Well, there isn't anything to eat in the van. Unless they brought food… Hold on. Get out of the bed and hide."

Silas rolled out of bed, rushing to stand behind the door as Julianna dashed into the closet.

"Agh! Take that, you mitherable mutha…"

Silas grabbed Victoria from behind and tried to wrestle the cricket bat from her before she could inflict more damage to his faux polar-bear skin bedcover.

"Wha?" she screeched and turned around, shocked by his sneak attack from behind.

Seeing her gap-toothed gasp, Silas laughed, losing control just long enough for her to wriggle out of his clutch.

She grabbed the bat again, ready to swing it at his head. "Where ith thee?"

"Give it up," Oscar said, pointing the Walther paintball gun he had taken from the kitchen.

Startled, Victoria stepped back and eyed them both, wondering which man to strike first. "No way!" She repositioned the wooden club on her shoulder, her fingers flicking in and out as she clutched it tighter.

"That was rude," André bellowed, rubbing the back of his head with one hand as he strode into the room. He saw Oscar and grunted, shoving him in the back, pushing him into the window.

Oscar reached out to stop from going through the large pane of glass and

479

the gun fired as he inadvertently squeezed the trigger. A bright blue paintball flew out, hitting Silas on the side of the head, the impact of the point-blank range knocking the older man to the floor.

Hearing the shot, Julianna burst out of the closet, hand raised high clutching one of Silas's shoes.

"Uh-oh," André said. He dropped his food-filled backpack and ran thunder-footed out of the room and down the stairs.

Tori remained hidden behind the decorative plant in the hallway, Oscar's smartphone in her hand, and video recorded the big man's exit. As soon as he was out of sight, she sidled toward the bedroom and the cacophony of chaos.

"You bitch!" Julianna yelled as she rushed across the room.

Tori stepped in just as Julianna was ready to bring her Florsheim weapon down on Victoria's head. She saw Tori in her peripheral vision and paused her assault. She backed up, took a deep and ragged breath, and composed herself. "You're lucky she came in, Victoria."

"Oh, don't stop on my account," Tori said, tapping an icon to stop recording. She stuck the phone in the pocket of her hoodie. "Go for it."

"No, no," Victoria begged, dropping to her knees awkwardly.

"Watch her," Oscar said, seeing the evil glint in her eye.

Tori looked over and saw Silas on the ground, a paisley mix of vibrant blue and blood-red sliding down the side of his head to pool beneath his face.

"Heh, heh. Thot by the kid," Victoria laughed.

Thwap!

Julianna's right hook sent the villainess to the ground, her lower jaw askew, the dark of her missing tooth stark against her remaining yellowed teeth and lolling pink tongue.

Dazed, Oscar cautiously stepped over the scrawny woman in black to get to Silas. "Is he alive?" he asked, hovering over his mother as she anxiously whispered words of hope and fear into the unconscious man's face.

Tori rushed to Silas's other side with a washcloth. She wiped the colorful smear from the point of impact, looking to see if anything had penetrated the skin. It hadn't. "No cuts," she said.

Julianna composed herself quickly at the good news and checked for a carotid pulse.

"It was just a paintball," she repeated, this time loud enough for the others to hear.

"Even blanks in guns can kill a person," Tori said without thinking. "I mean…"

She looked at Oscar, white-faced, now clutching the curtains for support, plump silent tears falling, stunned.

"There!" Julianna said, finding his pulse. "He's alive. He said he didn't want the police involved, but we have to get him to the hospital."

"What's going on…? Oh, my!" Leanne said, clutching her robe and coat around her tighter.

Luther gently moved his wife aside and knelt beside Julianna. "Let me check."

He rolled Silas's head to either side, looking for signs of bullet entry, then pulled both eyelids up. He looked at Julianna, fixing her fearful gaze with his calming one. "Why didn't he want the police involved?"

"That…that bitch was a liaison from almost forty years ago. He didn't want her or anyone else to know…" She paused and whispered in his ear, "To know he owns all this."

"Yeah, she's my biological grandmother," Tori said. "but I sure don't want to claim her. She must be some sort of genetic anomaly."

"She's an effin' freak of nature is what she is," Julianna said. "And wanted by the law. Silas said there are warrants out for her arrest and, for some reason, immigration wants her, too. How are we going to get Silas to the hospital and her… Get her out of here? Sorry, Luther, my brain's a scrambled mess right now."

"Don't worry about her for now," Leanne said. She rolled Victoria over and set her foot in the middle of her back. She pulled the tie from her robe and held it up as if it was a golden rope. "I've been tying knots since I was a Daisy Scout. She won't get out of this one. We can dump her at ICE or the police department, whichever is closest."

"What about the other guy?" Julianna asked.

"He's long gone," Tori said. She looked back at Oscar, ready to ask if André had hurt him, and saw he was still ashen. "Mama, I think we need to take Oscar to the hospital, too. I think he's in shock." She looked at Julianna. "And she's not too far behind."

Luther stood up. "All right, Leanne. You're in charge of the hospital run. I'll drag this bag of bones to the first place full of folks wearing shields. Son," Luther said to Oscar. "Son, son," he repeated, putting his hand on Oscar's cheek. "Clammy. You called it right, Tori. You help your mama."

"Oh, wait," she said. Tori pulled her phone out of her pocket, tapped a few times, then said, "Cop station two miles away. Turn right at the bottom of the hill. Can't miss it. I hope."

"Don't worry about me. I may be a male, but I'm not afraid to ask for directions."

"Julianna, I need you to carry Silas. Can you hoist him under your shoulder?" Leanne asked.

Julianna looked from her son to Tori, then to Leanne. "I'll be okay. The keys to the Caddie are on the hook by the back door. You drive, Leanne. Tori, you help her get Oscar to the car. From what I remember, the hospital is two blocks from the police station." Julianna put on her shoes, then squatted in front

481

of Silas. "Come on. Let's go," she said and lifted him as if he was a child.

***

"You don't need my name, do you?" Luther asked the sergeant. "I don't mind bringing the trash to you, but if you don't put it on any documents, her buddies can't come after me. She's a real tool, I hear."

"Yes, she is, Mr. Doe," the detective said with a wink. "She tried to murder her own daughter." He shook his head, looking down at the printout of international crimes she had been involved with in the last ten years. "Here. Tell the missus or your girlfriend or whoever, thanks for restraining her."

Luther accepted the sash from Leanne's robe and stuffed it in his pocket. "Well, if we're done here, I have to go visit a friend in the hospital. Thanks for keeping her. Oh, and we certainly don't want her back."

"Yes, sir. Hope all goes well with your sick friend."

"Me, too," Luther said, not bothering to correct him and say he was injured, not ill. "Me, too."

***

André walked down the street, rubbing his arms, chilled in the late-night winter air without a coat or hat.

"Hey, there! Need a ride?"

A black Mercedes sedan pulled up alongside him, the back window rolled down. "You look like you could use some warming up, sweetie," the middle-aged man said.

André looked from the man calling out to him to the driver's window. A grim-faced driver was staring straight ahead, emotionless.

"Oh, don't worry about him, sweetie. We could do anything back here and he wouldn't mind."

"Buy me dinner first?" André asked.

"Dine in or take out?"

"I don't care as long as it's hot and I'm not paying for it," André said.

"Ooh, then we have a deal because it'll be hot and I'm paying for it."

***

"What's the patient's name?" the receptionist asked.

"Silas Priest," Julianna said.

She looked up at her. "Are you his wife?"

"Um, no. We're...dating."

"Practically engaged," Tori said, grinning. "Oh, and I'm not his wife either, but I'm his granddaughter. One of them. There are three of us. We're triplets..." She saw the woman frown, so pressed her lips together, forcing herself to be still.

"Can we have someone look after him, too. He's my son," Julianna said, watching Luther try to urge a confused Oscar into a wheelchair.

"Oh, and I'm not his wife either, but we're dating," Tori said with pride, stepping over to put her hand on Oscar's shoulder, pushing him back down to a seated position.

"And what about you two?" the nurse asked Luther and Leanne.

"Oh, we're married," Leanne said. "But we consider it dating. She's our daughter." She patted Tori's shoulder, creating a link of diverse genders, ages, and ethnicities: tall, dark and concerned; blonde, bouncy, and chatty; seated, stunned and silent; a silly senior couple; plus one gray-haired man laid out in the back room with a triage nurse.

"But you didn't bring the other two?" the receptionist asked.

"Triplets? Oh, no. They were adopted to other families," Leanne said.

"Thank God," the dour-faced woman said. "Everyone but you," she said nodding to Julianna, "go sit down. I think I recognize the name Silas Priest. You," she handed Julianna the clipboard, "fill out this information on your...son?"

"Yes, he's my son," Julianna said. She exhaled in despair and added, "My only one."

"Thank God," the receptionist repeated, then looked up with embarrassment. "I'm sorry. It's been one of those nights. I'm sure he'll be okay. He's not on drugs, is he?"

"Absolutely not!" Julianna leaned down and got in the woman's face. "If you can't handle this job, then I suggest you find another one. And if I'm correct, you're a clerk. It isn't up to you to diagnose or evaluate patients, is it?"

"No, not my job. And yes, ma'am, I'm the receptionist."

"Fine. I'll do my best to be the polite parent and girlfriend involved with two of the hospital's patients, and you pass out clipboards and perform data entry. Deal?"

"Yes, ma'am."

"You sure told her," Tori whispered to Julianna when she sat next to her.

"Grr..."

"Sorry."

Julianna grunted and set the paperwork down. "There are only two men in this world I care about and they're both in the emergency room of a town I'm not familiar with. I have no one. I'm totally ungrounded, untethered..."

"You have me," Tori said, clasping the top of her arm. "And I'll stay with you and be your tether. I promise."

Julianna grimaced, picked up the paperwork, and tried to read it, her eyes glazing over. She set it back down. "Silas and I were just talking about that. If we were to go forward in time, we needed someone to come back to. The word I use is anchor, but tether is pretty much the same thing." She picked up the clipboard and tried again.

"You're wrong," Tori said, then squeezed Julianna's arm until she looked at her. "It's *when* you go forward in time, not *if*."

"You are so much like him."

"Yeah, I know. Ain't it great?"

She picked up Tori's hand, turned it over, and looked at it. "See this line up the middle? Not everyone has one. It's a fate line." Julianna opened her hand and pointed to the same spot. "And I have two. Weird, huh?"

"Weird as in cool," Tori said. "Now, finish those forms. I'm going to see what she meant about knowing the name Silas Priest."

Tori waited until the receptionist was finished with the police officer, then stepped forward. "Excuse me. Would you explain to me what you meant about recognizing the name Silas Priest?"

"You're the granddaughter, right? The triplet?"

Tori nodded, tight-lipped.

"You're the only blood relative here tonight, correct?"

She nodded again, her eyes starting to fill with moisture.

"He's been here before. He has a rare blood type. He donates on a regular basis. He's one of the hospital's unsung heroes. As that tall woman said, it's not my job to diagnose, but if he ever needs blood, there might be a problem."

"Because he's the one you'd be calling, right?"

She shrugged a shoulder. "Would you like to go back and see him? I'd like to let her back," nodding to Julianna, "but I can't legally."

"All right," Tori said, wiping under her eye with a knuckle to make sure a tear hadn't escaped. "But if you have any control when they send my boyfriend back, could you put him in a room right next to my grandpa? It wouldn't be illegal but would be mighty convenient."

She nodded and smiled. "I'll see what I can do. Here, put on this name tag and I'll take you back."

Tori hung the lanyard with the words Family, Visitor, Silas Priest around her neck, then followed the receptionist as she swiped her access card across the security card reader. When they got to the room, Tori clutched her escort's arm. Her grandfather was laid out in a pale hospital gown, the faint green tinge of the cotton drape accentuating his own poor coloring.

"Is he going to be okay?"

"Probably. Most people who come here do go home eventually. The ones who don't get to the hospital are the ones who don't make it." She pointed to the white plastic bag on the chair with his name on it. "Those are his personal belongings. You might want to take any valuables home with you."

Tori nodded then stood by him, holding his hand as the monitors blinked and beeped on a steady basis. A butterfly bandage covered the end of one eyebrow, a huge orange and rose-colored lump beneath it. "You're going to be okay. I promise."

"Not your call," he mumbled.

"Oh, of course it is! I'm your granddaughter. You have a whole lifetime of promises and parties and piggyback rides you owe me."

"Don't know about the piggybacks…"

And then he was out again. Tori looked up. The line on the graph had gone up when he spoke but was now back in the lower range, bouncing on a steady basis.

"Up and down is good, straight is bad," a man's voice said.

"Who are you?" Tori asked then looked at the badge. "Jarryd?"

"That's my name. I'm just the nurse. The doctor will be here soon. They're going to look for clots or aneurysms or little black ants…"

Tori giggled despite her fear. "How long?"

Jarryd snorted. "Have you ever heard of the phrase 'hospital time'?" She shook her head. "Probably because they're still trying to figure it out."

She laughed again, still weak but feeling better to have someone in the room with her.

"You're the granddaughter, right?" She nodded. "Make sure you take any of his valuables with you. Not that we have gangs of bandits roving the corridors…"

This time, she laughed out loud. "Okay, I promise. I'll do that while I'm trying to find a constant variable for hospital time."

Jarryd patted her on the shoulder. "I'll be back shortly. Keep him company. Talk to him. I don't know what just went on, but you got his vitals going in the right direction. Keep 'em up."

"Will do, Jarryd."

Tori waited until the nurse was gone, then set the bag of clothing and other personal items on the table. "Well, he said talk to you." She paused, tongue-tied, and looked around the room for inspiration. "I don't know why that's suddenly a problem," she said, her speech stilted. "I guess it's because I have to carry on both sides of the conversation. Then again, I'll just pretend you're my ventriloquist dummy. Do you like that idea, Silas?"

She laughed nervously and asked. "Do you want me to stick my hand up your shirt and make your mouth work?" She dropped her voice an octave lower, pretending to be him. "No, your hands are cold. How about you be the dummy and I'll be the puppet master?"

Tori frowned, her little theatrics falling flat. "I guess not this time. Well, they want me to check and see if you were carrying a million dollars in your pajama pockets, Grandpa." She dumped the contents of the bag on the chair then picked them up and rummaged the pockets before folding his clothes and setting them in a neat pile. "Who carries a wallet in their pajamas? See, nothing."

She had replaced everything into the bag when she looked up and saw his jacket on the coat hook. "Now, let's see if you have any treasures in there."

Silas's eyes fluttered but Tori didn't see them. He was unconscious but aware, in a sleep state so deep he couldn't move or talk but could breathe. He pulled in a deep breath and tried to snort with the exhale, but didn't have the strength.

"Well, look what I found, Grandpa. Your wallet. Do I have your permission to look through here? I know I'm your next of kin, but I want to make sure you don't keep one of those 'In Case of Emergency' cards…"

Huff!

"Grandpa? You heard me?" She stared at his face, then realized his chest was rising more than a usual breath would require.

Huff!

"Okay, okay. That takes a lot of energy. Let's do like the movies. One blink for yes, two for no. Or is it the other way around? No, no. Let's keep it one for yes, two for no. Now, do you understand me?"

Blink.

"Cool. Now, right now, all I want to know is should I look in your wallet?"

Blink.

"Gotcha." Tori carefully pulled all the cards from his wallet, looked at them, then put them in a neat pile on his belly. "How about that, Grandpa. Our first card game."

Silas's belly went in and out rapidly.

"You're laughing, I know you are," she said, then looked at his eyes.

Blink.

"Is this our special man, Silas Priest?" the very short man in a clean but tattered dingy-white lab coat asked.

"Yes…" Tori answered, frowning as she checked the non-official looking man over.

The man was at least a head shorter than she was, clean-shaven but wearing his hair long, drifting over his worn collar in oily strands. Tori sniffed, wondering if he was a vagrant who hadn't bathed or someone emulating men from centuries ago. He had an earthy smell that was intriguing but in no way foul or disgusting.

"Ah, that will do," he said, taking the bag of belongings from the plastic chair and setting it in the corner. He looked at her and nodded, his mouth pulling aside as if to smile but not quite bringing sincerity to the gesture.

"Who are you?" she asked.

"I'm Mast…um…you may call me Doctor Simon. I'm a specialist here."

Tori's eyes widened as she recognized the near slip on his name. "I think you're Master Simon…" she said accusingly, her eyes squinted, fixed on his for his reaction.

She couldn't have made a stronger impact with an eight-pound sledgehammer. His mouth opened, gasping for words that wouldn't come, then he felt for the chair and sat down.

Tori smirked and set her hand on his shoulder. "It's okay. I'm a friend," she whispered.

He quickly shrugged out of the familiar touch and scowled at her – suspicious but not wanting to leave the room.

"Oh, and I'm also his granddaughter. I'm one of triplets!" she bragged. She realized she was no longer whispering. "Can you fix him? My boyfriend accidentally shot him with a paintball gun. I mean, at the time he was trying to protect his mother and someone shoved him and it went off. It wasn't on purpose. He feels really, really bad about it. Can you maybe erase his memory or something?"

Simon pursed his lips together thoughtfully, then patted the pocket of his jacket. "Whose memory? Your grandfather or your beau?"

"Can you do both?"

He opened his lab coat and verified the contents of his jacket pocket. "Only one. You do know he can hear you right now, don't you?"

Tori nodded. "One blink for yes, two for no." She grinned. "And he just breathes real fast for laughing. He understands funny, too."

"That's good to know. Now, if you'll let me check him out…"

"Here, I'll move the chair around for you. I want to help."

Simon started to tell her he didn't care to have assistants, but her wide blue eyes of concern warmed his ancient time-traveler's heart. Not many of Silas's bloodline were left. She might be special, too. It was better to keep her as a friend.

The two worked together with limited chatter, Tori intentionally biting her lower lip to keep from asking him what he was doing or telling him she was friends with another time traveler, too.

"Now, I have one question for you and then I'll have to ask you to leave the room."

Tori inhaled deeply, ready to beg to stay, then blew out the breath. Sometimes it was best to be quiet and observe. She nodded without a word but kept the pout.

"What's the boyfriend's name?"

"Oscar."

"All right. Go ahead and leave." Simon saw she was reluctant to go and tears were ready to fall. "My dear, I'm going to use a little – shall we call it, medicinal powder? – and say a few *encouraging* words to Silas. I don't want you near either of them."

"Fairy dust and charms?" she asked, wiping under her eyes and nose with the back of her hand.

He canted his head to the side, lifted one shoulder, and softly grunted an affirmative.

She leaned down and gave him a long, hard kiss on the cheek, then scurried out of the room, pulling the door shut behind her.

Simon reached up and rubbed the side of his face. He blinked rapidly, trying to figure out what felt odd. "So that's what a kiss feels like. How soon we forget."

***

"Tori," Julianna called out. "We're over here."

Tori looked from where she had been to where Julianna was. Opposite sides of the emergency rooms.

Julianna recognized her glare of scorn as she walked toward her. "The receptionist apologized all over herself. She said she tried to get us close so I could check on Silas, too, but it wasn't possible. How's he doing?"

Tori nodded and shared a weak smile. "And Oscar?" she asked.

"They gave him some anti-anxiety medication and said to keep him away from any excitement for a few weeks. Oh, and that means no snowball fights for a year. At least. Airborne projectiles are a no-no."

"Got it. Can I see him?"

"Tori, what aren't you telling me? I've never heard you so quiet in my life. Well, even if I've only known you for a couple of days."

Tori held her hand up for her to wait, then stepped into Oscar's room. He was asleep. She pointed to the chairs across from the nurses' station and Julianna followed her there.

"Remember when you were talking about fairies and Master Simon?"

Julianna nodded, her eyebrows crowded in concern.

"He's the one seeing to my grandpa right now."

"Wait. What?" Julianna pulled Tori's chin up then looked in her eyes, checking the dilation for any signs of drugs or insanity. "Are you okay? I think maybe you need a doctor, too."

"No, I'm fine. I kind of recognized him. I asked him to erase Grandpa's memory of Oscar accidentally shooting him…"

"You what?" Julianna screeched, then looked around, offering a weak smile of apology to the only person – a janitor – who appeared to have heard her. "He can do that?"

"He said he's going to try. He could only do one, though. Oscar will know he accidentally shot him but Silas won't. I figured since he was already kind of konked out, it would be easier than messing with Oscar. He's going to be okay, isn't he?"

"Oscar? Yes, I wish you'd chosen the other way. I think the only problem Oscar's going to have is leftover guilt. Silas won't care. He's already one of the most forgiving people who've ever walked the earth."

"I'm sorry. I didn't know," Tori said.

Julianna wrapped her arm around her and pulled her close. "I'm sorry I said anything. It was a flip of the coin decision to make. I'm feeling a little anxious and unsettled, too. If you had chosen the other way, I probably would have found a reason for it to be wrong, too." She pulled out of the hug and looked at Tori. "You know, you're the closest person I've ever had to a daughter." She squeezed her close again. "And it sure feels great."

"You're not the only mother I've ever had, but even having three feels great, too."

***

"A triplet, eh?" Simon said as he looked over Silas. "I guess if there was any doubt that your rare blood type was a fluke, producing triplets even a generation down the line should be another mark in your favor. Or disfavor."

Simon took a small piece of folded paper out of his pocket, opened Silas's mouth, and put a twist of flower stamen under his tongue. "Remember nothing of Oscar, my friend. Nothing."

Chapter 15: Recovery

Tori jumped up and tried to get the short man's attention, frantically waving goodbye. "There he goes," she whispered hoarsely to Julianna.

"That's Master Simon?" she asked, standing to get a better look.

Simon turned around to offer a silent farewell to the granddaughter of Silas Priest, then looked beside her and saw Jane. He blinked twice. No, not her. Tall enough, the same features, but too fair. This one must be her daughter.

He raised his hand in a brief salute and left, waddling behind a male nurse, making use of the other man's access privileges to leave the secure section of the hospital.

"He looked like he recognized you, Julianna."

"I thought he did at first, too. Did you see that little shudder, though? I think he's seen my mother and thought I was her. We look a lot alike."

"Yeah, I look like my birth mother, too," Tori said. "Oh, and they told me to take home Grandpa's personal, I mean, his valuable stuff. They didn't want to be responsible in case bandits came through. This is all he had."

Tori handed Julianna the wallet, studying her face. "He had a few hundred dollars in cash, but I think the most precious item was this." She held out her hand, showing her the ancient Greek drachma drilled with two holes.

"Oh, yeah… It is," she said, adding a soft chuckle of approval and a nod.

"Is this what you need to travel?"

"Yup, and we need another one – one for each of us. That's what we're up to as soon as he gets healthy, a coin hunt." Julianna looked Tori in the eye. "Still willing to be my anchor, Little Miss Tether?"

"Yup."

"And look after Oscar?"

"My pleasure. Oh, and where are you going?"

"We're going forward five years to 2015. I think I know where to find my mom and da. I…um…have to tell them I'm sorry." She held Tori's hand. "I don't care if it's a parent, a friend, a teacher, or someone you accidentally bumped into, never wait to apologize. You never know what tomorrow will bring."

"Like today?"

Julianna looked toward the room Silas was in. "Like today."

"Miss Priest?" a woman asked impatiently as if it was a second or third time.

Tori looked up and saw the name tag read Doctor Johnson and the pinched-face crone was staring at her. "Priest? No, I'm Tori Greene, but my grandfather is Silas Priest. Are you looking to speak with me? I'm his next of kin." Tori almost made an introduction to Julianna, but by the dour look at the professional's face, she didn't want to be bothered.

"Would you like to chat in a private room? I'm here to discuss your grandfather's release orders and plan of care."

"No, here is fine. Actually, my friend will be helping me, so it's good if she hears it firsthand. Proceed."

Julianna chewed back her laugh as Tori gently putting the medico in place then sobered up and listened.

"There is a blood clot right behind the point of impact. Normally, this doesn't happen with paintball injuries. However, if the balls have been stored for a long period of time, it's possible the contents solidified. The projectiles are denser, more like a real bullet. We want to take him in for an MRI to confirm what we saw on the x-ray. I have to tell you, it's a little dicey."

Tori looked over at Julianna and mouthed, 'Dicey?' then turned back. "So, you took x-rays as soon as he got here?"

"Yes, before he even got a room. If there's any internal bleeding, we have a baseline. We can see exactly how much worse it is."

"Or better," Tori offered, leaning forward. "I mean, because it is possible to get better, not worse, right?"

"I suppose…"

"Look, lady," Tori said, standing up and towering over the seated doctor, "I don't know where you studied medicine, but you should get a refund. Anyone with any brains at all knows in healing the body, you never underestimate the power of hope or the destructive force of despair. And you can quote me on that."

"And you just said release orders and plan of care. Is he going home with a potential aneurysm or are you keeping him here for observation?" Julianna asked, hands on hips.

"Oh, wrong papers." The doctor looked at Tori, ignoring the dark angry woman, hoping to intimidate the younger, blonde female in front of her. She pulled her clipboard close and rattled off generic instructions off the top of her head. "Either way, he is to rest, but if he can't be wakened, call an ambulance right away and we'll readmit him."

"I think he'll stay right where he is until we get the MRI results back," Julianna said, rising. "And if anyone has a problem with that, we'll call his lawyer."

The doctor's neck craned back to take in Julianna's height, her stern words suddenly registering as the second blow of a one-two punch. "Right," she said and got up and left.

Jarryd the nurse walked up to Tori. "Thanks. It's about time someone put her in her place. She's about one season shy of retirement and making all of us miserable. She upsets the families who take it out on us."

"What do you do?" Tori asked.

"Tell them we understand and ask them to please file a complaint and let the administration know. We can't do anything."

"Yes, you can," Tori said. "And you're doing it right now. You're taking care of the sick and injured and giving the families hope."

"Thanks," Jarryd said. "Oh, and cool beans on that quote you came up with. I think I'll make it into a label and paste it on all the status whiteboards. We all need to remember that about hope and despair. If you two want to grab a bite, I'll call you when they're done with the MRI and have the results."

Julianna nodded to Oscar's room. "My son is in there. I think he'll be ready to leave soon. At least, I hope so."

"Yup," Tori said, "there's that wonderful four-letter word again. Hope."

Bzz. Bzz.

Tori looked down at her phone and saw the text message. 'How's it going?'

'Good. Be right there.'

"I'm going to let my folks know what's going on. Coming?" she asked Julianna. "I think he has us covered. Oh, and I wrote my cell number on the board in Grandpa's room. Just in case he wakes up."

The women stopped and turned back when they heard Silas roar from across the hall.

"No, I do not want an MRI. I don't need my head examined!"

"Oh, my," Julianna said, leading the way to his room.

Despite her head start and long legs, Tori beat her. "Grandpa, you be nice to these people," she scolded mockingly, her face shiny with tears of joy and a wide smile.

"Tori?" he asked, confused. "Why am I here?" He looked up and saw Julianna, her eyes wide with fear and uncertainty. "Are you sure you shouldn't be the one in bed, sweetheart? You look like you're ready to be sick."

"You remember me?"

"Of course, I do. Both of you. What?" he asked and smiled mischievously, "did I fly in a tornado and land in Oz, Dorothy?"

Tori looked at both of them, unsure about what he had said. The smile on Julianna's face, though, showed it was an inside joke and his mind was clear.

"So, if I know who both of you are, then it's okay to put on some clothes and go home?" He grabbed the back of his hospital gown. "What they put me in is a *little* breezy on the south end."

Julianna laughed and cried at the same time. "All right, but I have to stay here a little longer. You and Tori go on back. Luther and Leanne are in the waiting room."

"Luther and Leanne?" he asked, then blinked, thinking. "Oh, yeah. Your parents, Tori. I'm so glad they dropped in on their way to visit old friends on the east coast."

Tori stole a glance at Julianna. She was as confused as she was. Evidently, there were a few side effects with Master Simon's fairy dust cure.

***

Two days later

"I haven't felt this great in years," Silas said, bouncing around the kitchen, flipping bacon, slicing potatoes and dicing onions. "I hope everyone's hungry because we're having a breakfast feast!"

"Mom, are you sure he's going to be okay?" Oscar asked. "He keeps asking me who I am."

"I think it's selective amnesia. It has nothing to do with you."

"If you don't tell him, I will," Tori said.

"Tell me what?" Oscar asked, looking from her to his mother.

Julianna huffed. "The doctor didn't want you to get excited so I wasn't going to tell you anything."

"Yeah, but not saying anything is more upsetting," Tori said. "So spill."

"I don't want you to get mad because it has to do with time travel and you always get wound up…"

"Mom, just tell me, all right?"

"When that paintball pistol accidentally discharged…"

"When I shot Silas, you mean," Oscar said.

"Accidentally discharged," Julianna repeated firmly, "it seems the paint in the ball had solidified. It inflicted more damage than normal. Brain trauma."

"Yeah, I remember the blood and you carrying him like a child to the car."

"It didn't look so good. Well, it just so happens an old…as in very old…"

"Ancient time traveler," Tori spit out. "Speed it up or my folks will be here and we'll have an audience."

"Tori, you tell me," Oscar said.

"This Master Simon did some mumbo jumbo and fairy dust and made Grandpa forget you ever shot him. Except I think he did a little too much mumbo or dust or something because he keeps forgetting who you are. The good part is, Grandpa will never know you hurt him. Can you deal with that?"

"God, I love you, Tori," he said and pulled her close. "Yes, I can. Mom, you try to protect me too much."

"Well, I suppose that's why the Lord made both mothers and wives. Or girlfriends."

"You had it right the first time. Tori and I are getting married soon. Very soon."

"Yup, and we don't want anything fancy. Just legal. And our family. Especially my sisters. And…"

"Everything good over here?" Luther asked, carrying a tray of drinks in his hand.

"Nothing's plain around here, is it?" Oscar asked, taking a crystal goblet of orange juice with a wedge of sliced strawberry on the side.

493

Luther grinned then frowned at Julianna. "Are you sure he's going to be okay? Whatever it is they gave him in that hospital, I'd like a drop or two."

"Maybe they gave him some Fountain of Youth water," Tori said, then giggled into her hand.

"If they did, I'm all for it. He's like a puppy with that boundless energy."

"Tell me about it," Julianna whispered into her goblet, smiling.

Luther sat down beside his daughter. "Drink up, Tori. It has lots of vitamin C."

Tori took a glass, ready to salute. "Grab a cup, Grandpa. I'm toasting."

Silas took his goblet and lifted it. "Go for it."

"Here's to friends and family and all the good memories we'll make from this day forward."

"Here, here!" everyone toasted.

"Here, here," Oscar said softly and put the strawberry in his mouth. "As long as he doesn't forget Mom and Tori, that's good enough for me."

Chapter 16: Trial Run

Later that day

"Mom, we've been back from the hospital for less than six hours and he's already asked me four times who I am. I'm sorry, I thought I'd be fine, but I can't take it."

"Oscar, it might take a while. He has head trauma."

"I know, and it's all my fault. I talked with Luther and Leanne. They're both cool with Tori and me leaving with them. I made a call to the Youth Advocate Council. They said we can start our volunteer work any time we're ready." Oscar took a deep breath. "And believe me, I'm more than ready."

"You were ready a long time ago. Yes, go ahead and pack. If you need anything, you still have the credit card. Make sure you pay for gas and a few meals for everyone along the way."

"I'd ask if you're sure you'll be okay without me, but by that dreamy-eyed look you have, I can tell you're still in honeymoon mode."

Julianna felt her face warm but grinned in pride rather than feel embarrassed. "Do you know how good it feels to have an open relationship with you?"

"Yes, I do; it goes both ways. I'll be fine. I don't know if you've noticed or not, but I think Luther thinks of me like a son. He's even called me that a few times. We got along great working together in Oregon last summer, but this just feels...different."

"Mutual respect goes a long way. Will you all be staying for dinner?"

"Sorry. Luther and I talked about it. He's fine with leaving right away to beat the traffic."

"You'll hit it no matter when you leave."

"I know, Mom. And so does he. Luther's just considerate that way."

Julianna pulled Oscar close and rocked him back and forth like a baby. "I'm going to miss you."

"Hey, I'll always be in your heart. Besides, you have a new life ahead of you. Young love, even if it is about twenty – or forty – years late."

She kissed him on top of the head. "Having no secrets feels so great."

"Yes, it does. If you don't mind, I'm going to skip saying goodbye to Silas. It just hurts too bad, seeing him ditzy like that."

"Well, thank God he's only that way with you. Here's hoping it's temporary."

"Speaking of keeping secrets, Mom, Tori said you sort of had a plan... Were you going to tell me about it?"

"Yes, but I thought I had a few months, or at least weeks, to get the details worked out. Since you're leaving for I don't know how long, I'll give you the outline now. Tori knows the basics, but sometimes she goes off on a tangent and

495

misses the main point when explaining it to others."

"That's for sure." Oscar double-checked his chair for broken glass shards and sat down near the boarded-up window. He looked up. "I'm ready – shoot," he said, then squeezed his eyes shut in embarrassment. "I mean, let me have it."

"See, your sense of humor is already covering for your insecurities. The big plan is Silas and I will go to 2015 to see my parents. We might make a test hop for a few hours, but I'll let you or Tori know. Before we do anything, he'll have legal paperwork drawn up so Tori's designated as the caretaker. She'll have power of attorney for everything he owns. He'd like it if when we're gone, you two stay here."

"Two? You don't think he'll have a problem with me, a stranger?"

"I'm sure he won't. Doesn't. Before the accident, he liked you. I don't plan on leaving his side, so I'll remind him that you're Tori's beau if he forgets. Or when he does."

"Good, because I won't be going anywhere without her."

"It sounds like you plan on spending the rest of your life with her?"

Bottom lip stuck out in determination, Oscar nodded. "As soon as we can, we're getting married. I mean, we have to establish residency here in Massachusetts, I think. So, you plan to leave from now, 2010, and you'll skip forward to 2015?"

"Yup. We'll only age a few seconds in the time you and Tori and everyone else will have aged five years."

"Wow. A lot can happen in that much time. Just think of where we were five years ago?"

"Thanks, but I'd rather not," Julianna said dryly.

"Yeah, come to think of it, me neither. So, what do Tori and I have to do?"

"Don't change the locks or access codes to the garage and keep the tags on the Cadillac current. Oh, and you might want to take it for a spin once a month or so just to make sure all systems are go. Silas and I will pop in, say hi and tell you how it went, then grab the Caddie and drive to North Carolina to see my parents. Simple, right?"

"So, if you're going to stop by and say hi, why do you want to make sure the locks aren't changed? Won't we still be here?"

"I hope so! Look, I know what date we're aiming for, but if we're off by a month, or even a few years, we don't want to be stranded. Cash we can take, but it's a lot easier if we already have wheels and a home to come back to. Besides, if we miss by even a few hours, you might be out shopping or something."

"Sounds good." Oscar stilled and looked into his mother's eyes, not saying a word.

"What?"

"I want to remember you as you are right now, Mom. And say how sorry I am for not believing you. Man, life must have been miserable, knowing what

496

you do and not being able to tell anyone."

"Meh. I had you to keep me busy for most of that time. Now you have a life and I have the companion I've always craved."

"Well, that much is obvious." He patted her hand. "Take good care of him. He's a great guy....even if he can't remember who I am."

"Yes, he's the greatest. Well, at least next to you."

✳✳✳

One week later

"There! That's exactly what we need," Silas said, pointing to the picture.

Julianna enlarged the image on the computer screen. "Except for the holes, but you can drill those." She sat back, lips pursed, her arms crossed under her breasts, a scowl covering her face.

"What's wrong. I thought you wanted to do this."

"I do. But obviously something's bothering me. Silas, how much do you remember about last week?"

"It snowed?" He shook his head. "I'm sorry. I don't know what you're referring to."

"Do you remember seeing Luther and his family?"

"Of course, I do. They came to Vickie's wedding. Tori let everyone know I was her grandfather and therefore Grace's father. I got to see Ria and her family again..."

Silas stopped talking when he saw all emotion drain from her face. "That's not what you wanted to hear, is it? I mean, did I miss something important?"

"Yes and no. Let's not worry about it now." She sat up straight and pushed her hair back in frustration. "Go ahead and make arrangements to inspect the coin. I want to make sure this isn't some scam."

"Are you sure you're okay? You ask me a variation of that same question every day. I'm about ready to print it out and just hand it to you."

"Nah. Don't worry about it. I guess I'm insecure and want to make sure you healed completely."

Silas rubbed his fingers over the spot near his eyebrow. "It's just barely tender. When Victoria or André grabbed my paintball gun and popped me in the noggin with it, I was more worried about you. But you and Tori doctored me up and I was good to go."

"Whoa. You never said that before."

"What?"

"You don't know who shot you then?"

Silas took the strand hair she had moved behind her ear and twirled it around his forefinger, then leaned in and kissed her full bottom lip, slack with shock. "What difference does it make? We're here, together, with a plan. Those two scum are gone out of our lives forever."

"Where?" Julianna asked, a smile growing, her eyes now bright with curiosity.

"Don't know, don't care," he said. "Do you want to go upstairs and celebrate finding a coin?" He took the original drachma out of his pocket. "I'll flip you for who gets to be on top."

She took the proffered coin with a grin, happy that he'd remembered more of the events from the week before. Maybe he *was* getting his memory back. Now *that* was worth celebrating.

***

One week later

"That's it?" Silas asked, looking around at the budding trees. "Are you sure it worked? Everything looks the same."

"Did you drop your coin or lose focus?" Julianna asked.

Silas shook his head, looking in his hand to verify he still had the drachma.

"Then it should have worked. Grab a newspaper and check the date. Hey, I wonder if cell phones grab the info automatically like when you fly to a new time zone?" She looked at her phone and laughed. "Mine says critical system update needed to connect to the network."

Silas checked his. "Mine does, too. But hey, look on the bright side. These batteries lasted a year without a charge."

"Now that should be a world record. All we need is to find a paper to verify the date, then pop back home. No one will even know we left."

Silas hemmed and hawed for a moment then said, "Well, except for Tori…" He turned and looked around. "Where's a newsstand when you want one?"

"We may be in New York, but we're on the outskirts of Bethel, and you won't find so much as a convenience store to buy one."

"Let's start walking and see if someone offers us a ride." Silas looked up and saw the sunrise peeking over the hill. "This way. Walk away from the sun until noon and then let it warm your back until it sets."

"Maybe next time. I don't want to be gone that long. I only want to verify we can travel – make a safe round trip – then go home and get ready to see my parents."

"Good idea. Hey, look over there! Come on." Julianna and Silas jogged up the road a few hundred feet to a cluster of mailboxes in varied shapes and colors. He looked inside a long narrow red container placed next to them and took out a rolled-up newspaper. "March 21, 2011. We made it a year. I can't see a reason we can't make it to five, can you?"

"Sounds doable. Let me see that for a minute, please."

She opened it up. "Japan earthquake toll continues to rise," she read aloud. "Crap. Another disaster."

"Are you thinking your sister's ex-boyfriend has something to do with it?"

She shook her head. "Catastrophes have been happening since… Well, that's pretty much how the world began, isn't it? With a big bang? Much as I'd like to blame Storm for everything, I can't. Still want to, and now I'm more determined than ever to stop him."

"Whoa, wait, Jules. I thought we were going to see your parent so you could apologize. Do you have a hidden agenda?"

"Well, yes and no. Yes, to hidden, but it's not really an agenda. Rumor is there's a bag of coins stashed at my folks' new place."

"Coins, as in drilled ancient silver drachmas?" Silas asked, re-rolling the newspaper and returning it to its weatherproof housing.

She nodded. "Yup. That's another reason I chose the date. I want to retrieve them before he shows up and starts locking. With that many coins, he could equip a whole army of mischief-making minions…and I don't mean the cute little yellow guys who talk funny."

"Little yellow guys?"

"Believe me, you'll know who they are soon enough. Now, let's go home."

"Stop for breakfast first? You know, I'd like to celebrate my first time travel experience with at least a cup of coffee and a pastry."

"We're only halfway there. We have to make a safe return for it to be considered successful."

"Do we have to go back to the exact time? Couldn't we skip over all the mud and slush of spring break up?"

"Well, since I wanted to go to September tenth, 2015 for the 'big trip,' we might as well try a smaller increment in date deviation. How about a month – April sixteenth? That way, we can skip tax day."

"Sounds good to me. I sent my return in the first week in January, so I'm good."

***

One month later by the calendar
One hour later by biological clocks

"Well that worked out well," Silas said. "We're home." He rubbed his chin. "And we weren't even gone long enough for my whiskers to grow."

Julianna looked around and saw the cherry trees were blooming, all the ice and snow was gone, and a fresh flush of green grass was overtaking the golden-brown carpet of a dormant lawn.

Silas looked at Julianna, standing frozen as a Greek statue at the end of the driveway. "Was it that ridesharing car? I mean, we could have chanced it with hitching a ride but…"

"No, I'm just scared." She looked at the post that housed the security keypad. "They changed it."

Silas ran his fingers over the bricks. "Nice job of covering up the old bullet holes." He felt the side of the structure and noticed his override system was still there. Would it still work if a new mechanism had been installed? "Try the code.

You do remember it, don't you?"

Julianna snorted a quick laugh. "It's only been a day, sweetheart. Dementia usually takes a while," she said then gasped, remembering how quickly Silas had lost his memory of Oscar. "Well, it usually does."

"Does that mean you're not going to ask me about yesterday again?" Silas asked, one eyebrow raised. "I mean, you haven't so far today."

"Actually, I'm not. Nothing but looking forward today. Oh, and just a suggestion. When we get a chance, we might look up the news highlights for the last month on the internet so we're current. I haven't lived in this era before. Who knows? Maybe something big happened?"

"Go for it," Silas said, pointing to the keypad.

She keyed in Tori's birthday and the gate swung open.

"Home again," Silas sighed. "Let's go see if the walls inside are still standing."

Before they got to the porch, Tori and Oscar were running down the drive to welcome them home, arms open, Tori squealing like the winner of a Miss America pageant.

"We were worried about you," Oscar said. "We went out there every day for two weeks, but Tori told me to chill out. If it was her, she'd wait until spring to come back."

Silas and Julianna looked at each other with suppressed grins of guilt. "Well, obviously it was a great idea, or she wouldn't have had it, too," Julianna said. "That's my girl."

"Oh, and speaking of your girl, how about legally gaining a daughter?" Oscar asked. "We want to get married soon. Like as soon as possible."

"What about your youth corps group?" Julianna asked, then raised her hand to stop his answer. She looked at Tori again, this time carefully. "Let me guess, there's a reason you want it right away and part of it has to do with her taking it easy for the next what...eight or nine months?"

"See," Tori said, "I told you we wouldn't have to tell her, that she'd guess right away."

"Well, I always knew he wanted to marry you. I think I figured that out the first time I saw him beaming when he talked about you on the phone. You're positively brilliant with that pregnancy glow." Julianna looked at Oscar. "You are too, but yours is marred by a gray smear of doubt about how you'll do as a father."

"How...how did you know? I mean, I don't know if all guys feel like the same way, but I didn't exactly have the best role model in the world."

"Hey, I'm your mother, aren't I? I know everything about you. You'll be fantastic."

Silas watched the back and forth banter, content to be an observer, impressed by how a month had been spanned in less than a minute. Tori's boyfriend was going to be her husband. He was glad she had found someone. The young man…

'I'm your mother, aren't' I?' she had said.

He's Julianna's son? Silas's knees started to buckle. *That's why she keeps asking me about yesterdays.*

He took out his phone and opened up his calendar app. He quickly typed in 'Oscar is Julianna's son' and hit 'repeat as daily reminder.' Something was wrong with his memory, but not with his brain. He'd fix it right now, one way or another.

"Hey, Grandpa, isn't your birthday next week?" Tori asked.

"Um…"

"Today's April sixteenth," she whispered.

Silas took a breath and answered, "Then, yes. Well, a few more days than a week. It's April twenty-fifth."

"Cool. Let's have a party. And before you can say anything about getting older or whatever lame excuse you can scrounge up for not having a celebration, remember, it's the perfect way to get all our families together."

"I'll say okay to the party, but let's announce the wedding at the same time," Silas said.

"How about a compromise. Can we just tell *some* of them?" Tori asked. "Our *condition* is still a secret. I think my papa threatened to emasculate Oscar if he bedded me without being married first."

"Okay. I'll leave the wedding announcement part to you two." Silas sniffed under his arm and shook his head. "If you don't mind, I think I'll go freshen up. It's been a month since I've had a shower."

Julianna copied the movement. "Nope, it's not us. I think that car we came in had one too many air freshener trees in it."

***

"It's okay, Mama," Tori said. "We'll all be here, and that's all Oscar and I care about. White weddings are overrated. I think they're for the mothers of the brides, not the brides." She looked at the pile of bridal magazines her sisters had given her, leftover from their weddings. "Well, maybe some brides, but not me."

"I'm fine with it, too," Oscar said. "Everyone we care about is already here for Silas's birthday. Tori and I got the license and he's an ordained minister. Shoot, he already performed the ceremony for his other two granddaughters. Might as well make it all three sisters."

Leanne wiped her face again. "It's just you've always been my baby."

"And I always *will* be. That's not going to change. I wasn't going to say anything, but you're going to be a grandmother. You'll have babies to play with before you know it."

"Babies? You're having twins? Triplets?"

"I don't think so. I mean, I'm just a little bit pregnant…"

"No such thing," Luther said. "I'm glad I overheard it. It's the easiest way to find out." He looked over at Oscar and huffed. "I guess my threat can go out the window since you planned on marrying her anyway."

"We would have been married six weeks ago if we hadn't been waiting to make sure Silas was going to be okay. That seems to be his new bad habit, scaring the dickens out of us. First, the head injury and then a week later, disappearing just like that." Oscar snapped his fingers. "*Poof!* He and Mom, gone without a trace for a month."

"But they're back now," Tori said firmly, "so on with the show."

"Oh, and my mom wanted to add a little color to the event." Oscar handed a package to Luther and a bag to Leanne. "I guess you could say this is a costume wedding. No tuxes allowed, though."

Leanne looked in the oversized sack he had given her. "Oh, my! This looks just like my old hippie uniform!"

"She had them made based on what she remembered and the old photographs. Go ahead and change." Oscar looked at his watch. "Show starts in an hour."

Luther clutched his box close but didn't open it. "Come on, Rapunzel. I'll help you fix your hair. Here's hoping Julianna allowed for the few inches that forty years of your homecooked meals added on."

***

"Vickie! Ria! Grace! Oh, my God! Where's a camera. We need to get pictures of us," Tori said, squealing. "I haven't seen you in...in..."

"Since two months ago at Vickie's wedding," Grace said, "but to me, that's about fifty-nine days too long."

"Hey, Other Mom," Vickie said, "We all live within a couple of hours drive from each other. You pick the day of the month, and we can fill the calendar with rolling mothers-and-daughters reunions."

"Are you sure your moms won't mind?" Grace asked. "I mean, they brought you up..." She looked at Ria and grinned. "Well, except Ria. Chuck had help for a few years, so I guess I'm your only mother, even if I never changed a diaper or bandaged a scraped knee."

"Okay, Other Mom," Tori said sternly but with a smile, "I'm going to blame your moodiness on my pregnancy hormones. Knock it off, already. We all turned out fine."

"Yes, you did," Grace said, "but I have a few of my own lady-hormones kicking in. We're pregnant. Dusty and I are having twins...at least."

"No way..." Vickie said. "At your age? But you're going to be a grandmother in eight months."

"And you're getting little brothers and or sisters in seven. And hey, I'm only thirty-seven. I'm still plenty young enough to have at least one more pregnancy after this one."

"Depending on whether we want to go through more in vitro," Dusty said. "Hey, girls. Looking good in your sixties retro gear. How do I look?"

The girls' biological father, Dusty, a handsome brown-haired man, turned around in place, hippie beads dangling around his neck, full-sleeved pink paisley shirt, and hip-hugger bell-bottom pants covering his sockless sandals.

"Anyone up for a love-in?" Luther asked, announcing his presence. "Look at this." When he twisted back and forth, the fringe on his vest swung out nearly a foot. "I feel so groovy, man…" he drawled.

"Mama?" Tori gasped, seeing her mother standing in the doorway. "Your hair! It's so beautiful. Shoot, you could go as Lady Godiva and not get arrested for indecency. It's like a blanket over you."

"Her silver shield," Luther said softly. "Leanne, you're as gorgeous today as you ever were. No, wait. Even more so."

"Oh, you really should have that cataract surgery, Luther."

"No, my eyes are fine. The cloudiness is the gilding from loving you all these years, gold and silver streams of love, sparkling with memories of passion, joy, and tenderness. Of moments shared together, of everyday events made special by your nearness."

"Wow, Luther. You just kicked up the standard of saying sweet nothings to the ladies about fifty feet higher," Oscar said, Dusty and the other men mumbling agreement.

Luther looked at Oscar and winked. "You can call me Dad, Son."

"Thanks, Dad. I'll do that."

Chapter 17: A Woodstock Wedding

"Dearly beloved, we are gathered here today to witness the marriage of these two fine young people, my granddaughter, Tori Lynn Greene, and Oscar Rickman Shaw…"

A loud wail interrupted Silas. He paused to let Leanne compose herself. Luther was beside her, sniffling into a bright red bandana, patting her back with his free hand. His gentle reassurances, though, had gone astray. Leanne's knee-length hair – and the flowers and ribbons weaved into it – were now snarled with the beaded fringes of his vest. Grace, wiping her own tears on the puffy shoulder of her granny dress, was on Leanne's other side, trying to unknot the elderly couple. Her hands, though, were heavily bejeweled with costume jewelry. She was like Brer Rabbit and the Tar-Baby, now tangled in the mess as much as Luther.

Dusty had promised himself he would keep it together, letting the attention go to Luther and Leanne, the couple who had adopted Tori. His emotions had rejected the memo, though, and his lower lip was trembling, tears slipping through his lashes. To wipe them away would prove their existence. He sniffed and realized no one at the wedding cared whose blood ran through whom or which names were shared. They were all family. His family. He wiped his face on his pink calico shirt and hollered, "You go, Tori and Oscar!" hoping to give Grace time to straighten out Leanne and Luther.

"Tori! Oscar! Tori! Oscar!" the small clan joined in. Silas watched from his impromptu podium of a barstool seat stacked high with journals draped with a vibrant tie-dyed length of fabric. Pride bloomed warm in his chest. From over fifty years as an acknowledged bachelor to a member of such a diverse and passionate family. He took in the brilliance of Julianna, his special lady friend. Nearly a head taller than those around her, her long hair was accentuated with colorfully beaded braids, her grin showing she was as content with her collection of oddball relatives of choice as he was.

Silas turned back to Grace, Leanne, and Luther. When he saw they were no longer tied together, he raised his hands to silence the chanting. "As I was saying, my lovely granddaughter, Tori Lynn Greene, the daughter of Leanne and Luther Greene and a person most special to Grace and Dusty Rhodes; and Oscar Rickman Shaw, the son of Julianna MacKay Shaw, a person most special to me…"

Julianna's eyes sparkled as she clutched Dusty's other arm. "You tell 'em, Silas," she whispered.

"…to honor and respect each other, through good times and bad, whenever and wherever life takes you?"

"I do," Tori said.

"And do you…"

Did he just say whenever? Julianna looked at Grace and Dusty, then Luther and Leanne, then across the aisle to Tori's triplet sisters and their husbands. If anyone had heard Luther's unusual variation of the wedding vows, their faces didn't show it.

"I do," Oscar said.

"Then by the power invested in me by the Commonwealth of Massachusetts, I now pronounce you husband and wife."

The hugs, kisses, and crying overwhelmed the room, but it was Tori who called it back to order. "I have an announcement to make," she said, stealing a glance at Oscar, then fixing her gaze on Silas.

Oscar paled. He wasn't ready to announce his impending fatherhood yet. Tori's two sisters had already been married a few months and they weren't pregnant. He didn't want this to be a race.

"I just want to say a special thank you to my grandfather, Silas Priest, ninth-generation Mayflower descendent of Degory Priest. For those who know him, he's a man of many talents. But being clever or a great cook or exceedingly handsome…"

Tori paused, waiting for the anticipated laughs and applause to finish, then continued. "All these assets are pale in the rainbow of life when it comes to class. Oscar and I asked for a short ceremony. We wanted the service to be fun, with family and close friends, but legal. The way we figured it, the shorter the ceremony, the more time for celebrating. But what he did in less than one hundred words was to acknowledge the two people who gave me and my two sisters life. And he did it without lessening the importance of the parents who brought us up. Who thought that something which started so grim could come together so beautifully? Thank you, Mama, Papa, Other Mom, Other Dad, and all my other biological and emotional family members."

Oscar looked at her with pride at her generous words, sighing in relief that she hadn't spilled the beans.

"Oh, and thanks, Grandpa," she said, interrupting the applause, "for giving my husband, me, and the rest of our family…" Tori patted her flat belly, "a home to stay in while you and Julianna go on your grand tour."

The group clapped, hollered, and whistled as Oscar turned beet-red, suffering the backslapping from his sisters-in-law's husbands.

"Don't worry about it, cousin," Rick said. "Vickie and I were waiting until after the hubbub of your wedding to announce our new addition."

"Um…" Evan interjected.

Rick and Oscar looked at the other newlywed husband who was now a sickly shade of puce. "I guess I can say something now, then," he said reluctantly. "Ria's pregnant. Surprise!" he added softly with a weak smile. "Oh, and I hope you guys don't get morning sickness, too."

"Is that what's wrong with you?" Rick asked.

"Uh-huh. Ria's fine, it's only me who's miserable. Our wives may not have known each other growing up or done things together then, but they're sure making up for it now."

"No kidding," Oscar said. "Oh, in case you haven't heard, Grace is pregnant, too. Silas is getting two – at least – grandchildren from her and Dusty, and then at least one each from his granddaughters."

"Yeah," Rick huffed. "All within a few months of each other. That's a lot of messy diapers."

Oscar started laughing, then shook his head and grinned broadly, recalling an earlier conversation with his mother.

"What's so funny about messy diapers?" Rick asked.

"Not that. I keep finding packs of condoms all over the house. I asked Mom if Silas was giving me hints or something. She blushed scarlet – which is hard to do when you're as dark as she is – and said they were for her and Silas. They...um...liked to be spontaneous and she is still fertile."

All three men burst out laughing, then turned to find Silas. He was still at the podium, speaking with Dusty. The three young men all gave him a thumbs up. "You're next, old man," Oscar shouted across the room.

Silas paled, knowing they were teasing him about becoming a father. He feigned a wide-eyed look of confusion. "Who are you?" he asked, then laughed before Oscar could reply. *"Que sera, sera,"* he added, not caring if his glimmer of anticipation shone through.

"What will be, will be," he said softly and smiled at Julianna. *Sometimes being careful doesn't work when you're a Fertile Ferdinand.*

Chapter 18: The Real Deal

Two weeks later

"Are you sure you don't want to wait a month?" Tori asked.

"Why? We already discovered we could play around with the calendar," Julianna said. "Besides, you don't want us running around this place, bumping into each other at, ahem, inopportune moments. There's no reason to confine yourselves to the guest house. If you're here all the time, you're just a few rooms away from work. I still think it would be easier if you converted one of the bedrooms into a second office. You don't need to share the same one."

"It feels more like a business this way," Oscar said. "You don't know how much paperwork is involved with getting people off the streets and settled into jobs and homes, finding medical services, and such. I can look up and ask her a question rather than sending an email."

Oscar stopped when he saw his mother look down her nose at him. "Hey, what can I say? I like being around my wife. I get the idea you and Silas enjoy each other's company a lot, too."

"Hmph. Just a little bit…" she admitted with an embarrassed grin.

Tori rose from her desk and moved into Julianna's arms. "I'm going to miss you, but I'm glad you have the opportunity to get closure. Who knows, when you go back to see your folks, maybe your sister will be there? You'll get two wishes for one."

"Three," Oscar corrected, coming to stand on his mother's other side. "She has two parents."

"Yes, she does," Tori said. "And I have…" she paused to count on her fingers, smirking at Julianna. "Even if I had a dozen mothers, I'm still going to miss you when you're gone."

"I'll miss you, too," Julianna replied. "Silas and I are leaving in the morning. He's getting the Caddie checked over and fueled up right now. Oh, and he's packing a few clothes and such in the trunk. I don't think they'll get too stinky, sitting in a car for five years."

"Don't worry, Mom," Oscar said. "I'm sure Silas has already planned for that and has everything in an airtight container. I can't believe how selfless that man is. I swear everything he does is for someone else. Be sure to make time for something you know he wants to do, okay?"

"Absolutely."

✳✳✳

Silas awoke at five-thirty as he always did. He looked over and saw Julianna, her eye twitching as she smiled in her sleep. He took his smartphone from the bedside table and opened up the calendar. Two items showed. 'Oscar is Julianna's son' and 'Departure Day.' *Her son? She has a son?* He noticed the little icon. At some point, he had set this as a daily reminder. *Crap! Am I getting senile?* Then he looked at the other event: Departure Day. *Now that, I remember. There has to be a reason for setting 'Oscar is Julianna's son' as a daily repeat. Best to trust myself and not delete that reminder.*

He put the phone back and snuggled into Julianna. As always, her arms pulled him close. "Mine," she whispered. He felt her tense then relax.

"Are you okay?"

"Oh, yeah. I just remembered what day it was," she answered, her smile growing as she sighed in satisfaction. "D-Day."

***

The ride to Bethel was an emotional patchwork of pained, awkward silences, giddy recollections of joyous past events, and soft-spoken words of hope. Once they were at the copse of oak trees – the site of the portal – their farewells began.

"I'm glad you let us bring you here rather than get a rideshare," Oscar said. "I knew where the site was because Tori and I came here looking for you when you didn't come back right away the first time." He shifted in his seat, took a deep breath, and looked at his mother. "Don't think I'm being weird or anything, but I want to see what it looks like when you *go*."

"Me, too," Tori said. "But what I really want to see is you coming back. Can you take a quick trip in and out – or is that back and forth? – for me? I mean, for us?"

"Tori, I don't know how many times I can do this," Julianna said. "It doesn't hurt, but what if it deteriorates the body somehow? You know, like wearing out your favorite shirt by washing it too many times? I want to be respectful of it. Just remember, today isn't a final good-bye but more of a 'see ya' later' farewell."

Silas reached out and put his arm around Oscar. "Make sure you take care of that great-granddaughter of mine and her aunts and cousins, too."

"You sound pretty sure we're having a girl."

"And my sisters and Other Mother, too?" Tori asked.

"Family tradition," Silas said. "You're all alpha females. From my experience with strong women, they only beget more strong women. I don't think you two could build a boy if you tried."

Oscar chuckled. "Oh, we'll try all right. Not to have a son, but to have a big family. We were both only children..."

Tori raised her hand and interjected, "Brought up as an only child. Sorry, Oscar. Go ahead."

"And as long as we can give our children what they need emotionally and physically, we want plenty."

"That's all well and good," Julianna said. "Just remember there are literally thousands of children out there without families. You can always bring a few of them into your lives. I know my parents did. I can tell you from my own experience, all of us – siblings, parents, and the foster and adopted kids – were happy with the arrangement."

Oscar looked at Tori. "Well, we'll save room for another build-it-yourself baby, just in case we get a second surprise."

Tori patted her belly. "Yes, she's a surprise, but not unwanted. You just chose your own time, didn't you, darling," she said looking down.

"They always do," Julianna said.

"One more hug and squeeze and then we're out of here. If I stay any longer, I'll want to go back to the house with you two," Silas said.

"Ah, Grandpa. You and I know you wouldn't let Julianna go anywhere without you."

"Oh, he would," Julianna said. "But not for long. One way or another, we'd find each other…even if it took twenty years or more."

***

"That's it? They're gone. They just walked through and disappeared?" Oscar asked.

"No, they didn't 'just' do anything. They had their coins and their focus. No wonder your mother wanted to keep them out of the hands of others. Someone with an evil agenda could create all sorts of chaos."

"Hey, Tori, did you ever wonder why they never found JFK's shooter? Someone could pull a disappearing act like that if there was a portal near Dallas."

Tori paled at the thought. She shook her head, stunned at the concept. "I don't even want to go there," she said. "I'm ready to leave. This place is sad."

"Only because they just left," Oscar said, holding her close, his hand stroking her back as if she was a skittish foal. "It'll be the happiest place on earth when they come back. Let's go home. Immersing ourselves in work and pasta should bring us out of this funk."

"I hope so," she said.

"Ah, there's your favorite four-letter word again, hope. Come on. We'll get an ice cream cone on the way home – drop-in or drive-through, your choice. That's better and faster than pasta."

"Deal."

***

"Um, since the leaves on the trees look a lot drier than they did when we started walking through them, I'd say we did it. At least for a few months. Try the phones again?" Silas asked.

Julianna wiped sweat from her brow, then reached in her pocket and grabbed her cell phone. This trip through was different. She felt queasy. Here's hoping it was nerves and not some weird cellular breakdown. "Mine says, 'Multiple updates required,'" she said, stingy with her words in case her voice was as shaky as she felt.

509

"Twenty-three updates required before this phone is functional," Silas recited. "Hmm. I wonder if those folks still get the newspaper." He looked up the road. "They do. Race you there!"

"Nah, I'll save my energy," Julianna said, then looked for a boulder or barricade to sit on.

Silas pulled the newspaper out of the now faded red tube. "September seventh, twenty-fifteen." He folded it back up and returned it, chuckling. "Ah, five birthdays have passed, and I don't feel a day older."

"Just as sweet and sassy as ever," Julianna said, hoping she sounded brighter than she felt.

Silas jogged over to the guardrail and sat down beside her. "Tired?" he asked and reached out to hold her hand, surreptitiously checking her pulse rate. It was weak, but not dangerous. Her hands cool but not clammy.

"Do I pass the physical, Doc?" she asked, a smile in her voice.

"With a strong C, maybe a B minus. Bad case of nerves?" he asked.

"Yes, I'm pretty sure that's what it is," she answered, looking away so he couldn't check her eyes for signs of fibbing, or at least stretching the truth soap-bubble thin.

"Well, you sit there, and I'll see if I can get someone's attention." Silas tried mussing his hair, then realized it was too short to make a difference. He frowned and stuck out his bottom lip with an exaggerated pout, then looked at her, hoping to elicit an honest smile. "How's this? Do I look pathetic enough?"

She chuckled as much from his silly expression as from appreciating his effort. "Yeah, that'll steal a second look and get somebody's sympathy engaged. If you don't mind, I'll stay here. My height isn't so intimidating if I'm sitting down."

Several dozen cars and transport trucks later, a gold-colored minivan pulled over for them. Silas waved heartily, then grabbed Julianna's hand to help her up. The driver saw her struggle and put the vehicle in reverse, cutting the distance by half.

"Where to?" the dark-haired young man asked Silas. "Oh, and Mac doesn't take up much room. I can easily fit two more, even with his mega diaper bag."

"Destination Plymouth, Massachusetts, but anywhere east of here is a good start."

"He's adorable," Julianna said, letting the redheaded toddler grasp her finger.

The driver stomped on the brakes at hearing her voice, halting his access onto the highway. He looked in the rearview mirror, for the first time seeing the face of the tall woman. "Jane?" he asked.

Julianna's eyes opened to maximum width and her jaw dropped. She stared at the man. "Do I know you?"

A sly grin crossed his face. "I've never met you, but I might know your

510

parents."

Julianna felt a warm glow of recognition begin. "Is that why you asked if I was Jane?"

He nodded. "Maybe I shouldn't say anything…"

"Um, do you two know each other?" Silas asked, his stomach turning flip flops with their sudden change from strangers to old buddies.

"He's never met me, but…" Julianna looked at Billy in the mirror again, then winked at Silas. "Did you say this little boy's name is Mac?"

"Nicknamed for his godfather," Billy said, smiling as bright as the rising sun on a clear summer day.

"Silas, our driver is Billy Burke Melbourne. Oh, and I'd like to introduce you to my older brother, Wee Mac." Jane bent and kissed him on the top of his head. "My da's surprise."

"Hold on, folks," Billy said, watching the traffic for another break. "This van's fueled up and we're heading to Plymouth! We're taking a detour, Mac."

Silas sat dumbfounded for a moment, the casual chatter between Billy and Julianna completely going over his head. "Can I interrupt you two for a minute? Julianna, would you give me just a more of background, so I know what's going on?"

"I've known Billy since I was a child, probably younger than Wee Mac. They haven't met me because technically, I haven't been born yet. I'm still about two years from conception. Anyhow, my da and mom and Billy are old friends. When Da bought Mom from the eighteenth century through the portal near Greensboro… That was what, two years ago, Billy?"

"Only one," he said. "What a trip, your mother riding in an automobile for the first time. It was this one, too. But I'm hogging the story. Go ahead."

Julianna took a deep breath, happy to be able to speak freely of time travel, comfortable with the company she was with. "There's some big secret – which I really don't want to know about – of how Wee Mac came about, but his birth mother died just after he was born. They had already agreed to put Billy's name on the birth certificate as the father: no blood test required. Billy and his husband adopted Wee Mac without a problem. When all this happened, Da was in the eighteenth century, meeting Mom and catching up with his grandparents. He didn't even know he'd sired a child."

"Surprise," Silas said softly, then blushed at his lame joke.

"Yeah, well, when he and Mom came back, they worked everything out with Billy. Da is officially Wee Mac's godfather. I saw Billy and Wee Mac every year until I left…"

Now it was Julianna's turn to be uncomfortable, her words and excitement stilled with the memory.

Trying to spare her, Silas turned the topic of conversation sideways and the focus on the boy. "So, this is your half-brother? He's a cute little fart."

"Fart," Wee Mac said, giggling at the new word.

"Pass gas," Billy corrected, then laughed. "Oh, what the heck. He's going to hear it plenty by the time he gets to school."

"And that's how come *you* know Billy," Silas said to Julianna, "but *he's* never met you. Wow. This is strange. No wonder you didn't want to say too much to each other at first."

"I just want to ask one thing. It's Julianna, right?" Billy asked, waiting for her nod. "Do I go bald?"

She chuckled. "No, you don't. In about eighteen years, you'll have the most intriguing silver streak running through your hair. And Wee Mac here…"

"Yes, yes…" Billy asked.

"He's going to be tall and smart, not necessarily in that order. And he'll have the most mischievous sense of humor. All I'm going to say about that is always look before you sit down. Peanut butter looks like something else when it's on the outside of your pants."

They all laughed out loud. Wee Mac repeated, "Pants," then stuck his thumb in his mouth and snuggled into his car seat, already worn out from the drive.

"Is Plymouth your final destination?" Billy asked, looking at Silas.

"That's where I live. We're picking up my car there and dropping in on the kids for a couple of days. That leaves us three to get to North Carolina. Julianna wants to be there by the tenth."

Silas noticed Billy frown, glance at his watch, then look up again.

"I hate to tell you, but today's the eighth," Billy said. "If you want to be in North Carolina, you're going to have to shave some time somewhere. We're about five hours out of Plymouth now. It's a long day or day and a half drive south from there to Greensboro. Even with two drivers, you'll have to take a few breaks. You'll have to make it a quick visit with the kids."

Silas took out his phone. Still no signal. "Damn," he hissed, then gasped in embarrassment and looked at the baby to see if he'd heard. The young mimic's eyes were shut, fluttering with dreams.

"Time travel mess up your apps?" Billy asked, nodding to Silas's phone.

"Yeah…"

"Here, use mine. The map function is already open. Go ahead and plug in your destination. I can reset it easy enough."

"So, Uncle Billy, what were you doing out here?"

Billy chuckled warmly at the designation. "I wanted to see where the original Woodstock Festival was before Mac and I started our first annual tour of Revolutionary War sites. His grandfather – yours, too – fought in the war, but I figured I'd just say he had ancestors involved in helping create the United States. Or something like that. In the last two years, I've found that no matter how hard you prepare, most of parenting is winging it."

512

"Ain't that the truth," Julianna said.

"Do you two have children?" Billy asked, looking from one to the other. He saw Julianna's face go blank, then quickly added, "Oh, wait. Don't tell me. If I'm going to see you sometime in the future, I don't want to know *anything*." He paused and added. "Well, except for the important stuff like whether I keep my hair or not."

She and Silas shared a grin, both relieved at not having to explain the complicated arrangement of Silas's daughter, granddaughters, and all those adopted parents and their spouses who made up their large but loving family.

Julianna brightened. She knew Silas had been on the sidelines of Grace's life, very much like her da's godfather relationship with Mac Melbourne. She ran her fingers through the sleeping boy's ginger hair. Strange but wonderful how things worked out. Her da's surprise, her half-brother.

"Benji and Jane's little girl," Billy sighed, then looked up at her in the rearview mirror.

Julianna heard him and caught his gaze. "Uncle Billy," she said.

"Nice meeting you."

Chapter 19: Arrivals

September 8, 2015

"It doesn't look like anyone's here," Julianna said.

"You're being paranoid. I mean, cars aren't usually in the driveway when we get home." Silas got out of the van and walked around to the access panel and punched in the code. The gate swung open and he got back in.

"Go ahead and pull up to that side, if you will, Billy," he said. "We can go through the garage."

Billy glanced in the rearview mirror to see how Julianna was faring. She looked scared, nervous, *and* paranoid.

"Ow, JuJu," Wee Mac said, pulling up on her index finger to loosen her grip on his wrist.

"Oh, sorry, honey," she said and let go, gently patting his hand in apology.

"It feels like we're in an old sixties black and white TV series," Billy said. "All that's missing is the eerie music."

"Doo de doo doo…" Silas sang then got out again and reentered the code at the door.

"Do you want to come in and meet everyone?" Silas asked brightly.

"Um…maybe not," Billy said, glancing back at his son. "I don't know how to explain this to him. He's young but seems to pick up on a lot of what's going on."

"Do you think he'll want to be a detective like his daddy?" Julianna asked, her funk disappearing as she talked about her favorite 'kin,' as she always called Wee Mac.

Billy's chest puffed in pride. "I don't care what he does as long as he's honorable and does it because he wants to, not has to."

"Ah, spoken like the world's best dad." Julianna leaned in and whispered, "That's what he always called you."

He grinned, then his face fell. "What about Peter?" he asked softly. "He's still around, right?"

Julianna's voice returned to normal. "Oh, he calls Uncle Peter 'the world's best pop.'"

He sighed in relief. "Thank you. I don't think I want to know even a little bit more. Too much room for misinterpretation. You have it from here, right?"

She looked around to make sure. "Silas. Silas? Where are you?"

The throaty hum of the Cadillac turning over let them know where he'd gone. "We're all set to go after we say hi to the kids," he shouted, standing beside his car.

"Then this is goodbye for at least two years," Julianna said. "Do me a favor, remind me of this when I'm about six or seven…or whenever you think I can handle it."

"How about four or five? I'll bet you're a bright little girl," he said, stepping out of the van to give a proper farewell.

She reached around and gave him a hug that ended with a hard kiss on the cheek. "You've just met me, but I haven't seen you in over twenty years. Weird how I miss you and yet I'm a stranger to you."

"Not weird at all," Billy said, giving her a hearty squeeze back. "I'm just grateful for the preview of what a wonderful woman you become. Take care of that man of yours. Something tells me he's a keeper."

"We met at Woodstock," she whispered. "But don't worry. It has nothing to do with you and your trip there. Oh," she gave him a firm kiss on the other cheek. "Give that one to Uncle Peter next time you see him. You don't have to tell him it's from me, though. I know when I'm sixteen, he still doesn't know about us and time travel. He suspects something's odd about our family but always shakes off hearing any details."

"So, I guess this means you're heading for your tour of historical sites with the young man, then," Silas said, offering his hand to Billy.

Billy shook it heartily. "Never too early," he said. "I figure if I start now, maybe it will make it more personal to him later."

"Just like giving skis to a two-year-old," Silas said.

"Yup, that's on the list of winter activities in a few months," Billy said. "Take care of this woman. I probably won't see her as an adult again."

"Yes, but you'll love me as a little girl."

Billy reached up and wiped at his new-sprung tears. "I have to go. I don't want to even think about telling Mac why I'm crying. It's going to be hard enough to tell him who you are."

"Just tell him we were nice hitchhikers," Silas said. "Nice meeting you, and thanks for the ride."

Billy nodded, then got back in the van. "Come on, sport. Time for American History 101, the Pilgrims and the Mayflower. The Revolutionary War will have to wait a while."

Julianna waved goodbye, surprised she wasn't crying but Billy was.

"Are you all right?" Silas asked.

"Yeah. Seeing him is like a vibrant dream, the kind where you have to pinch yourself to find out if you're awake or not. He was here, but he wasn't."

"But you'll see him again, right?"

"Yeah. Hey, let's go scout around and find out where Tori and Oscar are. I want to see if I have a granddaughter or a grandson."

Ten minutes of calling out plus a thorough investigation of the garage and guest house revealed a large playroom with lots of children's toys plus three single beds and a crib distributed between three bedrooms.

"Five years and four children?" Julianna asked. "My boy's been busy."

"Your boy?" Silas asked. "You have a son? I thought we were here for Tori and her husband, Oscar. Didn't I just marry them just a few days ago? I mean, a few days before we left?"

Julianna groaned deep in her throat, holding back the scream of frustration. *I thought that 'forget Oscar' crap Simon had brainwashed and fairy-dusted him with had worn off. Is time travel screwing him up again?*

"Silas, I'm going to tell you again," she said slowly and deliberately, "Oscar is my son. Okay? Please don't forget. Again."

"You said again twice. Does that mean I forget all the time? Sorry, I'm sure it does. Do I forget anything else or just that? I'd hate to think I have dementia."

"No, just that," she said, easing up on her severe tone. "Excuse me, that sounded rude. Let's leave a note for them then go. It's really sad being here in an empty house. I'm sure there's a good reason, though."

"Well, dear," Silas said, "from what I see, I bet they're having another baby. The nursery is stacked with newborn-sized diapers and clothing, and the other three bedrooms look like the children's maid hasn't been here for a while."

"They'd never have a maid."

"Exactly. If *your son*, Oscar, has been busy tending to three youngsters and a very pregnant wife, I doubt he'd care if the older children made their beds or not. He'd be more concerned if they were clean and well-fed."

Julianna chuckled, remembering her mother when the twin boys were born, dealing with her and Mali at the same time. "Semi-clean and at least fed cereal with milk," she said. "Don't forget to leave a note."

Silas stepped into the playroom filled with building blocks, toy cars, and a shelf unit of art supplies. He shuffled through that and found a tablet with paper pre-printed with picture-framed edges. He tore a piece from it then set the pad back. He wrote on the back of the page in blue ballpoint pen, 'Sorry we missed you. Grandpa'

Silas chewed on the end of his pen as he stared at the note, trying to remember what else he was supposed to say. He saw a picture on the table drawn by a child. It was a red-crayon rendition of a person with sticks for arms and legs, lots of straight-lined fingers, and a big circle for a belly. 'MOM' was written at the top of it.

"Oh, yeah," he whispered and added 'and Mom' after Grandpa. "Don't forget again. Oscar is her son, Oscar is her son," he repeated then wrote it on the inside of his wrist. He turned to leave and saw Julianna, standing in the hallway.

"Check it out." He picked up the picture from the table and handed it to her.

"Mom," she read. "Oh, my God! Her child drew a picture of Mommy. Tori's pregnant again."

"And that's why they're gone. I'd say they've been *very* busy."

She handed it back. "Leave the note somewhere you know they'll find it and let's go." She sniffed back tears. "I'll meet you in the car."

Silas went to the kitchen. A young family always seemed to visit the fridge more than any other place. He looked at the refrigerator door, already covered with children's art. He resisted the urge to take the drawing of a blue dog – or horse or hippo – for himself but did use one of the fruit-shaped magnets to affix his note to the door. As he was leaving, he saw it. A plate of brownies.

"Bet you can't eat just one," he said, lifting the plastic cover and taking a piece. He popped it in his mouth, then grabbed two more. "One for my Jules and one for the road. Thanks!"

* * *

At that same moment, across town

"Just one more push and she's outta there," Oscar urged. He turned back and looked into the hall. "Okay, kids. Do you want to see your sister come out?"

"Nah, we're good," Hope said. "Hey, boys, I'll trade you this doll for one of those cars."

Huff, huff, huff, huff. "Leave-them-out-there," Tori blurted as one word, then pushed. "Catch!"

The midwife was ready but had to nudge Oscar out of the way when he leaned in at the last minute. "Excuse me, Dad," she said.

"Oh, sorry." He stepped back, then looked over her shoulder, biting his lip with a mixture of fear, eagerness, and excitement.

"One more push…" the midwife said.

"I-know-I-know," Tori grunted.

"And there she is." The midwife pulled the baby out the rest of the way. "Well done, Mom. Another perfect little girl." She suctioned the birth fluids from the baby's nose and mouth then set her on Tori's belly and bent to finish her work.

Two minutes later, the baby was cleaned up and swaddled in flannel, ready to meet the rest of the family. "Here you are, Dad," the doula said.

Oscar sniffed, unbidden tears dribbling down his cheeks just like when he'd held Hope for the first time. "Do we want to name her now or later?" he asked, then handed her to Tori.

"Ah, she's so cute," Tori answered, ignoring his question. One hand on her new daughter's back, Tori leaned to one side and looked out the door. "Let's get me cleaned up a bit more before bringing them in. As long as they're not *too* quiet, they're good."

"It's okay to be sad. I miss my mom and Silas, too," Oscar said. "They'll be back. You just have to have faith."

Tori grunted, partly from an afterbirth pang, mostly from hormone-enhanced anger. "We have other things to consider. Did you hear from my dad today?"

517

Oscar shook his head and bit his bottom lip. "He said there wasn't any cell service out there. Next time he was in a town, he'd call. If he knew this one was coming early, they never would have started the tour."

"Yeah, well, I told them to go ahead. The baby would come with or without them. Dammit." Tori saw his wide-eyed but silent admonishment. "Dammit because I told them to go when I should have asked them to wait. I love you and the kids, but for once, I'd like a grandparent here when a baby was born."

***

Two hours later

"Okay, kids, I'm fixing dinner again. Do you want chicken salad, scrambled eggs with veggies, or tuna surprise?"

"What's tuna surprise?" three-year-old Andrew asked.

"Yeah, huh?" his twin added.

"It's canned tuna with mayonnaise and the same vegetables I'd use for the chicken salad or eggs. You just get to choose your protein."

"Rock, paper, scissors," Hope said. "One, two, three."

Hope's open-handed paper gesture covered Jamison's and Andrew's rocks. "Okay, Dad. Let's go with the chicken tonight. Need help?" the perpetually helpful girl offered.

"Nah, I got this. Why don't you take the boys in the playroom and build something?" Oscar asked.

"Sure thing." She pulled the new piece of paper off the fridge with one deft tug. She'd color the back of it so she wouldn't have to bother Dad to get the tablet down from the top shelf. "Come on, guys. You build the castle and I'll be the princess in the tower."

***

"I'm sure this is the way," Silas said, rubbernecking to get a better glimpse at the street signs whizzing past.

"It doesn't look the same," Julianna said. "I think we should have taken a left at that exit in Trenton this morning. Why don't you pull over and ask at the gas station?" She looked over his shoulder at the gas gauge. Seeing it was still half full, she changed her tactic. "I need to make a pit stop, anyhow."

"Can you wait just a little bit longer…"

"No. I'm uncomfortable. Please, just let me take three minutes to pee and for you to ask the way to Lynchburg. From there, I know it's pretty much due south without any interchanges."

"I'm sorry. Look, I'll pull in here and check the map again. Would you get me a big cup of coffee when you're done?"

Julianna huffed then changed it into a cough. "Sure. Black?"

"Add a little cream and a lot of sugar, if you would. I don't want to take the time to stop for lunch." Silas looked up, realizing he had unintentionally

518

made another decision without asking her. "Unless you'd like to?"

"I'll grab something when I get the coffee."

Julianna splashed water on her face after she'd used the bathroom and washed her hands, hoping to perk herself up. She was tired but had dozed just outside of Plymouth. Poor Silas had been driving for over twelve hours. He'd been up for at least thirty-six.

She grabbed the first sandwich she saw from the shelf and fixed a tall super-sweet coffee with extra cream in it for him. If he wasn't going to eat, at least he'd have calories to run on. "Excuse me, sir," she said to the convenience store clerk. "Can you tell me how far we are from Lynchburg?"

"Quite a ways, ma'am. Once you get to Richmond, you can follow the signs and take Highway Sixty right to Lynchburg."

"Whoa, wait. Richmond?"

"Yes, ma'am," he said. He took out the oft-refolded map from under the counter and pointed to the red circle. "We're here. Richmond's just a few miles south, and then you take Sixty over to Lynchburg."

She unfolded the map one more section. "Or we can keep going south on Eighty-five and hit Greensboro without taking any exits. Thanks," she said, handing him a twenty-dollar bill. "Keep the change. You just made my day."

"Back at ya, lady," he said, pushing up his Dallas Cowboys ball cap. "You made mine, too."

Julianna walked up to Silas's side of the car, handed him the coffee, then came around and got in. "Good news and bad news. We took the wrong exit way back around Trenton. Good news is if we stay on this road, we'll wind up in Greensboro. From there, I could find my way blindfolded. Let's not worry about that yet, though. Drink up. I don't know if my stomach's burning from excitement or fear, but I have tuna on wheat and a box of milk. I'm ready to roll."

"Me, too," Silas said, then put the Caddie in drive. "Me, too."

Chapter 20: The MacKay Manse

Silas slowed as he approached the destination. "It's up ahead. You can see the roof from here."

"Stop, stop, stop," she said. "I know where we are now, for sure. I'm not ready yet. Pull in under those trees. That's where the state stockpiled rock for road repair."

"By the looks of it, they still do. Do you need a moment?"

"Yes. I want to take it all in. I mean, you know how a surgeon steadies himself, sort of prepares before he goes into to do an appendectomy or whatever?"

"I know the principle. Priests and preachers pray, actors meditate, athletes stretch…"

"Okay, okay. You got it. Roll down all the windows and turn off the engine. I want to hear the sounds of this place."

Silas did as she asked, then listened with her. The gentle squawks and chirps of birds, the rustling of grasshoppers in the weeds, and the wind blowing through the dried bamboo peppered the otherwise stillness. "Not so quiet, eh?" Silas whispered.

Julianna turned in the seat, the squeaks of the cushion against her clothing suddenly seeming loud. "Amazing, isn't it?" he added.

"You see that stand of bamboo? Da's going to transplant it to our place as a windbreak. I think he did it so he could watch us from the house and make sure he knew where we were. Not that he needed line of sight. All Mom had to do was listen for us. That woman could hear a cockroach fart."

Silas chuckled. "I'd sure like to meet that woman."

"You will…if all goes right. Okay. I'm ready. Let's go."

Silas started the Cadillac and pulled back onto the two-lane road. "And there it is."

"Oh, my God," Julianna gasped in horror. She looked at the shabby, weather-beaten building then at the phone's map again. "That's it? I mean, it has to be, but really? That's the MacKay Manse?"

Silas glanced at his map, then up at the number scrawled on the paint can lid wired to the fence. "Indeed, it is. You did say your father bought this place as a fixer-upper, right?"

"Yeah, but… Wow, I have a new respect for all the work he put in. I never saw pictures of the original place. Man, what a dump!"

"Meh," Silas mumbled. "Nice big chunk of land. Looks like there's some water down that way, too."

"A creek that runs all year. How'd you know?"

Silas grinned. "The green trees. Everything else is parched. I'd say by the dry vegetation that it's quite verdant in the spring and summer."

"What?"

"By the height and density of these weeds, the water had to come from somewhere. Since I didn't see irrigation equipment or ditches and furrows, I'd say it was from natural rainfall."

"I'm always amazed at how much you see and how little most people do. Hey! There's a car out front. I don't know who that is, but I'll bet it isn't my parents. Keep going up to the next driveway and park about halfway down. That's commercial acreage and no one's ever there except when it's time to seed or harvest."

Silas pulled in and shut off the engine. "Stay put. I'll go see who it is." Not hearing a reply, he looked and saw her eyes were wide in fear. "Hey, I got this, okay?"

Julianna nodded, dozens of scenarios going through her head, none of them good.

The noise of the idling muscle car parked out front covered the sounds of Silas wading through the tall grass and weeds toward the house.

From the edge of the overgrown field, he watched as a red-haired man – even taller than Julianna – pulled the rickety screen door off its hinges and stepped inside. Now more curious, Silas ran to the house and stood beneath the window, listening. The man was angry, cursing in Swedish or Norwegian. He caught a word. Norwegian. The intruder's heavy footfalls headed for another part of the house. Silas stuck his head through the glass-less window and peeked inside.

He was in the kitchen now, looking up. *Whoosh!* Silas watched as the man jumped into the attic – no stairs or ladder required. *Thump!* More curse words, boxes and or furniture being kicked around, and then running steps. Silas moved back into the brush and watched as the man leaped out of a window at the back of the house, as agile as a cat jumping off a three-foot fence. The man dusted off his hands, strode back to his bright-yellow Camaro without so much as a backward glance, and sped off.

Silas stood up, looked inside again, then headed back to Julianna and the car. This had to be Mali's ex-beau Storm, looking for coins. If it was, Julianna might be in danger.

Julianna and the car were gone! Returning to the house – hoping she had driven around to pick him up – Silas heard a vehicle approach. It wasn't his Cadillac or the Camaro, though. It sounded like a truck.

Two tall men got out of the huge late-model pickup, both redheads. *What is it with all these giant red-haired men?* The one with fairer skin was leaning through the truck's open window. "...Just hit the horn if ye need me."

Silas moved aside, hoping for a better look. *Yes! With that accent, it must be Benji. And he's speaking to Jane. Yes! Yes! Julianna's parents are both here. She's going to be ecstatic… Oh, shit! Where'd she go?*

He backtracked to where he had parked. She still hadn't returned nor had she moved the car further up the driveway. *She'll come here eventually, I know she will. I hope she will.* He looked up again and saw Jane, sitting by herself in the truck, fanning herself with a magazine. Time to make an introduction.

Silas wiped his face with the shoulder of his shirt, ran his fingers through his hair, then took a deep breath. *Like a Priest before a sermon.* He chuckled at the play on names, then walked up to the side of the truck.

"Hi, I'm…" he began, then stopped when he saw how scared she was. Jane scooted away from the window, her eyes wide, little gulps confirming her fear. She reached out and smacked the steering wheel, pounding it everywhere, finally finding the horn button.

"I'm sorry I frightened you," Silas said, then moved away.

"Step away from my wife!" Benji bellowed as he strode towards him.

"I'm sorry. I'm truly very sorry," Silas said, taking two more steps back. "She looks so much like my fiancée. I mean, my friend," he stammered. "Well, I was going to ask her to marry me soon. Very soon. Maybe even this evening." He paused and took a deep breath, oblivious to the rage in the fairer man's eyes. He squinted at the other man again, wondering who he could be, then shook his head. *Sleep deprivation. Are there really two Benjis or am I hallucinating?*

Trying to compose himself and restart the conversation on neutral ground at the same time, Silas looked up at the dilapidated house in awe. "She said this was the place."

"Who did?" the darker Benji without the Scottish accent asked.

Silas looked from him to the man he was certain was the real Benji, verifying they were two different people. Their physical forms were very similar. Other than the accent, they even sounded alike. One had African heritage, though, and the other did not. Or not enough to show.

"Just a sec," the man without the accent said. He stepped between Silas and Benji and opened the truck door for Jane.

"I've never met anyone who looks like me," she said, her hand on second man's arm as she gracefully straightened to her full six-foot-four inches.

Silas half-smiled, half-grimaced in return. "Your children look like you," he said sheepishly, shrugging one shoulder.

Jane's legs buckled, but the second man was ready and reached out for her, pulling her close so she could compose herself.

"My mother?" the man asked softly, his eyes bright with excitement.

Silas watched confusion overtake the second man's features but was unsure of what to do or say, so stayed mum.

"My mother was here?" he asked again, shaking his head. Then his indignation and voice exploded. "You know my mother?" he shouted at Silas.

Silas's mouth opened and shut, fatigue and uncertainty slowing his explanation.

The man snorted, frustrated at not getting an immediate reply. "Well?" he bellowed.

Silas looked at Benji to see his reaction.

Previously angry, Benji's rage had now been replaced with a mixture of puzzlement and fascination. Now it was his turn to shrug. "What he asked," he said, nodding to the other man. "Answer him."

"Let me back up a little. Or a lot, depending on how we're measuring *time*," Silas said.

Jane and the men looked back and forth between each other with an identical curiosity.

"*When* did you come from?" the non-Benji male asked.

"2010. Just a short five-year hop forward. Oh, forgive me for not introducing myself. I'm Silas Priest from Massachusetts."

"What are you doing here?" the man asked, continuing the interrogation.

"Now, before I answer a lot of questions – and I will answer them all," Silas said in his most congenial but no-nonsense tone, "may I have the pleasure of knowing your names?"

"Mac MacKay. This is Benji MacKay and..."

Mac paused his introduction and stared as Silas went ga ga, back gazing at Jane.

Silas felt himself grinning as if he'd just met a movie star. "So, it is you, isn't it?" he asked. "I mean, do I have the pleasure of meeting Jane MacKay?" He picked up her hand, not sure whether to shake it or kiss it.

"Am I supposed to know you?" she asked and stepped back, holding her hands behind her.

"I never had the honor," Silas said, "although I've heard what a charming and beautiful woman you are. Yes, your beauty is beyond description..."

Benji stepped between Mac and Jane, mumbling an 'excuse me' to Mac. "Ye'd better not be makin' a pass at my wife, especially with me standin' right here," he said, his arm around her protectively.

"Oh, I'm so sorry. I think that came out wrong. I haven't slept in nearly forty-eight hours. Julianna and I drove all night and day from New England." Silas looked back to the porch. "If you don't mind, I'm a bit light-headed, sleep-deprived, dehydrated... What I'm trying to say, is can we sit on the porch? A bit of shade would be welcome."

Mac came up to Silas and helped him to the porch as Benji moved some barrels around to serve as seats. "Hush about Julianna for now, all right?" Mac whispered.

Silas took a deep breath and nodded. "Who are you? I feel like I'm in a dream."

"You're not. I'm Mali's son, Julianna's nephew. Benji and Jane are my grandparents, and yes, I'm from your future. Kick back and chill for a bit. The show is about to begin."

Silas leaned against the wall. Jane was next to him, a stoic look on her face as she watched a small sports car come up to the house. Soon, Mac and Benji were speaking to a short man with a toupee, discussing the purchase price of the property. Words flowed in and around Silas, dreams stumbling over reality, events and conversations distorted by lack of sleep and too much sugary caffeine. His head jerked up from a slumped over position several times, then the scent of Julianna brought him about.

"Do you smell that, too?" he asked Jane.

"I do," she said. "It smells like flowers."

Benji sniffed, turning his head to follow the scent carried on the gentle breeze. "It's coming from down there," he said.

Mac jumped over the steps and picked up a pink floral scarf. He sniffed it. "It smells like lilies of the valley."

"Actually, it's a perfume called Lily of Lourdes," Silas said, accepting the piece from him. "Put your hands out," he said.

Mac gave him a quizzical look but did as he was told.

"I don't have a worktable," Silas said. "If something's in here, it will fall into your hands, not onto the ground."

"Sounds like you've done fieldwork before," Mac said.

"My nickname's Sherlock. I guess it's considered a hobby since I've never charged for my services," he said and carefully unwound the fabric.

Benji and Jane watched the proceedings. "There!" Jane said. "Look, there's something written on it."

"Coins 4 J," Silas read. He folded it in half and shook it over Mac's hands, hoping a scrap of evidence would drop. "There! Grab it before the wind catches it."

Mac held onto one long curly dark-brown hair. "Do you recognize the scarf?" he asked, looking at Silas.

"It's Julianna's. So is the hair, I believe. It must have flown out when the window was rolled down."

"Let's put this whole conversation on pause fer a moment," Benji said, looking between Silas and Mac, then back at Jane to make sure she understood his reference. She nodded that she did. "I asked ye before and we were interrupted by me makin' the agreement to buy this place, so I'm asking ye again: who is Julianna to me and my wife?"

Silas turned to Mac, one eyebrow raised, asking, 'Which one of us should answer?' Mac shrugged, so Silas replied. "She's your daughter. And also my fiancée or girlfriend, depending on her answer…when I get a chance to ask her."

"I thought Mali was our daughter," Jane said, her hand gently touching her lower belly.

"They both are," Mac said.

"Julianna's your second born," Silas added. "By the clock, I met her six months ago. By the calendar, it was five years. She came back from 2032 to 1989, looking for Mali. She's never found her as far as I know. I mean, I re-met her at a wedding. We recognized each other from Woodstock in 1969."

"But you just said she went to 1989, not 1969," Benji said.

"She took a detour, looking for Mali. It didn't pan out," Silas said. He looked at Mac, his new associate detective. "Does 'Cash 4 J' mean anything to you?"

"You really need to get some sleep, Silas," Mac replied. "It says coins, not cash. Big difference."

"Especially when it comes to time travelers, aye?" Benji said.

Silas groaned softly and shook his head.

"What?" Mac and Benji asked at the same time.

"Julianna and I had a drachma for each of us. She said she had hidden a bag of them here at the MacKay Manse a long time ago. That's the other reason we were coming here – to get them."

"Well, where are they hidden?" Benji asked. "We'll give him those and get her back."

"It's not that easy," Silas said. "Even as ditzy as I'm feeling right now, I don't believe he really has her. I think this is a fake ransom note, meant to make us retrieve the coins for him."

"If he doesn't have her, where could she be?" Benji asked.

"Maybe they're still here. Where did the girls hang out when they were younger?" Mac asked Jane, then winced in embarrassment. "Shoot! I'm sorry. They haven't even been born yet. You wouldn't know, would you?"

"Well, maybe I would," Jane said with a sly grin. "If I lived here as a child – and I did over two hundred years ago – I'd be out there at the trees, playing in whatever water was available, enjoying the shade."

"Now that's some clever thinking." Silas said. "Let's go find Julianna."

Benji paused and mused, "Julianna."

"I've never heard that name before," Jane said, "but I like it."

"It reminds me of a dear friend, my Uncle Wallace's stepfather," Benji said. "Julian Hart. Yes, even if ye hadna told me about it, I'd lean toward choosing the name Julianna fer a second daughter."

"Then let's get moving and see what we find at those trees," Silas said. "And if Julianna's there, the second thing I'm going to do is ask her to marry me."

"What's the first thing?" Mac asked.

"Make sure she's all right and not in danger."

Twenty feet from the trees, they all heard it. Giggles from two females coming from up high in the branches, and then a 'shush' admonition. "Someone might hear us," one voice whispered.

"Julianna!" Silas hollered, running to the source, ignoring Mac's warning to be discreet.

Thump!

Julianna dropped out of the trees. "Shush!" she repeated. "He might still be here."

"Who?" Silas whispered.

She looked around to see if he was alone, then saw three people come forward slowly, each one staring at her as if she had a purple horn sticking out of her forehead. "Mom? Da? And who are you?"

Thump!

Another woman dropped from the branches, also agile despite her forty-something years. Mali.

Silas inspected Julianna, patting her shoulders, pausing his wellness check to cup her cheeks, and ask, "Are you sure you're all right?"

Benji held Jane close as they watched, stunned. They were seeing their daughters for the first time as adults, completely passing – and missing – their infant through teen years.

Silas was down on one knee. "You're sure you wouldn't mind being married to an old man with gray hair?"

Julianna squealed again and this time, grabbed him by the elbows and pulled him to his feet. "Gray hair, blue hair, or no hair – yes! I want to marry you."

Silas heard Mali and Mac bickering. Something about Storm and a legend or a curse pertaining to a son. He didn't care. From what he understood, Mac was Storm's son. It was his and Mali's problem. Julianna was here with her parents and they could reconcile. Mali was safe and – after a few days or hours of reconnecting and apologizing or whatever time traveling families did at reunions – he and Julianna could return to good old 2010, Grace, Tori, her sisters, and all those babies that were due before summer of 2011.

"Excuse me," Silas said, putting on his peacekeeper's shawl. "If I may offer an observation. If the legend is true, I would think that this Storm person would try to eradicate all of his progeny, not just Mac. Julianna, how do you know he has another heir?"

"Because he's my son."

"You have a child?" Silas asked, his voice ending on a high note of surprise.

"Not again!" Julianna hissed. Her eyebrows narrowed and she bent to look him in the eye, determined once and for all to permanently impress the fact somewhere in his pickle-loaf brain. "You know him. A few months ago, you performed his wedding ceremony. Remember Oscar, your granddaughter Tori's husband?"

"Oscar, yes. But he's white..."

"Ergh!"

Silas put up his hand, hoping to calm her, then noticed the inside of his wrist. 'Oscar is J's son' was written so only he'd see it. "Do I have dementia?" he asked.

"No. It's complicated," Julianna said, resigned to a life of constant reminders. "Let's just say you had some selective hypnotism and I can't seem to reverse it."

"Oh, that's easy enough. Maybe I should get this tattooed, then?" he asked, showing her his penned crib note.

Julianna laughed. "No. How about if I just stick around and try not to get bitchy when you forget? Oh, and maybe update your phone so it'll show up on your daily calendar. Worked before."

Chapter 21: Homecoming

Twenty-four hours later

"Are you sure you don't want to go back to 2010? You're positive about staying in 2015?" Silas asked. "I mean, it is the only way you can catch up with everyone. Storm's neutralized. Benji and Jane have a plan. Mali and Mac are sticking around to help them build the MacKay Manse. I guess we could return to the time you left, but I'd be totally lost. At least, for a while. It would be pretty odd arriving in 2032, though. You left as a sixteen-year-old and if you suddenly showed up…"

Julianna cleared her throat and said, "Older?"

"That's a good way to put it."

"I'm positive. True, we'll miss Tori and Oscar's first years of parenthood, but I'm sure they took lots of pictures. I don't care how we explain being gone. Maybe we can tell everyone else we got stranded on a desert island."

Silas shook his head. "You look too good. I think we'd either be emaciated or wrinkled from too much sun, rather than looking like it was only yesterday – not five years ago – since we'd left."

"This should be easy then. All we have to do is drive north to get on with our lives. No trip through any time portal trees required," she said.

"Just a few hours of drive time and a couple of tanks of this era's high-dollar unleaded gasoline. Oh, and a new driver's license next month for you."

"Expired already? That I can handle."

"Especially since you'll need a new one anyhow."

"Why?"

"Because you told me you'd marry me. I was sort of hoping you'd take my name."

"Julianna Priest. Sounds good to me."

"Me, too. Come on. One more round of farewell hugs and kisses, and we'll hit the road. Our next MacKay family reunion should be a lot easier to manage."

"And I'll get to see Uncle Billy again!"

***

The next day

"Hey, I know who you are," Hope said. "You're my other grandma." She looked at Silas. "And you're my other grandpa! Hey, guys, our other grandma and grandpa are here."

Two little boys, their skin as dark as obsidian, their faces identical except for the odd shapes of their heads, bounded into the room. "Hi, Other Grandma and Other Grandpa," they said, chattering over each other.

"Go ahead and give them a hug," Hope directed. She saw their reluctance and huffed. "Like this, guys." She reached around Julianna's knees and squeezed tight, almost toppling her. Silas saw what was coming, and as soon as the young girl neared him, held onto Julianna to steady himself.

"When we dropped in a while back, I saw something with Hope written on it. Is that your name?" Silas asked, now squatted down to her level.

"You were here?" she asked. "We didn't see you. Were you playing hide and seek and forgot to tell us?"

"No, I left a note and put it on the refrigerator. Oh, and I took a few of those brownies," Silas said. "They were delicious," he whispered.

Hope heard her father come into the room. "See! I told you I didn't eat them," she said.

"Mom? Silas?" Oscar said, tears welling. "Oh, thank God you made it. I was afraid you were going to stay and we'd never see you again."

"Stay? We're all in the same time now," Julianna said. "We were in North Carolina, visiting my family there."

"So, you had a chance to catch up with your parents?" he asked, sniffing and patting his pockets for a handkerchief.

"Here, Daddy," Hope said, handing him a box of tissues.

"And my sister," Julianna said, stepping around the little boys to hug Oscar. "Oh, how I missed you and it was less than a week for us." She looked down at the children, wide-eyed with wonder at the new people who were making Daddy cry.

"Oh, and no doubt you've already met Hope. You were right about little alpha females. She runs the house if Mom and Dad are busy."

"You're always busy," Hope said. "But that's okay. At least you're always here," she added, looking up at Silas with a scowl of reprimand that quickly turned into a giggle that sounded just like Tori's.

"Oh, and here are the boys, Jamison and Andrew," Oscar said, putting a hand on each of their shoulders.

"Yeah, look at this," Hope said. "Do it, guys."

The boys stood side by side then bent their necks toward each other, matching the tops of their heads. The odd shapes meshed almost perfectly.

Oscar shrugged and grinned sheepishly. "They were conjoined twins. Abandoned at a hospital in Haiti. We sponsored them as foster parents for about..." Oscar paused and nodded to Hope, giving her the go-ahead to finish the story.

"About two minutes and then I said we should keep them forever." She put her hands on her hips. "It might be the only way I'd get brothers. But even if my baby sister had been a boy, I wouldn't give them back for nothin'!"

"You have a baby sister?" Julianna asked.

Hope dashed to the refrigerator and took the yellow magnet with googly eyes off her masterpiece. "See, there's six of us now," she proclaimed. "And I can write my whole name now, too."

She gave him her crayon-created picture of a stick figure family. There were three children, a dad, and a mom holding a baby, all standing under a rainbow of at least ten colors and signed Hope Priest.

"That's you?" Silas asked. "Your name?"

"Uh-huh."

Silas looked at Oscar, one eyebrow raised.

"Hey, now you can't forget who I am, right, Dad?"

"Is he Dad or Other Dad?" Hope asked.

"Doesn't make a difference," Silas said, "as long as Dad's in there somewhere."

"Just made it easier with this place and all," Oscar whispered. He looked up and saw his mother's sterned-face silent admonition and grinned sheepishly. "Well, as long as we're all being honest, Tori and I both wanted to honor you. And thank you for all you've done for us. Plus, I never really had an emotional bond with Hugh's heritage. He was constantly scolding and belittling me for not being man enough to carry on the Shaw last name. And so I'm not."

"Well, I can tell you now, I'm highly honored," Silas said, pulling Oscar close and patting him on the back, sniffing back tears.

"Oh, and check out the back of this masterpiece," Silas said, turning over Hope's family portrait.

Oscar gasped. "Why didn't I see this? 'Sorry we missed you. Grandpa and Mom.'"

"Oops," Hope said.

Oscar ruffled her hair. "Don't worry about it. Just ask before using paper with writing on it, okay?"

Silas grinned at the gentle parenting. "So, where are your mother and sister?" he asked Hope.

"We're right here," Tori said.

A bedraggled woman, barely recognizable, was leaning against the bottom of the stairwell. Wrapped in an oversized pink terrycloth bathrobe, a small flannel-wrapped bundle over her shoulder, she looked like she'd had a rough time, her face puffy from crying.

Silas enveloped her with a cautious hug, gently kissing the top of her unkempt hair as if he'd found a long-lost treasure.

"Okay," she said to Oscar, wiping her face on the sleeve of her robe. "Her name is Faith."

"Did we miss something?" Julianna asked. "I mean, I know we missed a lot but…" She turned to look at Oscar, now holding one boy in each arm. Hope had come over and was holding onto Silas's leg.

"This time's been rough," Oscar said. "Crazy hormones, her folks out of town and unreachable…"

"Her grandfather and mother-in-law God only knows where…" Silas said, sniffing.

530

Ding, dong, ding.

Hope and the boys raced to the front door. "My turn," Jamison said. Hope held onto Andrew's shoulder and waited for a split second, then helped her other brother tug the door open.

"Grandma! Grandpa!" all three shouted, bouncing over each other to find a leg or hand to grab onto.

"Mom?" Tori called, walking toward them, Oscar at her side, baby Faith now in his arms. "I thought you were in China looking for ancient strains of citrus or something."

Leanne took the baby from Oscar. She pulled the blanket down to see her sleeping face, ooh and ahhed, then kissed the top of her little blonde head. She showed her to Luther, then cuddled her close.

"Meh, those plants have been around for centuries," Leanne said. "Another few months won't make a difference. It was a bit of a tussle, convincing the tour leader to drop two from his manifest and let us fly back, but at the last minute, two Americans came up, waving cash in the air."

"Yeah, some rich old fart with the buffest boy-toy I've ever seen," Luther said.

"I couldn't believe it," Leanne whispered to Tori. "The old guy kept calling him sweetie, saying how Buddy was going to like China, too, then giggling."

"Don't tell me," Silas said, "the big guy's name was André?"

"Yeah, as a matter of fact, it was," Leanne said. "The old man kept going on and on about André and Buddy, but we never did see Buddy."

"Well, that's a good thing," Julianna said.

"And how was your trip? Did you bring back some good news for us?"

"It was fine," Julianna said "The good news is we won't be going anywhere for a while."

"Except," Silas said boldly, his single word getting everyone's attention, even the four and younger crowd. "Except to the altar. I asked her to marry me and she said yes."

"Hmph," Luther huffed. "Took you long enough. Five years and a world tour of coffee plantations to make up your mind? With someone like Julianna, it shouldn't have taken you even a month."

"I'm not complaining," Julianna said. "Silas and I have our own calendar, don't we dear?"

"From Woodstock in '69 to today, it seems like days, not decades."

Silas looked around the room and saw everyone had settled into little family groups. Content. Mostly. He was ready for complete contentment. "Hey, new grandma." Both Julianna and Leanne looked up. "The one whose name starts with J."

Julianna patted Leanne's back and stood up. "Yes, dear?"

"A porch chat if you don't mind."

"Okay." Julianna went outside while he told the little boys he'd be right back. She stepped down onto the first step and waited.

He came up to her and saw something was different. "Huh?"

"I just wanted to see what it was like with you taller than me," she said. "So, what's going on that you don't want the others to hear about?"

"That obvious?" he asked softly, nuzzling her nose to nose. Before she could answer, his lips brushed hers. "Mmm. A whole different set of nerve endings are getting stimulated."

"Well, don't let them get too happy. We have a lot of hours before bedtime," she said, then leaned in for another kiss.

After their kisses became more arousing, Silas forced himself to stop. He pulled away just enough to break contact. "When were you going to tell me you're pregnant?" he whispered.

"Hmph. How'd you know?"

"They call me Sherlock for a reason."

***

Hugo the thug snickered into the phone line. He put his hand over the mic. "Hey, Vinnie, it's the Killer Queen's baby sister. She's in a bind. Do you think we ought to help her?"

"Hell, no. I've heard about little Icky Vicky. KQ cut her off years ago. Tell her big sister hit the road." Vinnie laughed. "You know, hit the road like in 'got run over by a big rig' after shooting a cop?"

Victoria pulled the phone away from her ear and hit end. Another dead end contact.

She handed the borrowed cell back to the buxom guard. The dour-faced woman's foot was tapping threateningly, her other hand open, waiting to be paid.

"Do you think we can work something out?" Victoria asked. "I…um…smoked my last cigarette."

The guard pulled Victoria's chin up and looked at her, assessing her potential as a lover. "Maybe…"

***

Backwoods, North Carolina
Spring, 1681

"I know I had that coin. Where did it go?" Hugh said, sticking his hand in his pocket again. This time, his middle finger poked through. "Shit!" He bent over, picked up a fallen twig, and threw it into the bushes, startling a covey of quail.

"Damn! Damn! Damn!" He turned around in circles, looking for the stand of tall trees he had walked through. They were gone. All that was there were three scrawny saplings and wispy little twigs, all leafless. He crossed his arms in front of himself and rubbed the sleeves of his Yankees sweatshirt, trying to keep warm.

"How in the hell did I lose the road? It has to be here somewhere." He walked toward the edge of the forest, then back again. "Keep your bearings, Hugh. You must have hit your head or something, and you're still in the park. Time travel isn't real." He swept the ground with his cross-trainers again, looking down for the drilled silver drachma he had ordered online, just to prove to Julianna that it wasn't a magic token.

"Hmph!"

Hugh looked up.

An Indian in buckskins and beads was standing in front of him, his pony piled high with the gutted remains of an elk, a travois loaded with beaver skins behind it.

"Ya ta hey?" Hugh squeaked.

Just when you need help to prepare the meat and furs, the Great Spirit sends a slave. It's a good day. A very good day.

The End

Thank you!

Thanks for reading They Call Me Sherlock and making it all the way through The Whole She-Bang – Triplets: Three Aren't One Collection.

In case you didn't notice, this story also incorporates characters from THE FAIRIES SAGA and has a brief drop in from Hugo and Vinnie from **THAT TWIN THING**.

If you want to know more about Mac, Mali, Storm, Benji, and Jane, and what transpired while Silas was fighting sleep and confusion, check out **BIG MAC**.

To read the fascinating tale of Jane coming from the 18th century to the 21st, her story is in **THE GREAT BIG FAIRY**.

If you could take a moment, I'd appreciate a short review on Amazon, Goodreads, and/or BookBub. Other readers love knowing what to expect before picking up a book. Let them know how you felt about this one.

Thanks again!

Dani Haviland

About the Author

Author Dani Haviland started writing late in life and has been making up for lost time with a flood of works from sports, gritty women's fiction, time travel, and Sweet and Sassy romances to Unforgettable romantic suspense, Cute But Crazy rom-coms, and cozy mystery stories – with some short stories thrown in to round out the reading experience.

Dani is also the owner of Chill Out! Books, one of the publishers for **The Authors' Billboard**. Follow her on **BookBub** to make sure you get her latest stories.

Contact information:
Website: Danihaviland.com
Email: **dani@danihaviland.com**
Twitter: @dani_haviland, @gr8authors

I love to hear from readers!
Sign up for my newsletter to get the latest information on new releases, free stuff, and contests here.

Awesome readers group!
I have a Facebook Page for folks who are interested in early excerpts and insights into my latest books and box sets plus the latest from some of the authors and box sets I publish under Chill Out! Books. I'd appreciate it if you'd like the page. Drop in and see if I've remembered to add photos and excerpts of my works in process. **Dani Haviland & Friends Readers Group**.

More Books by Dani Haviland

THE FAIRIES SAGA SERIES

(Historical fiction/time travel, listed in order):

Kibbles and Bits: **FREE** ebook: Sample the early stories in The Fairies Saga stories with extended excerpts. Rind out how they got their crazy titles here, too.

Aye, I am a Fairy: (Book One) Young British lord finds himself entwined with a time traveling family and must decide if he should go back in time, too.

LOST: The Time Travel Romance That Started It All: (Book Two) The fun introduction to some of the very colorful characters from The Fairies Saga and Arlie Undercover. Find out how they're influenced by the fan-obsessive romance novel LOST by Lisa Sinclaire.

Naked in the Winter Wind: (Book Three) How does an older woman wind up as a young hottie in Revolutionary War era North Carolina?

Ha'Penny Jenny: (Book Four) More about the naïve and psychic young girl who was adopted into a time traveling family. Will her past catch up to her?

Dances Naked: (Book Five) Directionally challenged time traveler is rescued by Cherokee in 18th century. What must he do before the chief will show him to The Trees, the portal through time?

The Great Big Fairy: (Book Six) Very tall Benji grew up in the 20th century but was born in the 18th. When he finds a way to return to his grandparents in the distant past, he goes for it. Once there, he realizes he can't stay, but must return to the future.

Kidnapped! (Book Seven) The Scottish police officer would do anything to get his wife back...even trust the mysterious letter sent to him from his ancestor, a convict on The First Fleet into Australia!

Little Bear and the Ladies: (Book Eight) What's a bachelor trapper to do with all the females he rescues from the Hessian mercenaries? He'd better hurry and figure something!

Time in a Little Blue Bottle: (Book Nine) Elvis, Mark Twain, and the prime vampire are racing to get the bottle of Fountain of Youth water before sweet Bella and the youthful pickpocket. So why are time travelers Marty Melbourne and Master Simon interested?

Big Mac: (Book Ten) Fate and science said they should never have met but after that first touch, he knew he'd stay with her forever. Would the sudden appearance of the father he never knew be their doom – and the start of a pandemic?

Chasing Christmas: (Book Eleven) A young Cherokee is rescued from an abusive man and changes the lives of many in this 18th century America family.

Little Drummer Boy: (Book Twelve) Young Scout works to earn money for a home in post-Revolutionary War America but runs up against prejudices and snowstorms.

Never Too Young: (Book Thirteen) Scout and Ha'Penny Jenny have grown up, but will they be able to spend their life together, or will the past and ruffians get in their way?

Pool Boy Wanted: No Experience Preferred: (Book Fourteen) Young Benji has been a hostage and slave, but life gets worse when an older woman decides she wants him as her own.

Luke the Unexpected: (Book Fifteen) Love of classic motorcycles brought them together, but Luke and Holly have other challenges to face. Find out how their friend Benji got his stripes here.

Just Jenny and Scout: Four complete novels and three partial titles pull the life and love of Jenny and Scout together from the day they first met. Action, adventure, and a bit of romance in an historical epic of Early America.

TRIPLETS: THREE AREN'T ONE
(A potpourri of literary styles, all with strong characters)

The Set Up: Grace's story. A gritty Women's Fiction of how it all began.

Diamonds Aren't for Everyone: Vickie's story. A Billionaire Romance with mysteries and surprises.

That Magic Touch: Ria's story. A tender, heartwarming Medical Romance.

How Love Grows: Tori's story. A spunky young woman insists on doing everything her way. A Romantic Comedy.

They Call Me Sherlock: Silas's story. A young couple who met at Woodstock get a second chance due to creative use of time travel. Romantic Comedy.

The Whole She-Bang – Triplets: Three Aren't One Collection. All the stories in one set.

ARLIE UNDERCOVER SERIES
(Romantic suspense & Cozy Mysteries based in Alaska and Arizona)

A Stingray Christmas: (Book One) Anchorage detective on medical leave travels from Alaska to Arizona to see for the first time the son he'd fathered as an anonymous sperm donor. Great and rotten surprises await the cop with the smartest smartphone around.

The Biggest Heart Ever: (Book Two) When would Arlie learn that trying to do everything by himself could be deadly—and make Charlene a widow before they were married?

Always a Bigger Fish: (Book Three) Back in Alaska, Arlie finds out he's a target. Will vacationing detective Billy Burke (from THE FAIRIES SAGA) have information to help nab the scalper?

How to Fix a Broken Life: (Book Four) When Arlie's very pregnant wife is kidnapped by pseudo terrorists, will he be the one to rescue her or will a surprise hero come in to save the day?

Because You Said So: (Book Five) Something's amiss at the Port of Anchorage. Will Arlie be able to solve it and still be back in time to wear the Santa suit?

Heaven and Heartbreak: (Book Six) Sharing her child with a gay father and his lover was the easy part. Finding a woman for herself seemed impossible.

Crazy Ladies in Capes Debut: (Book Seven) Louie witnessed a murder – or did he? Are the senior women downtown responsible?

Never a Dull Murder: (Book Eight) Arlie has too many people trying to help him solve the murder of the baker in Witness Protection. Will his new gadget – or a hungry bear cub – find the answer?

Arlie and Company: All eight books of the Arlie Undercover series in one place.

THAT TWIN THING SERIES
(Romantic suspense series)

The Midwife's Son: The midwife refused her selfish patient's request to smother the scrawny twin and instead took him home to bring up as her own. Years later, will the two young men wind up in each other's lives despite the midwife's efforts to keep them apart?

Phoenix I'm Not: Will the billionaire's spoiled son be resurrected from the ashes of his former life of drugs and mayhem by love or be tortured and eliminated by the assassin sent by his mother?

Lost and Found Family: Separated at birth, these twins find they have more than genetics in common: they're both the target of killers who are willing to risk everything to take them out.

Peter Elph: A supplement to the story of Lost and Found Family, this short story is about a member of the Wagner family back in 1886 Tombstone, Arizona.

That Twin Thing: The Complete Collection: All four books in one place.

STAND ALONE NOVELLAS
(Contemporary romances)

Kit Kringle: An Alaskan Tale: Kay moved to Alaska for the wrong reasons, then decided to stay and start her own business. What she hadn't planned on were prejudices and falling in love.

Be My Angel: Wyatt's dream to help save the wild mustangs began with the purchase of a rundown ranch in western Oregon. What he hadn't anticipated was being mesmerized by a sassy woman in a wheelchair.

Three Are One: The post chaplain tried to help the young widow adjust, but would his feelings for her and the search for his lost sister cause problems?

One Arctic Summer: That unforgettable summer of 1994 in Barrow, Alaska, and the touch she never forgot…If she goes back, will he remember her?

The Polar Xpress: Will the California chiropractor get a first chance at romance with the owner of Second Chance Kennels when he is stranded in Alaska?

Too Fast For You: Ten years after Little League, two talented professional baseball players wind up on the same minor league team. Will she remember him? And will their friendship be ruined if she does?

A Plate of Christmas Cookies: World War Two got between them the first time. Will his adult children stop his second chance at happiness? Based on a true story.

The Wizard of Odds: Four co-workers get closer than they expected on a cross-country tour to win a bet and rescue some exotic animals at the same time. A Rom-Com.

The Purebred and the Mutt: The British auto enthusiast TV star meets the caretaker and mechanic at his American ranch. Could this Southern gal hold her own when they're confronted by a crazed fan? A Rom-Com.

Splendor and Surprises: Alaska Style – The Singles Collection Set One: All of the Stand Alone Single Romance stories that occur in Alaska in one place. Includes Three Are One, One Arctic Summer, The Polar Xpress, and Kit Kringle: An Alaskan Tale.

Cookies, Angels and Road Trips – The Singles Collection Set Two: A potpourri of sweet and savory romances. From Love at First Sight to Second Chances, lots of surprises and 'ah moments' plus a few giggles and guffaws. Included are A Plate of Christmas Cookies, The Purebred and the Mutt, Be My Angel, Too Fast For You, and The Wizard of Odds.

www.ingramcontent.com/pod-product-compliance
Lightning Source LLC
Chambersburg PA
CBHW072009020726
47501CB00006B/1743